On Silver Wings

On
Silver Wings

A Mystic Tale from Celtic Lore

Elfie Leddy

Pelican Pond

Published by Pelican Pond Publishing
Fine Fiction for All Ages
an imprint of Blue Dolphin Publishing, Inc.

For inquiries or orders, address
Blue Dolphin Publishing, Inc.
P.O. Box 8, Nevada City, CA 95959
1-800-643-0765
www.bluedolphinpublishing.com

ISBN: 1-57733-080-3

Library of Congress Cataloging-in-Publication Data

Leddy, Elfie, 1948–
    On silver wings : a mystic tale from Celtic lore / Elfie Leddy.
      p. cm.
    ISBN 1-57733-080-3
      1. Reincarnation—Fiction. 2. Women, Celtic—Fiction. 3. Women
    sculptors—Fiction. 4. Canadians—Ireland—Fiction. 5. Quests
    (Expeditions)—Fiction. 6. Ireland—Fiction. 7. Canada—Fiction.
    I. Title.

    PS3612.E34 O5 2001
    813'.6—dc21
                                                                    2001021310

Cover design: Elfie Leddy
Cover execution: Jeff Case

Printed in the United States of America

10   9   8   7   6   5   4   3   2   1

Chapter One

SHE FELT HIS GAZE glide gently over her face like a caress. Her breath caught in her throat as a warm flush spread over her body. Even though the anticipation was killing her she would savor every moment. The soft brush of his lips against her temple brought her back into the moment. Shivers of pure ecstasy rippled along her spine as he murmured words of love against her hair and lightly caressed the nape of her neck.

Pulling back slightly she gazed at him possessively, relishing all she saw. A lock of dark hair fell across his forehead and brushed one full and slightly crooked eyebrow. His sculptured nose stood proud, reminiscent of a Roman Legion captain from days gone by. As she gazed into his deep blue eyes she sought his essence, the source of such surprising tenderness, and felt again the waves of love that glowed from their center. How can the coolness of blue hold so much heat? Like fire held captive within ice.

She looked intently at the strong slash of his lips, swelled with expectancy. Distracted by a trail of heat as those very lips ran a soft line up her cheek into the tender fold of her ear, when he paused for a time on her lobe, she knew she could hold still no longer. She cupped his strong chin in her hands and gazed into his eyes; eyes that mirrored her own desire. She knew the kiss would come now, the melding of his lips with hers ... the bonding of two souls that had yearned for each other through time and space.

She felt the heat of his breath, faintly laced with the smell of cloves as he leaned towards her. Her lips parted in welcome and she could almost taste the sweetness before he even reached the soft moistness of her mouth. And from her core a tide began to rise and whorl through her in warm, soft waves.

A faint ringing off to one side momentarily distracted her, but she ignored it, willing herself to melt back into the sea of sensations. Once again the ringing thrust at her, more insistent now. Drawn back to the feel of his lips as they lightly brushed against hers, she embraced a rush of honeyed bliss, and drifted with the waves that were rapidly becoming rolling swells of passion. But the ringing became shriller.

In despair she watched the edges of her beloved's face waver and his features slowly lose distinction. "Nooo ..." she moaned.

Tannis rolled over, half smothered by the puffy eiderdown. As she groped for the phone she knocked over the stack of books perched on the edge of the night table. They thudded to the floor and shook her from her woolly-spun torpor.

"Damn," she mumbled, her lips still slack in anticipation of the kiss that was not meant to be. "Who is it?" Still groggy, she struggled to sit up.

"Are you my mother?" The questioning softness of the ritual greeting immediately identified the caller.

"Are you my daughter?" Tannis replied automatically, her lack of enthusiasm evident in her tone.

Damn! It was only a dream after all. But it was *the* dream, the one she'd had before. Only this time it had been so real she could still feel the light brush of his lips on hers. Of all the people to break the connection, it would have to be Linka.

"Whoops! Did I catch you at a bad time?" Her cheery tone held no apology.

"Bad time? Oh no. You just interrupted a rapturous dream. Nothing that would hold a candle to an early morning chat with my daughter right now. Feel free to sever what little romance I do have in my life." She didn't even try to keep the sarcasm out of her voice.

"You're so funny when you're grumpy, Mom."

"You woke me up."

Linka ignored the terse response. "You never sleep in. Do you know what time it is? It's after nine. I thought I'd catch you hard at it already, in the studio I mean." She giggled at her own pun, but receiving no response quickly added, "Sorry. So what's new with your dream-hunk?"

"Don't patronize me, you brat." She already regretted telling Linka about her recurring dreams. "Why couldn't I have a daughter I rarely see, like most mothers, instead of one who intrudes into my life almost daily ... and now it seems, even my dreams." To change the subject she asked, "So ... what's up?"

She tried to plump the pillows behind her without disturbing Mr. Muff and Ginseng snugly curled against her leg. Two pairs of feline eyes, one green, the other blue, shot her a steely look of disapproval. Stifling a yawn, she reached down to ruffle Mr. Muff's lion's mane and missed what Linka said. Ginseng saw her action as a signal to play and promptly pounced on her fingers, and a startled Mr. Muff. After a brief scuffle they separated, fur askew. Diverted by their mock battle Tannis laughed as they turned their backs to each other and casually began their morning wash.

Linka heard the commotion but didn't comment. The way her mother pampered her cats was disgusting. With the petulance of an ignored child she repeated her request. "Moom . . . I said . . . I need a big favorite. I have an appointment at the bone-cracker over in Kitsilano and my ride pooped out on me. Men! Could you take me? I thought we could make an afternoon of it, you know, do the mother-daughter-lunch thing and poke around in the shops. Whadda-ya say?"

Not only had her dream burst and she would never know how far this one would go, but now her first lazin' day in almost two weeks was shot to hell. After a week of sixteen hour days in the studio to finish the wall murals for the Los Angeles Gallery, she had looked forward to a decadent sleep-in and do-nothing day. Exhausted, she had forgotten to mute the ringer on the bedside phone last night. Well she was awake now, but didn't think she had the energy to do much of anything, let alone go out. She said nothing in hopes Linka would take a hint from her lack of response and make other arrangements.

Linka sensed her ploy but persevered. She didn't drive and hated buses so either took a cab or rode her bike, weather permitting. Today was definitely not a cycling day. She too had finished a big batch of work and needed a play-day. "We haven't had an adventure day in ages. Besides, I still have a favor token to redeem." Still no response. She softened her voice to the husky sweetness her mother found hard to resist. "I really *need* to spend time with you Mom." Still no response. Oh well, time for the heavy artillery. *"Pleeease?"*

True, it had been several weeks since they had done anything together, but why did it have to be today? Tannis rarely picked up her calls while she worked and had returned Linka's many messages with only two brief return calls. Irritated because her interrupted dream was her own fault, she knew it wasn't fair to take it out on Linka, but wasn't about to capitulate without at least one or two caustic comments. "The voice is a nice touch but just a tad too husky, I'd say."

"Gottcha. I'll make an adjustment next time . . . so how about it? Are we on?"

"It's not as if I have a life, right?" Tannis said. "Mothers just sit patiently in the wings, waiting for a call from their offspring so they can feel useful." She couldn't help but smile at the absurdity of that visual even remotely applying to her. "Oh, all right. I guess I can laze around tomorrow. But you're on notice that you've now used up your last favor token for the month, and, tomorrow is *my* day, so consider me unavailable for *any* reason whatsoever, capish?"

"Capish. Thanks mom. We're gonna have a super day, you'll see."

"Don't expect much above my mere presence. I'm truly beat. What time should I pick you up?" She glanced at the clock and wondered if she would have time for a bath or just a quick swish in the shower. Knowing Linka, she was already dressed, ready to go, and all but waiting for her ride out front.

"Half-tenish. See ya!"

A shower it would be. In spite of herself, a smile came to her lips as her thoughts stayed with her twenty-two year old daughter, Kalinka. A flood of happy memories followed her into the kitchen and replayed in her mind while she made coffee and prepared the cats' breakfast. She was still amazed at what a wonder of a child she had produced. Divorced since Linka was ten, it had not been easy to raise a daughter alone and develop her career besides. A few dismal memories flashed through her mind. But her single-minded commitment, and the joy she took in motherhood had anchored their light-hearted relationship with a deep bond of love. Since Linka's child-like exuberance had diminished little with adulthood, Tannis was often called on to act as a stabilizer. She could still, just by her unruffled presence or cooling hand of reason, soothe the heat of her offspring's mental confusion.

In the bathroom Tannis turned on the shower and stepped under the hot jet she loved. She leaned her head back, closed her eyes, and felt her mind drift back to her dreams. Since the first one, each subsequent dream had grown in substance and clarity, yet replayed the same encounter with the same man. He must be her soulmate, if there really was such a thing. Her dreams had always been vivid, but this dream was different somehow. It implied a different kind of reality, one she could not define yet knew for a certainty was no dream.

Adrift under the hypnotic pulse of steaming heat, she willed his image into her mind. It came quickly, along with every delicious sensation. Even the smell of him, a leathery, musk maleness lightly tipped with a tinge of cloves seemed to flood the air as if he stood right there with her. It was with a jolt that her eyes opened on empty space.

I am truly losing my mind, is what's happening here. As if to reaffirm her sanity, she began to soap herself vigorously. Due to her artistic nature she lived closer to the edge of reality than most people did. But this stretched the boundary of reason a little too far, even for her. Imagine ... responding physically to a dream-man as if he was real. Although her actions smacked of delusion, she clung to the lingering warmth of her physical arousal. Lacking a man in the real world, she had conjured one up in her dreams. *That's mighty mature.* But what harm could it do? All women fantasized to some degree. As she turned off the shower she was hit with an uncomfortable thought. What if these dreams were triggered by some hormonal imbalance heralding the upcoming change of life—menopause? No, she was much too young for that. She firmly dismissed that notion and attended to her ritual of beautification.

It took only moments to towel herself and dab her signature scent behind her ears and in the cleft of her upright breasts. Secretly proud of her breasts, she ran her hands over them and wondered idly what *his* hands would feel like cupped around their fullness.

"You're a sick puppy." Her statement brought a faint flush to the cheeks of her mirror image as she lightly applied mascara to her long thick lashes. Thankfully no one knew how these recurring dreams captivated her, not even her best friend, Josie, particularly not Josie. The important thing was, she reasoned, that she knew they were just fantasies and not real. Still ... a part of her wished they were.

It was ironic, she thought, as she brushed her teeth. She had a comfortable home, a great kid and wonderful friends, four precious cats, and enough money and freedom in her career to do what she loved best, and on her terms. Everything she could possibly want. Right? The only thing she didn't have was a man in her life; not that she needed one, of course. But ... she suspected her recent ache of longing could only be satiated by intimacy with a man; a longing consciously pushed aside but seeking acknowledgment through her dreams.

Men who had flocked to her because of her arresting looks during her more social years, had quickly lost their ardor when her iron-will surfaced; usually when she was supposed to 'put out'. She was neither frigid nor inhibited, far from it in fact. But in spite of the sexual freedom of the 70s, she had been adamant about keeping a relationship platonic until she could get to know a man without sex clouding the issue. Through her own perverse test of character, she had denied herself the very thing she sought. In spite of what they all said, men didn't really want a confident woman with a mind of her own. They preferred their egos stroked by the more pliable who used sex to establish and maintain intimacy. There had to be a man of character somewhere out there, besides in the pages of the romance novels she loved; a man of substance who sought the same in a partner. Romance novels were her one secret vice, a vice which only fueled her fantasies about men of integrity, depth and passion, persistent in their efforts to earn the love and respect of the strong women who captured their heart. Although she knew such traits were a fabricated ideal, she refused to compromise and settle for anything less. She knew what she wanted, but had hoped to find him in the flesh, not just in a dream.

Sighing deeply, she quickly blow-dried her hair then ran the pick through the ebony shoulder length curls. She then pinned back the sides with large combs, which accented her dramatic silver streaks but did little to tame her halo of curls. A jangle of cascading, tinkling earrings completed the look of a witch catapulted off her broom during a storm. Peaked eyebrows over large violet eyes reinforced the magical image. Only her delicate straight nose and lush wide lips reduced her slightly demonic appearance to something more whimsical, but nonetheless striking.

Tannis stood in only her black tights and scanned her closet. Feeling red today, she reached for a deceptively shapeless but well-cut silk tunic and slipped it over her head. Blazing with reds and purple threaded with subtle slashes of gold, the tunic caressed her back with cool lightness as she bent down to choose her footwear. Red kid boots, so soft they hugged her slender feet like socks, completed the ensemble.

She chuckled at the thought of Linka's reaction to her outfit. Her wardrobe, a raging tornado of strong colors, consisted of silky fabrics that screamed to be touched. Linka's taste in garb was another matter. She was a jock-babe through and through. Generally clad in comfortable sweatwear, she seemed to sense that the tentative pastel shades she preferred acted as a mere backdrop to an effervescent personality that needed no enhancement. Both her pale wardrobe and blanched apartment decor were in stark contrast to the rich colors her mother favored.

Her coffee mug in one hand and a slice of toast in the other, Tannis headed for the living room couch where the boys awaited their morning purring-time. The senior, twelve year-old Mr. Muff, graciously welcomed his favorite cheek strokes and purred softly as she ran her fingers through his long silver-edged gray coat and up the length of his luxurious tail. Impatient for his turn, Billy Bob, her enormous ten year-old orange tabby brusquely nudged him aside. After only a few firm strokes down his back, he tilted his head in enticement, flopped on his side, and insisted on a little belly rubbing from her, and finger nibbling by him.

Ginseng, the sturdy white youngster hadn't defined his personality yet. Only eight months old, he was still a curious, playful, and energetic kitty. Anything, even a light tickle under his chin, sent his motor trilling up and down the scale of kitty purrs. Too full of beans to sit still for long and satisfied with a quick but intense nuzzle, he bounded off her lap in search of the toy mouse he had misplaced earlier. Zoie, the Calico Queen of Bitch refused to budge from where she sat crouched on the corner of the couch, but hissed at Ginseng as he streaked by. The only female, her primary focus since her sudden arrival at their doorstep six years ago was to terrorize the boys under her domination, and jealously guard her 'mama' from threat; real or imagined. Her nasty disposition mellowed only for her 'mama' with whom she shared an inexplicable but deep bond of affection.

"O.K. gang. I gotta go." Sensing disapproval of her too-brief attentions when she rose to take her cup back to the kitchen, Tannis added, "You'll get double purring-time tonight, I promise." She couldn't imagine life without her constant companions, even prickly Zoie. It was pretty tricky sometimes dispensing equal attention to all, but well worth the effort. To her they were not just cats, but fascinating little souls who had gifted her with their friendship, each projecting an aspect of her own personality. Since she worked at home, they were tuned into her routine and knew when she was about to desert them. Tannis ignored the mournful faces from across the room as she threw on her jacket and said her farewells.

A low ceiling of cloud shrouded Lynn Valley with a gray blanket and morning mist smothered the tops of the fir trees pressed against the houses nestled into the surrounding hills. Merging onto the Second Narrows Bridge from the woodsy North Shore, Tannis scanned Vancouver's bleak inlet. It was a perfect day to poke in quaint shops and pretend the dullness common to early March didn't exist. Traffic moved sluggishly along the congested bridge lanes and Tannis found her mind had drifted back to the dreams which had begun about six months ago. Vague at first, like undefined longings that danced in wisps around her unfulfilled desires, a theme had slowly emerged; a replay of the same encounter with the same man. She didn't remember when she first knew he was her soulmate, only that he was her perfect counterpart. In fact, she wasn't sure there was even such a thing, but if there was, he was it. For with each dream, as his shape grew more defined and his substance more familiar, she felt like she had always known him. In a strange way it felt more like reliving a memory than experiencing something for the first time.

For he was the type of man she yearned for; strong, honorable, yet gentle. Clear on the qualities she required of a partner, she sensed he possessed them all. Her intuitive sense had always been strong and she trusted and never questioned it anymore. Intuition had nudged her towards the right choices at just the right time in all areas of her life ... except romance. That part of her was like a malfunctioning circuit that kept shorting out. Until the dreams.

Tannis was startled to find herself parked in front of Linka's apartment, a pink, three-story building perched on the western slope of Capital Hill. She had driven the familiar route in auto-pilot, her mind on the dreams. She shook herself as if to confirm she was awake. No matter how many times she drove in this auto-pilot mode it still startled her when she arrived at her destination without any memory of getting there. She peered towards the entrance and grinned as Linka burst through the front doors like a mini hurricane. All five foot three of her exuded health and vitality as she dashed down the walkway and yanked open the passenger door. "Ooh! I've missed you so much. Thanks mom, you're the best!" She lunged across the seat towards her mother for a sloppy hug. "You smell so good. Ouch!"

"Hi sweets. What's the matter? Neck hurting again?"

"Neck *and* shoulders, and just about everything else." Linka's grimace punctuated her discomfort. "I've been hunched over my light table day and night and forgot to do my exercises." She quickly raised her hands in mock surrender at Tannis' look of exasperation.

"Don't say it," she admonished. "I know I'm supposed to do my exercises. And I will," she added, rubbing the back of her neck. Whip-lash from a car accident the year before had resulted in recurring stiffness if she neglected to do her neck rolls and stretches during her often long hours at the light-table. To avoid further discussion on her neglect, she gave her mom the address of their destination then launched into a detailed run-down of all her activities since they last saw each other.

Her fresh face shifted like quicksilver, expressing each nuance of her intense feelings, while vigorous hand motions underlined each pertinent point. Left to babble happily or expound intense philosophical conclusions which changed on a daily basis, she would soon run out of steam or issues and settle down to a more interactive conversation. All Tannis need do was drive, listen, and throw in the odd 'Really' or 'Oh'. Today's topic was a rundown of how tit-useless men were and why her most recent companion, Jay, was now history. Tannis wasn't surprised. He'd lasted a good month longer than his predecessors.

"I'm convinced there isn't a man around you can depend on. All they're good for is the sperm bank. They expect you to be there for them, but oh, when you ask a teeny-weeney favor ... pfft! Well, I've made up my mind. I'm through with men."

"Until you meet somebody else."

"No. For ... ever." A firm nod emphasized the latter.

"Forever is a long time."

"I know, but so what. I mean, look at you. You're a perfect example of a completely self-sufficient, independent, and content woman. I have to admit you have the right idea. I don't know why I waste my time on these boy-toys. If you can fly solo, so can I."

Tannis shifted in her seat uncomfortably. Yes, she was quite the role model wasn't she, conjuring up a dream lover. "I am alone because I chose to dedicate myself to both my work and raising you after your father left. Both required a great deal of time and energy, particularly the latter. However, at forty-two, I do still have desires and don't plan to retire my vagina just yet." And what desires!

Linka shot her a surprised look. "Yuk, that's disgusting. I don't think of you that way. You're my mom for God's sake", as if that precluded her from having any sexual needs or passionate feelings. She was still surprised and discomforted by her mother's occasional vulgar comments. She couldn't fathom where they came from since both her mother's family and her own father's background reflected a refinement where such comments were unheard of.

What have I done, Tannis thought, amused at her little prude's reaction. She had obviously cloaked her own sexuality well over the years, so well in fact, she wasn't supposed to have any. Thank God Linka couldn't read her mind. Those years had been dotted with only infrequent dates, and just one sexual encounter neither Linka, nor anyone else for that matter, knew anything about. She had diverted her sexual energy to the creative focus required by her figurative sculpting, and it was her four foot nudes that transmuted her unfulfilled desires into seductive poses that hinted at her own cloaked sensuality.

Tannis deftly slid into a parking space left by a departing vehicle right in front of the wholistic clinic. She had to credit this as one of the more useful visualization techniques learned from Josie. A parking spot was always waiting for her wherever she went, generally right in front of her destination.

Linka abruptly stopped her critique of her friend's doomed relationship and peered up and down the street. She pointed at an ornate sign a few doors up from where they were parked and said, "Hey, look at that neat little cafe. The Kazbar. Meet you there after my session. I should be done in about half an hour or so. See ya." A violent slam of the car door, a swish of her long silky hair, and she was gone.

Tannis glanced through the front window of the Kazbar at the East Indian decor. A delicate tinkle of chimes set the mood as she entered and sat down at one of the small, bare wooden tables. She loved these intimate little cafes, perfect for solitary daydreaming or languid conversations over steaming Java. She ordered coffee from the smiling round proprietor and looked around leisurely, lulled by the low throbbing of Sitars and other exotic instruments that softly beat out their ancient cadence.

The charm of Vancouver's Kitsilano area was that the 70s had never really left. Small pockets, even whole blocks around 4th Avenue, still retained the flavor of the hippie era and offered sojourns into a gentler, earthier past. As she sipped on the mellow brew, she caught snatches of a ponderous discourse on altruism vs. objectivism from two older university types at a table on her right, both predictably clad in turtlenecks, jeans and elbow-patched corduroy jackets. A woman with a distinctly 'feminist' air sat alone at a table by the window, her nose buried in a thick book. Tannis sensed her broad bottom warmed that particular chair often, and felt the aura of her solitude as she raised her head and leveled a pensive gaze out the window.

A delicate young woman sat in the back corner of the cafe. Tannis hadn't noticed her when she first scanned the room, or the ornate poster pinned on the wall beside her proclaiming her a Tarot Card reader. The phrase 'not entirely present' immediately came to mind. Her gauzy flowered peasant dress, fine long hair and translucent skin reinforced the look of an 'earth spirit'. Tannis could hear her softly humming as she idly fingered the large crystal pennant hanging from a thong around her neck. As if in response to the scrutiny, she raised her head and their eyes locked briefly.

It might be fun to have a Tarot Card reading. Her last reading had been over three years ago when Josie had dragged her and Linka to a Psychic Fair. She would probably just get the usual assurances of good fortune, upcoming changes, and the appearance of a new man in her life. Vaguely specific and specifically vague, but nothing of value. It wasn't that she discounted readings completely, just that she didn't take them seriously. She had been told on several occasions she was 'hard to read', whatever that meant. What had amused her were the dogged attempts by those psychics to blanket their difficulty in reading her with vague predictions or just plain fabrications. She knew many were fakes because she had tested them. She'd offered incorrect information and asked bogus questions just to trip them up. Only twice had she been caught at her game, admonished, and then received what she considered applicable and valid information regarding her artwork. However, not one had said anything about her love life. Maybe Linka was right and she was meant to live alone. The thought that her initial infatuation with Linka's father would prove to be her only relationship put a grimace on her face. What the heck. She was in the mood for some fun.

As if reading her mind, the Reader, who had been watching her surreptitiously, smiled and waved her over.

Impulsively Tannis grabbed her purse and went over to her table. "Hi, are you expecting a client?"

"No. I wasn't scheduled to read today but my guides told me to come. I didn't know why, until I saw your aura. It's you I'm waiting for. Please, sit down. I'm Laura," she said as she moved her cup of herbal tea off to the side.

Oh brother. Spirit guides, no less. Maybe this wasn't such a good idea. Tannis unconsciously pulled in her aura and after a moment's hesitation, sat down. Too late now. She willed her face to go blank, and waited for the games to begin.

"What's your name?" Laura asked.

"Tannis, Tannis MacCrae."

"Hmmm." Laura reached down, and after rummaging in her needle-point bag, pulled a tape from its depths. She wrote the date and Tannis' name on the label before she slipped the tape into a small cassette player beside her. Tannis was somewhat reassured by the cassette. According to Josie, a taped reading usually indicated a credible reading.

"You're familiar with how this works, aren't you?" Laura asked. Without waiting for a reply she reached for the Tarot Cards. Her hand resting on the deck, she stopped suddenly and gazed into space. Then she made a small surprised sound and put the Tarot deck off to the side. "My guides tell me I must channel. They are most insistent. I already feel a whole block of information waiting. A moment please."

Bemused by this unexpected opening, Tannis watched intently as Laura closed her heavy-lidded eyes, inhaled deeply, then exhaled slowly. She repeated this process several times, then with her eyes still closed, reached for and pressed the record button on the tape deck.

"Yes. We have you found," she said, and took another slow, deep breath. After a short pause she began to speak, her voice slightly deeper and huskier than before. "Named after the Lady of Lianarth, renowned throughout the western region of Wales in the late 1400s. Tannis is a version of her name, Taenacea."

Tannis sensed a subtle shift in Laura during the silence that followed, and watched in fascination as she seemed to settle more deeply into some invisible place.

"You have the look of her. Hair to the ground and marked with wings of silver along each temple. When she draws on her powers, her wings are infused with magic. You are more familiar with her than you realize."

Tannis leaned forward with interest. This was not at all what she had expected. Her father had told her of her legendary namesake when she was a child. Lordy, that was so long ago she had almost forgotten. She assumed her namesake was just another mythical pagan deity, birthed from the imaginative yearnings of a mystic people. Until his death fourteen years ago, her father had recited countless tales of magical deeds performed by legendary figures dredged from Celtic lore, her namesake's among them. A historian, his specialty, the Druid's influence on Celtic Mythology, had inspired many of her early fantasy sculptures of wizards and goddesses.

Memories of her father softened her face. "Just before I was born, my father went to England and Wales to compile data for his book on Druid Sorcery." She had no idea why she was telling Laura this, but caught in a flood of memories, continued. "What was unique about his theory was that he believed the Druids, thought to be extinct in medieval days, were still active in remote areas. Contrary to mainstream historic belief, he also believed that many of the Druids were women. The story of Taenacea, the Lady of Lianarth must have impacted him in some way since he insisted I be named after her. He referred to her as a benevolent Sorceress and believed she, as well as many others branded as witches, were really practicing Druids."

Laura continued, her delivery slow and deliberate, as if Tannis had not spoken at all. The pauses between each statement grew longer, as if they were pulled with difficulty from a great distance.

"You know her well, yet she is hidden. Your connection to her will bridge time, by her own hand. It is no accident you bear silver wings as she does, for there is a Plain of Silver connection between you. Your dream is a memory which grows stronger. It is the face of your beloved you see. Destiny binds you together. The memory of a great love is awakening. Cycles of three hold meaning for you both."

Laura's pace slowed even more. She spoke with considerable effort, as if she could barely get the words out. "The dream is the doorway. Magic will take you through it and bring you the elements you need. Trust what your own hands call into being through your heart. The cycle begun seeks completion. Your souls are entwined. Water and dust will give him life. There are 12 strands of memory between you. You must bind them to you. Each must be incorporated into his image. What is left undone seeks completion. A girl child connects ancient memories and holds the key of three. There are layers to your Quest and this girl child is an important link. When the first strand is in place what you set in motion will realize its own fulfillment ... and your fulfillment."

Laura blinked rapidly as if to clear her vision and blindly reached for her cup of cold tea and took a sip. She looked dazed as she clicked off the cassette and coughed several times. Then she handed Tannis the tape. "Let me know how things work out." Her voice trailed off, as if she was not quite certain what had transpired herself. The Reading was over.

Tannis couldn't believe what she had heard. It was so ... strange, and not at all what she had expected. Not one statement applied to her life, except for the reference to her dreams. The rest of it was ... well, just plain weird, like a segment of the Twilight Zone.

"Here's the number of an old professor of mine at the University who's quite the expert on folklore, particularly from that era. I suggest you contact him." Laura said, the dazed look gone, replaced with clear eyes and a sweet smile.

Tannis' eyes widened and her mouth opened slightly. Lordy, she actually expected her to pursue this strange Quest. The tinkle of door chimes and fresh citrus scent wafting her way announced Linka's arrival and cut short her incredulous retort. Actually, she had no idea what she would have said. She quickly stuffed the tape into her handbag and greeted Linka with what she hoped was a normal smile.

"Wow, the bone-cracker sure did a number on me. See, no kinks." Linka rotated her head and gyrated her body to prove her point. Then she noticed the poster and the gal sitting across the table from her mother. "Did you have a reading?" she asked, piqued by this unexpected diversion.

"Just finished," Tannis said as she rose and smiled at Laura politely. "Thank you. It was ... interesting."

Linka looked from one to the other. Something was going on here. Not only could she feel it, but her mother had used that word—interesting. She didn't want to miss out on what she figured must have been a whammy reading judging by the stunned look on her mother's face. "Oh, can I have one too?" she asked impulsively.

Laura nodded as she handed Tannis a business card. "I wrote the Professor's name and home number on the back. It's best to call him in the evening." Then she smiled at Linka, "Yes I can read you. Sit down and relax while I get a glass of water to clear my aura."

As soon as the kitchen doors swung closed behind her, Linka leaned towards Tannis and whispered, "Choice! See what an adventure we're having. Out of the blue I pick a cafe with a Tarot Card Reader. 'Fess up. What did she say? Water to clear her aura? What does that mean?"

"Psychic cleansing I guess. She probably ..." Tannis stopped mid-sentence as Linka turned away and tossed her jacket over her own at their table, looked around the cafe, then plunked herself down on the chair just as Laura returned. Fishing another twenty out of her wallet, Tannis placed it on the table. "My treat. Enjoy!" As she walked away, she heard Laura ask Linka to focus on her questions while she shuffled the Tarot cards.

Tannis raised her empty cup when the proprietor appeared with a fresh pot of coffee. As she sipped the scalding liquid, she replayed her reading. Well. As much as she wanted to brush the whole thing off as implausible, according to Josie, channeled information usually came from a source relatively untainted by the reader's own biases. She had never heard anything quite so cryptic before, and that intrigued her. The challenge was in deciphering the meaning. Since she had to wait for Linka anyhow she would play with word associations and see where it led.

The statement 'water and dust will give him life' came to mind and immediately the word 'clay' popped into her head. Literally speaking, water and dust, loosely interpreted as dry dirt, creates mud, not much of a foundation for life. But symbolically, perhaps it wasn't so far off. She sculpted in clay, which was basically a type of mud combined with silicates and other additives, processed to produce a workable consistency. If she were to build a sculpture of her dream man in clay, she would, in effect, bring his image to life. Interpreted this way, the statement made a strange kind of sense, which pleased her, but raised other questions.

Her memory of him was more sensory than visual. How could she duplicate him from what she sensed he looked like? Would she need to have more dreams to duplicate his features which she had never really seen clearly? She was good at likenesses when working from pictures, but was a similarity enough, or would she need an exact representation? Based on her sense of what he looked like now, would she not just be making his appearance up to fulfill her own desire of what she wanted him to look like? And would his face be enough, or would she have to sculpt his whole body in order to bring him to life? And how was that supposed to happen, providing she could find these mysterious strands, and providing she was delusional enough to even try. Was he not was just an image in her dreams?

What were these strands anyhow? Events, emotions, or ... what? Although the reference to magic discomforted her, her mind again raced over what she'd been told. The girl child had to be Linka. If so, and if she did decide to pursue this Quest, she had no intention of involving her daughter. Such an undertaking would be precarious enough without sharing it with a 'space cadet'. Lord love her, but that's what she was. Bad enough she was considering pursuing this herself. Although she was intrigued by the metaphysical and accepted the paranormal as just another unknown aspect of reality, this was too much. What grown woman conjures up a dream man with clay and magic? It smacked of voodoo.

Visions of herself murmuring spells over a caldron prompted an involuntary giggle which attracted the attention of the other patrons. Even Laura glanced over at her. Caught in her mental imagery, Tannis didn't notice.

She could just see it; telling Linka about the Quest and asking her to help so she, the incarnate of an ancient Welsh Sorceress, could find 12 memory strands and incorporate them into a sculpture of a dream man she would bring to life with magic. Meet your new father, sweetie. He's from the past, but oh well, a good man is hard to find these days. Of course, she had absolutely no proof that this Taenacea, or her dream man had ever actually existed. Even if they had, the thought of reliving a dead woman's great love seemed a weak substitute for experiencing her own.

The trouble was, Linka would jump at the chance of embarking on such a bizarre adventure. Better to say nothing about her reading or the little nag would pester her until she did just what she had imagined herself doing just now. She'd best put it out of her mind. She glanced over just as Linka rose and unladylike growls from her stomach reminded her she was hungry. Some hot, spicy Indian food might just burn away her foolish thoughts. Expecting a word-for-word account of her reading, Tannis was surprised when Linka said only that her reading was in line with what was going on, with the exception of one glaringly inaccurate statement. Tannis knew better than to pry when nothing was forthcoming from her little Scorpio/Sagittarius. Generally she got much more than she wanted to know.

Over lunch, an adventure in cuisine featuring curried Eggs Benedict for her and a fiery carrot/curry soup that added luster to Linka's dark eyes, they covered a wide spectrum of topics—Linka's discarded suitors, when Josie would be back in town, Tannis' completed murals, Linka's submission for a photography re-touching competition, and the antics of the cats.

Although amused by her mother's feline updates, Linka thought her obsessed with her cats. It was the only quirk that marred her perfection, that and the odd unexpected vulgarity. Ever since she could remember she had been the mainstay of her life. Always supportive, her mother's belief that talent emerges through opportunity had allowed her to try just about anything that struck her fancy during her growing years. She realized now just how allowing her mother had been, for she had wanted to try every-thing. Linka also thought her gypsy-like beauty was worthy of gracing the cover of any glamour magazine. The sudden appearance of silver streaks along her temples when she turned thirty had startled both of them at first. When attempts to color the streaks failed, a mystery to both her mother and the salon who repeatedly applied color to no avail, she had pragmatically accepted this eye-catching addition and made no further attempt to color her hair, even when the streaks deepened into two wide bands of shimmering silver. Linka couldn't imagine her mom without them now. It made her look so exotic. Wiping a hot-food tear from the corner of her eye, she said, "I need your input on something, mom. You know that computerized system I told you about? What do you think about me getting it?"

"It's your decision, sweetie." Tannis preferred to stay neutral on the subject. Not all of Linka's brainstorms, of which there were many, reached fruition.

"It's a lot of money to invest right now. If I buy the equipment and software, which costs an arm and a leg, I clean out my savings and don't have a cushion in case I have a slow period, or something unexpected happens," she added.

"True. But this investment is in yourself." Linka was frugal with her money, in stark contrast to her flippant attitude towards life in general. Tannis knew this was a big decision for her, investing in a computerized retouching system, the cutting-edge in technology in her field. "What are the benefits? Would having the system save time, enhance the quality of your work and increase productivity?"

"For sure. Shelby's got one at his studio and says you can do stuff with it I can't even imagine right now—in half the time. My problem is ..." A frown creased her forehead as she gulped down her glass of water. "I just don't know if I have the patience to learn how to use the damn thing! I'm used to my light table and can just zip through my work in auto-pilot. I don't know if I can even learn such a complicated program."

"Of course you can." Sensing Linka had made her decision and just needed reassurance, she added, "To develop the skills of our trade we have to stretch ourselves. There's nothing wrong with your patience either. Look at the detail work you already do. Remember when I decided to do my own firing and built my kiln? I was unsure too, and a bit intimidated. I had to learn all about kilns, cones, temperature control, each a craft in itself. I was as comfortable as you are now just sculpting and letting others handle the firing end of things. But I'm glad I took the plunge and learned how to fire my work myself. Now I don't have to worry about breakage during transport, and I also have more control of the results. Building the kiln set me back too if you remember."

"I see what you're saying." Linka's eyes lit up, inspired by a new vision of herself completely proficient, her fingers whizzing over a keyboard as she manipulated a photograph on her large new computer screen.

"In light of your skill with just a brush, you'll be a wonder with this new technology. Consider it a tool. The talent is yours. You'll just have a new way of applying it. As a matter of fact, I have given it some thought and would be willing to lend you the money if you do decide to buy the system, at zero interest. Not as a favor, rather an investment in you and your business. Personally, I think it would give you a definite edge in the marketplace. Let me know what you decide." Her offer set a merry tone for their meandering through the shops along the street.

By late afternoon they were just ready to call it quits when Linka spotted a little bookstore called Knowings. Its fusty interior offered a wide range of spiritual and metaphysical books and related paraphernalia. While Linka scrutinized the display cases in hopes of finding a small gift for her friend Niki among the crystals, amulets and other psychic toys, Tannis wandered the back regions of the store. She had often accompanied her father on his hunt for obscure titles in similar small shops. She scanned the Esoteric titles for one that would jump out at her. That's usually how she found the most interesting books. As she scanned a half empty shelf, her eyes were drawn towards a thick leather-bound book lying flat on the shelf by itself instead of upright with those clustered at one end. She could have sworn the book hadn't been there during her first quick look. Curious, she was just about to reach for it when she felt something soft bump against her back. "Oh, sorry. I didn't realize anyone was behind me," she said automatically as she turned.

"Och aye, whell ... yea be seeing into yerself," breathed a lyrical voice.

Tannis had to adjust her eyes downward to meet those that twinkled back at her, and nearly laughed outright. Before her stood a plump little woman shrouded in a dark woolen mantle that reached right down to the floor. The woman was so short she looked more like a child wrapped in her mother's cape than an adult.

"It be the book of Sorcery, lovely," she sang. "Only those of the faith be seein' it." After a moment of intense scrutiny she breathed with what sounded like satisfaction. "Aye, yea be her. Questing are yea? 'Tis time."

Tannis was so taken back by this little personage her words barely registered. She smiled at what she thought was obviously a case of mistaken identity. About to point this out, her smile faded as a roar rushed through her ears and her head began to swim with a sudden assault of images, sounds and sensations; an old crone of diminutive stature whispering incantations, the tang of freshly cut herbs, the comfort of a man's protective arms around her, fingers of lightening from dark malevolent clouds, the grating clash of steel, the soft fuzz on a baby's head, a doe's liquid eyes, and the spine-chilling wail from a thousand throats suddenly silenced by a heavy shroud of mist.

A jerk shot through to the base of her spine, and it was over. Shaken, she stood facing the shelf and stared at emptiness where the old book had lain. Confused, her head still spinning with the images and impressions, she looked around blankly. She could have sworn she was facing the other way when the woman had addressed her. What was happening here? She heard the lyrical voice speak again but in a whisper, as if from a great distance. "'Tis the making of yer heart's wish." Then she felt something thrust into her arms. Tannis looked down at the package she now held. The bag of candles she had purchased earlier still hung from the hand that also held her purse and now clasped the package tight against her chest. There had to be some mistake. About to protest, she realized the little woman had vanished. She walked to the end of the aisle, peered down the next, and the next. But the little woman was nowhere to be seen. In fact, after quickly walking through the whole store, she saw only Linka and a little man fingering a crystal at the front counter, assuring the patient clerk that this was the crystal he resonated with and would purchase.

Her surroundings looked and felt unreal as if she was somehow disconnected from what she viewed. As if from afar she watched herself brush past Linka and rush out the door. Outside she gulped the damp air as she looked up and down the street. But she saw no one that even remotely resembled the little woman. Feeling a need to ground herself with something concrete she leaned against an antique lamp post and drew a few even deep breaths, reassured by the weight of the package which proved she hadn't imagined all this. The dizziness was gone, but she still felt oddly lightheaded.

"Hey, what's the matter? Are you OK? You flew outta there like a demon," Linka's concerned voice broke through her daze.

"Sorry. Oh, yeah. I just feel a little ... dizzy."

Linka scanned her face, noting her pallor. Her sculpting frenzy these past few weeks had definitely caught up with her, she reasoned. She must be exhausted. It wasn't unusual for her to work around the clock with only the occasional one or two hour snooze to rejuvenate herself while on a 'hot streak'. Then she saw the thick parcel. "What's that? I didn't see you buy anything," she said accusingly.

"I didn't. A lady gave it to me. Look, I know this sounds crazy, but the strangest little woman bumped into me, babbled something in a thick accent, handed me this parcel, then disappeared." She wasn't going to say anything about the jumbled images and sensations she'd experienced. In fact, she wasn't even sure it had really happened.

"No way!" Linka's eyes danced. "What is it? Come on, open it."

Tannis pulled the package tight against her body. "Not now. Come on, let's go. I'm obviously more pooped than I realize, sweetie." But she knew the parcel was meant for her. It felt heavy like a book and she suspected she knew which book, but not what it was or why it was given to her. The other thing she was certain of was that she'd had enough excitement for one day and was ready for her Saturday night ritual; a chilled glass of wine, soft music, and a long hot soak in her Jacuzzi.

Chapter Two

OLLING IN THE FROTHY SILKINESS of honey almond scented bubbles, Tannis sighed in contentment as she traced lazy circles on her raised knee. Zoie paced along the tiled edge of the deep sunken tub and batted at the popping bubbles, while the boys watched from their favorite spots. Soothing chords of Celtic Harp drifted through the bathroom door and half a dozen candles placed around the wide tiled shelf that framed the tub sputtered and flickered with the restless currents set in motion by Zoie.

Ah, this was the next best thing to an orgasm, Tannis thought as she carefully reached for her glass of wine. She savored the coolness as it slipped down her throat. As the tautness in her shoulders and upper arms unfurled with the heat of the aromatic water, she let her mind drift to the events of the day. Random words and images flashed through her mind in a swirl of sensations, and left a definite quickening deep inside her belly. She'd felt the same excitement while she replayed the tape of her reading earlier. Laura's words were now imprinted on her brain.

"But what does it all mean?" she asked out loud, as if her bathroom companions were privy to her thoughts. "O.K.," she continued, "Let's reason this through step by step. Fact: you have been dreaming about one particular man for months. You were told today he is your soulmate, and that you could bring him to life via water and dust by some undisclosed magical means. Speculation: you are the incarnate of a Welsh Sorceress and this dream man of yours was also her true love in that life. Fact: You'd like him to be real. Speculation: this will be the only man you will love, so if you don't pursue this Quest, you'll be alone for the rest of your life. Fact: That thought is making your uterus shrivel in protest."

She ignored the feline stares and took a small sip of wine. They were used to her voicing her thoughts. "Fact: were you to pursue this, your mission would be to connect 12 strands of memory from that life by experiencing them in some way. But apparently not alone. Your daughter is somehow involved, and holds three important keys to the puzzle. Damn.

21

Fact: you're obviously intrigued by this Quest and already thinking of ways to extract what you need from her without involving her directly. Speculation: the book you have yet to look at will hold the key to the magic you'll need." She immediately knew this was true, and continued, more animated now. "Fact: you have no idea how you know this, but you do. Speculation: you, rather me, Tannis MacCrae, apparently has the means to conjure up a flesh and blood man from a dream, and somehow zap him from the 1400s to the late 1900s. Fact: you are completely off your rocker lady, but ... if there's even a remote possibility it can be done, well ..."

So much for reasoning this through, Tannis thought. It still sounded bizarre. She suspected she was already hooked, for the most prevalent of her conflicting feelings was the rising excitement of a seemingly impossible challenge. "First things first," she admonished out loud. "One. Find out if this Taenacea actually existed. Two, call the professor, and three, check your father's notes. If you don't get confirmation from either source, it's probably just your imagination. If so, enjoy your dreams. You could do worse than a phantom lover, considering some women have no man ... and no erotic dreams either."

The issue was settled. She now had a plan of action. Boxes of her father's research notes were stacked in the basement and among them were bound to be references to her Welsh namesake, since he'd referred to her in his book. She'd look through them later in the week. As for the parcel, she'd check that out after her bath. Although the bookcases throughout her home were crammed with all manner of unusual first editions and oddities, most inherited from her scholarly father, she had a sneaking suspicion this book would not join them. She sensed it was directly related to today's experience. In the meantime, there was some serious, mindless, lazin' in the tub to be done. And since her uterus was probably going to shrivel anyhow, she might as well let the rest of her body follow suit.

She awoke with a start and glanced at the grandfather clock across the room through hazy eyes. Two-forty a.m. The heavy book slid from her lap as she sat up and extracted her legs from under a mass of furry bodies.

One of the French doors that led to her secluded deck was open and she shivered as a blast of damp cold air raised goose bumps on her bare arms. While she threw on her baggy sweater she did a quick body-count. Just as she had suspected. Zoie, immune to anything but her own will, had taken advantage of the open door and slipped out to unleash her nasty disposition on the neighborhood cats. The boys had learned not to cross her on the one firm rule of the house; positively no cats out at night. But not Zoie.

Tannis called for her as she walked around the deck and breathed in the moist night air. As she peered along the shadowy shrubs, she pondered the contents of the book she had been reading all evening. As soon as she unwrapped the parcel she recognized the book as the one she had briefly glimpsed in the book store. It was hand-bound, and very old. What caught her off-guard was a sense of familiarity, as if she had held it before, many times. She could see her own hands open the brittle leather cover, a cover still veined with faint traces of gold-leafing around the embossed title, *Magik Incantations and Potions*, barely legible now. She sensed other hands, yet her hands, leafing through it impatiently as if in search of a particular cure or spell.

The fine and regular calligraphy was not difficult to read once she made the mental adjustment to archaic English. She had poured over many such scripts alongside her father. Each page began with a scrolled title, like *Removal of Tumors of the Skin* beside an ornate square containing a baroque Celtic symbol. Below were specific instructions for the preparation of the ingredients and application of the remedy, along with the required spells. From what she had read so far, adding a few items to her already considerable stock of dried herbs would enable her to cure many of these afflictions. Although she didn't recognize some of the Latin names, she knew the book was a herbalist's gold mine, for each potion included precise measurements and detailed preparation instructions.

A poignant rush of warm memories enveloped her, of her childhood Irish nanny. Concerned over his wife's failing health and inability to cope with the demands of caring for an active toddler, her father had hired the middle-aged Maureen as a live-in housekeeper. With no family of her own, she had cared for her charges with a proprietary no-nonsense efficient humor. It was Maureen who had taught her to grow herbs and doctor common ailments with natural remedies instead of drugs, a practice she still adhered to. Maureen had also infused stability and liveliness into a house hushed by her mother's unpredictable moods and her father's distracted scholarly pursuits.

Tannis had only been three when her mother's nervous condition could no longer be ignored, and fourteen when she had died of a brain tumor.

Always high-strung, the pressure of its slow growth had intensified her debilitating spells. As close as she was to her father, it was Maureen who had mothered her as a child and steered her through her turbulent teenage years with a firm but loving hand. She'd been devastated by Maureen's sudden death from a stroke just days before her own wedding and considered it an ill omen, one which had proved correct. The marriage had been over within the year. Maureen, however, was still with her. Clay pots on window sills and the whiff of herbs always brought her to mind.

She suspected Maureen's Celtic heart would not discount the medicinal merit of dew from a spider's web picked at the stroke of midnight under a full moon. In surprise, she realized that much like her mentor, all she needed was a big black cauldron and whisk broom in order to hang a witch's shingle outside her door. She had everything else; the herbal concoctions and her feline elemental, four of them in fact. With this comical image, her calls for Zoie lost their edge and within moments a blotchy form streaked past her into the house.

She didn't go in right away. She wrapped her arms around herself as the magic of the night cloaked her in its mysterious shroud. Witchcraft permeated her very surroundings; the eerie shape-shifting of gently moving foliage from which ghostly faces seemed to peer; wisps of cloud that drifted across the moon, changing its face from benevolent to malevolent and back again in rhythmic repetition; and the faint undefined whispers of the night.

She felt a shiver run through her. Could desire alone create a manifestation of the magnitude she was facing? Or was it the beginning of a psychosis fueled by unfulfilled yearnings and unmet expectations—like her mother's. That disturbing thought always lay in the recesses of her mind. Did she have a genetic pre-disposition for instability? Nevertheless the tumor had almost been a blessing. Her mother had left this world through a medically sanctioned cause rather than the 50s stigma of a mental disorder. Still, it worried her at those times when she felt undecided, or out of control.

"No" intoned a voice in her head, but a voice which was not her own. She stood perfectly still, wondering if she had progressed to hearing voices. But she heard nothing more, just the sound of her own breathing. After a time she went inside.

When she reached down in front of the couch to pick up the fallen book she noticed a small piece of parchment lying underneath it. One side was blank, but what looked like a signature was scripted on the other side. The ink was so faded she had to squint and hold it close to the light in order to decipher the faded scrawl. It looked like LAGOHAIRE, and was preceded by several letters so faint, they could have been a D, or a U or even a V, and then either a broad M or two Ns or Us. She mouthed the possibilities ... Dum (that fit), Duum, Dvm (no, duds for sure), or Dunn. Dunn Lagohaire. That sounded right, much like a Welsh or Celtic name. Since both the D and L were capitalized, she thought the word could denote a titled surname, or geographic location. She would ask that professor when she called him.

A rush of longing washed through her, then faded as quickly as it had appeared. For a brief instant the name had struck a chord in her mind. The book was definitely scripted by a healing woman, which was unusual since not many people could write in those days. But she didn't believe the name on the parchment was that of the book's author for some reason. She fingered the edge of the parchment and instantly felt a sudden painful wrench pull at her fingers, a tug so strong she looked up expecting to see someone holding the larger portion of the torn parchment.

Now how did she know the parchment had been wrenched from her hands? And by whom? She had definitely experienced a powerful pull along the entire length of her arm, for it had left her with a slight ache in her arm. A cold knot of fear settled in her stomach. Quickly she inserted the slip of paper into the front of the book and put it on the coffee table. Willing her mind to go blank she doused the lights and headed for the bedroom.

Enough was enough. There were moments when Scarlett O'Hara's words made perfect sense. 'I don't want to think about it now, I'll think about it tomorrow'. What she needed was a deep, dreamless sleep, not weird sensations induced by fatigue and an overactive imagination. She remembered to mute the ringer on the phone and glanced out her bedroom window. Dawn had already begun to spread its pearly glow over the night sky. She was relieved that Sunday, already here, held no commitments. It was going to be a sleep-in day for sure, which she loudly announced to the felines already stretched over the bed's surface. "May a thousand fleas infest your coats if you dare wake me before noon!" She deftly maneuvered herself under the eiderdown and after a few minor comfort adjustments by everyone, all was still.

* * *

The mist swirled around her like cold fingers grasping and clutching at her cloak, seeking a path to the marrow of her bones. She stood pressed against the Tower as the wind howled around her and whipped her hair from beneath the deep hood that did little to protect her icy cheeks and watery eyes. So long... She had been waiting so long her blood had slowed to a sluggish trickle. In spite of the storm she had come with the signed Writ which would end her torment. She moved her stiffened fingers painfully, assured that the parchment was still cemented to the hand that clutched it in desperation.

"Where are you?" she screamed into the inferno. Tears of frustration froze to her cheeks as quickly as they fell. Her quivering limbs barely held her upright as gust after gust pounded her against the wall. And she felt faint. A dangerous lightness had crept through her, a lightness that could easily send her over the low wall and dash her onto the boulders two hundred feet below.

An ancient stalwart that rose from the western cliffs of her lands, the Tower of Aberayron had withstood the furies of countless storms that rolled in from the Irish Sea. But the vicious onslaught of this day's storm shook even these stoic walls. She had to hang on somehow. She bit down on her blue and stiff lips so the pain would keep her grounded. But still the lightness grew within her.

She barely heard her protest above the gathering vortex that threatened to pluck her from her precarious perch, just as a form emerged from around the side of the Tower, a man whose shape she knew. She should have felt relief, instead, after a moment of blackness, she heard herself scream. Before she could grasp what had happened, there was nothing but a bright light in her eyes, a crushing weight on her chest, and a bloodcurdling howl as she felt herself falling, falling, falling ...

* * *

Tannis' eyes flew open and she stared into a pair of green eyes round with panic, framed by a mass of gray; each hair standing on end as if an electric current had run up its length. All eighteen pounds of Mr. Muff were braced with stiff legs on her chest.

In a panic, she sent him flying off the bed as she sat up with a start. Her heart thudding, she glanced around to get her bearings, then ran her tongue over her rigid lips. She felt what seemed to be a blood blister on her lower lip, one whose origin she didn't even want to consider until she'd consumed at least one cup of very hot, very strong coffee. The digital clock told her she'd had about four hours of sleep.

She quelled the desire to bury her shivering body under the warmth of the quilt and quickly jumped up and put on her warm terry robe. Coffee would steady her jangled nerves; coffee spiked with a measure of the 12-year-old Scotch tucked away for emergencies. This definitely qualified as an emergency. Intent on scooping heaps of grounds into the filter with stiffened fingers she never noticed the agitation of her cats, or how they gave her a wide berth. Not one pestered her for breakfast as they usually did. In fact, suddenly not a cat was anywhere in sight.

After several scalding cups of her self-prescribed tonic, Tannis began to feel better. A hearty breakfast of scrambled eggs and toasted crumpets had also helped to bring back both her body warmth and comfort level. She leaned back in her favorite deck chair and looked around, determined to blot out her horrific dream.

The overhang of roof that covered half her deck enabled her to enjoy the outdoors regardless of season. On her right, the large studio she had designed herself when she renovated the house ten years ago boasted large windows alongside French doors that stood open, weather permitting. Her greenhouse was built against the back wall of this studio addition. Almost half of the left side of the large deck was walled with white lattice through which twined the strong stems of climbing rose bushes. Within the next few months the stalks and lattice would disappear under lush foliage and the delicate pinks of her Dr. Van Fleet and everblooming New Dawn English climbers. Large terra-cotta pots spaced along the perimeter of the deck would hold the various herbs she used for cooking and medicinal purposes.

The backyard of her large double lot was ringed with flowering shrubs and trees. Right now the barren soil in her flower beds hid the stalks of flowering perennials dispersed between low shrubbery. Starting with the emergence of spring bulbs, her yard would display an endless wave of changing color and design as each plant bloomed for its allotted life span. Tending her outdoor sanctuary was both a therapeutic delight and elemental expression of her creativity. Here she felt centered and here she could think with clarity.

And think she must, for what had started as a few loosely linked random events had taken on a life of its own. Everything was connected; the dreams, her reading, the Magik book, and the parchment tucked inside. It was this last dream which led to this conviction. Without a doubt, the man she had so briefly seen at the tower before her sense of confusion was also the man of her dreams. Suddenly she also knew it was his name written on the slip of parchment. No matter how she tried to shrug it off as coincidence or wishful thinking, she knew it with certainty.

A connection of some kind had been made when she handled the parchment, which had led directly to the dream, if it was a dream. For there was no logical explanation for the blood blister and cut on her bottom lip, which still felt puffed and tender even now. No matter how vivid your dreams, you do not wake up with real abrasions on your body. Maybe there was such a thing as time travel ... a corridor you could slip through under the right conditions; for that's how real the experience had been. Her feelings and memories of the dream were as crystal clear as yesterday's outing with Linka. And her blistered lip was very real, proof of some inexplicable experience. Her dreams had never before intersected her waking life in this way.

The memory of this last experience had not faded as did even her most intense dreams. She could instantly re-experience the event; the bone-chilling cold of the wind and her intense despair. Shivering at the memory she noticed that incoming clouds, heavy with at least one imminent shower, had already obscured the weak morning sun. She rose reluctantly and went inside. She would browse through the rest of the Magik book. She had only read through the first part last night, absorbed by the quaint and often horrifying maladies and cures of a more barbaric time. The writing, although legible, was cramped as if each parchment sheet was priceless. She waited for the last of the felines to respond to her calls, then closed the patio doors just as the first warning drops of rain splattered on the deck. The gloom outside set a perfect tone for an afternoon of witchery.

Tannis threw a few more logs on the dying embers in the fireplace and snuggled back under her fuzzy blanket. The lamp beside her cast lengthening shadows across the room and the deep resonant chimes of the grandfather clock confirmed evening was approaching. Resting her head against the deep plush back of the couch she drifted through the images of magic triggered by what she'd read. Spells for desires and curses, wishes and purpose all filled the second section of the book. Spells to attract and repel love were interspersed with specifics like ensuring the gender of a child and the most ancient of controversies; the removal of an unwanted seed from the womb of a compromised maiden.

Her mind twined around images of furtive forms that crept to the hovel of the local Wicca in the dead of night. Heads bent in secrecy, whispered yearnings would be exchanged for spells and paid for with whatever paltry means were available. Sometimes the price was high, but it was always paid. These, and herbal cures for physical ailments were the more harmless contents of this section. It was the contents of the third section which both disturbed and excited her. Here were incantations for experiences beyond her imagining; transforming of matter, shape-shifting, influencing dreams, illusions encompassing the sublime to the ridiculous, and lastly, methods to traverse the corridors of time in all its possible variations. What caught her attention in particular was the placement of objects into another time. If it was possible to do so, then someone could have planted these dreams in her mind and sent her the book from another time. If so, could it have been this Taenacea?

All this and more was possible according to the Magik Book. What had struck her right away was the 'Cautions' scripted at the bottom of these spells read suspiciously like warnings based on personal experience. According to what was written, people from different time frames could link with each other and even travel back and forth between their perspective time frames. But apparently, only if they shared a soul connection. She paused, uncertain if she wanted to follow this train of thought. It would imply she was possibly linked by such a connection to this Sorceress. And if so, this could be the beginning of a drama that would, with her willing participation, lead to its own undetermined conclusion. Maybe that's what Laura had meant; once begun, which it now might be, there was no stopping it. Perhaps she had already subconsciously agreed to participate. She must have, or why this morning's disturbing dream? The big question simmering in her mind was, who was orchestrating this drama, and why? Someone outside of herself, an aspect of herself in another life in order to rewrite their own destiny and balance karma, or herself, reaching into an illusionary past to fill a current void?

None of the options reassured her. If it was the first or second, she didn't like the idea of being manipulated by some Wicca Sorceress from the wilds of ancient Wales. She preferred to control her own actions and destiny. Besides, she knew nothing of this person's character or motives. All she knew about her was that the 'Cautions' implied some sense of personal integrity, speculation at best. But the thought of it being the latter was even more uncomfortable. It would mean she'd join the ranks of women with lowered expectations who grasped any mediocre relationship available to them. No thanks. She'd rather be alone than settle for less than she desired, or deserved. Her sudden obsession with relationship and being alone was discomforting. Two days ago she'd been perfectly content with her life and hadn't given it a thought. Now it was foremost on her mind.

To distract herself she opened the book again, intent on scrutinizing it from an artistic perspective. It was in superb condition. Then she noticed the first two pages were stuck together, intentionally it seemed, by tiny blobs of wax along the edges. Carefully she pulled the pages apart and read the inscription on the right hand side. At first she thought it was a poem, but after reading it through several times, it sounded more like a personal mantra, or a prayer.

> '*I arise today*
> *Through the strength of Heaven,*
> *Light of Sun,*
> *Radiance of Moon,*
> *Splendor of Fire,*
> *Speed of Lightning,*
> *Swiftness of Wind,*
> *Depth of Sea,*
> *Stability of Earth,*
> *Firmness of Rock.*'

Powerful and moving, it sounded like a personal ode to nature. As she mouthed the prayer, she got a sudden image of a woman in a long cloak, standing on the crest of a hill at early dawn. Her arms were raised in wide embrace, as if marshaling the elemental energies she would require for the coming day. She was struck by a discomforting parallel. Weather permitting, she herself mouthed a silent prayer of thanks and anticipation out on her deck each morning, but without the dramatic gestures. Certainly nothing as ritualistic and profound as this. This was more like a tribute to the Goddess of Life, the Earth, and the universe itself.

Secretly she agreed with what pagans believed; the God energy was equally expressed as a female energy, the giver of life. What felt like ancient memories buried in her genes began to stir with her intuitive flashes. How very odd, yet at the same time, not unnatural. Her involuntary "Hmmm" caused a ripple through the mass of cats lying around her. Still sleepy, they began to sit up, stretch, and throw her expectant looks. It was dinner time, and she was hungry herself. It was time to bring herself back to the present. But after dinner she would call the Professor.

As they followed her into the kitchen, she remembered their reaction to her this morning. It was as if they had sensed something alien about her, which confirmed something odd had happened. They had vanished to other parts of the house and hadn't resurfaced until just about the time the residual effects of her awful experience had disappeared. They had then wandered back into the living room and curled up around her. All except for sensitive Mr. Muff whom she had scared to death when she sent him flying off the bed. He stayed curled up on the bed in the spare bedroom until just a while ago.

She made a mental note to start a separate journal in which to record her feelings and impressions of these events and accompanying visions. If she was losing her mind, a record of her delusional experiences would cut down on the therapy she would require. She could give the psychiatrist her journal, ask for his assessment, and save herself thousands of dollars.

Joking aside, she would record both the Prayer and her reading to give her a point of reference for any information the Professor might have on this Taenacea, The Lady of Lianarth. For she was obviously the catalyst for these experiences. Memory was unreliable and often faded or changed subtly with each recounting. Documented, her experiences, beginning with yesterday's Tarot reading, would be unsullied by the editing of time or rationalization. She was somewhat an expert in the latter. Once it was all recorded, she could put it out of her mind and spend the next few days finishing one of her three busts in progress. Although she could afford to take a few more days off, she sensed she needed to ground herself right now. There was nothing like manipulating over a hundred pounds of clay to keep you present in the physical.

Chapter Three

"**D**ONE," Tannis breathed as she rose from her sculpting stool and wiped her hands on the damp cloth beside her. She tossed it aside and sighed with satisfaction as she gently massaged her aching shoulders. Up at 5 a.m., only quick dashes to the bathroom and regular refills of her water jug had interrupted ten straight hours of work. She was pleased with the results. One of her three works-in-progress was now finished. After a final scrutiny tomorrow, the young boy's likeness would join the wall murals in her drying room.

She loved the state of 'other-beingness' that infused her when she worked; when her hands moved over the pliable clay in almost undirected precision with an intent all their own. The clay and her own hands, as if knowing what the piece was supposed to express even before she did, often overrode the image in her mind and directed the emerging shape in spite of her efforts to construct a predetermined pose. She had learned to allow this early in her career. For if she worked intuitively and coaxed the piece along with a running dialogue, the results were always better than she had first envisioned, especially when it came to facial expressions.

Who are you and where are you from? What are you thinking and how do you feel? These were questions she would ask mentally while she worked. To her each piece was alive, with a history leading to this one frozen moment. This process allowed her imagination to capture the signature essence of her work; a life-like expression and presence. With her diversity of subjects from all historic eras she called her pieces "A Montage of Peoples Through Time." With life studies such as this piece, she would scrutinize the photographs she worked from to capture the elemental essence she wanted her piece to express.

Zoie and Billy-Bob circled the piece then sniffed it and rubbed up against its damp surface. Unconcerned, Tannis shooed her critics away. The scattering of hair left stuck to the clay would burn out in the kiln or in the case of casting, be sponged off when she was finished. She draped her work with damp rags and sealed it in a large plastic bag. Since her current three pieces would be cast in bronze, she would keep them moist until they went to the foundry. While she wiped down her tools and cleaned her work bench, she thought of her upcoming visit with the professor.

Her call last night promised a most entertaining and hopefully enlightening evening. Professor Osmond Harcourt would be delighted to walk her through Celtic Folklore, and yes, he knew of this Lady of Lianarth and would gather what information he had in preparation for her visit. Tannis could barely suppress her laughter as his words tumbled out in a quaint undeniable accent, as if haste were imperative. She could picture him muttering to himself while he gathered stacks of reference books in preparation of their meeting. But that would be later. Right now she needed a rejuvenating power snooze, then a shower, and something to eat.

When she pulled up at the address Tannis was not surprised by the Tudor style house wedged between similar older homes near the University. Mature, overgrown shrubs pressed against its sides as if to shroud the scholarly pursuits within. She conjured up an image of the man who would greet her at the heavy oak door, a game she played with herself before meeting anyone new.

From his voice on the telephone, she pictured him slightly frumpy and short, with wisps of hair flying every which way. Spectacles would be perched atop a prominent nose. In her experience, most scholars had prominent noses, as if better to sniff out subtleties others had overlooked. A little pompous, he would bustle around his fusty library while he searched for references to confirm a point in the making. A historian had to have a fusty library, and the multi-paned windows of the exterior indicated the likelihood of an antique cluttered living room and library inside.

She was just about dead-on in her predictions, except for his nose. Rather than being large, it was very bulbous and red, implying an appreciation for spirits. Professor Harcourt welcomed her with the expected pompous solicitude and ushered her past a dimly lit antique cluttered drawing room into a library even more fusty and cluttered than she had imagined. She declined his polite offer of a glass of Port, and sat herself in the winged arm chair he indicated. He pulled a decanter of ruby liquid from behind one of the tottering stacks of books on his desk and filled his own half-empty glass. He turned and hastily assured her he only imbibed occasionally.

Not quite sure how to begin, Tannis said, "I appreciate you seeing me professor. I must admit, I feel a little foolish about this."

"My dear, it's never foolish to explore the richness of our heritage. My goodness, were it so, I would be 'out of business' so to speak." He chuckled. To put her at ease, he recounted a tale or two of the legendary figures who had impassioned him to choose medieval folklore as his specialty.

Tannis liked him immediately. Here was someone who took every tale and fable seriously no matter how obscure, and like her father, deftly wove them into the fabric of history. Before she knew it she was telling him not only about her namesake, the Reading and Magik Book but also about the visions she had experienced since. She didn't realize how it might sound to him until she was finished, and immediately qualified herself.

"Nothing like this has ever happened to me before. I admit I'm fascinated by the possibility, but common sense tells me to verify if she was a real person before I let myself get carried away by my imagination," she said with a nervous little laugh.

"Hmmm ... of course, of course. How interesting." After a distracted sip from his glass he asked. "Tell me, my dear, do you believe in reincarnation?"

In spite of his nonchalant tone, Tannis squirmed under his suddenly pointed gaze. Deciding on candor, she said, "Yes ... I do. I believe our soul is eternal, so it would make sense that we've lived before. I've never experienced it myself but a friend of mine has had several past-life regressions and is convinced they're authentic experiences."

"Yes, well, Hmmm. There have been several documented cases of legitimate reincarnational memories," the professor conceded. "But by experts, under hypnosis, and in controlled conditions. Of course, most *claims* of past-life memories are triggered by a sense of familiarity or fascination with a particular era or historic figure. A fabrication of the psyche. Since the majority of these claims cannot be authenticated, I consider their validity questionable. Yes, very questionable. However, a colleague of mine, a clinical psychologist and hypnotherapist, has researched and documented several genuine cases in his time. With no small historic assistance from myself I might add." As if to add stature to his statement, he pulled himself up to his full five foot five height.

Lost in the memory of those cases he fingered a button on his plaid vest abstractly until Tannis cleared her throat.

"Oh yes. Back to you, my dear. Just give me a ... It's here somewhere." He turned and shuffled through the piles of books and papers heaped on his enormous desk. "I've been working in that era ... as a matter of fact, it's a favorite period of mine. More towards the politics of the War of the Roses.

Fascinating, but nevertheless ... same time frame ..." His words trailed off as his pudgy fingers rifled through a heap of bulging files.

Content to watch, Tannis snuggled deeper into the softness of the shabby library chair. The professor's small murmurs and occasional drawn out 'Ahh' reminded her of her father; though he had been a tall distinguished looking man. She still missed the cozy evenings spent curled up in his library chair, not unlike this one, as he spun tales of magical deeds by legendary figures.

"Ahh! Here it is." The professor turned and beamed his pleasure. With a large cumbersome book and files in one arm, and a small glass of Port in the other, he settled in the chair opposite her. He ignored the rude protest from the cracked leather when he shifted his weight to place his glass on the little round table beside him. He referred to several marked pages in the book resting on his fat thighs, then closed his eyes for a moment as if to correlate his thoughts.

He peered at her intently for a moment and said, "If there were an actual picture of the Lady of Lianarth, she would look much like you. With longer hair of course as was the fashion of the day."

This was the second time she had heard a reference to a similarity in their appearance.

"Tales say her ebony curls trailed the ground when loosened." He scanned her figure quickly as if taking her measure. "She would have been shorter and fuller than you. About five foot six I would say, but considered extremely tall for the times. As you probably know people were shorter then, men being considered tall at five foot five. Even more so among the Welsh, whose racial stature leaned closer to the earth than sky." Chuckling at his clever analogy, he settled back in preparation for a lengthy discourse.

"Her lineage was Irish, you know. From the DunLagohair area southwest of Dublin. Her great-grandfather's arrival on Welsh shores is documented you know. A fascinating story in itself." He hesitated, deliberating if he should elaborate, but chose not to. "Bloodlines were somewhat obscured by linguistic differences," he whispered, as if sharing a delicious snippet of gossip. "Then too, there were the hostage situations. Some titled hostages were never claimed or returned and lived out their lives among their captors. In many cases they intermarried, polluting the bloodlines even more than they were. At any rate, many of the Irish, Scots, Welsh, and of course English, were of mixed blood. In fact, the English Tudor line was of Welsh origin."

"Was it?" Tannis had never been able to get the English royal line straight.

"Very important in this case. It was Henry V who granted her grandfather additional lands and immunity for his property in the early 1420s with a Writ exempting him from the standard royal call-to-arms. That's another story as well, a rather mysterious one at that. Although King Henry died two years later, of dysentery I believe it was, the Writ was upheld by successive sovereigns. And why, you may ask?" Without waiting for a cue he continued. "You see, his widow, Queen Catherine de Valois, had an affair with Owen Tudor, a Tudor courtier of Welsh descent. Although she married him after Henry's death, Owen Tudor did not become king, rather remained the Queen's Consort. Nevertheless, he obviously influenced her partiality to the titled Welsh. Catherine's son also upheld the Writ, and so on, and so on.

The professor proceeded to list the reigning monarchs and those claiming rights to the throne during the 1400s. To ensure she had an understanding of the climate of the day, he digressed into stories of political intrigue and royal favors granted and withdrawn. Uncertain what was fact or his own interpretation, Tannis enjoyed his lively rendition of historic events. Reminiscent of her father, his words also painted vivid pictures in her mind. However, his meandering could lead them far away from her reason for being here. She would have to steer him back to Taenacea. The opportunity finally arose when he paused for another sip of Port.

"So, this Lady of Lianarth. She really did exist?"

"Most certainly," he responded, as if surprised she would have any doubts. "In both fact and fable, although her name has long been wiped from official church records. The Church did not care at all for her influence, you see. That's why her legendary reputation grew to such gigantic proportions in spite of being wiped from official records completely. You'll only find references to her in records like the Doomsday Book and privately owned manuscripts. As to the Tower of Aberayron ... so mysterious ... and tragic." The Professor paused. He dabbed his eyes with a crumpled handkerchief pulled from inside his vest which sent his glasses askew. Adjusting them, he fortified himself with another swallow of Port.

Confused by his ambiguous statement, Tannis was unwilling to break his train of thought. She suppressed her desire to ask just what had happened at Aberayron to cause his obvious distress. She could read nothing from his expression or eyes as he looked back at her intently. Then again, she didn't want to miss what he was saying. She could ask about this Aberayron later.

"Now, you must understand that the Celts were a very pagan and superstitious people. Christianity had not been embraced wholeheartedly, especially in remote areas, although for all intents and purposes they appeared to follow the teachings of the Church. Privately, however, the majority worshipped pagan deities of the old religions and only gave lip service to the faith of the land when necessary. Most annoying to the Church, who suspected as much, but had to rely largely on informants to name offenders.

"It doesn't sound like she had the best of reputations then," queried Tannis, a little disappointed.

"Stories about the Lady of Lianarth began to spread due to a combination of factors," he continued, as if lecturing to a class. "First was her unusual appearance and height and, as her father's only issue, she was groomed to inherit and manage his lands. Educated by private tutors, she could read and write in English, Latin, French, and her native Welsh. Also, contrary to custom, in spite of her beauty and the lands she would inherit as his only child, she was never betrothed. By her late twenties she was still not wed. All offers of marriage were rejected by her father during his lifetime, and by her after his death. Until her thirtieth year."

"That was unusual, wasn't it?" Tannis, intrigued by what had led to such independence at a time when women were mere chattels, bit back her desire to question him. She sensed she'd get more information if she prompted him gently rather than grilling him with too-specific questions.

"Very much so, considering her wealth. Needless to say this fact was a sore issue amongst the gentry, and particularly angered and frustrated her rejected suitors. In spite of her protective Writ some tried to take by force what she would not surrender through marriage, which resulted in on-going border skirmishes and raids on her lands after her father's death. Reputed to be as fearsome a warrior as any man, she often led her own troops into battle and quelled the uprisings very effectively. This too was considered unusual in light of her title and wealth."

Tannis could have sworn his tone held a faint note of disapproval. Well, well, this was some feisty lady to be sure, if his accounts were accurate.

"Now, what really fueled suspicion was that she was also a renowned healer, a Wicca. It wasn't long before her smallest healings were embellished into acts of Magic; both as miracles and hexings. The smell of witchcraft always hovered in the air and people were quick to blame crop failures, illness, death, the loss of livestock and any abnormalities of behavior or unusual acts of God on magical spells."

Reasonably conversant on medieval witch-hunts through her father's work, Tannis felt a familiar surge of impatience with the narrow-mindedness of the medieval era. She also had no love for the Church or its historic use of fear, guilt and violence, in the name of God, to enforce a doctrine geared to amassing wealth and power for itself.

"As I mentioned earlier, the Church was quite vigorous in its efforts to eliminate pagan practices like natural healing, and considered illness as the work of the devil or as divine punishment for sins committed against the Church's edicts. Someone had obviously fanned the whisperings of witchcraft against Taenacea. Perhaps a disgruntled suitor. In any event, she was credited with supernatural powers above and beyond those of a Wicca." The professor emptied his glass and rose to refill it again.

Tannis was puzzled. "What do you mean by 'beyond those of a Wicca'? I thought a Wicca was the same as a witch. The ultimate in evil," she added.

"Yes, and no, my dear. You must understand that Wicca was an accepted Celtic religion, the oldest in fact, reputed to joyously embrace every aspect of life from the elemental physical to the most sacred. Its emphasis was on the non-material, and the Wicca acted as both a healer and spiritual advisor to those around her. Through training in various esoteric disciplines, a Wicca strove to balance within her personality the elements of air, water, earth, and fire; the source of power on which she drew for her work. Traditionally, her craft included the use of herbs for healing, casting of spells, and in some cases, poisonous concoctions designed to induce illusions and delusions."

Perplexed, Tannis asked, "I still don't understand."

"What separates the two is application. A Wicca of the old religion is what you could term a 'white witch, or the feminine application of the Druid faith. Her work geared to helping maintain both the physical and spiritual well-being of the individual within the natural world and the cosmos, whereas those who diverged from the old faith into the use of 'black magic' were called witches. They would willingly kill with poisonous herbs and often formed covens to amplify energy for their deviant intents. Legend paints Taenacea both ways; as a Wicca, a true disciple of the almost extinct old faith, and also as a witch. Viewed with suspicion and envy because of her wealth and position, it was after those two streaks of silver suddenly appeared in her hair that consensus swung towards her being a witch."

Tannis involuntarily raised her hand to the side of her hair. "What do you mean, suddenly?" she asked, a little nervously.

"We need to backtrack a bit. As I said, Taenacea's ancestors came from Ireland, as did someone else. The Lord of Lagohaire, Garth MacCumal." He paused with a flourish to let this juicy tidbit sink in. "They were wed you know, shortly after they met. In her thirtieth year. But they rarely stood on the same shore. The management of his vast holdings in Ireland, and hers, just as vast in Wales, kept them apart a great deal. Her lands extended inland from Aberayron on the west coast of Wales to around Llanwrtyd Wells, about fifty kilometers east and about half the distance north to Rhayader, and the same distance south to Llandovery. Quite a substantial property in those days. She spent most of her time traveling her lands, administrating justice and quelling the unending disputes and raids along her borders. Thus her reputation as a fearsome warrior and swordsman as I said earlier."

"That's amazing." Tannis tried to imagine the size of her lands proportionate to the size of Wales. It hit her suddenly that he seemed to know a great deal about this Lady of Lianarth.

"Yes it was. Women inherited titles, but not land. Land was generally exchanged as dowry and deeded to their husbands as part of the marriage contract. Women didn't as a rule take up arms either. Many holdings were captured only because of this, by assaults launched during the absence of the Lord and his troops while he was off fighting at his outlying borders. Accounts of women leading their own troops into battle were more common earlier in Celtic history than in her era."

Backing up to where he had left off, he continued. "We don't know how they met, just that their wedding was recorded in the parish of Lianarth, the seat of her holdings. DunnGarth as he was called, was extremely tall as well, with very broad shoulders and dark hair usually tied back at his neck as was often the custom. Together, they made a stunning pair; both feared and revered, like a god and goddess toying with the lives of mere mortals, or so the stories imply. Marrying a foreigner so suddenly also fueled the suspicions of her countrymen, the Welsh being fiercely patriotic." Clucking his disapproval, he fortified himself once more.

Oh dear, Tannis thought. He'd better get on with it before he was thoroughly toddled. As if reading her mind, he continued at a brisker pace.

"Few could resist their charm or obvious love for each other; truly the stuff legends are made of. It's said on the eve of their nuptials the gods sent a storm that mirrored the magnitude of their passion, as if their very union had released Celestial energies. It was the lightning that was said to have hit her as DunnGarth planted his seed in her womb."

So she had a child. Tannis wondered whose child the reading referred to then: hers or Taenacea's.

"She disappeared the day after their wedding. When she returned a fortnight later her hair bore silver streaks down each side, starting at each temple and running down to the tips. Struck by lightning some said, marked by the devil in some unholy ritual others said. I believe the lightning story held sway because of the violent storm which lasted until her return. However, while causing much damage in surrounding areas, the storm left her lands and crops relatively undamaged."

"What about Garth? What did he think, while she was away I mean?" The mystery surrounding her namesake had definitely deepened.

The professor shrugged negligibly. "He left for his lands across the sea and the holdings were in the charge of her trusty steward, Master Eban, as they were whenever she was away from Lianarth. Titled husbands and wives didn't spend much time together except perhaps in winter when severe weather often prohibited all but the most essential travel. Most marriages were arranged in childhood and there was little love between couples, if at all. Old men often wed twelve-year-olds, with an eye more to material benefits than the appreciation of a comely wife. Arranged marriages among titled landholders were carefully negotiated and geared exclusively to extending holdings and increasing wealth and power.

"In spite of marrying for love and having a Consort to assist her when he was present, overseeing her lands was no small task. Records indicate she had about two thousand tenants. Her holdings had not suffered as great a loss of life as others during a resurgence of the Black Death. Just as her lands were protected by the Writ of Exemption, her people seemed to be protected by her magical powers."

Impressed by these numbers, Tannis tried to visualize how one woman could manage such vast holdings by herself. True, she would have assistance from appointed stewards and after her marriage, DunnGarth to some extent, but ultimately the responsibility for her fiefdom rested on her shoulders. Curious as to how he knew the number of her tenants, she asked.

"The Welsh, like the English and Scots, were great record keepers," he said. "Also the parish records throughout Wales are surprisingly intact in spite of the many Abbeys and Churches burned and pillaged throughout the medieval and subsequent eras. That's of course where local records were kept. Unlike England, Wales was left relatively untouched by the church's seizures and burnings. As a result Wales still has substantial archives in its Scholastic Centers, particularly the Nation Library at Aberystwyth in mid-Wales.

"By custom, a second or third son of the Manor was indentured to the Church. Since they were generally appointed as priests in their own parish or one nearby, they not only kept local parish records updated, but that of their own families as well. Since records tended to stay in the local parishes, a surprising number have survived. Many Manor Houses still display their historic documents; documents that date back well before Taenacea's time. You'll find many ancient family records crammed into the top shelves in the Manor's library. I've seen them myself." He shook his head in disapproval of such careless storage of priceless documents.

Tannis stifled a smile as she looked around the cluttered room. He could well have been speaking of his own surroundings. She felt embarrassed by her ignorance, particularly in light of her father's profession. But then, she had always been more interested in the tales themselves than their source.

"Records similar to the Doomsday Book were kept by the Welsh, Irish and Scots as well as the English, and were continually updated," the professor continued.

"I've heard of the Doomsday Book, but have to confess I don't exactly know what it is." The name had always sounded sinister, like some ultimate accounting.

"It's actually not a book per se, rather the name given to an ongoing collection of records initiated by William the Conqueror in 1066 as a greater survey of England. Designed to record land holdings, stock and other information required for the assessment of taxes, it contained a detailed account of the extent and value of each holding under English rule. The land was segmented into feudal groupings under Barons, Lords, and Clans. Officials were sent into each sector to ask specific questions and record the answers. The Doomsday Book was the original such record, although similar records called by other names, covered other regions and can still be found throughout the British Isles. You could say it was the first official census of the land and its people.

"So that's where you got your detailed information about Taenacea's holdings?"

"Partially. The records list the extent of each Manor's holdings; everything from the number of pastures, mills and plows to the further breakdown of the demesne; how many tenants were freemen or other such designations. Along with the parish records of births, deaths, and marriages, we can compile a reasonably accurate picture of a holding's worth and population at almost any given time."

Tannis was surprised by this extensive source but wondered how he had access to the information on one day's notice. About to question him, she realized she had missed what he was saying.

" ... she created quite a stir with her silvery hair and light eyes that were said to turn opaque when she put the look on you, as small a babe as she was. A changeling it's said ... spawn of the moon."

"Sorry, what was that?" Tannis asked, confused by the sudden change of subject. "Who caused a stir?"

"The child Taenacea bore DunnGarth." A sharp look indicated his disapproval, but mollified by her apologetic smile, he continued. "With both of them so dark of hair, speculation grew rampant over the paternity of this etheric-looking child. She was birthed under mysterious conditions on the road to Aberayron, with only a maid in attendance. Born with a caul over her face, she was considered either a spawn of the devil or a fairy child with magical powers. The first further fueled suspicions that her mother was a witch and bride of the Devil himself.

Captivated, Tannis leaned forward.

Spurred by her attentiveness, the professor lowered his voice to almost a whisper. "There's a story that she never cried or made a sound except when Taenacea went to battle. It is said she would wail in a high, monotonous tone, day and night, until her mother's return. Needless to say while she was a babe, Taenacea sent her Captain and Men at Arms in her stead after a few such unnerving incidents. Since nothing was known in those days of how Mother Nature can trick us with the recessive genes that pop up every now and then, whisperings about the child abounded. No one believed DunnGarth to be her father. Yet, no malice was borne against little Faye herself, just in case she was a fairy child."

"Faye." Tannis mouthed the name several times, relishing its lightness on her lips.

"Her hair was silver and hung straight down her back like a heavy silken cape. There's a Welsh song that was supposedly written about her called 'Faye of the Faeries'. It's quite charming really and if I remember correctly, a fine tribute to the last of her line. I can hunt it up for you if you like."

A slight chill wove up her spine when he said 'last of her line'. "What happened to her?" Tannis asked, feeling her throat constrict the moment the words were said.

"I don't know," the professor said as he averted his eyes and began to fidget with the files on his lap. "She vanished when she was about three," he mumbled. He seemed uncomfortable and hastily continued. "Her death was never recorded. Some say the Devil claimed his spawn, others linked her disappearance to the sea in some way. But individuals lost at sea were generally recorded as such after a period of time and her name was never among them."

Discomforted by the sudden tears clouding Tannis' eyes, he quickly glanced at his watch and clearing his throat, began to rise. "Well, my dear, I have an early appointment in the morning. Although I have given you an overview of the Lady of Lianarth, I'm still waiting to hear from several associates who have access to documents I still want to check. Perhaps you could come back, say Monday of next week? I should have more information for you then. And could you bring the Book and the parchment? If you don't mind, that is?" he added.

"Why yes ... that'll be fine." Her response had been automatic. She was more concerned with holding back the tears that threatened to pour down her face, embarrassed by this sudden feeling of vulnerability. Good God. She was reacting as if it was her child who had disappeared. She rushed through her thanks and let him hastily usher her down the dim hall and out the front door. He seemed as intent on getting her out as she was on leaving.

The professor stood at the front door and watched thoughtfully as she settled into her vehicle, then drove away.

Had she looked back, Tannis would have seen him almost quiver with excitement. He knew the Lady of Lianarth much better than he had implied. What had impelled him to share only a small portion of her story was to ensure Tannis' return, with the book and parchment. For if the book was verified as genuine, Tannis MacCrae possessed an object of antiquity more valuable than anything he had uncovered in his forty-odd years of research. It would provide the irrefutable evidence he required to complete his own book on a subject that had obsessed him for over two decades.

Tannis drove home in a daze. She should have been jubilant. Instead, she felt an impending sense of doom she couldn't explain. Taenacea, according to the professor, was indeed a real person, or had been, which changed everything. She felt like events had been taken out of her hands. This was no game and there was no turning back now. She was hooked. It wasn't until she was on the Burrard Street Bridge that she realized she had received a great deal of information, but no specific dates relating to Taenacea. Outside of her grandfather's Writ signed in 1420, she still didn't know when during the 1400s she had been born, or had died.

When she got home, she clicked on the answering machine and settled herself on the couch to allow for the ritualistic feline inspection that followed her outings. The boys just sniffed her legs but Zoie climbed all over her, intent on ferreting out alien smells, or worse yet, the scent of another feline which her charge may have traitorously touched.

Tannis lit a few fat candles as she listened to her messages, noting the progressive intensity of the three left by Linka. The first was a cheery, "Hi Mom, just checking in. Give me a call. Bye!", followed by a slightly more pressing, "It's me. Guess you must be busy. I've made my decision. Call me! We gotta talk." The third made her laugh out loud. "Are you my mother?" was the plaintive greeting in her 'I've been abandoned' tone. "You can't *still* be in the studio. Well, call me ... no matter what time it is. Don't forget. Even if it's late. Love ya."

She knew Linka would pester her until she got the scoop on her reading and found out what was in her package. The other two messages on her machine could be dealt with tomorrow. One was from Cal, her agent, and the other from Josie, who was obviously back in town. Lordy. It had been a while since she spoken to her, she thought, as she hit the auto-dial button on her phone beside Linka's name. For once she'd have an adventure as bizarre as any Josie had shared with her. But she wanted a chance to digest and record everything before she shared her tale. Deeply immersed in the metaphysical, she knew Josie would probably want to drag her right off to see a past-life regressionist she just happened to know.

"Mom, where have you been?" wailed Linka, who had snatched up the phone before the first ring was even complete. "Do you know I've been calling all day? We have business to discuss. Where were you any-how?"

"Hello to you too, sweetie! Yes, I'm fine, thanks for asking. Yes, I did have rather a wonderful day; lunch in Paris, skiing in the Alps, then a romantic dinner in Baghdad," Tannis quipped in a bored European-type accent.

"Get serious, Mom. By the way, what was in the package? And what about your reading? Anything good?" Silence at the other end of the line prompted her to add, "Sorry. I know it's none of my business. I'm just very interested. So ... how are you?"

"In possession of a life, and one incidentally, where I don't feel I have to make daily reports to my nosy brat, thank you very much. Actually, I spent a fascinating evening with an eccentric professor to get information about a certain legendary figure mentioned in my reading." She knew her carefully chosen words would give Linka little of the information she sought, and continued with relish. "The package contained a very interesting book I also don't care to discuss right now because it's late and I'm tired. But why don't you come over for supper tomorrow night, if you're free that is. I may just share a few snippets about a new development in my life."

"Oooh! You make me so mad!" Linka knew nothing would persuade her to say more when she took that tone. "OK. Around six? B.J. is dropping off some negatives for me at five so I can hitch a ride over with him. I'll bring a treat for the monsters."

"Like they need more spoiling." Tannis knew this unexpected offer was intended to ensure full disclosure. "Sure, but if you're planning to bring dried sardines, sweetie, just bring a few, not five pounds worth like the time you got them hooked on the stuff. I'm the one who has to suffer 'fish breath'. See you tomorrow, I love you, and good night." She chuckled. Linka's 'treat' ploy was as much to win the approval of her feline competitor, Zoie, as it was to put her mother in a talkative mood.

Linka was thoughtful when she hung up the phone. Something was definitely up. You didn't just get a package thrust in your hands in a metaphysical book store by someone who then disappears. As to the reading, if her mother had joked that it was the usual 'psycho-babble' she would never have given it a second thought. But she had said nothing. Besides, she had just said the package contained something important enough for a 'new development in her life'. Her mind went right to work on what this new development could be.

Tannis stared blankly at the flickering candles as she mulled over what she now knew of Taenacea. She was somewhat relieved Taenacea had not been an important historic figure. It gave her existence credibility, in spite of her controversial reputation. She had laughed with Josie over claims from people who had been well-known historic figures like Cleopatra, Abraham Lincoln, or Napoleon in a past-life. In fact, at one 'Come as You Were' past-life New Years party a few years back, they had seen more than one Julius Caesar and Cleopatra. Two of the four bearded and robed party-goers professing to have been Jesus were women. No wonder most people were skeptical about reincarnation.

Josie had gone to the party swaddled in the faded cadmium yellow silk robe of an impoverished Bangalore Priest, a rather voluptuous one at that. She had chosen medieval garb, complete with a long hairpiece that made her look more a witch than wholesome country maid. Funny she should think about that choice of both era and costume now. She got up and sat at her desk, and pulling her 'Quest' journal from the drawer, began to record what the professor had just told her about Taenacea. Although she used her computer for her household accounts and investments, she still wrote her journals by hand. The intimacy of scripting her innermost thoughts onto paper gave her thoughts the substance an impersonal computer screen never could. She would on occasion pick up an old journal and leaf through the pages for a nostalgic journey into her own mind's eye. What amazed her was how a subtle change in her perception now could transform her view of past events.

She suddenly realized how much she had hoped Taenacea had existed as a real person. She assumed the details of her life had been pieced together from folklore and the professor's own fanciful conjectures. Nevertheless, she was pleased she was real—with a much-loved husband and child. Journal in hand, she lowered herself onto the couch carefully beside the length of a sleeping Mr. Muff.

As an image of Faye came to mind, her throat constricted and unbidden tears rolled down her cheeks. She wiped the unexpected moisture from her eyes. She couldn't imagine what it would be like to lose a child so young. Hit with another wave of sorrow her hand reached for the comfort of warm fur at her side. An emotional link had been forged between herself and Taenacea, for this had to be Taenacea's sorrow she was experiencing. Along with the images triggered by the professor's words, she had seen pictures he had not painted, fractured images with accompanying sounds as well as moments of profound feelings interspersed with scenes frozen in a silent tabloid. And it was happening again, right now.

She saw him ride towards her on a large black stallion as wild as the hills around him, grinning like a love-struck boy ... a passionate embrace on a hilltop as the wind whipped their cloaks ... the grate of clashing steel as they fought side by side ... bloodied and bruised, her arms trembled under the weight of her broadsword ... Garth's tender murmurs to the babe he held ... the paralyzing cold of icy rain as she sought warmth in his arms ... then a moment of nothingness followed by a rush of impressions too quick to grasp before they dissolved into a swirling of darkness that faded into utter blackness.

She stirred slowly, numbed by the onslaught of disconnected impressions. It was almost too much sensation on top of what the professor had brought to life. Her eyes closed in protest as she leaned her head back onto the couch. Once her head cleared, she couldn't help but replay the images of Garth. His looks alone would satisfy any woman's fantasy. But it was his abiding love for Taenacea that impacted her the most, a single-minded devotion so palatable she could feel it.

The stroke of the grandfather clock marked her progress as she read her journal entries. She sensed she had no choice but to open her mind and embrace the memories of that life, however they would come to her. Ah, to experience the fullness of such a man. Whatever it would take ... build him in clay, a past-life regression, even magic spells—she knew she would do it. Her decision made, she addressed the deities in a shaky but dictatorial tone.

"OK spirits, or whoever you are. I'll do it. But I need your help. I'm not exactly a pro at this." Suddenly she remembered something Josie had told her, about spirits being playful and there being no time in their reality. "However, I am in control, so here are the ground rules. #1 - No interference in my work. I have to meet my deadlines. #2 - The cats are sensitive to my energy and I don't want them freaked-out like Muff was the other morning after the tower dream. #3 - I'll need a signal of some kind to identify each of these strand experiences." This last was said respectfully, but emphatically. She saw no reason why she shouldn't experience only the strands required to complete this Quest. She had no intention of meandering through unrelated events. Her intent was to direct her experiences to a swift conclusion, and claim her prize.

Willingness to venture into the unknown did not mean she could not keep her feet firmly rooted to the ground, no matter what happened. There was order in the universe, and she saw no reason why order could not apply to this situation. On impulse, she whispered a little prayer of protection Josie had taught her. She felt a little foolish now that her dialogue was complete, but a prayer couldn't hurt.

Chapter Four

SHE TRIED TO CATCH HER BREATH before the next swell of desire rendered her incapable of any thought other than release. They had so little time and she wanted to stretch each delicious moment into an eternity.

The insistence of Garth's attentions hinted release might come more quickly than she wanted, but she could not help but surrender to the snakes of fire his lips left burning on her quivering breasts. As he teased her nipples with his tongue in the slow circular rhythms she loved, a low earthy moan escaped her lips. She arched towards him to encourage his leisurely progress along her ribcage, over the soft swell of her belly, and down to the core of her need.

She clasped his head and locked eyes with him in perfect understanding. It was time for them to fly to the place where their spirits would join. "I will die with pleasure," she thought. "I will die in the arms of my beloved." A slight quiver of her thighs sent him an unmistakable signal of readiness.

Garth's eyes never left hers. He reared up smoothly and her heart melted under his loving gaze as he plunged into her with one spine tingling swoop. Crying out in primeval welcome, she grasped him tightly. Finally joined, they lay perfectly still for a time to allow their spirits to merge. Then, impelled by the age-old cadence of unbridled passion, slipped into a groove of movement and sensation both familiar and new.

"Oh yes, my love. Now." She grasped his buttocks as she strained to meet the final thrust that sent her spinning into a maelstrom of exploding lights and excruciating sweetness. Unable to contain such massive sensation, she melted into nothingness.

Some time later she drifted back to consciousness, her body still soft and flushed with the afterglow of her release. She brushed a mop of sodden curls off her forehead. It was always the same between them; this raw physical pleasure of coupling which led to an indescribable sweet joining of their very essence. And every time, another strand of shared consciousness solidified and strengthened the bond between them. But there was nothing spiritual about the massive weight pressing on her right now.

"Get off me, you heaving oaf," she gasped, "before you crush me. My body *is* corporeal you know." She pushed at his sweat-slick torso with little effect. Her bite on the lobe of his exposed ear however, induced an immediate response.

"Ouch. You vixen of a woman," he yelped in surprise. Then he settled beside her and rested his head on his bent arm. He almost feared how easily she inflamed him and how willing he had become to please her for just a look, to hear that throaty laugh, or catch the dance of the saucy dimply by her mouth. If she had cast a spell on him, he greatly feared that he delighted in being enchanted. He could no more resist the playful aspect of her nature than imagine his life without her. With a wicked look on his face he peered into hers. "I'll have to pierce you again with my mighty sword if you keep looking at me in that wanton way."

She read the intention in his eyes. "In your dreams, milord," she responded with a definite leer. "I doubt even so great a warrior as yourself can unsheath his sword again so quickly ... without my magic." She giggled and waggled her hips provocatively.

Garth swatted her thigh lightly, then trailed his fingers up her belly, around her breasts, and upward to rest upon her lush bottom lip. "Ah, my Cea," he whispered tenderly. His eyes searched hers for an answer to some inexplicable question. "Heart of my heart and soul of my soul. It almost frightens me when we join like this, when you look at me as if you see me always through newly awakened eyes of love. For it's as if you devour a piece of me, as I do of you. Will there be anything left of us, I wonder?"

She loved to listen to the musings of his heart. Pursing her lips, she pondered his question. "It is said Garth, that the deepest love is a pure surrender of self, whereby two become one in body, mind, heart and spirit, even through time. It is a small death of sorts, a death of separateness, yet a birth of oneness rising from that very death. To yield to the power of such a merging, each become stronger by gaining what the other has given of themselves in this meld of their spirits."

"Aye." He looked thoughtful for a moment, brows knit in consternation. But a faint twitch of his lips belied the gravity of his response. "So you mean that in time, with all this exchange of ourselves, I'll be walking around with your teats, and you with my manhood?"

"Ohhh . . . you beast." Taenacea glared at him then lunged towards him with punishing intent. "I would be cheated in the exchange, milord." The absurdity of her statement and image of his words sent both into gales of laughter and off the bed to land in a heap on the cold stone floor.

"Damnation, woman!" he bellowed as he grappled his way back onto the bed. He stopped abruptly to examine a skinned elbow and threw her an injured look. The quicksilver changes within her manner never ceased to surprise him. Not easily trusting of those without a consistent nature, had it not been for the constancy of her dedication to tasks, he would have thought her lacking substance. One moment she was soft and compliant, drawing strength from him, the next a vexation in her disregard of all but her own will. He felt like he would never quite know what aspect of her heart, wisdom, or strength would surface next. But it pleased him, even provoked him to uncharacteristic actions himself, in order to discover yet another layer of her depth.

Considering the battle scars marking his body, his concern for a lost bit of skin set Taenacea into another fit of hiccuping giggles as she sat on the floor splay-legged, breasts bouncing enticingly with each hiccup.

"You are a wicked witch. First you drain the juices from my loins, then you toss me out of your bed without a care," he moaned.

The woeful expression that followed his outburst propelled her to scramble back on the bed. She hugged his resisting form close and crooned her sympathies. "Oh, how I love this man," she thought. "With him I am complete. Were the very earth to shake, his strength and dependability would make me feel secure."

She stroked his hair lightly, then giggled as he buried his face between her breasts and began rooting for her nipples like a suckling piglet. This set her off again, which made his head bob up and down with each heave and hiccup. A sharp unexpected bite on her nipple prompted a squawk of protest. His willingness to embrace the humor in most situations delighted her, except perhaps right now. His nip had hurt. He was as wicked as she when it came to teasing, and like colts in a field of tender young grass they spent as much time frolicking as they did feeding their insatiable lust for each other. Speaking of which . . .

Some time later they lay entwined, each drifting in the landscapes of their private dreams.

She fluttered back to wakefulness slowly. Still languid with the after-math of fulfillment, Taenacea murmured small sounds of sleepy contentment as she reached for her beloved. Her hand encountered only empty space. He must have risen and lit a blazing fire in their chamber, if the warmth she felt on her bared torso was any indication. Icy chills usually permeated their chambers in late February, in spite of the leaded glass and heavy hangings that covered the tall narrow windows.

Well, she would enjoy these stolen moments of leisure before she had to face Garth's departure and her tasks for the day. Sighing, she wished for the thousandth time that he could stay longer, but the tides cared little for the needs of a woman's heart. Travel by sea this time of year was always treacherous, and she could not help but worry for his welfare. She mouthed the spell of safety for him, as she always did.

A sudden sound, one she could not identify, rang in her ears. It was musical and rather pleasant, although nothing she had ever heard before. Curious, she sat up and opened her eyes.

"Zeus. Where am I?" A sickening dizziness overcame her as an alien scene shimmered before her eyes. Undulating in ghostly waves, it faded before she could properly grasp what she had seen. Then a horrific tremor tore through her body and a queasiness churned in her belly. She squeezed her eyes shut and waited until the sensations settled before she cautiously opened her eyes again.

* * *

It took a while to quell her nausea. What had just happened? She distinctly remembered waking up as Taenacea, or was it as herself, Tannis? She wasn't sure. Her body had felt crowded, as if someone else was in it besides her; someone that had seen her room briefly, through her eyes. Confused, she looked down at her nakedness. Was it possible . . . tentatively she slid a shaky hand over her left nipple, and felt the tenderness left by Garth's playful bite. A flush warmed her cheeks and an "Ohmygod" escaped her lips as she realized she was also somewhat damp between her legs. The feel of this blatant evidence of recent love-making absolutely stunned her.

"Well, if I'm Taenacea, I've woken up in the wrong time, and if I'm Tannis, then how can I have signs of her exuberant lovemaking on my body?" She examined her body more closely. Several small bruises dotting the inside of her thighs caused another flush to heat her face. She sprang up, dashed into the bathroom, and scoured her naked reflection in the mirrored wall. With a sigh of relief, she confirmed she was indeed Tannis MacCrae, living in the year of our Lord, nineteen hundred and ninety-six. For a split second when she first woke, she hadn't known who she was.

This was definitely *not* a dream like her others. She had literally done it. Somehow, she had traveled to the past and made love with Garth. Not just once either. And what fabulous love-making it had been. His eyes had been glued to hers even as they climaxed together again and again. It was almost . . . cosmic, like nothing she had ever experienced before.

She had actually been inside Taenacea's body and experienced the richness of this encounter as Taenacea; physically, mentally, emotionally, and in ways she could not even describe. It was like being Taenacea totally, yet knowing that she was also herself, Tannis, experiencing herself as Taenacea. But Garth had not seen anything amiss, unaware another woman was sharing the body of his beloved. A very strange feeling indeed. Replaying the erotic memory several times, her initial surge of euphoria was momentarily tainted with a small smudge of dis-ease. Was this not an infringement of the most intimate kind? Yet . . . if she had been Taenacea in that life, then it was her own experience she was reliving. Wasn't it?

The tower dream had left its frightening mark because she now sensed it was incomplete, a mere glimpse of what she had yet to experience fully. This latest encounter, however, felt complete, a memory designed to connect her to her 'other self' and Garth, in the most intimate way. From a fantasy point of view, it was everything she could dream of and a wondrous conclusion of what her earlier dreams had implied. But this was no fantasy and she knew it.

Her mind reeled. If this was a memory strand, then in effect she had become Taenacea, or at the very least, merged with her so completely, there was no separation between the two. Was that the difference between dreams and time travel? She had thought you would remain yourself somehow, and observe the events around you like an invisible voyeur, not experience them first hand. And if it was time travel, then where was Taenacea while she was in her body?

The one brief moment when Taenacea had looked out of her eyes into her world had puzzled her. Perhaps Taenacea had been zapped into her sleeping body in the present while she was in her body back in Wales. If so, then the exchange could only take place while she was asleep, which seemed plausible and comforted her in a small way. But the moment of waking had been uncomfortable, like some kind of overlap had occurred just prior to each returning to their proper time-frame. She hadn't liked that at all, and hoped it wasn't a standard part of such an experience.

Then she remembered her rules. "Is this a memory strand?" she asked, and waited. A very clear tinkle of delicate chimes rang in her ears. She liked the pleasant sound of her confirmation and turned on the shower, satisfied one of her stipulations had been met so promptly. Good. She was in control.

She recaptured the delicious sensations of her dream, reluctant to wash away the physical residue of her experience even while it embarrassed her. "Gawd, you are a sick, sick puppy," she said with mock disgust as she glanced ruefully at her misted reflection. Then she turned away from the ghostly image and briskly stepped into the shower.

Dinner over and the dishes done, Tannis gently nudged Linka into the living room. Once both were comfortably settled on the couch, she wrapped up the monologue she had begun during dinner, careful to skim over the intimate aspects of her latest experience.

"It seems I've experienced two memory strands, one partial and one confirmed as complete by the chimes." She took a deep breath and tried to make light of the matter in case Linka thought her completely mad. "As crazy at it sounds, I'm enthralled by this Quest. Only I can't do it without you apparently. I have to consider that you might possibly be the incarnate of Faye, and that's why you're supposed to be involved. So . . . are you game to venture where no man has gone before and help me on my bizarre journey?"

Engrossed in editing the telling of her story, Tannis hadn't seen the swift succession of emotions that flitted across Linka's face as she listened intently.

"Awe ... some! Yup, I'm game." Linka breathed, then exploded into action. She leaned over to give Tannis an exuberant hug. Then she jumped up and clapped her hands in glee. "This is *so* choice, Mom. I'm with you for sure. It's just *so* romantic . . . a Quest to find your dream man. And I'm in it. So, what do I have to do? How do I make myself dream? Oh, I know. The book. We have to look in the book," she squealed, impatient to see this magical tome. "I can't believe that I was her . . . Faye . . . I must have been, your daughter in that life too, I mean. I just knew I would experience another life, just like Josie said." Undaunted by the fact that Faye's life had been infantile and brief, she concluded, "No wonder we've always been so close. This is just too cool." She flung herself back onto the couch with an enormous sigh of satisfaction as her mind conjured countless time-travel flights into unknown pasts.

Tannis had to laugh and shake her head as she pulled the Magik Book out of her bottom desk drawer. Suddenly she felt possessive, almost loathed to have anyone other than herself touch the book. She caressed the cover lightly before she reluctantly handed it over.

Linka accepted it gingerly, and under her mother's intense gaze, opened it with appropriate reverence. She stopped at the prayer at the front and read it silently, once, then again before she looked at her mother with awe. "This is beautiful. Like an Ode to Life itself." Wrinkling her brow, she said very slowly, "You know, I feel like I've heard this before. Over and over again. I knew what the next line would be even before I read it. And that third line . . ." her pace quickened as her finger tapped the book, 'Radiance of Moon'. It jumped out at me like it has a special meaning! This is too wild, Mom. It makes me think of Faye's birth. Do you think I could actually remember . . . being born as Faye, I mean?"

"Hmm. Maybe. What do you mean you'd heard it over and over again?" The statement peaked her interest and she wondered if the Magik Book itself had the power to trigger visions, just by being handled.

"Remember when you used to chant 'Itsy Bitsy Spider' when I was little? It was something I heard repeatedly." Linka said. "We sang it every night for eons, until I finally got sick of it, or hit my teens, whichever came first." A depreciating giggle and roll of her eyes indicated it had most likely been the latter. "This prayer feels just like that. And you know what? I got this flash of a woman standing on a hill with her arms in the air doing something while I looked up at her. Does that make any sense to you? Could it have been me as Faye, and you as Taenacea?"

Tannis was startled. Linka must have tapped into a visual association with the prayer. She had always been intuitive, in spite of her erratic behavior, particularly where the two of them were concerned. So in tune, often one finished a sentence the other had started. Just a look frequently answered an unvoiced question between them. During Linka's formative years, the subjective and paranormal had been discussed as openly in their house as the tangible and factual. Traditional fairy tales and children's stories were entwined with her father's mythical stories, stories which had often lulled both into fantasy dreams. When Linka was older, the three of them had spent many evenings speculating on the mysteries of the unknown. Linka's perceptiveness had frequently sliced through their conjectures right to the crux of an issue. Perhaps it wasn't so surprising that she was in sync with this reincarnational drama. "You could be experiencing a trace memory, as Josie would put it, of that life. According to the legends, you were born under a full moon."

Tannis watched Linka with affection and chuckled at her comments as she flipped through the book and stopped to read the occasional page out loud. Her father had seen to it that she too could read many of the ancient scripts he researched. "Oh, gross! Did they actually *do* that? Hmm . . . this spell would come in handy with some of the dweebs I've dated. Bats dung, ugh. Hey, look. Mom, mom, mom," she said, poking her finger insistently at Tannis' arm as if to punctuate the importance of her discovery. "Here it is . . . a spell for Conjuring Memories, and . . . " frantically she flipped the next few pages back and forth, "Locating Events and Mind Links in time!" The latter was said with immense satisfaction.

Ebony and honey-gold heads bent together as they poured over the incantations. "Thank God we don't have to hunt up any bullock droppings or eyes of newt." Linka quipped. "This whole last section contains spells where you only need candles, herbs, and a spiritual familiar. You've got that stuff already. But how come you need a familiar for all the spells in this section?"

"Cats have a consciousness closely aligned with ours. Since they're connected to the elements of both the natural and supernatural world, they function as a conductor to bridge the boundaries that separate the two realms."

"Got it! You sound just like Josie, by the way. Which of the cats are you going to use for your familiar?"

"Hold your horses. I hadn't thought that far ahead. Probably Zoie, I would think."

"No way!" Linka exclaimed. "God knows where she'll take you. She's definitely too mean-spirited and spaced-out to focus properly and act as a reliable facilitator. I'd say Mr. Muff. He's cool. Sorry mom, but I can't help it. I just hate her! She acts like a guard dog who owns you."

"Be nice now." Tannis chided. "She's really a darling, and of the four, she's the most tuned into me. Besides, if you didn't suck up to her as if you were jealous, she wouldn't go out of her way to torment you."

"Oh, give me a break! Me jealous of that flea-bitten splotchy mass of scraggly evil. Not I," Linka sputtered. She glanced around quickly to make sure the evil in question hadn't heard.

Tannis' look indicated that Linka's action proved her point. "And you wonder why she gives you such a hard time," she stated calmly. "For your information, she has no fleas, nor is she scraggly. She just couldn't decide between being a long or short-haired cat, so picked both." Changing the subject, she said. "Now, let's set some ground rules here. I'm not about to let you muck around with spells willy-nilly, and don't even think about asking me if you can take the Magik Book home!"

Linka's face fell. She was about to do just that.

"We're dealing with a power we don't understand, so restraint is in order," Tannis continued. "I suggest you jot down this 'Mind Link' incantation to forge a connection with Faye. If a link is established, you can try the 'Conjuring Memories' and see what surfaces. " Her tone implied there was no room for discussion.

Linka nodded. "Do you think I'll have the same type of experience you had? You know, feeling like I'm in Faye's body?"

"Who knows, sweets. But write the spells down to be sure you get them right." Tannis got a blank notebook from her desk drawer and handed it to Linka. "You might consider recording your experiences, especially any dreams you might have, like I do. I also suggest you establish your own ground rules, and ask for a signal to separate these experiences from your regular dreams . . . and delusions." The latter was said pointedly. Linka too easily read meaning into imaginative conjectures based on wishful thinking.

Linka threw her mother an unforgiving look, but copied the spells like a dutiful child while Tannis watched with maternal pride. Petite yet athletic, her daughter radiated wholesome energy, a vitality reflected in her animated personality. Impatient to feast on every delight the world had to offer, she darted from one thought and experience to another; relishing each, yet willing to replace it at a moment's notice with a new diversion. "It'll be interesting to see how these two meld," she wondered. It almost seemed like Linka was trying to make up for the life Faye hadn't completed, if she truly had been Faye in that life.

As if reading her mind, Linka said, "I can hardly wait to find out what happened to her. It's got to be something really mysterious, or else your little professor had one too many Ports and muddled his facts. Oh say, can I come with you on Monday? He sounds so cute. Besides, since we're in this together, I really should be there. He won't mind, will he?"

Tannis shrugged her shoulders. "I doubt it, although he may have trouble relating to you as an elusive little fairy creature from the past."

Linka stuck her tongue out at her childishly.

Suddenly Tannis remembered what had been simmering in the back of her mind. "Listen. You know I don't usually pry into your affairs, but I was wondering about your reading. Did the Tarot Card reader say anything about this to you? And what did you mean by her one inaccurate statement?"

Linka looked blank for a moment, then soundly smacked her hand against her forehead and exclaimed, "Man oh man! Now it fits. At first I didn't think much about it, because it was the usual stuff, you know, how lucky I am to have such a great relationship with you, bla, bla . . . money comes easily to me, bla, bla, and that I would soon meet a special man, bla, bla. But then she said I have caused my mother wretched sorrow and endless tears. Well, that statement didn't make sense. I thought she might be a few cards short of a full Tarot deck, and didn't take the reading seriously after that. I was kinda disappointed actually." Pausing to gasp for breath, she added in awe, "But now I wonder if she meant the sorrow you felt as my *other* mother, like when Faye disappeared. Oh, and she also said I had a big adventure coming up. At least she was right about that."

"Possibly." Tannis, lost in her own thoughts while Linka continued to browse through the book, was startled when she suddenly asked, "Hey, how come you got a taped reading and I didn't?"

"I didn't know you didn't have your reading taped. Maybe I need it because my reading was so ambiguous. In fact, I'm glad I have the tape. I would have forgotten half of what she said." Changing the subject completely she asked, "Have you decided to buy your computer equipment?"

"Yup. But change of plans. I'd like you to co-sign a loan at the bank for me instead of lending me the money directly." And hurriedly explained, "I have to establish a credit rating for my business at some point and a bank loan would do that, in spite of the fact that I hate the thought of paying any interest. I don't have enough collateral to get a loan by myself. I checked. Being a young, inexperienced, one-woman enterprise, the lending officer said my chances were zip, but with a solid co-signer, like my famous mother, the loan would go through, no problemo. The paper work is done and ready for your signature."

Tannis secretly applauded her decision. As willing as she was to help outright, she respected Linka's shrewd choice of a more independent indebtedness to the bank rather than a personal one to her. "I'm so glad you decided to go for it, and I like your approach. Tell me who I have to see, and I'll pop into the bank tomorrow morning."

"Thanks mom. I really appreciate your help. If all goes well, I'll be pulling out my hair in front of a computer screen in a few weeks." Linka moaned, then brightened. "Oh well, the future awaits . . . and so does the past. Weird eh?"

The clock struck eleven. "Now, my darling, our business is concluded and it's time to drive your little tush home. You've got some dreaming to do, and I need my sleep. My studio awaits. Just be clear about your intent before you leap willy-nilly into the past. And let me know what happens." She pushed away a sudden wave of uncertainty. Had she done the right thing by involving Linka? Well, it was too late now. Time would tell.

* * *

A few miles from the Keep at Aberayron her waters broke and sent a hot gush of liquid down her legs to soak the riding furs that had done little to ease the jarring motions of her mount. "Oh please Mother, not now," she pleaded silently. She longed for the comfort of a fresh clean bed and the helping hands of old Lil back at Lianarth.

It was too soon. The child was not expected for another moon by her reckoning. As reckless as this journey had seemed so close to her time her inner voice had nudged her towards the coast to scan for any sign of sails. Garth must be coming. Many times before she had followed her inner urgings and was waiting for him on the cliffs when he arrived. Confounded at first by her knowing, he now scoured the still distant shoreline from his craft for her solitary form upon the cliffs.

A searing shaft of pain gripped her lower belly and brought an unwanted moan to her lips. In the cool glow of the moonlight, she slid awkwardly from her mount and looked about her for a likely place to stop. They were alone, she and this silly chit of a handmaid who was to begin her service at Aberayron. The maid would be of little help, scared witless by the slightest rustle in the calm summer night. She wished she had sent her ahead with the small escort that would be within sight of the Keep by now. Caught off-guard by another clutch at her belly, her eyes were drawn to a small circle of sacred oak trees off to her left, which seemed to beckon her.

She pulled herself along in slow measured steps, her horse following behind with trailing reins. Taenacea quietly reassured the maid, whose eyes darted around in panic. "We'll be stopping here. My time is come, but there is no need for concern. See child, we will be safe here in this sheltered little circle. There is nothing to fear. Just tie the horses by the edge of the thicket and pull the furs from their backs to make a pallet for me. Then bring my satchel, and fetch a gourd of water from the brook I hear down that rise. I will stand watch until you return. Now go and do as I bid." She held back a grimace from another wash of pain until the maid turned her back to her. Her quiet tone had reassured the dazed girl enough to stumble to her bidding. It would not be long however before she realized the gravity of their situation and became totally useless. She would have to resort to spell-making.

She doubled over the next contraction, but breathing deeply, allowed the pain its intense but brief life. When the maid returned, they gathered twigs and branches for a small fire to heat the water; a small amount for cleansing, and the rest for the Mother's Ease Tea to speed the birth and help her womb contract.

Before long all was ready. She pulled herbs from the medicine pouch she always carried, and dropped them into the steaming pot to steep; black cohosh and coltsfoot, rosemary and a little chamomile; then a small amount of poppy for relaxation. Having first poured a little hot water onto the dried chamomile in the second drinking gourd, she added a liberal amount of poppy before she handed it to her maid. "Here child, drink this tea. It will keep the night chills from you. Sit and rest against this tree while I tell you about your new home.

To ease the chit she prattled in soft cadence about jolly cook in who's charge she would be, and how she would have little to do but tend and dry the herbs and help the other young girls in service at mealtime. All the while she watched covertly for signs of drowsiness. She had added a little too much poppy, but there was little time. The child could not be witness to her conjuring. She left enough suspicious tales in her wake as it was.

She breathed through another intense contraction then rose unsteadily and faced the moon, arms raised in reverence. After she murmured the spells she required, she awkwardly sank onto the bedding and sipped her tea. She glanced at the maid who now mumbled incoherently at the poppy induced visions in her mind. Taenacea took advantage of the little time she had to appraise her surroundings. Soon the demands of her body would render her oblivious to all but her task.

It was a fine setting for the birth of a moon child. The night was still in its mystery, with only faint whisperings from the wind that caressed the tree tops on this midsummer's eve. The light dew on the soft blanket of grass within the circle winked at her sweetly as she breathed deeply of the moist cool air. She began to fidget a little with faint stirrings of restlessness. It was time. She focused with effort on the benevolent face of the full moon directly overhead and breathed herself into a deep relaxed trance. She felt no movement inside her belly now, only an insistent pressure from within. Then all feeling was gone. She was outside herself and hovered over her body in gentle sway to watch the age old events unfold with interest. She saw it all, yet felt nothing.

Gentle ghostly hands massaged her taut belly while others rubbed salve around the birth opening to help her body stretch. Around her crooned the soothing voices of countless mothers who had come before; easing her task as they gathered to celebrate the emergence of a new life. Old Lil was right beside her, and smoothed her brow while she murmured ancient prayers. Lights danced above her lying form and Faeries darted into the tree tops to tease the forest spirits who also peaked out from behind leaves, rocks and scrub; too shy to leave their shadowed havens but enthralled by the ancient miracle at hand.

A pressure as strong as the twenty foot ocean swells that crashed against the seaward cliffs of Aberayron washed over her straining body and pressed it into the soft cushion of the earth. In one smooth thrust came first the head. With the second thrust the babe slid from her womb into the waiting hands of Lil, who delicately eased the cowl from the tiny face. Other hands tied and cut the cord and wiped the babe clean. For a long moment, every sound in the glade ceased. Her helpers faded back into the Plains of Silver as Taenacea settled back into her body and opened her eyes.

She sat up slowly to pick up the babe and look deeply into ethereal eyes that stared back at her with the wisdom of her celestial origin reflected in her unwavering gaze. Tenderly she cradled the tiny product of her deep love for Garth against her breast. Silent words passed between them as mother and child welcomed each other into their hearts. Gently she ran a finger over the silver down on the little head. She pulled herself upright and raising the naked babe into the air, said clearly,

"Child of my heart, child of the moon, child of the Faery Ring; I name thee Faye, and ask for you the blessings of the Spirits of this land. May they guide you, and guard you, and lead you through the enchantment of life. Soon you will see your father who has sailed from across the sea to meet you, and we will begin life as a family." Then she sank back onto the soft furs with her daughter cuddled against her and drifted into the sleep of pure motherly contentment.

Just before dawn Taenacea awoke. She lay her babe down on the warm furs, rose, and cleansed herself. A quick glance confirmed the serving maid was still sound asleep. She had forgotten all about her during the birthing, and hoped she had not woken and seen the magical events. Quickly she buried her afterbirth at the entrance to the dell as ancient offering to The Mother. This now would be a sacred place, marked by the blood of her womb, the elixir of life itself; a place near Aberayron where both could go for communion with each other and the elements of earth and spirit. Here she would teach her daughter timeless truths and the magic required for a charmed life. She picked up her sleeping babe, swaddled her in shawls and tied her snugly to her breast, silently giving thanks to the spirits who had assisted her.

With the child pressed close to her heart, she turned to the East and began her daily prayer; embracing the life-giving energies around her.

* * *

Gentle chimes teased Tannis back into wakefulness. Eyes closed, she lay perfectly still and savored the magical strand she had just experienced. She compared the two births, those of Faye and Linka. Both girls had entered the world with similar ease. Except Linka had burst from her womb with an impatient thrust, whereas Faye's arrival was like the smooth undulation of mercury. And while Linka's birth was aided by the gloved hands of a doctor and nurses in a sterile operating room, Faye had magically slipped into a moonlit night with the assistance of loving phantom hands.

As Taenacea, she had been present at the birth, but at the same time not; due in part to her spell- making and the powerful potion she had ingested. The experience itself was a mystery, one she couldn't explain or even understand. She could only remember parts of what she had seen while hovering above herself as Taenacea. Thankfully, this experience had left no residual marks on her body. A nervous giggle escaped her. She wouldn't know how she would have coped with milk running from swelled breasts.

This then was another complete strand, confirmed by the chimes that had woken her. But a strand so moving, she felt tears of pure love sting her eyes. There had also been a much smoother transition from one life to the other, without the jarring tremor or nausea as in her last experience. She felt only a slight queasiness in her belly. She liked this much better. No overlapping, and no freaked-out felines. She opened her eyes, relieved to see the boys lying around her legs fast asleep. Only an odd tail or whisker twitched in kitty dreams. Zoie, whose favorite spot was on the pillow beside her, had raised her head and looked knowingly into her eyes, as if aware of what had transpired. In fact, she looked almost smug.

So far, nothing too weird had happened, except for that one overlap. She still had six strands to experience, rather six and a half since the tower strand was not finished. She knew, for the chimes had not signaled completion of that nasty event. The tower strand disturbed her deeply and she kept pushing it out of her mind. Before she had a chance to examine her reluctance to complete that particular strand, the cats began to stir. It was time to get up, then call Cal. She had forgotten to do so yesterday. But first she would go to the bank as promised, to ensure Linka's loan would be processed quickly. Hopefully it would prove to be a blessing. With the diversion of her new computer equipment, Linka wouldn't get too carried away with her involvement in the Quest.

Chapter Five

"**S**O, HOW'S MY FAVORITE ARTIST?" Cal drawled. His relaxed tone belied the energy he expended to keep his stable of artists busy with commissions and showings in his local and American galleries. When Calvin Wilde took an artist under his wing, they had better be prepared for success, and the hard work required to achieve it. Only in Tannis' case did he make an exception. She proved to be more demanding of herself than he could ever be.

When he first met her, it didn't take him long to figure out that here was a woman who knew exactly what she wanted to do, and how. As well, her instincts for what would sell proved impeccable. At a time when the most fashionable tastes in the world of Art leaned to the abstract, her realistic figurative work had forged an unusual appeal among his select collectors and clients. He'd learned to trust her instincts, and uncharacteristically allowed her to determine how she was to be promoted. Had he not, he knew he would not be representing her at all. "Has your original concept won out for a change?"

"Fat chance. The client probably envisioned something more saintly, but this medieval woman is becoming more substantial than I'd originally intended. There's a lot more strength and power to the piece than I'd planned, but I'm curious where it will lead so I'm going with it, OK?"

"Fine by me, but I'd better check with the fellow overseas, the one who's handling the commission for the buyer." Cal chuckled, and added with puzzlement, "Odd situation, if you ask me. I usually know who I'm dealing with. In this case, it's all hush-hush. But babe, for those bucks, I'll do my super schmoose and get the go-ahead for you."

"Bucks already spent on a delightful little trinket for your latest paramour no doubt. I swear, Cal, the only reason you work so hard is you're a slave to your ladies; expensive and empty-headed ladies I might add, whose devotion you uselessly try to buy. Has it ever occurred to you that you're quite the catch and don't need to squander every cent you make on those silicone socialites who cling to your arm ever so briefly?"

"I'm a lost man," he drawled, rolling his eyes heavenward. "You're the only woman I've ever loved. But since you won't have me, all I can do is console myself with hollow imitations in the hopes my broken heart will somehow continue to beat."

"Oh, Cal, you're such a nit," Tannis chided affectionately. "You know I adore you, but I'm all wrong for you. What you need is some down-to-earth cuddle-bug who worships the ground you walk on. Your ego demands it. Besides, I have no intention of birthing a dynasty of Wildes for you on that sprawling ranch in Montana, which is what you really want and won't admit, even to yourself."

Cal sighed. He knew she was right on both counts. Her art was all-consuming, and besides, he would live in terror of losing such a treasure, were he to possess her. Ruefully he remembered their one romantic interlude after her first successful showing in his New York Gallery. All but one of her pieces had sported a red sold sticker by the end of the evening. Unexpectedly, her well-deserved euphoria had erupted into a passionate response to his advances when they celebrated at the hotel after the show; a response he had yearned for but which had completely overwhelmed him. Left scorched by a fiery intensity he could neither understand nor match, he found he still yearned for her, and believed he always would.

As if sensing his reaction that spontaneous night, she had used candor and humor to deftly transform an awkward situation into a cherished memory, and their relationship into one of trust and ease. Still smitten with her, Cal was secretly relieved that their working rapport was unaffected by their brief dalliance. It was a great deal safer. But he could not help comparing subsequent conquests to her, and finding them wanting. After ten years he still clung to the habit of thinking he was in love with her.

"Earth to Cal, are you still there? I said the murals are finished. Do you want to see them?" Tannis asked.

"Yeah babe, but I gotta run now. My phone lines are blinking like a Vegas Jackpot. Keep those fingers molding their magic, and I'll pop by if I get a chance. Just don't go running off with some knight in shining armor in the meantime." As long as she didn't fall in love with someone else, he could nurture the hope she might respond to him again one day. He suspected she never would but liked to keep the possibility alive.

Gawd, little does he know, Tannis thought ruefully, taken back by his unexpected statement. She wondered what had prompted him to say that. It was quite out of character. Though not exactly a knight, witching up a past love was not far off. That would really sit well with him, poor dear. She knew he still loved her a little, but her earthiness and inner strength terrified him as much as it attracted him. Cal was more comfortable admiring beauty and passion from a distance than actually experiencing it first hand, a quality which made him such an excellent agent and gallery owner. He could intuitively sniff out the most beautiful, unique, and unusual item and turn it into a prized possession for an outrageous amount of money.

After she hung up, she impulsively hit the auto-dial on her phone. Josie's cheery message of the day spewed in her ear as she waited for her friend to pick up. The little twerp insisted that every caller first hear her daily astrological forecast before she answered.

"Today the heavens will draw together loved ones as Venus moves into the seventh house of Libra. Nurture your relationships and have a magical day. You know what to do if I'm not in."

"It's me you crazed psychic. Pick up will you?"

"Hi," Josie panted. "I just this minute started the Jeep to come over. Some interesting aspects surfaced in the charts recently, in your sign in particular. Put the coffee on. I'll be there in ten or fifteen. See Ya!"

"Sure, why don't you come on over." Tannis said to the silence of the disconnected line. There was never a dull moment with that gal around, providing you could keep her grounded long enough to get and keep her attention. Her news would. Joking aside, Josie was the one person in the world she could tell anything to and get excellent feedback. When it came to insight into others, her intuition and perception was faultless. Only with herself were those perceptions flawed. If she could learn to apply her skills to her own personal life, it wouldn't be such a mess of shattered relationships. Tannis smiled as she loaded the washing machine and prepared a snack of fruit and cheese to nibble on while they inhaled their ritualistic cups of coffee. They had a lot of catching up to do.

Without warning, Josie breezed through the door and dropped her purse and bags on the tiled floor in the foyer; bags filled with reference books and god knows what other charting and psychic paraphernalia she never left home without. Her lengthy hug was accompanied by a deep, contented sigh. "Oooh! I've missed you, even though I have just had the most incredible experience of my life." She pulled back slightly and peered into Tannis' face with unmasked love.

"You look great. Something's up, I can see it in your aura. It's dancing with fire. But first coffee, then I have to tell you about my rebirth into the

Earth Medicine Wheel of Life." She settled on the couch, feet up and crossed, and reached out for the cup of steaming coffee Tannis placed before her. On hearing her voice, the cats ran in from all directions, jumped on her, and nudged for attention. Even Zoie allowed her a few strokes before she settled in her favorite armchair across from the couch.

The cats adored Josie. Ginseng had run off to find his mousie and returned to place the ratty toy at her feet in homage. Whenever she came over, they would nuzzle her and meow their tales of woe, knowing she would commiserate with silly dialogue. "I know," she would croon, as she did now, "The mama neglects you terribly. Nasty mama. Such a hard life you have, my puss-wuss's. Thankfully you have me who understands." Everyone concerned just loved this ridiculous ritual, knowing full well they were well-loved, well-cared for and spoiled rotten. She adjusted her position slightly as the boys snuggled around her, then launched into a recap of her latest sojourn.

"Remember Dean, the client I had just read for the last time we talked, the one who asked me out? Well, he told me he was going on a Shamanic Retreat and asked me to go along. I thought, perfect. We can spend two weeks together and commune with not only nature, but each other, if you get my drift. Man what a babe, but as it turned out, also a major weenie. I'll save that story for a male-bashing session. Outside of that unexpected disappointment, the retreat was fabulous. We ate dried berries and jerky, drank bark and herb teas, evaporated negative beliefs in the sweat lodge, experienced visions, and communed with the Earth elements through guided imagery. We even conjured up one major storm. Quite different from the East Indian retreats I've been on."

"Where did you go?" Tannis asked, amused at her friend's continuous efforts to find herself and connect with her inner self; a source she already drew from intuitively. But she could never convince Josie of what to her was obvious. Josie insisted she was still incomplete.

"Some place in southern Oregon. We actually lived like the natives had, in the open, with only our own hand-made shelter of branches to keep off the rain. I know, I know. You don't have to give me that look. Dean built mine for me, or I would have drowned. It rained a lot. But I think this time I really tapped into an important aspect of myself and found my center. Especially after my vision-quest." She gulped down half her coffee, and continued. "Did you know that in the Earth Medicine horoscope, the wolf is my animal totem. You're a salmon by the way. I'm studying the wheel of

life now and may combine it with my traditional astrological chartings. And
. . . my musical vibration is an F sharp, an octave above yours, the salmon.
Neet eh?" Her enthusiasm was evident as she fleshed out her newly
discovered philosophy and recounted the sacred rituals which had led to
her currently elevated state of enlightenment.

As she listened, Tannis marveled at how their literally accidental
meeting six years ago, when Josie had rear-ended her at an intersection, had
led to such a deep and satisfying friendship. She had never really had a close
relationship with a woman, outside of Maureen. She chuckled at her initial
resistance when Josie had ordained their meeting as no accident, rather as
destined through karma for some higher purpose. Higher purpose or not, it
had taken Tannis almost a year to disengage her natural reserve and allow
this persistent and mad-cap person entry into her private world, and heart.
Josie had rear-ended her in more ways than one. She seemed to know just
when Tannis was overworked or needed stimulation, and would arrive
unannounced to drag her off for an impromptu adventure, or to meet one of
the many odd but interesting people she knew. Through them, and her own
inquisitory nature, she experienced both the bizarre and extraordinary and
unconsciously strengthened her reliance on her own intuitiveness.

Tannis watched her friend fondly. Her dark brown hair hugged her
delicate head like a glossy cap, except for one long braided wisp that hung
down by her left ear. Its end was bound in a bright red string that sported a
silly little bell; to remind her to stay grounded, she would say flippantly when
asked. Usually clad in black tights like Tannis, she would wrap her petite yet
lush form in a puzzling array of unidentifiable layered tops she purchased in
either second hand stores or the finest of boutiques.

Her recent native experience was blatantly apparent today. She wore
layers of suede over something that looked suspiciously like a western tart's
camisole; all accessorized with a jangle of beads, claws and shiny things
which chinked on her many necklaces and danced from her ears when she
moved. Tannis thought her outrageously delightful. Her every whim and
pursuit was reflected in her ever changing wardrobe, one she could fortunately afford to indulge thanks to the substantial quarterly cheques issued
by her father's estate.

The subject of her scrutiny had stopped talking and silently returned
her appraisal, "Your turn. 'Fess up. Your chart and my vibes tell me
something awesome is afoot."

"Same-ol', same-ol', as far as work goes," she began, and filled Josie in on her creative status, Linka's latest proclamation of celibacy and intended computer purchase. Finally she told Josie about her impromptu reading and the Quest. She shared every nuance of her experiences to-date, and omitted nothing but the more intimate aspects of her passionate encounters with Garth.

Josie listened attentively. Throughout, she blinked rapidly and occasionally widened her sparkling brown eyes as she digested all she heard. She fondled her braid and chewed on her bottom lip abstractly as she leafed through the Magik Book Tannis handed her when she described her unusual meeting with the little lady in the bookstore. That was another thing about Josie; she could listen while she read a book and hummed a tune, and not miss a beat.

Concluding with, ". . . So, here we are. I'm committed to conjuring up a man from another life," Tannis refilled their coffee while a still silent Josie flipped through the pages of the Magik Book, eyes glazed in reflection.

When Tannis returned, Josie shut the book firmly. She looked at her evenly, then said, "You know, I could just hate you. I spend a bazillion dollars in mind expansion training, years studying every conceivable consciousness-raising methodology known to man, thousands of hours in intensive meditation with the world's greatest gurus, and been regressed under hypnosis dozens of time. And all I walk away with is knowing I had been nobodies, just putzes living uneventful lives in godforsaken places, never once to fulfill a grand purpose." She stared into nothingness for a moment before she continued. "You, on the other hand, have this romantic and exciting Quest just drop into your lap without doing a damn thing." Eyes heavenward, she intoned, "Hello up there. What did I ever do to piss you off."

"Oh quit whining, you goof, and help me out here. Let's put some of those bazillion dollars to work." Tannis quipped. Seeing the irony of the situation really did pain Josie, she added, "I need someone to help me, who knows something about all this stuff. I consider you the expert on the paranormal. Maybe that's your purpose in our relationship in this life . . . to guide me through my Quest."

Josie immediately brightened. Yes, perhaps *this* was the karmic mission her recent vision-quest had implied. She had been directed to "flow with the fish of the sea". Tannis was a Salmon on the same musical vibration as she, with only an octave between them. In the Earth Medicine Wheel, the Salmon was said to represent wisdom and strength of purpose. Perhaps some of the strange things she had seen in her hallucinatory state during her vision-quest was linked to her friend's surprising disclosure. She munched abstractly on a handful of crackers she had pillaged from the cheese tray and asked, "Did you catch the significance of there being twelve strands? Not seven or sixteen, or some other number, but twelve?"

"Should that mean something?"

"Of course it means something. Don't you find it interesting that your key number is three, the twelve being divisible by three, and your birthday is August 12; that Linka holds three memory strands, you've already had three memories, and you have nine to remember in all—three three's—your master number," she stated with a flourish.

"Trust you to zero in on that obscure connection. I didn't think you were into Numerology."

"Not in-depth, yet, but the whole thing seems to revolve around threes. Three people; Taenacea, Garth, and Faye. Faye being Linka . . . get it? Linked by Linka, who apparently holds three very crucial keys to complete the Quest. Hmmm. That in itself is unusual. Let's see your notes on the reading again. Like you, I'm better with hard copy than a tape."

"I see what you mean," Tannis moved to the back of the couch and looked over Josie's shoulder as she read the predictions from her journal. "I wonder if this numeric connection is the cycle of three the reader referred to?"

"I'd say so. And Linka must be considered the girl child, for now. Lord help us!" They looked at each other in mock horror and laughed. Josie sobered and said, "Don't be so sure you have a cause for concern. You know, Linka isn't as flaky as you think. She has an innate wisdom you tend to forget about, as well as a sharp mind, clarity of truth, and great intuitive powers. You still see her through your 'mother eyes', through which all the memories of her growing years taint your objectivity. I wouldn't worry. Her immense respect for you will keep her on track."

Seeing Tannis's skepticism hadn't diminished, she admonished, "Who pray tell was it that encouraged her individuality in the first place? You can't suddenly decide now that you don't like how she chooses to express herself when you were the very one to nurture it."

"I know, but still..." Tannis said quickly, piqued because Josie was right. But before she could add anything, Josie did. "So she's not the contained control-freak you are. Man, do all mothers want their daughters to be just like them? She's delightful just the way she is. Now, back to the Quest. Seems to me that Linka, as Faye, being the product of this great love will be the one who ties something together. You definitely need her."

"I am not a control-freak. I just exercise the choice of choosing how I live." Tannis responded automatically. It was an old argument between them, as was hers that Josie was really very sensitive and insecure, in spite of the bravado of her outward demeanor.

"Oh, and that's not control?" Josie quipped. "I see. Well, the year I spent climbing your hundred foot defensive wall had nothing to do with control, eh?"

"Nope. That was a test of character you eventually passed."

"Well, thank you madam. But let me tell you, I can hardly wait to see your iron-clad will challenged by events you *can't* control," she said smugly.

"Oh, but I can. In fact, I'm determined to. I don't see why I can't time travel in a sensible and orderly fashion. Thus my conditions." Her conviction wavered a moment when she saw Josie's sage smile. "The thing I don't get though, is the purpose of the twelve memory strands. Why do I have to experience them before I can manifest the man of my dreams?"

Josie glanced at the ceiling as if requesting celestial patience. Tannis really had no idea what she was dealing with. "From what I know, if you're going to bring him into your reality, you have to *find him* before you can capture his essence. I would think the strands imply pivotal events in Taenacea's life, in relation to herself, Garth, and Faye. You have to infuse him with substance before you can bring him into your current reality. Dust and water would be the clay you'll use to build him from your dream memories. You got that one right. But to be alive, he has to have a soul."

"Why not just Garth then? Why my memories as Taenacea, and Linka's as Faye?"

"Maybe it's collective memories that ground Garth in a time frame from which you can draw him to you, or maybe they're connected because they, rather you, are all aspects of the same oversoul. Have you an idea how many spirits are floating around in alternate realities, or doing their thing in other lives?"

"Nope, and I don't care." Tannis shook her head emphatically. "I think it's what you said first, the events that impacted the three of them in that lifetime. That makes more sense to me."

Josie's bell tinkled in agreement as she nodded. "So," she challenged, "How do you plan to direct yourself to where you want to go?"

"I'll just . . ." Tannis trailed off, a bewildered look on her face. "I have absolutely no idea. I guess I just figured because I've had these strands spontaneously, the others would happen the same way, or I would use the spells in the Magik Book to go back in time and experience the memories I need. But I don't have the faintest idea *where* I'm supposed to go as to dates and places, do I? Come to think of it," she said, as she rose and paced in front of Josie, "the professor didn't give me any dates at all. He just referred to the War of the Roses as having occurred in the same time frame. All I know at this point is that Taenacea lived near the west coast of Wales some time during the mid to late 1400s, and that about 2,000 people lived on her lands. But that could have been during her father's time, or when she was a child."

"Oh, there is poetic justice!" Josie exclaimed as she wiggled in glee. "It's not going to be so easy for you after all."

"You don't have to sound so pleased," Tannis shot back sarcastically.

"Well, if you think everything is just going to fall into place without some challenges madam, then you haven't accepted the fact that the universe has both a creative sense of humor and its own design. It operates under its own set of rules which, incidently, are not always in accord with our ideas about how things *should* work. Ask me, I know all about that." Josie stated. She sighed over her history of fractured illusions and dreams in spite of her psychic pipeline.

That was another thing Tannis loved about Josie; her ability to be candid about her own misfortunes, at least after the fact, if not during. She also had the irritating habit of instantly pointing out the very thing Tannis did not want to hear. She mused over the questions raised while Josie scanned the prayer at the front of the book and ran her finger down the page to count the lines. She looked up with dawning awareness.

"Bing . . . go! Do you realize you could have the memory strands right here in this prayer?"

"I could? What do you mean?" Tannis asked. She reached for her journal and scanned the page while Josie looked on. "But . . ." her voice trailed off.

"Apparently Wonder Woman here can time travel, but can't count. Go figure. How many lines are there to the prayer?" She assumed the tone of a mother patiently coaching a child.

Tannis ran her finger down the lines. "Ten. So?" Josie said nothing so she counted again. "There are ten lines all together. Nine, if you consider the first line an intro." Then it hit her too. She caught Josie's look of confirmation. "You could be right. If what I suspect is true, this is Taenacea's Magik Book. She wrote it, didn't she? It makes sense, especially after the feelings and visions I had when I first touched it. It's her prayer, and these must be the nine most important elements of her life. But how can the prayer at the front of the book represent important events in a life being lived after the prayer itself was written? Unless there was magic involved. Like the chicken and egg, which came first?" Josie beamed encouragement at the direction of her self-talk.

Tannis felt a mass of information settle into a pattern that fit, if magic was a prime ingredient. "But how can I be holding her book now? And the little lady. She's important somehow, and has something to do with all this. Could it be the book was zapped into my time by her? Or was it Taenacea herself that sent it here, as a guide to help unravel a puzzle, or finish something left undone? That would mean my prize, if I complete the Quest, is to get my own dream man, just like she did."

"Now you're cooking. And in response to your questions; magic, she's obviously a key, possibly, perhaps, I'd say so, and yes, you will be rewarded for your effort by claiming your man . . . and that'll be ten bucks please." Josie trilled. "Damn, I'm good! That was the fastest and easiest reading I've ever done." They burst into peals of laughter and hugged each other sloppily. Zoie, who was now stretched along the back of the couch near Josie, raised her head and glared at them in disdain, then closed her eyes firmly as if to banish the unsightly spectacle.

Josie looked from Zoie to Tannis and back again, then asked, "By the way, how's Linka planning to time travel without a familiar? In case you haven't noticed, she has no cat, and we know what an interesting relationship she has with yours, especially Zoie. So 'fess up, oh wise witch of Celtic lore, how's she going to manage that?"

"Good point, oh irritating friend of mine. Just keep throwing cogs into the wheel, why don't you?" Tannis quipped, in keeping with their silly mood.

"It's my job. I'm here to make your charmed life at least somewhat as difficult as mine. After all, why should you get the man of your dreams so easily, when all I get is a string of useless tits who have no appreciation at all for a beautiful, wise, spiritual, and incredibly sexy woman?"

"More like spinny and a tart if you ask me. And ... I wouldn't know about the sexy. You're not my type." Tannis threw over her shoulder as she walked into the kitchen to brew another pot of coffee.

"Oh, Tarbender," Josie hollered after her. "I'd like to order a glass of dry red please." If she had any more caffeine she'd have to be scraped off the ceiling. Besides, fortification of the grape was definitely called for at this juncture. Nothing she could have anticipated had prepared her for this. Her friend's revelation could easily become a case study of note, if properly recorded and verified. Her mind raced with the possibilities. But she would have to tread carefully.

Tannis pulled a half-full bottle of Pinot Noir out of the wine rack, and a chilled Moselle out of the refrigerator for herself. She grabbed two wine glasses and headed back into the living room. She'd better pick Josie's brain before they both got completely idiotic; although sometimes they came to the most astounding realizations while they goofed around. After a silly toast they read the prayer again, minds in perfect synchronicity.

"If the prayer is the key, how do I relate it to the memories I've had already?" Tannis asked.

"Use the same method you did to reason out the dust and water statement. It's all symbolic, but if you could connect one block of memory to one line, then you'd have a point of reference to work from," Josie replied, and reached for a piece of paper from the stack that was a fixture on the coffee table. She pulled a pencil from the fat ceramic jar that sat beside the stack and jotted down possible associations.

Like the mighty cat of the African plains, Tannis often took an afternoon snooze on the couch, especially if she was having a 'hot' sculpting day and planned to work into the night. After a meditation cycle, she would ask for inspiration and energy, and kept paper handy to record any impressions she might get from her dreams when she awoke. Many of her works had been inspired by dream images quickly sketched on awakening, before the memory faded.

"Do you think it's the word at the beginning of each line that's important, or the one at the end?" Josie asked, pen poised over the prayer she had copied onto a separate sheet of paper.

Tannis leaned closer, her eyes drawn to the words at the end of each line. The word 'Moon' seemed to shimmer slightly and she heard a faint tinkle of chimes. "The word at the end. 'Moon' just jumped out at me, and my signal went off just now."

"Faye's birth!" they exclaimed simultaneously. Josie chewed on her bottom lip as she did some mental calculations. "She was born in midsummer, so around July, which would make her a Cancer ruled by the feminine imaginative planet, the moon. There's a breast connection to the moon as well; Cancer rules the breast, and Leo, which is your sign, rules the heart. You said that you tied her to your breast, and the professor confirmed you lugged her around with you all the time." Josie jotted down these points while she ran a few other possibilities through her own mind. "I'll bet there's a strong influence from Neptune in her chart which would account for her 'fey' nature and affinity with the sea. Didn't you say she was supposed to be born at Aberayron on the coast?"

"Yes. That's where I was heading because I'd had an intuitive nudge that Garth was on his way. Faye wasn't due yet but Garth was determined to be back in time to greet his new child." Tannis marveled at how she knew with certainty that this was true. It was as if she could now flesh out events beyond what she had actually experienced. "There's something out of sync here," she added, puzzled by a thought that evaporated just before she could catch its meaning.

"Let's see if we can figure it out," Josie prompted, jolting Tannis back to the present. Then she added with a thinly veiled touch of envy, "You can wallow in your memories later, especially the sexy ones. The main thing now is to figure out how this works, then develop a plan."

Planning was Josie's passion. She loved to analyze and make lengthy notes about every facet of her life. 'To Do' stickers were invented just for her and covered every surface in her cluttered apartment which, in Tannis' opinion, aptly mirrored her state of mind. The problem was, she rarely followed any of the prodigious instructions so meticulously set to paper, and floated impulsively from experience to experience in total disregard of her previous intentions. She just loved the illusion of order her lists and notes gave rather than the tedium of application.

"Let's see . . . if we say the moon represents Faye and the whole birthing strand, it's going to be a lot trickier than I first thought. You're looking for events that would have had a deep significance to Taenacea on a soul level, like the birth of her first child, and her passionate relationship with Garth; events which shaped who she is, or was." Josie concluded.

"That's challenging enough if I had a pile of memories to choose from, which I don't," Tannis grumbled. This was getting complicated. How was she to get to know her alter-self well enough to understand what was significant to her?

"Use magic," Josie stated. "Isn't there a spell to direct yourself to a situation where you let's say, experience 'the stability of Earth'?"

"I wish! To use the time travel spell, I have to have a specific date or time frame, according to the Magik Book. I can't do that until I see the professor again. All I can hope for in the meantime is to have another significant dream." She cringed at the slight whine in her tone. Seeing Josie's sardonic look, she added, "Too easy, eh? You're just dying for me to try those spells, aren't you? Well, I'm not sure about all this magic stuff. In fact, I may not use the spells at all."

"You are and you will. You're just scared. An understandable reaction. But the fact is, you already practice the Wicca arts, so what's the big deal?"

"What are you talking about?"

"The herbs you grow, and all those remedies and concoctions that keep you so disgustingly healthy and young looking. And your garden." Josie stated.

"That's completely different. It's all holistic." Tannis retorted defensively.

"And a Wicca isn't? Spells are an extension of the same thing. Instead of just using growing things from the earth, the spells harness the elemental energy within the earth and cosmos, just like indigenous peoples did, of which I now have some experience. How different is it from the Shamans who marshal earth and animal forces?" She waved away Tannis' intended protest. "In case you've forgotten, everything happens for a reason. You're having this experience for a reason and Magic brought you the book for a reason. I'm assuming you are intended to use it, not just add it to your collection of first editions. There are no accidents in life, you know," she intoned. "Besides, you have all kinds of resources at your disposal. There's your father's notes, the professor, and you have Linka and me. Give me a day or two to finish my client charts, and I'll help you, as will Linka. The two of us can wade through your father's files and find anything referring to Taenacea while you play with water and dust in your studio."

Tannis liked her suggestion. In spite of her curiosity she felt overwhelmed at the thought of sifting through her father's daunting number of boxes alone. It would take too much time away from her work. Besides, she didn't have the patience.

Josie said she'd talk to Linka, since she was going to call her anyhow. Trailing Tannis into the laundry room, she launched into a more detailed account of her 'Shamanic Path to Self-Mastery'. While Tannis shook out the damp clothes and loaded the dryer, she deftly drew comparisons between Earth Medicine and Wicca applications. Tannis felt more at ease with the magical aspects of both disciplines after her discourse. When they settled back on the couch, Josie re-introduced her favorite topic; her love life, or rather the lack thereof. This was followed by a finite dissection of why her relationships always went kaput.

Four gongs from the grandfather clock reminded Josie of the stacks of charts left undone in her penthouse apartment. If she was going to devote time to this exciting new project, she had to clear her slate. She swept up her bags, promising to call Linka and bring her over later in the week. With a breezy farewell she sailed out the front door.

Used to her impromptu arrivals and departures, Tannis didn't bother to see her out. Left with plenty of food for thought, she decided to go for a walk to clear her mind and mull over their conversation before a few more hours in the studio. She was excited by what was happening with her current piece.

Chapter Six

BY SATURDAY, Tannis had transformed the rough build of her medieval lady into a piece possessing life and personality. At what she called stage three in her work, she focused on refinement, and smoothed the slightly leathery surface with damp sponges which created a marble-like finish. Since the piece would be caste while still damp instead of fired when dry, the finish now was crucial. Tannis stood back for a moment in appreciation. She slowly walked around her, pausing to view her from every angle. She felt the same brief sense of familiarity she had felt several times during the week. Then the feeling was gone.

A little over three feet high from head to hip, the female figure was noble, but far from saintly. She exuded strength and sensuality, particularly since she wore no wimple, or clothing. Tannis' hands had of their own volition added more and more clay to what had started as a more slender form.

Atop the voluptuous naked torso sat a face of paradox and mystery. The head turned slightly to the left as if in response to someone in that direction; the features commanding yet feminine. Her unique style of hollowing the pupils infused the large eyes with a compelling sense of life and almost discomforting depth of expression, yet the slight quirk on her lush lips enticed you to anticipate the witticism on the tip of her tongue.

A riot of wild curls loosely gathered at the nape of the neck, cascaded down her back and implied its mass would continue indefinitely had the body not ended where it did. With such an abundant cape, clothing seemed quite unnecessary and even the skirt she held lightly in one hand seemed ready to slip from her grasp. Caught in the act of disrobing, her brazen sensuality created a study in subtle contradictions.

Lush firm breasts lay softly on her ribcage, which in turn tapered into a delicate waist that fanned into the roundness of her hips. Her left hand loosely held the implied skirt and her right hand reached across her belly, palm up, as if to beckon someone to join her. Reminiscent of a more hedonistic time, the figure stimulated images of pagan worship long since replaced by the untouchable reserve of the Madonna-like statues more commonly depicted in the medieval era. The piece compelled tactile contact.

Well-pleased with the results, Tannis shrugged her shoulders in resignation. Once again her intent had craftily mutated into what the sculpture itself intended to be. Contract be damned. The specifications for the piece had left her oodles of room for interpretation. All she had been told was that the client wanted a medieval noblewoman around three to four feet high to fill a niche in the entrance hall of his estate. Since a more traditional full-body piece would have little impact amid the saints and classic busts in dim adjacent niches, she figured a naked torso would at least warrant a second look.

Her male and female were destined for entrance hall niches and the third, a child, was to grace a drawing room. "Wuppity-ding." Her outburst startled Zoie who lay nestled against a bag of clay on her work table. She tried to imagine what kind of person would commission three expensive pieces so carelessly. Probably an arrogant fat little man who had made millions on the commodity market and purchased a bankrupt estate and title in order to play the role of Lord of the Manor and impress his importance on weekend guests. Confucius had said, "Success give man big head . . . also big stomach." Her depiction of the client stuck in her mind.

"Gawd, I can really be nasty," she said out loud, and chuckled. Oh well, whether he appreciates it or not, she most certainly did. Carte blanche meant carte blanche.

She felt herself sag with fatigue, and draped the piece. She would have a sandwich and power snooze, then start on the medieval male. At today's pace, she could have the initial build completed. She would have to decide which of the stances roughed out on paper she would use, and a break now would garner her the energy to work through the night if necessary. She always constructed the armature and rough build in one shot in order to stabilize the point of gravity, then leave it a day to settle before she worked on it again.

Zoie and Billy-Bob followed her outside as she munched on her sandwich and scanned the yard for Ginseng. She saw him near the fence, methodically sniffing the earth as if prodding the birth of reluctant bulbs with feline encouragement. In spite of his efforts, only the crocus heads and other early bulbs heralded the beginning of another floral season. Mr. Muff, perched on the vee of the plum tree, observed in resignation for he knew there would be no dashing around the yard until the little white gardener was finished. She watched their antics a while, then called them in and shut the door.

Settled on the couch under one of the cuddle blankets always draped across the back she relaxed and let her mind wander. The cats, finished with their toilette, vied for the best spot between her legs and against the coziest fold of the blanket before they too settled for their snooze. Only Zoie sat crouched uncomfortably on her chest, her bottom nestled against her linked fingers, her face only inches from her own.

"Well, my little elemental, how about a journey?" Tannis quipped. "Take me to a medieval lord, one I can use as a sculpting model." Zoie maintained her slit-eyed stare as she closed her eyes and drifted away.

* * *

"Damnation! What is he doing here?" Taenacea breathed, and closed her eyes a moment in order to steel herself to greet the irritatingly pompous ass striding towards her; all five feet of him.

Lord Giles Kaylon picked his way delicately through the late winter muck, evaluating the surroundings, calculating what changes he would make once all this was his. Pock-marked cheeks and nose veined from too much drink accented the slash of fat lips that loosely resembled a leering grin. He ran his beady little eyes up and down the figure of the woman he approached. Her people paused in their tasks and watched with trepidation. A dark cloud seemed to gather around their mistress every time this neighbor arrived.

Taenacea's skin crawled in abhorrence. It took all her will not to smack his odious little face, and instead welcome him with some semblance of grace. "Greetings, Lord Kaylon," she uttered with considerable effort to keep the loathing out of her voice. "And what brings you to our Keep so early in the year? Were you not battling the Scots at your northern borders?"

"Quite, quite. But the enemy is persistent and has sent for reinforcements," he replied, and spit out a wad of phlegm for emphasis, which left a trail of spittle dangling from his chin.

He gets more revolting with time, Taenacea thought. "What has this to do with me, milord?" Her tone bordered on rudeness.

"I have need of your men to put an end to this threat against our borders." His tone implied he'd much rather march in and take what he felt was rightfully his.

He had once called her a witch, amongst other things, and Taenacea knew it burned him to the core that she had thwarted his greedy intents. "My borders are not in question, milord," she reminded him. "Only yours. Which has little to do with me."

The truth of her statement infuriated him. Giles was well aware that she cared not what happened outside her own borders, and biting back his desire to wipe the disdain from her face, changed his tactics. It took considerable effort. "Will you not honor the Writ of Alliance which impels us to uphold the peace of these lands?"

They had been through this time and time again. Taenacea responded with some asperity. "Yes. However, you know my holdings have always been, and still are, exempt from obligation to assist unless," she glared down at him, "we *choose* to assist. As the outcome of this difficulty on *your* borders poses no concern to *us*, I will not pull my men away from time with their families."

Taken aback by her blunt answer, Giles looked around in hopes of catching a glimpse of DunnGarth's men. He saw only a few in the Keep, slouched casually against the wall of the armory, but with hands resting lightly on their swords in readiness. He pulled himself up in a vain attempt at dignity and said, "Best I discuss this with DunnGarth himself. Where may I find him?"

"He is to return shortly, but will concur with my wishes, as you well know," she said lightly, and casually glanced towards the southern hills visible through the open gates as if he and his men would ride over the nearest ridge at any moment. She had no intention of letting this little prick know that he was not even on Welsh soil, but back in Ireland.

Red-faced with frustration and anger, Giles refused her watery offer of refreshment. He knew all he would get is the weakest of ales, not wine from her private stock. With a terse promise to return shortly himself, he retraced his steps and attempted to mount his steed with some dignity. He did not succeed. He also did not see the sneer Taenacea threw at his back, or the relief on the faces of her people. Had Taenacea known his thoughts as he rode away, she might have reconsidered the wisdom of her insolence, but the day's tasks of mucking out the Keep and checking with her Miller on the level of grains in stock wiped caution right out of her mind.

Giles Kaylon was fuming with hatred and frustration. There was no help for it; the Writ of Exemption would apply until the end of this year. Until then his hands were tied. Because of immense favors done in the past which had ensured the reign of that once benevolent English King, her holdings had been exempt from any call to arms by the crown for three generations. It was the continuation of this outrageous exemption that had prevented his own family from extending their lands southward and to the western cliffs at Aberayron. As well, her staunch refusal to support Richard of York's rightful claim to the throne could well be his own undoing unless he acted now. He had already assured his liege of her support.

"We'll just have to eliminate the problem. For only you and that strange slip of a child stand between me and my intents," Giles hissed as he bounced along with his fat legs sticking out from the flanks of his cantering mount. All his efforts to disrupt peace on her borders in order for her to seek his aid had failed. He would have to resort to a more personal attack. The time was ripe for a witch-hunt, and it would take little to ignite existing suspicions into a frenzy of fear among the stupid country folk. Seeds of distrust had already been planted and fanned by his spies. He'd see her burned as a witch, but first, he would have his way with her.

It was the custom before a witch-burning for a Magistrate to attempt to draw the devil out of the soul of the accused in cases of possession. As the appointed local Magistrate, he had the power to interrogate her both publicly and privately. A private interrogation would afford him the opportunity to rut with her and remind her of the true purpose of a woman. Then would come the torture that would rack her body with pain, but leave little in the way of telling marks.

She was a large and strong woman, but his men would hold her down, bribed by coin and the opportunity to spend their lust on her after he was done. She could accuse him of rape, but her outcry would be ignored. Everyone knew that seducing the accuser was a standard ruse used by witches with the Devil's own mark upon them. And by god, he would find a mark upon her, if he had to put it there himself! It would seal her fate in spite of her wealth and position. Not even a royal decree would be able to sway the people's lust for a burning. Once she and her whelp were gone, he would step in as her neighbor and ally and oversee her lands until the crown approved his petition to annex her holdings. Considering the large sums of his own gold and troops already placed at Richard's disposal, he was confident her lands would be his once Richard was crowned.

The Lady Taenacea had spurned his marriage and alliance proposals in favor of that Irish heathen from across the sea, and for that DunnGarth must die. It was nothing personal, he even quite liked the man. Nevertheless, it would not take many coins to arrange an unfortunate accident at sea, or on land. As to the child, her wanderings could easily propel her over the edge of one of the hidden gorges amid the hills ringing the northern end of her keep.

* * *

A cold shiver up her spine and a raspy scraping on her chin brought Tannis back into herself. "Holy Shit!" she exclaimed. She grabbed Zoie by each jowl once she had opened her eyes. "If that's your idea of a joke, I'm *not* amused." The Queen of Bitch flicked her tail in mild indignation before she lightly jumped to the floor and stalked away.

"OK, so you took me back to something important. But it's not quite what I had in mind." Tannis hollered after her. Her skin still crawled in remembrance of that swine. That Taenacea had to deal with such a horrid foe sent another shiver up her spine. The shiver was not just from meeting Taenacea's enemy in person, but from what happened afterwards. As Taenacea, she again experienced all her feelings and thoughts. But when Lord Giles Kaylon had ridden away, it was her own consciousness, not Taenacea's, that had followed him and made her privy to his evil intents. This was definitely a new development; the ability to read someone else's thoughts.

The piece of torn parchment came to mind. She wondered if it could have something to do with this latest experience. Had the piece been torn from the Writ Giles had referred to? But it was signed by DunnGarth. Would not Taenacea herself have to sign the document to make it legal? She thought again about the man whose intents to own what Taenacea had were stymied by the protective Writ. He was both horrible and dangerous. This was no game, but a life and death struggle in a time when enemies acted upon their vengeful desires. She had not heard the chimes yet felt the experience was very important. Once again she had more questions than answers.

"I can see you're going to be a great help, Zoie," she yelled. "Sure, run and hide, you beast. So you should." Ruefully, she realized that she had not been very specific in her request. Lord Kaylon was a nobleman, and she could sculpt him, not that she would want to. Point taken. She would have to be much more careful of her expressed desires, and much more specific. It almost felt like her every careless thought could come to life in some horrible way. She pushed away her paranoid thought. There was work to be done. She munched on an apple and tried to focus on the pose for her next piece. Her little jaunt into the past had given her nothing helpful in that regard. She browsed through a few of her art books in hopes a male stance would inspire her, but couldn't settle on anything.

As promised, Josie and Linka had come on Wednesday and Thursday to tackle her father's files. Sequestered in her studio, she had paid scant attention as they hauled the boxes into the hall outside the spare room. She heard faint giggles and the murmur of conversation when she went into the kitchen to get ice for her water jug, but had only stopped to chuckle at the occasional loud exclamation, assuming correctly the cats had offered their unrequested assistance.

After all the files had been stacked into teetering piles behind the closed doors of their work room, Josie drove Linka home. Thursday was another productive day after which they all had a leisurely dinner at Mykos, their favorite Greek restaurant. Josie and Linka would not be back until next week to continue with the files. Meanwhile, Tannis intended to ask the professor for specific dates. She had a suspicion nothing of import would be found in her father's notes but didn't want to spoil Josie and Linka's fun in looking. Besides, she quite liked knowing they were there, as long as they didn't intrude into her creative space.

The phone rang, but she just listened to Linka's desperate plea while it was being recorded. "Mom! Pleeese pick up. I have to talk to you." Tannis swallowed her mouthful of apple, then answered in her 'patient mother' tone. "Hi sweets. I'm all ears."

"You'll never guess what happened to me." Linka exclaimed after a dramatic gulp of air. "I was jogging last night with Rob, you know, the fellow from the gym I work out with. Well, there we were at the end of our run, in the pishing rain, right behind my apartment. I was just heading around the garbage containers when this little black thing I thought was a rat, latched onto my leg!"

"And was it?"

"Huh? No. Not a rat, a cat. Or should I say a kitten. A little black skinny thing with huge ears and enormous yellow eyes latched onto my sweats like there was no tomorrow. Soaked to the skin and howling like a demented lunatic." After only the briefest of pauses she continued. "Rob tried to pry it off me, but no way. Mom, it clung like a leech. He did get it off once, but it hissed and scratched and spit like nothing I've ever seen, not even Zoie, and jumped right back onto my leg. Sooo . . . I had no choice but to take it in for the night."

"Oh, I'm glad you did. Seems like a match made in heaven," Tannis quipped, not even trying to stifle her laughter. She stopped laughing when she realized where all this was leading. "No. Absolutely, irrevocably, and without a doubt, no. You will not dump this kitty on me; not for a lifetimes worth of 'favor' tokens. In case you haven't noticed, I already have four cats, with no intention of getting any more, so have a nice day and say good-bye."

"Geez Mom, are you PMSing, or what? I just thought you might be able to help find a home for it since you know a lot of cat people in your area." Linka wheedled sweetly.

Tannis was struck with a deliciously wicked thought. She kept her voice even and said, "Actually, I do know someone for whom this kitty would be perfect. Why not bring it over and I'll take a look at it? Should I thaw another steak, or do you have plans for dinner?" she asked, barely able to contain her glee.

"No plans other than to find a home for this little fiend toot-sweet. Sounds great," Linka said. Her mom would come through for her once again. She would probably be able to leave the kitty with her until a suitable home was found. "I'll tell you all about it. Be there in half," which was their code for half an hour.

Tannis popped a couple of potatoes in the oven to crisp bake. She hummed to herself happily as she marinated the two small but fat tenderloins, and slathered garlic butter onto two thick slices of French bread. She had just finished the salad and was sprinkling Parmesan cheese on top of the garlic bread when Linka burst through the front door.

Sensing a feline intruder, the three cats sitting on the counter beside her dashed to the door to investigate. The kitten saw the cats and scrambled up Linka's body in panic. "Ouch! Let go!" was followed by a variety of hisses, growls and ear-splitting kitty shrieks, and a frantic "Mom. Get this thing off me!"

Tannis wiped her hands and casually walked towards the foyer where Linka stood with her pony tail pulled down over her left ear. A little black object splayed on the top of her head frantically tried to grip the shifting mass of hair while it spit at the felines surrounding its human perch.

They in turn reacted to the intruder in a variety of ways. A wide-eyed Mr. Muff peered up in mild surprise and a curious Ginseng tried to climb Linka's leg to investigate. Billy Bob, secure in his maleness, glared at the newcomer for a moment, then flicked his tail and walked away disinterested. Only Queen Bitch Zoie stood braced in front of Linka, back arched in rigid indignation and dared this noisy intruder to take one step into her domain.

Tannis let loose a whoop of laughter which startled the cats and brought an irate flush to Linka's face.

"It's *not* funny! Get it off me. It's pulling my hair out by the roots," her bedraggled offspring wailed.

Tannis shooed the cats away and reached for the terrified kitten. She crooned to it softly as she disengaged it from her daughter's hair. Released from her tormentor, Linka dashed to the bathroom to repair the damage while Tannis cradled the wee thing until its little heart stopped hammering. She sat on the edge of the couch and examined the little bundle, speaking to it softly. "My, aren't you the sweetest little . . . " she tipped it over to peer at its privates, ". . . girl. Don't fret now, it's OK. No one's going to hurt you here baby."

The kitty, who immediately relaxed in Tannis' gentle clasp, examined her as well and began to speak in little chirps and trills. Her short, sparse coat of pitch black fur barely concealed painfully prominent ribs as her skinny front legs and unusually large paws began to knead on Tannis' wrists. Huge ears perched atop a pointed little face dominated by enormous amber eyes. She was a pathetic looking kitty, about four to five months old. Tannis' keen eye noted that with love and care, this little scrag-a-muff could well blossom into a beautiful sleek feline. She noted with interest that like radar, as soon as the bathroom door opened, the kitten's attention immediately swung to a more composed Linka heading towards them. With a look of utter devotion, the kitten sat up expectantly, ready to pounce on her beloved's lap the moment she sat down.

"It's a little girl." Tannis announced with satisfaction.

Linka saw the look on kitty's face and did not sit down, choosing to pace in front of her mother as she continued her tirade. "I named her Trix, temporarily of course. You have no idea what I went through last night. I had to sneak her inside and dry her off. I put her in the bathroom, but the minute I shut the door she started to wail. Mom, she made such a racket I had to turn the stereo up to try and drown her out which resulted in an irate call from Cranky Kremp." She rolled her eyes to emphasize the severity of a phone call from her cantankerous building manager. "You know I live in a No Pets, No Children complex, so I finally had to take her outta the bathroom and into bed with me, just to shut her up."

"Did that settle her down?" Tannis asked.

"Well, yeah," Linka answered reluctantly, determined not get sidetracked.

"She's only a baby you know," Tannis responded calmly. "How would you feel if you were abandoned, cold, wet and hungry, then dumped in a small room?"

"What did she expect, room service? I took her in didn't I?" Linka retorted, pressing her intent. "Did you find somebody?"

"Yes."

"Well, will they take her?" Linka asked hopefully.

"I would say so," Tannis said with a smile that tickled the corners of her mouth. "I don't think she has any choice in the matter, actually."

"What do you mean, she has no choice?" Linka asked suspiciously. On seeing her mother's enigmatic expression she stopped in her tracks and slowly sank down onto the other couch.

"It seems she's already chosen her new caretaker, don't you think? She could have clung to Rob's leg you know." Tannis relished the stunned look on Linka's face. "You said yourself she settled down as soon as she was with you. Besides, you've missed one very important detail in your enthusiasm over the Quest. You need your own feline familiar for spellmaking." She paused to let this point sink in. "Now you have one. So pout and get over it. Say hello to your new kitty and take her off my hands so I can put the steaks on the grill. There's no point fighting the obvious. I'll fix her something to eat."

She rose and placed the kitten onto Linka's lap and went into the kitchen. The two on the couch stared at each other; one in rapture, the other in disgust. Linka waged a mental battle but sensed she was defeated. She did not want a cat, but without a familiar, the spells might not work. The price of participation was high, but she wasn't about to miss out on a chance to time-travel. There was nothing to be done; she would have to keep the little nuisance if she intended to time travel, for a while anyhow. Yep, her mom was good—real good. She had known her desire to make spells would override her resistance.

Resigned to her fate, Linka quickly warmed to the intrigue of hiding her charge from the other apartment dwellers and the eagle-eyes of Crabby Kremp. Over dinner she discovered the first of kitty's passions. She was determined to sit on her lap during the meal no matter how many times she was removed. Once Linka relented, she delicately sampled each tidbit offered, which led to the discovery of her second passion; a somewhat bizarre, palate.

The resident felines glared at the little upstart, particularly Zoie, who realized her days of tormenting Linka might well be over. Ginseng, whose youth compelled him to shoot longing looks at the kitten, was ecstatic. Finally, here was someone he could both play with and dominate. By the time Tannis and Linka did the dishes, Trix and Ginseng were clamoring all over the furniture and were even joined by Muff and Billy Bob for a short but frenzied race around the house. The new addition had been accepted.

Sunday dawned fresh and clear. Only a few saucy clouds buffed along by tart sea winds marred the glorious March day. The air felt light with the prelude of spring and hinted at its approaching softness. With the patio doors open to let the morning air dance through the house, Tannis lazed in bed and sipped her morning brew. While the cats groomed each other around her, she caught up on her kitty chats; chats during which she shared her thoughts and plans.

"You know guys," she said as she stroked Zoie, "I have to get going on the medieval male, and I also want to start sculpting Garth. What do you say I make them one and the same?"

She took the pause in the group grooming as a sign of assent. "After all, the buyer won't know the piece is serving another purpose, and I have the feeling that all I have to do is sculpt him, not keep him." It was an ingenious idea. "Besides, I think I should work on Garth while I'm experiencing the strands." Chimes lightly tinkled in her head. "Ah, see . . ." she said, "I am on the right track." The signal was proving very helpful. It seemed to confirm her intentions as well as the completion of each strand.

The felines dashed in and out the open deck door while Tannis rearranged her studio. To make room for Garth, she rolled her female and another bust in progress off to the side. She had decided to build a head to hip male partner for her female, and wheeled in a stand strong enough to hold the weight of the clay. Six boxes of clay sat in readiness behind her as she began to build the armature.

Screwing together the support pipes and laying on slabs of clay was physically taxing. After she had stuck over 200 lbs. of clay onto the armature, Tannis stood back, sweaty and exhausted. She rubbed her aching shoulders and arms as she examined the pose critically. The rough form of a man was already evident. The pose was similar to the female, only his head turned slightly to the right and his arm reached across his belly in the same direction. His other hand implied it would later grasp an object in front of his waist although she wasn't certain what that would be yet. Six hours. It had taken her only six hours. "Not bad," she said aloud. Just looking at the strong form sent a shiver of anticipation down her spine, and the broad torso immediately brought Garth to mind.

The critical factor in the initial build was the point of gravity within the piece so it would not only sit in a well-balanced stance, but also not crack during the drying process. Since these pieces would go to the foundry for casting in a leathery state, drying was not as great a concern. The fact that clay had a memory was. Once the piece settled, subsequent changes like repositioning of arms would result in warping as the clay tried to recapture its original pose. Satisfied all was well, she draped Garth. "Now you just sit there and settle my love. Tomorrow I devote my entire day to you. But right now I need a break."

Tannis sat on the deck, cozy in her favorite oversized old sweater as she sipped her steaming mug of rose hip tea. When these commissions are done, I'm going on a holiday with Josie, she decided impulsively. Somewhere overseas. Her vacations over the last six years consisted of time spent in her garden with only the occasional long weekend away with Linka, Josie, or sometimes both. Her infrequent jaunts to New York and California for gallery shows had generally been quick overnight stopovers.

She and Josie had promised themselves such a trip for a long time, but either she was in the middle of preparing work for a show, or Josie was off on a Fire Walk, spiritual retreat, or trek to yet another energy point on the planet. Once she finished these pieces, she would have more than enough time and money to take a well deserved break. She made a mental note to check with Josie and tell Cal of her plans. She spilled her tea in surprise when Cal's voice drifted out from the house. "Well speak of the devil," she thought as she blotted the moisture from her lap.

"Hey babe, caught you slouching, eh," he said with a slow, lazy smile as he moved towards her. "I had an appointment on the North Shore and wanted to see how my magic gal was doing."

"I was just thinking about you, Cal," Tannis said as she received his affectionate hug. He settled in the deck chair beside her and updated her on pending contracts under negotiation and what was happening in the art world. Tannis appraised her friend while he moaned about the sudden departure of his latest paramour with his most recent client. With chiseled features reminiscent of the Marlboro man minus the swarthy complexion, Cal was a study in down home elegance. His full head of thick dark hair tipped his collar and sported a light dusting of silver at the temples which added a distinguished edge to his face. Deep set gray eyes under full lashes hid his innermost feelings. A strong nose braced a wide and full mustache, and added substance to his slightly narrow lips.

Six feet tall and lean, he moved with the smooth stealth of a jungle cat. With a little sun, a day's stubble and casual western wear, he could play the part of a rancher in town who tipped his hat to passing ladies with a laconic "Ma'am" while he looked them up and down under hooded eyes. But at the moment, clad in a soft suede jacket over a cream polo sweater, his lanky legs caressed by faded designer jeans, he reflected polished success.

She sipped her tea thoughtfully as he outlined his plans for a fall show. "No Cal," she interjected firmly, as surprised at her vehemence as he was. "I'm going to take some time off starting with a holiday this summer, after my work in progress is done. So don't schedule another show until next year."

Taken aback by her unexpected statement, Cal stifled his desire to object and mentally reviewed the impact of her decision on his plans. "No sweat, I can work with that. But tell me, what brought this on?" He was curious why the sudden desire for a holiday. Granted, she had worked nonstop for the last six years, but the decision to do so had been hers, not his. In fact, she had been so prolific, he had enough pieces in storage to do two one-woman shows, with plenty to spare. They had joked about it on several occasions and he had once said she could take a year off and not make a dent in her stock. Her current stock already included a whole new line of wall masks. Destined for next year's spring show in California, he could use them this fall if need be. Truth was, he just hadn't thought she wanted time off.

"I don't know, Cal, it just feels right now. Maybe I need to get a fresh perspective on my work and move in a new direction. Besides, Josie and I have been promising ourselves a trip for years. I feel a need to get out of my

insular world for a while and just be a real person, doing normal things."
Adding in her head, "or maybe experience a life in another era, as another
person, without distractions."

Tannis knew her decision surprised Cal. When he asked about the life
studies of Trudeau's boys, she immediately reassured him. It was an extremely prestigious commission. "Don't worry. I'm not taking off tomorrow.
Besides, I've done one of the boys already, and all three will be ready for
casting before I go. But please," she pleaded, "Don't take on any new
commissions unless the client is prepared to wait until later next year to get
it. Besides," she added with an impish grin, "you could use my absence to
boost my reclusive reputation if need be. You could even pretend I've
disappeared on some mysterious sabbatical."

She had a point, and her upcoming absence could further enhance the
aura of mystique her obsession for privacy had created. Then he remembered their client. "Before I forget, I did contact the agent for the three
pieces, and you do have carte blanche. For someone who's paying a five digit
figure per piece, the buyer doesn't seem concerned about approving preliminary sketches or what he'll actually get. But, I for one am extremely curious,
so let's have a look at what you've done."

Tannis shared her impressions of the mysterious buyer as they sauntered into the studio. Their chuckles at the eccentricities of the rich and
famous were fueled by wicked snippets from Cal while Tannis moved things
around and rolled the piece into the center of the studio. Then she removed
the draping with a flourish.

Cal stood immobilized by disbelief. Before him sat an almost perfect
likeness of Tannis! He turned to her in amazement, further shocked by her
bland expression and the dawning realization she had no idea that it was a
self-portrait of herself. Even with the sculpture's slightly fuller figure and
longer hair, there was no mistaking who this was.

Well, well, well . . . this was too rich for words. He looked at the detailing
on the piece, awed by her talent at making even herself look alive with the
still-damp clay. He could almost feel the taut muscles beneath the deceptive
softness of her skin, for the face and torso were perfectly finished. Only the
hands, lower portion of the hair, and base needed refinement. Stifling an
urge to reach out and cup one of the breasts, he turned to Tannis, whose
face now reflected her growing concern over his silence. "It's breathtaking,
babe! The best work you've ever done. It's so pagan it almost makes me want
to get on my knees and worship her."

Her ego mollified, Tannis chuckled, "She is pagan, isn't she? It happened all by itself, as if the concept sat inside me, just waiting to be built. I often got a really distinct sense of familiarity while I worked on her. But what I especially like about her is her strength."

"This is too funny," Cal thought, but he masked his amusement. Of course she would feel a sense of familiarity; she had sculpted herself. It baffled him how she could not know it. Only a woman totally unconscious of her own beauty could replicate herself without the vanity of commenting on the likeness. Just as he was about to point this out he was startled by a melodic voice right behind him.

"Here you are. Thought you might be outside . . . oops. Did I interrupt something?" Josie brushed past the man who looked vaguely familiar. Then it hit her. This must be Tannis' agent, Cal, whom she had never actually met but had seen from a distance at several of Tannis' gallery shows. Although Tannis rarely attended her own shows, she had. For some reason though, she had felt shy about approaching Tannis' agent. Since Cal only dropped by the house sporadically, they had somehow just missed bumping into each other over the years. Tannis had never said anything about how gorgeous he was, so she had never felt compelled to press Tannis for an introduction.

Cal stared at the energetic apparition of jangles that brushed past him and left a light scent of musk in her wake as she threw herself into Tannis' arms.

"Just popped in to tackle those files and hug my favorite pal," she trilled as she turned to look at the statue. "So, let's see what you're . . ." She stopped mid-sentence to look from the sculpture to Tannis, then back again. "You never told me you were sculpting yourself. And half nude, no less. Come on, what gives?" As soon as the words were out of her mouth, she realized it was not herself Tannis had sculpted, but Taenacea. Thank God she hadn't blurted out anything else. Tannis wouldn't have told Cal who this woman might be.

What followed was a comedy of errors, both in expression and gesture. Tannis looked at the piece in stunned surprise, then dawning recognition. A slow flush settled on her face. Josie looked at Cal with thinly veiled interest, and Cal looked just plain confused before his eyes locked with Josie's. Both burst out laughing at the absurdity of the situation, and at the confused look on Tannis' face.

Tannis shot them a dirty look and pulled back her shoulders in indignation. "Well, thank you very much," she retorted, "It's nice to know my friends find me so amusing. Josie, meet Cal, Cal meet Josie. Now please excuse me while I attempt to gather whatever shred of dignity I have left. I'll get us some refreshments. For your information, she doesn't look *that* much like me. She's a lot heavier and shorter than I am, her eyes are bigger, and her nose is slightly hooked. Mine isn't." Then she stalked out of the studio. Left alone, their laughter subsided into an awkward silence. They walked around the sculpture and covertly appraised each other like two circling alley cats. It was Josie who threw the first punch to test the measure of the man. "So, you're the elusive agent who works my pal so hard."

"Not me. She drives herself, which you should know if you're a close friend of hers." His statement sounded tart, so he added with sincerity, "I'm just lucky enough to be the one she allows to market her marvelous work."

Satisfied that he genuinely appreciated the genius of her friend, Josie relaxed a little, but felt somehow vulnerable. It was just like at the shows she had attended; she wanted to approach him, but something had held her back; something she could not explain. She read his aura while he walked around the piece again. His colors were clear; a good man, and a looker at that. From what Tannis had said, he was quite the ladies man, and she could see why. He was very attractive. She knew he'd never been married, and wondered if he was in a relationship, or available, or worst case scenario, gay.

A more composed Tannis returned just then. With a rueful smile she said, "OK guys, now that I feel like a total fool, let me cover this up and let's get into the living room. I can't believe I could unintentionally sculpt a likeness of myself and not even know. No wonder I felt such a strong sense of recognition about the piece," she said to Cal. She shot Josie a quick 'mums the word about Taenacea' look. Josie mouthed a silent 'gotcha' as they left the studio. If this was how Tannis wanted to play it, it was OK by her.

Cal sat himself on the couch beside Tannis. Josie sank into the armchair opposite which gave her a clear view of Cal while speaking to both.

Ever the gentleman, Cal got the ball rolling. He smiled at Josie. "I understand you and Tannis are planning a holiday this summer. Where to?" he asked. An awkward pause and furtive look between the two told him something was amiss.

Josie had no idea what he was talking about, but recovered smoothly. Tannis must have finally decided to take a holiday and told Cal before mentioning it to her, which smarted a little. But she waved her hand negligibly and said, "Oh, so you cleared it with Cal—good," as if their plans had hinged on that one detail. Warming to the prospect of actually taking a vacation together, she impulsively added, "We're doing the British Isles. As a matter of fact, there are some spots I want to pop back to, Stonehenge for example. I have a contact at the National Trust who can arrange to get us right into the circle. No one has been allowed to get close to the stones for years, you know. It's been cordoned off for ages."

Tannis smiled at the subtle game being played. It was always awkward when two close friends who knew of each other but had never met, finally did. Although both were special to her that alone did not guarantee they would like each other. Neither had pulled out their deadly weapons yet; Josie's cutting tartness, or Cal's disdainful politeness, which was a good sign. To reassure Josie she exclaimed, "Super. I just knew you could pull that off." Then she turned to Cal. "Josie's handling the itinerary. With her contacts," she couldn't help adding, "and planning abilities, our fabulous destinations will be mapped out in no time."

Josie shot her a quick 'I'll get you for that crack' look before asking slyly, "So, tell me, who is the lucky recipient of your half naked likeness?" She wondered how Tannis would handle being hit with something unexpectedly, like she had.

Her answer slipped out smoothly. "It's our mystery client, and he doesn't know she looks a little like me—and he won't." She looked pointedly at Cal and waited for his nod. "The chances of my meeting this buyer are about a million to one, considering he had somebody else commission the pieces on his behalf. Besides, it's probably only going to collect dust in some shadowy nook of his crumbling castle." She then preceded to tell Josie about her humorous impression of the elusive buyer in hopes of dissolving any remaining tension.

"I don't think your work should collect dust anywhere, especially *this* piece, but it's not for me to say what you do with her." Josie said peevishly.

Cal was bemused. He didn't know quite what to make of this snippet of self-possession, or the mysterious undertones of her comments. Her bizarre appearance with all those clinking things around her neck was not his style. It was also difficult to determine what the rest of her looked like under the layers of stuff that swaddled her almost to the knees. But she exuded a strange kind of appeal, and as Tannis' best friend, he suspected a keen intelligence lurked under her ditsy exterior.

Just then the front door crashed open. A sudden blast of cold air washed over them, accompanied by ear-splitting howls interspersed with some very irate and human curses. Tannis wondered what Linka was doing here. Interesting. It would be the first time her three favorite people were all in a room together. Curious this should happen today; Cal meeting Josie for the first time, and all three together for the first time.

"Help. Trix is driving me nutso, Mom. She thinks I'm her personal, full time entertainment unit. I can't get any work done so thought I'd bring her over to play. Hey, Josie, and Cal. How's my Daddy-O? You two finally get to meet. Cool. You'll love each other," Linka exclaimed, giving both a beaming smile before she turned back to her mother. "Gee thanks mom. Have a party and *not* invite me," she chided. Her feline passenger Trix, scrambled from the tote bag as soon as she placed it on the floor and scooted towards her waiting pal, Ginseng.

The next half hour was an exercise in futility. Trix and Ginseng tore around the house like lunatics. Josie relished the story of how Linka got her kitten, delivered from the perspective of both mother and daughter, and Cal was smart enough not to get in on this 'chick thing' happening around him. Rarely had he been within a circle of such uniquely different women. He watched them with amused perplexity: The Gypsy, the Flake, and the Jock.

The air buzzed with chatter which seemed to change topic from one moment to the next. Yet, even when they moved to the kitchen where efficient and ineffectual hands prepared a tray of snacks, not one word was missed and every question was answered. He realized something else too. Not since he was a boy on the ranch in the care of Mexican domestics, could he recall women together who so openly showed affection for each other. Although there was no end to the snide remarks and sharp witticisms that flew between the three, they were delivered fondly and accepted light-heartedly. The only cattiness evident were the furballs who streaked through the room, for now the boys had joined the kitty fracas. Cal grinned with pleasure at the sudden outbursts of heart-felt laughter. Secretly he loved the bedlam, and found it oddly comforting to be part of this chaotic happiness. That was it—happiness—something he only experienced on his recently rare visits to the ranch. More accustomed to the jaded and contrived pleasure expressed by his moneyed clientele, he was reluctant to leave this atmosphere of genuine warmth. But leave he must.

It was great to chat with Linka again, for he hadn't seen her in months. Adopted by her as a favorite uncle, she had labeled him Daddy-O. When they had first met ten years ago, Linka tried to ignite her mother's romantic interest in him, but after a particularly enlightening reprimand from Tannis, resigned herself to his current role as special friend. When Cal did reluctantly rise to leave he hugged Tannis and Linka lightly. After a moment's hesitation he also exchanged a somewhat stiff hug with Josie; a hug from which she quickly extracted herself to turn and dash to the bathroom.

Linka shot her mother a 'what's with her' look, but before Tannis could do more than shrug Cal was gone and Josie was back. She said nothing about her sudden departure, instead, launched into a complicated explanation of how they would proceed with the files. When Linka mentioned she was going with her mother to see the professor the next evening, Josie, feeling left out, flipped her braid in irritation and said, "I don't see why I can't go if Linka is going too."

"He'll think Taenacea and her troops have descended on him, that's why." Tannis said, "I want to get specific dates and also find out more about this awful Lord Kaylon." Both aired their views after Tannis described the horrid little man, and the unusual experience of knowing what he was thinking after he left the keep. They speculated on just how he fit into Taenacea's life until Josie changed the subject.

"By the way, how can Linka use a kitten as a familiar, considering what happened to you with Zoie, an adult cat?" she asked, curious. "God knows where she might end up!" She had difficulty imagining Trix as the transformer for time travel.

"I was thinking the same thing, Mom." She hadn't, but Josie's inquiry made her suspicious of her mother's explanation.

"She found Linka didn't she? Trust me. She knows exactly what to do. That's why she showed up. As Josie would undoubtedly confirm, its destiny," Tannis stated. "Besides, my experience was my fault not Zoie's. I wasn't specific enough. So let that be a warning to you," she admonished her daughter.

"Hello! Am I four years old, or what?" Linka retorted. "I don't plan to do any time travel yet," she lied. "Not until she knows who's boss here. Any spell making I do now would be to try and tranquilize her. My place is wrecked. I can't believe something so small can do so much damage without being seen doing it! It's like I blink, and zap—a magazine is shredded into a thousand pieces."

Her response was eyerolls and chuckles. She sighed deeply and glanced at her watch. Then she rose and went over to the phone. There was no sympathy to be had from these two. "Trix!" she hollered, "We're outta here. The mama's gotta work in the morning." She stopped in her tracks. She couldn't believe she had just said that. She sounded just like her mother— a crazy cat lady. Josie was staying so she called a cab, then went to hunt up her errant charge.

"I'm free Tuesday Josie. To go through the files. Call me. See ya tomorrow, Mom," she said and gave both a hug before she headed out the door with Trix peeking out from her tote bag.

Barely able to constrain their laughter, they watched the cab pull away, then let loose. "That girl is a hoot." Josie exclaimed. "I'd say Trix is meant for her. Who would have thought she'd end up with such a little skittle-ball. And for all her huffing and puffing, she's going to become just as nauseating with Trix, an appropriate name by the way, as you are with your brood. It seems the Quest has unleashed some unusual twists and turns in our lives already."

She caught Tannis's speculative look and responded with an emphatic, "Don't even think it. I have no intention of now, or ever, getting a cat. Since I don't plan to do any time travel I won't need a familiar, so stop with the look. Besides, you know I'd be a lousy mom the way I just up and leave when I feel like it. Now, let's go have a good look at Taenacea."

"You really think that's who she is?" Tannis asked.

"Isn't she? Both the reader and professor told you about the likeness, so it's got to be her, since you insist it isn't you." Josie said.

"I never thought about it while I was building her, but you could be right," she said with growing excitement. Well. Her decision to build Garth in a similar stance made sense. It seemed the lovers were an inseparable pair, even now destined to be together.

"I want to see your other stuff too, especially those Egyptian murals you've just finished. Then I want you to tell me everything you know about that luscious man, Cal, whom incidently, you've been hiding from me, you witch. I think I'm in love." She kept her tone light and responded to Tannis' "Oh brother, here we go again" with a sexy wiggle as they sauntered into the studio arm in arm.

Chapter Seven

IT WAS NOW MIDDAY. Forgotten was her disturbing night of jumbled dreams where cats ate from the table and a howling Josie clung to Cal's leg. Giles Kaylon had strutted through her house, then outside into the Keep where he instructed builders to rip down everything, especially her unsightly greenhouse. A host of scraggy kittens shredded the rolls of parchment which littered every surface and Cal led in a troop of short, fat clients to bid on a sculpture of her naked and warped torso. Josie ran around looking for her lists. The plane was waiting and she didn't know where she was supposed to go.

Handling clay always calmed her, and considering the Freudian aberration she had awoken from, some vigorous clay pounding was just what she needed. Its cool smoothness quickly soothed the muddled residue of her dreams and while she worked on Garth she told him everything, even newly remembered details she had not actually experienced. By the time she spoke of the odious Giles, Garth's face was roughed in and his torso defined.

Zoie rose from her favorite studio spot at one point to jump up on the platform and sit on the opened bag of moist clay. From her perch on the bag she hissed at the boys who trampled across the work bench and batted sculpting tools onto the floor. But Tannis was oblivious to both her surroundings and the cats' antics. The sky had cleared and shafts of watery sunlight from the two skylights in the ceiling highlighted the contours of Garth's face as she worked on his features. Needing a break to clear her blurry eyes, she caressed his cheek lightly and went outside.

Yoga exercises loosened the tightness in her neck and shoulders and several deep breathes of the loamy dank air cleared her head. Back in the studio, she felt a sudden desire to wrap her arms around Garth and feel him. Impulsively she grabbed the splattered old smock she sometimes wore and put it on. Then she cranked up the platform until she was almost eye level with the sculpture.

She closed her eyes and imprinted his dream image in her mind, then clasped him lightly and ran her hands over his back. A slight tingling in her fingers urged her to knead and press. Up and down the arms, around the chest and ribs, and down the lean muscled belly, her inner vision directed her hands to duplicate her memory of his body. Soon, discarded blobs of clay lay on the floor, many squashed flat by her feet as she moved around the piece.

Finally her trance-like state began to diminish and a groan of discomfort from knotted muscles induced her to stop. She stood back to view the results of her impulse. In all her sculpting years, she had never done anything like this. Like mental Braille, an unseen force had guided her hands to replicate the man of her dreams. Most of Garth's body was ready for final smoothing and only his hair, hands, and the area around the base required more work. She glanced at the wall clock. Three hours had reaped results generally not achieved in triple the time. The resounding gong of the grandfather clock in the living room abruptly brought her back to reality, and reminded her of other obligations. For a moment she stood perfectly still, in awe of what she had done. She wondered if the state of other-beingness she had just experienced could happen at will. A gentle tinkle of chimes assured her it could. Mollified by her confirmation, she wrapped Garth and left the studio. What she needed now was a rest, then it was off to pick up Linka and see the professor. In order to encourage him to answer the questions she had prepared, she intended to gift him with a fine bottle of Port, if there was such a thing.

The gentle therapy of a soak in the tub dissolved the aches in her arms and shoulder blades. Tannis was so relaxed after her bath it took only moments to fall into a deep dreamless sleep, and when she awoke two hours later, she felt completely refreshed. She gave Linka a quick call to let her know she would be over shortly, fed the cats, tucked the Magik Book and parchment in her tote bag, and drove to the nearest Specialty Liquor Store.

The clerks knew nothing about Port, so she used price as an indicator of quality and chose a Portuguese Fonseca. "This had better be worth it," she thought as she paid the fifty-six dollars, plus taxes. The professor's life probably consisted of little outside of history and tippling. Her offering might entice him to be more forthcoming with what she needed right now: specific dates.

"Hi Mom. Mooove! I can't open the door with you right there," was the frustrated greeting as a crouched Linka tried to shoo Trix away from the open apartment door. "Trix just oinked out on a heap of smoked salmon and cream cheese—my supper. Gawd. I'll be glad to get out for a while." She straightened up and brushed a lock of hair out of her eyes, more like the harassed mother of several preschoolers than the caretaker of one kitten. Trix rubbed against Tannis' legs in greeting, let loose with a hysterically warbled meow, then dashed away.

Tannis noted the basic elements of Linka's apartment were still intact, like the furniture, but most of her attractive ornaments were nowhere in sight. What really changed the tone and smacked Tannis in the face was the riot of colorful balls and cat toys that littered the room. It looked like a veritable pet store. "Good lord. You know she won't play with half of this," she admonished.

"I know . . . now. Talk about a short attention span." Thankfully her mother didn't comment further. "She'd still rather shred magazines, books, and plants. She also clawed the hell out of my candles. They're now toast. The mini-blinds are this afternoon's passion. She loves the way they twang when she jumps on them."

Tannis noticed a few missing potted plants and suspicious dark spots on the pale sandstone hued carpet. Her gaze stopped in a corner where once a lovely Areca Palm had fanned its froths over the back of the creamy white couch. Now only a few chewed and frayed strands hung dejectedly over a carpeted cat activity centre. The multitude of fluorescent colored toys attached to the corners of the impractical construct seemed a poor substitute to her.

"How did you get all this stuff in without being seen?" she asked. Once Linka set her mind to something she gave one hundred percent, but even she had outdone herself this time. Hopefully she'd soon realize it was her time Trix needed, not all this stuff.

"I conned Rob into taking me in his truck on Saturday. We hauled it in late at night. I figured he owed me since he was the one who first suggested I take Trix in for the night." She leaned towards Tannis and whispered, "We'd better go while she's distracted," as if there was a remote chance of leaving without Trix noticing. Trix did follow them to the door, but sat amid the jumble of shoes as if she knew this outing was a necessary prelude to her upcoming task. They arrived at the professor's door in high spirits, due largely to Linka's recount of Trix's cute antics over the past few days.

"Portuguese Fonseca? For me? How thoughtful," the professor exclaimed, almost giddy with excitement. He would soon hold the Magik Book, and sip on the most delectable of Ports while he examined it. Tannis' daughter was delightful, and he felt his nose tingle from the fresh citrus scent that wafted towards him when she moved. He found two glasses, smaller than his, and insisted they sample the Port. With a slight tremor, he took a delicate sip from his own and sighed in rapture as the ruby liquid snaked down his throat. Then he leaned against his desk, arms folded across his rumpled vest, and waited as Tannis pulled out her notebook and a pencil. Like students in a private classroom, mother and daughter gave him their full attention.

"First, I have been able to verify records still exist regarding several legalities pertaining to Lianarth, Aberayron, and most importantly, Taenacea's Irish lands. Fascinating, and quite an unusual situation for the times." He paused for dramatic effect as much as to put events in proper sequence. "As I said before, Taenacea and DunnGarth's families both originated in Ireland. However, therein lies a much more complex link. I found several documents, one of which deeded the holdings of Lagohaire to what would be Garth's grandfather, William MacCumal. Like the other two documents from earlier periods, it states his family was to hold the deed under crown sanction for thirty years, or until such time as a descendant of his married a descendant of the original owner's line, the Lagohaires." He paused dramatically and added with a flourish, "And that was exactly what happened when Taenacea married Garth."

Linka, quick on the uptake, asked, "So the title and land in Ireland were Taenacea's, as were the lands in Wales, and by marrying Garth, she reclaimed what had been hers all along."

"Exactly," the professor exclaimed. "But for quite unusual reasons. There had been an ancient bond between the two families going back well before Garth's great grandfather's time, yet I could not find one record of marriage between the two families prior to Taenacea marrying Garth."

"What kind of a bond?" Tannis asked, surprised by a rising sense of inner excitement.

"It all started with their ancestors, two chieftains in the twelfth century who joined forces to oust the troublesome owner of the land which lay between their two slightly larger holdings. Unusual in an era when most holdings were small, yet fought over with barbaric savagery. Whatever the reason, and some say there was a tragic tale of love involved, these two families worked the new tract of rich farmland together and shared the yield. Joined by this communal tract, they each had one less border to defend, and in time, shared other goods and services. Combined manpower also enabled them to defend, and increase the size of their holdings. You could say they formed a peaceful coalition that lasted for hundreds of years."

"Did Taenacea know about her heritage in Ireland before she married Garth?" Tannis asked.

"There is no mention of it in any Welsh records, so I would think not," the professor replied with a shrug.

In her heart Tannis knew love bound their union, in spite of the lands Taenacea would inherit. Before she had a chance to ask, Linka did. "When did she find out?"

"Garth must have told her on her wedding day or thereabouts because he sent a petition to England requesting royal approval before proceeding with the Writ of Transfer."

"What was the date on the document?" Tannis asked quickly as he paused to take a sip of Port.

"DunnGarth's petition was dated prior to their marriage in the summer of 1482. Another letter to a Magistrate in Ireland shortly after confirmed royal approval and requested the Writ of Transfer be filed. The second letter was dated just after their nuptials were recorded in the local parish." His eyes darted from one to the other as they both began to speak, and he held up his hand as if to fend off a barrage of questions, adding, "In spite of his own love for the land, one thing in Garth's favor was that he took it upon himself to search for any legitimate heir to title when others before him had assumed there were none. He had heard of this ancestral member of the Lagohaire family rumored to have landed on Welsh shores. It was what led him there, and to Taenacea herself."

Tannis was elated. Finally she had a date. Linka, more interested in herself, asked, "What about me? Did you find out anything about Faye and what happened to her?"

"All in good time, young lady," The professor would not be dissuaded from a topic he found fascinating and stoically continued with his clarification of why the original Irish Writ was so unusual. "I'm speaking of the Irish lands now. You see, to ensure that the joint holdings of the two families would receive equal attention and protection, the Writ stipulated both lands be held in the stewardship of first one family for thirty years, then by the other until such time as two of their offspring married and the holdings finally become one."

"I don't get it. Who appointed the caretaker when the deed changes hands? The Crown? And what if the caretaker decided not to honor the Writ, or was killed?" Linka asked, perplexed.

"This notion of theirs was poetry in motion," the professor replied, beaming at his play on words. "You must understand. Land was everything, for it represented power and prosperity. Raised to honor the Writ and appreciate its benefits, the caretaker was often the eldest son, but always the most responsible appointed by joint agreement of the two families. Since thirty years roughly represented the length of a caretaker's adult life, ravaging the adjoining lands would be like robbing his own grandchildren of their heritage. Nothing was to be gained."

"With fewer defensive battles to wage, this arrangement maintained and increased their holdings and wealth. Since the deed was transferred to the family title, the death of a caretaker would have no notable impact, and another steward would be appointed in his place." He paused to rub his hands together and mumbled, "Now where did I put those documents?"

"There's still something I don't get about the title exchange," Linka said, "Was it legal?"

"Precisely why I want you to see these documents. For the answer is right here." He turned to Tannis. "Could I see that slip of parchment, please?"

He scrutinized it carefully then compared it to one of the documents he held in his hand. Then he waved them over. "See here. What confounded me about the title was how the Writ could legally pass between two families with different names, using only one name on the deed." His eyes darted from page to page as he explained. "Here is the signature of DunnGarth on a copy of his letter to the Magistrate dated 1482, which matches the signature on your piece of parchment. However, this is what I want you to see." He lay several documents on top of each other so only the signatures and dates at the bottom showed, then placed the slip of parchment on top of the first and said, "Now, compare all four and tell me what's different. I've placed them in chronological order with the most recent date on top." He moved back slightly and gave them space to examine the signatures.

Tannis scanned the signatures and noted the dates, 1482, 1392, and 1303. Her eyes lingered on the slip of parchment with Garth's signature, verified as genuine by the professor. Beside her, Linka exclaimed in exasperation, "The dates and writing is different but the names are the same. I don't get it."

"I thought so too at first," said the Professor. "But if you look again you'll see Garth's signature has the prefix Dunn, with a double 'n' denoting his ancestral line, the MacCumals, whereas the next one down is spelled with only one 'n' so it reads Dun, for the original DunLagohaires. The next one reverts back to the double 'n', and the last one is signed with only one 'n' again." He took a deeply satisfying breath at his own cleverness and concluded, "Don't you see? It was so subtle I almost missed it myself. The last title holder was Taenacea DunLagohaire. Working backwards that would mean DunnLagohaire represents the MacCumals, which meets legal requirements and denotes which family is acting as caretakers."

"So the MacCumal name doesn't show up in any documents then?" Tannis asked. She thought it strange they would agree to legal anonymity.

"Because the Lagohaire holdings were originally double the size of the MacCumal lands. A small price to pay for the benefits reaped, I would say. But their name boasts a fame all its own." He reached for a thick book on his desk. "The warrior chief, Finn MacCumal is part of Irish lore. You may have heard of the tale. Known as the Finn, he was considered the defender of Ireland's shores. I'm not saying Garth's family are the legitimate descendants of the legendary Finn, as many claim to be, or if he had ever actually existed. The Irish, of course, swear he did. But here," he handed the book to Linka, " I've marked the section on the Finn and several songs and other legends that could be linked to Faye and Taenacea." He turned to Tannis and asked, "Now, may I see that Magik Book of yours?"

As Tannis handed him the book, a shudder racked her body. She suddenly felt so clammy and ill she thought she would have to vomit. She rose and asked where the washroom was. Once there, after a series of dry heaves and feeling only a little better after she splashed some water on her face, she returned to find both Linka and the professor engrossed in the books each held. Still queasy, she sank into her chair and took a small sip of Port to steady her nerves. The taste wasn't nearly as abhorrent as she'd imagined and surprisingly her queasiness began to subside. Only the occasional rustle of paper now punctuated the silence. She was about to prompt the professor when her vision suddenly blurred and a rapid succession of images flashed before her eyes.

A young boy walked with a deer along a narrow mountain path, then was surrounded by huge hunting dogs, their fangs bared. A Viking held a bloody dripping head in each hand, and a kneeling blonde-bearded man wept at the side of a young maiden lying upon a funeral pyre. Then everything went black. Startled, she thought she had cried out in protest, but neither the professor or Linka appeared to notice. As suddenly as the visions had begun, they stopped. She felt just fine again. She wondered if handling the Magik Book had triggered these visions, as it had with Linka. But the image of the Viking confused her. He didn't fit in with the other images somehow.

She jotted her impressions down in her notebook and had just finished as the professor reverently closed the book in his hand and said in unabashed awe, "What I am holding here, my dear, is a genuine book of magic. Scripted by Taenacea I'd say." He relished a surge of satisfaction. What he had suspected was correct. She *had* been a witch. "It's most unusual, however," he continued, "to see any written spells from that era, particularly bound into a book. Nothing of the like was found when Margery Jourdayn, England's most famous witch was burnt at the stake in 1441. I suspect because she was illiterate, like others of her ilk. But this one . . ."

He stifled his inner excitement and continued in what he hoped was a matter of fact tone. "I'm surprised at the superb condition of the book. Although the embossing on the outside is faded, the inside is as fresh as if it had just been written. I'll have it authenticated by one of my colleagues who specializes in carbon dating of paper and ink, but I am positive it is genuine."

"No!" Tannis' voice reflected her panic. She had the feeling that should the book leave her possession, it would cease to exist. Fighting down an inexplicable annoyance she added, "I don't care to have it authenticated. You may examine the book again of course, but only in my presence."

Linka's eyes darted from one to the other. Uh oh! Her mother's voice held a steely edge she recognized. She quickly glanced at the professor. He looked absolutely stunned, then noticeably annoyed.

He was not only stunned by her words, but also by the sudden surge of rage and frustration that caused his face to redden. For a moment he even felt an urge to do her harm. At least she had not denied him further access, but her arrogant tone infuriated him and he felt resentment settle in his belly like a leaden ball.

"As you wish," he said curtly. "But if this book has been transported through time, you must consider its historic importance. I might also suggest a past-life regression to confirm your connection with the book, and with Taenacea." Forcing himself to use a more congenial tone he asked, "Have there been any new developments since last week? Any new dreams?"

Tannis had not missed his reaction to her outburst and felt a moment of revulsion as his anger played across his face. The sound of chimes, accompanied by an unsettled feeling in the pit of her stomach caused her to hesitate. Something had shifted between them. "I did meet Taenacea's neighbor, Lord Giles Kaylon. But only briefly. He came to pay his respects to Garth." She omitted any mention of the reason for his visit and Taenacea's dislike for the man. "Do you know anything about him?" she asked. She didn't like what she was feeling and wanted to change the subject.

Sensitive to the shift of energy in the room and surprised by her mother's evasive reference to Giles, Linka closed her book and watched them carefully.

"Oh yes." His demeanor changed immediately. "Lord Kaylon was a powerful man and staunch supporter of Richard 111 of Gloucester. I must say he merited more historic attention than he received, even though Richard was defeated by Henry VII, the leader of the Lancaster Party. Their definitive battle at Bosworth Field in 1485 ended the War of the Roses and in time, united the two royal houses. However, Lord Kaylon did play a key role in English efforts to reconcile Wales to the Union of England. He was a man of vision. Unfortunately his countrymen, particularly the Welsh patriots, considered his efforts a betrayal, as did Taenacea, even though the annexation of Wales was inevitable."

Tannis could have sworn he took the fact that Giles had been slighted in the annals of history personally. The unpleasant image of the arrogant little swine came to mind, so she quickly changed the subject. "Do you know when Taenacea was born and died? And Faye?"

Hearing her 'other' name, Linka sat up attentively.

"Yes, well . . ." What he had been about to say died on the professor's lips. He knew, but didn't want to say. If he did, he was afraid Tannis would never come back, and he couldn't let that happen. He had to see Taenacea, er, Tannis again. And he had to get her book. He had noticed how intrigued Linka was with the Book of Fables still on her lap, and saw a solution to his dilemma.

"Yes, well, what I meant to say was that I'm still waiting for some rather crucial transcripts. These things take time. I will contact you the moment I have the information." He turned to Linka. "Please feel free to take the fable book home, young lady. I see you have some fascination for it, and you can return it when I see your mother next." The last was added with a flourish as if Linka was graced with the loan of some priceless treasure. "And you may keep these copies of the Writs if you like," he said to Tannis as he pulled them from his desk and handed them to her.

Tannis rose and grabbed the documents before he changed his mind. She wanted to leave, now. She had been put off twice now, and had no intention of coming back just to get embellished snippets of history. Any further contact with the professor would be by phone. She sensed he was withholding information, but had no idea why. Well, if she could not get it from him, she would get it elsewhere. Occupied with her own thoughts, she missed his look of loathing when she picked up the slip of parchment and held her hand out for the Magik Book. He released it reluctantly and managed to mask another surge of resentment behind a watery smile. Linka's polite thanks and farewells made their departure only a little less awkward.

This time he did not stand outside the door as they got into Tannis' Cherokee. Instead, after a hasty farewell, he slammed the door and leaned against it, breathing heavily. He was thoroughly confused. Oh dear," he whispered. "What has happened here?" The passionate rancor just experienced was completely alien to his nature. The instant when her arrogance almost caused him to do her bodily harm frightened him. Certainly he had felt moments of envy when a colleague was credited with finding something he had missed, but irrational fury, never. It was the book. He wanted the book, yes, but his intense reaction when it was withheld had been most inappropriate. Perhaps he had been working too hard, or his sleepless nights had fatigued him to the point of emotional instability. Whatever the reason, he would have to take care. He could not afford to alienate her, and he feared he might have just done so.

As soon as Tannis pulled away Linka asked, "OK, what was that all about?"

"What was what all about?" Tannis asked innocently.

"Oh, come on. Like I didn't feel the charge between you two when you told him he couldn't keep the Magik Book. And you told him nothing about how gross that creep Giles was either. How come? You got all evasive."

"It's just your imagination working overtime, sweets. I was curious what he'd have to say about Lord Kaylon. I guess I got frustrated because I didn't get a chance to ask all my questions, and . . . still don't have Taenacea's date of birth or death."

"You aren't tired, you're just making excuses because you don't want to talk about. Don't think I don't know. But you did get the year of Taenacea's marriage, whereas I got sweet-tweet outside the fable book." Linka moaned.

Tannis thought for a moment. "You do have a date. If you were a moon child, a Cancer like Josie says, you would have been born in June or July of 1483." Which also meant Taenacea was married in September or October of 1482, if Faye was a premature baby," which she had suspected.

"Then we both have a date since it's only the year we need, right? For the spells I mean. In the meantime, I have a whole pile of fables to read. These stories are fascinating and there's only one or two I remember grandfather telling."

Distracted, Tannis barely heard her recount some of the tales and declined her offer of tea when they reached her apartment. She was far more disturbed than she wanted to admit. For when the professor had touched the Magik Book, something unpleasant had been unleashed. Just thinking about it made her very uncomfortable.

The next morning, Tannis gave Linka a quick call to see if she was still coming over, and when. She had a hair trim scheduled and some errands to run. Linka answered in her 'I'm a little low' voice.

"How's my darling girl?" Tannis asked.

"Tired and yucky, a shrub unit of the scraggiest kind," was the dejected response. It had been raining steadily since last night. Unless a strong weather system blew in from the sea, the clouds, held fast by the north shore mountains could weep dismally for days.

"A perfect day for rummaging through files," Tannis said briskly. "I have to go out for a bit, but I'll leave the key for you in the usual spot. You can cuddle up in front of the fire if you like. I'll make us some hot chocolate when I get back. When's Josie picking you up?"

"Anytime now," Linka stated, only marginally cheered by the thought of the sinful beverage sipped before a roaring fire in the company of two of her favorite people.

When Tannis returned from her errands she plopped her dripping umbrella into the ceramic cylinder beside the large potted palm, and placed her grocery bags on the tiled floor while she hung her jacket in the closet. She ran her fingers through her damp curls then picked up the bags and descended the two steps which led from the tiled entrance into her sunken living room. She glanced down the hall on the right which led to the bedrooms and on her left to the guest bathroom, laundry room, and pantry connected to the kitchen. No cats ran to investigate the contents of the rustling plastic bags for they all lay sprawled around the living room. Billy-Bob and Ginseng raised their heads in a sleepy slit-eyed welcome, then stretched deliciously and curled into a new position.

She savored the prosaic scene of her beloved domain as she walked to the kitchen. A cheery fire crackled in the fireplace set into the middle of the floor to ceiling bookcases along the right wall. She had made the large tiles around the fireplace herself and glazed the Moroccan relief pattern in ivory, burgundy, and navy blue. She had also hand-tooled the large Sacred Round, an antiqued ceramic Mayan calendar which dominated the wall above the mantle.

Against the low wall separating her living room from the hallway, a glossy-leafed Peace Lily brushed against the Riesener mahogany roll-top desk where she scripted her journal entries and attended to her household and business ledgers. Two large sofas and an oversized armchair covered in a puma colored suede-like fabric were accented by a profusion of ethnic cushions patterned in rich mulberry, cinnabar, navy, and creamy white.

Tapestry shaded lamps cast their soft light from the rare, ebony-inlaid medieval trestle stools she used as end tables. Unusual relics sat atop the long oak-joined Tudor side table placed against the back of the couch facing the fireplace. Linka and Josie sat on the floor, their backs resting against a sofa, silent in their absorption. They paused to throw her a distracted wave, then bent their heads back to their task. The surface of the enormous low coffee table in front of them, its square top inlaid with beaten brass was now heaped with stacks of files. Only a tall grouping of fat beeswax candles rose above the bed of bulging folders.

Exotic flavors blended in subtle opulence as firelight twinkled on the brass and gilt surfaces of objects displayed in the bookcases and around the room. The back wall, a few feet behind one of the sofas was paned glass. Matching paned French doors on the left led out onto the deck, and a row of large tropical plants in glazed ceramic pots sat in front of the length of bare wood framed windows. The solid six foot fence around her back yard eliminated any need for drapes, although she did on occasion roll down the shades while taking an afternoon snooze. An etched glass door on the far end of the window wall, also framed in wood, led directly into her studio.

She glanced to her left at the mahogany grandfather clock in the corner beside a late seventeenth century Portuguese chair. The richly tooled, embossed and incised leather was fastened to the walnut frame by large brass nails. She always felt a thrill when she looked at this beautifully preserved chair purchased at an estate sale at a ridiculously low price.

She brushed past the oak baluster-legged dining room table set against the dwarf wall separating the main living area from the Chef's domain. She placed her grocery bags on the well-lit island counter and began to empty them. She loved the airy, rustic flavor of her kitchen. Both the floor and countertops were tiled in a matte mocha terra-cotta. Many of the oak cupboards had no doors and displayed rows of glasswear and her own colorful hand-painted dinnerware. Glass jars filled with dried fruit, pasta, and nuts sat along the back of the counters alongside small appliances. Ethnic collectibles and ivy plants ranged along the top of the cupboards.

But what dominated the kitchen was the oversized island with its six element counter top stove, above which hung gleaming copper pots and pans attached to the rack beneath a beaten copper ventilation hood. She commented on the outrageous price of some of her purchases as she emptied her bags but got neither sympathy or a response of any kind. Neither Josie or Linka cooked.

She glanced between the ferns hanging from the broad beam above the dwarf wall at the absorbed pair. Then she made hot chocolate and prepared a platter of sandwiches. The carpet in front of the couches against which Josie and Linka leaned was as littered with files as the coffee table. She ran a caressing eye over the cats nestled against the pillows on the couches and smiled when the boys raised their heads briefly to sniff the sweet chocolate. Trix, who had earlier singed her tail on the open fire while investigating this new wonder, was curled against Ginseng's belly and briefly twitched her own little black nose.

She handed each a thick ceramic mug topped with whipping cream sprinkled with chocolate shavings. Then she brought in the platter of sandwiches. "There's no place to put this so grab a few. Then it's self-serve from the dining room table." She curled up in the armchair nearest the fire with her own frothy beverage and listened to Linka recap her magical tales while she munched on her own sandwich.

"I wanted to wait 'til you got home to tell you about the fables relating to us. Oh, I filled Josie in on our visit with the professor. Ummm, this is yummy." Linka licked the creamy froth from her upper lip. Tannis relished both the childish image and her unique mode of storytelling.

"The book has some stories where men win their lady love with acts of valor, against unbeatable foes like dragons, gargoyles, and Wizards. But mostly it's tales of slaughter and war. I'll read you the song about Faye the professor mentioned." She did so, then shared several excerpts from other tales.

" . . . they must be talking about her, Faye I mean. The way she's described is just like you said, Mom, from your dreams. Isn't that song neet? And get this, she had an affinity with animals, for they always followed her around, like in this line, 'dancing aft' with legs of four, most times one but oft times more'. I bet she had her own elemental."

"Cats are not the only country animals with four legs, you know," Tannis responded with a touch of sarcasm.

"I know that! But in this other story, they talk about the faery child with her black puss guardian. She might have had a black cat, just like me," she stated defensively.

"Maybe Trix is a reincarnation of her black puss," Josie teased, "since we're getting all caught up in parallels here."

"Nothing would surprise me anymore," laughed Tannis. The unexpected and unpleasant change in the professor's attitude came to mind, but she pushed it aside.

"You think?" asked Linka, her mind on more significant matters. "But look here, this is what I really wanted to show you. When I read it, the words jumped out at me just like the word 'moon' did in the prayer. I've found my three strands," she said with a flourish. "Three candles illumine every darkness; Truth, Nature, Knowledge. It's from the Triads of Ireland, and has something to do with the Plains of Silver."

"What's the Plains of Silver?" Josie asked.

"Sort of a magical place of visions we go to when we dream. To get inspiration. Do you think these three strands are mine, Mom?"

"It's not so much what I think, but what your gut tells you. What's interesting is that you do have a thing for candles."

"I sense the candles are your connection," Josie said. "Just like the nine lines in the prayer are your mother's strands, your strands could well be these three; the elements of truth, nature, and knowledge."

"That sounds awfully broad to me," Tannis said. However, the candle connection was interesting since Linka had made her own for years. Her apartment was graced with many beautiful clusters, or had been before Trix's arrival. Tall church candles, some encrusted with gold and silver foils and some with pressed flowers, leaves and delicate ferns embedded into the wax contrasted with those she molded into balls, pyramids and other shapes she had marbled with sparking metallic veins. Tannis had quickly grabbed the ones Linka considered rejects and clustered them throughout her house, particularly in the bathroom. She loved to bathe by candlelight. The three beauties which rose amid the files on the coffee table were also a gift from her talented daughter.

"I find it strange that although Taenacea lived in Wales, she's almost more connected to Ireland. Didn't the reader say there were layers to the Quest? Linka told me about the family coalition, and the Writ. It might be important to explore the Irish connection."

Tannis considered Josie's comment as she got up to check her journal entries, taking a detour to grab another sandwich. "Yes, she did say that. Maybe because that's where it all started. To reach the end, we may have to start at the beginning." She wondered if the plain connection mentioned by the reader referred to the Plains of Silver Linka had mentioned.

"I think my strands are to do with the past, with the family history. Especially since Faye didn't live that long," Linka said sagely.

"Clever girl. I agree. Truth and knowledge implies you'll shed light of something important, but I don't see where nature fits in just yet. That's the one I find very broad." Josie mused.

"The Writ and the coalition would refer to how the families managed their lands I'd say. Maybe there was something unusual about it other than their alliance. At least you have a date to work with now, your birth. I'd see where that takes you first," Tannis said, then shared her frustration over the professor's abundance of peripheral information, but lack of specific dates.

"The dates you want would be in the local parish records. He might not have access to them yet," Josie said. "Anyhow, you have the year of Taenacea's wedding to work back and forth from. What more do you need?"

"I suppose. Anyhow, I have work to do," Tannis said as she rose, reluctant to break their cozy ambiance. But her fingers tingled with a desire to mould. "Let yourselves out when you're done, unless you find the dates I'm looking for. Only then may you disturb the genius at work," she added with an imperious wave of her hand.

When Tannis emerged from her studio the fire was reduced to glowing embers and the files were cleared away. She could hear the steady drum of rain on the deck outside as she read the note Josie had stuck on a pencil in the jar on the coffee table. It confirmed they had found references to Taenacea, but no dates. She rekindled the fire and placed her 'Crescent Moon' disc into the player. The plaintive call of Orca whales and the light strumming of harps set a reflective tone as she prepared her supper.

The meal eaten and dishes done, she decided to examine the strange feelings the professor had triggered. She turned off the lamps and lit the candles she had moved to the center of the coffee table. Focusing on her intent as she stared into the flame she took several deep breaths and cleared her mind. She allowed random thoughts to fly past without scrutiny and waited for that empty space in her mind from where images surfaced. She saw Giles' odious face emerge, then slowly dissolve, only to be replaced by the professor's. Both appeared and disappeared several times in quickening succession. Then came a brief moment when the two faces merged and rested one on top of the other, and she knew. They were one and the same!

Until now she hadn't noticed how much alike they looked, not that such similarity was a criteria in reincarnation. There was often a strong resemblance along the eyes and bridge of the nose, according to Josie, because the memories of the soul are stored within the eyes. As an artist she compared the two, focusing on the features beneath the coarseness of Giles and the sweetness of the professor. Now the resemblance was not only striking, but so obvious she wondered how she had missed it.

Their bodies were basically the same although Giles' bulk was softer and sloppier than the professor's, and his nose larger. The professor's lips were narrower and smaller and he had more hair. She realized it was the nature of the two men that made them appear so different; at least until the professor's anger appeared. When his anger surfaced he lost his befuddled sweetness. Then she had reacted to him the same way Taenacea reacted to Giles, as if they were one and the same.

In light of her discovery, the question now was not if the professor was really the incarnate of Giles, but whether he knew he was. Had handling the book triggered a memory of his other self's emotions, fleeting as they were? To meet a counterpart from Taenacea's life changed everything, especially since it was such an odious one. She didn't know how to handle this new development. She'd have to sleep on it.

Putting the Quest firmly out of her mind she watched several figure skating competitions she had recorded over the past month. She had two tapes worth and watched both while she brushed the cats. She liked to guess the winners before they skated, and was usually right. But mostly she just enjoying the varied dance programs of the pairs and the increased level of skill in executing the jumps in the men and women's singles.

The next morning she called Josie. She had received no answers to the questions posed last night regarding the professor/Giles incarnate. In fact, she could not even remember her dreams.

"Hi there! Today the stars say, watch your backs! Neptune is in retrograde. If you're not wary you may be condemned to repeating the past," the machine intoned in Josie's 'doom forecasting' mode. Shaking her head in disbelief, Tannis identified herself and waited for Josie to pick up. "What do you do," she quipped, "take drugs and record the daily message before dawn?"

"No and yes. You know I have insomnia, but sounds like I hit a nerve," Josie shot back. A call from Tannis this early meant something was afoot.

"Actually yes. I need input. Interested?"

"You bet! Hang on a sec, I'm in the middle of smudging and I have to blow out my candles." She dropped the phone which clanked loudly in Tannis' ear.

Almost afraid to ask what this latest ritual was for, Tannis waited until her pal breathed into the mouthpiece. "OK, I'll bite. What are you smudging now?"

"Myself—sexually. In preparation for the possibility of a new relationship," Josie stated, hoping for more specific prompting.

"And do the stars indicate there may be another victim on the horizon?" Tannis drawled, determined not to let Josie steer the conversation to Cal.

"It's always good for a gal to be prepared so if a new prospect walks into her life she won't be bogged down with the energies of every other man she's ever slept with. I recommend everyone do so when a relationship is kaput. I'm just catching up because I've overlooked it for a while," Josie explained in a manner that implied she had simply forgotten to manicure her toenails. Before she could launch phase two of her ploy, Tannis interrupted with a description of her visual experience during her meditation. "Do you think he knows he's the incarnate of Giles?"

"Well, I wasn't there, but no. At least not consciously. From what you say, it surprised him as well. What do you think triggered the sudden change?" she asked.

"It had to be the Magik Book. He was different after he handled it, when I came back from the bathroom."

"You left him alone with it!" Josie exclaimed.

"I felt so sick all of a sudden, I thought I was going to throw up."

"Well, you had no way of suspecting anything and now the damage is done. For all you know he could have mouthed a few of the spells and unconsciously evoked his connection to Giles. Tell me, is he into reincarnation?"

"He gave me the impression he was, providing it was experienced through controlled hypnotic conditions, and verified historically. He did say he helped a friend who researches past lives so he must think some claims are valid," Tannis said.

"Considering how hell-bent Giles was to burn Taenacea at the stake, and we don't know if he was successful, you can imagine what a coupe it would be for him to get his hands on her Magik Book," Josie said. "It would prove she really was a witch."

"A healer and Wicca," Tannis corrected defensively.

"But according to him, a witch," Josie retorted.

"What's that got to do with me now?" Tannis wasn't sure she liked where this was leading, further discomforted by the lengthy silence before Josie answered.

"If karma between them wasn't resolved history could repeat itself, that's what. In which case you don't want him to know you're on to him. Gives you an edge. On the other hand, if fortune is smiling on you as it usually does, you have an opportunity for karmic resolution."

"By letting that nasty little man irritate me all over again?" Tannis sputtered.

"It's not so simple. There's two sides to every story, and your side is still incomplete. From the sounds of it, you were a pretty tough cookie and who knows what you did to him."

"My God, Josie, he probably had me murdered," Tannis exclaimed.

Josie remembered what Linka had told her. "Not you. Taenacea maybe. Reason out the political motives. Giles supported Richard and had already promised your troops to his cause. We know this now. You obviously supported Henry's claim to the throne, so your opposition would have struck a serious blow to his ambitions. What I find interesting is how he thinks Giles was denied well-deserved glory. He may subconsciously try to grasp for himself what was denied him before. As a historian, possession of a book we know he can prove to be genuine could achieve that, and propel him to the pinnacle of academia."

"He has to get it first," Tannis said flatly. She didn't like what she was hearing.

"If he gets his hands on it, you have no way of proving it's yours. So whatever you do, don't let it out of your sight. Does he know where you live?"

"No, but I think you're overreacting. It's not as if he'll hire someone to steal it. He may just be experiencing flashes of past life memories he'll write off as imagination." She had enough problems without fabricating threats where none existed.

"I wouldn't count on it. What you're forgetting is lives are lived simultaneously, not consecutively. The emotions felt are real and very strong because they are happening now, in the ever-present. I know from my own past life experiences how intricately they affect each other," Josie stated. She was dead serious.

"A soul experiences innumerable lives in a variety of historic time frames—but all at the same time, so to speak. In each life the soul is so focused on that particular reality, it's not usually aware of its other lives." She paused to try and explain her point clearly. "The memory of another life, which bleeds through to conscious awareness from another time frame, does so because it's relevant to the life it intersects. Linear time is just a three dimensional perception that's already been breached in your case. Karmic lessons apply to all aspects of the whole soul. Actions from the past can affect you in the now as much as your actions and feelings can influence the past. Think about that for a minute."

Josie's point was sobering. But Tannis wasn't sure she entirely believed it. Linked by this Quest, the dangers from the past could well affect her life in her present, which would make the reverse true as well. If she pissed the professor off now, could it escalate their animosity in the past? The concept was difficult to grasp and overwhelming if true.

"The forecast could have been written for you, and probably was," Josie muttered. She would check up on this professor herself. "I'll call a friend of mine who has at least as much credibility as he does and see what he comes up with. We'll find out quick enough if he's playing games. Besides, since I'm not in the picture directly, I am at your service in all other ways, Milady. We probably won't need the professor anymore with my connections. Who knows, this could be a book in the making."

"Absolutely not! I appreciate your help, but a book is out of the question, so don't even think it," Tannis stated emphatically.

Josie gushed reassurances to a prickly Tannis. What she didn't tell her was that she had already started writing the draft for the book. The seed had been planted right from the start, when Tannis had first told her about her dreams and the Quest. Since she couldn't have such an exciting experience herself, she would write about it. All the years spent amassing her vast storehouse of knowledge could be incorporated in this documentary. It covered a wide range of metaphysical experiences outside of reincarnation itself. If need be, she would camouflage it as a novel. She had met a publishing editor in London last fall and had jotted his name down somewhere. She would send him a proposal and outline. You never knew.

Fueled by her intent, she bid Tannis a hasty farewell and sat herself down at her computer. She pulled up the Quest file and began to pound on her keyboard, all thoughts of smudging and Cal forgotten.

Chapter Eight

TANNIS WAS CONFUSED. Rather than ease her mind, she found Josie's explanation of simultaneous time difficult to grasp. Like most people who believed in reincarnation, she thought time *was* linear, and any past lives one had experienced were finished. Apparently not. One thing was clear; when she was in the past herself, she experienced everything as fully and completely as she did her life right now. Mulling over what she'd heard, she gave up any thoughts of sculpting and decided to escape back into Taenacea's reality. Rather than fearful of the consequences, she was more intrigued than before. A visual of the little lady in the bookstore drifted into her mind. Thinking about her evoked the same feeling of warmth she experienced when thinking of Maureen. There couldn't be any harm in trying to locate her.

This would be the first time she would consciously time travel to a specific date for a specific purpose, and excitement at the prospect caused flutters in her belly. She got the Magik Book and memorized the proper spell before she lay down on the couch. Zoie, who had been crouched on her favorite chair, padded over as if waiting for her summons. She settled on her chest as she had done before. If the little lady was important in Taenacea's life, she would surely have been present at her nuptials, so she focused on her wedding day in 1482.

"OK my friend, let's see if we can find our little Welsh lady," she said softly. She envisioned her in her mind as she stated her intent and whispered the words that would initiate her launch. A sharp tug at the base of her spine, a flash of blinding light and she felt herself pulled upward and into a bright swirling vortex which propelled her along its length with nauseating speed.

* * *

118

Her feet clung to the ground, toes curled within her boots to try and keep a grip against the winds that tore at her and the sudden wild gusts that nearly knocked her to the ground. Propelled forward by a persistent voice in her head, she struggled towards her destination. It was nearly midday, yet the skies were blackened by the storm which had gathered on her wedding night. The wind at her back drove her forward, then without warning, changed course and pounded her backward as if to impede her journey or test her fortitude.

In a trance, unaware of the electrifying fingers of lightening that snapped branches and sent them crashing to the ground around her, she heard only the familiar beckoning voice. "Ye're nearly there, Cea. This way now." She moved off the worn path and turned sharply to her right, urged towards a wooded area in the distance. Stumbling over soggy mounds and rocks slick with rain, she found a gap in the underbrush and followed the narrow path into its center; a calm mossy circle of grass. Like celestial walls, the trees muffling the sound of the storm. Within the enclosure the sky around the full moon above was studded with stars. Beside a large flat-topped oval slab of stone stood Lil, a smile of welcome on her broad smooth face. On the ground beside her a small fire crackled under a steaming pot, seemingly suspended in mid-air.

"'Tis time for Awakening, my Cea. From yer bed of fire, with a new life within, ye heard the call. Come now. Drink this posit and we'll begin," Lil said with a face gone serious.

Taenacea smiled wanly at her trusty nurse and teacher and forced down the vile tasting concoction. She felt only a faint stirring of fear. She had known the Awakening would come, but not that it would draw her from her bed of rapture to brave the ferocious storm that had gathered during her joining with Garth. Her time to walk through the fires of the Wicca rites and bind with The Mother was at hand. For this she would sacrifice the mortal illusions held dear 'til now.

To her would come the white light of Healing by touch once her ego burned to cinders; the sight of foretelling once she could look at the darkness within each soul with compassion; and spells that would move her through the corridors of time and consciousness, providing her faith in the Mother was stronger than her indomitable will. As old as the land itself, her knowings would awaken from a place beyond time, from the Plains of Silver.

She would learn to draw from this universal source of intuitive connection and marshal the energies of air, water, earth, and fire. She would develop spiritual communion with animals to hear their teachings, and learn the specific uses of herbs for potions. And there would be more, things so secret, only her soul would remember.

She barely felt Lil's light tap on her shoulder as she handed her a twisted, soggy root and said as if from afar, "Chew on this 'til yer lips are numbed."

With eyes already glazed from the potion, she obeyed and felt her body slowly flush with heat. Warmed into a comfortable stupor, she did not feel the invisible hands that plucked her clothing from her so craftily that in a blink, she stood naked. Caressed by the moonlight's alabaster light, her unbound hair rippling behind her, she drifted to the stone. It took both a moment, and a lifetime. With a trusting look at her mentor, she lay down upon the uneven slab of rock. She heard only the beginning of the Ceremonial Chant before her eyes closed in surrender to The Mother.

What was said and done and where she traveled she could not remember clearly. There was only one point in her rites when she became acutely aware of a sharp pain on each temple, as if lightening had pierced her very skull. An infinity of timelessness passed before she was teased back to wakefulness by a caressing hand on her brow. She opened her eyes, feeling like she had closed them only an instant before. As she slowly sat up she knew she was changed. Infused with a fullness she could barely contain, a knowing so deeply entrenched, its presence within her psyche filled her very being. What now felt almost too expansive to contain would soon become commonplace and undetectable.

She had only faint recollections; the face of an old Crone so ancient it almost appeared young, then become the face of all women, of all ages. That and strange images of herself in a setting so alien, words could not express what she had seen. The voices of a thousand spirits of feminine knowing had whispered their secrets in her ears, and seared her heart with a joy and pain so profound, she knew them as one and the same. She had walked with death and knew it to be the seed of renewed life.

"You did well, my Cea, for the mark of the Mother's darting eyes is upon you. The wild passions of her knowings now flow in your veins. Cherish this gift, and do it honor. Drink this, then sleep. There is much I must teach you." Lil said to her mind, smiling as Taenacea looked around for her clothing. "There is no need. The Mother will warm you with her heart." Lil was right, for even though she was wrapped in her old thick blanchet, Taenacea in her nakedness was just as warm.

Half a moon passed, and each day began with the chewing of the root before Lil showed her the world as it really was, seen through Wicca eyes. She was taught the secrets of elemental power and how to embrace and accept earth's endless rhythms. Nature's hidden bounty fed her body, and its spirits her soul. Every night they drew from the powers contained within ancient sites, rode on moonbeams through alternate realities to dance among their stars, and joined with the joyful consciousness within all things. Lil took her forward and backward in time to show her probable wonders and horrors not even dreamed of in her own reality.

When the end of their time drew near, Lil no longer gave her the root. She was often silent and gazed upon her charge with troubled eyes. With each passing day Taenacea noticed Lil gained a growing transparent quality, seeming less substantial somehow. On the last night, and she knew it to be the last, she had to concentrate to focus on Lil, and not on what she could so clearly see behind her.

Lil looked intently at the splendid woman before her marked by the Mother with silver streaks spiraling down from each temple. "'Tis done," she said. "There is only one thing left perhap', and for that I will come to you through time." Her form began to flicker and waver. "Your Prayer of Life is a gift from The Mother. Speak it each dawn and you will be blessed as you experience the nine strands of understanding ordained for this life. You must script your magical knowings and bind them together, then hide it well. If needs be, move it to the Plains of Silver for safekeeping."

Her voice reverberated in Taenacea's mind as she said, "Remember my Cea, use your powers well, for as you are blessed, all you see, will be. Let it be the Mother's eyes you choose. Guard thoughts fueled by all else, least it become so. The Mother walks with you." That said, she sat against a nearby tree, pulled her cloak tight, and went to sleep. Deeply moved, Taenacea lay down as well, wrapped only in the warmth of The Mother within the magical circle of her Awakening.

It was the chill that woke her. She sat up, her body damp with a fine beading of morning dew. Bemused at how solid she felt compared to her previous lightness, she looked around. She saw nothing to mark what had taken place. No faery stone and no fire. There was no sign of anything within the circle to mar what nature alone had seeded. And no Lil. She intuitively knew there never would be again, not in a corporeal sense. Perhaps there never had been, although she had been seen by all. Magik had manifested her, a magic that had weakened as her task reached completion. She had simply faded back to the Plains of Silver from where she had sprung.

A great sadness clutched at her heart and brought tears to her eyes. For the first time in her life, she was truly alone. Oh, she would see Lil again in the place where dreams, enchantments and magic lived, but never again in the flesh; this woman who had been with her from the moment she was born. Pushing back a wash of tears, she squared her shoulders. It was time to imprint her life with all she had learned.

She donned her clothing and fastened her cloak at the neck. The storm had passed and left behind a freshness of air she inhaled with greed. Every fiber of her being responded to her surroundings with a richness never before experienced. With reverence she raised her arms to welcome the dawn with the Prayer that passed her lips for the first time, and would do so every day for the rest of her life, except for one dark interval.

* * *

The rest of the week passed in a blur. Detached, as if in an altered-state, Tannis watched herself work and perform her daily activities from a fuzzy distance. Her response to Josie and Linka's discovery of a wealth of information linking her counterpart's activities to Druid rituals was only a distracted, knowing smile. She hardly knew what she did those few days. By Sunday morning she began to feel more like herself again, more focused in her own reality. It seemed almost as if the residuals of the potion she had ingested during Taenacea's Awakening had dulled her own outer awareness while it stimulated her inner perceptions. For she had experienced a whole block of memories besides those of the Awakening itself.

Her first realization was that using spells didn't guarantee she would end up where she wanted to go. True, she had been propelled to the right time-frame, but not to the wedding itself. She felt a deep sorrow at Lil's departure and knew her presence at the Awakening had been an apparition of the most unique kind. The feeling stayed with her all week, along with a deep respect and awe for the ritual she knew to be a very special and most secret initiation into the Wicca faith. Aware of a small shift within herself, she realized some of what Taenacea had experienced had also filtered into her own consciousness.

The way life and particularly the Goddess energy within women was honored and nurtured by the Wicca faith struck her with force, and stirred the intuitive core of her own being. In comparison, her sense of self was only a watery version of a much greater awareness she now wanted to investigate. The feeling of her heightened senses was incredible. There was now more reason than ever to take a holiday. It would not only give her time to explore this new aspect of herself, but an opportunity to see powerful ancient sites she remembered visiting during her journeys with Lil.

The chimes had signaled the Awakening as another memory and introduced her to Lil; a woman who had been with her from the moment she was born. Lil, the little woman in the bookstore, who looked almost exactly like she had in the woods. She had come to her like she said, "through time if need be" to bring her the Magik Book. That must have been why Lil had become serious and slightly troubled near the end of the rituals. She must have known about the probability of this Quest, known even then Taenacea's counterpart in the future would need a book not yet written; all to somehow complete her beloved Cea's life strands. But what had gone so wrong in her life to make it necessary to do so?

Like the chicken and the egg, which came first? The interlocking events that affected each time frame made more sense if the two lives *were* lived simultaneously. Actions in one life could affect the other since both realities would be planned with a co-operative theme. But she would ponder this complex theory another time. What she did know was that how she perceived 'time' had definitely changed.

Funny. Lil had called her Cea from the time she was a babe, the same pet name Garth had used when they were alone. It was also more than coincidental what Linka had read about the Plain of Silver. The Plain of Silver was mentioned throughout Irish folklore, though not believed to be real. Through her own experience she knew it was. The Awakening also explained Taenacea's silver wings. She was marked with stripes earned during her rites of passage as a Wicca. It didn't however, explain her own. Unless . . . had it also been a cross-over event? She had said nothing to Josie or Linka about her first directed time travel strand, surprised her spaced-out demeanor had gone unnoticed.

Her mind drifted back to the other memories triggered by the Awakening as she puttered in the greenhouse, her hands gently thinning the rows of seedlings in her flats. She remembered the story as told by Lil, of how she had purposefully appeared the day Taenacea's mother went into labor. There had been no mention of where she had come from, however. She could see the events in her mind's eye. The midwife was busy at a neighboring croft while her mother writhed in the final stages of delivery. The men folk clustered around the stables in the keep, and the worried women wrung their hands as they consulted amongst themselves. Her distraught father paced about and snapped at everyone in his path to ease his own helplessness. He could do nothing for his beloved young wife. The keep was in an uproar. Into the confusion walked Lil. She brushed past the frenzied occupants and found her way to the bedside of the Lady of the Keep.

Nearly all life and blood had seeped from the slight, pain-wracked body that had already labored too long. Lil shooed everyone from the chamber and went to work. For all her skill, there was little to be done for the mother. But the babe would be saved. With her last thrust of love, her mother expelled the child into the waiting hands of Lil, this stranger who promised to care for the babe forever. The wasted woman looked trustingly into Lil's eyes and drifted to a gentler place, her purpose fulfilled.

From that moment on, Lil was mother and guardian to the child named Taenacea. Amid the rituals of death and with the whole keep in mourning, no one noticed Lil slip out at night with the babe, or that it was days before she returned and took her place in the household as her nurse. Overwhelmed with the loss of their Lady, no one thought to question her right, and by the time her father emerged from his sorrowful isolation, she was as much a part of the household as the babe.

Tannis saw Lil gently teach her to revere both the bountiful and fallow cycles of the earth. Her father, whom she loved but shamelessly manipulated, could deny his stubborn and precocious offspring nothing. She ran wild in the hills and brandished her miniature broadsword as vigorously as any local lad. Her father had retained a private tutor to teach her to read and write in English, Latin and French when she was only ten. As he would a son, he encouraged her horsemanship and skills with the blade. And, before her fifteenth year, she was as knowledgeable in the management of their lands as he. There was no question these lands would be hers with his passing.

Tannis embraced the visions which fleshed out the greater part of Taenacea's youth and early adulthood. She also understood the pact made with Lil not to wed until she met her destined partner. Because she requested it of her father who loved the wildness of her spirit, he refused repeated marriage offers from the neighboring Giles and other greedy suitors. He not only considered them barbaric and incapable of caring for his people and lands justly, but could not stomach the thought of any of them bedding his precious child against her will. He had loved his departed lady as deeply as she had loved him, and he wanted the same for Taenacea.

Her father anchored her days with purpose, but it was ageless Lil who taught her the most valuable skills in secret places at night. From her she learned that spirituality consisted of three aspects; remembering the past and utilizing the energy and knowledge of one's ancestry, understanding and working in harmony with the natural world, and applying spiritual intentions to one's everyday reality. Through Lil's tutelage, she had become adept at divination and the reading of nature through bird flight patterns and cloud formations. She could also read the reflections within water and other elements in order to understand the prevailing energy patterns within her surroundings. With Lil she had also gone into the woods to learn of the most sacred; the power and uses of her bleeding time, emerging a woman in every sense but one. And it was Lil who knew it was time to meet her destiny and sent her to Aberayron where she would meet her soul-mate, Garth. Tannis could recall nothing of their first meeting, and efforts to direct herself to that event failed. All she got were fuller images of how Taenacea administered her people and lands after her father's sudden death.

The meeting with Garth must be a strand to be experienced at another time. Her journeys seemed to follow their own pattern, aligned with her growing awareness and questions, but impervious to manipulation. In spite of what she had told Josie, she found she could not control events. Even what had occurred in the studio this past week was out of her control. She had worked every day, but had no memory of it. In retrospect, it felt like she had barely worked at all.

When she emerged from her trance on Sunday morning the results left her speechless. Both Taenacea and Garth were finished. Not just roughly, but completely; finished in all their finite detail, and ready to be crated and transported to the foundry for casting. All she need do now was regulate their moisture until they were picked up.

To say she was stunned was an understatement. It generally took at least a month of concentrated effort to complete one piece of their size. The majority of that time would be spent in refining details like the hair, eyes, hands and clothing. Instead, she had completed two pieces in under three weeks. She vaguely remembered talking to Taenacea about the Awakening while she worked on her. The finished product now reflected her new understanding of the complexity and mysticism of this woman. She didn't remember working on Garth at all, but he too emulated a depth of character as if sculpted through Taenacea's intimate understanding of the man.

When she removed the draping from the pieces that sat about two feet apart on their pedestal stands, she had gasped. Before her sat perfection; life studies so beautiful and dynamic, she could barely believe she had created them. Tentatively she ran her hands over the pair. Beneath the coolness of the leathery clay she could almost feel the heat of their love as they reached towards each other. She was often moved by some of her work, but nothing had ever impacted her like these did now.

She didn't know how long she walked around them to touch a curl, run a finger over a bottom lip, or trace the contours of Garth's exposed chest. His shirt opened nearly to the waist seemed to billow with the teasing of the same soft wind that ruffled the strands of hair escaping the loose thong at the back of his neck. He held a roll of parchment in one hand, and the thumb on his other hand loosely looped his ornate belt. A slight smile of anticipation was set in a face of strength and character, and his eyes crinkled warmly at the corners as he gazed at Taenacea.

Taenacea too boasted fine detailing. Caught in the act of disrobing as if for a spring bath in a meadow pool, her expression appeared to urge her lover to join her. Her hair cascaded down her back wildly, the curls scored to give the illusion of sheen and movement. She held the corner of a loosened skirt that appeared to slip from her hips, and her other hand reached towards Garth, frozen in a moment of gentle beckoning.

Mesmerized, Tannis couldn't stop looking at them. She got her camera and began to take pictures from every possible angle for her portfolio; first together, then individually. She wanted to capture them in raw clay before the foundry transformed them into effigies of bronze. Conjured from the nether world, their deep gray color made them appear not quite human, yet too solid to be ghostly. Grounded in her own consciousness again and infused with euphoria, she left a message for Dan who handled her transports. She also left a message for George at the foundry. She had specifications for the patina she wanted to discuss with him.

Unable to contain the expanse of her own awe she also left a message for Josie that said simply, "Come over if you can," then draped the pieces with damp cloths and took a long shower. Clad only in a plush bathrobe as she toweled her hair, she left the bedroom to investigate the aroma of freshly made coffee. As she padded through the living room, she saw Josie rummaging through her kitchen cupboards.

"Do let yourself in, and please make yourself at home. Breakfast? Help yourself," she said with irony, not surprised at how quickly Josie had high-tailed it over.

"You said come, so what's wrong with now? Heard you in the shower and thought I'd feed the body. Been feeding the spirit, but missed breakfast this morning. How's about I fix us an omelet?" Her casual tone didn't fool either of them. She was dying to find out what the call was all about but knew the explanation wouldn't come until Tannis was ready.

Tannis watched her add items to the pile of ingredients already on the island counter. "OK, you can do the omelet thing, but only a plain one for me with just cheese and 'shrooms." Although Josie rarely deigned to cook, when the bug bit her there was no telling what the results would be. She had the most adventurous ideas about cooking, and within her dishes raged an unusual variety of ingredients. Even with instructions to keep hers plain, Tannis knew the fold of her omelet could hide unexpected surprises, anything from gooey marshmallows to burnt chili peppers. She would make toast, and could just eat that if the results were too terrible.

She leaned against the dwarf wall and ran her fingers through her still damp hair as she updated Josie on the latest strand and filled in the details of Taenacea's life as a child and young woman. Then she tried to explain how odd she had felt all week, and what had happened in the studio.

Josie listened as she chopped, ground, and tossed tidbits to the cats on the counter and a more polite Mr. Muff sitting by her feet. "Seems to me you were in another dimension all week. You know, the Plains of Silver. That's how you could manipulate time the way you did." Josie chewed at her lip, then added, "You know, I always wondered about something. I suspect all great artists go there, to the Plains of Silver, I mean. They just don't tell anyone about it, or even know it themselves in most cases. Their dilemma would be how to take credit for something that was created through them, not by them."

"Interesting deduction. I've wondered that myself, watching interviews of famous artists and writers on TV. Did you ever notice they aren't able to talk about some of their work in detail, yet can go on and on about what inspired others?"

"Like they don't even know—my point exactly," Josie stated. "What a hoot, eh? Probably many of them are tormented by not understanding the source of their own creativity. Instead of realizing all inspiration and ideals are drawn from a collective universal consciousness and embracing that source, their egos can't handle it. They end up going nutso, wallow in booze or drugs, or stop creating at all."

"If what I'm going to show you is the result of my connection with the Plains of Silver, believe me, there's no conflict. I think I've just reached a major turning point in my work," Tannis declared.

"That-a-girl. Just think how prolific you'll be. Why, you can whip up, say, thirty pieces in four to five months, then take the rest of the year off and travel the world with me," Josie shouted above the hum of the mixer as she beat the egg whites. "We can explore the wonders of the world and every energy point I've missed, especially since I'm sure you've been there before. It'll be like a trip down memory lane for you. You can teach me things about Wicca and the proper use of feminine energy, I'll bet!"

Tannis took the bowl out of Josie's hands and deftly folded the egg whites into the creamy mixture.

She watched the two fat omelets sizzle in the side-by-side pans and smacked Josie's hand as she tried to drop some hot diced peppers onto her mushroom and cheese omelet. She decided to test her pal's resolve. "Just think Josie, we can travel for years and years, maybe even forever. Just two Godlettes on the loose. Who needs men, right? After all, we have each other."

Josie sobered. "Well, just until I meet my perfect man. Then, friendship aside, you're on your own," she said as she flipped the omelets over and buttered the toast.

"That's what I love about you—your loyalty. At least until a man appears on the horizon" sniffed Tannis in mock devastation, which set them off again as Josie sloppily scooped the golden omelets onto the brightly glazed plates. They threw barbs at each other between bites, ignoring the felines who hopped back onto the island counter to sniff out the little chunks of cheese purposefully left by Josie amid the other scraps. There was no such fun to be had when the mama cooked, but when Josie cooked, she just cooked. Clean-up was not part of the cooking experience.

Just then the doorbell rang. Tannis got up to check her peep hole. It was Cal. He hugged her, surprised by Josie's cherry greeting from the table and curious about the contradictory odors wafting his way. It was unusual for Cal to drop by on a weekend, unless. . . no, he couldn't be here in hopes Josie was. But as incompatible as they seemed to Tannis, there might just be something going on. Lord help us, she thought, but all she said was, "Sit yourself down, partner. Have I got a treat for you." She got another plate and scooped some of Josie's and her omelet onto the plate and set it down in front of him. "Try this. Josie made it."

Oddly pleased by Josie's presence, a sentiment she obviously shared, Cal heard the challenge in Tannis' tone. With a faint smile he pierced a very small piece and tentatively placed it in his mouth. Two pairs of eyes focused on him as he chewed and swallowed self-consciously. He sensed this was a pivotal point in his future relations with both women. After the initial onslaught of jumbled flavors what remained was a pleasant tangy taste. He'd always had a yen for spicy Mexican food, and this was definitely spicy.

"Hmmm, quite ... intriguing," he stated, and proceeded to clean his plate with deliberate concentration, hoping his actions would fend off further inquires since he would have trouble finding words to actually describe the taste.

The challenge met and passed, Josie promptly dumped another large chunk from her plate onto his and threw him a 'let's see if you can handle more' look.

"Lord help us," thought Tannis as she excused herself to shoo the cats off the counter and get dressed. The man was a goner now, for the ultimate gamut had been thrown and accepted, and now Josie would reel him in. She'd seen it all before. As for Cal, having shown his willingness to play, he'll be bound and gagged before he even knew what hit him. Lots of luck, buddy, Tannis thought affectionately. This should be some roller coaster ride for as long as it lasts. Oddly enough, Josie might just be the ticket to prompt Cal to actually participate in a relationship. He was a big boy now and should be able to handle getting singed by her fire-ball pal.

"Come see what I've done," Tannis said when she returned. The pair followed her into the studio, chatting lightly until she removed the draping from her work. The air of unity the clay pair exuded stunned them into silence. Josie's face reflected her longing to find a soulmate as Taenacea had. She was the first to stir and walk around the pieces to touch a surface here and there.

Cal's face reflected a multitude of emotions before he did the same, the foremost being one of such complete resignation that the finality of it clutched at Tannis' heart. What she had not been able to convince Cal of with words, the sculptures had through their unity. What he saw was not a medieval woman, but Tannis, Tannis with her ideal mate. A door closed on the hopes she would one day want him the way he imagined he still wanted her. Thankfully, Billy Bob's indignant meow as he skidded into the studio then dashed out again broke his sorrowful reverie.

Stirred to his soul, his inner turmoil cloaked, Cal drawled, "Babe, they are some pair. Wherever they came from, you have definitely tapped into an incredible new source of inspiration." He missed the quick warning look Tannis shot Josie and was baffled by the nervous giggles his comment triggered.

Sensing his discomfort, Josie piped up, "It's a chick thing so don't even ask." She gave Tannis a great big hug and whispered in her ear, "They're exquisite. We have to talk." Part of her wanted Cal to leave so they could discuss the sculptures openly and part of her wanted him to stay. Elated by his unexpected arrival, she was convinced the vibes of her own desire had drawn him here. While Tannis discussed the patina with Cal, she sat on the sculpting stool, her eyes on him as he listened intently and made notes on his pocket computer. The synchronicity of their working rapport was apparent and she noted Cal always made sure he understood what Tannis said, another mark in his favor.

". . . so I want these two poured in the gold colored bronze. Oh, and remind George to order that pewter silvery alloy he told me about if he hasn't done so already. That's for the third piece." Tannis said.

"You're planning to pour the child in silver?" Cal asked. He wondered why she had chosen a finish before the piece was even built, something she had never done before. "It'll skyrocket our costs. . . but hey, I don't have a problem with that," he amended quickly when he saw the stubborn set to Tannis' jaw.

"I just hope George has enough gold alloy at the foundry for both pieces. He was only expecting Gar. . . I mean, one piece. The second wasn't supposed to be ready for another three months," Tannis mumbled, annoyed at the slip, which Josie caught.

"He told me a shipment had just been delivered when I called to check on pouring dates. Besides, we have a five month working schedule for each. If there's a delay with the second pour, the client will still get it earlier than expected," he added, glancing at his watch. "Gotta run. I'm setting up a show at the gallery." Without knowing why, he turned to Josie and asked, "Do you want to come along and see another creative genius at work?"

Everyone, including Cal himself, was surprised at his invitation. Caught in the worst kind of dilemma, Josie was torn between a desire to stay with Tannis and to take Cal up on an invitation extended without any prompting from her. She shot Tannis a quick 'I know you'll understand' look. "I'd love to. I haven't been in a gallery for eons!" she exclaimed. "Should I follow you in my Jeep or do you plan to come back later, in which case we can take your car?" she asked, hoping for the latter. She wanted a ride in his snazzy silver Jag, and to have the pleasure of spending part of the evening with him as well.

"It would be nice, but I haven't received an invitation yet."

Tannis saw his hopeful look, and feeling sociable after her week of isolation, said, "Consider yourselves both invited for dinner. Any requests?"

"Stuffed veal," Josie stated without hesitation.

"Stuffed veal it is, now go and play kiddies. I have to pick up some things then don my Chef's hat. Cal, you can provide the spirits," she added merrily. A celebration was in order after what she had achieved this week.

Dinner was a relaxed and jolly affair. Tannis was concerned Josie would blatantly pursue Cal, but in fact, she did the exact opposite. Cal had already taken the bait so she was completely relaxed and absolutely charming. Cal got a sampling of her intellect as she spoke knowledgeably on many subjects and appreciated her genuine attentiveness when he spoke. Tannis threw in only the odd comment, happy to listen as she watched the two forge a comfortable ambiance.

The meal, accompanied by a Folle Blanche and Sauvignon to suit both white and red palates, was declared 'excellento'. It began with, was interspersed with, and ended with heartfelt toasts. By the time the clock struck twelve, all three were a little giddy.

"A toast to the fat little fart who's paying for this 'xpensive champagne and doesn't even know it!" Josie said as she puffed out her cheeks and leaned back on her heels, trying to look both fat and pompous. Her uncontrollable giggles signaled the end of the evening. For someone, even though they drank sparingly, was charmingly tiddled.

A lingering hug and furtive whispers at the door between Cal and Josie indicated a tryst was being arranged. After Josie dreamily shut the door she informed Tannis she had better stay the night and went to the spare room she had long since claimed as her own. Meanwhile, Tannis slipped into her studio for another look at the couple.

I know nothing about you Garth," she said softly, "Who you were and how we met. Your life is an empty slate outside of the small bits I've seen when you were with Taenacea." She felt a warm arm encircle her as Josie, wearing a voluminous flannel nightgown, came to stand beside her. "You're almost loathe to let them go, aren't you?" she whispered.

"In a way, but mostly just amazed at what I've created," Tannis chuckled. "I'm just checking to make sure they haven't disappeared on me. Pretty silly, eh? I'll take more pictures once they're bronzed but I want to imprint them on my mind just as they are," she said as she covered them. They wandered back into the living room arm in arm.

When Tannis brought up the subject of Cal, she was surprised by Josie's perceptive evaluation of him. The fact she was so calm and reflective signaled a new and more realistic attitude than Tannis was accustomed to seeing. In the past, when the 'love bug' nipped her, she would gush with love-struck euphoria, exalting the perfection of her newly proclaimed soulmate 'el nausea'. When the relationship fizzled and after a period of devastation and depression, she would spring back, blithely chalking the whole thing up to 'another bloody learning experience'. She had expected the same euphoric launch with Cal.

"He's very nice, but lonely under his slick persona. Somehow lost and thirsting for something meaningful. I'm not sure if he knows it on a conscious level yet, but I do. Gently nudged by the right person, I wouldn't be surprised if he allows himself to reconnect with his country roots." Tannis had told her about his ranching background. But before she could envision a future with this delicious man, there was something she had to clear up. "By the way, did you catch his expression when you first unveiled your work?"

"Which one? Seems to me there were many." Tannis hoped this wasn't leading where she thought.

"The one where he looked as if he had lost something precious and had resigned himself to the fact. Any ideas, seeing as you know him so well, I mean?" Casting her a speculative look, Josie waited.

Tannis hadn't told Josie about their short affair years ago and wondered if she intuitively knew. Treading carefully around what she considered a delicate subject, she replied, "Let's just say there was a time he thought he was deeply in love, like I did with my ex, Brad. But a relationship requires more than the passion of one partner to flourish. Maybe seeing Taenacea and Garth made him realize he needs someone more compatible to build a life with." A long and knowing look passed between them. "Hell, we're *all* looking for the perfect mate, aren't we? Look at me. My search is taking me into the past, for God's sake," Tannis added lightly.

Josie knew Tannis had probably been the object of Cal's love. She knew too well how one could feed their own desire for someone entirely inappropriate. Of course, Tannis was entirely wrong for him. Determined to forge her own destiny, she was too strong-willed to repeat the role of helpmate to a man's ambitions. That's where they differed. Unlike Tannis, she knew she couldn't maintain direction in her life by herself. In truth, she lacked an elemental drive for independent self-expression. Innately loyal and supportive, she needed a shared goal, a partnership of intent for a sense of stability and security within herself. She needed a man to give her purpose.

She appreciated the fact Tannis' response was honest, if somewhat ambiguous. After all, it might not have been her at all. She would assume it wasn't, but knew that even if it was, Tannis had managed to turn what would have been a one-sided infatuation into a lasting friendship. Besides, it had happened a long time ago, before she had met either one of them. The topic closed to her satisfaction she asked Tannis to remember everything she could about the Awakening ritual. She scribbled in her notebook without an ounce of guilt, in spite of her hidden agenda. She did however check to make sure her aura was tightly tucked in so Tannis couldn't pick up on her deceit. "Which one is it?" she asked. "I'd say lightning, wind, or earth."

"At first I thought earth because of the Wicca rites and Lil's teachings about nature's elements, but I think it's lightning."

"Because of the hair? Wow, that must have been something! I can just see her walk back into the keep with those silver streaks, cool as can be. I bet her people were freaked when they first saw her," Josie said, shaking her head, "No wonder they thought her a witch."

"The hair, yes," Tannis said dreamily. "I felt something happen to my temples. More importantly," she frowned slightly, "it's what the streaks represent; Taenacea's rites of passage."

"Like a shift or quantum leap in consciousness and increased spiritual awareness?"

"Something like that, but more like a concentrated light teaching. Only in this case it was more like a lightning teaching," she added with a giggle.

"I'm beginning to see the subtleties of how these events connect. This one certainly did change you and impact your life then, and could do so now as well, I suspect." Writing furiously, she concluded, "That makes four strands."

"Three for sure. The Tower strand isn't finished yet, which unfortunately means I still have to experience it." She shivered lightly. "I really don't want to, Josie. I have a horrible premonition it has something to do with my demise, like it's the final memory strand."

Chapter Nine

THE QUEEN OF DRAMA, Linka, left only one message on Tannis' machine. It stated she was absolutely swamped, and would drop by to share the bazillion incredible things that had happened to her once her work was done.

She must have experienced her first time travel experience, Tannis concluded. She wished she was a valium-taking-kind-of-gal, because she would definitely need something to survive the upcoming narrative. She brushed her speculations aside and focused on the slender young form her hands were busy shaping. Her mind drifted back to Sunday night's dream, the night when Josie had stayed over.

The by-product of her dream travels still amazed her. While she was fully in Taenacea's body, she experienced everything as her; but once the experience was over, she also knew the minds of those around her, providing their thoughts were about her. As disconcerting as knowing another's thoughts was, thankfully the skill didn't apply to the present, only the past. Once a strand was experienced, a conduit to that aspect of her life stayed open and allowed re-entry at will. She had already gone back to relive many of the events experienced to-date. She did so now. Proficient after countless such excursions, she felt only a momentary flicker up her spine as she focused on her intent and smoothly shifted her focus to the past.

* * *

It was her wedding day. Taenacea, wide awake before the first light of dawn, glanced at the shadowy heaps of sumptuous cloth draped over the ornate chests filled with wedding gifts. Although some were sent from the King, most had come with Garth from Ireland. She smiled in exasperation, and mentally chided him for his generosity in spite of knowing her careless disregard for worldly adornments. It was the man she wanted, not his wealth. That she had herself.

135

Under the considerate and sober rule of Edward III, nobles at court had
begun to display their prosperity with clothing trimmed in rich furs and
jewels. Taenacea, secluded and disinterested in court fashion, roamed her
lands with freedom of spirit and movement. She chose the practical and
simple skirts, tunics, and surcoats of the country folk over the confining
headdress and tightly bound kirtle of the gentry. Dressed as she was, she
could easily be mistaken for one of her vassals but for her height. Although
her lineage was as long and noble as those at court, she chose to wed Garth
as a woman of the land in her own Chapel, not as a titled Lady at court. The
rich velvets and other fine fabrics received only a distracted glance as she
arose. She had already claimed the most precious gift of all, the fabric for her
wedding dress. With only her chalon thrown over her nightdress, she crept
from the Keep. There was something she must do before the inhabitants
stirred and began preparations for this afternoon's feasting.

On the top of a nearby hill still shrouded in the damp mists of pre-dawn,
she said a prayer and thanked The Mother for this season's bountiful
harvest. She then asked her to bless this day of her nuptials. Winter's
approaching nip could be felt in the air as blustery winds cooled the
lingering warmth of fall. Soon it would be the fallow time; a time of only
essential outdoor labor. Her people would be occupied with spinning and
weaving, repairing tools and carving as they sat beside their small crackling
fires in the company of loved ones.

She stood in silent reverence on the sodden grass and allowed earth's
instinctual knowledge to seep through her being. The watery sun gained
strength and substance; then burnt away the mists while brisk winds drove
the heavy clouds over the horizon. Before too long the sky was clear.
"Thank you, Mother," she whispered. Accompanied by joyous bird trills,
she headed down the slope to her private pond, where she would bathe as
a maiden for the last time.

Back at the Keep, enticing aromas and the chill from the icy water drew
her to the kitchen hearth for a meal of warm bread and cheese washed down
with fennel wine. Then she dashed up to her chambers to dress.

Garth had arrived the day before, but as was the custom, could not look
upon his bride prior to the nuptials. He had sent more gifts to her chambers
and with little else to do, spent the day grooming his steed, playing with the
children, and jousting with the men folk but half-heartedly so. Sobered by
what was soon to transpire, though never questioning his inner confidence,

he suddenly felt nervous on the threshold of entering a joining with someone whose strength he felt surpassed even his own. Finding this in a woman was a strange feeling, particularly in one so beautiful. He also knew his desire to live with such a woman, both revered and feared, would complicate his life. But he had given it much thought and was prepared for the sacrifice of remaining in second place while on her lands in all areas but those relating to supporting her decrees. He had quickly realized he could learn much from her land-husbandry and apply it back home. Though this would be viewed as weakness on his part, he cared not for the opinions of any other than Taenacea's. The depth and passion this woman would bring to his life was rare, and he would strive to remain worthy of her respect. The decision made, he knew their time together to be brief, and did not want to lose one moment in idle activity. He was expected to join the men for a night of riotous drinking, but to their disappointment, stayed for only one malt. He wanted a clear head for the morrow. Later, on the narrow cot in the Marshall's quarters, in spite of the sound of boisterous revelry around him, he drifted into sleep.

Garth finally saw his bride at the small Chapel of Lianarth, a short distance from the Keep. Clear eyed, he awaited the only woman he could ever love, a woman not only beautiful, but possessing a mystery and quintessence to gratify a lifetime's curiosity. He had not seen her for five months now except for a brief glimpse the morning of his arrival. She had quickly dashed up the staircase, but not before he heard her throaty laugh. He now stood impatient outside the chapel doors, ringed by his men and a large crowd of her people. His breath caught in his throat as she approached.

The sun was behind her as she walked towards him like a golden goddess, her gown whispering enticements as it caressed her lush form. Her hair, lightly bound with gold and silver ribbons flowed to the ground behind. From strong shoulders fell a simple gown of cloth of gold over which fluttered a gossamer surcoat adorned with embroidered silver and green flowers at the neck, sleeves, and hem. An intricately woven gold and silver belt, dotted with twinkling emeralds, hugged her hips. Its long strands swayed gently in time to her measured steps.

Although he relished every detail of her wedding gown and was touched to see she had transformed his betrothal gift into the stunning surcoat she wore, it was the radiance of her smile that sent a quiver of joy and desire through him. That this woman would be his was almost too much to believe. He squared his shoulders with resolve and swore a silent oath to the deities that sustained her. He would do everything in his power to deserve worthiness in her eyes, and theirs. He would protect her, cherish her, and put at her disposal all his holdings and wealth. Without hesitation, he would give his life for her.

In the dim chapel, wherein wafted the sweetness of beeswax candles, amid the body-warmth of their trusted friends, and under the approving eyes of old Lil, he pledged himself to the Lady of Lianarth, and she to him. Their eyes locked deeply as they privately sealed the irrevocable nexus that bound them together for eternity in mind, body, and spirit.

Later, under a blazing sun which flushed already jubilant spirits, hundreds of people were gathered for the feasting as hundreds more streamed in from all corners of her holding. Trestle tables within the Keep and great hall, and those outside in the surrounding meadows, groaned under the weight of the harvest's best victuals. The vassals who came to celebrate their lady's marriage brought more food as well as gifts lovingly made by their own hand. Kegs of fine imported wine, rarely tasted outside her household, oiled the celebration into frenzied merriment. Along with high spirited dancing, traditional marriage ditties grew increasingly bawdy. Even the reserve of the disgruntled from her outlying borders was quickly dissipated by kegs of chilled ciders, fiery malts, and potent wines.

Of all the neighboring nobles present, only Giles Kaylon hung back. His terse congratulations to the newlyweds barely met basic cordiality. As he brooded over the loss of these prosperous lands, his mind worked at seeking ploys to exact vengeance for his thwarted attempts to obtain the holdings he coveted. It was he who should have been the groom, not that foreigner. Late in the afternoon, glutted with food and drink, he approached the Consort of Lianarth. The title to these lands was still officially held by Taenacea and protected by that idiotic Writ of Succession and Exemption. Signed by Owen Tudor in 1420, the Writ was honored by the royal house to this day, nearly sixty-two years later. How their current sovereign could allow such a stubborn and witching woman freedoms hard-won by men, baffled and infuriated him. As a woman, her purpose was for rutting. As his wife, she would have been kept docile by continuous childbearing and beatings. Instead, although married now, she still managed one of Wale's largest holdings by herself.

He could get nowhere with the bitch, but perhaps DunnGarth could be persuaded to see the benefit of an alliance, particularly since he was much away. He seemed a congenial, if not ambitious sort. Intending to ingratiate himself as a worthy and concerned ally, Giles approached Garth and pulled him aside. Not until later, as he strutted away, confident he had planted seeds for a great alliance, did he realize perhaps this was not so. Although Garth had concurred with the need for an alliance, he had committed to nothing outside a willingness to discuss the matter again. The damn Irish were so glib of tongue, one never knew what had actually been implied or said. Then again, he may just have been distracted by the thought of ravishing his new wife. Perhaps he could be held to his word when his lust had been satiated.

Garth watched him stumble away with relief, impatient to rejoin his bride. He knew well the danger of antagonizing this pompous, albeit powerful little man, but had no desire to mar his golden day with dangerous intrigue. Having heard of his underhanded dealings and ruthlessness from others, he intended only to divert Giles' attention from Taenacea to himself. He hoped he had convinced the greedy little prick his willingness to consider an alliance once he became more familiar with their alleged border disputes. Then, he had implied, he would not be away much and they could discuss relations at length. The ruse would buy him time to find a more permanent solution to current tensions.

Garth was confounded by Taenacea's intense dislike of Giles. True, he was odious; and true, he wore his avarice like a mantle. But her revulsion, only lightly cloaked by civility, hid an arrogant rage he feared could erupt into thoughtless action and result in disastrous consequences. Whatever the source of her powers, she walked in light. Only Giles could bring out a darkness in her so profound, even the skies grew caliginous over their heads during their confrontations. Pulled away from his dark thoughts by the erotic sound of her throaty laughter, he went to join her.

The great hall was bursting with revelers who had moved in from the meadows at dusk. Those who could still stand wheeled about unsteadily, offering raunchy wedding night encouragement. While Garth and Taenacea mingled good-naturedly among their well-wishers, they exchanged teasing smiles and covert caresses in agonizing foreplay. Finally, duty met and both weak with anticipation and longing, they quietly slipped away to consummate their long awaited union.

* * *

"And this was the product of that wedding night," Tannis exclaimed, as she sat back to critique her work. Her mind flew back to the night of this child's conception, where the unseasonable golden day had been replaced with a voracious storm. Forks of lightening snapped branches, and winds tore them from the trees as they blasted across the foliage of her lands in devastating waves. The stormy weather had not abated until Taenacea emerged from the Faery Ring a half moon later, reborn as a servant of The Mother, and carrying the corporeal seed of a celestial union within her womb.

The sculpture of a life-sized Faye lacked the chubby softness of most babes of three. Slender of body, thick long hair hung down her back to her waist. But it was her face which held the viewer captive. It was a face both innocent yet ancient. Her large eyes were raised skyward and appeared glazed, as if in commune with the gods themselves, and her small mouth was slightly open as if anticipating a wondrous surprise. In her arms she held a crest, its bottom nestled in her clasped hands and the rounded top edge resting against her chest.

Puzzled, Tannis stared at the crest. She had no memory of making it, and hadn't the slightest idea what she would imprint on the blank surface. The way things were going, it wouldn't surprise her if its purpose were revealed in a strand, and transferred to the surface in another trance-like session. From her perspective it seemed an odd item for a child to hold. Constructing Faye had also defied time, proving Josie's prediction of accelerated productivity true. Were this pace to continue, she could build twice as many pieces in half the time, and have more time to herself. But to do what? Meander through a past life in perpetuum?

She wiped her tools and covered Faye. Enough of this. As much as the past obsessed her, she was still rooted in the present. Her house needed attention. She smiled wryly. Even Taenacea had to muck out the keep once in a while in spite of her household staff.

While Yanni's 'Night at the Acropolis' cranked in the background, the spring breezes chased her through the house as she cleaned. The cats were eager to help too. They hissed and challenged the vacuum, batted her dusting feathers, and pounced on the wet mop as she wiped down the terra-cotta floor, all the while executing joyful leaps as they streaked in and out the open doors. It was great fun. Their outdoor dashes tracked in fresh trails of muddy kitty prints the mama would make disappear with a miraculous swipe of her mop. Finished, Tannis closed the deck doors. The cats scattered around the house to wash residual soil from their paws while Tannis went out for groceries.

Although she liked to buy her meat and vegetables fresh, her freezer held an assortment of basics like leg of lamb, roasts, ham shanks, steaks and breast of veal. Impromptu dinner parties were never a problem. Her years of dining Brad's unexpected clients had established the habit of a well-stocked larder and freezer. A quick stop at the Quay Market for fresh vegetables, and her shopping was done. There'd be just enough time to throw together a Shepherd's Pie and pop it in the oven before Linka arrived.

The brat was late, so she enjoyed a cordial of Drambuie as she listened to the soft strains of piano music before the front door crashed open and a positively vibrating Linka flew in. With feline radar, Ginseng was at the door to greet his pal before Trix had even hopped out of the kitty tote. After a tender nose kiss, they were off, and scampered around the house with Zoie in hot pursuit.

"That was a week from hell!" Linka exclaimed. "I swear it's feast or famine. Either I just have a few boring portraits to touch up, which takes a blink, or a hundred oriental eyes to open in one gigantic wedding portrait. This week was eyes."

She pulled a notebook and the fable book out of her bag and set them on the coffee table before she filched Tannis' drink and plunked herself down in her favorite corner of the couch. She took a small sip and wrinkled her nose in disdain.

"How can you drink this stuff? You and your sweet wine and cordials." She jumped up to check the freezer. Sure enough, there rested a frosty bottle of Silent Sam, her personal favorite on the few occasions she did have a drink. She dropped some ice cubes into a tumbler, then splashed in a little vodka and a lot of orange juice. Back on the couch, she took a satisfying swig of her drink, then launched into her tale.

"Are you ready for this?" Without waiting for a reply she continued. "Weeelll . . . it started on Tuesday. I went over the spells and read the marked sections in the folk tale book which filled my mind with visions of magical deeds by larger-than-life characters. I says to myself, 'Self, you might as well go for it.' So I did a relaxation cycle. Trix sat in front of me real quiet-like and watched my contortions, as if waiting for further in-structions. I was doing the lotus position, but I'm out of practice, and got all messed up. I think I pulled a muscle or tendon. Next time I'm gonna lie down and do it."

Tannis got up to check the pie in the oven and got herself a glass of water while Linka continued to prattle.

"Anyhow, I felt this rush going up my body, a snap like a giant elastic, only it came from inside me, then total darkness. Suddenly I got zinged through this whirling tunnel and pfft! I walked out of the tunnel, right into another life. Man, was that ever weird. Not just the tunnel thing, but finding myself in another life, like an episode of The Outer Limits. Only I wasn't Faye like I thought I'd be. I was another girl, about eleven or so, 'cause I already had budding breasts under this scratchy tunic-thing I was wearing. Did it ever feel freaky. Not that my fried eggs are much bigger, but *those* definitely felt different, and not like mine at all. I felt different, yet I knew I was still me."

She paused a moment to relive the sensations and find words to describe how you can be more than one person and still know who you are. She drew a blank. Besides, her mother would know what she meant. "Nothing was like I thought it would be. I mean, not that I had any point of reference, but I kind of assumed I would be Faye, and expected to see what you had described. You know, the keep, Lianarth or Aberayron. But everything was different. I knew I was in the wrong era, but not until later. Anyhow, that was after the dream, when I checked it out at the library. I landed in a much earlier time frame, not in Wales, but in Ireland, around the tenth century."

It took a good half hour to recount the tragic tale of the young maiden, Fiona, who was betrothed to William MacCumal, fifteen years her senior. On hearing the name, Tannis twigged that this dream could signify one of the first connections between the two families, if this Fiona was a Lagohaire. She paid close attention to her daughter's disjointed ramblings just in case.

"Fiona was betrothed to William when she was a child. The first time she ever saw him she loved him on sight and followed him around like a little puppy. Since she was the only girl child to live past her first or second year for generations, a dream to unite the two families looked like it could come true. That had been the curse of the Lagohaire family for eons apparently. All their girl babies died for some reason.

"Anyhow, Fiona was really tiny and skinny, with silvery hair, much like Faye from what you've said. But she had some kind of wasting-away disease—probably leukemia, I'd say. That's hereditary, isn't it? Anyhow, she used herbs to fight her illness, but it only slowed down the process. Mom, it felt like she was doing everything she could to make it to her nuptials and live long enough to bear her sweet William a child. I got flashes of her instructing her nurse to pick special herbs and make fortifying teas she drank faithfully. But to no avail. She kept wasting away."

Linka's voice had taken on a chanting quality as she continued. "She was still beautiful, in spite of being so skinny and sick. She liked to be carried to her favorite spot in a nearby meadow if it was warm, and would sit there for hours with wild animals gathered around her. It was so sad. By the time she was ready to wed she could barely leave her chambers 'cause she got tired so easily.

"Tragedy struck the night before the nuptials. It was awful. Because of her delicate health, William had come to her for the ceremony, contrary to custom. He was in a panic when he heard how ill she was. He was so worried about her, he snuck into her chambers at night to give her his mother's betrothal ring as a special gift of luck, since she'd had a long and happy life wearing it. What he found was his beloved lying by the cold hearth, dead. She hadn't made it after all."

Linka's eyes held a suspicious glossy sheen and Tannis winced at the catch in her voice. She knew too well the emotional impact of such a journey into the past, and how personal the feelings were. What she did find interesting was that unlike herself, Linka used the second person tense in the telling. She could see how it would not be an easy thing to speak of your own death in the first person.

"I suspect William looked a lot like your Garth, with his dark hair and broad shoulders. He was really tall too, but had a beard. Well. Something inside of him just snapped when he found her dead on the cold stone floor and he just lost it! They said his cry of anguish could be heard throughout the countryside, and echoed through the valleys all night long. I heard it, and it sounded like he was being ripped apart. The next day, instead of Fiona sitting at his side on the wedding dais as his wife, she lay in waxen repose on a funeral pyre, dressed in her silver wedding gown, all but her face covered with summer flowers.

"William knelt by her side the whole day, sobbing as if his heart was broken, and allowed no one near her. Finally that night, her father got some men to drag him away. A bunch of men had to hold him while they torched the pyre. During the burning, William got away and vanished, and was never heard from again. Some said he threw himself into the flames of their love, but others reported he rode to the coast and threw himself off the cliff. And that is the end of my first time travel experience."

So, the brief flash she had must have been of the funeral pyre scene, and part of this ancient story. But it was something else that Linka had said, that intrigued her. "How do you know what was said, or what happened if you died during the dream?"

Linka replied with relish. "I wondered if you'd pick up on that. Because . . . after I died, which was no biggie, kinda cool actually, I floated above my own body. I was a little dazed, but saw and knew stuff that happened after I died, a little like watching a movie." Then she glanced at Tannis a little more contrite. "You know what that's like, mom, 'cause you've experienced it yourself."

"Well yes, but certainly not right off the bat. I'm really impressed it happened to you first time around," Tannis stated with appropriate awe.

Linka took a moment to bask in the glory. "Does that mean I'm now a little witchlette?" She giggled at the startled look on her mother's face as much as to ease her own emotional tension. Then she sobered and said, "You know, I never thought I would ever experience anything like this. Not only to become another person and know what they think, and what their body feels like, but afterwards, knowing it was really me in another time and place, but still me. Then there's the other stuff, the visions and memories after the actual experience. Talk about a trip. I still can't believe how I could feel, smell, taste, and touch everything as if it was happening right now, here. Now I know how hard it was to explain when you first told me about your dream. There is a difference between this time travel or whatever you call it, and a sleeping dream. I know, I was actually there!"

Tannis nodded in agreement. The experience could not be put into words. "Any ideas as to why this event, or what it means?"

"I just know these two have to be ancestors of Taenacea, or why would I have this experience? After I tell you what happened next, well not right away next, but after that, you'll see how it all ties in."

Her efforts to create an aura of mystery while munching a piece of celery failed. Tannis didn't miss the little innuendo, but pretended to. "So what did happen next?" she asked calmly. Linka's next adventure was delivered in her personalized jargon, between mouthfuls of Shepherd's pie.

"Now, this trip is really wild 'cause it starts with just a voice telling the story," she began. "Man, this pie is awesome, mom," she mumbled, momentarily distracted. "Anyhow, it started with this voice telling a story, only I couldn't see who was telling it. Everything was black at first. Then I started to see little bits and flashes of what the-voice was saying. Then more quick pictures, and suddenly I was right there. Only this time I watched the events, but didn't participate. That was weird too, like some massive movie screen in the sky, but I was watching from the inside of the screen, yet wasn't actually part of the action. Anyhow, get ready for Ms. MacCrae's visually experienced version of the legend of Finn, Warrior Chief of the Fianna."

She stopped. "I could just give you the fable book to read if you aren't familiar with the story, and you could return it to the professor when you're done. Or do you want to hear my version?"

The thought of contacting the professor decided Tannis. More importantly, she knew better than to tarnish Linka's relish of the telling. She had listened patiently while her own events were recounted, and outside of common courtesy to do the same, she knew the importance of sharing such an extraordinary experience. "I want to hear it from you sweetie."

"Great! OK, here goes. In ancient times Finn defended the Irish shores from a mega big invasion from the seas and became like a God to the Irish. He wasn't just a war monger, but quite the hunter too on his lands in the Leinsters Hill of Allen, I think it was." Fork still in hand, she got up to check her notes, then continued.

"Yep, that's it. The same area the professor said. One day he was hunting and heard a horrible racket up ahead. He came around a corner and found his hounds had surrounded this delicate little doe. It just stood in the middle of a circle of ferocious dogs, staring at him with liquid gray eyes, which was unusual in itself since deer eyes are brown. The doe wasn't even scared, and just calmly looked at him, as if waiting for him.

"The Finn thought this strange behavior an omen, being superstitious like they all were, and called the hounds off. When he headed home, the doe followed, surrounded by his now less-than-ferocious hounds who ringed her like her personal guards or protectors or something.

"Later that night, after boozing it up and telling his men wild lies about the doe incident, he fell into bed. But just before he fell asleep, pfft! The doe stood by his bed and looked down at him with those liquid 'doe' eyes, no pun intended."

A throaty chuckle from Tannis as she visualized the events gave Linka time to take a badly needed gulp of air.

"Well, she was so beautiful that the Finn smiled at her with genuine love. And pfft! The doe vanishes and in her place stands this awesome looking babe. She reminded me of Fiona and Faye, 'cause she had that same silvery, faery look to her. Anyhow, it was love at first sight. His loving smile from a pure heart, even though he was a ruthless killing machine, had broken the spell an evil wizard had put on her 'cause she had spurned his advances, the wizard's I mean." Linka paused and sighed with contentment at the heaping plate she had demolished, but carried right on as she trailed her mother into the living room. The dishes could wait, but Tannis' curiosity couldn't. "How did she escape the wizard and end up in the Finn's woods?" she asked.

"She managed to get away with the help of one of the wizard's hounds who was tired of being kicked in the ribs all the time by the old grouch. He chewed through the ropes of her cage, and she headed for the hills. When the wizard discovered her escape, he vowed to get her back. But that's for later." Linka knew her mom was hooked, so drained her glass and sauntered into the kitchen for a slow refill. It wasn't often she had her mother at her mercy and intended to make the most of it. Her plan worked.

"Get your tush in here and tell me what happened," Tannis demanded with mock severity. A quick glimmer of something flashed through her mind, something to do with this story. But it was gone as quickly as it had come.

"Well, like I said, the Finn dude was ga-ga over this gal. The feeling was mutual, they were married, and the Finn became a changed man. Because she had been turned into a doe, she had this magical affinity with animals and made him stop hunting, then fighting, then killing; all the stuff that made him a hero among his countrymen before. He spent his time worshipping her of course, and talked to the animals as they walked around the woods and communed with nature, an activity considered mighty uncool in those days.

"One day he had no choice but to do battle with these really nasty characters 'cause his borders were at major risk and he could lose all his lands if he didn't get off his butt. While he was gone the wizard showed up and captured his bride, intending to turn her into a doe again. But she was about to have Finn's baby, so he couldn't. Instead he just locked her up until it was born. He took the baby boy she named Oisin deep into the woods and left him to die. Only he didn't, die I mean. An old hermit couple found him and took him in. But by the time he was six, they were almost blind and too senile to take care of him, so he ran into the woods and lived on roots and berries. The animals looked after him, particularly one. He was into animals like his fey mom. When he was older, hunters would sometimes see him walking the mountain trails with a doe at his side. And guess who the doe was?"

"His mother?" Tannis queried.

"Yep! She had escaped from the wizard again with the help of the same trusty dog who had run wild in the woods since her first escape, but who kept an eye on her from afar. One day Oisin gets separated from the doe and surrounded by hounds, just like his mother had. Only they weren't friendly at all. Just before they were about to pounce on him and rip him to shreds, the Finn, a haggard recluse now, rides up and calls them off. Something about the boy reminds him of his long lost bride, so he takes him home with him. The doe magically disappears, having seen Finn reunited with his son at last, even though he didn't know it was his son. And that's the story in a nutshell."

Tannis had trailed along visually, comparing it mentally to Irish tales of this Finn, and was startled by the sudden end of the tale.

"What do you make of it, mom? Why would I experience a fable that probably never really happened? And what's it got to do with Faye?"

Linka's questions hung between them. "What's the first thing that came to your mind when it was finished?" Tannis prompted.

"That the two stories are connected, even though this Finn thing happened, if it even did, hundreds of years before Fiona's lifetime."

"So you don't think it's a memory strand?" Tannis asked.

"Well, yes. That's the funny part. I do," Linka replied, and added quickly, "because I got the signal."

"Like chimes or something?" Tannis wondered why Linka brushed over her confirmation so quickly.

"Not exactly chimes. You know how dense I can be sometimes. I didn't want to miss recognizing the signal, so I programmed another sound, which I got. Trust me, it's a strand." She tried to change the subject but Tannis was too quick. "What kind of sound?"

Linka looked shamefaced for a moment, then replied airily, "Oh, just a foghorn."

Tannis thought it appropriate, considering that's about what it took to get her up in the mornings. Her daughter had never been a morning person. She couldn't resist asking, "A big one, or a little one?"

"OK, you've had your fun. Be serious. What do you think?"

Tannis considered all she had heard while she made a pot of herbal tea. Suddenly the quick flashes she'd experienced at the professor's made sense. Curious, she asked, "Which of the three illuminations do you think this was?"

"Knowledge. It could be any of the three, but my gut tells me knowledge."

"Hmm. I saw some of those scenes myself, during that 'psychic moment' as you so flippantly called it, at the professor's."

"You did?" Linka asked, puzzled, and just a little deflated.

"After I came back from the bathroom. They were so quick, I couldn't make sense of them. I saw a man kneeling by a funeral pyre, a young boy walking with a deer, and some other stuff that doesn't fit yet." She paused as a possibility began to gel in her mind. "Since I saw flashes of your story, I wonder if it's connected to my story as Taenacea. It's the time frames that don't make sense, unless . . . symbolically, the three women represent a pattern; you know, different lives connected to one family line. But I don't know how that works." Her theory was quickly picked up by Linka.

"Ask Josie. She knows all about this soul stuff. But for now let's suppose they're linked to Faye, or the soul of Faye, as you would say. Ouch. It's pun night tonight." Before Tannis could respond, Linka had another inspiration. "Maybe it's important because it explains a thread that runs through the family line. Do you realize what it would mean if we could prove they're descendants of the Finn? I wonder if anyone has ever been able to prove a fable real, with concrete evidence I mean."

"I don't know, and I wouldn't call our experiences concrete evidence," Tannis said, " but I find it hard to believe Taenacea could be connected to an Irish legend. That's pushing it a little in my books. Besides," she added wryly, "confirmation via a spontaneous past-life time travel experience is not considered proof."

" OK, I get your drift, but I don't care what anyone thinks. It all has to do with uniting these two families. I just know it. Maybe they're all the same person, or soul. I bet Garth is the reincarnation of those other two, William and the Finn, or why would he look so much like them? All this would classify as knowledge, wouldn't it? Like you said before, we may have to go back to the beginning before we get to the end," she said triumphantly.

"You could have something there, sweets, but we'd better check out this William and Fiona union historically, to see if there's really a family connection. I doubt there are records from their era, so don't get your hopes up. The professor as much as said Wales had the greatest number of preserved records, compared to the rest of the British Isles." Just the mention of his name made her uncomfortable. She didn't want Linka contacting him, so quickly added, "You can give Josie a call since she's now the official scribe and researcher for the Quest. Gives her a chance to make more lists. Besides, she would know if there's a soul connection. This is getting too complicated for me." Bad enough she had to sort out Taenacea's life without bringing in other eras, and other souls connected in some metaphysically overlapping way.

Linka was thrilled Josie would be more involved. "She really digs this romance stuff. You know she's a closet mushbox." In her mind, they were like the Three Musketeers now, on a grand adventure.

Mother and daughter sat in silence, lost in thoughts of their individual dreams. The Quest was taking subtle and complex twists and turns, part in reality, and part in whimsy.

Linka, who savored her active role in the Quest wondered if her mother also drifted into endless replays of her dreams, as she had since her first experience. She had not been entirely honest about being swamped with work. She had been swamped because she had spent most of her time daydreaming, fleshing out her experiences, and relishing her new secret life. She didn't want to break their companionable silence, but knew she had to share her final experience with her mother. Might as well get the icky part over with. Besides, it was the best of all, she assured herself.

"There was one other thing. But mom, promise not to get mad. It turned out OK. Since this is more personal, I wanted to tell you about the other stuff first. And before you lecture me on irresponsibility, I promise never to do it again."

Her statement signaled a bombshell. Tannis braced herself, and waited.

"Before I did anything, you know I was feeling a little down," she began. "I felt even sorrier for myself after the Fiona thing, wishing I could meet some really neet guy who would love me like William loved her. Before I knew it, I was mouthing the conjuring spell, with thoughts of a great love in my mind." She winced at the pained look on her mother's face, but continued stoically. "All hell broke loose! zap! poof! and all that stuff, and suddenly I was this Viking-type chick with long fat braids bouncing off my buxom breasts. I was in some really primitive and cold place. The visions popped all over the place with bits of this and that. But the really important thing, which I didn't know was important until later, was this dude who charged into the filthy little village where I lived. He bellowed my name like I was his property or something." Seeing her mom shift impatiently, she decided to skip the details and just touch on the most important aspects of the experience.

"What's important is what he looked like. He was huge, like your typical, fantasy Norse God with long, blonde hair, a beard and piercing blue eyes. Only his hair was matted, he was filthy, and he smelled. He looked like a barbarian but with really gentle blue eyes. Anyhow, I think he raped me. But I liked him, even though he scared me. In fact, we loved each other in some weird kinda way. Then everything faded and went black."

Peevish that Linka had discounted her warnings not to mess with the spells, Tannis kept her face rigid and waited for the rest.

Linka sensed her disapproval and tried to smooth over her faux pas. "You'll get why I had this dream when I tell you what happened the very next day. When I got home from a consultation at the studio, gardeners were topping the trees around the apartment. I was bagged, so I made a latte and drank it outside on the deck still kinda in a daze." She paused dramatically, then lowered her voice. "Something made me look at the tree being topped, and that's when I saw him. This huge guy was hanging from the tree, swinging a power saw like it was a toy. He looked just like the Viking—cleaned up. I mean, he has this long gorgeous, shiny, thick hair, but tied back in a ponytail. The cool part it's exactly the same length as mine. And he has the same soft blue eyes, a really nice face and smile, 'cause he smiled at me. The only thing this guy has —which my dream Viking didn't—is tattoos covering his arms. But anyhow, I got so rattled when he smiled at me, I dropped my mug over the balcony." She rolled her eyes in disgust, before she concluded, "And that's how I met Sam. He comes down from the tree and picks up every last chard, one thing led to another, we talked, he came upstairs after he was done working, and . . . we've seen each other every day since," she finished, glowing with bliss.

"I see." Tannis was momentarily stunned. Her first thought was, why can't I just dream about a man and then meet him like Linka apparently had, instead of going through all this Quest stuff? Her second was, a biker! Just great. Ashamed at her involuntary pang of jealousy and snide impression of someone she hadn't even met, she said, "Obviously I don't need to say anything about your careless use of spells. You know now, firsthand, this is real power you're dealing with."

In spite of her concern, what was done was done. "However," and this was said with considerable effort at first, then more charity, " I am really impressed at how easily you were able to transport yourself." Nevertheless she couldn't help but blurt out, "Tattoos?"

"Sam was a biker for a while in his teens and regrets the tattoos. He just likes bikes, and still has this awesome Harley he's rebuilt." Before Tannis could voice her concerns, she rushed ahead in justification mode. "It's not like he's some greasy, big-gut biker or anything. He *owns* the landscaping business and its two trucks, and has four guys working for him year-round. Rebuilding Harleys is his hobby. This is the fourth bike he's done, and he sold the other three for mega bucks.

"Riding is a real rush! I know what you're thinking, but don't panic. Sam already bought me leathers and a helmet. Can you imagine? I mean, how many guys would do that just so you're protected?" she asked, still in awe of her luck.

Tannis couldn't envision Linka as a biker babe. Well, her beliefs about acceptance would be put to the test. She had always been an atypical mother, with no preconceived expectations for her daughter, or so she had thought. She trusted her judgment, offered gentle guidance when consulted, and hoped everything would turn out OK. Nevertheless, her reaction to this bombshell indicated she just might have some motherly expectations as to who would, or would not be an acceptable companion for her offspring.

The development of Linka's career proved her daughter's judgment was sound. Tannis still marveled at the larkish emergence of her talent for negative retouching. Linka had been hired as a receptionist at McGrath's, a small but very exclusive photography studio. Her curiosity had propelled her to retouch discarded pictures during her lunch break. That was when her intuitive talent emerged. Caught in the act by the owners, her ability was instantly recognized. A supportive young couple, they gave her a chance to try her hand at retouching a few customer's negatives. As her skill improved, she was promoted to assist their in-house retoucher. When that gal left to get married the following year, Linka got her job. Her work was so good that about a year ago, with the endorsement of the studio, she had left to start her own home-based retouching business. She now contracted her services to many of Vancouver's most prestigious studios.

What did Tannis proud was that, in spite of being swamped with orders from the other studios, she always gave priority to McGrath's orders, in appreciation for their support and role in the development of her craft. Busy establishing her business, her relationships leaned more towards casual dating. She recycled her men so fast Tannis had stopped trying to figure out who she was dating. This was the first time she sounded genuinely interested in someone, rather than flippant. All that really mattered to Tannis was that this fellow treat her treasure well. She shifted gears and asked, "And what does Sam make of Trix, and vice versa?"

"Call it a grudging truce. Lots of glares directed at turned backs, including mine, but no major fracas so far. But guess what Sam did? Since I don't want to leave Trix when we get a chance to go for a day trip on the bike, he came up with this cool idea for a cat-box for the bike, so Trix can go with us. We took her out already, but the wind nearly whipped her away, so he has to construct something that will protect her, and give her a chance to see at the same time."

This man definitely intrigued Tannis. The lengths he was willing to go to please her brat were uncommon. Her curiosity piqued, she asked, "Will you bring him around some time so I can see the box for Trix and make sure it's safe from a cat person's point of view?"

She was surprised when Linka said, "Actually, I was gonna suggest one of your super meals. I've been raving about your cooking, and sculpting. Besides, he wants to see your garden. I've been raving about that too."

A Sunday dinner date set, they lapsed into silence. Finally talked-out, Linka stuffed her things in her bag and looked for Trix while Tannis called a cab. After Linka left, Tannis sat out on the deck for a while. Her mind replayed all she'd heard tonight. She would reserve judgment on Sam until after she met him. The other, Taenacea's possible connection to a fabled past gave her an idea. Maybe she would trace her own family tree, to discover its origin. Her parent's genealogy charts, a project started by her mother, were still tucked in the bottom of a trunk of her mother's personal effects. She had only glanced through the trunk once. Embarrassed by the hodgepodge of memorabilia meaningful only to a discordant mind, she had never opened it again. It might be time to do so now.

She would keep this particular project to herself, but she would ask Josie to look into Taenacea's ancient lineage as well. She would know who to contact to have a professional search done. If need be, she would use this contact for her own search. It would be interesting to see if there was a connection between the Lagohaires and MacCumals, and the Finn, in spite of what she had said to Linka. But, she was getting carried away by speculation. Her priority was to complete her strands, not make a historic discovery that would have little affect on the Quest's inevitable outcome. She could see how a less than disciplined mind could easily get caught up in imagining all kinds of ancient ties. The psyche was a delicate instrument, and knowing was not always the balm one supposed.

Chapter Ten

THOUGHTS OF LAST NIGHTS' CONVERSATION on her mind, Tannis sipped her morning coffee out on the deck and noticed for the first time since her sculpting frenzy that spring had arrived.

She savored the annual awakening of her garden. She watched Ginseng tenderly nose the crocus and cyclamen while Mr. Muff patiently padded behind him. Miniature daffodils cloaked the flower beds like a yellow quilt embroidered with a riot of longer-stemmed, multi-colored tulips. Beneath the shelter of the trees and hydrangea and rhododendron bushes, peeked the waxy heads of hyacinth. Her eyes scanned the boxwood, Irish heath, lavender, lilac and juniper bushes, noting which would require pruning. She loved the vibrant pockets of color: blues and reds of anemone, the pristine white of narcissus, the multi shades of early spring iris, and the white and pinks of chionodoxa. The glorious display of summer blooms over the upcoming months would change the landscape of her garden until late into the fall.

She felt a sudden pang at the thought of missing this panorama while away on her holidays, but depending on how things went with Linka and Sam, she just might have found someone worthy of caring for the garden in her absence. Conversation would tell if his business was based on large profits from coastal beautification because of demand, or a real love for growing things. Only the latter would be acceptable.

It made sense to ask Linka to house-sit, especially now that Trix expected to come over for regular kitty visits. She made a mental note to do just that. With a cat of her own, Linka could not really refuse to babysit her mother's cats. That concern off her mind, she inhaled the soft sweetness of the gorgeous spring day and surrendered her thoughts to the past.

Taenacea's wedding day was her fourth complete strand. Everything about it was golden: the sudden appearance of the sun, her wedding dress, even Garth's garb of emerald green and deep gold velvet. To marry the man she so passionately loved could only be considered a golden moment in her life, and rich extension of life's bounty. But she still had no idea of how they had met, other than knowing it had been at the urgings of old Lil. Just how had this Irishman found his way to Welsh shores?

She wanted just a little more time outside before she headed into the studio for the day. She lay her head back against the chair, closed her eyes, and relished the tickle of the light breeze on her face. The occasional throaty caw from airborne crows concerted with the shrill chirrup of a descending flock of bush tits. Her mind focused on Garth, she felt only a gentle tug and quick shiver up her spine before her descent through the spiral.

* * *

"Yea must go to Aberayron. The folk whetting their appetites for accusations of witchery will soon look to other matters if yea are gone," Lil said.

"It's foolish. I save a life and what do I get for my efforts? Whisperings of sorcery from even the woman whose child I save," Taenacea said with ill-concealed impatience. It was always the same. Each of her healings would eventually be stalked by suspicion, until the next urgent calling for help only she could give.

"Yer pride blinds yer understanding."

"You know it is not so. I covet no glory for The Mother's work," Taenacea retorted, pained by Lil's sharp retort.

"Aye, but folk will 'na thank you for shedding light on the darkness of their hearts. This you must embrace too. The child was near dead, if not so for a time. Folk being what they are point the finger when faced with their own fear and ignorance," Lil replied as she patted Taenacea's cheek with affection. "Now gather your things, for you must leave for Aberayron at first light. Something wondrous awaits you. 'Tis time."

Taenacea complied with Lil's urgings, knowing her sight to be more far-reaching than her own. It was just that she had come from there not a week hence and still had much to do on these lands in preparation for harvest.

Somewhat reluctant she did leave next morning at dawn in order to arrive by late evening. Soon her spirits lifted. Riding through her lands always made her feel both invigorated and humbled. She loved this land and the people under her care: from the tall hills and crags to the hidden meadows and open grasslands where the well-tended cottages of her people sat amid fields now ripe for harvest. She could always anticipate a wave and shouts of greetings, a cool flagon of wine or ale sipped outside the small cottage of one of her folk, and icy water from a nearby brook to wipe the dust of the ride from her hands and face. In the hedge and stone-walled fields ranged cattle, sheep, and the sturdy ponies native to the region. The surrounding pockets of dark, lush woods were home to all kinds of game, especially wild hare, which made the excellent stew her countrymen favored.

Closer to Aberayron, the landscape became more craggy and sparse, with large outcroppings of rocks and boulders littering the scabrous ground. The grass here was long and coarse like wild wheat, and lay almost flat to the east from the constant battering of ocean winds. But it was the first smell of the sea and its salty bite which sent a thrill through her as she rode towards the towering cliffs upon which had sat the old castle of Aberayron. Only the Tower still stood proud, for the castle was long since all but destroyed by ancient battles.

A new Keep had been built about six hundred yards inland at the edge of a sloping valley protected on the western side by the cliffs upon which the old Tower still sat. The hewn rock from the old castle ruins had been hauled to the new site with carts pulled by the hardy Highland ponies. Now, many of the folk who previously had to walk a mile or more from their homes already lived within the protection of the massive new Keep.

She greeted the housekeeper and steward, and after a rich repast of hare pie and wheaten bread retired to her new chambers. Along with the kitchen, her chambers were already fitted with the comforts her wealth could provide. She pulled back the heavy tapestry drapes and looked out one of the seaward windows. In spite of the thick paned glass barring the biting winds entry, she shivered with cold as she searched the murky night, but for what she did not know. No sail dotted the choppy sea beneath the glow of the moon, and even if it had, what would it have to do with her? No sea-wise sailor would anchor in the treacherous little bay that lay beneath the Tower.

Sometime before light, an insistent knocking on her chamber door awoke her with a start. It was unusual for anyone to be up before her, except for the baker whose fresh bread was set to rise well before first light. Quickly she donned her clothing and pulled her warm cape tight around to ward off the icy morning chill. She followed the stable boy, Liam, down to the great hall where trestle tables and sitting benches still leaned against the rugged stone walls.

"My lady," he began haltingly, thick-tongued by the excitement of his news. "There be a ship come in late evening a little up the shore, and a boat that Fisher Bill be finding. Wrecked it was. Gone aground on the rocks on which they find a man. He be in a bad way. Fisher's wife did the tending of him for the night, but his fever be high and she canna do more. They heard you was back, and they be bringing him to yea now." This was a long and deliberate speech for the shy lad who found it easy to speak with his four legged charges, but more difficult to converse with the two legged kind.

"Thank you Liam. Tell them to bring him in here by the hearth, then go and tell cook to feed you," she said kindly. "But first, perhaps you could have a word with Nellie. Ask her to help you start a fire in the hearth, and begin spreading fresh rushes." Taenacea knew young Liam was sweet on Nellie, but her mother the cook was too vigilant for them to do more than cast longing glances at each other. It was only her occasional request for assistance that drew them to the same tasks for brief times. She held in silence Nellie's blurted feelings for Liam, and although she often helped along a stumbling romance in the making, she preferred to let the hearts of those involved forge their own pace without well-meaning nudgings.

After a mug of warm herbal tea, she saw a cauldron of water set to boil on the blazing fire, and gathered strips of sheeting and other items she might need. It wasn't unusual for a seaman to be brought to her for mending brawling wounds since ships anchored a little south of her at New Quay, or further north at Abersystwyth. But a sail so close to her land other than in passing was open to speculation. The little bay on her shore was ringed with treacherous shoals and jagged rock known to sink even the hardiest of craft.

It wasn't long before the litter arrived, sagging with the weight of the unusually large man upon it. He must be taller even than she was, she thought as she quickly scanned the still form covered with a coarse blanchet. She asked them to lay him by the fire and inquired of his condition and what had been done by Fisher's wife. The pallet bearers knew to wait before scurrying to the kitchen for a hot meal. With keen eyes, she examined the still form and noted the flushed skin and damp sheen of sweat upon his face. When she bent her head to his chest and felt the pulse at his neck, she knew him to be raging with a fever that would soon burn the breath from him unless she could bring the fever down quickly.

She rubbed her hands together to charge them with The Mother's light and began a more detailed examination. She held her hands inches above his body and waited for the tingling feeling or surge of heat which would indicate his injuries. She cared little for the superficial cuts and bruises on his hands and face, which was also swollen and distorted his features. It was not his appearance she cared about, and these small injuries would heal quickly. What she sought was the unseen. Only one deep gash on his head would need cleansing and sewing, and the crudely bound break on his left leg would have to be set before he regained consciousness. She waved the bearers over and instructed them to help her remove his clothing and carry the litter. Once he was naked, she covered him only with a light blanket and had them follow her to the river rushing down the slope of the ridge encircling the meadow.

She led them to the little pool that lay hidden by a screen of trees—her own private bathing place—fed by an icy mountain stream. She removed the blanket and had the men pull out the padding upon which he lay. Then she had them lower the pallet into the pool until only his head and neck remained above water. They stood miserable in the frigid water and grudgingly held him down so he would not slide off. She ignored their discomfort and strange looks and watched quietly while his flush turned a pasty gray and he began to shiver violently. Still she waited. When his lips were blue and his teeth chattered, she had them pull him out and cover him tightly with the dry blanchet she carried. Back at the Keep, he was quickly transferred to a warm pallet and placed beside the roaring fire. Only then were the men released to the bountiful warmth of cook's nutriments.

Covered only with a clean sheet and light blanket, she left her patient to the fire's restorative warmth and left to mix a posit for the fever. All the while he had not stirred, for he was unconscious from the nasty gash on his head and the shock of his icy submersion. With the help of Liam and her steward she then set his leg and bound it rigidly with lamb's wool, linen, and bark held fast by straight sticks and dampened leather strips that would tighten as they dried. She then cleansed and sewed his gash and dressed the other abrasions on his face.

Once the posit had slowly dribbled down his throat, Taenacea eased his head back on the pillow and rose with weariness. She had done all she could. His healing would now be in the hands of The Mother. She left Nellie at his side with instructions to call her should there be any movement from her charge. In the kitchen she drank a flagon of well water and munched on a warm meat pasty, then went outside to rejuvenate herself in the warmth of the late summer sun.

Her eyes followed the slope of the meadow down to the farmlands nestled within the harsh surroundings of forested ridges, craggy rock, and windswept plateaus. She proudly watched the doll-sized activity down the slope as the blustery winds drove random shouts and the aimless bleating of sheep her way. The little stone cottages with tightly thatched roofs sat in companionable clusters, separated only by small walled gardens and animal shelters. Taenacea never tired of surveying the growing prosperity of her lands, or the overall contentment of her people. It took patience to teach them to accept many of her radical methods, but continual bounty from lands previously considered barren earned her compliance and a cautious respect.

Her success was based on crop rotation and fertilization with seaweed. As well, her knowledge of enrichments contained in the soil kept her people fed when those on neighboring lands went hungry. When it came to the husbandry of her lands, she stood firm. It would be done her way, utilizing the cycles of the natural world and the spiritual influences of the celestial bodies. Her initiation had included the mastery of interpreting the signs and auguries of the natural world in order to live in harmony within it. It mattered not if her people understood her directives, as long as they followed them to the letter. To ensure this end, she had hand-picked one land steward to oversee each pastoral area, all of them versant in the basic understanding of the signs of the natural world, each accountable only to her. This is who she went to see as she travelled her lands to check on their progress. As well, herbal supplements provided by a midwoman in each community supplemented dietary deficiencies when fresh produce was scarce. She was aware that had it not been for the benefits reaped from doing so, many more vassals would have been disgruntled by her uncompromising and to their mind, strange, dictates.

The frantic call of her name pulled her back to her duties. An excited Nellie was jumping from foot to foot at the gates, gesturing her to come quickly. She smiled, thinking her patient must have blinked or moved a finger, since her instructions specified the report of any movement. But with the extra measure of sleeping potion in his drink, she had not expected him to waken until after the evening meal.

Bending down to the still form on the pallet, she noted his natural coloring had returned and realized he was sleeping a deep, healing sleep.

"He was after opening his eyes for a moment and looked at me woeful like. Then he closed them again. So I called for you, as you asked," Nellie said, eyes sparking with excitement.

Taenacea thanked her for her keen observance and sent her to collect vegetables for cook. Alone with her ward, she scrutinized him closely for the first time. The bruising aside, he was an impressive man. His dark wavy hair was long, but trimmed in the style of a gentleman for all its filth now. The high brow implied clarity of thought, and a straight nose stood noble above the sensual lips of a wide mouth, now somewhat laxed by sleep. His chin was square and solid, giving his face the symmetry of strength and resolve. Though his eyes were cloaked by heavy lids, she imagined them blue, pleased by the etched lines of easy and frequent laughter at the corners. Although paled from illness, his skin implied both the swarthy tinge of a man of the land and the brine-buffed look of the sailors she had ministered on occasion.

She scanned the breadth of his wide shoulders and muscled chest, coated with a dark matting of hair that tapered down to a narrow waist under the blanket covering his lower body. She remembered his long expanse of leg, well muscled calf, and powerful thigh while setting the break. A sudden stirring of appreciation for his form brought a tingle to her belly and warmth to her cheeks. Her hands had not felt alien upon his body and she stifled an urge to run her fingers along the ropes of several old battle scars. She also sensed she would like him a great deal.

She shook her head to clear it of this strange thought and left him to his peaceful slumber as she went out to the kitchen gardens. Today she and Nellie would replenish Aberayron's medicinal stock of healing herbs. With more people living in the Keep now, their previous supply was inadequate. As they worked, she patiently instructed her bright young apprentice in the proper picking times, drying and uses for the herbs. This way Nellie would be able to care for minor ailments and injuries and as her knowledge grew, attend to all but the most severe illnesses in her absence.

Hours later, the smell of roasting meat and bubbling broth enticed them towards the great hall. The afternoon had passed quickly and she wanted to check on her patient. Carrying a heaping basket of freshly picked leeks, carrots and cabbages, she was surprised to see her guest now lay propped on one elbow as he stroked the head of her hound, Ruftar while watching the preparations for the evening meal.

His eyes were blue, a deep, unfathomable blue. She stood very still in the archway of the Hall, Nellie speechless at her side. She had no time to wonder at the somewhat shocked look on his face or why his mouth hung open slightly, as if seeing something of amazement. She stood in a circle of such warmth she never wanted to leave.

For a moment or eternity, she could not tell which, her eyes locked with his in a recognition of such impact, she was struck dumb. It was as if she knew him, had always known him, and would know him forever. It was that complex, yet that simple. She felt a slight shift within her, a relief so profound it was like having finally reached a yearned for destination. He was simply for her, whoever he was. She mouthed a silent thanks to The Mother and Lil, for her urgings to come here now. She never questioned what she felt was destined.

As she handed her basket to Nellie and asked it to be taken to cook, her eyes never left his. Then she smiled at him. "I see you have met with the approval of Ruftar our most ferocious hound."

"Aye, he be that for sure," he replied in a resonant voice that sent the old, almost blind canine into an ecstatic quiver of pleasure. Blind he may be, but deaf he was not, and a compliment said with such assurance was most welcomed at his age. Feeling the dog's joy vibrate under his hand, a slow smile spread across the man's face. He looked straight at her and inquired, "And would the Lord of this fine Keep be about, for I'd like to be making my thanks to him." A lilt to his voice confirmed Irish origins, yet its lightness bespoke culture.

"You are looking at him, and thanks are of no consequence," quipped Taenacea in kind, used to the stranger's assumption.

He wrinkled his brow, but hearing his error was lightly received, asked, "And what might be the name of this great Lord I am unknowingly addressing?"

"Lady Taenacea of Lianarth, and Aberayron where you lie. And whom may I be addressing, kind though somewhat sea-battered Sir?" she replied with an impulsive, and saucy curtsy.

Her action caused those in the hall to pause in their tasks and watch this unusual banter. Though always hospitable to strangers, their Lady usually held herself in more reserve until she had taken the measure of her guests.

Her unexpected playfulness held them captive, and many a furtive look was thrown towards the hearth as they went about their business.

Though a little befuddled by the weakness from fever and ache from his injuries, Garth was not often struck dumb. He had heard about this holding prior to his departure from Ireland from the cleric who had confirmed the Irish ancestry of its lord. The cleric had also shared vague but discomforting stories of its current mistress, implying she was a wicked, albeit, powerful old woman considered a grave enemy of the church. Expecting to travel inland and confront a crone in the seat of her holdings, he was surprised to find himself lying at the hearth of its mistress, a woman whose beauty and presence rendered him speechless. Not expecting a lightness of greeting more common back home than on these shores, he could not help but respond in kind.

"Garth MacCumal, Lord of DunnLagohaire from across the sea, cruelly washed ashore on this fine holding, at your service. 'Tis a disadvantage I be finding myself at, for I am unable to bow, being naked as a babe under this covering."

Taenacea's giggle was followed by shocked gasps around her. "I know. For it is not long since I attended your wounds."

A flush raced across his cheeks before he inquired with a twinkle in his eye, "Then would it be asking too much for my clothes, so as not to offend the sensibilities of these kind folk?"

"I had them washed, crusted as they were by the sea salt, but the kitchen fires should have dried them by now. I'll send someone to fetch them, and you some broth meantimes." An open-mouthed Nellie was sent scuttling for the clothing and told to fetch a mug of hot broth and fresh bread when she returned. Taenacea excused herself and went to change her own dusty clothes.

As she undressed, she marveled at the quick recovery of her patient, and whispered his name several times. Garth, Garth MacCumal. It had a comfortable ring to it and did not seem at all foreign. In fact, it sounded familiar, although try as she would, she couldn't place it.

She had taken more care than usual with her appearance and chose a bright red surcoat over her fine white tunic and violet striped linen underskirt. With her hair she could do nothing. She ran her fingers through the tangle of ebony curls that little could tame, and finally just looped her long tresses twice before carelessly binding them at the back of her neck with a sturdy leather strand. Then she left her chambers and lightly descended the broad stairwell that led to the Hall.

Garth was not only dressed, but had slit his trousers with a knife to allow for the bulk of the bindings around his broken leg. He now sat leaning against a bench by the hearth, looking with longing at the food being carried past him to the tables where the folk were already seated. They in turn threw him speculative but friendly glances amid their whisperings.

He immediately broke into an appreciative smile upon seeing her. As she moved towards him he sat up straighter, but flinched in doing so. She noted much of his pallor had gone and marveled again at his recuperative abilities after such a severe fever. "I see the broth has brought your strength back," she said, sweeping the expanse of his partially exposed torso with a lingering glance.

"Very tasty, the four mugs I had. But my strength would be better served with more hearty fare," he responded, eyes on the plates of steaming meats, pasties, cooked greens and warm breads passed before him in succulent procession.

So pathetic was his longing, Taenacea could not help but laugh. "Perhaps you would care to join me at the table?" she asked. "Tongues would surely wag at my lack of hospitality should you expire from hunger at my fireside." A few of the lads jumped to assist, and managed to get him settled into a high backed chair beside her. But not without a great deal of low cursing and awkwardness due to his size and rigid leg.

There was little wrong with his arms or stomach however, for he heaped his trencher high with a healthy serving from every dish as it passed. Eating with steady deliberation, he filled his plate twice more. Finally satisfied, he took a deep pull from the flagon of wine before him, and sat back with an enormous sigh. "That be the finest meal a starving man could wish for milady," he said, turning to her with a mock torso bow.

"I am pleased these few morsels you managed to swallow were to you liking, milord," Taenacea responded, with an obvious emphasis on the word 'few'. "And what is it that brings you to our shores?"

"A family matter. I have hopes of finding someone with whom there are matters to discuss relating to the lands of Lagohaire." He expected a barrage of female questioning, instead received a waiting silence that propelled him to continue. "While rowing from my ship moored just beyond your bay, a sudden squall sent my boat towards your shores before I could put out to sea again. I remember a large wave, then nothing until I awoke." He touched his head gingerly and winced. "It appears I must thank your folk not only for my rescue, but you again milady, for your healing care." He glanced down at his leg which stuck straight out under the table. "A most unusual binding on the break, for it feels snug, yet not unbearably tight."

Taenacea nodded in agreement. She had listened carefully for any hidden meaning and found he spoke clean and true. She had uncharacter-istically also very much enjoyed looking at him while he spoke, thus her silence. "Yes, I find the dried leather to have a tightness allowing enough movement so not to restrict the circulation of the limb, thus speeding the healing."

The tables were being cleared around them and folk began to leave, if reluctantly so. Taenacea also rose. "You need rest. I'll prepare a posit to ease the pain and soothe the stiffness you will feel on the morrow." Seeing he was about to protest until a sudden flinch of pain washed over his face, she stated, "It is the posit I gave you earlier that made you feel so well on waking. It's effects are wearing off now."

The same lads who had assisted before hung back to help him back to his pallet by the fire and hopefully hear more of where he came from. With a look that brooked no argument, Taenacea instructed both lads to stay with him for the night. Although still warm during the day, the nights were cold so close to the sea and the thick walls of the Hall held their own year-round chill. They could take turns sleeping while they kept the fire going, but first they had other tasks to complete, she reminded them.

She prepared a soothing tea for Garth and sat with him silently as he sipped its healing warmth. All the while he looked at her in silence across the top of his mug. She couldn't remove her eyes from him, and after a few half-hearted attempts, no longer cared to. Mesmerized, they stared openly at each other. A wordless understanding had been presented, explored, and accepted. Finally, when all had been said with their hearts, Taenacea rose. "Sleep well, Garth," she said softly.

"You as well, Taenacea," he replied. His voice lingered on her like a caress that sent delicious shivers up her body even as she reached her chambers. And so began the happiest three weeks of her life. With their silent agreement made, they could now get to know each other with ease, for they both knew their lives were linked forever.

Garth lay awake long after Taenacea had retired, the softness of her farewell running through his mind. After replaying every moment of their interaction, he realized he had reached a pivotal point in his life. His single-minded dedication to the care of his lands these many years had been lightened with many enjoyable dalliances, but none which touched his heart and soul as their meeting just had. Jested by his companions for the trail of broken hearts left in his wake, he realized he had met a woman like none other. He was somewhat discomforted to realize it would be she who would determine his worthiness of a kind of relationship he could hardly imagine but felt ready for. He feared her strength and mystery a little, and knew she would not be wooed and tamed with sweet words. After much deliberation he concluded no artifice could be applied, for she could see into his true nature. Discomforting as that was, what she found in the recesses of his soul would determine his fate. He could do no more than open himself to her, and hope she found him worthy.

The first week, not a kiss passed their lips, only longing and caressing looks. Taenacea would not allow him to stand or walk so Garth sat on the outside steps of the great hall and watched the bustling activities around him. He asked questions of the passing folk who quickly lost their shyness of him and he spun silly Irish tales for the children who boldly clustered around. By the end of the week he began to hobble around with a crudely fashioned, but effective crutch.

The second week, their longing looks were accompanied by small touches and teasing familiarity as she ministered to his healing wounds. She would break from her tasks to sit with him for a meal, and soon there would be laughter, always laughter. And in the fire-glow of the evening, she quietly told him of her life and her soul's work. She shared what she could of her intuitive heart, and veiled only the deep wisdoms of The Mother, not meant for men's knowing.

Soon Garth moved around with a walking stick and swinging gait that kept him apace as her constant companion. She showed him her surrounding lands, told him of Lianarth, and introduced him to her people. It was obvious to all they were smitten with each other as they trod the land further afar each day, she with her measured stride, he with his listing gait. Many of the womenfolk felt the stir of longing as they watched the pair stand on the cliffs by the great Tower; Taenacea leaning back against Garth's chest as his arms encircled her like the most precious of objects.

It was here he told her of the ancient family Writ and his intent to hand over the care of his lands in Ireland. They had not known in Ireland that a daughter had been born to Nevil Lagohaire in Wales. Hearing of his death and thinking him childless, they continued the guardianship of the lands as decreed by the Writ. Unexpectedly, word had come through a traveling cleric about the unusual inheritance of lands by the daughter of an Irish Lord, believed to be of their line. It was the mention of the Irish Lord which had drawn Garth to Wales to investigate the report, but all-seeing fate which thrust him right into the hands of whom he sought.

Taenacea told him of her own Writ of Exemption, earned through her grandfather's personal bravery in saving the sovereign's abducted son from certain death. The continuance of the exemption allowed her to focus on the prosperity of her holdings without diversion from unnecessary warring and expensive king-making intrigues. But it was the practical annual gifts of enormous sums of gold into royal coffers that encouraged successive sovereigns to uphold the Writ.

In the chill evenings they huddled close before the fire and spoke of their lands, exchanging husbandry techniques, or just jested playfully like happy children. Her folk came to love DunnGarth, as did the children, the hounds, and even the troupe of mousing cats that usually trailed only Taenacea. Like a god and goddess, their love made them appear larger than life, and their joy in each other left a trail of smiles in their wake.

By the third week, their mutual passion was palpable and yet, not so much as a kiss had passed between them as they teased, laughed, and opened the secret windows of their souls. Although his leg was still weak, he spoke of impending departure. At the end of the week the bindings that fettered both Garth's leg and their mutual lust were removed. They were sitting by the Tower enjoying the lingering rays of the sun when Garth broached the subject of his leave again.

Taenacea had made her decision. Garth would continue the custodianship of her Irish lands as he had done before they found each other. Processing of the Writ of Transfer would be only a legality. Her choice would keep them apart a great deal, but duty warranted such personal sacrifice. She could no more leave these lands than turn her back on The Mother, or cut out her own heart. She risked much, but could not do otherwise. Their betrothal sealed, and a wedding date set for the following year, an unspoken signal passed between them. The time had come to pledge their love and taste the nectar of each other's lips.

The last few days had been torturous in his attempts to maintain constraint. Amid their serious discussions over the self-imposed separation required by this arrangement, he could not help but think only of her lush body. His restraint had been difficult enough to this point, but now, with his impending departure, he felt like the fire of his need to claim her as he own could no longer be denied. He was hard pressed to keep his mind on her words, for the scent of her as she leaned close and the softness of her breasts pressed against his arms inflamed his senses. At this moment he was willing to agree to anything for just a taste of her. But an intuitive knowing of this woman cautioned him to pledge his love with tender actions not unbridled lust.

"Ah, my Cea, my love. It pains me to leave you so soon, but we must both attend to duty." Garth crooned, as he gently lifted a stray curl from her neck. He began to caress her lightly, his fingers dancing down her neck, across her breastbone, over her shoulder and down her arm, finally tracing a soft design in the palm of the opened hand laying in her lap.

She could hardly breathe when he picked up both her hands, and with her palms up, placed a soft kiss on each wrist. That small action, so simple and yet more intimate than anything she could have imagined, ignited forks of desire throughout her body.

She felt his gaze glide gently over her face like a caress. Her breath caught in her throat as a warm flush spread over her body. Even though the anticipation was killing her, she would savor every moment. This was the most incredible dream come true . . . The soft brush of his lips against her temple brought her back into the moment. Shivers of pure ecstasy rippled along her spine as he murmured words of love against her hair and lightly caressed the nape of her neck.

Pulling back slightly, she gazed at him possessively, relishing all she saw. A lock of dark hair fell across his forehead and brushed one full and slightly crooked eyebrow. His sculptured nose stood proud, reminiscent of a Roman Legion captain from days gone by. She paused a moment, seeking in his deep blue eyes his essence, the source of such surprising tenderness, and felt once again the waves of love that glowed from their center. "How can the coolness of blue hold so much heat?" she thought, "Like fire held captive within ice."

She looked intently at the strong slash of his lips, swelled with expectancy. Distracted by a trail of heat as those very lips ran a soft line up her cheek into the tender fold of her ear, when he paused for a time on her lobe, she knew she could hold still no longer. She cupped his strong chin in her hands and gazed into his eyes; eyes that mirrored her own desire. The kiss would come now, the melding of his lips with hers . . . the bonding of two souls that had yearned for each other through space and time.

She felt the heat of his breath faintly laced with cloves as he leaned towards her. Her lips parted in welcome and she could already taste the sweetness before he even reached the soft moistness of her mouth. And from her core a tide began to rise and whorl through her in warm, soft waves.

He drew her head closer and gently kissed her, then explored the sweetness within and accepted her own searching with a groan of pleasure. Demanding more, he crushed her to him and felt her fingers knead the muscles of his neck with insistent appeal. The dance of demand and withdrawal continued. They kissed deeply, then lightly, teasing each other into an almost unbearable frenzy, both knowing the final surrender would be withheld until their wedding night.

He cupped the heaviness of her breasts, and lazily circled her nipples, already proud and quivering with the need of him. He lowered his head to them, and gently flicked each tip with his hot tongue. Her groan of guttural pleasure spurred him to even more tender ministrations behind her now loosened hair which cloaked them and kept secret their gestures of love. Each imprinted the memory of what would forever be savored in their hearts, this first encounter that must sustain them until they were together again.

When restraint had reached its limit, Taenacea pushed him away, and panting like a bitch in heat, attempted to collect her garments into a semblance of propriety. Her abrupt withdrawal drew groans of despair from a rumpled Garth, then hearty laughter as he watched her trembling hands vainly try to tie her bodice. One nipple peeked saucily over the edge of her blouse and he could not help but reach out and give it a gentle tweak. He received a sharp smack on his hand.

"Yea're a bitch at best, and a witch at worst, my lass. Teasing a man to distraction, then acting like a proper Lady!"

Still flushed, but the errant nipple deftly tucked back in her bodice, she answered with some asperity. "Well then, you poor wee fishie, so helplessly swept to my door by the sea, why not just go. Leave if you must. Go away and your torment will be over." She carelessly waved her arm in the general direction of Ireland, even though her heart constricted with the pain of his imminent departure.

Garth rose and pressed his hands over his heart, his eyes heavenward in mock despair. "'Tis broken my heart is. I'll go then, and wailing with longing for more you'll be, as soon as my sails you 'canna see." He made a face at the absurdity of his rhyme as he reached for her hand and pulled her up against him. Having tasted her, he could not bear to leave her, but knew he must.

For a long moment they clung to each other, fused by a desperate need so newly found and too quickly severed. Then they linked arms and made their way back to the Keep, silenced by the enormity of their self-imposed sacrifice.

* * *

Tannis stirred and opened her eyes, paralyzed by the yearning tugging at her very being. She strained to go back as if a return to the past would ease her longing, but the light tinkle of chimes signaled the end of this particular journey. The sheer erotica of kissing and relatively tame foreplay amazed her. Not even the best of her remembered orgasm could compare to what she had just experienced. Her cheeks flushed with the replay, and as she looked around almost with guilt, she caught Zoie's disapproving glare.

"You're just jealous, you little turd! If you weren't so picky, you could find your own stud-puss. Then you'd know what it's like!" she retorted. She laughed when Zoie jumped down from her perch on the railing and stalked away, ragged tail straight in the air.

She indulged in a dreamy replay to test the experience against the prayer to see which line it was. It hadn't escaped her that her first hazy dream and those which followed had been a teasing preamble to this strand. She was hit with a sudden thought. Had her first dream been anything other than this erotic enticement, she may never have taken the Tarot Card reader seriously and pursued this Quest. She grinned at the craftiness in the choice of inducement. The deities had chosen the one unsatisfied aspect of her life to trigger receptiveness, her desire for a relationship of substance.

Then she knew. It had to be Splendor of Fire, this passion ignited the moment they met, drawn together by destiny to kindle a flame that had burned through time itself. She had experienced five strands already, and with Linka's first, six were now complete. She was halfway there. The thought sent a quiver of excitement through her. Still flushed with memory, she felt like she would burst if she did not share this wondrous experience with someone. She placed a call to Josie, idly wondering if the Horriblescope of the day would again reflect her experience. The truth of it was, the experience was so wonderful she just wanted to talk about it.

"Hi there. Things are heating up for all the signs. Get ready for the ride of your life, but stay grounded or you'll get swept away. Happy day!"

"Oh, for heaven's sake, Josie," she said after her pal's chipper greeting, "do you mentally spy on me before planting these digs on your machine?"

"Gottcha again. Maybe you'll finally surrender to the power of Astrology and accept the fact the stars *do* influence our actions. But, your skepticism aside, what's the scoop? You're not just calling to pick on me, this I know," Josie retorted.

"Am so. And . . . I've just experienced my fifth strand." She launched into the story of her meeting with Garth, relishing the graphic telling and omitting not even one torrid detail. A part of her was surprised at her desire to share such an intimate experience, something she never did. She couldn't help herself. It was too delicious for words. By the time she was done, they were both breathing heavily, carried away by the sheer romance of the interlude.

"Holy shit, as you would say, but not I, as I don't swear like a fishwife. Makes me want to grab the first man I see and go for it. But then again, it would never be anything like that," Josie chortled, then added, always with a view to profit, "Tell that one on the 900 line to love-starved divorcees and we'll make a fortune."

They giggled at the image her statement brought to mind. Tannis asked if Linka had called yet with news of her strand. "No? I'm sure you'll hear from her soon enough. Far be it from me to deprive you of the pleasure of her unique version of time travel."

"Thanks a heap." Josie groaned. She tried to wheedle some highlights from Tannis to no avail.

"Enough with the questions. I have to go finish Faye. Call me after you talk to her, or pop over, OK?"

In the studio, she threw on her old smock and went to work. The mild spring breezes danced through the open sliding doors as she lost herself in the detailing of Faye. Her hands worked swiftly and surely while her mind drifted back to her meeting with Garth. Not only could she remember more details of their first encounter now but his thoughts were also open to scrutiny. It had been the same for him, this instant recognition. From the moment he set eyes on her he was captivated, and by late evening beside the flickering firelight, after much deliberation, and in spite of being still somewhat afraid of her, he never doubted he had found what he had sought in a mate.

As the next few weeks unfurled, Garth marveled at the openness, competency and complexity of this incredible woman, who drew from his such a desire to explore her depths. He felt challenged, invigorated, and secure in her presence. Unlike with other women, he was able to speak from the heart and translate his love into tender actions. She deserved no less. If there was such a thing as a perfect match for each man, it was she for him. Her mystic aspects, veiled from his understanding, he knew to be elements of ancient women's wisdom and connectiveness to earth elements. Esteem for her grew daily as he watched her administer her people with honorable justice, and her lands with a modus operandi of intuitive reverence.

The sudden stillness of her hands, now resting loosely in her lap, pulled Tannis from her reverie. Surprised, she realized she had finished Faye, excepting the blank slate she held, its edges bordered with a Celtic design she didn't remember doing either. Before her a faery child seemed to hover lightly on her clay base. Just a hint of naked foot peaked out beneath the soft folds of the simple gown she wore. Flowers at her feet gave the impression she stood in a summer's meadow, from which she had plucked the bloom tucked behind one ear.

Tannis chuckled when she saw the face of a kitten peeking out from behind one fold, a kitten with the look of Trix whose large ears perked attentively at its mistress. Now that the piece was all but finished, she understood her intuitive desire to caste Faye in silvery alloys. The soft pewter color would glow as if caressed by moonbeams, and enhance the child's elusive charm. As she covered Faye, her thoughts flew to her parents. In spite of the fact Taenacea had known of her acquisition of substantial lands in Ireland before her betrothal, Tannis knew it was love and destiny which bound them to each other.

Chapter Eleven

TANNIS HAD ALMOST FINISHED the second bust of the three young boys that marked the end of her current commitments. Her new auto-pilot trance begun while working on Taenacea, Garth and Faye, proved available on command and was not exclusive to her special trio as she had first thought. While her hands wrought their magic, her mind could wander freely. It always took her to the past, to her other life.

She wondered if any of those places still existed, like the old Tower or at least the new Keep at Aberayron. She was surprised by her desire to see if anything had survived the ravages of time. She had to find out. Knowing Josie, a trip to Wales would definitely be on their agenda.

She glanced at the photograph of the young lad her hands duplicated and was reminded of her young stable boy Liam, then Nellie, then all the other folk as real to her now as Linka, Cal, and Josie. She wondered how Garth had reacted on first seeing her silver wings. Did Liam and Nellie get together? What happened to Lil and who was she? A real person or a spiritual apparition? There were so many unanswered questions, particularly regarding the Tower strand. What happened that dark and stormy night? A small part of her was curious and a large part did not want to know. Then there were the other flashes she'd had, the ones her travels had not yet explained.

She sprayed the bust with a fine mist of moisture and realized it reminded her of the brief flash of mists and sound of wailing. She was now so obsessed with her Quest, her Welsh life seemed more real than her own. She even thought of herself as Taenacea in her mind, and realized she recounted her experiences in the first person. She had given little thought to Linka's new relationship, or Josie's for that matter. Josie had said nothing of how things were progressing with Cal. Was she so absorbed in herself she hadn't bothered to inquire? In her defense, she realized this was a once in a lifetime experience she could not be faulted for relishing. Josie, if anybody, would understand. Still, feeling a little guilty she decided to remedy the situation and give her a call.

A cheery "Hey, girlfriend" from the object of her thoughts startled her. Josie waltzed into the studio and gave her a huge musk scented hug.

"I know, I know. I'm not supposed to interrupt the genius at work, but it's time for a break with your number one pal. Besides, I have oodles to tell you. Since you're too discreet to ask, I'll spill my guts without prompting."

Tannis disengaged herself and exclaimed, "Get out of my head already! I was just going to call you, you annoying little psychotic." She draped her work, tied up her bag of clay and washed her hands in the utility sink. "OK pal, let's do the go-juice marathon outside. You have the deck."

Josie completed her kitty ritual and assured Billy Bob his ratty old toy mouse would be replaced by her next visit. She pulled a mess of papers out of her tote bag and waved them at Tannis. "What I have here in my hot little hand is proof, my girl," she stated dramatically. "But first, what's with the Tattoo man?"

"So Linka did call you. Well, hang on to your G-string. She's bringing him over for dinner on Sunday, after which I will make a full report." She firmly changed the subject, as only a Leo can do, and asked, "Any thoughts on her strand experience and unsanctioned journey?"

"Seems to me she is the key to a saga. What hit me was her leading role in the continuity of an overall love theme, on a soul level. As Finn's love she started the earth consciousness mandate, as Fiona she kicked off the family sage, and finally as Faye and the product of your eternal love for Garth, she represented a conclusion to a plan. I'm still working on the soul connection. However, she being a key player, I concur her strand represents knowledge." She shot Tannis a questioning look, as if waiting for her to see something she hadn't yet realized.

"Then why isn't she the main character this time? Why isn't she Taenacea, and this not her Quest?" Tannis asked.

"Didn't work before, did it?" Josie stated. The look on Tannis' face indicated she had no idea what she was talking about. "Souls tend to reincarnate together in what we call soul groups to learn their lessons. Usually there's an overall theme designed to reach a specific understanding. A time-frame is chosen, geared to offer a rich environment within which the souls have an opportunity to learn individual lessons as well as the group lesson. That's why you are drawn to people in this life you've had interactions with in other lives. You know, like meeting someone you feel you already know well, or have strong reactions towards you can't explain, before you even have an interaction to warrant such an emotional response.

Elementary reincarnation, but I'm getting off track here." She put the pile of papers still in her hand on the little cedar table beside her, and went into the kitchen to get more coffee. She returned to a pensive Tannis, hunched over in her chair, and faced her companion.

"In this larger drama, the fairy-gal and macho man match didn't work. They must have figured a stronger personality such as Taenacea was needed. Different star matings create different results due to the intrinsic personalities inherent within each sign. On a soul level, Linka's role could have been to assist in the development of the family theme in order to establish Taenacea's inherent mind set. Soul memory is recorded genetically you know. Every experience of each ancestor is pooled within the DNA and soul memory of their offspring. Therefore Taenacea's unique predisposition towards land management was encoded by her past, and her Wicca faith allowed access to this pool of knowing accumulated by her genetic ancestry."

It made a strange sort of sense to Tannis and implied a definite theme, an experiment still being played out, but on a grander scale than she could absorb just yet. She must go to Wales and Ireland and see for herself, and said so.

"Since we'll be just next door, I would have suggested we pop over and see if we can find any physical evidence of Taenacea's life. Besides, it's *our* holiday. We can go anywhere we please."

Tannis grinned. "Great. I'm ready for a complete change of scene." Then she glanced at the pile of papers beside Josie and asked, "OK, so what's this proof you have."

Josie grabbed the papers and donned her 'serious researcher' expression. "Your little professor *is* holding out, but first let me backtrack a bit. I contacted Professor Eastman whom I met during a regression retreat, and who still has the hots for me I might add. Of course he was more than delighted to help and provided these goodies. He too is an expert on that particular era it seems. So here's the scoop.

"First, Giles, embroiled in the major political events of the time, namely what led to the conclusion of the War of the Roses, played both ends against the middle. The little fart was up to his ying-yang in intrigue. Openly loyal to the reigning King Edward III and selectively supportive of his son Henry's claim to the throne, secretly he backed Richard, the Royal House of York's crown candidate. Henry, leader of the Lancaster Party was a descendent of the Welsh Tudor line and beat out Richard at Bosworth in 1485. When Henry was crowned King of England later that same year, he actually united the warring houses of York and Lancaster by marrying Elizabeth York and . . . bla, bla, do try to stay awake," she said, seeing Tannis' glazed look of disinterest. "This is the stuff of political intrigue, history in the making right under your Wicca nose I may add. You were smack in the middle of it, and not as indirectly as you thought."

Her comment captured Tannis' attention. "Now to the proof. Apparently there is a somewhat 'underground' cache of surviving manuscripts available to those in the know. But not as inaccessible as you were led to believe. Secondly, Bernie, Professor Eastman, confirmed most of what you were told by your professor, and more. A copy of the 1420 Writ signed by Henry V resides in a private collection that holds other supposedly nonexistent Tudor relics as well."

So, her instincts had been right. He had not told her all he knew. But why? Not wanting to rehash Josie's speculations on that subject, she asked, "Do you have a copy of this Writ?"

"Yup." Josie handed it to her, and added, "And . . . I found out Taenacea was born August 13, 1452 and Faye July 16, 1482. Notice a connection?"

Tannis thought a moment. "Only that you were right about Faye. She was Cancer, a moon-child and . . .oh, I get it. Taenacea is a Leo, like I am."

"And . . ." Josie prompted. But Tannis just looked at her blankly. She saw no other connection.

"I wager had her mother had proper midwife assistance, Taenacea would have been born on the 12th too, instead of the 13th. A moot point, but interesting. Anyhow, Bernie found parish records showing an extremely prosperous yield from Taenacea's lands on a consistent basis from 1471 on, especially when compared to surrounding areas."

"Is that important?" Tannis asked, puzzled.

"It is since it happened to be the year after her father, Nevil Lagohaire died and Taenacea took over the husbandry of the land. It seems her powers kicked in right away. Bernie said there were still resurgence of the plague then, and some of her own people had died. She only had half the manpower it took to work so much land. Incidently, her parishes recorded much fewer plague deaths than surrounding areas. It was as if her lands were charmed, which grew more evident after her marriage and silver wings initiation." She pulled another sheet of paper from her stack and handed it to Tannis with a flourish. "And this, my dear friend, is a copy of the marriage record issued after crown approval."

Tannis felt a myriad of emotions as she lovingly ran her hands over the names. Garth Brien MacCumal and Taenacea Fiona Lagohaire, wed October 17, 1482. This confirmation made it almost too real. She did a quick calculation and wrinkled her brow, perplexed. "Unless my math is totally off base, Faye was a month premature. Gawd, even the healthy, full term babies didn't always survive in those days. A fleeting memory made her add, "I was surprised and frightened when the pains hit. It was too soon. I would have never taken the trip so close to term."

"That's why the need for magical assistance at her birth, I would think." Josie said. "Besides, you had used your own powers since the Awakening, which, if you hadn't realized yet, happened in a time warp. You were only gone two weeks in real time, but her gestation could have been accelerated while you were in your alternate reality, resulting in a healthy, full-term child. Which brings me to my next item."

Tannis asked her to hold that thought while she went into the kitchen to make sandwiches. Josie trailed along and flinched pieces of meat and cheese she dropped for her four-legged pals. Back on the deck, Josie filled her in on Bernie's other discoveries. It seemed he was intrigued by this steady increase in crop yield, especially during a time when crop failures and pestilence raged in not only Wales and England, but Scotland and Ireland as well. And there sat this 'Camelot' of abundance. No wonder Lord Kaylon was dying to get his hands on it.

Josie wiped some mayo from the side of her mouth with her finger and leaned towards Tannis. "And this is where the little fart rears his ugly head again. All that stuff about Giles is true. He was covering his fat little ass all around so whoever won the crown, he would be right at their side to reap the benefits of his allegiance. In fact, he even had a thing going with Scottish claims to the throne. He was one piece of work."

"How did all that tie in to Taenacea?" Tannis asked.

"Since food was a premium commodity in keeping troops fighting the cause, he was willing to do anything to get his hands on Taenacea's stores. Thus the border raiding of her lands, orchestrated by none other than himself. It was all a scam. His men stole her grain and livestock to feed Richard's army as well as his own troops, out fighting for all the other crown hopefuls."

"How on earth do you know this?" Tannis asked, feeling a surge of rage at having her lands raped in that manner. "If he was so secretive about it, there wouldn't be any records of his actions."

"Of course not, but someone who was there and party to his doings would know, wouldn't they." Josie stated with relish. Her words hung in the air while Tannis absorbed their meaning.

Tannis scanned all the possibilities, but could not come up with a likely candidate. "So who was it?" she finally asked.

"None other than Bernie himself. That's why he was so eager to help. Talk about synchronicity. I knew there was a reason I called him instead of several others I could have contacted. He wasn't my most favorite choice you know, what with our unsatisfactory past, and the price I will have to pay for his insights."

Tannis ignored her implications and prompted, "So who was he in that life?"

"None other than poor Richard himself!" Josie said with a flourish. "I say poor 'cause he got his royal ass whipped at Bosworth Field and lost the crown. He's still a little sensitive about that memory."

Curious, and not certain she could swallow the convenient appearance of yet another historic figure, particularly one of such note, Tannis asked, "Does everyone you know believe in reincarnation and have regressions, or what?"

"If they don't when I meet them, they do by the time I get through with them," Josie retorted with the smug conviction of a self-appointed zealot. Then she added, "Your skepticism is plastered all over your face. I told you souls reincarnate in groups. Besides, what gives this whole thing legitimacy is that I wasn't there, and I'm your best friend now."

She had a point. Less interested in Bernie having been Richard, her attention once again focused on Giles. Once again she became incensed by the actions of the horrid little man as scenes of battles at her borders rose to her mind's eye. At times she led her troops alone, at times with Garth at her side. When the culprits could be found, the battles were bloody. The cause of such bloodshed suddenly impacted her and she rose and began to pace in front of Josie.

"Why, the little turd! Those battle scenes I saw were all related to that little weasel. It was his raiding we quelled, his men we fought, and his avarice a thorn in my side. He comes a'calling to offer assistance in squashing his own raids, pushes for an alliance to ensure a foothold in my lands, and all the while plots my demise." Her harsh laugh didn't sound like her voice at all. "No wonder he hated me so. I stood in the way of his cause, slaughtered his men in battle, and under the protection of the Writ could not be openly eliminated."

She stopped suddenly as another thought hit her. How could she miss something so obvious? She didn't realize she spoke aloud. "And there I was, a Wicca. With all this power at my disposal, I had no idea what was going on right under my nose. It seems I thought I was uninvolved, yet I probably fed half the troops in the War of the Roses," she spat bitterly.

Josie ginned. "Seems that way. Oh, chill out! Even a goddess of your magnitude had to have some mortal challenges. Don't forget, you had lessons to learn too. So your 'sight' was a tad selective." Seeing Tannis was truly upset, she added ironically, "Aren't we getting a little carried away here? I mean, it was her life, not yours."

Her comment hit home. Aware of her unreasonable agitation, Tannis looked off into space and tried to explain. "I know Josie, but the more of her I experience the more she's inside me, a part of me. It's like it *is* happening to me. I know I say 'I' when I talk about her. Not just because I go back into her life and live it, but it's almost as if now she's shifted into my reality as well. I feel like we're merging and becoming one. I even catch myself thinking like her sometimes. It's not like I think. Do you under-stand? It's as if her life has more substance than mine right now." She looked worried, and suddenly asked, "Am I going nuts here or becoming an obsessive neurotic?"

Josie had noticed subtle shifts in her friend. At times she caught a staunch assurance in her tone, stronger than her natural confidence. At the same time, she seemed a little more unsure of herself. Small cracks had begun to appear in her carefully orchestrated and controlled existence. She could have pointed out any number of subtle changes, but instead she grasped her friend's hands and responded to her genuine concern.

"Nuts. You? No. You are the most grounded, most balanced person I know, so put that silly thought right out of your mind. Listen to me Tannis. You are so unconscious of your own courage you don't know what you've done. You don't realize you are a Trailblazer, experiencing journeys in consciousness that most people only dream of, or are too timid to even explore. Of course it's all strange and you're bound to feel confused and out of your element. You're not just out of your element, you're out of your usual reality."

That was an understatement. Tannis looked only a little mollified, so she softened her voice and continued with her assurances. "You're teaching me so much by allowing me to be part of your experience, for which I thank you. I'm beginning to understand how a soul can merge realities to become simultaneously aware of other aspects of themselves through their other personalities. The Plaeidian channelers suggest it's normal, that if we were fully cognitive of ourselves, using the other 90% of the brain and consciousness lying dormant within each of us right now, we'd all be aware of all our simultaneous lives. We'd be able to not only handle it, but accelerates our growth by utilizing even more hidden aspects of ourselves. That's what being fully conscious implies. It's what you're trying to explain in a way, how that feels, right?"

She reserved judgement on the Plaeidians, but yes, it was what she was trying to explain. "I guess, but let's not get into that now." Josie could well launch into a whole explanation of the Plaeidians. "My head is already spinning. Did you find out anything else about Garth?" she asked, diverting the focus from herself.

"Not on him personally, but his family per se, yes. Bernie needs more time to research Irish records. There's apparently an extensive private collection covering that era he has a lead on, but the owner spends all his time abroad and he hasn't been able to track him down yet. He thinks he can get copies of the actual Writs, can you believe it," adding with a grimace, "although I may have to agree to an evening of wining and dining to get those."

It was a perfect intro for a change of topic and Tannis' next question. "I thought you and Cal were possibly an item?"

Josie responded with asperity. "Hello! Glad you dropped back into the real world enough to notice such a small detail as the major romance of my life." She ignored the childish tongue stuck out at her and continued with relish. "It just so happens that everything is moving along so fine. Suffice to say, I am *sooooo* glad I smudged." A dreamy look, reminiscent of a Cheshire cat who had just slurped up a dish of thick cream settled on her face.

Tannis didn't miss the innuendo and teased, "Why you little tramp. On the first date too, I bet."

"Yep I was, and did," Josie said without shame. "I had to make sure he'd want more, since he seemed a little hesitant at first, although I don't know why. Besides, I could tell, he wanted me."

Tannis laughed along with her but cringed inwardly at her friend's casual attitude towards sex. She could see how Cal would be curious, but wondered what magic Josie spun to keep him coming back for more. Embarrassed by her mental intrusion into such intimate territory, she grabbed Josie's arm and dragged her into the studio to show off Faye. While Josie ooed and cooed over her sweetness, Tannis asked her opinion on the blank crest. With a start, Josie spun around, dashed out the deck doors to her pile of papers, and rifled through them. With her bell bouncing she returned with two sheets.

"I knew there was something I forgot. The family credos. I haven't looked at them closely myself and was gonna wait until I had some other stuff before I gave them to you, but my vibes say now is the time." She pushed aside a cluster of sculpting tools and lay the sheets down side by side. The copies were poor quality and had notations with arrows pointing to various spots on the crests themselves. Some of the lines were broken, and they had to peer closely to get a sense of the whole picture. In silent agreement, Josie scrutinized one and Tannis looked at the other; that of the original DunLagohaire line.

"This motto here above the two lions says 'I Will'. I can't make out the Celtic symbols but those sketches at the bottom look like berries of some kind and the middle portion could be a rising sun."

Josie nodded in agreement and compared it to her own sheet. "This one must be the MacCumal crest. It says 'I Am' above two birds—eagles I think. The background looks like fire, or flames and these flowers look like dandelions. Wait, Aries," she exclaimed excitedly. "Which makes your crest Leo. Well, I'll be danged. The families took on astrological credos."

Tannis looked blank, so she said, "I know it sounds hokey, but no wonder it never worked. The ancient efforts at uniting the two families, I mean. If Fiona was also a Cancer, like Faye, and let's assume she was, it couldn't work. Cancer and Aries—never. Fire consumes all but itself. A fire sign can only mate successfully with another fire sign. It would take a Leo, Sag or another Aries to create a lasting match. Which you are . . . Taenacea is, or was. Don't you see? It's like this whole family drama played out with the wrong elements. Even evolved souls have lessons to learn. They had to work at this, to get it right." In awe of her discovery, her mind made connections with lightening speed. "Since Aries represents the Awakening and Leo The Ripening Time, the two joined could be a union of cosmic completion."

Tannis looked at Faye silently, absorbing Josie's theory. Humbled by the weavings of destiny and cosmic activity beyond her comprehension she looked at Josie, and in a moment of perfect attunement, understood. "Faye holds the unity of both in her hands. The crest. The two credos." Delighted with this deja vous moment, she relished their special loving bond. Then something clicked inside Tannis' head. She nudging Josie aside and looked intently at the two sheets of paper. Without a word, she reached for her bag of clay and with a lump in one hand and sculpting tool in the other, began to deftly mold the blank crest, oblivious to all but her task.

Josie checked the time on her wristwatch instinctively, then watched her friend work in silence. When Tannis was almost finished, she tip-toed into the kitchen and returned with a glass of wine for each just as Tannis smoothed the last raised surface with a fine, wet paint brush. She placed the brush into the water jar where others soaked and rose to rub her neck. Josie's voice slowly brought her back to the here and now.

"Thirty-six minutes. It took only thirty-six minutes to finish the crest. Those damn threes again. If I hadn't seen it with my own eyes, I wouldn't believe it. Talk about flying fingers in auto-pilot! Now I know what you mean by trance accelerated time. Girl, you are a wizard." The last was said in awe as she absorbed this new aspect of her friend. She handed Tannis her glass and toasted her, then looked closely at what Tannis had molded.

The crest finished the piece without overpowering it. Divided in half by a rising sun the words 'I Will' were scrolled above the flaming sunbeams. Along the bottom leaves were intertwined with raspberries and dandelions. The motto 'I Am' was scripted between two lions reared up towards the two eagles which capped the first credo with their protective wingspan as they looked down from the rounded peak. "Well," Josie breathed, "I don't know where you got the idea, but it's exquisite. It's the perfect finishing touch."

Tannis couldn't agree more. Fragile Faye holding the delicate but powerful crest did complete the piece. She glanced at Josie with deep affection. "I guess I'll keep you around, as long as I get the occasional trigger like this."

To which Josie retorted with a grin, "Twenty bucks, please. Rates just went up. And having once again waved my magic wand, I'm off. You are absolutely exhausting to be around for too long. My energy is zapped. Now do your job and finish those strands girl, before I die for want of knowing." She took only a small sip of her wine, gave Tannis a quick hug and went out to the deck to collect her stuff. As she sailed out, she called over her shoulder, "I'll call when I have more stuff from Bernie."

Her sudden departure, something Tannis was used to, left her feeling flat this time, like a huge balloon of energy they had ridden together had suddenly deflated. She stood silent for a moment and stared at Faye, waiting for something to happen. But nothing did. With a sigh and the resolve of a disciplined artist, she covered Faye and carefully rolled her away. Then she pulled the stand with the unfinished young boy towards her and went to work.

By supper time the piece was done. Like his completed brothers, he required only a final smoothing once the clay was more leathery. She knew all three would be ready for casting mid-week and decided to call George at the Langley foundry to let him know. She wondered when Cal would be back from his New York Gallery while she waited for George to pick up the phone. Since she had only scheduled the pick up of two pieces, George hadn't scheduled these three for casting until mid-June.

She greeted him affectionately and explained her dilemma. "I don't want to mess with your casting schedule, but I'll be away in June. You know how hard it is to keep the pieces at the right moisture level once they're leathery. Is there anything you can do to help me."

"You have to be the queen of timing, Tannis. A booking I had, a multi-piece park statue just got cancelled and I have the alloys you need in stock. Not only can I pour the boys, but I also have the alloys to pour your other pieces. Will the boys be the usual dark bronze color?" he asked.

"Yes. But make the oldest boy the darkest, and the other two each a shade lighter for contrast. I'll mark the pieces. And George, you're a sweetie," she added sincerely.

"Oh, well . . . anything for you." A quiet man, George knew her words were no flattery, but genuine appreciation of his workmanship. He cleared his throat and added, "The silver alloy is on the way. Cal called to let me know and arrange pickup for your pieces. I'll have it by the time your pieces are delivered. I'll call when they're ready to buff."

Tannis insisted on being there when his men did the fine patina on her work to instruct them where to accent the highlights. "You bet," she said.

After finalizing some details, she hung up. The realization that Taenacea, Garth and Faye would be gone in a few days hit her, and she rushed back into the studio. When their coverings were removed, she scrutinized them individually, then really looked at all three together again.

A surge of excitement tickled her belly. The strength of Garth and Taenacea reaching for each other created a perfect backdrop for the delicate Faye. Placed between but slightly in front of her parents, she completed a trio emulating tangible power. Alas. This was how they should be placed once cast. Visualizing the ideal tableau, she could almost feel the living presence of the two golden figures and their elusive silvery child, bound together by infinite love.

Without warning her throat thickened and tears began to slide down her face. She felt overwhelmed by a conflict of emotions: deep longing, sorrow, and such excruciating joy she felt unable to breathe. Standing alone in front of the trio she surrendered to the onslaught, her mind blank and incapable of thought. All she could do was feel. And as suddenly as it had begun, it ended. She felt a tingling at the top of her head. A slow warming floated down her body in one undulating wave as an immense feeling of satisfaction accorded her creativity its due. It was her competent hands which had translated celestial inspiration into these exquisite finished products.

She wiped her face on the sleeve of her smock and covered the pieces. With mechanical efficiency she cleaned her work area, and when finished, headed into the bathroom for a shower. That's when inspiration struck. She would combine her Sunday dinner party with a private viewing for her friends. Cal should be back. As for Sam, if he could survive the evening he'd prove the substance required to handle her daughter. Refreshed after her shower she left dinner invitations for each member of her extended family on their answering machines, a useful technology only the stubborn resisted.

She put a selection of celestial CDs into her player and brushed the cats while she planned her dinner menu. Unable to decide on a single main dish, she settled on a barbecue. Weather permitting they would eat outside. If it rained, the meat could still sizzle under her deck's protective overhang. Lost in thoughts of the accompanying dishes, she almost missed hearing the phone.

It was none other than the professor. "Hello, my dear," said the hurried voice. "So sorry to disturb you. I have some information for you and hoped to pop by this Sunday evening with my associate to . . . er, show him the book, and ah . . . share my findings. Would that be convenient?"

Shocked by the unexpected call, Tannis could barely ask, "Professor, how was your trip?" Her ears began to ring and she felt decidedly strange. How did he get her unlisted number?

"My trip? Ah, oh yes, splendid, yes. Quite splendid. Shall we say Sunday then?" he said, sounding somewhat flustered, as if forgetting he told her he would be out of town for a week.

In a voice laced with ice and sounding little like her own, she heard herself say, "No. Sunday is not convenient. In a week or so would be better. I'm behind in my work and cannot spare the time." She winced at the lie but could not bear to see him now.

"Oh, I see," he sighed with obvious disappointment. Trying another tactic, he wheedled, "This associate of mine is a very busy man. Very difficult to pin down you know. And the records I want to show you must be returned. I need to see your book again, to confirm something with my associate. Are you certain you cannot make an exception under the circumstances?"

"I think not," Tannis said rather tartly. The little fellow was making a great to-do over this. If he thought she would just drop this hot item into his lap he had another thing coming. A little surprised at the intensity of her resentment, she amended slightly. "Really, I do appreciate your efforts on my behalf, but work comes first. I'll call you to set up a more convenient time. Good-bye." That said she quickly hung up.

It wasn't fair to be annoyed with him personally, but she couldn't help seeing and hearing Giles when she spoke with him now. He had not been deviously inaccurate, just guilty of omission. But why? To get his hands on the Magik Book of course. As well, his proprietary attitude annoyed her as if only he could uncover important information. Since she possessed an expansiveness of spirit she had little time for the posturing of self-important people. Almost overnight he had acquired the less desirable traits of his counterpart in her eyes. Quickly she shrugged off these unpleasant thoughts. It was definitely a pajama and 'cuddle up in bed with cats and a good book' night. She would do just that, and finish a romantic adventure started before her own began.

By noon on Sunday the house sparkled and the open doors enticed the brilliant shafts of spring sunlight to play indoors. Her cooking was done and only the green salad needed to be made. The smell of baking ham tinged with the pungent bite of green onions and garlic wafted past Tannis as she greeted her first guest with a big smile and hug.

"Oh, yummm. It smells so good in here. 'Fess up, what's on the menu?" Josie asked as she thrust two bottles of Pinot Adour into Tannis' hands and headed into the kitchen to investigate.

Out of habit, Tannis inspected Josie's attire while running down the list of edibles. Josie was doing the country maiden-slut look. A pleated cotton camisole edged in lace, whose open top buttons exposed the valley of her lush breasts, topped a full skirt. Dancing with a sprightly country print, the skirt's ruffled hem was also edged with lace. Combined with heeled ankle boots, a cameo at her neck, and some tiny dried flowers attached to her grounding bell, her outfit looked relatively virginal. Until she bent over to stick her face into the fridge and Tannis saw the red garters that held up black fishnet stockings. She couldn't help commenting, "Are the stockings a welcome-home present?"

"Just a reminder that there's more here than meets the eye," Josie retorted airily. Distracted by what she saw in the fridge, she exclaimed, "Is that Malakoff Torte. Gawd, you haven't made that sinful concoction in ages."

Their wine poured, they were just heading for the deck when a horrible roar shattered the quiet of the neighborhood. Growing louder it finally settled right outside the front of the house. They went out front to investigate where a sputtering roar hit them afresh.

In the middle of the driveway sat an enormous Harley Davidson bike, sun glinting off the chrome and sparkling cherry red body paint. Astride the monster of a bike sat a monster of a man. Clothed in studded black leather, he was in the process of removing his helmet from which spilled a silky cascade of honey golden hair. Mesmerized by this larger than life scene, they heard a familiar voice pipe up from behind the wide shoulders of the driver.

"Hi Mom! Hey Josie! Isn't this just choice?" screamed Linka, unaware the engine had been turned off. She grabbed at her chin strap, impatient to remove her helmet and release her own golden tresses. Clad in black leather jacket, chaps, boots and gloves that matched her partner's garb, she scrambled off the bike.

Any comment Tannis or Josie had been about to make was cut off by what they saw once Linka had dismounted. For behind her, attached to the back of the bike by a chrome rack sat a cherry red box topped with a see-through plastic dome. And from this bubble peered the precocious little face of Trix.

"Isn't it too cool?" squealed Linka. "Sam had it made. She loves it. See, it has air holes on the sides so the wind doesn't get at her. She's used to her collar and leash now. Well, sort of. So we can take her anywhere with us. We've already been to Horseshoe Bay this morning." This all rushed out while she tried to peel the thigh hugging chaps off her jean-clad legs. Jeans?

Josie must have read her mind because she nudged her and whispered, "Biker babe alert, biker babe alert." It was too much for Tannis. She burst into peals of throaty laughter and was immediately joined by Josie who was barely been able to stifle her own merriment.

"What's so funny?" wailed Linka, looking from one to the other as she unzipped her jacket. She turned to Sam who had also disembarked and said in a pained voice, "Let me introduce these two lunatics. In the wild green tunic, my mother, Gypsy Lee Tannis, and her best friend, Calamity Josie in the square dancing outfit. This is Sam."

Tannis and Josie curtsied in unison and received a withering look from Linka that set them off again.

Decorum would have been restored had Trix not decided she wanted out. Tannis was just ready to extend a warm welcome to Sam when she caught sight of Trix bobbing up and down in the box. Josie noticed the bobbing action too, which set off another fit of giggles. Tannis pointed her finger at the box behind Linka, but her gesture went unseen.

"Mooom! Josie. You two are so rude. What is so funny?" Sam leaned down to whisper something in Linka's ear and with a horrified, "Oh-MyGawd," she hurriedly unlatched the bubble lid and picked up a squirming Trix who had an agenda of her own. She had seen Ginseng, who was eyeing the smelly object his pal had arrived on from the safety of the front door.

Sam's, "pleased to meet you, ladies," said in a deep voice was in complete accord with his sun-bronzed Viking image. An impressive six foot five, his leathers had the look of a warrior's battle gear. Unruffled by the antics around him, he seemed to enjoy them, if the twinkle in his piercing blue eyes and smile within his pleasant mustached and bearded face was any indication.

Tannis led them inside and through to the deck. She immediately liked her daughter's Norse God who walked through her home with confident stride and appreciative glances at his surroundings. Still waters have depth, she thought as she quickly jumped out of the path of two flying furballs, Trix and Ginseng, who streaked past her leg then darted across the deck and into the yard. Out on the deck Linka shot Sam some silent signals with facial gestures and ill concealed hand movements. Tannis wondered what was up, but didn't comment as she went to get Linka's juice and a cold beer for the Viking.

Shed of their riding leathers, Sam and Linka were leaning against the back railing of the deck when Tannis returned with the drinks. She paused a moment to look at the pair. A muscular, bronzed man with flowing hair the same length and shade as Linka's, Sam wore jeans and a white Harley T-shirt that strained across his chest. Her petite, lithe daughter was clad in skin tight jeans and a very short sweat top that just brushed her ribs and left an enticing band of taut flesh bared to the caress of the breeze. So, sweats weren't totally out in the new look her daughter sported.

Drinks delivered she went back in for the appetizers. Placing them on a deck table in the shade, she watched an animated Linka give her man the grand tour of her garden. Her observation was shattered by Josie's sardonic, "Are you done with the 'prospective son-in-law evaluation'?"

"Oh for heavens sake Josie. I have a right to look at the man," Tannis said as she lowered herself into the deck chair beside her companion.

"Uh huh."

The garden tour complete, Sam and his attachment sauntered back onto the deck where Tannis and Josie sat. "That's quite the garden you have Tannis, if I may call you that? Or would you prefer Ms. MacCrae?" Sam said as he lowered himself into the chair beside her.

"Tannis is fine, but thank you for asking." Ah, he was courteous. Good.

"It's been a while since I've seen such artful planning that looks like everything placed itself naturally. I can hardly wait to see it in full summer bloom."

His comments, obviously based on knowledge, endeared him to her for life. Glowing with pride she turned and asked his opinion on a new grafting technique she had seen on television. They discussed natural fertilizing techniques, sparred over the best hybrids each had produced, and compared varieties of roses best suited to their coastal climatic zone. Meanwhile Josie and Linka were huddled in their own intense conversation. They paused occasionally to shoot the two quick furtive looks interspersed with conspiratorial giggles.

Engrossed in their conversations, no one noticed Cal walk through the doors. He paused to enjoy the scene and shot the large stranger a speculative glance. Alerted by inner radar, Josie raised her head and welcomed him with a careless, "Hey babe! Grab a brew and park it here," as she patted the seat beside her. When he returned with a beer Cal, clad in cowboy boots, jeans and a plaid shirt, sat down. Side by side, they looked as if they had just come from the set of a Western movie. The obvious similarity of their garb induced laughing gibes. Amid jests, introductions, and questions, the cats sprinted between their legs and extended their own greetings. Cal was prompted to share his adventures among the Rich and Famous of New York, then Paris and London where he had successfully tied up some very lucrative deals.

"You didn't book anything for me, did you?" Tannis asked pointedly.

"No. I did however show your slides to some interested parties who are now panting to outbid each other for the first of next year's commissions," Cal drawled. "By the way, when are the pieces going to the foundry?"

"Next week." Tannis had little time to say more. At the mention of her mother's work, Linka leapt up, grabbed Sam by the hand and tugged at him to follow, saying, "You gotta see the awesome stuff my mom does. Can I show him what you're working on?" she asked Tannis, more as an afterthought, and already halfway through the doors into her studio.

They were gone before she could open her mouth or rise from her chair. Curious as to Linka's reaction, she decided to let them view the grouping in private. She told Cal about her call to George then excused herself and went into the kitchen to make the salad. She could hear Josie's and Cal's voices weave a companionable cadence outside, but from the studio she heard not a sound. She looked up from slicing cucumbers as Linka and Sam walked into the kitchen with strange looks on their faces. They had been gone a while. Curious how Linka would couch her response since Sam knew nothing of this Quest, she received his compliments with grace, although the long appraising look he leveled at her before it made her squirm a little. But it was Linka's response that really floored her and froze her knife in mid-chop.

"It's almost freaky mom, like Taenacea and Garth are alive. But seeing them together like that is absolutely awesome. And Faye is perfect. I just got shivers up my spine when I saw her. And that choice crest. Where did you get the idea for that? Hey, now that you're done your stuff, would you do Sam from his Viking life. We'll pay," Linka said excitedly. Then she smacked her forehead. "Wow! I just had a halogen moment. Why not do a whole line of reincarnational people? We could all have regressions, pick a life, and you could do a sculpture. Isn't that a cool idea? After you do Sam, that is."

Tannis' mind raced. Did Linka tell Sam about the Quest? She must have. For a moment she was angry at having a stranger privy to her personal experience. It's one thing to share this with family, but him? If not, he obviously knew of his Viking life. He must think them all mad.

"I had to tell him, Mom. Not just 'cause it's cool, but how can I find my other strands with him around if he doesn't know what I'm doing? Besides, since his own regression, he sorta thinks there might be something to this, 'specially since he's now atoning for how badly he treated me in that life."

Linka's apology answered some of her questions, but raised others. "You had a regression?" she asked of Sam. "With whom? When?" Even as the words left her lips she knew the probable instigator sat right out on her deck. She just didn't know when to quit, that one. She laid her knife down and addressed Linka. "Let me guess. When you called Josie, she just happened to know a regressionist who could take Sam back to verify that life. She suggested it would be a good idea, being there had to be karmic purpose behind your meeting. You of course agreed, she arranged it, poor Sam had no say in it, and here we are. Right?"

Their faces and a chipper voice behind her as Josie sauntered in confirmed her suspicions.

"Guilty as charged. But now we know this relationship is about karmic payback. Sam really was a nasty dude. He slaughtered her father and brother, threw their severed heads at her feet, then carried her off as his prize. They had a tumultuous relationship and she finally killed herself in belated grief over the beheading thing. Actually, which she won't tell you, it was because he took up with other women. This time around, he has a chance to win her heart without butchery and opportunity to atone for his womanizing with undying devotion to this little brat here."

Her blithe explanation brought a flush to Sam's face and smug look to Linka's. Sam valiantly cloaked his feelings about this public outcry of previous transgressions as he pulled Linka close and grinned sheepishly at everyone. He looked so contrite they burst into laughter.

Tannis rolled her eyes and exclaimed, "I don't know from nothing! Get out of my face you motley crew of space cadets. Excepting you, Sam, to whom I can only say, welcome to the psycho club." She ignored them as she continued with her slicing, her mind on what had just transpired. The three trailed back out to the deck, seemingly unconcerned by her blunt dismissal.

Honestly. This whole thing was getting out of hand. It was one thing to share her unique and romantic experience with a women, but for a stranger, and a man at that to know was discomforting. *I just hope Josie doesn't decide to tell Cal.* As that horrifying thought hit her, she hollered for Josie to come help her. She then proceeded to explain in no uncertain terms that no matter how many orgasms Josie had, under no circumstances was a word about the Quest to pass her pillow talk lips. She listed the various penalties for any breech of this command and made Josie swear her compliance on her best set of Tarot cards. "Now get out of here, you troublemaker," she said as she shooed her out of the kitchen. The utterance of several lethal spells from the Magik Book came to mind, but she quelled them.

Josie hoped to placate Tannis so called Cal and took him into the studio. He found it hard to drag his eyes away from the trio as they discussed their impressions and agreed on the impact of the grouping. When Cal looked at the other two busts, he shared his amazement at the likeness to the boys he had met himself on a trip to Ottawa. He was puzzled by something else. When he left a week ago, only one head was started. Now both were ready for casting, and the third roughed in, according to Josie. Whatever transition Tannis hoped her trip would trigger, it looked to him like it had already occurred. He had never known her to work so fast, with such detailed results. Excited by the potential, he was more than willing to sanction time off for the balance of the year if she asked.

The barbecue was an undeniable success. Unwanted helping hands in the kitchen, impeding more than assisting, near collisions as trays were carried out, and crafty cats using this mayhem to beg tidbits from accommodating guests kept laughter dancing in the air. Sam and Cal, both in barbecue aprons, argued over the readiness of the sizzling steaks and shot their gals teasing smiles. Dinner chatter was lively as bowls passed between gesturing hands were quickly emptied by the two men who worked their way through an extraordinary amount of food. The red puddles of blood left on their plates by oversized, rare steaks reminded Tannis of another meal, where Garth had also eaten with concentrated relish. She smiled at the thought that even through time, men changed little. Linka would have to stock more than cottage cheese, carrot sticks, and tofu in her refrigerator if this sweetheart stuck around.

And sweetheart he was. He not only jumped attentively to her brat's every whim, but melded into the relaxed bantering like he belonged. He and Cal hit if off right away and many a helpless look at the antics of Josie and Linka indicated they were both in the same boat—sunk! She felt only a momentary pang of separateness. It was not jealousy, rather an ache for her own completion. But that would come in time. For now she would relish the company of those that filled her heart.

Another session of too many people getting in each other's way had the dishes done and put away. They now sprawled contentedly under the soft glow of night torches spaced along the side of the deck. Each of them had a cat on their lap. Tannis noted gentle Muff had chosen Cal and Billy Bob, firmly entrenched on Sam's knee, purred in time to each stroke received. Trix hung over Linka's thighs, dead to the world, and Ginseng idly chewed the tie strings hanging down the front of Josie's blouse as lazy conversation drifted between them. Zoie, crouched on the corner of the railing, ignored them all, eyes on the patio heater that sent waves of warmth their way.

It was nearly eleven when the chill air prompted departure. Farewells said and hugs exchanged, Linka and Sam went through the ritual of donning their leathers for the ride home. A sleepy Trix was placed into her padded box after which Linka quibbled with Sam over the best way to attach a large container of leftovers to the bike. Finally seated, a roar brought the bike to life underneath them and the stillness of the night was shattered for a time as the Harley backed down the driveway and disappeared down the road.

Tannis cringed only briefly at what the neighbors might think as she bade an affectionate good night to a dreamy Josie and Cal, already lost in their own private world. Josie would leave her Jeep and pick it up tomorrow. When the tail lights of Cal's car vanished around the bend, taking with it any sound of human intrusion, she stood outside her door a while and breathed in the night air. She was tired but satisfied. It had been a good day. With no thought other than a night of blissful sleep, she went to bed.

Chapter Twelve

"MOST DEFINITELY NOT! I will not have you pull men from my fields under guise of my endorsement to fight your battles. If anyone is to rally my men, it is I, or Garth—not you." Taenacea stared at her enemy with open loathing. She could not believe he had done so, and admitted it openly to her now, as if she had no say in the matter.

Garth, who stood back from the shouting match which had pulled him from the stables, stared at his wife's coiled anger with growing trepidation. Never had he seen her like this. He sensed something in her composure had snapped and to safeguard any foolish action on either part, signaled his men to readiness. He held back but continued to watch her, alert to the slightest sign of trouble. Ramrod straight with clenched fists, she looked ready to pounce as she towered over the squat Lord Kaylon. Loose hair flew around her face, and lit by the sun, gave the appearance of sparks flying from each silvery strand.

Giles had his own difficulty in containing his temper. Being so publicly dressed down by this spawn of the devil, his face had taken on a sickly puce coloring.

Taenacea's eyes were black with rage. "And furthermore, it seems each time you come to our aid, the raiders vanish into thin air, whereas when we go alone, there is a battle to be had, and usually won." Her implication hung between them. She was beyond thought now. "And . . . I find it odd that half the men we slaughter or send to heel, bear your standards. If you gave half the attention to your lands as to your greed, you would not find need to raid your neighbors." There. Her suspicions had finally been voiced.

Aghast at such open accusation, one that could not go unchallenged, Garth hastened towards the pair before his own efforts to keep the peace were trod to dust. Giles had turned about and walked a distance away. His shoulders quivered with indignation as his hand clutched his sword with deadly intent. When he raised his other hand to call his guards, Garth quickened to his side, and inwardly loathing the touch of him, pressed his arm down as he spoke soothing apologies.

192

During Taenacea's tirade, dark clouds had gathered overhead and obscured the sun. A chill mountain wind swept into the courtyard and whistled through the open walkways in a hissing punctuation of her anger. Everyone within the keep froze, and wondered if this time they would see their frightening Lady strike down her adversary with magik. The tensions sizzled and stirred the clouds above into dark swells. Even the birds were stilled as Taenacea paced back and forth like a she-lion. Her skirt swished like an angry tail as she glared at the backs of the two men. Blinded by the blackness of her heart, she was unaware of the gathering energies above her.

Garth eyed her as he spoke to his companion with carefully controlled persuasion. Giles would have none of it and resisted his appeals and physical stricture. He moved as if to pull his sword as he spit out his indignation. Seeing the action, Garth's men moved closer. Giles' men, still mounted just outside the gates, edged their horses nearer, but would do nothing unless ordered.

The sudden appearance of little Faye and her black kitten broke the clutch of Taenacea's rage and proclivity for conflict. The child stood between the two in wordless comprehension and looked from one to the other through slate colored eyes. Guided by insight, she knew to stand between them.

Her innocent presence finally registered in Taenacea's mind and drew her back to some semblance of control. Nothing must happen to her child. In a shaky but gentle voice, she called her to her side.

"Sweet Jesus, Mother of God," Garth breathed, as he steered Giles further away from his wife and child. He saw Taenacea clench her jaw and threw her a silent appeal before he leaned down to his resisting companion. Crossing himself inwardly for his upcoming deceit, he explained, "Inexcusable yes, but what's to do. A woman's time of flow oft brings on madness. Just this morn she thrust me out of my own chamber with rantings and ravings of infidelity with a chambermaid."

"Are you a milksop then?" Giles spat, "to let a women treat you so. The devil's in her. Should the church hear of her bewitchment of you and your compliance to her every mad whim, you too will be marked. I may not be able to intervene should it come to that," he boasted, his rage momentarily diffused by his sense of self-import. "There's already talk of witchcraft against her and you could well be named as Satan's servant, defending her as you do."

"You are right," Garth said, in outrage. He was outraged at a threat this man would instigate himself, and used it to his advantage. "Be assured she will feel the back of my hand and bite of my belt. She'll not be riding proud for a goodly time. Man to man, I would ask the matter be left to me, by one as gracious as yourself. I can see I have been too indulgent a husband. As to the issue of our borders, I will address the matter at once and send word of a meeting between us. For now, I shall post my own patrols . . . to assist you of course," he added with a slight tightening of his own jaw.

Giles nodded sullen agreement and threw the demonness a smirk. He would like to do it himself, but was mollified by her impending punishment at the hands of her husband. He would speak further on the subject with Garth, for women needed regular beatings to keep them pliable. Garth was not such a bad fellow after all. Just a little naive as to the proper way to rule his roost. When he was mounted, Giles rode away quickly. Let him beat her black and blue for a time, for he would still have the final retribution.

Faye had drifted off as soon as the tension had diminished. Still peevish from the encounter, Taenacea waited for Garth to approach, then snapped, "I heard you. How could you say such stupid things. And how could you even touch that vile man. Now you're playing a dangerous game. How am I to fabricate bruises when he comes back to gloat? You know he only seeks an opportunity to steal even more from us, just as our own King does. In fact, I wouldn't be surprised Giles waits in hiding, follows the raiders, then robs them of our crops and livestock. I can't prove it, but I know it."

Her tirade tested his patience. Never before had he seen such wildness in her eyes or heard such venom in the bite of her words. "Cea, my lass. Think. I know what you say is true, but we agreed we must keep peace between us until Henry is crowned. For he is more dangerous than you know, and that is no jest, my love. It sickens me to speak as I did, but would you have the blood of your child on your hands, before your people? And would you be charged with witchcraft and burnt by the zealots, your child as well?"

She still simmered with anger, but his words cut to her heart. That she must be tested so was almost unbearable.

"It's not so much a threat while at your side my love, but I worry for when I'm away." He moved closer and pulled her stiffened form into his arms in hopes of soothing her.

Calmed a little by his comforting, she looked at him and said, "It's not the crop and livestock I mind losing, Garth. You know I would share with any who ask for aid. It's the taking of lives I mind. The burning of homes and senseless killing, not just of men, but women and children is what turns my blood cold."

This he understood, for he felt it too. Garth reflected on the loss of over one hundred of her people along the borders this last two year, many of which she had known by name, a few of which he had.

"What protection is the Writ if the likes of Giles, and even Edward, sworn to honor it, are the very ones who raid me to feed their troops?"

"Aye. It's the battle between Richard and Henry that's soured the King's honor, lass. His hold to the throne is near ended and he's lost consideration for his supporters' vested interests. With his need of gold and troops these past years, his caring for his people is all but gone." He felt helpless in the face of forces mightier than his own, but determined to do something. "I will go to Henry and get the Writ renewed myself. We know he will be our next King. I shall pledge the Irish lands to ensure not only his seal, but more visible protection. The coffers of my own estates will surely hasten his victory. Gold will buy the allegiance he requires."

"No! I cannot let you do so, Garth. As much as these lands mean to me, I will not risk the sacred trust of our Irish lands by raping them of what has been built by the gods themselves," she replied forcefully. Exasperated beyond belief, she added, "And you will not offer up your own wealth, or estates. I will not have it, do you hear. I will find another way."

Her mind spun, and beneath the swirl festered her anger at the cause. Fatigued by the constant fight to keep her borders intact and the endless drain of energy to keep Giles at bay, she surrendered to her emotions and spat, "Oh, what's the use. Leave those at the border to their own defense and let Giles do what he will. I send no more troops in aid. I will fight him no more. Let him take the lands adjoining his and perhaps he will leave me in peace. *I wash my hands of it all.*" The last was said with such force, the impact of her words frightened even her for a moment.

She felt torn. Given the Irish lands as her sacred heritage, she took her duties to heart, although it was Garth who sailed and saw her wishes executed. She would not threaten those lands, or Garth's for these she stood upon. She loved this land of her birth with a passion and would die to uphold the nourishment of every inch of it. But it was so massive, with so many people dependent on her guardianship. It took much from her, in spite of her trusted stewards and faithful troops. The scope of her commitments hit her, and for the first time she was afraid.

Although she had never set foot on the soil of her Irish holdings, she knew she would risk as much for them. But her feet stood on this soil, and the firm hold she'd had on it now seemed fragile at best. She must salvage what she could. Then it came to her. She turned to Garth and said, "A Gathering. We must call a Gathering, to give our people the choice to move within our protection, closer to Lianarth, or stay where they are and take their chances with a less benevolent proprietor."

Garth was puzzled at her reasoning. "You'll be leaving them to squalor and death. You know Giles will take what he will without mercy. The very men that fight for you now will be on the lines against you as he battles to claim even more of what you have. They will die, Cea, for we must defend what's ours."

But she was stubborn in her position. "Let them decide their fate for once, not me. We can better protect what's left if our holdings are smaller." As if to soften her harsh decision, she added, "Besides, we have so much already Garth, both here and across the sea. See that the word goes out."

It was drastic, but a fair plan if her folk were willing. He felt no need to question her wisdom in spite of an inner sense of dis-ease. He would stand by her as he had always done. "I'll dispatch word and call the Gathering for a fortnight from now. And I will still see to the Writ's renewal. With Giles closer, we will have need of royal support." The sooner Henry was on the throne, the sooner peace could be restored. He would hasten the prospect with his private wealth in spite of Taenacea's objections. He could do what he wished with it, and he wished to ease his wife's pain. Still he was uneasy. He kissed her gently and instantly felt the sear of passion rush through him. Lord, but his need for this woman threatened to consume him, even under such tense conditions. He pulled away with reluctance and went to speak with his Captain. He would draft the Appeal for Renewal this very day, spiced with an offer from his private coffers. His best men would be sent to ensure it reach its destination, the others to take word of the Gathering.

The following week his men returned and reported there would be over five hundred men at the Gathering, eager to hear the Lady of Lianarth's solution to the raiding and killing. They would bring their families and make a feast: wives to cook, daughters to dance and select worthy suitors, and sons to pit themselves against others in the games of strength and swords-manship. Only one person knew there was more than this plan afoot. Her shadow followed Taenacea constantly, but unable to speak of it, she simply waited.

The petition had been taken to Henry. His march from the south towards Bosworth was rumored to bring him close to their lands. Garth's men would ride south to intercept him there. To speed things up, Garth had scripted his name and placed his seal below Taenacea's. All that was needed to make this document legal was Henry's signature and seal.

While they prepared for the Gathering and directed the loading of food stores on the carts that would follow their small entourage, Fay became very agitated. She clung to her mother's hand or clutched at her skirt as she strode through the Keep and gave her orders. When her mother's patience wore thin, she ran to her father, who hoisted her on his shoulders and carried her along as he gave directions to those being left behind.

Concerned, Garth spoke with Taenacea but her mind was on the Gathering. She paid scant attention and assured him it was only because Faye knew she was not to go with them. Her tendency to wander off, even in the night here at Lianarth or Aberayron was of no concern, but could prove dangerous in unfamiliar places. After all, she was only a babe of three.

The night before their departure Faye crept into their bed, something she rarely did. She clutched at their hands and stared long at their sleeping faces; first one, then the other, as if memorizing them for all time. Garth and Taenacea woke to those slate eyes, now opaque, staring into theirs with fierce intensity. When they arose, she clung to both their hands and would not let go. It made dressing and eating the morning meal awkward. If they let go even for a moment, she would wail as she had when she was a tiny babe and Taenacea went to battle.

By the time they were ready to mount, the child was hysterical, and their nerves frayed. Scooped into the ample arms of cook who held firm, she began to screech like a banshee. Discomforted, Garth turned to Taenacea and asked, "Have you no seeing about this odd behavior?"

"No," she lied. She had not thought her brief but dark flash of foresight important, eager to be gone and settle her matters. "Nothing came to me. She's just been with us together for a long time, and now we leave. I will take her to Aberayron when we return." She voiced her decision again. "Yes, we will go to Aberayron." But worry vexed her and she took more time than usual with her soft farewells, as did Garth. They were a distance from the Keep before Faye's plaintive wailing was no longer carried by the wind.

No one noticed when late that night, clad only in her nightshirt, the child crept silently out of the bed shared with cook and slipped away, intent on her own purpose. Used to her appearances and disappearances, none were aware she had not been seen for a whole day, until the following evening. Afraid, they began to search the Keep and their torches lit up the night as they combed the nooks and crannies calling her name. 'Til late night they searched, and defeated they straggled back for a little sleep, only to renew their search in the morning. The thought of not finding her, or finding her injured or dead had every able-bodied person scour even the deepest crevices outside the Keep. Further and further afield they moved: calling, always calling.

For days the calling of her name filled the air, but no sign of her was found. They widened their circle but found not even a torn scrap of her gown. It was as if she had vanished into the mists behind her odd eyes. To send a message would do no good, for the importance of their Lady's presence at the Gathering was evident to all. All they could do was search and pray the deities would shield the child from harm. They dared not think of what their Lady would do if she was not found.

Taenacea felt uneasy throughout the journey. When they stopped for the night, she could not sleep, but thought it to be concern over the Gathering or her resentment at the reason for it. The right choice made, she felt uneasy nevertheless. She still simmered with rage against Giles, against his past deeds and future intentions. Having lost hearth and family, many at the Gathering would lay the blame at her feet. She must brace herself against it and make them see the sense of her suggestions. But it was not an easy thing to ask them to leave the soil rooted with the labor and bones of their ancestors. Her disease did not abate, but she pushed it down, until she heard a sound that made her scalp tingle and sent a wave of panic coursing through her very being.

She and Garth had ridden ahead, their escorts screened by the falling mists behind them. They had nearly crested the rise which overlooked the valley, and instead of the friendly murmuring of a large crowd, the air was filled with a horrendous wailing. Carried on the wind, the sound wove through the curtain of the evening mists. Wailing, amid a deathly silence that should not have been. She glanced at Garth in panic. He too sensed something amiss. They urged their horses to the top of the rise, to sit immobilized by the eerie scene below them.

In the valley, where they should have seen the flicker of fires and shadowy forms moving to and fro, there was only a stillness so absolute, so horrifying, it took a moment for the truth of it to sink in.

Mutilated bodies covered with blood littered the ground like discarded husks of corn at harvest. But these were not husks; they were the bodies of her people. The scene flickered on and off as the evening mists began to cloak the valley floor in ever changing waves. But it did not go away. And the wailing, the almost imperceptible wailing of the thousand tormented souls whose bodies lay scattered across the entire length of the valley, did not abate.

Stricken, Taenacea looked at Garth without comprehension. What? Why? What in God's name had happened? Taenacea slid from her mount without realizing she had done so, and began a slow descent into the bowels of hell. Around her the wailing and moaning rose and fell as she became muffled within the misty cloak. With wretched deliberation she moved among the dead. There were fathers and sons, brothers and nephews who would never see their children grow. The hands of the mothers, sisters and daughters no longer held the warmth of comforting. All lay silent in death; the only movement, a faint flutter of a lock of hair or piece of clothing. And not a creature of The Mother stirred, as if shamed by the carnage, all were gone from this place.

She fell to her knees. "Ayeee! Why, Mother . . . why?" she cried, imploring the heavens for the Sight to know. And it came, swiftly. Images began to swirl in the mists around her, images of her people moving in life, their thoughts intent on the Gathering, anticipating her arrival. Then came a darkness, and within it, another scene.

Giles Kaylon had fed his thirst for vengeance as he rode from her Keep. The witch spoke as if she had known his actions, but could do nothing to him within the confines of her own Keep. Nonetheless, his plans for revenge were fired anew, in spite of the beating she would receive at the hands of her husband. She must die now, and with her the foreigner and the strange child. By the time he reached his own cold hearth, his plan was set. His relish of his cleverness was interrupted by his scouts, with news of a large Gathering planned on her borders.

"May Satan curse her, and him too!" he snarled as he pushed the trembling scout away to pace off his agitation. It was obvious they planned open warfare; a Gathering could mean nothing else. Reports of the heavily laden carts following meant only one thing. The coverings hid weapons and armor. So, the witch planned an attack under guise of a Gathering, as reported by his scout. Then a battle he would give her, by Zeus! He quickly calculated his strength in numbers. With his own men, those hired for border skirmishes, and the troops dispatched to aid Richard only a day's ride away, he would more than match her strength.

She would not arrive for a few days and his men could be ready to march by the morrow if he acted now. It took less than a day to reach the hills that ringed the meeting place from his Keep. A message sent to the other troops would have them back at his side a day later. All thoughts of his previous plan left his mind. The element of surprise was on his side, and for once he could act openly. He intended to strike swiftly and slaughter every last one of them. Later he could say she had ambushed him. Who would know otherwise, for they would all be dead, her troops in this battle, his later, in Richard's. Afterwards, he would offer his men for the first wave of footmen. None would survive. They meant nothing to him. Loyalty could be bought as needed with only a little coin.

He strode outside and set his plan into motion. He told his men the Lady of Lianarth was dead. In his own twisted mind she already was, and because his words bore his conviction, they believed him. His troops were well equipped, well fed, and well rested. Prepared for the royal battle with the fruits of their last raiding, they were further fueled with promises of land, and the inducement of title. It took less than two days to reach the hills that ringed the meeting place.

Meanwhile his scouts, weak-willed men enticed from Taenacea with promises of wealth and title, mingled with the crowd in the valley, warmly greeted by those who had not long ago been their friends. They were to assess the strength of weapons, but it was a friendly Gathering, and the men carried only the small dagger that never left their side.

The scouts' report did not deter Giles from his thirst for blood. Indeed, the opportunity for a certain victory was better than hoped. He would have the element of surprise and little if any resistance. Before Taenacea's men could retrieve their weapons, they would be dead. And for once the blasted mists would be in his favor. They would strike in the still of late night when mists shrouded the valley floor and muffled the sounds of death. The sentries, lax in their anticipation of threat, would be the first to fall to the stealthy slice of his men's daggers.

And so it was. With the stealth of malevolent demons, they swept down and systematically cut the throats of every man, woman and child. Then, cloaked under the deadly mist which hid the expanse of the butchery even from their eyes, they silently crept away.

As she spiraled back into her body, Taenacea's horror knew no bounds. The fault was hers; the death of these thousand souls on her head. Had she not been so blinded by rage against Giles, she would have known what her careless words could set in motion. Her Sight only came through channels clear of the turbulent emotions, and the rancor of her thoughts had blocked her Knowing.

Before her lay the results. She had misused her power, and for it her people had died. Not just her men, but her women, and the children. Mother help her, the children. For the intent had not been to slay them, but the mists were so thick, the culprits could not see whom they slew, so slew them all.

It was more than she could bear. The vehemence of her own words, 'I wash my hands of it all' reverberated through her mind. With those words, and others said with similar force, she had closed her heart, and her sight. Overcome by a grief and guilt so heavy she could not breathe, she knew she was lost.

She never felt the strong arms that carried her leaden weight out of the valley, placed her gently against a tree up the slope, and tucked a warm robe around her rigid form. Her eyes did not see him search the field for even one spared soul. When he found one old man hidden in some bushes, she did not know the man named Giles Kaylon as the culprit before he too died of his wounds. She knew only she was the cause. She was unaware he sent his men the following morning to inform the families back home, so they could tend to the burial of their loved ones. And she never felt the tender caresses, or heard his own retched sobs as he held her through the night and helplessly watched her life's spark flicker and fade; to take refuge in a deeper place than he could reach.

The mourners they passed on the journey back, those left behind who now trudged to their sad task, were but shadows to her. Their faces, tear-stricken and taut with accusation raised not one quiver of feeling, and their sobs were not heard. She saw nothing, heard nothing, felt nothing, held captive by the monotonous sound of wailing as it imprinted itself on her soul.

The cart she lay upon must have lulled her into sleep for a short respite, but as she thought this, the abysmal wailing started afresh, only now with a more feral tone. She kept her eyes closed and prayed for blessed release from the sound, yet knew it would never come.

* * *

Tannis opened her eyes in shock, face stretched tight with the immense grief she felt. The wailing came from Zoie, who sat by her head emitting low moans of sympathy. Or was it censure? Never in her life had she felt so shamed. Sickened by her part in the horror, she wanted to throw up. As the bile rose in her throat, she scrambled off the bed and lunged towards the bathroom. Pain-racking heaves brought little relief, and she poured a glass of water with hands that trembled.

"Lordy!" she breathed, unable to wipe the grisly scene from her mind or stop the faint sound of wailing she still heard around her. A light tinkle of chimes reminded her this too was a strand; a strand of great importance. In spite of her inner denial, the scene replayed itself in slow-motion and great detail, again and again.

Clutching at the walls for support, she staggered to the kitchen on shaky legs but stopped by the dining room table. Through the windows, the pre-dawn mists that often cloaked the North Shore looked too much like her dream. But it wasn't a dream, it was real, like the other journeys she'd been more than willing to embrace. Shivers raced along her limbs while she made a pot of coffee, and when she was done, there were more grounds on the counter than in the filter. But her visions did not abate.

With Taenacea crowding inside herself, she hovered somewhere be-tween the present and past. Her mind raced with thoughts generated by both of them as she searched for understanding. OK. She had misused her power. But could words alone create such havoc? She remembered all too clearly the vengeful thoughts she'd had while raging at Giles. In spite of knowing the danger she had surrendered to their power willingly. Then too was the impatience with her people, the fatigue of always caring for them. She had worn the mantle of her responsibilities without question and with loving commitment up to that point. Why had she surrendered to self-pity at such a crucial time? And the battles. There was no end to the battles to defend her own. What of her fortitude? She had stated she would leave her people to their own devices rather than sacrifice the smallest abundance of her lands to protect them.

And so it was. The heavens had decreed her wishes true by the faculty of her own words and intense desires. This was no small power Taenacea had, and up to this point, she had used it well. So well, in fact, the magnitude of energy at her disposal had not been evident, even to herself. Lil's parting words in the Faery Ring came to mind, the warning to use her power well, for 'what yea see, will be'. What else had she said? 'Guard thoughts fueled by all else, least it become so'. Yes, that was it. Her thoughts had been fueled by the emotion of anger, self-pity, and frustration, not the clarity of a pure heart. The gift received at her Awakening was as enriching as its price was harsh.

This journey had to be the 'Strength of Heaven', a morbid lesson in misdirected thought. The implications were sobering. Were her own thoughts now as powerful and vulnerable to manifestation? Linked as she was with Taenacea, it would behoove her to take greater care. Not that she was the sorceress Taenacea had been, but. . . .

The Magik Book must not leave her hands again, and the spells therein, verboten to everyone, especially the professor. If he was the incarnate of Giles, the power within those pages must be kept from him. A man who could do this, was capable of anything. She would send it back to the Plains of Silver, but not until the Quest was finished. Until then it would remain under lock and key.

The Quest. Her mind flew back to Taenacea and the disappearance of little Faye. On top of the slaughter of her people, she would return home to more sorrow than a mother could bear; the loss of her only child. She had not forgotten the child's mysterious disappearance. She tried to recall more but drew a blank. With sinking heart she knew that memory was still to be relived. This was Taenacea's dark hour, and hers as well. After several cups of hot weak coffee, she pulled herself together. Still shaky, she dressed and sought diversion in work.

By noon the third boy was finished and the faces of the other two sponged smooth. When the youngest was smoothed tomorrow, she would be truly finished. The horror of her last journey was kept at bay while in her creative space, but now it unfurled again and replayed itself. The faint wailing of the thousand murdered souls echoed in her ears until she could bear it no more. She had to do something, or lose her mind, so she dashed from the studio and reached for the phone.

The sound of Josie's voice as she intoned the daily Horriblescope released the tears held back by will alone. She caught only two words of the message. Retrograde influences. By the time Josie answered, she was weeping outright and could barely speak. She didn't have to. Josie was on her way.

It was into Josie's soft arms she fell, and her shoulder her own tears soaked. Finally spent, she pulled back and with quivering voice recounted her tale. When she reached the exhaustive end of Taenacea's experience, she waited in hopeful silence, as if for absolution.

Shaken herself, Josie breathed, "Oh Tannis." She didn't know what to say. But when she saw the fresh rush of tears roll down her friend's stricken face she sensed clarity, not sympathy was needed. "Well, girlfriend, seems to me in every life some tears must fall, and you got yours in one heck of a whammy. But remember, emotions aside, destiny is ruled by its own purpose. This was supposed to happen, did happen, and there's nothing you can do about it, in spite of how devastated you feel. You simply made a choice based on emotion rather than reason, and now it's history.

"But since you feel responsible for the death of all those people, it's 'Wallow in Misery' time," Josie announced as she glanced at her watch with a twinkle in her eye. "For the next fifteen minutes we will blame, guilt, cry, pluck our hair from our heads—well, at least pretend to—rend our clothes, wring our hands, and generally wallow in self-pity for the fiendish results of your human actions. Ready?"

She sprang from her seat, fell to her knees and began to moan and wail, "It's all your fault! You did it on purpose you cold, heartless witch," and a host of other silly accusations as she distorted her face in torment and writhed on the floor in what were to her, gyrations of agony. She interrupted her performance to grab a dishcloth from the kitchen and placing it on her head, began to pluck at it as she moaned. The cats, totally freaked by her absurd behavior scattered to seek refuge elsewhere.

Tannis was stunned. At first the accusations stung. But soon the tears which ran down her face stopped, and she laughed in spite of herself. This was without a doubt the most ridiculous thing she had ever seen Josie do.

"Laughter? Is that laughter I hear? How could you, you evil witch. You're supposed to do penance for your guilt of remembering something another you did, in another life, five hundred years ago. But it's your fault she did it, you know. Come on, get with the program. You could at least slash your wrists in atonement for *her* choices."

Which brought Tannis back to her senses and able to see the experience more objectively. "For heavens sake, stop it. You look ridiculous. Besides, you sound demented," she said as she wiped her face the tissues Josie held out to her.

"Not bad. That only took three minutes. I'm glad, 'cause I don't know how long I could have kept it up. How could women carry on like this for days, sometimes weeks or even months? Guilty recriminations are both draining and stupid. Feel better?" she asked, as if she had just dispensed an aspirin and glass of water.

"Much better, Dr. Idiot. As they say, 'thanks, I needed that'."

"At least you know what the wailing soul thing was all about," Josie stated pragmatically as she went to get a cup of coffee. Her first sip made her grimace, and she sloshed the contents of her cup into the sink followed by the contents of the pot. This marathon of emotional healing required more bracing fortification.

"I can't believe what happened here, not the experience itself, but my reaction to it," Tannis said as she grabbed a filter, placed it in the waiting basket, and deftly scooped a generous portion of coffee into it.

"It was just too much for me. The emotional intensity of this Quest is definitely accelerating. I'm feeling it more deeply now and Taenacea is getting stronger—stronger in my reality. It's as if I absorb more and more of her with each journey. Is that possible?"

Josie propped her elbows on the counter as she watched the brew drip and thoughtfully worked her bottom lip. She sighed. "I don't know. We have no guidelines for this kind of experience. I guess the closer you get to completion, the more intense your link with her becomes. When you experience so much of someone else's life on an emotional level, they're bound to become integrated with your own. She had some kind of power though," she said with reverence. "I don't know if I could handle it the way she did. God knows what kind of havoc I would wrought, based on my emotional desires sometimes." She shuddered at the thought. "It confirms how many of our own traumatic events are perpetuated by undisciplined emotion based on the universal truth that thought creates reality. I do agree you have to keep that book out of everybody's hands but your own," she said emphatically. "I'd tell Linka about this too. Hearing it should be warning enough. There's no telling what she could unleash with her thoughts, particularly since the energy behind her little desire brought Sam into her life so quickly. Man, talk about instant manifestation!"

Which brought to mind the information Bernie had shared with her last night. He had dropped by after a regression, fresh with insights into his life as Richard.

"Bernie confirmed most of this when he came over last night." Seeing Tannis' unasked question, she added, "No, nothing on Faye's disappearance yet." She proceeded to tell Tannis the incident in the valley, the slaughter at the Gathering was later justified as an act of self-defense by Giles. He told Richard he had been intercepted by his scouts with news of Taenacea's death on his way to Lianarth to parlay with Garth. He said he was warned her troops were assembled in a nearby valley, their carts loaded with arms. From there they would storm his lands. Taenacea had been seen marshaling aid in her outlying areas, and since sightings of her were always reported, real or imagined, he was believed.

Richard remembered hearing conflicting stories about what had actually happened in the valley, some from the few surviving butchers themselves, when in their cups. But clever Giles saw to it they were placed on the front lines at Bosworth, and their inevitable death ensured the real truth was never know.

By the time the battle at Bosworth was won, the slaughter in the distant mists of Wales was all but forgotten. But the Welsh loyalists remembered and hardened their hearts at the treachery for the English cause. Attempts to incorporate Wales under English rule would be resisted with renewed truculence and English Lords who owned Welsh lands would find no peace or compliance for a long time afterwards. The Act of Union would not come for another fifty years, and did little to wipe resentment from the hearts of Welsh loyalists.

"To this day the valley is said to be haunted and on misty nights in mid-May they say you can hear the faint sound of wailing. It became known as the Wailing Valley, a reminder of what can happen when mortals anger the Gods, as Taenacea had. Some stories imply it was divine retribution for trying to become too God-like, others that it was her pact with the Devil, the surrender of a thousand souls for the protection of her lands. Regardless, the event provoked outrageous new fabrications about her magical power."

"These tales didn't help Taenacea's image as a benevolent Wicca," Tannis said ruefully. "I can see now how legends are made, and embellished by fear, superstition and imagination. The irony is the grain of truth even in their ravings."

"No kidding. Now that you've been declared a legend, what's next on your agenda?" Josie asked. More accepting of human frailty than her exacting friend, to her mind, the matter was just another learning experience in man's ongoing understanding of his own consciousness.

Tannis hadn't thought about what she would do now, and looked blank for a moment. "I dunno. My work's done. I just have to smooth the last boy and then they're off to the foundry on Wednesday. I might just dedicate the studio to Christmas gifts, and spend time in the garden. I have annuals to plant," she said with little enthusiasm.

"*And* experience the rest of your strands, *and* start getting excited about this awesome holiday, *and* shop for new clothes! Yep, I'd say you have nothing to do," Josie retorted. Assured her friend was grounded in her own life once more, she made her usual abrupt departure. "Thirty bucks, please. You pay premium rates for wailing and gnashing of teeth. Also, I expect to see at least half a dozen new clothes in your suitcase by the weekend. We've got a holiday happening, girl, and don't forget you'll be traveling with the Queen of La Mode." She lifted her perky nose in the air and strutted out in imitation of a model's absurd gait.

After Josie left Tannis scripted her instructions for the foundry, as she had told George she would. This attention to detail ensured she would get exactly the results she envisioned. Although her work sat draped around her, the studio felt as empty as she did. She was used to the emotional lull between batches of work, a time of nothingness when her batteries charged for her next wave of inspiration. But this hollowness was amplified by her recent experience. She needed activity, something to divert her lethargy and stop her mind's roaming. While she cleaned her work area in preparation for her next batch of creations, her visions receded. But she could not scrub away the lingering taint of Taenacea's guilt.

After a light dinner and some restless channel surfing, she took a long, soothing soak. Later, she lay in bed relaxed and dreamy. During her bath, the memories had been stilled, as they were now. Trouble was, without them, she felt like she did not exist at all.

Chapter Thirteen

THE MISTS DISSIPATED UNDER A BRIGHT SPRING SUN and took with them the residual effects of the Wailing Valley. A restful sleep without dreams left Tannis invigorated and in a sassy mood. Her fingers tingled with a desire to create. She would make her Christmas gift for Linka. She got a fresh box of clay and went to work.

In a few hours the rough build of a kitten, a life-sized Trix with huge ears sat before her, one raised paw supported by a clay prop. Her tilted head gave the impression she asked to be picked up and the huge eyes above the pert little nose made her chuckle. Although the clay was gray like most of her working stock, when Zoie jumped up to examine the work in progress, her hackles rose in surprise before she realized it wasn't actually Trix. Her reaction confirmed its likeness. Trix had been built so effortlessly, she wondered why she had never thought of sculpting her own cats and decided she would do so after her holidays.

Chimes from the front doorbell signaled the presence of a stranger. She paused in her work, assuming it was canvassers and waited for them to go away. But an insistent second, third, and then fourth press of the ringer decided her. She wiped her hands and reluctantly went to see who it was.

She opened the door to the annoyed face of the professor and a tall skinny man who looked decidedly uncomfortable. What on earth was *he* doing here and who was his crane-like companion? Seeing him instantly triggered an uncomfortable knot of apprehension in her stomach. She made no effort to hide her annoyance.

"Professor," she said coldly, "I don't remember giving you my address." Her tone implied his presence was clearly unwelcome.

Before he could reply, his tall companion interrupted in a reedy staccato voice, "I'm afraid it's my fault, Ms. MacCrae. I'm Bernie. Professor Bernie Eastman . . . a friend of Josie's. It was she who gave me your address and suggested I come see you. I'd like to discuss an important matter, to do with the Quest. It won't take long, but it concerns all of us." He fumbled with his already askew tie, and implored her to grant them entry with his eyes.

Josie again. This time she had really gone too far. She had no desire to discuss her business with her arch enemy, a resurrected Richard, or even King Henry himself. After yesterday's experience, none of them were at the top of her favorite people's list. But curiosity about Bernie's presence won out, and she stepped aside. "Very well. Come in and say what you have to," she said flatly. She would hear him out but that was all.

She noted Zoie took an instant dislike to her surprise guests and slunk around the perimeter of the room swishing her tail as she cast wary glances their way. Finally she settled on the edge of the mantle, but kept her gaze glued on the professor.

Bernie eyed the many relics around the room before he sat down. "My, you have some wonderful things here. Genuine I see. And the books . . . " He threw the bookcases a longing look. It was apparent he wanted to browse, but protocol and the reason for his visit kept him seated. Reluctantly he pulled his eyes away and said, "You see, not only am I a friend of Josie's, but of Osmond as well. I am the associate he mentioned to you. I am also a clinical regressionist, with a special interest in folklore and reincarnation."

"Why didn't you tell Josie you knew the professor?" Tannis asked bluntly.

"She never mentioned his name. She only referred to him as the little professor. Many professors I know are of shorter stature than myself. I had no reason to think it was Osmond until he called me, quite agitated I may add. He asked me to regress him to a life he thought he may have lived in Wales, as Giles Kaylon. He was upset because of the volatile emotions he felt towards you," Bernie explained.

Tannis could see why Josie was not enamored with Bernie. His voice was annoying, as was his abrupt, querulous manner of speech.

The professor threw her an appeal for understanding, but she ignored it. So, he had not known of a reincarnational connection prior to handling the Magik book. It was what had triggered his memory, just as she'd thought.

"I did the regression the same evening, uncertain if his speculation was correct. It was. After the regression I called Josie but she was out. I left a message but she didn't get back to me until late last night. She told me about your experience and suggested that I drop by and see if I can assist you in resolving your concern over the . . . ah, shall we say, odious behavior of Osmond here." He chuckled nervously at his attempt at humor, and added, "It was my decision to bring Osmond along, not Josie's. I know the difficulty

I had in reconciling my past life as Richard. That's why I feel dialogue will enable the two of you to resolve your feelings. Yours in particular, Ms. MacCrae."

Tannis was not pleased Josie had given out her address without asking. That little psychic was like a giant octopus whose tentacles reached into too many verboten places. But her irritation was tempered by the fact she had not suggested Bernie bring the professor. Bernie had done that on his own.

"As Richard, I did know Giles. But I had no idea he had incarnated as an associate of mine this time around. Not until he called and told me about the resentment he still harbored towards you. Nothing like that had ever happened to him before. I know him. It's not in his nature to feel such, shall we say, uncontrollable agitation. He asked me to regress him to that era and see if he had been Giles Kaylon." He threw Osmond an unfathomable look. "After I regressed him, there was no doubt both you and I knew him well."

Tannis could have sworn he harbored resentments of his own. An uneasy silence hung between them. The professor looked at her beseechingly and said, "I most deeply apologize, my dear, for the distress I caused you, then."

She didn't believe him and had no sympathy for his discomfort. The slaughter was so fresh in her mind his presence inflamed still-raw emotions. Suddenly she shot out of her chair and paced before them in agitation. It had to be said. "How could you just slaughter 1,000 people in their sleep? They had no weapons, and half were women and children. It's a perfidious crime. You were the only scourge in my whole, entirely too short life!"

As stunned by her expressed rage as the two men, she sat down abruptly, and took a deep breath. She was doing the same thing Taenacea had. She must not give history a chance to repeat itself because of *her* lack of emotional control. As much as she wanted to vent all her rage, she held herself in shaky reign.

"Your reaction is exactly why we need to work this through," Bernie stated. "I already explained to Osmond how residual feelings, particularly those as emotionally devastating as yours, do carry over into another life. They've done so with you. The professor here seeks resolution. I'm sure you do too, Ms. MacCrae."

She wasn't so sure, but forced herself to listen with a semblance of openness as they both recounted their memories and justified their actions.

Their view gave her an entirely different picture of Taenacea, describing her as rude and ruthless, arrogant and stubborn, and a less than ladylike taste for blood on the battlefield. The air crackled with the release of ancient energies, but she willed herself to say nothing. The phrase 'don't do it', 'don't do it' reverberated in her head until the tension was unbearable. Abruptly she offered them tea, for no other reason than to give herself a chance to leave the room and still the mantra of caution still beating its warning in her head.

It proved difficult to look into the eyes of her adversary; eyes that mirrored his cupidity from the past. Why, the little prick thought himself justified in taking what was hers, she fumed, even now. To this point they had not discussed anything beyond the Wailing Valley, but she felt a burning desire to do so. When she returned with the tray and cups of tea had been dispensed, she smoothly introduced the question she'd been dying to ask. "And were you the cause of my death?" she asked with deceptive calm.

The professor almost spilled his tea at the unexpected question, but lulled by her apparent calm, answered bluntly, "Yes."

"How?" she asked hoarsely.

Bernie had not missed the tension under her deceptive composure. This was not going at all like he'd envisioned. There had been no dialogue indicating a desire to understand past events, just a palatable rage Osmond's 'yes' now accentuated. "Since you haven't experienced that memory yet, I strongly advise Osmond not to elaborate at this time," he said, and looked at his companion pointedly.

"I must know what happened at the Tower!" she exclaimed, irked by his arbitrary interference.

"I understand," Bernie said, suppressing his impatience with her stubbornness. This situation could get out of hand if he didn't intervene. She needed time to assimilate his point of view before confronting her adversary. "You must listen to me. I have some experience in these matters. The depth of your emotional reaction indicates you need time to come to terms with your feeling about what happened. More importantly," he added with particular emphasis, "Josie would agree with me. Your experiences are spontaneous, which goes even beyond my knowledge of regression. I would be very cautious about tampering with the past."

"And how is knowing, tampering?" Tannis challenged, irritated by his condescending tone.

"There's no way of knowing how foresight of your death prior to reliving it within the context of your Quest, might in some way affect, or even change the past. That in turn could effect the future, meaning your present."

"It probably *does* need changing, considering he wanted me dead, and had the deed done, by his own admission," Tannis said coldly.

"No. In most cases I wouldn't be concerned. In this case, I am. Think for a moment. Even the scope of what you remember is changing. The level of intensity and effect on your own life now definitely is. Josie mentioned your devastation. If I've learned anything in my research of past lives it's that we are only aware of a very small aspect of how it changes us. Your own experience proves this," he emphasized. "I have never heard of this type of link without hypnotic assistance. I've also never heard of an object being moved through time. I refer to the Magik book I have yet to see."

The logic of his words would have diffused her, but the mention of the book only enraged her anew. She knew she would have to relive the Tower strand to completion, but hoped, as Bernie had admonished her not to do, to change it somehow with foresight. For she knew without a doubt the Tower was the place of her untimely death. But the mention of the Magik Book firmed her resolve to keep it out of their hands. Suddenly she didn't know if she could trust Bernie either. As a historian or past-life regressionist, or whatever he was, he too could claim accolades, were it in his possession. It seemed deceit surrounded her, even now. A chill washed over her as she stood up and looked at them through the eyes of her nemesis.

"Be that as it may, but under no circumstances will my Book be discussed, now, or ever. It belongs to another time. Gentlemen, I thank you, but now I must ask you to leave. There are other matters requiring my attention. Once the Quest is completed, I will contact you. Until then, I bid you a fine day."

The finality of her words brooked no argument. She strode to the front door, opened it, turned to them and waited. In those few moments, her two amazed guests caught a glimpse of the awesome power of the woman whose life was under discussion. For even Tannis' voice had changed to one of dictatorial authority. A shadow behind her made her hair appear longer, and her silver wings seemed to flicker around her face with tiny sparks. Or so they thought, as they mumbled awkward farewells and heard the door slammed at their backs. During their hasty departure, she had not moved; just glared at them in disdain.

Tannis leaned against the back of the door. "Whoa. What just happened here?" she asked aloud. For in that brief interlude, it had been Taenacea who dismissed her guests, while she, Tannis, had watched from a portion of her own consciousness. She was stunned by the presence of Taenacea within *her* being. The transition had happened swiftly, and without warning. She had not even felt the light click in her spine which usually signaled a change of reality. But she still felt the iron-clad resolve of her counterpart's personality. Shaken, she felt drawn to the warmth of the sun on the deck. She needed to examine this new development and dissolve the chill she felt. It was the only indication of her sudden shift in consciousness.

This was the first time Taenacea had intruded directly into her reality, outside of that one moment of waking when she had looked around her bedroom in confusion before they had both settled back into their own time frames. Then she was only a flickering presence. Now she was very present, and had used her body for her ends. Had her own indignation propelled her here? Could she do that? Could she know what her counterpart Tannis was doing? Had she been about to perform a blunder whose repercussions could affect them both? Her head swam in confusion. It seemed she could do nothing anymore without stirring up yet another aspect of what had appeared to be a relatively manageable experience. The rules had changed and her perceived control of the Quest had slipped. It was one thing to pop into Taenacea's consciousness, but quite another to have her nudge her way into her own. Well, screw it! Saturated with the inexplicable, she went inside and impulsively called Linka.

"You sound down, mom. Are you OK?" she asked, not fooled by her mother's watery affirmation that she was fine. "I'll have you know your daughter is a genius. I'm getting the hang of playing with this stuff ... I had another strand ... and ... my new computer system is set up, and I'm playing with that too. Hey, why don't you come over. It's been ages since you visited, and Sam's barbecuing on the deck. He's going out later to look at a bike so we can have a private chat, How about it?"

The invitation sounded like just what she needed. Curious about the status of their relationship, she also wanted to see Linka's new retouching system. "I'd love to," she said, adding, "Should I bring anything?" A dose of the ordinary and concrete was more palatable than resolution, understanding, or the Quest itself right now.

"Yep! My favorite mom in the whole wide world. Don't forget her," Linka tossed back.

Tannis was glad of her impulsive decision to go. She needed to get out. As much as she loved the seclusion of her home, right now it harbored ghosts from the past and the residue of her unwelcome visitors. Besides, she wanted to see if Sam had become a permanent fixture in more than Linka's heart. Her suspicions proved likely when she parked and spied a big barbecue and stacks of boxes on the balcony. If he wasn't living here yet, he was at least storing some of his things on her brat's balcony. Knowing how Linka loved the spacious elegance of her apartment, she wondered if more than his clothes or toothbrush, would give evidence of cohabitation.

Sam greeted her at the door with a casual, "Hey, babe. It's a famous artist on our doorstep." Hair pulled back into a ponytail, he sported a large chef's apron with 'Eat My Grits' in large block letters across the front. He waved a bottle of Moselle and beckoned her to enter with the corkscrew in his other hand.

"Hi yourself, Mr. Grits," Tannis replied with a grin.

A flurry of noise from the kitchen distracted them both. A loud "No. Saaammm! She's nabbed a shrimp" was followed by a scuffle and streak of black with a pink jumbo shrimp firmly clasped in feline jaws as it scooted past them down the hall.

"Mom," Linka shrieked, "do something!"

"Not my house, cat, or problem," she retorted as she followed Sam into the living room. Prepared for a minimal change in decor, she stopped in surprise and absorbed the transformation. The living room was now a study in black and white, accented with chic splashes of color. One of Linka's couches was replaced by a sleek black leather sofa and on the wall behind it hung a huge rectangular print of a sparkling blue Harley Davidson bike. It dominated the room, yet blended, its metallic glints softened by the new Areca palm beside the couch.

The coffee and end tables were new too; a golden oak with clean lines indicating good taste and fine craftsmanship. At one end of the massive coffee table sat a cluster of flower pots. Purple African violets, red Gloxinia and snowy dwarf Chrysanthemums added spring lushness to the room. Her eyes scanned a large grouping of floral photographs on the side wall; each a close-up of just one or two vibrant blooms. But what drew her was the addition of a six foot long aquarium containing only water and sea coral, but no fish, atop a sturdy oak frame that matched the tables.

Before she could comment, Sam handed her a glass of wine and Linka gave her a hug from behind. After a nuzzle against her back, Linka exclaimed, "Isn't it choice? Sam had it 'specially made. He's just getting the tank ready for the fish, which he'll introduce a few at a time. It's quite the process, when you do it properly. So, whadya think?"

Tannis sensed her question was about more than the change in decor. "It works for me! The room's lovely and it's about time you two quit dragging your butts and got serious," she retorted, to which they all burst out laughing. Sam excused himself to attend to his culinary tasks. Halfway to the kitchen he bent to scoop up Trix and pop her into the deep pocket at the front of his apron. It was obvious whatever reservations the two had initially were resolved.

Linka took her to the spare bedroom and showed her the computer system and scanner, set up beside her old light table. Her work station had previously been set up in a corner of the living room, but with her new equipment and the addition of Sam's stuff, this arrangement made more sense. She watched fascinated as Linka played with a face on her screen, and showed her how she could erase blemishes and make other cosmetic alterations.

"I'm really slow and can only do some of the basics. I still use my light table for my orders, but I figure in a few weeks I should be able to start doing some of my work digitally. Sam's a slave-driver, and makes sure I spend a few hours every day on the system. I think he's kinda interested in playing with it himself, so as the pro in this household, I'd better master my craft." The picture on the screen was an old photo she had scanned into the computer for practice. Embarrassed by her ineptness, she shut down the terminal and said, "Oh, Sam's designing me a huge adjustable drafting table for airbrushing. I'll be able to do the large pieces I can't do by hand and brush. Speaking of creating, can I come to the foundry, when you go to check the polishing? I've never been, and I want to see my family in bronze before they get shipped, OK?"

A little surprised, Tannis remarked, "Sure." Warmed by her daughter's request, she knew the reason was not just pride in her mother's work. The pieces were personal to her too. "I'll ask Josie if she wants to tag along. She's never been either."

Back in the living room, enticing aromas drifted from the kitchen and deck as Linka detailed every item Sam had integrated into 'their' place. "He won a prize for each of those flowers in the prints. And wait until you see the tank when it's done. We'll have a bunch of tropical fish that'll blow your socks off. I know, I've seen his books. I never realized how much I like tropical fish, until now that is," she gushed.

Funny how love opens us to new experiences and interests, Tannis thought. She noticed the kitty toys which had dominated the room before were now reduced to charming accents as they spilled from a low basket beside the couch. A colorful crumpled blanket at that end of the couch also provided a cozy bed for the little minx.

Linka caught her mother's approving glance. "I know. It's much better now. She sleeps there at night, unless I need her as an elemental. And she adores Sam as you can see, even though he talks to her like a neo-nazi general. She minds him, not me, and she's *my* cat," she emphasized with more pride in her pet's adoration than malice at not being the object of it.

Sam's meal was simple but delicious. Shrimp lightly sautéed in garlic butter and perfectly grilled filets were accompanied by an oil and vinegar salad, fluffy baked potatoes, and a fresh baguette they ripped into chunks and smeared with butter. Tannis toasted the cook, pleased that he could, or he would surely starve. For all that Linka had watched her mother's culinary skills, she had never shown an interest in developing her own, thus rarely cooked. It was apparent Sam didn't mind and had begun his atonement.

Tannis savored the meal, as well as the way Sam and Linka teased each other, quips underlined by affectionate consideration. Sam could well be willing to put down roots, based on his references to projects in the works for Linka's studio and experiences they wanted to share. The airbrushing equipment Linka wanted desperately was expensive. But he had checked it out himself and if his 'babe' needed it to grow in her craft, she'd have it. His moral support was evident, and she sensed his conviction would lead him to purchase the equipment for her if she couldn't do so herself. Since she had no support from Brad in her early sculpting years, she knew how fortunate Linka was. She had conjured herself up a gem.

While they did the dishes, Sam explained how he had customized the bike in the picture. It had been his first, one he had rebuilt himself and sold for a tidy sum, but not without reluctance. His joy had been in the doing, more than the profit.

"Where do you do the work?" Tannis asked.

"My buddy has an automotive shop in North Van I use in the evenings. He does all my mechanical work. That's where I'm going." He removed his apron and added, "I'll see you gals later," as he literally threw in the towel. Linka laughed as she scooped it off the kitchen floor and aimed a swat against his departing back.

"Before you get started, I have to warn you again about the spells," Tannis said once she was settled on Linka's couch. No matter how soft, she didn't care for the feel of leather. She gave Linka a recap of her strand, the implications of Taenacea's misuse of her powers and a more emotional rendition of her unexpected company than she realized. "I'm serious, sweets. You got a wonderful man out of your 'play' but be sure you're not emotionally overwrought in any way if you intend to use the spells."

Although she nodded in agreement, Linka thought her mother was acting paranoid over the spells and unreasonable in her dislike of the professor. It was she who needed to use caution, since it was her energy directly linked with Taenacea. But her experience had been horrid enough without censure from her daughter. Diversion was called for and she had just the thing. Another strand.

"This strand was so beautiful and magical, mom. It was a combination of three different time periods which reinforced our family's affinity with nature. Remember Finn and his lady?" she asked, "Her name was Maeve, and Josie was right about her earth-energy influence. Maeve taught Finn and his people how to work with the natural rhythms of the land while she was around. Her attitude took seed and surfaced sporadically through their line until the Writ was established. I came back as Fiona with the same intention, and finally as Faye. By the way, did you know Faye was mute?"

"She was?" Tannis said, surprised. "We had such a strong telepathic link I always knew what she was thinking. Until the last time I saw her, that is. There were no need for words between us. I spoke to her but didn't think it odd she never answered since she spoke directly to my mind."

Linka spun a tale that led to the credo by which the two families would bind their lands. "So it was Maeve, and me as Fiona and Faye, who energized land consciousness in those around them, through our 'fey', pardon the pun, knowing. Energy being what it is, the land responded to this respectful nurturing. Another interesting twist; we were all practicing Druids. *That* was the underlying theme from which the family credos and the Writ sprung."

"Really." Tannis was puzzled, but pleased her father had been on the right track. "But Taenacea was a Wicca," she said.

"She was. But Wicca were the feminine counterparts of Druids, focused on the healing arts, which supports grandfather's theory. They emerged when the Druids went underground. Maeve was a Wicca too. The ancient Druids were very reclusive and worked with energy in their secret temples. It was the Wicca who acted as ambassadors of the faith. They went out and interacted directly with the community by becoming their healers and wise women."

"Oh, right." Something else Linka had said nagged at her. "Did you say you were Fiona and Faye, but not Maeve?"

"I did. I only watched her life during my first strand, remember? I knew I wasn't Maeve. *You* were Maeve, the instigator of this whole love thing between the two families while the nature theme took root in the family's' consciousness. The influence started with you and slowly grew, with a little help from me along the way, to ensure the concept was well entrenched in the family genes."

"The three acted as anchors to keep the Druid theme on track. Josie figured it was something like that. But I wonder why I can't remember my life as Maeve. All I got were the flashes about Finn."

"I think you have enough on your plate, don't you?" Linka said. "Besides, I'm the historic vehicle here, and my foghorn confirmed this as the nature strand. Maeve's role is important only as the historic initiator. Anyway, could you really handle experiencing *another* life right now?" She could see her point was taken. "So, now I have two of my illuminations. I wonder what the last one, Truth, will be?" she queried, hoping for the glazed eyes which indicated Tannis was tuned in on a psychic level.

"I don't know, and if I did, I wouldn't say. You too have to experience what you must firsthand." Her own desire to have foresight into her Tower strand came to mind again, and her face clouded as she speculated on how Giles had orchestrated her demise.

Linka winced as hatred and bitterness distorted her mother's beautiful face. "You know I'd never criticize you mom, but I think this hate-on you have for Giles, and now the professor has gone too far. I understand your pain, but you're not being entirely rational about the whole thing." She had caught her mother off guard, and pressed her advantage. "I mean, from what I know of history, most men were just like him, and his attitude was typical of the times. *Everybody* was trying to screw everybody else, fighting and seizing each other's lands and just killing anybody that got in their way. It was only *you* and *your* holdings that were different. I mean, there you were, in your own little bubble-world of Druid and Wicca energized perfection, insulated from the real world around you. A perfect cop-out. You said yourself Garth was like you, different from all the other men you knew. But he was a Druid too, like the Finn and William were. It's like you lived by *your* rules and faith, and forgot the rest of the world didn't. You judged them by your own criteria."

Tannis registered the truth in Linka's passionate censure. "Point taken. Not that it excuses his actions, mind you. But Giles was like everybody else; the King, the noblemen, all plotting to take what wasn't theirs. Just about everybody was corrupt. Maybe I *was* living in my own bubble-world as you put it, but if I was a Druid, if we all were, we had a mission; to teach alternate ways of living by example. I failed to do so, because of him."

"OK, but so what?" Linka retorted. "From what Josie's told me about karma, and how each life is a continual learning experience in which we take on different roles, maybe you were an evil person in another life, and Giles was the good guy. Maybe this was his payback life, or maybe it's a lesson you two have worked on for a long time and never reached resolution because you're both strong and stubborn. Seems like the professor is trying to reconcile with you now, but you're unwilling to do so." Out of breath and speculations, she drained her bottle of carbonated water.

"Considering his obsession with the Magic book, I don't think he's here to make amends. I think he'd like nothing better than to get his hands on it and use it to make himself famous, in spite of how contrite he acts. I just don't trust him," she added, as her fingers pulled at the fringes on the cushion beside her.

"You'll have to come to terms with him sometime, as you so sagely remind me when I try to evade an issue. Seems to me that's what you're doing. Besides, he can't get his hands on the book. You sent it back, didn't you? Say, how did you do that?" she asked, but the look on her mother's face indicated she'd never know. "OK, never mind. However, since you're the much better person, it's up to you to instigate a resolution. You don't want this thing between you to go on life after life, do you?"

"I'm not exactly thinking about future lives just now. I can't even handle one past life it seems," Tannis stated sardonically. She was sick to death of being criticized for her unwillingness to be objective and forgiving, so changed the subject. "By the way, how did Sam take to his regression? You never really said."

"He didn't say much, only that his dreams had never been as vivid as his regression was. He usually doesn't remember dreams. He's still getting flashbacks but won't talk about them. He's curious though, 'cause he sometimes asks me things." She didn't elaborate what things. "He does want his bust done as a Viking. Oh, get this, his name was Tonketh then, so I'm going to call him Tonka if he's out of line, as a reminder. Anyhow . . . will you sculpt him? We'll pay the going rate, so it'll be strictly business, not a favor," she added in a no-nonsense tone.

"You can't afford my going rate you nit, no matter how many Asian eyes you open this year, or next. But take pictures of him and I'll see if I can tap into his Viking life. You know the routine: front, sides, back and a slow revolution of close-ups. But I will make no promises," Tannis replied affectionately. This was the first time Linka had asked her to sculpt anything. Since she had already started the kitty for Linka, Sam's bust could be their joint Christmas present. But she wouldn't start him until after her vacation. Linka's suggestion about reincarnational life studies sounded interesting and might prove lucrative. Sam could be the prototype for just such a new series. If it went well, she'd mention it to Cal. Besides, she was ready for a change of venue. She could call them her 'as you were' series.

Linka updated her on Crabby Krepps the landlady who was no longer a problem. Tannis had to laugh as she recounted how the discovery of Mrs. Krepps' secret now made them co-conspirators. Linka didn't have to worry about her landlady's reaction to her new feline roommate since she had one herself. It seemed Trix had got out one day, followed her downstairs, slipped into Mrs. Krepps open apartment door, and become fast friends with her cat, Mr. Wetherbee, an old, nearly blind tom enchanted with Trix.

"The problem is, I had to make a deal to take Trix down twice a week to play with Mr. Wetherbee. But, as they say, a gal's got to do what a gal's got to do. Besides, she's really not so bad. Kinda lonely. She has three kids that never see her. They just phone to see how close to croaking she is or if she's senile enough to be put away. Can you imagine? They can't wait to cash in on her investment portfolio. Sad eh?"

Tannis agreed, thankful her only daughter cared to include her in her life. Too many young people didn't, and her neighbors on the one side suffered the same fate. Old and alone, the sweet couple always mentioned anticipated visits from their children whenever she called in to see if they needed groceries. In their early eighties, neither drove, so she sometimes ran errands for them when she went out. Visits from busy offspring were eagerly awaited, but rarely occurred.

Life was tough at times, regardless of the era. Tannis suddenly felt depressed. Sam wasn't back yet, but she knew Linka still had work to do so bid her a fond farewell. As she merged onto the Second Narrows Bridge her thoughts went to aging. At least the couple next door had each other. Who would be her companion once she was old and arthritic hands could no longer mold clay? Gawd. What brought this on? Firmly she pushed those thoughts out of her mind. It was a long ways off yet.

Mentally she calculated the status of her strands. There were only three more, rather three and a half. The Tower strand still needed completing. In spite of her revulsion, she needed it to finish the Quest and claim her prize. She wondered if they would come before her holiday, or await more familiar soil for completion.

She'd forgotten to ask Linka about house sitting. Considering Sam would be caring for her garden, no small task in summer, she wanted to ask him personally. Providing her pieces were poured on schedule, they could leave as early as June. Their return ticket would be open, and how long they vacationed depended only on their whim. She knew Cal would eventually draw Josie home. Since her pets and home would be well cared for, what would draw her back?

When she got home a message on her machine from George assured her the castings would be done on schedule. Another from Josie said she was going to the ranch for the weekend with Cal and wouldn't be back 'til Tuesday but to keep that evening open for her. Things seemed to be moving along for everyone but her, who still had to thrash through events from a past life—events decidedly more unpleasant than at first.

An uncomfortable thought hit her. Maybe her resistance to resolution would prevent her claiming her prize. All her strands would have to be experienced before she could meet her soulmate, the Tarot reader had said. She must be destined to meet him overseas then. But how? And where? She imagined a range of possible scenarios. Frustrated, she gave up. If it was meant to happen, it would without her trying to second-guess destiny.

The next day she finished Trix and set her aside to dry since this piece would be fired, not cast. Last night's dreams had offered her nothing but a rather confusing montage of meetings with all kinds of men, under all kinds of conditions, not one of which even remotely peaked her interest.

Still in sculpting mode, she decided to do some quick studies of Taenacea's Welsh country folk. She would make them about two feet tall, a comfortable height to work with, that would shrink down to about eighteen inches after drying. By the end of the day she had roughed in six figures in various rustic poses. Like relics from the past, the people she had loved gained shape and substance under her confident hands.

Aberayron's jolly cook, head thrown back in laughter as she clutched a large bowl on her ample hip; Lianarth's shy Liam, forelock in face as he leaned against a bale of straw, and Etline, her steward's wife from the parish of Lianwrtyd south of Lianarth, who sat on a bench as she dreamily nursed her child from one swollen, exposed breast. Two young lads from the village at Builth crouched in intense scrutiny of a frog one held in his hands; a grandfather from the cottages at Lianarth, back bent from years of toil sat smoking a pipe, and her prodigy Nell, hands clasped with her younger sister in dance, skirts whipped high by their merriment.

She felt like a little girl playing with her dolls as she grouped them in a charming country scene. Or perhaps this is how the Gods played with the lives of mere mortals. She addressed each by name as she checked the props which held up any extended limbs, then lovingly covered them. She would keep these for herself and set them on the half-wall by the dining room table where she could see her Welsh vassals from both the kitchen and living room.

Her dreams that night were pleasant snatches of country life at both Aberayron and Lianarth. But when she awoke she knew somebody was missing in her tableau. With the same rust colored terra-cotta clay she had used for the six others, by late afternoon she had rough-built the Lord and Lady of the Keep, as well as their faery child, Faye. Now the grouping was complete.

A familiar figure under her hands, Taenacea stood proud as she grasped the cloak the wind billowed behind her. Garth appeared to direct some kind of activity and stood legs spread wide, one hand on his hip, the other pointing. And little Faye was captured mid-stride as she clasped a bunch of flowers in one hand and reached to the sky with the other. When the piece was leathery, she would perch a small bird on those delicate fingers and make it look like it had just alighted. Although roughly built yet, she had already captured their likeness. She placed these three slightly before the others and looked at the frozen tableau of another life, another time. A shiver of excitement ran up her spine as she envisioned the finished products.

These nine pieces would be hollowed and fired, then finished with only a transparent wash of color in the hair and garments, as if faded with the passing years. The natural patina of the terra-cotta clay would reinforce their earthy origin.

Prompted by a clear vision of the finished product, she spent the rest of the week in a happy trance as she completed them one after the other. Her anger receded under the warmth of fond memories as her hands deftly molded the familiar figures. Some of her people would now live in another time, in more concrete form than just memory.

Chapter Fourteen

A S SHE GENTLY CUPPED THE ROOTS of a geranium plant with one hand, about to press the soil around it with the other, a distinctive shiver up her spine signaled an upcoming shift in consciousness. She looked up from her task and felt Taenacea try to focus through her eyes. The scene blurred. Finally her eyes readjusted and settled on a different expanse of colorful blooms.

* * *

Since her return from the Gathering, her comatose state had persisted. Garth had brought her here to the edge of the meadows in hopes nature would take a hand in healing the devastation of her sorrow.

When they arrived back at Lianarth Taenacea had wanted only to go to bed, pull the covers over her head, and fall into a sleep so deep, the wailing could not pierce it. On their journey home she had rallied just enough to respond when addressed, abet vaguely. Hovered on the edge of a chasm of despair, the news of her precious child's disappearance plunged her into its depth. She staggered against Garth and allowed her fragile hold on reality to slip away. What little spark of purpose could ignite her healing had been smothered by the devastating news of Faye's disappearance, and she lapsed into the gray netherworld between life and death.

For a week she lay immobile within the shroud of her bedding, She opened her lips only enough to allow a small trickle of water or broth down her throat as she stared at nothingness with unblinking gaze. Garth, almost demented with grief, held her for hours and spoke reassurances in a vain attempt to quell her sorrow, and his own slide into despair. He never left her side, but she did not see or hear.

The second week she allowed herself to be fed, washed, and propped up against her pillows like a boneless doll. Not a word had passed her lips, nor would she meet the gaze of her beloved or those who cared for her. At first

Garth cared little about her lack of response. He knew the harshness of the judgment she would place upon herself, for he would have done the same. He could do little more than be with her, croon his love to her and see to her every need until such time as she was ready to emerge

Garth left her side for longer periods and did what he could to keep the necessities in muted motion. With her energetic leadership removed, it was all her remaining folk could do to see to daily needs. Many were in mourning for their own loss as well as hers, uncomfortably aware of the rising tide of resentment which had taken root throughout her lands. Within the Keep, the guilt of allowing her child to slip away kept folk isolated by their grief and attentive to her needs. She did not notice, or respond.

During the third week, she rose from her bed one morn and lifelessly took back the reins of her stewardship. But it was with deadpan face, sunken eyes ringed with black, and hollow voice that she gave her instructions. When she finally ventured outside the protective walls of the Keep, it was to sit in solitude upon a rock, or aimlessly retrace her own tracks which led nowhere but in an endless circle. Unaware of the tension around her, she had not shed even one tear.

Garth was truly worried. He knew it would take time for his beloved to reconcile the slaughter in the valley, but because of their deep bond, he felt at a loss why she would not turn to him for comfort and support as she always had. Numbed as he had been by the scene which greeted them, he knew he could not match her devastation over what had occurred. He had done what he could, consumed by the thought of killing Giles. Were it not for her deadened state, and his concern to get her back to the safety of Lianarth, he would have ridden out immediately and done just that. But the disappearance of Faye, who was his child too, ached as fiercely in his heart as hers. When he could bear to tear himself away from his wife's side, he had searched himself in places thought overlooked by others, but like they, found not a trace of her. He had never before in his life felt so helpless.

As he watched her phantom wanderings, Garth firmed his resolve to ride after the messenger he'd sent to meet with Henry. He would seek the seal himself and inform Henry of the deed done at the Gathering. He would demand royal retribution, at whatever price. Someone would pay for his wife's deadened heart, for with it, his own life had no meaning. Her atrophy would not go unavenged. Tormented by her unresponsiveness towards him, he helplessly watched her self-imposed isolation. As she gave her orders each morning, she did so more out of habitual rote than real awareness, for she had done the same each day for most of her adult life. In the shadows of the night, he pulled her wooden body close and tried to infuse it with his own warmth, all the while crooning his love in hopes of eliciting even a small response.

He sought his own comfort in the fires that had always infused them with renewed life, and hesitantly traced the dance of their loving on her cool form. But he received only abstract compliance. Not a kiss, not a touch, not a flicker of desire was forthcoming. He could not force what had been so willingly given, instead stilled his own need and just held her close and waited. Still she held her agony in stubborn abeyance and not one word of the slaughter passed her lips.

Perhaps the safeguard of the signed Writ would draw her from her detachment. For seeing the empty shell of this once vibrant woman whom he loved beyond measure, crushed his own spirit. He would do anything to bring even a flicker of life to her eyes. Right now he would welcome uncontrollable rage. Anger would at least reflect a revival of her passionate essence. So he told her of his plans to find Henry himself, and see justice done. Henry would be close to her southern borders now and his own absence would be short. He promised to send word when the royal seal was obtained and to be sure, drafted another petition in case the first was compromised by a disgruntled vassal. She attached her signature above his without a flicker of interest.

He glanced back at her solitary figure on a small rise outside the Keep before he left, assured of her safety at least, if not sanity. Giles was said to be on his way to join Richard and marched on English soil by now. He also knew that Taenacea, gripped within her shadow world, would not leave the sanctuary of Lianarth.

In his absence her folk came used to her aimless and ghostly wanderings, much like her child's had been. Each day she went further afield and walked silently through the meadows, untouched by the swell of its bounty. Her hands aimlessly caressed grasses and blooms as she sat in the fields, or unconsciously clawed the bark of a tree as she leaned against it with unseeing eyes. But almost imperceptibly, The Mother's healing began. As her bare feet pressed against the earth's carpet, the essence of The Mother flowed to her through the timeless process of renewal and nudged persuasively at the protective shroud of her dejection.

As she watched the antics of the young animals, a deep yearning for her own child registered and unfurled, and a few hot tears finally trickled down her sunken cheeks. The Mother soothed the weight of her shame with the visible reflection of renewed life all around her. Another day, as she lay on her back in the fields and gazed at the scuttle of clouds that rolled past, she remembered her Awakening and heard the whispered voice of Lil upon the wind. "Awake Cea, 'tis time." The loving insistence of her words drifted through the barrier of her guilt and ignited a small spark of life within.

The change was slow, and to others, hardly perceptible. But each day a little more life coursed through her veins, and more color tinged her cheeks as she tentatively reconnected with her surroundings. On a soul level she felt the pulse of earth's endless transformation—from life, to death, to life again. As the truth of her loss registered, a sage awareness of the fragility of joy translated itself into a new appreciation of both her loss and blessings. She acknowledged the expansive flow of consciousness, dependent on death itself for renewal. If there was nothing of substance within the human experience to cling to, there was the unending stability of the land. People would come and go in light or darkness, but the land in its wisdom stayed pure in its seasonal transformations. Without censure or recrimination The Mother exposed the dark side of earth's fallow seasons as openly as its bounty: two halves of a whole spiraling in ever-changing completeness.

That night she dreamed for the first time. She awoke with only a vague memory of being drawn along a silver cord into the waiting arms of Lil. But their journey on a strand of consciousness—remembering much, forgetting a little, and forgiving a lot—imprinted itself on her soul. When she woke, she still felt broken, but the seed of renewed purpose had been firmly rooted during her celestial journey.

With pragmatic acceptance, she realized 'what was, IS'. She was not yet done with life, in spite of her emotional desire to be so. The sorrow of losing her child could never be erased, but could be assuaged by time and the satisfaction of nurturing new life from the land and her people. The slaughter at the Gathering would forever be etched in her heart and its lesson imprinted on her soul. When she walked the land now, she tentatively extended her aura to draw strength from The Mother, a strength needed to withstand the aftermath of her own carelessness. Her shame would diminish only with time and a renewed commitment to life. But she held tight the deep core of bitterness against the man she felt responsible for the fracturing of her idyllic existence.

Only at night would she allow heaving sobs and burning tears to cleanse her inner agony. But she wept for her child, her people, and the loss of her own soulfulness in private, and would not reach out for succor. Since the slaughter, her morning prayer had gone unsaid, but now she again paid her tribute to life. Only now she rose to greet the dawn with the bittersweet humility of renewed respect through painful understanding.

* * *

Linked to the earth through Taenacea's prayer, Tannis settled back into herself. She looked down at the fragile stem of the plant in her hand crushed by the intensity of her experience: crushed like the spirit of her counterpart. As the chimes tinkled, she thought deeply about what her latest strand meant. "What power we have, yet how little," she sighed. For a moment she felt Taenacea stir within her to briefly look upon her little 'Camelot' and wondered how she perceived this orderly, but small plot of land. Did she compare it to her own immense and wild lands?

Inevitably it's the earth and heavens that hold sway over the velleity of humanity through its power to destroy and rejuvenate without judgment. She realized this was the 'Stability of Earth' strand, its lesson linked with the 'Strength of Heaven' strand. Humanity can build, create and nurture, but it was our own manifestations which draw us to a deeper understanding of the intention of life. Our soul remembers its connectiveness and purpose, though we may not. Beneath the joyful and sorrowful events we create, we're reminded that all just IS, in spite of our ego's resistance and penchant for control.

That being the case, she had six flats of annuals still to plant. She returned to her task, saddened by the harsh and painful process of awareness. Conscious living was painful, as painful as it was uplifting. Her dramatic Quest was but a small thread in an eternal tapestry of interlocking design. But damn it! This was her thread, and she resolved to play her part well.

The phone rang just as she finished stacking the empty flats and her tools away in the greenhouse. It was George. Her pieces would be ready for polishing in two weeks. He had run an extra shift just for her and scheduled three of his best craftsmen to polish her pieces at the same time. Good. Josie could now arrange a departure date for their trip.

She washed the soil from her hands in the rain barrel and viewed her efforts. The gently filtered sun dabbled the leaves of Begonias clustered in the shady side of her yard. Elsewhere, yellow calendula were spaced behind golden rows of dwarf marigolds, bordered by white alyssum. Once these filled out, the staggered arrangement of blooms would offset the leafy ground-hugging and bushy perennials. The large ceramic pots on her deck which usually housed her herbs were now filled with bright red geraniums. The white cascade petunias and blue lobelia she'd planted around the edges would eventually spill over the sides of the pots in lacy bloom. She had transplanted the herbs from those pots into their own bed beside the greenhouse. Zoie sat contentedly in the midst of her herbs, as if she knew these plants were aligned to the magical aspects of her mama.

Tannis intuitively knew the healing energy of soil, and relished the feel on her hands and bare feet. She always gardened in bare feet unless digging over a bed. Then she'd slip her feet into a pair of muddy old gumboots. She never used gloves when working the soil either. But now her hands and feet were caked with drying soil. She went in to shower, and while her hair dried, caught up on her Quest's journal entries, adding her perceptions of the most recent strand. When she was done, she stopped next door to see if her neighbors needed anything from the store before she popped down to the mall for groceries. When she returned and the groceries were put away, she sat down at her desk. She reached for the genealogy charts she had pulled from her mother's trunk, along with the ghosts that clung to them.

Her father's line, primarily of English and Welsh descent had been traced back to 1704 and her mother's to 1641. She scanned the notes for clues to her mother's origins which appeared to be predominately Irish. She hadn't known that. What also impacted her was the succession of sons born through her mother's line, with only a few daughters surviving to create new family branches. Nearly all of them had the initials d.s.p. for 'died without issue' or d.s.p.s. 'died without surviving issue'. It seemed a repetition of the old Lagohaire legend and confirmed her belief she was linked to Taenacea's ancient family line. But could she prove it? All she had to work with was intuitive knowing and her time-travel experiences.

Further scrutiny showed numerous changes in the spelling of the family names, something she would have to keep in mind when looking for more ancient records. A file folder of documents proved the information gathered to-date came from a wide range of sources. References to regnal years, the commencement of reign of a particular monarch, civil registrations, parish registers, church records, tithes, wills, and deeds, all pieced together the genealogy before her. Several disputes over wills and marriage settlements over the past three hundred years had also been documented through the Chancery Records.

That's where she'd start—with Giles Kaylon's family claim to a large portion of her Welsh lands. The difficulty would be in the spelling of old names of parishes, but as she knew the boundaries from memory, she could mark them on a current map and the researcher could translate the names to their appropriate counterparts. She pulled out a yellowed invoice from the company which had prepared the family history. She wrote a letter to Braith & Timms in Oxford, England, and inquired if they could continue their search. From these records she could not tell if their efforts had been exhausted, or if the project was abandoned because of her mother's illness. The dates indicated the latter was likely. Since the last correspondence had occurred over twenty years ago, she included the old file number to assist them in locating the file, if it still existed.

Inspired by the sources available for such a historic hunt, she scanned the various letterheads for a likely place to initiate an idea that had just popped into her head. She remembered a book of her father's from the Irish Archives which listed ancient pedigree families, and knew the names Lagohaire and MacCumal could be variations of such ancient families. She got the book and checked the listings. Several possibilities existed. Further scrutiny found the coat of arms for a likely family name—O'Legothhar— was a lion. Excited by her discovery, she drafted a letter to the National Library of Ireland in Dublin to inquire if a pedigree family tree already existed for that name. No point reinventing the wheel. She listed possible variations of the Lagohaire and MacCumal names, and referred to the geographic location of their land holdings, suggesting the MacCumals most likely originated in the Allen Lake area in Northern Ireland.

She typed up both letters on her computer, addressed them, then walked to the mailbox to send them off. There, it was done. She would say nothing of this to Josie or Linka. Josie had taken her father's notes to her apartment and was still working with them. As for Linka, the charm of sifting through a scholar's notes had been replaced with a live-in companion and a new computer. As for her, scrutiny of her family tree and attached notes would make interesting bedtime reading once she was back from her holiday.

Tuesday marked Josie's return. Since the little minx could fly through the door at any time, Tannis got an early start in the studio. Her figures were leathery now, so she removed them from their armatures and hollowed them out carefully then glued them back together with the paste made from dry crushed clay and vinegar. While the spring breezes tickled her neck and curls, she refined and detailed where needed, careful not to knock and break the extended arms. This was the most fragile stage of production, but since she had refined the appendages prior to drying, she could avoid any breakages.

It was past six when she finished the last piece and covered it with plastic punctured with air holes to ensure slow and even drying. She left the curly scrapings on the bench and floor, and leaden with fatigue, took a shower. She had just sunk into the couch with a glass of juice in hand when the front door opened and a perky voice trilled, "A solitary drinker, eh, tsk, tsk. Pour me one and I won't squeal."

Tannis smiled at the apparition which danced her way accompanied by the jingle and jangle of a mass of golden wrist bands and long clinking earrings. Like a Conchita from a Zorro movie, Josie was clothed in a low-cut almost transparent peasant blouse tucked into a swirling skirt of lace flounces. Cinched at the waist with a woven sash of fiery red linen, the sash's fringed edges bounced against the skirt's flounces as she threw herself into the arms of her best friend.

Tannis barely had time to put down her glass and stand up before wafts of gardenia enveloped her in Josie's fragrant hug. Then Josie pulled back and twirled around several times for effect. Tannis rolled her eyes and went to get Josie her drink. "I thought you went to Montana, not Mexico! Or has there been a government coupe I'm not aware of?" she asked dryly.

"Montana, and no coupe. We had this incredible festival dinner with a Mexican theme. I liked it and decided to stick with it." Unabashed by her outrageous costume, she asked, "And how have you been? Oh hell! I don't want to hear yet. I already know you have oodles to tell me. I do too, and I'm going first." She lifted her glass in a toast and said, "Cheers," then plunked herself down on the couch. The cats immediately zeroed in on her for attention. She ruffled their coats tenderly but cut short her silly cat-chat.

"It was simply marvelous," she breathed. "And the ranch . . . ! Did you know Cal owns over 300,000 acres of rolling hills dotted with cattle, pastures, and lakes?"

"No, I didn't. I knew he raised horses so figured it had to be a few hundred acres or so."

"Hundreds of thousands, and it's a working ranch. The hacienda is sprawled in a broad valley. The house is a dream right out of a western movie with heavy oak beams and filled with huge old Spanish furniture. Its got a long shaded porch across the front where you can sit in sagging rockers and sip lemonade by day and star gaze by night. Cal doesn't just raise horses, he raises Arabians; the most beautiful creatures you ever saw."

"So you had a good time?" Tannis asked.

"Good is understated, and only three glitches to report," Josie said with a cheeky twinkle in her eyes.

Tannis knew to wait. Josie was bursting to tell, and did.

"The first was no biggie. Having ridden yaks in Tibet, camels in Egypt, and even lamas in Peru, I figured a horse would be no big deal, even though I've never ridden a horse before. Wrong!

"Cal brought out a docile old chestnut nag, thinking it best before I tackle a livelier Arabian. Sparky, which she may have been in her younger years, decided to have her mid-life crisis the minute I settled in the saddle. Stubbornness was the quality she amplified, and the ride became a battle of wills; stop and go all the way," she chuckled.

"By the end of the day I was butt-raw and fed up. So I had a chat with her in the stables and explained exactly what would happen if she didn't get over her crisis before the next day's ride. Message received, and the following afternoon I graduated to a nice little Arabian mare, who, having been duly warned *before* I got into the saddle, was most cooperative."

Tannis could just imagine the telepathic conversation between the two. She had never ridden herself either, but assumed a certain amount of cooperation was necessary. "And what was the next trauma, no doubt as quickly dispatched as the first?"

"It was no biggie either, a bonus as it turns out . . . at the big party. All the neighboring ranchers came to oink out on hot spicy food and four inch mega raw steaks as they prattled on about people I didn't know, and talked stock. I don't mean the Dow Jones either, I mean the four-legged kind. There was no end to conversation about bloodlines, breeding, semen banks and stud markets." She grinned wickedly. "You know how I get when I'm

out of my element. I started reading a few auras just for fun. Then I threw
in a few snippets here and there to spice things up a bit, but they're not quite
ready for me down in cattle country."

"You didn't? Cal must have been mortified. Do they always have
celebrations at the drop of a hat?" Tannis asked. Secretly she loved the way
the stuffy and rigid set off a signal Josie couldn't ignore, like a red cape to a
bull.

"Only for special occasions, which it was. As to my readings, no
problemo! I just changed focus. Instead of dropping personal info, I diverted
my talents to their stock. You know, which bull would father the best
younguns', what mare to breed with what stud . . . that sort of thing." She
said as she sat back smugly.

"So, can we expect some interesting mutations south of the border? "
Tannis asked.

Josie shot her a dirty look. "I had them eating out of my hands, and
lining up for readings, but covertly of course. A bunch of them pulled me
aside to ask when I would be back, and if I do chartings through the mail."

"You are too much. How did Cal handle this? Do I still have an agent
or did you bury him somewhere out on his lone prairie after his stroke?"

"He's very much alive, thank you. You know Cal. He's always looking
for ways to cash in on a new commodity. I believe he's found it." Josie
retorted, but with a nervous little edge to her voice.

"That's a relief." Tannis said. She had caught the edge in Josie's voice
and wondered if it related to her third disaster. "So what's the third and final
faux pas?"

"Well . . . a funny thing happened on the way to Loredo! I have to
backtrack to the first night. We went to bed and started to make love. It was
pretty hot stuff. Then Cal stopped. I mean, you know, he couldn't. I thought
I was losing my touch and redoubled my efforts, but no dice. Well natch, my
antenna went up, and after some rather uncomfortable prodding, at least on
his part, I finally got the scoop." She smiled fondly at the memory, and
continued in a dreamy voice, out of sync with the embarrassing situation
she'd just described.

Tannis was curious, yet not sure if she wanted to know.

"It was so romantic. What created his impotence was the fact we were
under the roof of his ancestral home, lying in the very bed he was conceived
and born in. Don't tell me tradition and family heritage don't influence us.
Anyhow, the bottom line was that only Wilde brides had lain in that bed for

over six generations, and since I wasn't one, he couldn't proceed to ravish me."

"And," Tannis prompted.

Josie took a leisurely sip of her wine and stared into space as she relived the memory.

"Don't do this to me. You can be wicked, do you know?"

"I've been called worse." Josie relished Tannis' frustration and continued, but slowly. "Point of decision. To screw or not to screw, that was the issue. With the family legacy hanging over his head, Cal did the right thing."

Tannis was silent. She thought the impossible wasn't possible. "You don't mean . . . no, you didn't."

"Did so! He proposed and I accepted. We got out of bed calm as you please, got dressed and drove into town to wake the magistrate who sleepily mumbled our nuptials, without his teeth in. Our nuptials were witnessed by his beaming wife with curlers all over her head and one flannel encased tit hanging out of her velour robe. Nevertheless, I presume it was legal, so say hello to Mrs. Josie Wilde!"

Josie pulled out the hand kept hidden behind her voluminous skirt and flashed it in front of Tannis' face. On seeing the enormous sapphire, Tannis realized it was true. They had known each other less than a month, and now they were married. But then Taenacea and Garth had met, and by the end of the day knew themselves perfectly matched. But that was different, or was it? She didn't know how she felt about the bombshell Josie had so calmly dropped but after a moment of stunned disbelief, leapt up and hugged her friend tight. Then a thought hit her. "How could you? We promised we would be each other's maids of honor should either of us marry. I could just strangle you both."

"I know. I told Cal you'd be pissed. But what could we do? It felt *sooo* right! Besides Cal couldn't touch me without this sanction, and it was inevitable. Don't worry. We'll do the formal thing since I want to experience the whole virgin-white-bride ritual with all the trimmings. Then you'll be my maid of honor. Fair enough?" Josie could afford to be flippant, secure in the knowledge her pal would understand. She did.

"Well, OK," Tannis said, but smacked Josie's hand lightly before scrutinizing the ring. She then insisted on hearing every detail of this bizarre surprise. The celebration party Josie had alluded to made sense now. It was a wedding celebration. First they toasted the bride and groom, then the Arabian mare Josie had renamed Chimes because her silvery tail and mane reminded her of Tannis' silver streaks and Quest, Tannis suddenly burst out laughing. "My Gawd. Do you realize you are now Josie Wilde, as in a 'wild bride', which you are? Most appropriate I'd say. And tell me, does Mr. Wilde have any idea what he's in for?"

"Nope, and I have no intention of enlightening him. He has no idea how good I will be for him. Seriously. He's already shed a huge chunk of that jaded veneer he's armored himself with. Deep down he might be scared out of his wits at what's a'commin', but he's looking forward to the ride, no pun intended," Josie giggled.

"I'm just surprised because it all happened so fast. I also have a confession to make. When your eyes first lit on Cal, I thought you two were the most mismatched couple on earth. I gave the relationship about a month. I was wrong, and I'm sorry," Tannis said.

"I know that you nit, and commend you for holding your tongue. You're allowed the occasional miscalculation. After all, you don't work with the stars. I do. The key word being 'earth'. By earthly standards we *are* mismatched, but our compatibility is based on more heavenly alignments," Jose retorted with her 'wise sage' look. Then she became completely serious. "For the first time in my life, I've found someone worthy of a commitment. I won't run from this relationship, like I've done in the past. They were just practice runs anyhow. *This* is the real thing. I'm also assuming you'll throw my words into my face, should I stray from my intent."

"You bet," quipped Tannis, inwardly praying it would never be necessary. She hoped Josie had finally found the security in partnership she'd always sought. Then another thought hit her. What about the holiday? Now that Josie was married, their upcoming plans were probably out. She couldn't help feeling disappointed and realized she now really wanted this holiday, despite her lack of outward enthusiasm. "I guess the holiday's off," she said.

"No way, Hose! Scheduled as planned, so relax. Cal will be bopping all over the continent and can meet up with us when he can get away. Is that all right by you?" she asked.

"Of course. But you're newlyweds," Tannis retorted, "You shouldn't be having a separate vacation already. That's for when the romance has faded, not when its just begun."

"Listen to Ms. individual expound on 'shoulds'. If you think this is to be a traditional relationship, forget it," Josie said. Then more seriously, "Although Cal takes priority in my life now, he does not come between me and my pal, and those are words from his lips as well," she emphasized. "This is a partnership, not enslavement. I don't expect him to stop what he's doing either, excepting the bimbetts that is. Fidelity is absolutely unnegotiable."

Tannis couldn't help injecting, "On his part only, or yours too?" She got a dirty look for her efforts, before Josie continued.

"He'd like me involved in the schmoosing end of the business in time, having first-hand experience of my charismatic effect on people. That's why he wants to meet up with us overseas. He intends to utilize my skills with some of his prickly clients. But I won't interfere in your business relationship with him."

Tannis was relieved. As much as she loved Josie, she would brook no interference with her work. She asked about their living arrangements and plans to begin the Wilde dynasty. "Hang on to your britches, gal," Josie said. "First the holiday and the church wedding. Then perhaps I'll consider retiring to the sprawling acres of Montana to claim my stall beside the other brood mares," she protested, and added they would both keep their separate apartments. Since Cal would be away a great deal, she would stay put in hers for the time being.

"Besides, it'll drive him mad with desire if we're apart. Think of the homecomings!" she said as they headed for the kitchen to forage for snacks and brew a pot of tea.

Wrapped in sweaters against the evening chill, Tannis recounted her experiences under the glow of the deck lamps. Her voice cracked with the telling, and although much calmer than before, there was no mistaking the emotional impact of her memories. Had the evening been misty, her recount would have been even more chilling than it was. Josie listened attentively, but said nothing until Tannis unveiled her nine figures in the studio.

"Contrary to what you may think, marital bliss has not dulled my vast abilities; in fact, they are tremendously enhanced," she said as she walked along the side counter and peered at each piece thoughtfully. "Bottom line: your experiences are more integrated, you are more aware of your power, hers and your own, and resolution with Giles *has* to occur once you've completed all your strands. Particularly the Tower strand, the one you are so stubbornly trying to avoid." Then she added flatly, "There is one figure missing in this grouping, and you know who it is. By the way, these are fabulous. So soulful, I can almost read their eyes."

The mere possibility of who she referred to enraged Tannis. "Not on your life," she stated emphatically. "I will not add that vile little prick to my group. Never."

"Yes you will, because of what they all represent. He too is a part of that life, of what made you who you were. The enormous surrender and sacrifice it will take to build him is what will ensure your own karmic resolution. Whether you want to accept it or not, he played just as important a role in your life as these folk did, more so in fact. By including him, you may just lose the load of guilt you're carrying."

Tannis looked at her friend with resentment, "Do you realize what you're asking of me."

"Probably the hardest thing you've ever had to do," Josie replied with a deadpan face. "Now, pull yourself together, lose your indignation, and don't let one little weasel get the better of you. You did that once. You gave your power away to him, and look what happened. This is all about changing just one small strand in the tapestry of time: your mutual attitude towards Giles. It's an opportunity to absolve her of a guilt that's still very real on a spiritual level, because it's coming through you. Get it? So stop it. I mean literally— just stop it."

The truth of Josie's words smacked her right in the face. She was stunned by their impact as they registered, and humbled by their simplicity. Just stop it. Stop energizing the pain, the rage, the whole agonizing memory. Stop reliving the horror and the guilt, and the should-haves. She had fed those emotions every time she relived them, as Taenacea had. She could decide to just stop. In fact, she must do so, and would. But she would not concede to sculpting Giles just yet.

As if reading her inner dialogue and satisfied by her decision, Josie diverted the conversation to more pleasant things. After Josie had agreed to come to the foundry, and insisted on spending the night, Tannis updated her on Linka's relationship. But by midnight their conversation was interspersed with long silences and shameless yawns. Within the hour both were in their respective beds, lulled to sleep by the purrs of their bed companions.

A quick cuppa at Linka's started their trip to the foundry. Josie had exacted a promise from Tannis to say nothing about her marriage. She wanted to spring the news on Linka in her own unique way, via her huge heirloom sapphire clustered with diamonds. She took in every detail of the new apartment decor, noting the smooth blending of their furnishings which enhanced each other without overpowering either—a telling reflection of their relationship.

Although Josie liked him, she couldn't quite figure Sam. He had taken to the regression and the bizarre antics of their little clique calmly, yet had revealed little about himself. When asked, Linka had said he rarely saw his parents, and his sister never. But she would not say why, which meant she knew. His silence implied either repressed emotions, or a well-balanced individual. She couldn't help but wonder what had transformed an obviously very physical ex-biker into a sensitive nurturer of flora. Time would tell, as would the astrological chart she intended to do. The main thing for now was that Linka was happy. And that she was, as she prattled on about Sam, Sam, Sam. So much so in fact, she hadn't even noticed her ring even though she had almost punched her in the nose with it.

In the Cherokee, Linka slid their cameras across the back seat and sat smack in the middle behind Tannis and Josie, elbows propped on the back of their armrests as Josie recounted her adventure in Montana. She waved her sapphire right under Linka's nose again, but got only a, "Hey, cool ring. Is it new?"

"Yes. I would say my *wedding ring* is rather new," Josie retorted pointedly. Tannis could barely stifle her laughter as she watched the truth dawn on Linka's face, and annoyance flush Josie's.

"No Way!" Cool. I'm glad it's you that nabbed him. Oh, this is so romantic," she gushed. Her congratulations were followed by all the reasons why she really wasn't surprised. "I told you guys you'd love each other, didn't I?" she added smugly. After checking out the ring, she couldn't help but compare Josie's euphoric descriptions of Cal's attributes with Sam's, and launched into verbalization of them all.

It soon became a game of one-upmanship. Tannis thought she would vomit. It was one thing to be happy for her best friend and daughter, another to listen to this nauseating stereo rendition all the way to Langley. "Well, hallelujah. Love rules!" She had intended it a joke, but a tartness was evident in her tone, and she quickly amended, "Oops! Just a moment of natural jealousy from your local spinster."

Tannis' remark surprised Josie. It always amazed her how sensitive unattached women were to the joy of those in a relationship. Old programs die hard, and even in liberated women, a partner still enhanced her sense of status and self-worth. Conversely, most women in a new relationship felt only a little guilty, and a lot smug, although the latter was usually kept under raps. But she didn't. "When you finish your Quest and claim your prize, you too shall join the gushing brigade. Wait and see. It's not our fault you chose such a complicated but dramatic way of finding your true love. And yes, love is what it's all about," which led to the lyrics of 'All You Need is Love', followed by a discourse on the true meaning of love and self-image, and ended in a hilarious description of the mind-set of Montana Ranchers and their obsessive love of bloodlines.

Tannis turned off the highway, and about a quarter mile down the service road turned into the entrance to the Langley Foundry. She drove along the gravel driveway past the cottage and office, and pulled up beside the warehouse attached to the foundry itself.

Her heart skipped a beat as she disembarked and glanced through the shop doors in anticipation. The large rolling doors at the front and back of the shop were open to the sun's beams which highlighted a haze of fine metal motes within the shop, yet shadowed it's contents. She could hardly wait to see her pieces. George greeted them at the doorway with a smile and cautioned them to watch where they walked as they entered the surreal interior of hanging hoists and hulking equipment. The bite of metal tickled her nose as Tannis looked for her pieces. Illuminated by overhead lights, three wooden trolleys with chains loosely attached to the ceiling crank rack high above, sat in the middle of the shop. Her sculptures sat on these trolleys.

Tannis strode over to the trio and began a minute examination of each. She knew the clock was ticking for the three men appointed to the finishing, but she had to take a moment to relish their transformation. They were breathtaking! The golden bronze of a more substantial looking Garth and Taenacea bore every detail of her painstaking finish and the form of Faye looked like a slender silvery waif, even in metal. The casting seams and imperfections had already been ground away and their surfaces were now smooth. She took her time and scrutinized each carefully, first close up, then from varying distances in order to determine what required highlighting. Only then did she tell the men what she wanted. She watched them reach for their grinding tools and begin. Josie and Linka stood behind her, a little intimidated by the noise as the men began their work.

George, who had waited for Tannis to finish, pulled them away and led them out of the shop into the clean air. Behind them, the grinders squealed as the three figures were already cloaked in a swirl of flying metal filings. He steered them down the short gravel path that led to the small cottage by the entrance to the foundry. "Minnie's been chomping to see you. She has fresh coffee brewed, and baking as well. The fellas will be awhile. I'll come get you when we're ready for the acid application."

A silver haired, wiry woman of undefined age sprang through the front door amid a rush of canines in all shapes, sizes and colors. The smaller ones leapt up in yappy greeting while the larger dogs wagged their welcome more sedately as they sniffed the scent of felines on Tannis and Linka with disdain.

Although George, the grandson of the man who started the foundry was the boss, this little woman was the generator that powered their enterprise. When her tiny form strode into the foundry, the men quivered in trepidation, for only the most stoic and gifted craftsmen survived her demands of excellence. Exposed to her own family's steel fabrication business all her life, her own short-lived career in metal sculpture reflected her love of the medium. She had met George during his apprenticeship at her father's firm, and enthusiastically embraced her role as his helpmate when George's father passed away. Knowing herself to be only a mediocre artist, she willingly gave up her craft to cast the work of more gifted artists than she.

It was Minnie who had seen Tannis' work many years ago in the Los Angeles Gallery and approached Cal for her casting business, and it was Minnie who had prompted George to give her work special attention and priority. That foresight, along with the excellence of the finished products had brought them both recognition and fortune, though the latter was not evident in their humble abode. It was reflected in the best equipment, alloys, and craftsmen in the business, and in results which established them as the foremost artistic foundry on the west coast. In spite of casting for other well-known Canadian and American artists, Tannis' work was still given priority.

"You've done yourself proud, Tannis. Very strong, those two!" she hollered amidst the noise from her four-legged entourage. She shooed them away abstractly and added, "Whoever your companion is out there, I hope he's real. Now come on in and introduce me to your friends here." Her comment indicated she was aware of who the woman in bronze was.

During a feast of warm muffins and fruit filled sweet rolls washed down with Earl Gray tea, the conversation revolved around Josie's marriage, Tannis's talent and Linka's craft and retouching equipment. While Minnie expounded on her views on the necessity of good equipment, George came to get Tannis. They were ready to prepare the mixture that would highlight Taenacea's hair.

Under George's watchful eye an acidic mixture was prepared and carefully applied with a brush where Tannis indicated the highlights should be. While the topical did its work Tannis checked on Garth and Faye's progress, then returned to Taenacea. They repeated the process. When she was satisfied, she watched as Taenacea's hair was cleaned, waxed and buffed. The result was astonishing. Although not actually silver, the sun reflected off the bleached gold streaks with silvery glints.

Subtle highlights on Taenacea's face and torso added a glow, as if her body was warmed by sun strokes. Garth's flesh sported a sun-bronzed glow, contrasted by the highly lightened surface of his opened shirt.

But it was Faye that had undergone the greatest transformation. The unique new mixture of silvery alloys gave her form a surprising translucent and mother of pearl glow. Her hair, almost silvery white, contrasted with the soft pewter of her skin and lightly antiqued folds of her dress. The crest and base appeared more defined by the application of a darker antique topical. This combination of shades made her appear to hover above the base, rather than rise from it.

"You've hit on something here, Tannis," George mused as he squinted at the results with pride. "I was a little worried we couldn't produce the effect you wanted, but this alloy has a greater range than I anticipated." He knew the topical mixtures influenced the results, relieved their ad-lib adjustments to the formula had worked. He recorded the formula mentally, pleased at how this particular alloy reacted to the acid topical. He admired Tannis' instincts and willingness to try something new. The job could have easily been botched by the application of the acidic compound to an untried new alloy.

A whistle signaled lunch break, but rather than go to collect their lunches, the men gathered around the trio which had been rolled closer together for Tannis' viewing. She ignored the whispers and speculative looks, absorbed by her own reaction to the finished products.

It was a strange moment for Tannis. Beneath a satisfied sense of completion lurked a wrenching desire to cry, as if a part of her was splitting away, never to return. As if by celestial design, sunlight appeared to ring the trio in a protective halo. She wanted to capture the illusion and quickly left to get their cameras.

While she and Linka took pictures, the men headed for the picnic tables beside the front doors where Minnie stood waiting with a large stock pot of soup. She ladled it into their bowls as they opened their lunch buckets and drew out their sandwiches. Hot soup, or hearty stews in winter were a perk Minnie knew kept her crew warmed to their tasks.

"If you're satisfied, they'll get their final polish and be shipped out by the end of the week," George said. "Arrangements have been made for pick-up at the airport. They should be airborne by the end of the month."

Tannis leaned against the shop wall and took a sip of her own steaming mug of chicken soup. "Any idea where they're going," she asked him curiously as she scooped a spoonful of fat noodles into her mouth.

"To the airport is all I know. The client's plane is picking up the crates, but no destination is logged on the manifesto yet," he said with an uncaring shrug of his bulky shoulders.

Tannis knew George cared little for clients or destinations. His world was here. But she wanted to know. Struck again by the whole mysterious undertones of the commission, the picture of her illusionary client wiped further speculations from her mind. What did she care anyhow? While Linka and Josie distracted the men from their meal, she slipped back into the shop to look at the busts of the three boys. Their seams had not been ground down yet, but the casts looked good, and she liked the slight difference in color of the trio. She gave little thought to the fact they would grace the home of a past Prime Minister of Canada, but took pride in the knowledge they were an accurate likeness of his sons.

Life-studies were just a lucrative aspect of her craft. Her real love was building pieces from the creative folds of her mind. She had a final look at her spectacular trio from the past and again envisioned them placed in a natural outdoor setting instead of some dark indoor nook. For fun, she energized an outdoor location as she touched each. There was no harm in wishing, and her intense desire might affect their placement. But it was not for her to say. Chagrined by her obvious possessiveness, she left to hunt up Josie and Linka. She found them in the foundry where a fresh caste was being poured. Distanced from the intense heat of the molten metal they watched the process a while, then said their farewells.

It was over. She took one final look at her trio and knew a piece of her would go with them to their unknown destination.

Chapter Fifteen

CHESTNUT AND HAWTHORN TREES backed the aged oaks that bordered the crushed gravel drive. The large truck slowly lumbered along the shaded avenue. Beyond, lay a great expanse of rolling emerald lawn. The drive veered slightly to the left. Joe O'Dwyer caught a glimpse of his destination before he pulled the truck into a large courtyard. Paved with ancient flagstone, the courtyard was flanked by a low stone wall on the left, separating it from the velvet downslide of emerald. Water lay still within a large, three-tiered fountain directly across from the massive Manor House on his right. He whistled in awe.

"Jaysu," he thought, "A right fine place, it is." He backed up close to the main doors, careful to steer clear of the fountain on his left. He stopped the truck, opened the door, and hopped down. His three hastily acquired helpers alighted from the back of the truck and peered around with interest as he swaggered up the low wide stairs under the impressive high portal. He picked up the enormous brass knocker and dropped the lion's head heavily. Manifesto in hand, he waited for someone to open the massive double oak doors.

No one came, so he knocked again. About to drop the knocker a third time, he stepped back quickly as the doors swung open. A large red-haired fellow whose freckles almost obliterated his ruddy face, peered at him, then squinted at the truck in puzzlement. "And what be you wantin' this fine day?" he was asked in the brogue of country folk.

"A shipment from overseas, looks like," returned Joe, liking his friendly demeanor. This would be Nell's man Seamus, no doubt.

"Sure, but we weren't expecting that for a month or two. And then only one," he said mildly as he read the manifesto. Puzzled, he scrawled a large S. MacCumal on the appropriate line.

Joe shrugged his shoulders. "I dunno. So where will yeh be wanting the crates? Have yeh the men to move them or should the boys here be giving yeh a hand? There'll be no charge for the helpin'," he added quickly, hoping

Seamus would comply. He was curious over what these rich folk would have shipped from Canada. It wasn't often he delivered fine goods. His usual run was from the brewery to surrounding pubs. He'd only chanced on this job while having a pint at the pub in Ley Node. For the driver who was to make this delivery had the drive shaft dropped out of his truck part-way to the airport. In hopes of a few extra pounds, Joe had collected a few men from the pub and offered to pick up the crates at the airstrip. He'd have a story to tell for the night's pint, providing he got to see what was in them crates.

"Ah well, 'tis sudden to be sure, and prepared we're not," Seamus said as he scratched his thatch of fiery curls. He turned and called into the interior of the house. "Bryan, come see!" Only the faint strains of an operatic aria could be heard, so he bellowed again, "Bryan!" He turned back to Joe. "'Tis lucky the man himself is here. He'll be telling yeh what's to do."

Joe peered past Seamus, but covertly like. He'd heard of the dark one who was rarely here and had only caught a glimpse of him from a distance once before. He would be the Lord of the Manor.

"Quit bellowing like a bullock. I heard you," quipped a cultured voice with only a faint lilt of accent. The voice belonged to the tall, impressive looking man who strode through the door. He cuffed Seamus' arm lightly in passing. Arresting blue eyes spoke of command and presence, but the crinkles around their edges betrayed a well used sense of humor.

He scanned the manifesto, and raised his eyebrows in surprise. "You might as well bring the crates down, seeing I'm here." He glanced at the Rolex glittering on his wrist, and added, "Let's have a look then. I have an overseas call to make, then I'll be back. You can open them up right here in the courtyard." He turned smoothly and vanished into the house, thoughts on business matters.

Joe responded, elated they would unveil what was inside. He moved the truck forward a little to make room for the unloading. Even with the four of them, it took some time to slide the heavy crates first onto the hydraulic ramp, then onto the flagstone. Seamus had jumped in to help and strained along with the rest of them. All five were puffing and wiped the sweat of early summer heat off their brows when they were done.

"Would a pint help the task then?" asked Seamus, his own lips parched from exertion. Nonchalant nods indicated the men's assent. He disappeared into the Manor House and returned shortly, arms laden with bottles of stout. Meantime the men shuffled about, cigarettes hanging from their mouths as they scanned the seemingly endless expanse of well-tended grounds. It wasn't often they were offered refreshment. The dark one brought out more bottles, but had none himself. He scanned the manifesto as they pulled deep from their pints and chatted casually about weather, the races, and taxes. Crippling taxes had many large estates such as this open their doors to tourists in an attempt to keep them family owned, but this was not the case here.

Their second pints were downed at more leisurely pace, but after Bryan paced around the crates a few rounds, the men swallowed quickly and went to collect their crowbars. Joe had them carefully pry the top and sides off the crate nearest, and throw the straw packing he pulled away himself into the back of the truck. He unscrewed the bolts that held the trolley firmly attached to the base of the moving crate. The men then strained to roll it towards the two standing on the broad stairs. A nod from the dark one, and he pulled away several layers of puffed packing plastic. Then he too stepped back.

They stared at the faery child who gleamed strangely in the shifting sunlight. A few clouds had scuttled across the sun and cast shadows which seemed to make her shimmer and ready to float off her base.

Something clutched at Bryan's throat as he looked at the child. He couldn't explain it and cleared his throat, discomforted by the constricting sensation. This wasn't what he had expected. Although he had seen the artist's work in a private collection and initiated the commission because of it, he had imagined he'd get a medieval cherub, not this mystic, slender child.

He looked above her head, his eyes drawn to the bare fountain at a distance behind, and instantly knew she must be placed at its center. There was nothing there now, the old cluster of cherubs long since ravaged by time. This silvery apparition, not quite angelic, but definitely celestial, would be perfect. She belonged outside rather than in the drawing room where he'd thought to place her. She belonged under the sun and its shadow play. His decision had been intuitive, and he never thought to question it.

Whoever this MacCrae artist was, she had created the piece as if knowing a perfect setting awaited her. Fleeting images of faery rings on moonlit nights raced through his mind, followed by a momentary surge of longing for something he couldn't name. It happened so fast he blinked, and wondered if it had happened at all. Then he realized the silence around him.

"Open the other one," he said as he pointed to next crate, his voice strangely hoarse. It occurred to him the crate should be taller if it contained a life size medieval man or woman. Impatient to see just what it did contain, he moved closer, a curious Seamus at his side.

When the final wrapping was removed, he stood immobile, stunned by the vision in gold. The woman of earthy and seductive beauty took his breath away. In naked splendor she seemed to reach towards him, about to throw a teasing comment his way. He listened for it, then realized it would never be heard. His head swam and his ears rang. A loud "Sweet Jesu!" from one of the men muffled his involuntary groan.

Seamus, who was still looking at Faye, spun around when he heard the exclamation. He also stared, mouth agape. "Mither of God! 'Tis like the Queen of the Faeries, but more corporeal like," he exclaimed as he moved closer. He almost laughed outloud when he caught the look of worship on Bryan's face. The men had also clustered around, though not too close, and openly gawked at first her breasts, then her face, then her breasts again. One of them even smacked their lips in appreciation as they shuffled about.

Seamus looked from the faery child to the pagan goddess, then to the one remaining crate and wondered what could be inside. Bryan was staring like a half-wit at the golden women before him, so Seamus signaled Joe to open the last crate.

Bryan was oblivious to his surroundings. "If she were real, I'd claim her as mine," he thought, as a rush of something undeniable wound through him. The sensation was gone quickly but left behind a heat that raced through his veins. He couldn't keep his eyes away. A loud gasp after the sound of cracking wood drew his attention back to the last piece. He caught the smirks on the faces of the men as his eyes fell on the reason for the stillness, and found himself looking into a face he knew well. A shock rippled through him so forcefully, he almost staggered from the impact of seeing his own face stare at him with humorous confidence.

"Sweet Jesu! You sly one, it's himself that's standing before me," exclaimed Seamus, baffled his reclusive brother would commission a bust of himself. Placed like they were, the pair seemed to reach towards each other. From the look on his face, his brother thought the same.

Bryan's mind whirled. How could this be? How could the artist know what he looked like? And the pair looked as if they belong together. Who was she, this golden woman? And who was this artist? He realized he knew nothing about her. For a moment he was angry. This had to be some sick joke. He hadn't commissioned a bronze of himself. He didn't know what to think, an unusual state of mind, but he intended to get answers. He would speak to the agent himself. Uncomfortable as he was, he took in the fine detail of his own likeness with pride. There was no question; the artist was good. She had captured his image perfectly, but as another personality, an ancestral Bryan clothed lightly in an open shirt and holding a parchment as he beckoned to his mate.

Now why would he think her his mate? He felt foolish for his thoughts, but secretly savored the impression as he walked around the piece. It wasn't so much that she had captured his likeness, it was that she had captured the essence of himself. She had captured what he had long kept hidden and flagrantly display it for all to see. Taut with mixed emotion, he instructed the men to pack up and go, adding Seamus would see to a little something extra for their efforts. He wanted them gone, even Seamus. He needed to be alone to deal with the shock and sort out his milling thoughts, a state of mind he did not care for.

When the truck had vanished around the curve in the drive, Seamus, though bursting with questions, slipped away to leave Bryan to collect himself. It was obvious the poor bugger had been thrown a cog. He'd hear about it soon enough.

The silence was punctuated only by sporadic birdsong and the faint bleat of sheep from distant pastures. Bryan circled the three sculptures, then rolled them closer together, facing the front of the Manor. He sat himself on the front steps to really study them.

They were spectacular! Never had he been so moved by a work of art, let alone three. This was almost personal, the reaction the pieces drew from him. In fact, it was *very* personal. He gazed first at the woman, and admired the strength behind her enticing demeanor. That she was beautiful there was no doubt, and that his hands itched to cup those lush breasts and span that small tight waist was also not in doubt. What was in doubt was that there could possibly exist such a wondrously wild creature anywhere in this world.

He had known many beautiful women. Some he'd shared a night with, or more. But always a lack of something undeniable prevented him from pursuing a lasting attachment. Although he appreciated them all and enjoyed the interludes of companionship they provided, something missing cautioned his heart to remain closed. He had not known why, but now he did. The reason sat before him. Only a woman such as this could capture his heart, and had. The problem was, she wasn't real. She was a sculpture.

He pulled his eyes away and turned his attention to his own likeness, a little more comfortable with the mirror image now. How could an artist capture what had only been shared with Seamus and his partner Lorne? She had not captured the Bryan MacCumal he showed the world, but the Bryan he would be were he living here instead of jetting between his private offices on the continent. How was that possible? Even in a sitting, were he to have commissioned a bust, these aspects of himself would not be known. But one person had captured them, sight unseen.

The moment he laid eyes on the statue of himself he'd known he had been running from himself. Damn! His mind settled on the arrangement made long ago, an arrangement that kept him from his birthright. Twenty years of staying away in order to keep his heritage intact. As the eldest, the title of Lord of Lagohaire had passed to him at twenty-one, as had the legacy of unpaid taxes and threat of foreclosure. His father and grandfather had been more enamored with winnings at the races than financial management. Their heritage stretched back to the tenth century and comprised one of the 7 septs, descendants of Leathlabhor, prince of Dalriada, one of the originators of the Irian race. The title should have gone to the earthier younger Seamus, whose love of the land made him a natural guárdian of the family estate. But without money, good husbandry alone could not create solvency. His own talent for making money had. And then there was the scandal. Even now, it still stung. He quickly pushed that memory away.

An arrangement had been made between them. Seamus would see to the estate's care while Bryan made a lot of money to clear it of debt. The debt had been cleared long ago, but caught in the momentum of his own Midas touch, there was always one more lucrative deal to put together before he felt ready to settle down and return to his birthright. Without a mate to encourage nesting in preparation for a family, the call of his lands went unheard.

Their original two hundred and fifty thousand acres in Laoighis which spread into the counties of Kildare, Kilkenny, Carlow, and Wicklow, had remained intact until the 1970s. He had immediately deeded one hundred thousand acres along the perimeters to the counties as natural parks when tax demands could not be met. The public now enjoyed the relics of Irish ruins as they stumbled on aged abbeys amid the many shades of green rolling hills. Dotted with pockets of virgin forests, deer and other small game still roamed free in this protected track of woodland.

He had reluctantly surrendered more acreage on his northern borders to the encroachment of the expanding suburbs of Dublin and DunLagohair, one of the most popular yachting harbors on the Irish coast. Bryan himself had a spry little yacht moored there called the Enchantress, used more for the leisure of his select clients than his own. DunLagohair was also the ferry terminal between Ireland and Wales. Tourists flocked in ever increasing numbers from Holyhead, many to visit the controversial little community of Ley Node at the south west tip of his lands. As he thought about his yacht the 'Enchantress', his eyes fell on the golden beauty before him, and he decided it a most appropriate name for her. For she was wild and untamed, a woman that could stir the blood in a man's veins like a sudden ocean swell.

He had taken many chances on the road to independent wealth, but none as chancy and without hope of making money as Ley Node. Several years ago Seamus had been approached by an organization with a unique approach to crop and stock production; sound and energy resonance. Excited by the concept, Seamus had persuaded Bryan to meet with the project coordinator, Jane Higgins. Her seven years at Findhorn and clarity of purpose had convinced Bryan. With Seamus' enthusiastic support, Bryan had provided financial assistance and the use of twenty-five hundred acres at the southwest tip of his property. Now, five years later, the unique community project received as much attention as Findhorn in Scotland for the immense size and quality of its produce. The livestock, fed by pasture and grains grown on-site using natural fertilizers, was now also in great demand by select restaurants in Dublin.

The foundation staff, artisans and other occupants of the village lived in rustic stone cottages cleverly upgraded with modern amenities. Wary at first about Jane's suggestion to build cafes, craft shops and Bed & Breakfast facilities, their addition two years ago proved astute. They not only generated enough funds to justify their existence, but added an idyllic flavor to the village which also attracted a different kind of attention. Several of the moneyed clientele who had purchased exquisite artisan items within those shops or spent a few nights in the Bed & Breakfasts, now funded the Foundation's new initiatives with hefty annual donations.

Of the remaining acres, the Estate rested on a central ten thousand, ringed by small efficient farms that provided produce and meat for the estate, local markets, and select city restaurants. As practiced for hundreds of years, good land husbandry was balanced with just enough technology to ease the work. Lorne, his partner, had thought this altruistic project a folly at first, but now promoted it as an environmental corporate asset which enhanced their reputation as an eco-conscious investment conglomerate.

"I must spend more time here," Bryan thought. He'd been afraid to admit his disenchantment with the endless acquisitions and mergers, his stock and trade for over twenty years. Certainly it had been both profitable, and necessary to keep taxes current and the family estate not only in good repair, but thriving. But he had little time to enjoy the fruits of his labors, a point Seamus always drove home during his brief visits. In his mid-forties now, Bryan knew it was time to settle down and consider marriage and family. But with whom? He had found no one remotely suitable and thought himself destined to remain alone.

His eyes swung back to the golden Enchantress and he wished her smile was for him. Unused to such longings, he smirked at the thought of a mid-life crisis some men experience at about his age. Or was it just a natural pause in life, a time to evaluate past achievements and ponder new directions? If so, he had reached that point. But he wouldn't dwell on it, and turned his thoughts to the artist, intrigued by how a stranger from across the sea could shatter his anonym.

He had never understood how collectors could hoard works of art and hide them away to be caressed and consumed by their eyes alone. Now he did. He now too felt the possessiveness of coveting something that stirred him deeply. Were it not for his good sense, he would whisk the pieces into a vaulted shrine of his own.

But like the faery child, the man and woman's shrine was the land under open skies. The thought had floated into his mind, settled, and taken root. He looked around, and knew where they would be placed: at the front of the Manor, on the two unadorned blocks of granite on either side of the stone steps. They would face the fountain, but be turned slightly towards the main doors in welcome. On leaving, a guest would appear to be invited to enjoy nature's bounty outside. Excited by the prospect, he rose to find Seamus and have him arrange to have them mounted. With characteristic resolve and a burning curiosity not felt for a long time, he knew he must meet the artist. Lorne could set up the appointment with her agent.

He found Seamus out back by the lake and suggested a stroll. The hounds who had frolicked in the brush, loped ahead of them and bayed their excitement. Bryan put a companionable arm over his brother's shoulder and told him where he wanted the sculptures placed. Then he shared his unusual reaction to them and recent awareness of having reached a crossroads in life.

Seamus listened attentively. "In spite of what yeh say, yeh'll be off again then?" He knew his brother, and missed the rare talks such as this.

"I have to. It's what keeps this ours," Bryan said hollowly as he waved his arm wide to encompass their surroundings.

"Ah yes," Seamus agreed. He threw Bryan a keen look. "But when be enough, enough? D' yeh hear? Le Node pays its own way, the estate coffers are brimming, and yeh're a rich man, outside yeh business worth."

Bryan shifted uncomfortable and drew away. What Seamus said was true. He had no reason not to come back now, outside of being alone and without a partner.

As if reading his mind, Seamus said, "Yeh heart and roots are here, though yeh mind's elsewhere. To be sure, 'tis time yeh found a lass like my Nell, and thought of some wee ones. There's great comfort in the arms of the right woman. Yeh'll not find a woman of the land where yeh've been looking. Yeh know how a man alone can take to the drink or gamblin' in his bitterness," he added, as if seeing the estate slowly slip into the cash registers of the local drinking establishments, as many had.

"There's no fear of that, my friend," Bryan retorted, and punched his brother's arm lightly. "Speaking of which, when will you make an honorable woman of Nell and give those carrot topped bastards of yours their rightful name?"

"Ah yes, when yeh settle down and meself can leave to build a huge barn to house the wee monsters." Seamus laughed heartily at the thought of his offspring hanging from the rafters of a barn. They had lived in the old servant's quarters back of the kitchen since they took to caring for the estate.

The thought of feisty little Nell, a round and bustling hellion with hair even brighter than his brother made Bryan smile. Her face matched his, freckle for freckle, and heart as well, despite her tempestuous outbursts. She was much like their mother had been and refused to marry Seamus until she had her own home where she would rule supreme. But the arrangement with Bryan had kept her caring for the family seat, while her heart yearned for her own. The monsters Seamus spoke of were the delight of his life, next to Nell. With school nearly out, the six bobbing figures, whose hair color ranged from strawberry to burnt mahogany, would soon shadow their father's every move. Like the Pied Piper, they would follow him about, taught in his gentle deliberate way to respect and love the land on which they ran wild.

As the brothers walked side by side, the fickle hand of genetics was evident. For their height was all they had in common. Seamus was a large man, at six feet. Broad of shoulder, his arms and legs stood firm like solid oak trunks, and his ample girth reflected dependability, and a particular appreciation of good food. His bulk housed a purposeful nature, softened by a calm acceptance of the rhythms of life. Only Nell could ruffle his thoughtful composure and test his patience.

Bryan, a throwback to more ancient and recessive genes brought to mind the term 'Black Irish'. Blue eyes with wavy black hair, his swarthy complexion hinted at shipwrecked Spanish origins. A few inches taller than Seamus, and built like a Greek God, he looked a modern-day buccaneer. Only his sword play was that of high finance whose victories swelled Swiss bank accounts.

By nature he was deeply sensitive and as rooted to the earth as his brother. But he kept his feelings hidden beneath a cool mask of aplomb. The heart of him emerged only under the warmth of his brother's ease, or in the privy of his friend and partner, Lorne Stonebridge. Theirs was a relationship based on complimentary skills and trust each recognized at their first meeting. As a duo, they had become a powerful force in the business world. But outside the boardrooms they shared a rare camaraderie of few words, yet perfect understanding.

It was Lorne who had arranged the commission with the agent, acting on an impulsive request from his partner and friend. "I want something medieval for the estate from that artist I told you about. Three pieces; a man, woman and child. Pay what you have to. Two for the niches in the foyer at the house, and a cherub type piece for the drawing room." It was also Lorne who had long handled the shrewd investments of both his and Bryan's assets which listed them among the rising billionaires, in both business and private fortune. And it was Lorne who acted as the public front for their conglomerate of enterprises, giving Bryan the privacy he needed, particularly after the scandal. It was Lorne who had fed the paparazzo's speculation so well, they believed him to be the sole proprietor and his silent partner only an investor from the company's early days.

As they wound their way along the front of the Manor, the sun caressed the sculptures in the courtyard with its departing glow and gave the golden bronze a flaming copper cast. So breathtaking was this orange blanket of light that Bryan lingered outside after Seamus went in. After a moment's hesitation, he walked over to the Enchantress. As he gently ran his hands over her body, he imagined the heat of the metal to be hers.

For an instant he thought he felt a heartbeat; and sensed a presence so strong he imagined her alive. Guiltily he pulled his fingers from the breast he had unconsciously caressed and lay them lightly on her shoulder. A shudder ran through him as he did so, but was gone instantly. He must be imagining things. He shook his head to clear it of these mad thoughts and went inside; but not before one backward look at his Enchantress.

* * *

Tannis sat with eyes closed as she dreamily caressed Garth's small torso. It was naked to the waist. Suddenly she felt a wash of heat around her heart and breast, then an unexpected touch on her shoulder. She flinched and opened her eyes to see who had touched her. She was alone. A deep breath stilled the sudden quickening in the pit of her stomach, but she waited expectantly for something to happen. Nothing did other than the light ring of chimes. For what reason she did not know, for the sense of being touched was now gone as well. She had also not been transported back in time so continued with her delicate sanding.

She had been thinking of Garth while she ran her fingers over the sculpture that needed no more attention. Careful girl, she thought, now's not the time to lose your grip on reality. She picked him up and placed him beside Taenacea and the other dry and sanded pieces. Her kiln could fire three at a time, and when the first six were done, Taenacea, Faye and Garth would go into the kiln together. She could have them all finished before she left on holidays. As reluctant as she was to build Giles, she would do so tomorrow. Perhaps if she imagined him as a benevolent professor she could actually stomach sculpting him.

She had never worked on anything she detested, and wondered if she could. She suspected it would take a sip or two from her medicinal bottle of Scotch to enable her to do so. But that was for tomorrow. Now she had to vacuum the dust from her sanding, then go and pull those precocious young weeds which had sprung up almost overnight. Ginseng, eager to assist, sat waiting in anticipation of the first pull of her hand hoe. As she smoothed the soil, he first sniffed the damp loam, then patted the ground with his kitty prints.

Her knees black and damp, Tannis rose and laughed at Ginseng, who looked like he was wearing black socks. She scooped up her unsuspecting companion and carried him to the rainwater barrel outside her greenhouse. He howled in protest as she washed his dirty paws, then scooted into the house at high speed. But later, when Tannis lay soaking in the tub, all was forgiven and he sat companionably on the edge of the tub.

Tannis woke from a night of confused dreams wherein Giles and the professor superimposed on each other as they alternately railed at her and patted her hand affectionately. They stormed through her house to hunt up the Magik book, then swore in a court of law they were unaware of its existence. Not a very optimistic start to her 'day of Giles' as she called her unpleasant task. In case it might be needed, she carried the bottle of Scotch into the studio with her, intending to only have a small sip. Impulsively she splashed a small amount into her coffee. A buzz-on might get her kick-started. She giggled to herself in a most demented manner, then grabbed a gob of clay and flung it carelessly onto the bare armature. The lump stuck and she laughed again.

Throwing the clay made her feel better, so she slapped more and more on until she had a short blob, which needed only a little modeling to loosely resemble the person it was to be. Years of skill won out, and she carefully worked the lump to smooth out any existing air pockets and give it shape. The absurd image of Giles, walking towards her in the muck of the Keep, came to mind. She'd use it as a mental model to create a caricature of the pompous little ass. In keeping with her mood, she exaggerated his girth and piggy face.

While she worked her hand crept surreptitiously towards the bottle of Scotch. She was so caught up in her view of what a silly little man he really was, her growing giddiness transformed her rage to humorous disdain, and she was unaware of just how many times her hand had crept towards the bottle.

A while later, she began to talk to him and vented her conflicting emotions, concluding with, "So, you silly liddle pric', and I'm shur it is. You think you can intiminate me, do you?" Her voice had risen, accented by a noticeable slur. "Well, les jus make shurr doze odioush rolls of fat are apparen, and les jus add a liddle bid more fad to the roll hangin over your belly, sal we."

Tannis was unaware there had been a witness to her ludicrous monologue. She had not heard Linka's entrance, or even sensed her as she stood in the studio doorway in time to catch her dialogue wind down.

"Holy Shit! You're pissed, Mom!" Linka exclaimed, both horrified and amused by the scene. She stared at her mother's guilty face, then at the half-empty bottle of Scotch beside her. The Scotch bottle usually only came out when someone had a bad cold. Mixed with strong tea and lots of sugar, two cups of this tonic induced the sweats which, after a good sleep, resulted in a clear head in the morning. Her mother paused, sculpting tools in hand, lips slack, similar to those suggested on the fat little man she was building. "It's not even noon, for God's sake. What *are* you doing?"

Tannis peered at her daughter blankly. With an attempt at dignity she replied, "I am not." She offered her explanation in a deliberate attempt at sobriety, "I wuz jus worken on Shir Giles and needed a shlight tonic to help, thas all." Suddenly realizing she was tiddled, she mouthed an exaggerated 'oh', deliberately put her tools down on the bench, and burst into a fit of giggles. The look on Linka's face was too funny for words. Why, she looked just like a mother about to scold her errant offspring.

Linka shook her head in disgust, but sprang forward as her mother began to wobble when she attempted to rise. She grabbed her unresisting arms and firmly propelled her into the living room. One push nudged her onto the couch, and her own momentum keeled her flat and muffled her trill of, "I'm doing silly gilly, I am, I . . . mfmph." After one giant sigh, she passed out.

Linka covered her with the throw blanket and tucked the arm which hung limply on the ground against her side. With a maternal sigh she returned to the studio and deftly wrapped the piece she recognized as Giles, as she had seen her mother do. Ah, that explained the booze. She tied up the bag of clay and wrinkled her nose as she capped the bottle of Scotch.

The silence in the living room was punctuated only by the grandfather clock's subtle tick and an occasional snuffle-snore from the couch. She laughed at the absurdity of her mother's solution to an abhorrent task. As she bent to check on the zonked form, she caught the strong whiff of alcohol. She must have downed a lot of Scotch. It would take a while to sleep it off so she left a message on her own answering machine for Sam, telling him where she was. She might be here a while, so she scanned the bookcases for something uplifting to read. She picked one of the 'Chicken Soup for the Soul' editions and curled up on the other couch.

Trix, who padded over to greet her second mama, wrinkled her little nose at the offensive smell, then looked around for her playmate. Locating him, she streaked out onto the deck for a fine game of hide and seek, and later, a lazy snooze in the afternoon sun.

The aroma of coffee and cooking drew Tannis back from her swirling, fuzzy dreams. She opened her eyes reluctantly, looked around, and wondered why she was on the couch. The moment she tried to sit up she remembered and clutched her pounding head. As she planted her lifeless feet on the ground she blanched at the form which flitted around her kitchen. "Gawd no. Not Linka," she breathed, flushed with embarrassment.

Linka caught her movements out of the corner of her eye. "I see you've developed an new sculpting style," she retorted as she poured a mug of coffee for her mother. She handed it to Tannis with a 'long-suffering maternal look' and added, "I wouldn't recommend it as a regular approach. It's a good thing I popped by or you'd be totally soused." With a malicious giggle she added, "And to keep this lapse our little secret, is worth . . . oh . . . at least ten favorites tokens, or it's off to the paparazzi I go."

"Five tokens, and screw the paparazzi," Tannis mumbled thickly. She was thankful her head was still attached to her body as she wobbled to the bathroom. She splashed cold water on her face and gulped two glassfuls of the same then tottered back to the living room, grateful to sink back onto the couch. Her head felt attached, but now it seemed her body had decided to drift away with a nauseating lightness triggered by the aroma from the kitchen. "What are you doing?"

"An omelet. Sam taught me. He says it's a basic every girl should know how to make," Linka replied chippily. "You probably just had your usual piece of toast this morning and something in the belly might do you good."

"I see. After years of trying to entice you to cook, to no avail I may add, one word from Sam and you're ready to take on Julia Child," Tannis sniffed.

"I was just a kid then mother," came the reply, as if she were now a wise old woman. But to mollify Tannis she added, "Actually, I was going to ask you to show us how to make some of your terrific dishes. You know, my fave stuff, to carry on the family tradition of yummies."

"So now it's dynasties, is it? You're spending too much time around Josie," Tannis mumbled as she carefully made her way to the dining room table. "So what brought you around today?" Gawd, she felt awful. She didn't think she could eat a bite.

Linka handed her a fluffy omelet which immediately collapsed into a quarter inch pancake on her plate. But since her mother ate some, it musta tasted OK. "I brought over the prints of Sam for the sculpture. I also developed our pictures from the foundry and want you to see them before I do the touch-ups."

"Ummm," Tannis mumbled in response. She realized she was hungry and quickly demolished the flat, tasteless omelet as well as two pieces of toast washed down with two more cups of coffee. Feeling better, she rinsed the dishes Linka had left on the counter, her hands still a little shakey, wondering how it took four mixing bowls and a variety of other unrelated utensils to make one omelet. "Is Trix here too?" she asked.

"Yep. She's outside. Neither her nor the others, which incidentally all trooped in to sniff you, are impressed," she said as they scanned the pictures.

Tannis shrugged. What's done is done. Besides, she was much more interested in viewing the prints, some of which were excellent promo shots. Even so, Linka pointed out the areas she would enhance on the negs before the pictures would be processed again. Tannis looked over the pictures of Sam, then took them into the studio and tacked them on her bulletin board. She pointedly averted her gaze from the wrapped figure on the bench, and gingerly picked up the bottle of Scotch and carried it into the kitchen. Trix was at the door, already in her tote bag. "Off already?" she queried, as she watched Linka tie her runners. "Thanks darling, for everything." An explanation of some sort was in order, but all she said was, "Sorry. I'll tell you about it some time . . ." she finished rather lamely.

"No sweat. Remember the ten tokens. Love ya . . . you lush," Linka replied cheerfully as she gathered up her portfolio and breezed out to wait for her cab.

"Five," Tannis hollered after her, and winced at the echo in her head. She called in the cats and lay back down, for it seemed only a horizontal position stilled her persistent dizziness. She closed her eyes gratefully and let the swirling mass of black and gray weave through her head. She felt unusually cold, and after a particularly severe wave of shivers, wrapped the blanket tight around her body and willed herself to sleep.

* * *

Even as she clutched her cloak tight, the icy blasts found entrance and forked through her in chilling shivers. Taenacea wobbled as the wind's force pressed her back against the wall. The message from Garth had said to meet him at the Tower at Aberayron. He must have scrawled the message quickly for it bore no seal, but eager to assuage her guilt, she paid it no mind. Besides, his messenger had handed her the Writ, affixed with the royal seal above her own name.

Baffled by the reason for it, she scanned its surface quickly and mentally sent Garth her thanks, a gratitude she intended to express more physically once he was back and they were safe. The messenger, eyes downcast and face cloaked, had mumbled something about returning to his regiment and left right after handing her the parchment. She sensed a stealth in his manner but gave it little thought. She left immediately, without an escort, so as not to alert enemies of her intent by the waggle of a careless tongue. Most would think she just rode to attend to an illness in a distant cottage.

Since the slaughter and her return from the netherworld, Taenacea had become acutely aware of the dangers around her, seeing them even where none existed. She sensed enemies amongst her own people and acted with care to counteract the mistrust behind the sullen responses to her directives. The signed Writ would go a long way to assuage this resentment.

During her solitary journey, she kept a watchful eye for movements in the brush. She did not believe harm would come to her personally, but kept cautious of sudden movements. This proved difficult when a storm began to gather around her. The winds rose quickly and soon tore at her. They almost plucked her from the saddle as if the elements, not just her people, were gathered against her. Head bent against the wind, she reviewed the messenger's words. Why would Garth want to meet her at the Tower? Was he heading back to his lands right afterwards? Why not Lianarth, where news of the Writ's sealing could be more easily spread? And why did he not bring it himself? What had detained him? Had he gone on with Henry to Bosworth for some reason?

She had almost decided not to come, thinking he would return to Lianarth if she was not at the tower to meet him. But she owed him much and the need to put an end to her guilt was great. Now that she was ready, she was impatient to do so. She would have met him in England, or crossed the seas to Ireland. As the Writ accompanied the messenger, she had proof it came from his own hands.

She would speak her guilt, share her sorrow, and show her gratitude once home again. He had set aside his own pain and stood by her during her darkest days, doing what he could to bring her back to life. She flinched as she remembered her withdrawal from his succor. She had given him not one thought and let him leave to find the King on her behalf, without even the smallest gesture of love. Suddenly she longed desperately for her husband, for the deep love they shared and the passion which would ease their loss. Perhaps they could have another child, more to help the healing than to replace their lost Faye. But even her fiery thoughts of shared love couldn't penetrate the unforgiving cold.

She rode past the sealed doors of the new Keep to the Tower and tied her mount to a cluster of saplings that would afford her steed a small measure of protection from the sudden deluge of lashing rain. Garth must not be here yet, for she could not see his mount. Slowly she began to ascend the Tower steps to wait his arrival.

On the open coastal cliffs the storm was a vicious inferno as the wind tried to tear her from the Tower. Head bent against its force, she clutched at the seams of the freezing granite blocks and dragged herself upward. A mist swirled around her like cold fingers, intent on a path to the very marrow of her bones. The wind howled as she paused, pressed against the Tower, and whipped her hair from beneath the deep hood that did little to protect her icy cheeks and watery eyes.

She had been there now for what seemed an eternity. Hour after hour she waited. So long. She had waited so long, her blood had slowed to a sluggish trickle. But she had promised, promised to wait, to finally release her torment. To come here alone was dangerous, but Garth had instructed she do so. She moved her stiffened fingers, assured the parchment was still cemented to the hand which clutched it tight.

"Where are you?" she screamed into the inferno, tears of frustration freezing to her cheeks as quickly as they fell. Her shaking limbs barely held her as gust after gust pounded her against the wall. And she was feeling faint. A dangerous lightness had crept upon her, a lightness that could easily send her over the low wall and dash her onto the jagged boulders at the base of the Tower. An ancient stalwart that rose from the seaside cliffs of her lands, it had withstood the furies of countless immense storms from the Irish

Sea. But today, even it seemed to tremble. She had to hang on somehow, so she bit down on her blue and stiff lips for the pain to keep her alert. But still the strange lightness grew within her.

"Nooo . . . " She barely heard her protest above the gathering vortex that threatened to pluck her from her precarious hold just as a form emerged from around the side of the Tower; a shape she knew as intimately as her own, wrapped in a cloak that did as little to keep the icy winds from him as hers.

Her smile of welcome took forever to stretch across her face. As if in slow motion, she reached for him and sought the safety of his arms. His warmth enveloped her for but a moment, then he pulled her down beside him on the stones. Protected a little by his bulk and a sudden lull in the winds, she kissed him feverishly with numbed lips and whispered words of love.

"Oh, Cea, my foolish lass," Garth breathed into her neck. "I brought the signed Writ to Lianarth. Why did you ask me to meet you here, in this storm?" he asked, as he reached clumsily beneath his cloak to pull out the parchment. As baffled as he was by her message, his relief at being with her was evident in his gentle chiding. He wanted only to take her away from this place, to the safety of their chambers, and his arms. Though he thought her message odd when it had arrived, he saw it as a sign of her emergence from her deadness. He would do anything to recapture even a portion of her life-spark. Used to her strange ways, he did not think to question her request.

"What do you mean? I did not ask you to meet me here. I'm here because of your message, and the Writ requiring your signature to be final," she replied. A sudden clutch at her stomach made her not only faint, but ill. Something was very wrong. They looked at each other in confusion as they exchanged parchments and tried to scrutinize them by the sporadic forks of lightning that pierced the darkness. But they could see little other than a wax blob representing the royal seal above her name on both.

Suddenly the hackles rose at the back of Taenacea's neck. Primal instinct alerted her to danger. She looked up and saw a moving mass of blackness stealthily surround them. And like a demon from the bowels of hell, her squat enemy took shape behind Garth. Giles! The wind had once again begun its assault. Before she could even form a sound, he lifted his arms and plunged a sword deep into Garth's back. His powerful thrust, fueled by the rage of frustration and aided by a gust of wind which had pressed him forward, found its mark. Had Garth not been crouched to protect her from the elements, he could have fought him off. Not even aware of his presence, he had no chance against this sudden attack.

"No!" she screamed in horror as she watched Garth's face contort, first in surprise, then pain. He reached his arms back and vainly tried to grasp the sharp rapier. Before he could even reach it, the other dark forms fell on him and dragged him away from her towards the edge of the tower wall.

Her mind raced with almost painful clarity. In a second she realized what had happened. Giles had stolen one of the two parchments, the one sent by his messenger, and lured them here to their death. Perhaps there was something she could still do.

"Wait! I'm here. I came like I said I would," she screamed. As Giles' form loomed over her, she frantically tried to reason with him. "Here, take the Writ. I'll give you the lands, all of them. I'll sign them over to you. But for the sake of all that is Holy, leave Garth be. Kill me if you must, but not him . . . oh Mother of God . . ." she babbled incoherently. She shoved the Writ towards him and knew from his face he could not hear her pleas above the shriek of the wind and fury in his heart.

Almost frothing at the mouth, his eyes glazed with the lust of the kill, Giles ripped the parchment from her hand with a yank that sent a surge of pain shooting up her arm. Instinctively she clutched the small remaining piece in the palm of her hand.

He would kill her now, she was certain. Faintly she heard him scream as he shredded the parchment, "Witch! I have you now. There's no signed Writ and no protection. It's all mine now, mine." As she watched the pieces scatter to dance an insane dance in the wind, the storm collected directly overhead. She jumped as the lightning shot darts of sulfuric fire at the Tower and the thunder cracked and boomed around them in celestial rage.

Then suddenly she felt calm. He would kill her now. Soothed by a rising faintness and the feeling she could float away, Taenacea closed her eyes and waited for the final blow. Her lightness increased and pulled her upwards, to hover above herself. She could feel nothing anymore as she looked down on herself with curiously. From beyond the veil of another reality she heard not a sound, but saw all. She watched as Giles beckoned his men while she knelt on the cold wet stones, head bowed to the inevitable. Everything she loved was gone: Garth, Faye, and her lands. There was nothing more to do, to fight for, to live for. She was calm in her readiness.

She watched the men pick her up, drag her unresisting form to the edge of the walkway, and heave it over. She watched as her body hurtled towards the jagged rocks below, and saw but did not feel the impact on the jagged rocks. She watched it all from a quiet distance above herself, encased in the warmth of white light.

Her body now lay limp and ragged upon the rocks, blood trickling from her head and the side of her mouth. She looked at it sadly. Sensing movement, she watched them drag Garth awkwardly down the winding stairs, his body limp and heavy with his own loss of blood. She watched them drag him to the prominent point of the cliff and roll him over the edge. Her soul sighed in sorrow. Then they dragged her own lifeless form to the edge of the same outcropping and rolled her over it as well.

The thrashing waves drew their bodies into its bed and the undercurrents pulled both beneath the boiling surface. Above, the wind screeched its protest and clouds thundered against each other in fierce protest. With a deliberate fork of deadly intent, she watched one icy finger of lightning strike the Tower at its base. In spite of withstanding such storms for hundreds of years, the aged stones were hit with such force, the structure surrendered and slowly began to crumble.

When it was done, a great stillness settled over the jumble of stones as both wind and rain took a pause. Only one curved, six foot piece of wall and a few broken stone steps now led to the black cover of sky. A silent witness, only this effigy held the horror of what had transpired upon its broken cluster. As the scene dissolved, Taenacea sighed a deep regret, and after one last look to imprint her soul, she felt herself drawn upwards along a silver strand. A soft, almost indiscernible tinkle of chimes accompanied her departure from this earthly plane.

Chapter Sixteen

TANNIS LAY IMMOBILIZED. She knew with certainty Taenacea was still inside her consciousness. So merged were they, for a moment she relished the fullness of being more than one. Linked as she was, the slight feel of rising continued and pulled her upward to where Taenacea had gone. Once there, she knew all there was to know about the woman she had been, and could be. Every nuance, thought, and feeling melded into her being. She knew the purpose underscoring her life, a life that was hers as well, separated only by the illusion of time.

She didn't know how long she lay there but was relieved this final horror was now over. In spite of her initial resistance, she accepted her and Garth's death at the hand of Giles with a calmness she would never have imagined. The paper dragon fear constructs is always much greater than the event itself.

The strand finished, she sensed Taenacea was now gone too. She stirred and sat up, but felt somehow empty with the absence of Taenacea's consciousness. Her own seemed to rattle within a space designed to hold much more than her own paltry sense of self. The Tower memory finally complete, she knew it to be both the Swiftness of Wind and the Depth of Sea, their final resting place. It seemed appropriate. The sea had brought Garth to her, and the sea had swept them both away. Taenacea had chosen it over the land she loved in order to be with him.

The next day she did nothing at all. She didn't answer the calls from Josie, Linka, Josie, Cal, and then Josie again. As she drifted through her memories, she felt the delayed emotional intensity whenever the Tower strand replayed in her mind. A turbulent weather system had swept in, held fast by the coastal mountains. She sat in front of a fire most of the day and watched the images of that life flicker between the flame's fingers. Outside the rain pounded the deck in unrelenting rhythm; a fitting backdrop for her replay. The cats, as if sensing her need to understand this experience, lay quietly around the room without even one quibble among themselves.

The total merging with Taenacea had again resulted in a blood blister on her lower lip. She licked its tenderness thoughtfully, assured she had again traveled to the past in body, not just in spirit. A heightened intuitive sense of the connectiveness of all things, including the hidden portions of herself infused her being. Now she could finish Giles without resorting to alcoholic assistance, a condition she did not care to repeat.

She smirked at how tickled Josie would be on hearing that story; a story probably already relayed with relish by her brat. Then an urgent sense of having left something undone washed over her. She glanced around in panic. Her eyes rested on her desk, where the catalyst for Taenacea's power was still locked in a file drawer. She knew what she must do and jumped up to get the Magik Book.

For a while she leafed through it, unconsciously memorizing a spell here and there. She held the parchment Taenacea had clutched in her hand in death, and felt its residual vibrations race through her veins. She knew they must both go back, back to whatever dimension had held them in abeyance until they appeared for her. As she re-read the Prayer, she realized all but one of her strands were completed. She sensed the ninth would come overseas. Linka must have completed hers, thus the phone calls. Her last Strand, Truth, once revealed, would add a final dimension to her understanding of a life cut short. That's what her message on the machine had said. As if sensing her mother needed time alone, she had said she would not come over until tomorrow.

Perhaps the last strand was connected to something she would see or experience in Wales. The Firmness of Rock may well be the standing walls of one of her Keeps. It seemed likely traces of Taenacea's life still remained. She wondered how she would feel about such a visual confirmation and knew she would not have long to wait. With a last lingering caress over the surface of the prayer, she closed the book and placed it on the coffee table in front of her. She then lit some candles she placed on either side in a shrine-like arc. She relaxed and prepared her mind for the incantation that would whisk it back from where it came.

It happened so swiftly yet with such fluidity, Tannis was stunned, and almost disappointed. She spoke the incantation as she gently touched the Book and felt a surge of energy rush through her fingers, through her body, and up through the top of her head as if sucked through a funnel. The edges of the book began to shimmer and somehow crystallize into vibrating specks of dancing light that grew fainter and fainter, until with a blink of her eye, the Magik Book was gone. Had she heard the chimes faintly, or just expected to? Uncertain, she knew she had done the right thing.

"Well . . . it worked." In awed shock of what had just transpired, she trembled slightly as she stared at the empty space between the candles where the book had lain. Shakily she got up and tossed another log on the fire. "That's as close to making Magic as I ever want to get, thank you very much," she mumbled as she raised her eyes to whatever celestial beings had orchestrated this incredible event. Suddenly exhausted and numbed by the mystic events of this day, she curled up on the couch and instantly fell asleep.

She awoke early next morning, still on the couch. The room was permeated with the smell of wet ash, for the rain had continued all night and fallen through the open flue. She jumped up, feeling surprisingly revitalized, and opened the deck doors wide to a clear blue sky and saucy morning sun. As she made coffee, she tossed the felines a cheery good morning then hummed a springy, but tuneless melody.

Amazed by how experiencing such a horrid death could leave her feeling so good, she scooped the wet ash into a bucket and shut the damper. Still humming tunelessly, she took the bucket of ash out to the compost, then took a bracing shower. Later, clad only in her robe, she sat outside with her coffee to let the sun and breezes dry her hair.

She ran her fingers abstractly through the ends of her curls. Her hair had grown long these past few months and now reached the middle of her back. She wondered if hair growth could be energized by time travel, or her meld with Taenacea. She shook her head vigorously and decided she liked the feel of it. She's have the ends trimmed lightly, but the additional length would allow her to pull it up on her head. It would be handy for the trip.

Later that evening, the roar of the bike announced the arrival of Linka and Sam long before they actually did. Trix accompanied them as usual. Sam sat as silent witness to the telling of Linka's Truth strand; his private thoughts masked behind a calm but attentive demeanor. Tannis said nothing of her Tower strand, curious if Linka would. The 'Truth' of matters would now be revealed, no doubt with dramatic flair. Before Linka began, she gave her mother a long, searching look. "There's something different about you, Mom."

"Different? How?"

"Oh, I dunno. Sorta like you're you, and then you're not. You look . . . oh, I don't know." She saw Tannis' startled look and quickly added, "Maybe it's just that your hair is longer . . . cool." Then she launched into her tale, enjoying center stage.

Her strand had consisted of a series of images and thought forms. "The thoughts were like peeking into people's heads and seeing one intention played out fully," she began. "There were oodles of those. I had to wait 'til they were all done to figure out the 'Truth' of what they represented. But I know I got it right cause my horn blasted. Since you've experienced a lot of what I saw, I'll just spit out the Truths themselves. That's what Sam said I should do, rather than go into the details of each flash of experience."

Tannis threw the silent Sam a grateful look.

"First. The family does originate from the Irish Finn, who wasn't just a folklore hero, but a real person who became immortalized in time. The MacCumals were his direct descendants and comprised one of the seven septs, or families. Lagor is one of the principal names of another sept, a branch of which settled in Kildaire, Kilkenny and primarily the county Laoighis. A branch of the MacCumals settled nearby and this became their primary family seat. We may not be able to prove it, but we know it's true. Second; that's where the family saga started. Third; you were Maeve, and I was Fiona and Faye. Our joint task was to set this whole family coalition in motion like we thought, on a soul level of course. I was someone else as well, but that's for later," she added flippantly but would not elaborate. "Four. There were two signed Writs." Tannis sat up, attentive. It was as she had suspected.

"One had Henry's seal, and the other Richard's. A man at the Keep, one of Gile's spies, overheard your conversation with Garth about the Writ and him going to get the royal seal. The spy reported this to Giles who immediately rode to Lianarth that same day, intent on slaying you in your beds that night to prevent you getting it signed. He figured without it, he'd have no royal impediment to taking over your property.

"He was hiding by the river with his men, setting his plan. Faye overheard him while she was wandering nearby. He had already intercepted the first Writ before it even reached Henry and already had Richard's seal on it. He just didn't know how to use it to his advantage." She paused to take a gulp of air, then continued.

"Remember, Garth had written up a second Writ, with the addition of the enticement of gold from Ireland, the one he took to Henry himself. That's the one he had signed by Henry and took back to Lianarth. Another of Giles' messengers met him halfway there and told him he must meet you at the Tower immediately and alone. It was a matter of life and death, and he was to bring the Writ with him. That's how he was lured there. You of course were enticed there by another messenger, believing him to be sent by Garth because of the note and Writ. Which, by the way, you never looked at closely. You didn't notice you had the Writ with Richard's seal."

She was right. Not only had it been too dark to see, but she had assumed she had Henry's seal and didn't look at it closely. The cost of her assumption had been her life. Whatever Giles had originally intended for them, he had seized the opportunity presented by the two Writs, a safeguard that had actually orchestrated their demise. Linka's silence pulled her out of her musings. She seemed embarrassed, and fidgety before she continued.

"Five. The night I vanished was a stupid accident I set in motion myself. By the way, you didn't seem so broken up about that, or at least you haven't talked about it much. Anyhow . . . " She held up her hand to ward off her mother's defensive rebuttal. "Keep in mind I was just three and as gifted as I was, still reasoned like a child. I didn't want you to go away, which you did . . . you know, to the Gathering. That night I decided to follow you, but I got confused as to where you were going. While I was shrieking, I remembered you saying something about going to Aberayron, so thought that's where you went. So that's where I went. I actually made it there while everyone was still looking for me around Lianarth." She shook her head in disbelief at the tenacity of the child she was.

"You see, the night before I had a dream about never seeing you again. That's why I spent all night looking at you both and why I had the screaming fit when you left. Also, I knew what Giles was planning, but since I couldn't talk, I couldn't tell you about it."

Tannis couldn't help but interrupt. "You actually walked all those miles to Aberayron without being seen by anyone?"

"Yep!" Linka retorted. "I didn't get there until three nights later. I was hungry, tired and lonely. The Keep doors were shut tight because it was stormy, and remember I couldn't call out. So I had the bright idea, if I waited on the cliffs like you always did for Garth, somehow you would both appear.

After all, Garth always came when you stood there. So that's what I did."
She saw the stricken look on her mother's face and waited for the question
she knew would be asked.

"You died there, all alone?" Tannis whispered.

"Stupid really. I got too close to the edge of the cliff trying to look for a
ship, and a gust of wind sent me over. I don't remember the actual dying
part, but I do remember being tossed about on the waves and laughing. The
transition of death was so smooth, I didn't even know I was dead when I got
pulled down to the bottom of the sea. I seemed to stay there for a long time,
and played games with the fish until you and Garth came down. I guess that
part was magic, or an after-death experience manifested by my childish
desires. Anyhow, that's why there was no trace of me, or you two for that
matter."

"So." Tannis said slowly. "We were all taken by the sea, the purpose of
the Depth of Sea strand." She felt saddened at the senseless death of her
faery child. Faye had slipped out of Taenacea's body in her life-giving fluids,
and slipped into death within Mother Earth's fluids.

"Number six. You'll love this one, Mom," Linka said. "Giles died a
deserving death." She paused dramatically for a moment, relishing her
mother's look of satisfaction.

"He went back home after he killed you both to plan the takeover of
your lands. He'd already sent his spies, accomplices, and messengers to the
front lines at Bosworth Field so thought his secret was safe. He decided to
have a big feast with the food his raiders stole from you, to celebrate your
demise. Drunk with victory, he ate and ate as if he was devouring you. He
also drank so much he fell unconscious. Here's the poetic justice. His body
rejected his gluttony, and while he was unconscious, he vomited, and
choked to death on his own vomit. Choice, eh? His greed did him in. I just
love universal paybacks."

Tannis took a moment to gloat over his demise. She did not let on she
already knew. It had come to her yesterday. She had stood, invisible beside
him as he ate and drank himself to death. "It *is* poetic. The very thing he
coveted, killed him. Those mouthfuls of food he ingested were all he ever
got of me." She had at least been spared the indignity of having him use her
body. The thought still triggered a shiver of disgust.

"Hear, hear. Footnote," continued Linka. "Since their bodies were
never found, Taenacea, Garth and Faye slipped into the world of legend,
with all kinds of wild conjectures about what had happened to them,

especially after Giles was found dead. But, keep in mind, there was the War of the Roses thing happening just then, and not too much attention was paid to the four deaths until later, excepting by her own people. They were the ones that fueled the legends."

Curious, Tannis asked, "Did you get anything on what happened after? To the land, I mean, in Wales and Ireland."

"Yup. Henry defeated Richard and was crowned, which both Taenacea and Garth knew beforehand. King Henry and later his daughter, Margaret Tudor, honored the Writ. They sent a series of barons to oversee each of the holdings. Margaret later passed the lands on to her son, James I, who claimed the Welsh lands as his after he became the first Stuart King. He'd heard about the reputedly magical aspect of this land and for a while kept one of his favorite mistresses there. But it wasn't long before the land suffered crop failures and blights like the rest of the country. Poorly managed by indifferent stewards, James lost interest in the holdings that seemed to have lost their magical quality and divided it up amongst his barons and lords."

She jumped up to replenish their drinks, but continued. "Ireland fared better. Stewardship was claimed by a relative of Garth's who happened to be at court. He was a cousin named Seamus who came down from the north lake area with a pack of relations in tow. Since there were no known Lagohaires after Faye, the land was claimed by the MacCumal family. They still own it, I guess." Her story complete, Linka sank back onto the couch, triumphant.

Tannis took a few moments to digest what she had heard. "Well," she said with a note of finality in her voice, "I guess that's it. The Quest is over, at least the reliving of the past part. And that's the truth of it," she added sagaciously. Somehow she knew the Stability of Earth would come later, without any time travel.

Sam, who had sat silent while stroking Ginseng at his side and Trix on his lap, said with apparent awe. "I'm amazed at how calmly you've taken to this 'time travel', Tannis. I found my own experience unsettling, and it was just one past-life regression. But I certainly don't discount your experience. I'm just baffled by how you're able to discuss past-lives and time travel as if you were talking about something mundane."

"Believe me, it's not mundane to me," Tannis retorted dryly. "I've been pulled through the wringer side-ways, and my own beliefs have been stretched to the limit." She paused, then added, "But you know, there is more to life than we perceive. I know that now. I guess we expect a grander vision than seeing ourselves make big mistakes in other lives."

Linka jumped to her defense. "But it was grand. And romantic, and sad, and horrible, and wonderful and mystical all at the same time. I feel like I now have deep roots that stretch way back in time. It gives my life a whole new meaning, and purpose. Don't you feel the same?"

Sam and Tannis chuckled at her intensity. Tannis shook her head at Sam in a 'short of a fuse, but you gotta love her' look, both in agreement that it was this very quality that made Linka so lovable. Still chuckling, Tannis said, "Well sweets, it was another life and another time. It doesn't mean you're carrying the genes of that line now, just the memories."

"How do you know?" Linka shot back. "How do you really know? Besides, subjectively, based on my experience, I do. I mean, if I traced our family line I know I'd find proof." And with a determined look she added, "And that's exactly what I'm going to do."

Both Tannis and Sam groaned in unison at her statement. Tannis thought it odd that both Linka and she had decided to trace their roots. Linka would probably lose interest in the idea, and like so many of her brainstorms, this one would never realized fruition. Nevertheless, she'd say nothing about her own private search. Absorbed with matters of the heart, Josie had most likely forgotten about her intended search of Taenacea's bloodline as well.

"Very funny." Linka protested indignantly. "Just wait. By the time you're back from your holidays, I'll have our whole family tree done." She shot Sam a pointed look and added, "And . . . don't think the Maxwells are exempt from scrutiny. I have to know where your roots are too. Being a landscaper, you of all people should understand the importance of roots."

The mention of gardening gave Tannis a perfect opportunity to broach the subject of house-sitting. Both Linka and Sam were enthused and Sam immediately launched into a discussion of what she wanted him to do. Linka interrupted continually with questions about the cats, most of which went unanswered since Tannis intended to go over their care after she'd prepared a detailed list of instruction.

Deep in thought, Tannis barely heard the roar of the bike's engine after they left. She needed time to reconcile what she had herself experienced with Linka's information, then refocus on her own life and upcoming plans. For all intents and purposes, the Quest was over . . . leaving her what?

The next several weeks passed in a flurry of activity. The felines sensed something afoot and became increasingly grouchy. It wasn't just the increasing number of phone calls and visits from Josie, Linka and Sam with Trix in tow, it was the presence of two large suitcases in the bedroom which swallowed up a steady succession of 'mama smelling' clothes.

Tannis, in an attempt to shake herself out of a dull 'it's done, but I don't feel complete' mood, continued her work on Giles, surprised her previously volatile feelings had decreased dramatically. She had transformed the crude and garish caricature of Giles into a more realistic portrait of the man, yet retained his pompous stance and air of self-importance. With his stomach thrust out and a sneer within the puffy flesh of his piggy face, the piece was amusing. A pudgy hand rested on a walking stick as if its length could add stature to the bulk it supported. It only served to emphasize his squat form. Though he appeared asinine, at certain angles a glimmer of dark intent shadowed his eyes with a devious cast.

Giles was placed slightly off to the side of her happy grouping of country folk, his malevolence apparent. All the pieces needed now was to be fired and their color wash applied. Linka's Christmas gift, the likeness of Trix, was safely tucked under her counter away from prying eyes. By the time she got back, it would be well-dried and ready for sanding and firing. Sam would be her first new project, once her holiday was over.

A week before their departure, Josie sat at the dining room table and poured over the travel brochures and her scads of notes. She continued to present an unending variation of destination options. Tannis left to turn down the temperature of her kiln and when she returned, Josie was still talking.

". . . at least one full day in Findhorn, I'd say, 'specially since we have to see the battlefield of Culledon and the Loch Ness Monster," she said, certain Nessie would rear her head just for them. "We can spend a little time in Scotland, right?"

"You don't have to break my eardrums. I'm back. And yes, whatever. I told you to decide. I will trail in your wake, receptive to surprises, something you're very good at," Tannis retorted testily. They already had this conversation innumerable times over the past few weeks.

"But there must be someplace special you want to see," Josie asked, undeterred by the irritation in her pal's voice.

Tannis was irritated, and fed up with going over and over an itinerary that was sure to change regularly. "You're driving me crazy."

They were already scheduled to see a long list: Stonehenge, The Ring of Brodgar, the Druid's Alter, Callanish Circle in the Outer Hebrides, the great Avebury Circle, the Healing Stone in Cornwall and the Maen Llia Stone in Wales. Of course there were numerous other mounds, burial sites and ancient energy points called keys, as well as the Welsh leys. These meadows or cleared strips of land that crisscrossed the Welsh borders linked all the surrounding sites in an energy grid who's purpose was still unknown.

They'd have to be gone six months at least to take in all the ancient sites. It was obvious her concept of travel was much looser and impulsive than Josie's. But she'd better say something, or Josie would continue to pester the point. Thoughts of Wales lent growing conviction and enthusiasm to her request. "You know me. I'd be happy to just plan our agenda each morning. There is one thing I do want to see and that's my lands. I want to see if there's any ruins left, like the Tower at Aberayron." She squared her shoulders in an unconscious imitation of Taenacea and added firmly, "And I want to see the Lagohaire lands in Ireland, or at least where they may have been."

"A given, and it's a done deal. I'm way ahead of you, girl. There's a neat place in that region of Ireland I just heard about from Cal called Ley Node. One of his clients told him about it. It's similar to Findhorn, but they work with stock as well as vegetation and have re-created an authentic village where everyone practices age-old crafts. It's quite the attraction and I've already tentatively booked a Bed & Breakfast there."

Josie rubbed her aching neck. "Rest assured, by the time we're done our jaunt, there won't be a single sacred site in the British Isles we haven't seen." She threw her arms wide in emphasis and added, "In fact, we'll be so steeped in Celtic lore and ancient energy, we won't need a plane to get back. We'll just magically zap ourselves home."

That's what Tannis was afraid of. "I don't have to see them all, you know," she retorted dryly as she ambled to the kitchen for more coffee.

Trailing her into the kitchen, Josie thought she must still be dealing with her death memory even though her earlier melancholy had lifted somewhat. "You know, I can't get over Giles stabbing Garth and just throwing you off the Tower. His original plan was to have you burnt at the stake, after he had his way with you. Seems like his desire for your demise was greater than his desire to ravage you."

"Tell me about it." Tannis shuddered. "I don't know if it was celestial intervention or karma, but his rage got the better of him. The fact I was already out of my body when I died had more impact on me than the death itself. I didn't feel a thing—just watched myself shed my physical form with fond disinterest. I wonder if that's what death is really like, or if we'll ever know," she said, still in awe of that aspect of her strand. The subject has been discussed many times since her experience.

"I think it's how it would be for all of us, if we changed our beliefs about death. It's only our fear and resistance that makes it so traumatic and painful. Oh, which reminds me, Cal got a call from overseas. Your 'client' left explicit instructions for Cal to return his call immediately, if not sooner. But Cal's busy getting ready for his buying trip and I told him to hold off until he gets back. The little fart probably wants an entire harem after seeing your naked sculpture," Josie giggled. For in their minds, the buyer was a lot like the fat little Giles.

"Not in this lifetime. Tell Cal not to call him until we get back. I don't even want to think about work until then." Realizing she had not participated in the planning or been particularly enthusiastic about the holiday itself, she assumed a bored socialite tone, and said, "I am now a jaded lady of leisure traveling the world with her trusty, if somewhat eccentric companion, whose task is to sift through the thousands of men who will swarm around me in order to find my Garth counterpart."

Josie, glad to see Tannis showing some interest, took a dramatic bow, closed her eyes and clasped her hands in prayer. In her best 'priestess' voice, she intoned, "By the grace of the Goddess, I swear to leave no stone unturned in the Quest to find your Garth, even those of Stonehenge. And should I fail, I will retire my astrological charts and tarot cards forever, and resign myself to breeding a copious new generation of Montana Wildes for the rest of my life, or at least until my uterus collapses."

"Ha. Some sacrifice," Tannis replied with a chuckle. Her upcoming journey felt more real since her bags were packed, excepting a few last minute items. She wondered how Josie found time to shop while absorbed with their itinerary, and asked.

"Oh, I'm only taking a few things. Since I am a bride, I have a whole new trousseau coming to me. I will have both Mr. Wilde's, his wedding present to me, and my own Gold Card to play with. Besides, since the flamboyant Diana, Princess of Wales has stimulated the English fashion industry, I intend to buy most of my stuff there. Some awesome new designers have emerged, and I have my eye on a few of hers."

"Humph." Tannis had her doubts about the styles the tall, svelte Princess had adopted these last few years suiting Josie. But one never knew. She had herself bought several long, gauzy peasant-style summer dresses that buttoned up the front, unlike anything she usually wore. She thought them delightfully fresh and cool. They would be comfortable for sight-seeing as well as appropriate for casual dining.

Unlike the clothes-a-holic Josie, she had only bought a few new things herself and looked forward to purchasing fall and winter items, especially the wools of Scotland. She still preferred the comfort of her leggings and loose tops, but had bought a few pairs of white slacks and leggings. She also invested in a new raincoat, a necessity no matter what time of year you visited the British Isles. A lovely loose, light nylon in burnt cinnamon, she loved the way it rustled and shimmered with her movements. Once they reached England, she planned to get a pair of rain boots to match. Her many pairs of soft kid boots lay folded flat beside her sandals, runners, tights and light jackets in one case, while the other held her new dresses, vibrant tunic tops, undergarments, evening wear, toiletries and jewelry.

Plans continued to be made in spite of the change of venue which accompanied all of Josie's best intentions. Cal was directed by his bride not to return the client's calls, and his secretary given specific instructions to politely inform him Cal would be in Europe for the next two months. If there was a problem with the order, final payment could be withheld until his return.

Tannis had their tickets safely tucked away in her travel purse along with their passports. A less than orderly Josie had been know to lose such important items on her own travels. It wasn't long before Tannis' feeling of hollowness dissipated under the excitement of their impending departure and her efforts to keep Josie focused.

Link and Sam stopped by daily, each time bringing a few more personal items, and stayed for supper most evenings. Tannis and Sam took turns cooking with a suddenly attentive yet inept Linka underfoot. They also took over the feeding and care of their new charges under Tannis' watchful eye.

Clasping her copious lists of 'Things to Do', Linka leaned on the deck railing and watched her Norse God weeding the garden, relishing the dark bronze of his back as his muscles rippled in cadence to his task. She laughed

at Trix who watched Sam, then furiously dug a huge hole where he had
smoothed the weeded soil. Her eyes returned to her list and darted up and
down the pages of her mother's typed notes, now almost obliterated by her
own copious footnotes.

"How much dry vitamin supplement mixture do I add again? Half a
teaspoon or a full one?" she hollered.

Her shouts drew Tannis out on the deck. She'd had enough. She firmly
grabbed Linka by the shoulders, stifling a sudden urge to slap her. This
insanity had been going on all week. "Will you please stop it. We've been
over this a thousand times. You'll be just fine. You've done a good job all
week." Her assurances hadn't diminished the worried frown on Linka's face
so she added, "Besides, Sam will be here."

Sam's name produced immediate results. Linka relaxed her crinkled
forehead and gulped with relief. "Oh yeah. I forgot. Everything will be OK
then. I just don't want to screw up, that's all." Certain all would be well, she
tossed her lists on the nearby chair and dashed from the deck to jump on the
back of her unsuspecting mate. Her bear-hug resulted in a brief tussle
punctuated by her shrieks of protest when Sam began to tickle her. Tannis
chuckled at Ginseng who spit his indignation and leapt into the air at the
sudden interruption of his rhythmic task.

The last few days before departure were bedlam. Sam and Linka had
already moved in and Josie spent more time here than she did at home. Her
itinerary changes were ignored by everybody but Sam. He was fascinated by
her ability to change a three-month schedule in ten minutes without
missing a beat. But the constant activity and noise grated on Tannis' nerves.
She needed time to herself and went into the studio, locking the door
behind her. She would do the patina on her country folk. Focused on her
task, she shut out the shouts, bursts of laughter and other background noise.
In a row of small jars, she added color pigment to clear medium for the
earthy violet, blue and green shades she envisioned in her mind. Then she
brushed the color on the bisque clay surface in successive coats, until she
had the desired intensity. Once the paint had dried, she waxed then with a
light shoe polish, which antiqued the folds and crevices, as well as acted as
a protective sealant.

Like artifacts whose colors mellow with time, the contrast of colored
and bisque clay was further enhanced by Garth and Taenacea's glossy mass
of curls. A crafty brushing of powdered silver dabbed in medium, left no

doubt as to the silver streaks that ran the length of Taenacea's curls. She had also duplicated the hair color of the other country folk; black, brown, and red, contrasted with the blonde of the girl whose hands Nellie clasped as they danced.

When she was done she felt more relaxed and balanced. Several knocks at the studio door had gone unanswered, but when she unlocked it, everyone trooped in to examine the pieces and compliment her on their impact. Cal, who had dropped in while she was working, was the only one who didn't know abut the Quest and significance of these folk. Too date, Josie had kept her promise not to tell. He ran a speculative eye over the work he considered a departure from her usual style.

"Where did you get the idea for these? These three," he said, pointing to Taenacea, Garth and Faye, "are obviously duplicates of the commission pieces. But what about the others? They seem to belong with the trio, even that funny little man over there." He looked bemused at the uncomfortable titters that followed his query.

"Oh . . . they're probably from a past life, or something," Josie commented wickedly as she grabbed his arm and deftly changed the subject. "So, where in Britain do you think you'll be able to meet us?" He too had obviously been deluged with her ever-changing plans from his swift expression of irritation.

"Babe, given your itinerary, which you probably won't even follow, I may never see the two of you again. Just leave messages for me at the hotel. I'll check in regularly," he chuckled. "That is, providing you secure the Hampshire as your home-base."

"Don't worry," Tannis laughed, "We'll be staying put for a few days between sight-seeing jaunts—at the same hotel. You can check for messages and leave numbers we can reach you in case we miss each other. I'll look out for your bride. Contrary to appearances, *one* of us has her feet on the ground."

A dirty look from Josie was followed by a pragmatic shrug. "Just give me your itinerary, oh husband of mine, and with my antennae, I'll find you."

Since everyone was in a 'don't worry, everything will be fine' mood, Sam assured Tannis her home and cats would be well cared for, Linka assured Sam she had it all down pat, and Josie assured everyone she was a mature married woman now and wouldn't lead Tannis astray. Her statement didn't reassure anyone.

The same chaotic scene was repeated on a sunny Sunday, the day of their departure. They were all at the airport, for it took all available hands to roll in the 'few things' Josie was taking. Tannis' two suitcases and carry-on tote looked insignificant beside Josie's six budging cases which resulted in a stubborn battle of wills over weight restrictions at the check-in counter. The Indonesian clerk repeatedly intoned the regulation weights allotted each person, whereas Josie repeatedly tried to negotiate a trade-off with Tannis' underweight baggage. A compromise was reached only because the young clerk was ready to burst into tears of bafflement at Josie's total disregard for the rules. One bag was run through as Tannis' and two discarded, but not until Josie stubbornly pulled its contents out and calmly rearranged her cases.

This unexpected but charming scene, complete with dainty lingerie and other wispy items carelessly flung over open lids, diffused many an irate passenger in the line-up behind her. Some thought it a TV set-up like Candid Camera, and preened in case of hidden cameras. By the time she was done, they realized no mike would be thrust in their face. She shrugged and threw them a charming smile as she handed Cal the empty case and finally checked hers in.

"How can you stand by so calm about her outrageous antics?" Linka asked her mother as she clutched her arm tightly. She suddenly realized her mom was really going away, and for a long time.

"I'm used to it," Tannis responded. "Not much Josie does surprises me anymore, sweets. Besides, look at the smiles she leaves in her wake. She probably made their day," she chuckled. She felt Linka's clutch and responded to her aura of abandonment with a gentle, "I'll send you postcards every single day. You'll be able to track our travels and add them to your binders of stuff you so loosely call a family diary." Unlike herself, Linka was a packrat of memorabilia.

She glanced over at Josie and Cal, and smiled. Glued together in a deep erotic kiss, their intimate farewells drew considerable attention. Tannis hugged her glassy eyed daughter tightly and whispered loving assurances. Once she could extract herself from Linka's emotional clasp, she accepted a warm bear hug from Sam.

"Don't worry, Tannis. I'll look after everything. You just have a great time, and find those Welsh lands. I want to hear all about it when you get back."

Cal had finally extracted himself and was next in line. Since he would see them overseas, he gave her only a light hug. Josie and Linka's exuberant farewell embrace nearly knocked her over and was accompanied by excited chatter from both. Busy with their last minute reminders, they missed most of what the other said.

When Josie sashayed through the metal detector arch, it squealed its protest at the scads of chains and metal ornaments draped on her person. She calmly removed them all, and spilled the contents of her huge purse and tote bag, which also prompted a series of squeals, on the conveyer belt. She was eventually declared clear of threat, but only after the uniformed authorities were convinced her divining rod was not a secret weapon smuggled into the Queen's country to put an end to the young Royals' marital strife.

Many of the same dumbfounded fellow travelers who had witnessed her repacking scenario were held up again. They hoped this personage would be ensconced in first class, and those destined for first class feverishly hoped she would be seated elsewhere. It would be a long 9–10 hour flight.

* * *

Bryan sat restlessly in his private jet, awaiting take-off. Disappointed by his attempts to reach the agent Calvin Wilde, he needed to walk off his frustration. Not one of his messages had been returned. All his calls received the same polite response from a secretary whose composure was unaffected by his threat of legal action, which he knew was ridiculous. Personal frustration didn't warrant such an inappropriate attitude.

He knew he was starting to make a fool of himself. Unanswered messages only left him more determined to get hold of the man. Calvin's inaccessibility revived the mystery surrounding the identity of the artist and her exquisite model. If he had to hire detectives to track him down, so be it. How hard could it be to find an art agent? As soon as he reached his London office, he would call Lorne and have him hire someone. Then he could attend to his business dinner at the London Carvery without mental distraction.

He realized he was obsessed, an obsession which grew in magnitude since the three sculptures had been mounted outside his ancestral home.

He had stopped back at the Manor twice since they were mounted. They looked as if they belonged, as if they had always sat there, which only fed his desire to find the artist and the model.

Both times he had been drawn outside at dawn. He watched the early light shift over the figures and give substance to the ghostly faery child, now encased in a light mist from the fountain's gentle spout. An adjustment in pressure had the water lap lightly at her base, and the spouts on the larger lower level of the fountain surrounded her whole form like a moist halation whenever they came on. He had made the adjustments himself, pleased with the results.

But it was always the golden Enchantress brought to life under the glow of dawn that held him captive. During the warmth of the day the sun flushed her with living vibrancy as if infusing her body with its heat. And each evening at sunset he watched her life slowly ebb away to heighten the mysterious depth of her expression. He made a habit of gently brushing her sun-heated back, breast or hand and often ran a lingering finger along the warm lushness of her lips.

Obsessed he was, to be sure. Perhaps if he met the artist, probably some eccentric elderly woman attempting to recapture her youth through these mystical figures, he might both satisfy his curiosity and end his obsession. He had already shifted appointments to spend more time on the Estate, and he knew Seamus wondered at his inane excuses for returning so often. But embarrassment prevented him from giving a reason.

Even his business dealings lacked his usual keen attentiveness of late. In the middle of negotiations or a business call, his mind would wander to his Enchantress. The image of her beckoning hand stirred a longing within himself which distracted him to the point where he had begun to overlook details not previously missed. Lorne must have noticed, but had said nothing, yet. Like some legendary Temptress, the Enchantress beckoned him to an unknown fate. At the moment, his fate was total mental confusion.

His mind flew back to his father and he squirmed uncomfortably. Was he to repeat a pattern which had ended in tragedy? No. He would not let that happen.

* * *

The plane circled high over the crystal city of Vancouver, bound for the Arctic route to London. Josie waited impatiently for the seat belt sign to blink off, then jumped up and went to have a word with the pilot.

Tannis sat back comfortably in her chair, unconcerned by her pal's sudden disappearance. She could hardly believe she was actually airborne, on her way to England. She noted the majority of the first-class passengers were businessmen intent on getting some work done during the long hours ahead. She would do what she could to keep Josie occupied, and thus cause minimal distraction.

Josie returned, satisfied the pilot and co-pilot had the proper lunar conjunctions aligned to their signs. She rifled through a handful of brochures, then tossed them in her lap and sighed with pleasure. "Driving around should be fun but we don't want to miss anything, especially the castles and traditional tourist destinations," she said wistfully.

"We can miss some of them. Perhaps we should join one of those excursion tours rather than putz through the countryside without a clue as to where we're going. After we do the London scene, that is," Tannis said. "I hear they're wonderful, with knowledgeable guides to give us a complete history of the sites. We can just sit back in a luxury coach, and look out of large windows while we get the rundown." She hoped to prevent Josie from driving at all, if possible. A maniac behind the wheel, thoughts of her on bumpy, winding country roads in a mini as she had apparently done in the 70s, terrified her. But she had to tread lightly. Josie was sensitive about her driving. Liking her comfort, she just might respond to the luxury of a first class tour bus.

"If I can ride a yak in . . ." Josie began, deftly interrupted by Tannis' sing-song completion.

". . . Tibet, a camel in Egypt, a donkey in Peru, and now an Arabian in Montana. You think you can traverse the British Isles in a mini, driving on the wrong side of the road? *I don't think so!* At least your beasts of burden knew the territory; a rental car does not." She took care to keep her voice playful and light.

"Don't think I don't know what you're trying to do," Josie shot back, knowing full well her erratic style of driving was not appreciated by her best friend. Tannis usually insisted on driving when they went anywhere together. She sighed dramatically and left the issue unresolved, just to annoy her and keep her guessing. Their beverages arrived while Josie scanned their flight companions. Covertly, she did quick readings on the businessmen closest to them.

The male passengers had thrown appreciative glances at the pair. The tall one who crossed her long, black-tight clad legs with unconscious ease, filled their minds with thoughts of Latin moonlit nights; for the riot of curls that escaped her topknot to hang in charming disorder around her face, enhanced her seductive dark eyes and full mouth. The little minx beside her exuded her own unique femininity. A light suede jacket edged in hanging medallions opened on a lacy chemise. The jacket's rows of medallions jingled in competition with the jangle of necklaces draped over her generous breasts. Along with the silly tinkling bell attached to her decorative braid, she stirred memories of an abandoned and more exuberant youth.

Josie sensed their glances and responded to the scrutiny by a spontaneous introduction to herself and Tannis. Within half an hour she had them all named, charted and enthusiastically sharing tips from their own travels in the British Isles. Over dinner, all thoughts of business wiped from their minds, several of them participated in a lively discussion of abstract art vs. realistic, galleries, Montana breeding stock, Egyptian antiquities, divining, continental cuisine, astrological compatibility and current best sellers.

Exhausted by the whirlwind of the last few days, Tannis closed her eyes gratefully and took a snooze after her meal. Josie used her shut-eye as an opportunity to catch up on her notes for the book she had decided to write as a novel; the book about the Quest. As a novel she could embellish the importance of her own involvement. She pulled her laptop from her tote bag, opened the OSW file, and began to type.

A photographic memory helped her re-enact conversations and flesh out the completion of the Tower and Truth strand. She added the miracle of her own marriage and pre-travel hilarity. She even managed to work on her story line notes and put everything away just before Tannis began to stir. Tannis went to freshen up, then joined the lively conversation, casually dropping droll and snide witticisms, delighting the men with her throaty laughter. By the time the plane circled in preparation for its descent, Josie had added more than a few names and numbers to her personal black book and Cal's potential clientele list. She handed out several cards to promote Cal's Gallery and artists, ensuring Tannis' name was placed at the top of the list.

When the conversation returned to a comparison of popular styles of art, Tannis felt reassured her semi-isolation and focus on her craft over the past several years hadn't dulled her conversing abilities. She enjoyed these discussions, eager to hear views on the fickle tastes within the world of art. Sobered by an intruding thought during their descent, she leaned towards Josie and whispered intently, "I don't care what you have to do, but please see to it we don't spend the next two weeks in customs as the x-ray machine scrutinizes every item you own, *capish?*"

"*Capish*," breathed the sagacious Josie with an exaggerated wink. Whatever she did worked. When they emerged out of customs at Heathrow, they found themselves right at the exit, marked 'way out', leading to the parking lot.

"This is 'way out'. Trust the English to digress from acceptable 'exit' signs," commented Josie.

They were immediately claimed by a small, slight gentleman who identified himself as John Stout, Cal's English emissary. They suppressed their giggles at the absurdity of his name, for he was less than stout and barely tipped five feet in height. He briskly led them and their cart of luggage to a waiting silver Mercedes he fondly called the 'Merc', and whisked them off to their hotel in the heart of London.

Stout, as he was called by his charges, informed them he, who knew the British Isles better than anyone, would be their personal guide, and they, the beneficiaries of generations of Stout knowledge. They tried to keep up to his fast patter and did little more than glance out the windows at the blur of passing images.

They pulled up to the Hampshire, a lovely Edwardian Hotel in the heart of Leicester Square, where Cal always stayed when in London. Stout ushered them to the front desk and introduced them to a tall distinguished gentleman behind the counter. His face instantly broke into a genuine though somewhat unpracticed smile upon hearing the name Wilde.

"Ladies, my pleasure," he exclaimed in a modulated accent. "Welcome to the Hampshire. Mr. Wilde has been a regular for many years, and we're delighted to include his lovely bride, congratulations extended, and companion into our family of, shall we say, *special guests*." His emphasis on the latter made them feel very exclusive. "If there's anything you need, ask for me directly. Nigel's the name. I shall be at your disposal during your stay, as is John here," implying their every whim would be immediately gratified.

Josie raised her eyebrows. She then smiled at Nigel sweetly, and launched into a list of essential items she hoped the hotel could provide; first priority given to a coffee maker and bean grinder for their room. Neither could function without their bracing morning go-juice.

Their suitcases awaited them in charming adjoining rooms. The tasteful and distinguished decor in soft gray, rusty pumpkin, peach and cream tones, was set off by a large oval window set into a four foot alcove. Sheer curtains were framed by lively cabbage print drapes that looped gracefully on each side, and matched the bedspread. A large vase of English summer blooms wafted their mixed scents from a round antique table centered in front of the window. On either side were antique chairs, whose silky stripes matched the settee and footstools across from the bed. Inviting a lazy afternoon tea by the window, or a quiet evening reflection on the day's activities, the decor bespoke of refined elegance.

Josie dashed through the door of the adjoining room and declared the private bathrooms between both serviceable and charming. "It's perfect. My room's in shades of blue and apple green, my colors. Since this will be home for a while, let's order a bottle of champagne to celebrate the beginning of our holiday. Then we can get all gussied up for dinner. Cal made 9:00 p.m. reservations for us at the London Carvery . . . surprise! . . . which gives us plenty of time to sip, bathe, dress, sip, and even snooze if we need it, which I don't."

"Sounds like a plan." It was obvious to Tannis there would be many more prearranged events, so she'd better get used to having them sprung on her. "I see Cal has already greased the wheels by arranging for our little shadow, Stout," she added. They speculated on how such a little snippet of a man, barely five feet tall and weighing no more than six stone, Josie informed her proudly, could be named Stout. Josie had done her homework on English weights, money, and other essentials.

"I guess it's his way of keeping tabs on his beloved bride. He told me about Stout a while ago. Stout's his London contact because he knows the country. He's been employed as his proxy buyer for over eight years now 'cause he hears about all the yummy private estate sales from his family. There have to be hundreds of Stouts in the country, mostly in the service industry, so they're in the know and call him when a sale's afoot."

When the champagne arrived, they uncorked, poured, and toasted the beginning of their excellent adventure in front of the fresh, fragrant blooms.

"'Ere's to a bloody great time!" trilled Josie, in a poor imitation of Stout's Cockney accent.

"Cor, but a right bonker of a time it'll be," Tannis retorted in kind, her accent not much better. They looked at each other fondly and wondered what surprises awaited them.

The original London Carvery, the art deco restaurant where they would dine, was located in the Forte Regent Palace Hotel. Tannis twirled around in her deep violet calf-length silk dress. Unbuttoned to above the knee, an enticing expanse of bare, creamy leg flashed into view as she did her turns for Josie. Her hair was loose and wild, her only accessory a pair of gold amethyst-encrusted loop earrings and small evening purse in violet rhinestones.

Then it was Josie's turn at center-stage. Shed of her usual layered apparel, she looked deliciously naughty in a tight little black number which not only hugged her lush breasts, but emphasized her tiny waist. Her dress stopped dangerously close to her tight little tush and gave way to an expanse of slender, black silken legs. Ornamentation had been toned down to one black velvet band around her neck, one large, brightly colored and highly lacquered fish that dangled from the ear opposite her bell braid, and a bunch of plastic bracelets that chinked on her arm in a riot of purple, magenta, turquoise and yellow, which matched her fish.

They looked rich, pampered, and ready to melt the coolness of even the most stoic Englishman's heart. They both carried wraps; Tannis' a pale shade of violet and Josie's a shrieking magenta which drew many an eye in the Lobby as they waited for Stout. Since they were only going a few blocks, they would walk to their destination. You only drove in London if you were a sadist, Stout informed them. You walked if your destination was nearby, or took the tube if it wasn't. A car would only wiz you past where you wanted to go on London's primarily one-way streets. Tannis was relieved to hear a mini could not be 'let' these days and was only a fondly remembered relic from the past.

A fine drizzle accompanied their dash into the bustling lobby of the Forte Regent Hotel. They melded into the steady stream of native and international guests who chose the hotel for its affordability and location, overwhelmed by the diversity of global accents they heard. Stout led them down a long hall off the reception area and past several small shops and a pub.

"I'll be in 'The George' having a pint," Stout said, as they headed to the end of the corridor, and the large wooden doors of The Original Carvery. The moment they entered, they were transported into the era of the roaring 20s and 30s, and knew they were completely overdressed for this 'all-you-can-eat' smorgasbord style restaurant. But it was their first night in London, and they didn't care. Seated smack in the middle of the room, Tannis and Josie played their 'where they're from, and what's their story' game, playfully honing their perceptive skills even while they ate.

Across the room sat two businessmen, oblivious to their surroundings. One was calmly attentive to the other who bounced in animated rhythm to the figures and percentages which streamed from his lips. Bryan would not usually patronize such a place and was here only at the specific request of his guest, Graham, a young commodities genius who had almost doubled his personal investment portfolio over the past two years. Because of this, he would have sat on a park bench if Graham had asked.

Bryan was not altogether displeased with Graham's choice. He appreciated the anonymity such a high turnover restaurant afforded. Dinner over and business concluded, as he listened to anticipated projections for the coming years, he glanced around the room idly, mind on a different type of figure. His eyes fell on a mass of black curls which framed a striking face in the distant center of the room; a face strangely familiar. Before he could take another look, a party of diners between them rose to leave and obstructed his view while they stood in lengthy farewells. When they were gone, so was the face which had captured his attention.

The flicker of recognition had jolted him, but he wasn't sure why. He shrugged off a now familiar tingle throughout his body as his thoughts turned to his Enchantress. He wondered if her form still held the heat of the day or if she'd already been cooled by the evening's chill. He'd much rather think of her than the statistics Graham continued to present. He'd had enough, and ended the meeting with a polite but firm, "Do it, and send the prospectus to my office. Now, if there's nothing else, I have to run. A pleasure as usual, and the bill's been taken care of. Keep up the good work buddy. And book the yacht when you want. I'll let them know to expect your call." His mind on his seductive Enchantress, he picked up his raincoat and left.

As he hurried through the crowd, he stopped to allow another patron to pass and bumped into someone behind him. For a moment he felt like he'd been hit in the gut, and then the feeling was gone. When he regained his footing, he charged through the doors without a look backwards or acknowledgment of the accidental encounter.

Tannis, who paused near the doors to inspect a particularly lovely patinated and enameled bronze Femme-fleur figure on a marble base, was caught off guard by a sudden bump from behind. It felt more like she had been hit in the stomach with a sickening crunch than jostled by someone. When she regained her balance she turned to see who had jolted her, but caught only a brief glimpse of the back of a man in a raincoat before the doors closed. The sickening feeling was gone and she was left with only a slight uneasiness in her belly.

Attributing the quiver to sensory overload, she made her way back to the table. She tossed Josie a hasty explanation when asked why so pale, paid the bill, and hustled her companion out of the restaurant with undue haste. Telling Josie to get Stout, she rushed outside, eyes darting up and down the street. She had no idea what she was looking for. Feeling foolish, she leaned against a light post and waited for her companions. Her queasiness gone by the time they got back to the hotel, they laconically discussed their upcoming six days of sight-seeing in London while they got ready for bed.

Tannis missed the warmth of furry bodies snuggled against her own, and conjured up Garth's face, seeking solace in his memory. She tried not to think about meeting anyone, instead, would trust destiny. In the meantime, she intended to enjoy herself. The hands of fate would deliver him to her if it was meant to be. Still, the words 'meant to be, meant to be' lulled her into sleep.

Chapter Seventeen

A CONTINENTAL BREAKFAST washed down with their own familiar tasting coffee kicked off their first day of sight-seeing. Although prepared to enjoy all the delights of cuisine and beverage native to England, both Tannis and Josie had tucked a supply of coffee beans and instant cappuccino into their cases.

They tossed Nigel and Stout a cheery hello at the front desk, then took their first stroll on the Queen's soil with Stout in tow. Down Picadilly under a clear cobalt sky across which scuttled only a few wispy clouds, they paused at Fortnum and Mason, renowned for its food halls, where each shop bore the Royal Warrant Coat of Arms above its doorway proclaiming Royal approval. As they continued down Knightsbridge, Josie disappeared into every boutique en route to emerge with a bag. Tannis went into a few shops too, but preferred to walk ahead with Stout, all ears to his tales of London life.

The key tone for the afternoon was 'culture,' after which they hopped a double-decker bus back to the hotel. Josie, of course, had to clutch the outside handrail and hang from her precarious perch as she had seen actors do in movies.

Groans of pleasure punctuated the foot massages they exchanged once back in their rooms before they drew their baths. They left the adjoining doors open so they could converse back and forth while they soaked away their aches in the hot, frothy water. They concurred that sensible footwear was a must for the rest of their London trek.

Tannis caught a glimpse of the new clothes which littered Josie's bed, thankful she had her own room. Her own purchase for Linka was already neatly wrapped and addressed, ready to be expressed to her biker-chick back home. She envisioned her in the soft, creamy, leather pant suite and matching lace-up bustier she had bought for her. Her mind still on clothes, she chided her pal through the doorway. "You'd better take it easy with the shopping. It's only day one, and even Cal's coffers have a bottom. We haven't even hit Harrods yet, where you're bound to spend a fortune . . . or any of the other boutiques London is famous for."

Her response was a flippant, "My man says he wants me to have fun. Besides, I want to experiment with some new looks before all I can fit into is a muu-muu when I'm pregnant with all those little Wildes."

Tannis was amused by Josie's passion for an ever changing wardrobe which reflected a myriad of moods and styles in keeping with her current interests. Her impulse purchases were usually only worn once or twice, then never seen again. But she knew Josie not only recycled them through consignment shops, but also donated bag fulls to the local women's shelter at the end of each season. She wondered if her odd assortment of retro and just plain weird stuff lightened the mood of some abused women. Possibly, since new drop-offs were eagerly awaited.

A chatty room service meal preceded their night cruise on the River Thames, where they gawked at the beautifully lit Big Ben and Houses of Parliament. Later, while Josie chatted on the phone to several local acquaintances, Tannis wrote her first few cards to Linka. She also recorded her impressions in her journal, as she would do throughout the trip.

Day two was dubbed 'Royal Hob Nob Day'. The changing of the Guard at Buckingham Palace, and the stately towers of Westminster Abbey were duly appraised under a briny sky. Tannis was more impressed by these well-known landmarks than she thought she would be. Fortunately the weather held, except for one shower later in the day when Stout led them to the Tower of London to gape at the Crown Jewels. Josie's knowledge of gems was soon apparent, and one of the Beefeaters willingly fleshed out their historic origins.

On the third day, a morning of sightseeing was followed by another afternoon of shopping. After a meander through the vibrant markets of Petticoat Lane and a rifle through the crazy fashions of Chelsea's Kings Road, Josie embarked on some serious bargain hunting in Camden Market, where antiques and curiosities kept her gold card busy and Stout cussing.

Here Tannis purchased several small items herself, but her mind was more on the past than what the present offered in ways of wares. Her attempts to draw Josie away from her shopping frenzy failed, so she gave up and leaned against a stall post to watch the people around her. Suddenly she had an idea. She would take pictures of people with interesting faces or unique posturing, and use them as models for what could become a new line of country folk, similar to those she had sculpted from her Welsh life. She would use these faces, but sculpt them in medieval garb.

As she moved up and down the street she photographed some faces that were dour, and others etched with tenacious good-will. Pleased with the contrasts, she looked for more and found the lean and embittered, the broad and content, and others less easily defined, but unique to her eye. Completely absorbed, she jumped when Josie grabbed her arm and declared herself shopped-out.

"Not likely," Tannis exclaimed, realizing it was already late afternoon. "The only reason you're quitting is because the shops and stalls are closing. Speaking of which, my tummy rumbles say it's time for dinner."

The next day was surrendered to Harrods. The gleaming letters of its name across the top of the entrance welcomed the spending of an obscene amount of money within its ornate stone walls. When they finally returned to their hotel, again laden with boxes, bags, and Stout in tow with more, Tannis announced firmly, "That's it. Tomorrow is a 'no shopping' day, *capish?* We're doing something that doesn't require the use of your gold card. We're going to do something outside." To which Josie agreed, on the condition they do the 'chicks on the town' thing tonight. Revitalized by dinner, a shower, and a slinky new dress from Harrods, Tannis trailed the effervescent Josie as they popped into several night clubs. Although swains gathered around them like bees swarming to honey, none had the look or essence of Garth, not that she was looking, of course.

Heavy-eyed from last night, they staggered down to the lobby. Stout declared they had got 'butchered' as the Cockneys would say, but showed no mercy and set a brutal pace as they strolled through Regent Park. Refreshed by their walk, they wandered through Madam Tussands. Tannis felt like the jolly green giant among the diminutive wax figures, much like Taenacea would have among her own country folk.

"It appears you had some sense in your choice of clothing in Wales," Josie commented dryly as she pointed out one board-like bodice. "Considering the stiffness of these costumes, it's a wonder women could even breathe, let alone do anything else. Of course, the rich never did. I don't even want to think about what those bodices did to their breasts." Eyes round in horror, her loud comment drew shocked looks from the cluster of staunch royal supporters beside her. Back in the hotel lounge, they munched on a plate of chips while they continued to discuss the stature and personalities of the Royals they had seen. But once Stout joined them, the conversation shifted to plans for their upcoming excursion.

Stout had received very specific instructions from Cal. His eyes darted between them as they argued the merits of driving themselves vs. hopping a tour bus. Josie of course was for driving, Tannis for a tour bus. "Well luvs, here's my say. I can drive you in the Merc, or arrange for seats on a fine Globus Bus leaving Saturday. All you ever wanted to see in merry England in 14 days. When you get back, I'll take you round my England and Wales in the Merc. We'll do B & B's and dear Stonehenge and all that on your list." Cal had told him Tannis was particularly interested in taking some time in mid-Wales and seeing some of the better Neolithic sights.

"You'll see what's missed on the tour, and can enjoy the scenery without worry about driving," he concluded, waiting with bated breath for their decision. His usual means of transport while scouring the country for art was his old panel van. He hoped they would go for him driving the Merc, a flash car to do the run of the land in.

Tannis jumped at the offer, and shot Josie a 'no argumento' look. "We'll do the tour," she stated firmly. "If you can get us on at such short notice. Then you can drive us to Wales, say two or three days after we get back." She turned to Josie and added, "Remember, we have a date with destiny at Stonehenge on the Summer Solstice, so we have to be back on time."

A relieved Josie agreed, and dunked her last chip into the heap of ketchup on her plate. Her pedestrian's taste of English drivers had killed any desire she may have had to drive. She just wanted to keep up the charade to annoy them both. Besides, she had gone to great lengths to arrange their private viewing of the famous megalith and refused to take a chance of missing out because they were lost.

Stout knew Cal would be relieved and silently thanked the saints, and Tannis. He excused himself and went to confirm the seats already tentatively booked. He was pretty sure Josie was just taking the mickey out of him with her stubborn refusal to concede. Cal had assured him Tannis would likely win out on this point, as she had.

The following morning he arrived at their suite door with a thumbs-up for the tour and detailed brochure which Josie immediately snatched out of his hands. Clad only in her robe, she raced back into her room, jumped onto the middle of her bed, and compared the tour's itinerary with her own. Stout was right. The tour would cover nearly everything they wanted to see.

Tannis seized the opportunity to slip downstairs and have a word with Nigel about their rooms while they were away. Nigel heard her out then provided the ideal solution. While on tour, their possessions would be stored in a storage closet then moved back into their rooms the morning of their return. The same arrangement would apply to their Welsh trip, unless instructed otherwise. Tannis also inquired into crating and air cargo costs. Josie would have to ship a great deal of her purchases back home.

"You're a perfect sweetie. Thanks," Tannis said, relieved their $300 a night tab would be reduced to a nominal storage fee while they were away. For all her lists, it was these small details Josie missed and her more frugal nature caught. Back in her room she told Josie of the arrangement and began to pack what she would take on tour, and what would be left behind. While she did so, Josie's Stonehenge friend called to confirm their private viewing and arrange their pick-up time on the designated morning. Later, dinner was interrupted by a call from Cal which sent Josie flying into her own room.

Tinkles of laughter and low murmurs drifted through the open door while Tannis, packing done, wrote cards to Linka. Each card bore either her own keen perception of the pictured attractions visited, comic notes on Josie's antics or funny captions from each location. She took the cards down to the front desk and left instructions to mail two cards each day in the order specified. She wondered how everyone was faring at home and thought nostalgically about her cats. With Sam there she knew all would be well, but she still particularly missed their warmth at night. Back upstairs she offered to help Josie pack up what she would leave behind, hoping the good weather would hold during their tour.

It did. After a heated tiff and numerous cups of coffee, Josie's luggage was reduced to one large case and several 'totes' for essentials like her laptop and the makings of her daily face. Her one case pulled behind, Tannis and a grumpy Josie joined the forty other people that milled around the large white and red Globus.

First on the bus, Tannis claimed the two front seats in order to have the benefit of the large tinted windows at front and sides. Josie immediately introduced herself to both the driver and tour director. She informed Tannis that "he's a sweetie from Yorkshire, a dependable Capricorn so we'll be safe," and that Maggie, their tour director "is an Aquarius, like me, so we'll have lots of fun." She then settled into her seat beside Tannis and scanned the passengers as they boarded.

The healthy age mix of lively folk had them guessing their origins until their first stop at Hampton Court Palace, the lavish home of Henry VIII, As they strolled through the magnificent Great Hall, the kitchens, and outside in the ornamental gardens, Maggie shared juicy snippets from King Henry's flamboyant reign. As Josie predicted, Maggie proved a delightful guide. She also looked charming in her smart red suite and matching pillbox hat over a gleaming fall of mahogany hair. Not only was she entertaining, but when Josie added her own outrageous comments, Maggie looked to her for additional tidbits that had their companions hooting. Maggie knew she had a live one in Josie and intended to utilize her as such.

When they alighted at Stonehenge, they were shepherded through the gift shop and out the other side for controlled viewing. Stonehenge could not be seen until they were above-ground again. Tannis' heart raced as she set eyes on the stones about two hundred yards away. So powerful was this ancient circle, everyone lowered their voices as they stood in mute awe, jostled by the wind that raced across the flat grasslands.

Maggie shared the more popular speculations of Stonehenge's origin, including the tale of how Merlin had brought the stones from Ireland where they had graced the top of a blue mountain range in tribute to ancient giant gods.

"Hundreds of noblemen had gathered on the Salisbury Plain for a peace parlay fated to fail," she said. "And fail it did, for they were all cruelly slain by those who preferred the fortunes of war and discord. In tribute to the courageous intentions of the peacemakers, Merlin magically transported the stones from the Emerald Isle and placed them over the sight of the slaughter. The stones of Stonehenge, a dolerite blue-tinged variety of sandstone professed to be harder than granite, are also said to possess healing properties, even to this day."

Tannis, who had been standing a little off to the side of the group, felt a grounding settle over her, as if this particular megalith stimulated a deep memory of her roots. She saw flashes of her life as Maeve, and others she could not identify, others who had touched many such stones and trod other sacred places, just as powerful but not as famous. She was unaware these stirrings would solidify as she trod this ancient soil, touched timeworn castle walls, and stood within mystic circles. For now they were merely faint stirrings within her soul's memory. Startled by Josie's voice, she felt disoriented for a moment, then cringed as her friend expounded her own theory of Stonehenge's origin and purpose.

"It was built by the Pleiadians, a giant race known as the Lyrians, from the Pleiadian star system. They lived here about 15,000 years ago and used the site as an energy conduit temple. It was used both for planetary energy manipulation rituals and as a doorway, or portal which intersects other realities. The portals are dormant now of course, but only because we don't know how to use them." The disbelief on many a face didn't deter her from continuing.

"As our original ancestors, when earth was seeded by the Pleiadians, the Lyrians were the giant race who also inhabited and built the life-size statues of themselves on Easter Island. They were never finished because a distant, warring galactic race threatened their culture, which prompted them to pack up and leave in order to divert the aggressor's attention away from this gem in the universe. These stones are all that's left of the original temple which stood on this particular energy site," she added casually, as if she remembered exactly what it had looked like then.

Had her presentation not been so light, Josie's rapt audience would have written her off as a lunatic. But although some retained their quizzing and skeptic looks, most accepted it as just one of many other wild theories about Stonehenge's origin. Tannis grabbed her pal's arm and pulled her off to the side to chide lightly, "Give them a couple of days before you totally blow them away, will you."

"Relax," Josie said. "I thought I'd throw in the truth . . ." She stopped abruptly, and scrutinized Tannis' face. "You look different."

"Waddya mean?" This was not the first time she'd heard that comment of late. Linka had mentioned it too.

"I'm not sure yet, but 'fuller' somehow. That's it. You look and feel fuller. Could be a twosome happening here. Hmmm . . ." She peered at Tannis again, then abruptly turned to Enid, a young Norwegian girl, to answer her question about the Pleiadians. Happily she launched into a detailed account of that star system's ancient connection to planet Earth, or Terra, as those blue-skinned terrestrials called planet Earth.

Josie had invited an elated Enid to join them for dinner and some more galactic chit-chat. Tannis sat back, embroiled in her own thoughts as Josie prattled on about Earth's terrestrial heritage. She had definitely felt vibrations and sensations at certain spots in some of the cathedrals, mostly in the tucked-away corners the energy of the tourists' hadn't yet diffused.

Later in their twin-bedded room, Josie recorded her impressions of their first day on her laptop while Tannis did the same in her journal. Josie paused and peered at Tannis thoughtfully. "Stonehenge was definitely the high-light of today," she said. "Can you imagine what our private viewing will be like when we're actually going to be inside the circle? The energy in that ring must be spectacular, tangible even. Especially at dawn."

Tannis agreed. "I felt something today, even standing two hundred yards away," she said, remembering the shift within herself and resulting connection with the land itself.

As if mirroring her thoughts, Josie asked, "Maybe now that you're standing on ancient soil, you'll be more closely connected to your Wicca and Druid roots."

"Possibly. But lord knows what that will do to me. I'm not sure I want to experience this vacation through some ancient haze of altered conscious-ness," Tannis mumbled as she squirmed in bed, seeking a more comfortable position on the somewhat lumpy mattress.

"Just instruct your higher self to allow it, and at the same time let you stay alert to your current experiences," was Josie's matter-of-fact response before they exchanged sleepy good nights.

Although it was standard procedure to move back two seats each day, the girls were told next morning they could stay in their front row seats. Maggie intended to keep the live one close, especially since their traveling companions raised no objection. As they passed through Dartmoor, an eerie landscape of granite tors and scrubby hills, Tannis felt an almost magnetic tug pull her gaze northward to Wales.

But it was the crossing of the 3,240-foot Severn Road Bridge into South Wales, and the intended stop in Cardiff that set Tannis' heart racing. Although considerably south and east of her lands, she felt the pull of her ancient roots. While the group visited Cardiff Castle and the stately civic buildings of the Welsh capital, she dragged Josie away to wander through the streets and shops by themselves. She wanted to capture the flavor of her people while walking among them.

Wrapped loosely in a new woven shawl dyed in muted earth tones, her hair streaming out behind her, Tannis strode confidently through the streets. Her cheeks sported two bright spots of color placed there by the brisk sea winds that blew through the port city. As if recognized as one of their own, the eyes of many residents followed her sprightly progress. Josie had trouble keeping up to her stride and finally leaned against a stone building, defeated. When Tannis stopped and looked back, she waved her on with a "No can do. See you back at the hotel for dinner. I'm going shopping."

That night they sampled their first traditional Welsh fare, beginning with Welsh Rarebit, a strong cheddar, beer, and egg sauce over toasted bread. The flavor tasted familiar to Tannis although she had never had it before. Leek soup, rabbit stew, and a tender leg of lamb with roast potatoes followed. They had Creme Brule for dessert, a cool molded cream made with milk, molasses, and almonds sprinkled with nuts. Considered a French dessert, the Welsh had favored this dish since medieval times, and claimed it as their own.

Over dinner Josie bitched, "If you don't slow down on our walk-abouts, you'll be on your own from now on. I have enough trouble keeping up with your long legs without you increasing your stride with this new 'it's my land' attitude. *There!* Grievance aired. At least this one is. I don't imagine you can do anything about this lava bread, can you?" She swallowed her small mouthful with a sour face. "Seaweed, yuck! Did you really eat this stuff back then?"

"Yes. At Aberayron. Not only did we use seaweed to fertilize the land, and even hauled it to Lianarth in carts, but Lava bread was a nutritious staple on the coast, especially because it traveled well," Tannis responded, unaware of the quizzing looks from two of her dinner companion, looks Josie caught.

"Family used to live on the coast in the Bay of Cardigan," she explained to Arthur Crown and his cheery wife, Jean who sat across from them this evening. In her opinion, Jean should have been named 'comparison chirps', considering her busy-body demeanor. Oblivious to the fact no one listened to her for long, Jean's comparison prattles usually faded into a not-unpleasant background twitter.

Arthur, a retired history professor, patted his wife's hand affectionately as she turned to her other dinner companion, the elderly widow from Des Moines, Iowa. She listened patiently as Jean compared every blade of grass and building seen so far with something much grander back home in Louisiana. Arthur, a man of both culture and curiosity, shared his interest in folklore with the girls, his initially tentative nature becoming more bold under their prompting. He even touched lightly on the legend of the Lady of Lianarth before he concluded with, "So, I believe that outside of embellishments due to the verbal retelling of these tales, most are probably more accurate renditions of history than history would have us believe."

He received very emphatic nods of agreement from Tannis and Josie. Enid, a convert to the unusual now, vigorously nodded in agreement. She had swiftly claimed a seat at their table, intent on shadowing Josie, her new guru of fascinating information.

Next morning, they traveled north through 'The Valleys' which had fueled the Industrial Revolution with its iron ore and coal. The Wye Valley in Brecon National Park was declared deserving of its reputation as the land of salmon rivers and Welsh mountain ponies. The name, Maggie said, was taken from the distinctive flat-topped plateaus of the Brecon Mountains themselves. The spectacular gorges riddled with caves and waterfalls had been forged by limestone erosion.

They stopped briefly in Ludlow's medieval market town where a dreamy Tannis barely registered the activity at the Wedgewood China Factory at Stoke-on-Trent. She was caught in the mystic musings of her homeland, saddened by their impending departure. They would stay in the port of Liverpool for the next two nights and from there tour to surrounding areas on day-trips. She wasn't particularly looking forward to it. To Tannis' delight, they went back to Wales through the Horseshoe Pass the very next day, to the riverside town of Llagollen. Famous as the gathering place for minstrels, the town hosted an annual contest called the 'Eisteddfod'. Literally meaning 'gathering', the Eisteddfod attracts participants from all over the world, and provides a dazzling display of folk music and song and dance.

Their last stop in Wales was at the site of Plas Newydd, home of the eccentric 'Ladies of Llagollen' who were reputed to have created a stir with their cultural societal. Behind their residence sloped a partially wooded hill on whose barren top sat a crumbling ruin. Alone outside while the others viewed the Manor House, Tannis looked longingly towards the southwest. Less than fifty miles away lay the borders of her own lands. She sensed the ground she was standing on could well be the holdings of Giles Kaylon, or even the south western borders of hers. Lost in the past, she stared blankly at the hilltop and didn't sense Josie until a soft caress on her arm pulled her back to the present.

"So close, and yet so far, eh? Let me tell you, if this is what your lands are like, I can understand your desire to come here. It's magnificent! We'll be back before you know it, and then you can wander around, or sit and moon to your heart's content. But right now we're holding up the tour," she said gently, affected too by the land which held her pal captive.

Passing through Hawkshed and the Old Laundry, the home and source of inspiration for the favored children's author, Beatrix Potter, brought back memories for Tannis. When Linka was little, she and Tannis had become so caught up in the delightful tales, they often played out the stories and pretended they were the animals. The series still sat in her bookcase back home, waiting to share their magic with another child, hopefully a grand-child.

Unexpectedly she became more pensive when they crossed the border into Scotland. Her mood lifted only slightly when they arrived in Glasgow, which proved more of a center for the arts than the center of industry as had been expected.

Tannis and Josie left the group and went to see the acclaimed Burrell Collection, Art Gallery, and Museum in nearby Kelvingrove. By now Maggie and their tour companions were used to them striking out on their own. They looked forward to Josie's hilarious recounts, generally more interesting than their own activities. Tannis' dry and witty rendition of their adventures were also well-received, especially when they focused on Josie's antics.

The next day was slated as a free day. They had seen so much, Tannis was suffering from sensory overload. Further exhausted by Josie's incessant chatter, she enjoyed a delicious sleep-in instead of going out for breakfast with Josie, and announced she was going shop-snooping by herself. After a quick lunch in a pub she wandered through the stylish arcades and fashion filled shops, clear on what she intended, which was to buy a range of the finest to the hardiest in woolen wear.

Thrilled with her new collection of sweaters, long woven skirts, jackets, cape and three shawls, she got back to the hotel in time to join Josie for dinner, and a taste of Glasgow's surprisingly lively night life. Aching feet forgotten and rejuvenated from a day spent alone, she tried her hand at a Scottish reel in one rowdy pub, but refused many of the drams of Scotch sent her way to entice her to participate in more. She had no intention of getting 'butchered' on Scotch as she had when sculpting Giles.

The tone of the next day was gray. Tannis, swaddled in her new charcoal cape which matched both the sky and her mood, felt thoroughly depressed. She boarded the bus behind Josie, sluggish and uncertain why so grim of spirit. Following the 'Bonnie Banks' of Loch Lomond where the open moors sloped gently down to the waters edge, she had said not one word until they entered the Highlands via the bleak beauty of Glen Coe, the site of the treacherous massacre of the famed MacDonalds.

Her dreams last night had been as murky as the skies were now. Tannis felt overwhelmed by the oppressive air of perfidy that hung as heavily here as it had over her own Wailing Valley. That's what everything reminded her of today in spite of being in Scotland, the Wailing Valley. Later, as they crossed over to the Isle of Skye, her morose mood deepened. The Clan Donald Center's guide droned on about its thirteen centuries of Clan history, a history not dissimilar to that of Wales. In her opinion, the efforts of the Scots, Welsh and Irish to forge their own national identity had resulted in centuries of bloodshed with the encroaching English, often with each other, and even amongst themselves.

Lost in her brooding, she did perk up a little when they reached Loch Ness, though with little help from the oppressive drizzle and chilly wind. It was Josie that drew her from her mood for a short time by intoning a loud chant to lure the monster Nessie forth. When spiritual incantations and even mortal appeals failed, her explanation brought smiles to her companion's faces, including Tannis.

"The lunar alignments are not ideal today," she said. "Since Nessie has to move through a corridor of time from an intersecting world, the time portal being underwater, she can only appear under specific astrological and energy conjunctions. That's why she's so rarely seen." Her outrageous explanation baffled even Enid, her most rabid disciple.

Gloominess settled over Tannis again when they traversed some of the most awe-inspiring but lonely landscapes imaginable. Shattered mountain tops, open moorland, and dismally dark woods were blanketed by a leaden sky and steady drizzle. At Inverness they shivered as they stretched their legs before boarding and heading for Culloden Moor. As Maggie recounted the history of Bonnie Prince Charlie, and the slaughter which took place here on his behalf, Josie looked for recognizable landmarks with rising excitement.

It was in this part of Scotland that Diana Gabaldon's heroine Claire and hero Jamie Fraser had played out their passion as depicted in her novels. And it was on this very moor that Jamie had fought reluctantly, albeit savagely beside his own men and relatives of the MacKenzie Clan for their Bonnie Prince. The battle had been all for naught. Back on the bus Maggie and the others paid rapt attention to Josie's recap of the book as she described the Battle of Culloden. And for once, Jean, the queen of upmanship, could not find a battle in Louisiana to compare.

While her bloodthirsty dinner companions discussed well known battles and slaughters over blood oozing cuts of prime rib, Tannis, her plate untouched, brooded in silence. She stared with revulsion at the puddle of blood seeping into her potatoes from her red slab of meat. The thought of her own slaughter memory squelched what little appetite she may have had. She wondered if she would be able to find the valley once in Wales and if so, would she hear the wailing again as she had after reliving the slaughter?

Josie was aware of her grim mood but didn't quiz her until they got back to their room. "Today was really a low for you, wasn't it?" she asked.

"Yes. I think because so many lives have been sacrificed for the power and greed of so few. Maybe it just impacts me because of my own Welsh memories and the futility of the battles I fought myself. And for what? Oh . . . I dunno." Josie did not respond, so she continued, warming to a chance to share the feelings kept buttoned-up all day.

"Especially here, where life was harsh in this incredible but lonely beauty. Like in the movie *Braveheart* or *Rob Roy*, most men simply wanted to live out their lives on their own little tract of land without conflict. Instead they were swept up in the obligations of Clan and personal honor. All orchestrated of course by the powerful few, intent on placing their chosen candidate on the throne and padding their coffers in the process. Most folk didn't care. They just wanted their own identity, a reasonable life, and to be left in peace."

Josie suspected she was hearing Taenacea's, not Tannis' views. Since Tannis was now pacing in front of her in obvious agitation, Josie censured, "And what was the Lady of Lianarth doing at the time, may I ask? Was she not herself fighting for the fiefdom of her little kingdom, of which she was the uncrowned Queen?"

Annoyed by Josie's challenging critique, Tannis barked back defensively, "That's different! At least I didn't raise armies and march all over other people's land trying to win the Crown for England. What I did was to maintain peace and prosperity for my own people."

Giving scant attention to this weak argument, Josie exclaimed, "Maybe, but with your well-deserved reputation as a mighty warrior, *I for one* wouldn't have wanted to meet with your savagery in battle." To diffuse Tannis' rising agitation, she changed tactics and asked in awe-struck tone, "Weren't you ten feet tall, oh Scourge of Lianarth, with lightning bolts shooting from your silver strands, and sparks flying from your eyes with every scornful glare? Didn't the ground burst into flames behind you as you vanquished your enemies?"

Teased out of her intensity by the absurdity of the image, Tannis smiled weakly, then retorted, "Not exactly. I was only eight feet tall. But I had breasts the size of laundry baskets, a basket for each that is. And it was snakes that spit electric venom from my streaks when somebody annoyed me. One look from my fiery eyes would instantly incinerate any poor bugger that incurred my wrath."

"Should I let our tour companions know to tread lightly around you then?" quipped Josie, relieved their conversation had taken this silly turn.

"They know already," Tannis grinned wickedly. Her earlier gloom lifted. "Didn't you know there were originally *forty-five* in our group besides ourselves? Now of course there are only *forty*," she added with satisfaction. She swished her robe around her legs to emphasize just who was responsible for their reduction in numbers. Their giggles continued well into the night and resurfaced at breakfast the next morning, which drew envious looks from their companions for secrets not shared.

They were still chuckling sporadically as they crossed the heather clad moors to the Spey Valley for a tour of a whiskey distillery. During their lecture on the ancient art of converting barley, water, and yeast into a heart warming liquor with a silent kick, Josie loudly proclaimed that whisky was also known to aid in the production of clay asses, and asked if she could buy a Case-lot for her friend's future creative initiatives. The embarrassment on Tannis' face made her companions laugh in spite of not knowing the reason behind the remark.

That evening, the whole group enjoyed Highland dancing, bagpipes, and a regional specialty, the Ceremony of the Haggis. Although the Ceremony was great fun, only Tannis and a few other hardy souls actually ate the stuffed sheep's gut. She found it delicious, and had several helpings.

What occurred next had both their companions and the locals talking for days. The incident started with Josie harmlessly chatting to a huge bullock of a red-faced Scotsman. He had made some belittling comment in response to their discussion on the correlation between size and power, so Josie calmly challenged him to a demonstration of real power vs. his brawn version. Humoring her, he agreed. His rugby team buddies nudging closer to watch what would be to them an obvious victory for their goalie. Closing her eyes for a moment in concentration, Josie then rose to her tiptoes in order to reach her opponent's upper torso. Using only her forefinger, she marshaled her energy into that one finger, and pushed the three hundred pound hulk of a man to the floor as easily as tipping a feather in the wind.

During the stunned silence that followed, she turned on her size six heels, wiped her hands in satisfaction, and rejoined her gaping companions. Behind her the shocked Scotsman, his face three shades redder than before, was helped to his feet by his mates. Ignoring the jibes and barbs thrown his way, he strode to the bar and ordered a double Scotch, straight up. More than one covert but baffled look was thrown their way during the rest of the evening, and when Josie made several unnecessary trips to the bar, the group parted in silent respect.

"I really get annoyed by these blokes that think just because you're little you're helpless and tit-useless!" she exclaimed, as if commenting on a minor annoyance.

Their last touring day was definitely an ABC day. They only glanced at the quaint medieval town at Stow-on-the-Wold in the Cotswold Hills, were left cold by Sir Winston Churchill's burial place in Bladon, and didn't lose their 'glazed' viewing mode until at the college buildings of Oxford. There they walked through the backdrop for the movie *Shadowlands*, starring Sir Anthony Hopkins and Debra Winger. Both had seen the movie innumerable times. Disappointed, Tannis couldn't sense the layering of centuries of scholars or feel the hushed reverence of passing students and professors like depicted in the movie. It was impossible to pick out the professors in the pell-mell of noisy activity around her, and the students were anything but reverent, many rudely jostling them as they dashed past. Their final stop was a visit to the Queen's favorite residence, Windsor Castle, which still bore the signs of its recent ravage by fire.

By late afternoon the bus pulled back into London with its cargo of satisfied but exhausted passengers. Although an evening celebration was scheduled for the group, Tannis and Josie declined and said their good-byes while the luggage was unloaded. Theirs was claimed by Stout, who was not at all surprised by the addition of four new suitcases. When the trunk was full, he piled the rest into the back seat of the Merc, which barely left enough room for their owner, Josie.

Their rooms, the same adjoining suites as before, were waiting, along with their personal possessions neatly in place. Ignoring the disarray of tour luggage, after a quick shower they rushed downstairs to meet Stout in the dining room. After they ordered, they gave him their souvenir gifts, a genuine Scottish Tam to keep the chill of his thinning hair from Tannis, and two bottles of Scotch to keep the chill from his bones from Josie.

Touched by their unexpected consideration, Stout relished their unique rendering of the tour's highlights. These two had wormed their way into his heart and he had missed them while they were away.

When Nigel came off duty and heard Josie's unmistakable laughter, he paused at the entrance to the dining room. Tannis spotted him by the doorway and waved him over. Seated beside Stout, he too was enthralled by the girls' recap of their tour. He also enjoyed the envious looks from several male diners. The ladies' laughter had lightened the atmosphere in the whole room. The two were clearly not jaded socialites, rather, enthusiastic and perceptive visitors who appreciated the history of the land Nigel thought the finest in the world. Reluctantly he excused himself. He had to work the early morning shift.

Nothing was planned for the following day other than a sleep-in and 'lazing around'. Their whirlwind tour had finally caught up to them, and they soon trailed back to their rooms.

*   *   *

In a cluttered little alcove at the end of the hall at Braith & Timms, Charles Thornton nervously flicked the ash off the end of his cigarette. It landed beside the ashtray on top of other heaps that had also missed their mark.

Bloody Hell! Marjorie had found out about his affair and tonight was to be the reckoning. It just wasn't fair. The stupid bitch cared for nothing but the busybody gossip of her tea klatch's spying within the neighborhood. But she had actually surfaced from her favorite pastime long enough to call his office late one night. The night he was not where he was supposed to be. In her bull-doggish way, she prodded all the secret niches of his private bureau, and found a small evidence of his dalliance, the proverbial matchbook men insisted on pocketing in cheap bars.

It wasn't as if he did this regularly. In fact it was only the one time. A fling with the file clerk down the hall, which had obviously been as disappointing for her as most things in life were for him. His dour face reflected his bland little life and tedious job—digging for evidence of other people's illustrious ancestry. He was married to an equally unappetizing and bland little woman he'd lost interest in long before their modest nuptials. And every night for twenty-one years he had trudged home to his dull little house, excepting once.

Marjorie was a subtle shrew who had doggedly squashed any spark of initiative or self-worth he might have developed. When he had first seen her stride briskly along the country lane he thought her fresh and healthy, a supportive type of helpmate. He had sadly been wrong. A few short years later, he could barely stand the sight of her tightly-corseted figure as it wheezed out cutting gossip each night while he ate a soggy and unimaginative dinner. It was not that he would regret losing her, but possessing little personal drive, he didn't know if he would get a flat as close to his workplace as theirs was.

Marjorie had said nothing, just thrown him inexplicable looks until, in her own words, she was ready to 'have it out'. He'd been in a dither all week, forgetting to make calls and overlooking specifics his dogged attention to detail would normally never had missed. But he was distracted by his worry.

He reached to butt out his half-smoked cigarette and knocked over a teetering stack of files. Bloody Hell! A mass of papers fluttered to the tiled floor beside his desk. Now he'd have to spend an hour putting them back into their proper folders. It took more than an hour, and with still a handful to go, Charles began to scan them quickly, rather than read them carefully to ensure they landed back in their proper file. As he clutched the last bundle, his fingers grasped a newly opened but unread letter from the 'IN' basket beneath the stack. He scanned it quickly. It was a request to search out the Lagohaire name. The request for immediate attention to the search on the Lagohaire family of Ireland was accompanied by a substantial retainer in hopes it would speed the search.

Charles placed Mrs. Wilde's letter at the top of the Lagohaire file, intending to tackle it right after lunch. He had begun the search on this name already, for another client from Canada. Apparently this request was also on her behalf, but by an author. Unlike the first request, this one was accompanied with a payment. He would send the data to the Hampshire in London where Mrs. Wilde said she would be staying for at least another month. The other party would receive photocopies, pending receipt of the required retainer. He made a mental note to write and inform her, but worry over this evening's impending row wiped it from his mind.

Chapter Eighteen

BRYAN MACCUMAL WAS FRUSTRATED and on a mission. His last visit to the Manor had done nothing but add questions to those already cramping his mind. He'd arrived late last night and was up before dawn to watch the sun awaken his Enchantress. Startled by Seamus' tap on his shoulder, he accepted the thick steaming mug of tea gratefully.

"Enslaved, are yeh then," Seamus asked in a hushed voice as he watched the faery child turn pearly and the pair by the front steps golden with the morning's light.

"Losing my mind is more like it," retorted Bryan. He made a sudden decision to share his weighty thoughts with his brother. With only minimal embarrassment he told him of the events leading up to his current obsession and growing desire to relinquish his jetting, wheeling and dealing life. He wanted to take back the reins of his family home.

Seamus felt the uncharacteristic longing that permeated his brother's voice. "Tis a pickle yeh're in for sure, what with her being only of metal. As to the mystery of the making of the pieces, have yeh noticed the crest? 'Tis the old family crest the faery child is after holding."

"Our crest?" queried Bryan as he strode over the fountain which had been turned off for cleaning. He hadn't looked at the crest closely, thinking it an imaginative ornamentation. But on closer examination, he recognized it as theirs. It contained the eagles, dandelions and flames of the MacCumals, deftly combined with the lions, raspberries and rising sun of the Lagohaires, but as they had been hundreds of years ago according to the family legend and pictures depicting the ancient crest.

It was his great grandfather who had removed the Lagohaire elements from a crest which represented a coalition long abandoned. That's why Bryan hadn't recognized it. His grandfather, with a passion for Irish lore and history, had spun the tale of the ancient family bond many times. But the lads had been young, and both he and Seamus had long forgotten the details. Bryan vaguely remembered being told by his own father of his

304

resemblance to the mysterious Garth, a trend which surfaced every three generations or so, as if to recapture a chance for a union between the two families. Only there were no female Lagohaires anymore, and hadn't been for hundreds of years.

Seamus interrupted his thoughts with a speculation. "Maybe the artist heard of the legend and was after hunting up the crest in hopes of impressing yeh."

"Possibly, if she knew I was the buyer. But Lorne placed the order for me. Not even her agent knows I'm the one who commissioned the pieces." That's what perplexed him.

"Ah weel, 'tis a mystery for sure, since they look like they was made for just the spot they be sitting in," Seamus replied. "Had any luck in finding her out then, the artist?"

"Not yet. But I think Lorne may have tracked her agent down in Paris. I'm off to meet with him tomorrow. Then I'll be in London for a few days." With a look of determination, he turned to his brother and added, "I want you to clear the site and start building Nell's home, right away. I've been selfish about keeping you here so long, and I'm sorry. I'll be winding down my business and be home to stay by fall. In the meantime, you can expect to see more of me. I have a lot to learn before you're gone from here."

Though a great smile broke across Seamus' face, all he did was nod and say, "Aye. It'll be a joy to Nell on hearing it. But it's only a mile or so away I'll be from the manor. Yeh can almost bellow, and I'll be hearing yeh."

When he arrived at his office in Paris, the first thing Bryan received from his secretary was an urgent message from Lorne. He called him back before he even removed his jacket.

"Hey buddy, good news. Calvin the agent is staying at the Novotel Bagnolet. I've already left a message for him saying, "No pay, refund expected, and pieces being returned if you don't contact ASAP," Lorne said.

"That'll get his attention, you sly bastard," retorted Bryan with satisfaction. He felt only a little embarrassment at creating such a fuss over what would probably turn out to be only an imaginary figure. "Arrange dinner for the three of us tonight will you. I want to find out what's going on here. You're coming, aren't you?"

"I wouldn't miss this. Are you planning to tell me, or are you going to keep me in the dark about what this is all about?" Lorne asked. His partner's sudden fixation on finding this agent intrigued him. After Bryan told him what he had told Seamus, not sparing himself in any way, Lorne chuckled and said, "So, a dame's finally got to you, even though she's not real. Well, well. And when do I get an invite to meet this silent Enchantress and see what the artist did with your ugly mug?"

"Maybe next weekend, if you can tear yourself away from your own number crunching obsession," Bryan retorted.

"That obsession as you put it, is what keeps you so filthy rich, and don't you forget it," Lorne retorted with pride. He briefly updated Bryan on some other business and promised to leave a message for the agent concerning dinner. He felt better knowing what was going on, but still didn't understand Bryan's distraction. He found it hard to believe he was hooked on a piece of sculpture. His partner needed a break. He had not mentioned several of the deals Bryan had negotiated lately were riddled with loopholes, loopholes which could have cost them millions, loopholes he had quietly closed.

Several hours later at the Novotel Bagnolet, Cal mulled over Lorne's brutal ultimatum. Damn! He'd planned to surprise the girls in London for dinner at Quaglinos, and then spend a much needed night with his bride. He missed her more than he thought he would, annoyed his plans would be postponed for one more day. It also meant shifting his whole appointment schedule around.

In spite of his irritation, he'd have to take care of this matter first. For not only were the two previous payments spent, but it was now a question of personal credibility; both his and Tannis'. Never before had a client been unhappy with their purchases. Although the threatening tone of the message could just be a ploy by an irascible client, he couldn't take the chance. He left a message for Lorne saying he would be there, lucked out when he called London to change his dinner reservations at Quaglinos, and after leaving a message for Josie, took a shower.

As he soaped himself, he thought about his wife with longing. He wanted to clear his mind of this matter before he saw her. Her antennas would immediately sense something was amiss. Besides, when it came to her friend Tannis, there was no telling what she was liable to do if she felt her pal slighted or harmed in any way. He'd better have something positive to report when he did see her. But for the life of him he couldn't imagine what the problem was. Confident of a swift resolution, he stepped out of the shower and dressed for dinner with care.

* * *

After a decadent sleep-in, a groggy Tannis rang for brunch while Josie showered. They sorted through their stuff and arranged for some to be boxed and shipped back to Canada. The task completed, Josie was eager to find out what Stout had planned for their Welsh sojourn and went down to the lobby to hunt him up.

All thoughts of Stout flew out of her mind when she picked up their messages, most from Cal. She scanned them quickly, her lips softened by a smile. It was the last one that sent her racing back upstairs. She burst into Tannis' room and waving the message slips, shrieked, "Babe's coming to London! Just for one night, to wine and dine us. Then he has to go back, but guess where he's taking us. To Quaglinos, the place to eat in London. OhMyGawd! We have to get special gussied up for this one."

"When, and why gussy up special for this one?" Tannis asked, pleased Josie would have a night with her husband before they went to Wales, but not thrilled about having to go shopping again."

"Tomorrow night, and because some of the Royals eat there. We have to scour Harrods again, nothing else will do. Something really hoity-toity in case we meet up with one of them. Maybe even Princess Di. Are you with me?" she asked, eyes-a-glitter with a sudden vision of a totally new look for herself.

"Can you at least wait until I'm dressed?" quipped Tannis, clad only in her favorite nightshirt. It was covered with photo images of her cats beneath the "I'm Purrfect" imprinted across her chest in large bold letters.

"I guess. But hurry, 'cause it's 'chicks with gold cards' time," she squealed as she dashed back to her room. When she returned, Tannis was dressed in an oversized long white shirt and her signature tights, garb easy to get in and out of. A light golden tan acquired back home while gardening, and hair carelessly pinned at the sides gave her a distinctly exotic look.

"By the way, we're all set for tomorrow. Dennis left a message confirming he'll pick us up at 2:00 a.m., the middle of the night if you ask me. We'll be standing in the middle of Stonehenge before the sun begins its ascent on the summer solstice, unlike the hundreds of other people who have to look on from outside the barriers. Thank you, yes, I really am good. Now ... let's go shopping!"

Tannis' thrill of excitement was more from the stirrings felt during her first visit to the site than the thought of shopping—again. Those stirrings had triggered a quickening that accelerated every time she stood beside, or touched the megaliths seen on tour. Knowing she had been a Druid, and knowing the stones were a holy site built by the Druids, she wondered what would happen once she actually stood inside the ancient circle. She set those thoughts aside and tried to focus on their expedition with some enthusiasm, for Josie's sake if not her own.

An Art Nouveau vision of a dress, right out of the 20s, was her choice. Draped over a mannequin with long curly hair similar to her own, she knew it was perfect. They found it almost right away on the way to Harrods, in an exclusive little boutique missed during their first day's stroll down Knightsbridge.

It was breathtaking. The bias cut gown, delicately layered in silk and gossamer fine lace fell from the shoulder to mid-calf. In the softest shade of cream, a hint of violet silk peeked out from under the slinky lace layers. Although sleeveless, one shoulder was capped with lace that draped diagonally down to the opposite hip, forming the first of three layers. When she modeled it for Josie, the lights caught the 101 craftily embroidered sequins and sent tiny sparks of silver and violet glittering along the undulating edges of the layers.

"You look like a modern day Guinevere in that dress. It's perfect for you," Josie exclaimed, awed by the contrast of the ethereal dress to Tannis' swarthy skin and dark hair. It took several hours and several cuppas at Harrods before Josie finally settled on a style for herself. "I've decided on the Audrey Hepburn look," she proclaimed, pleased with the anticipated contrast to Tannis' mystical gown. And it took another hour to find just the right dress; a simple, well cut little number with a hem that stopped discreetly at the knees. "This is it. I'll only need one stunning piece of jewelry, black silk stockings, and toppling high heels to bring me closer to Cal's look of utter amazement at how sophisticated I am. After all, I have to look the part of the wife of the most prestigious art dealer in the world," she added dramatically.

Harrods willingly surrendered two expensive pairs of shoes; black silk with gold spikes for Josie, and delicate satin cream for Tannis, accessorized with two frothy lace fans that clipped into the front of the low-heeled pumps. At the jewelry counter they found the amended two pieces of jewelry for Josie, a four inch wide bracelet of Black Alaskan diamonds studded with pearls, and matching earrings that hung in a twinkling cluster and caught the glint of her sparkling dark eyes. Here Josie also found the crowning touch to Tannis' outfit; an Art Deco headband, inset with amethysts, pearls and sequins, which perfectly matched her dress.

"This one's on me. Now you're the reigning Queen of Art Deco, which by the way, is the theme at Quaglinos. No need for thanks. It's your early birthday present. Happy Birthday!"

"Thank you, and I accept. It's beautiful," Tannis said, reinforcing her appreciation with a big hug. Exhausted but exhilarated they scrutinized their purchases back at the hotel. Tannis remarked cheekily, "You exceeded your stated quota of jewelry. I knew you would."

"This is the thanks I get for buying you a gorgeous present, and no mention of the enormous sacrifice on my part, in not buying the matching necklace for my outfit? *Oi vey* ... I should have more friends who break my heart," Josie quipped back in a perfect 'spoilt brat' whine. She was far more interested in how she'd arrange her braid in keeping with her new look, and waved away Tannis' thanks for her birthday gift with a flick of her hand.

* * *

A stunned Cal shook the hand of the man who was the spitting image of Tannis' sculpture, pony-tail and all. He barely managed to contain his shock at first seeing him. Professional suave camouflaged his confusion while introductions were made and by the time he had seated himself and ordered a double scotch, he felt more composed. He wondered what was going on, but asked smoothly, "I understand there's a problem with your commission, Bryan?"

His composure made Bryan feel foolish for a moment. "No problem with the quality of the work. In fact, it far surpasses my expectations." He could see the quizzing 'what then' on his guest's face. "What I have a problem with is that an artist in Canada, who had never met me and did not know I was the buyer, was able to sculpt an exact likeness of me. And you have to admit it is a remarkable likeness. What I have a problem with is that she also incorporated an ancient family crest of ours, long since in disuse, into the crest the child is holding. Perhaps you could explain how this is possible,"

Bryan replied. He wondered if he sounded as foolish as he felt, but nevertheless watched Cal's face carefully.

Cal was at a total loss. He hadn't know what to expect, but certainly not this. He remembered he had noticed some odd looks and overheard strange comments between Josie and Tannis, looks and comments begun, but quickly stifled. And he knew which of the two could be made to tell. Bryan and Lorne were waiting for his response. His mind flicked over several responses, but decided that candor was the best policy. In fact, now that he had figured out who his client was, a very reclusive and wealthy man who was Lord of one of the largest privately owned estates in Ireland, he knew candor was his only option. This man would tolerate nothing less.

Several *Fortune* articles had been written about him years ago regarding some kind of scandal. More recently he remembered articles about his partner Lorne's swift rise to two-digit billionaire status. He had believed what the articles had implied, that Lorne, the only one photographed for the past ten years, was the sole owner of their powerful empire. So . . . the reclusive partner only hinted at did exist, and with his estates in Ireland, be worthy of three-digit billionaire status. It was none other than Lord Bryan MacCumal who sat across from him right now, impatient for an explanation.

"Frankly, I'm at a loss too, Bryan," Cal said as he met the even gaze of the shrewd blue eyes across from him. "I had no idea the subject of her sculpture was a real person. Ms. MacCrae doesn't do many likenesses anymore so I don't know what to tell you. I'd be annoyed too, if this happened to me," he added, and received a nod of agreement from Lorne. "But, I do know someone who may know, someone I'll be seeing tomorrow in London, after which, I may have some answers for you."

Bryan saw Cal was sincerely at as much a loss as he. His discomfort somewhat minimized his own and brought a twinkle to his eyes. "Then it appears we've both been duped, once again by the fairer sex." More seriously, he added, "Nevertheless, I would like to meet the artist. I'm sure you can appreciate why under the circumstances. Can you arrange it?" He hoped he didn't sound too eager.

Some instinct made Cal wary of giving too much information before speaking with Josie and Tannis. "Actually, she's on sabbatical right now," he said smoothly. "She won't be able to be reached for a while, but as I said, I'll see what I can do."

Bryan had no choice but to accept his statement, and decided to enjoy the meal. Perhaps through casual conversation he'd be able to glean more information about the artist herself. To get the ball rolling he discussed other art purchases, artists and trends. He was keenly aware Cal was being elusive whenever any reference was made to Ms. MacCrae, for he focused more on her skills than her as a person.

In spite of what had drawn them together, by the end of the meal the three men discovered they had interests and contacts in common. They also not only respected, but genuinely liked each other.

Bryan was nevertheless surprised to hear himself say, "You, your wife and her traveling companion will have to come to the Manor while you're here. Just let Lorne know at the office when, and I'll meet you there. He's been dying to take the yacht out for a sail but like me, needs an excuse." He liked the idea of spending a few days with these two and Seamus, providing he could talk Nell into entertaining Cal's wife and her friend while they went sailing.

He had gleaned no more on the identity of the artist, and at one point when he had compared her to another gray-haired eccentric artist, he received only a curt, "Silver, not gray," and confirmation that she was independent, copiously creative, single, and very private. In Bryan's mind, this only strengthened his earlier impression she was an older, feminist-type recluse whose art was her passion.

* * *

Tannis was far away. Her lips slightly parted as if in readiness for a kiss, she journeyed through dreams that recaptured her passion for the only man Taenacea had ever loved. Their 1:30 a.m. wake-up call shook her from these erotic dreams of Garth. Reluctant to waken she kept her eyes shut until she remembered why the alarm was set. Stonehenge. She jumped up quickly, washed her face and ran her fingers through her hair. Then she donned a long, woven skirt over her boots, topped it with a long knit sweater and her now favorite shawl purchased in Cardiff. It wasn't long before she was dragging a very sleepy Josie through the silent lobby.

They had prepared for this special day with a very light dinner. They also drank only lemon juice in water before retiring and on waking, knowing lemon increases the body's acidity which allows for more sensory receptiveness. But without their coffee, both offered Dennis only a hazy greeting as they piled into his vehicle. Josie crawled into the little car, a far cry from their comfortable Merc, and curled up in the back seat as best she could. Tannis, knees almost under her chin, watched the dim shapes slip past in anticipation of their destination. Already she felt flutters of excitement, although it could have been fear, for Dennis was as erratic a driver as Josie.

Many of the hundreds already gathered for the solstice eyed them curiously as the guard checked their papers and led them through the gift shop and onto the site itself. When they emerged, the mist swirled around them, adding mystery to the silent darkness of pre-dawn on the wind swept plain. Across the boundary ditch, the circle appeared much larger than expected. About a hundred feet in diameter, the so-called doorway stones loomed sixteen feet high. But it was the remains of the five doorways called trilithons, which had once made up the outer horseshoe, which rose to a height of thirty feet.

While Josie slowly walked the perimeter, Tannis approached the megalith called the Heel Stone. It stood outside the circle in perfect alignment with the center of the circle, and in the exact spot on the horizon where the sun would rise today on the morning of the summer solstice. She couldn't see the people through the mist which now ringed the great circle, as if to protect them from prying eyes. Then Tannis entered the circle and stood at its center, her eyes closed, waiting ...

She didn't have long to wait. The bottom of her feet began to tingle as a surge of energy rose upward through her body. At the same time she became aware of a strange clicking noise coming from the stones around her. Soft at first, the clicking sound grew stronger and louder. The clicking quickly changed to a whirring that spun first around her, then within her, until her feet felt only lightly connected to the ground within a vortex of sound.

Surrounded by a halation that caressed her with warmth, she felt the spinning and whirring increase its intensity and transform itself into a cylinder of light; light which lifted her off the ground in a motion so gentle, she was barely aware she was afloat.

Intuitively Tannis allowed the funnel to pull her through to its center; to the Plains of Silver. A knowing of all that was, is, and would be, shimmered through her mind like quicksilver. Yet she was aware of every detail of every aspect of every nuance she experienced. Embraced within the magical place where time intersected upon itself, she saw the unending patterns and possibilities of existence. Transported for a moment or an eternity, she felt a firm tug at the base of her spine. Then she was pulled through the funnel once again, and back into her body. The visions receded slowly as the whirring wound down to a clicking noise and as if cut off by some universal sword, all was still once again. Only the wind moaned as it swept the grasslands and caressed the stones as it traversed the stillness around her.

Disoriented for a moment, she opened her eyes and blinked. The fiery ball hovering over the horizon lent distinction to the silhouettes around her. She paused to the allow the experience to settle within her as she watched dawn break. She now knew with certainty that she, Tannis, and not Taenacea, had touched the inexplicable force known as earth energy, channeled through her by this ancient and powerful conduit.

Fully cognitive of her surroundings but still in awe of her extraordinary experience, she turned towards a stunned Josie. Stunned, because not only had she heard the clicking and whirring sound, but she had also seen Tannis lifted off the ground within a ring of light. And she had hovered there until the sun had fully cleared the horizon. Then she had watched her slowly drift back to the ground.

She looked deep into her friend's eyes amazed by what she saw there. It was as if another person was in there with her; a merging of two women; Tannis and Taenacea. Was her hair suddenly longer, or had she just not noticed its growth over the last few months? Were her eyes slightly larger and darker or was that an illusion of dawn? Whatever had happened, Tannis had definitely undergone a transformation.

This was also a personal moment to cherish, a moment for herself. She looked back towards the horizon as the red disc hovered directly over the Heel Stone for a time, then continued its ageless ascent. Under its fiery gaze, the mist evaporated and left a steely sky that transmuted the pre-dawn flinty blue stones to a lighter gray-green shade and disclosed wildflowers dancing in the grasses surrounding the site.

"This has been the most awesome, incredible experience I have ever had," she whispered.

"Ummm," was all that a distracted Tannis murmured as she began to walk reverently from stone to stone. Josie watched her place a hand on each one in turn and smile enigmatically as she did so, as if in response to what she felt.

Why, she's thanking them, she thought in surprise, and quickly followed suite. She immediately noticed certain spots on the stones felt different somehow; tingly and warm. She began to seek these spots out. In residual confirmation of their activity moments before, each stone held one warm spot her hand soon found as instinctively as Tannis' had.

Both were so engrossed in their benediction, Dennis' voice startled them. His "Well ladies, was it as mystical as desired?" signaled it was time to leave. He had watched from afar, and shot Tannis a bemused look. He could have sworn he saw her hover above the ground, but reluctantly credited the illusion to the shifting mist and his own wistful desire to witness something profound after so many years spent studying this site. The mist, a crafty illusionist, seemed to hug the inside of the circle, disappointing many of the visitors who had traveled from afar for the solstice. Closer than the viewers outside the barriers, he too could only faintly see the stones within the unexpected shroud. Shaking his head at how this circle could so easily bewitch you, he ushered them through the barrier, the gift shop, and back into the parking lot.

Once they had driven up from the parking lot and were again on ground level, they looked back at Stonehenge. They could see the circle clearly now, hardly believing what they had just experienced. Each were lost in their own thoughts. Dennis wondered if he had really seen what he thought he'd seen; Josie determined to keep a keen eye on the duality emerging in Tannis; and Tannis, impatient to see her lands and test her new ability to connect with the Plains of Silver. Because that is where she had gone, but in a more complete way than when she sought creative inspiration. And in that vast storehouse of timelessness, Taenacea's knowledge had imprinted itself on her consciousness.

Back at the hotel they ordered a hearty breakfast, and when it arrived, Josie discussed her individual experience at length. Tannis responded with only a few murmurs as she ate mechanically, barely tasting anything. Josie, bursting with the question foremost in her mind, finally blurted out, "I could have sworn you levitated back there. You hovered at least a foot off the ground from what I could see."

"Yes, and I did," stated Tannis calmly. "I was pulled through a primal energy vortex. The vibrational change caused the elevation. I can't explain why, but this had to happen before I go to Wales." Still distracted by the residue of her experience, she felt only partially present. She could see herself as she spoke and moved, as if an invisible voyeur of her own actions. Curious. Like deja vu, only the feeling impacted everything she said, or did.

"I think so too," confirmed Josie lamely, aware of the scant attention Tannis paid her. "However, before you float off completely, we have a date with Cal tonight. I want you present, for dinner at least." Interrupted from saying more by a knock at the door, she jumped up to answer it even though it was Tannis' door.

"*Babe!*" she shrieked when she saw who stood there. Her impatience forgotten, she flung herself into the arms of her husband and rained frantic kisses all over his beaming face. Cal scooped up his bride and twirled her around with unabashed glee. A cute expanse of bare bottom under her frothy short robe made a few enticing revolutions before he set her down and acknowledged Tannis.

"Hey, Tannis . . . you look great," he exclaimed over Josie's head as he took in her own scantily clad form. "Did I interrupt a lingerie party?"

"No, you nit. Hello to you too. We did the Stonehenge thing at dawn and are now just doing our nails and stuff for tonight. I hear a handsome swain is to escort us to dinner," Tannis responded with the same sense of deja vu. All this had already happened, and she was just repeating her lines. As they chatted she realized that even when she consciously changed what she thought she should say or do, it had already been said and done. Before long she saw Cal run his hand erotically over Josie's bare bottom in response to the rising sexual tension between them.

"My nails are dry so I'm going to take a nice long walk in Kensington Gardens. You kiddies will just have to amuse yourselves while I'm gone," she stated as she ushered them into the attached suite and shut the door. She dressed quickly, wanting to be gone before their passionate reunion. She left none to soon.

Their welcome complete, Cal and Josie relaxed as they sipped on the champagne Cal had ordered. Josie turned to him lazily and admonished, "We didn't use anything cowboy, and I feel kinda ripe just now. Do you have a problem with that?"

"No ma'am. Do you?" he responded laconically. He played with her braid and thought about his seed which may already have settled in her womb.

"Not me, as long as I can shop 'til I drop and wear everything at least once. I guess I can happily graduate to designer muu-muus once I'm as big as a barn," she replied cheekily. She rubbed her lower belly gently and crooned, "Swim little cowpoke, and make your pappy a happy man."

A little concerned by her air of certainty, Cal said, "If it, er doesn't take, it's ok by me. I don't want you to get your hopes up and then be disappointed. We were just kidding around, right?"

"Nope. It's happening, so I won't," she said with conviction. "A woman like me knows these things. Besides, the conjunctions are right, so your first born will be ..." she paused to do a quick mental calculation," ... an Aries. A fire sign possessing the qualities of a pioneer, the primary characteristics being leadership and courage. The Aries motto is 'I Am', just what we need to start this dynasty."

Cal shook his head, perplexed by all this Astrological stuff and pulled his little minx close. He cradled her gently before he broached the subject he wanted cleared up before Tannis got back. He straightened up a little and settled against the copious pillows Josie had added to the meager room quota. "A funny thing happened in Paris last night, babe."

"What?" mumbled Josie, half asleep and content to follow her baby dreams.

"I shook hands with, and then had dinner with Tannis' sculpture," Cal said, watching her face carefully.

Josie wrinkled her brow. "What sculpture?" She had no idea what he was talking about.

"The male from the trio she just finished."

"Oh. You mean he's mounted in some restaurant in Paris? Weird," she said, wondering where the other two were. "I thought they were all going to some tycoon's castle somewhere."

Slowly and deliberately, Cal said, "They were, and did. They went to an estate in Ireland, actually. But what I meant was, I shook hands with the man himself, the spitting image of the sculpture. And he was definitely not mounted in the restaurant. He was in fact seated across from me; a breathing, eating, drinking and talking real person. Now ... you wouldn't happen to know anything about that, would you?" he asked casually.

Her mind whirled and Josie breathed, as much to herself as in response, "You mean he's real?"

"Very much so. And very annoyed at how a complete stranger could not only sculpt his likeness without permission, but also duplicate his family's ancient crest. You know, the one held by the child. Any ideas how Tannis did this, or why?"

This was too delicious for words. Josie leapt up, straddled his waist, her face lit with excitement. As she hugged him she squealed, "She did it! Yee gads ... she really did it!"

Cal winced from the blast of her response in his ear. He placed his hands firmly on her shoulders and tried to contain her bouncing and squirming, which had begun to stimulate a certain part of his anatomy. Reluctantly he pushed those thoughts aside. "What did she do, other than piss off an important client, which in itself is a first."

"Tannis conjured up her man. She had to sculpt him first though. It was the Quest ... man, I can't believe Garth is real," she babbled. "Tell me, what's he like? Who is he? How did you meet?" She was so excited she had just blurted it out she realized too late. "Now I know why Taenacea's inside Tannis. She had to be here to make the connection. Wowzers!"

Cal, confused and irritated at her seeming uncaring for the gravity of the situation caught a momentary look of guilt on her face and asked, "Who are these people? What Quest? I think you'd better backtrack and tell me what the hell is going on here. Because, babe, you obviously know."

Josie cringed at her faux pas. She weighed her pledge of silence to Tannis, which had just been broken, against the enormity of this new development. Confident that once Tannis had her man all would be forgiven, she told Cal everything ... even her intent to write a book about her friend's experience.

Of all the possible explanations he could have imagined, this was certainly not one he could have anticipated. Slightly dazed by the matter-of-fact account of magic, past lives and time travel, yet intrigued by the story itself, he interrupted her several times to ask questions until he had the chain of events straight. After his momentary sense of loss, what surprised him most was to discover Tannis, whom he thought he knew well, had a hidden mystical and romantic side. That Josie was mystical and rather eccentric he knew and accepted, although he didn't understand it. He just delighted in her as a whole, in spite of her metaphysical attitudes which still baffled him.

But Tannis had always been open and straightforward, well grounded in reality, or so he had thought. With her, what you saw was what you got, or so he had believed. Until now. To find out she was a closet romantic was a surprise. Well, well. He chuckled, and remembered several furtive moments in the studio, including her complete unawareness when she had sculpted herself. It made a strange kind of sense in light of what he just heard.

"So she had no idea she was sending 'herself' and their child or the likeness of him to none other than a reincarnation of her ancient love, the man who commissioned the pieces," reiterated an amused Cal. Privately he wondered at the chances of such a coincidence happening without intervention from some invisible hand of destiny. Maybe there was something to all this past-life stuff. He still didn't believe it, but the way Josie had told it, it made you wonder if it was possible. Further speculation was interrupted by Josie.

"You mean that this Bryan was the one who commissioned the pieces?"

"Yes ma'am, through his partner Lorne. Our buyer is none other than the current Lord Lagohaire of Ireland, Bryan MacCumal, the reclusive genius behind the Emerall Corporation. A billionaire extraordinaire, somewhat of a mystery, but a very nice fellow. By the way, we're invited to visit his famed estate for a few days, you and I."

"Does he know she's here?" she asked, hardly believing this delicious opportunity.

"I told him you were traveling with a friend, a companion, but not who it was. She's invited too. But don't worry, I kept her identity a secret even though he pumped me about the artist who could duplicate him, sight unseen. He was really angry at first. He's a recluse you know. So much so he's had Lorne, his partner, front the company for him. He and Tannis certainly have something in common: an obsessive need for privacy."

Josie's mind reeled with connections as they clicked in place. Her eyes glazed as she furiously chewed on her lip, thoughts filled with possible scenarios for their meeting. It was time for both of them to emerge from their respective cocoons. Decision made, she said intently, "Babe, destiny calls. We have to get them together, but romantically, in keeping with the Quest. It's only fitting you and I, her best friends, are the ones to orchestrate it. I'm convinced our purpose is to reunite these soulmates. Do you realize they've been searching for each other for hundreds of years?"

Cal thought this a little dramatic, alarmed at Josie's intensity of purpose. These type of arranged events, blind dates if you will, never went well.

Josie scoured the possibilities, with an eye more to her role, and how it would read in her novel. "We have to have a plan. They can't know anything about this of course. And Tannis has to do her Welsh 'connecting with her roots' first. I sense that's important. Anyway, we don't have time to do anything before then, to do it properly, that is. But we can have some fun for now. We need something to entice them and lead up to the grand finale ... something romantic to peak their interest and get their juices flowing. Tell me everything you know about the man so we can figure how to use this invitation to the Manor to our advantage," she commanded imperiously.

Cal tried to dissuade her as she explored and rejected several scenarios. Then she exclaimed, "I've got it. Here's what we're going to do . . ." An alarming thought crossed her mind when she had laid out the plan, and she said, "Tannis is getting too knowing for her own good right now. She may pick up on something. We'll have to be really careful and throw her off the scent. She's getting so she can read me like a book. I'll use the baby thing if I have to, OK? Hopefully thought she'll stay as spaced out as she is right now and won't suspect a thing." Details settled and his last few objections brushed aside, she shifted gears.

Pointing at Cal's pelvic area she breathed huskily, "I understand you had a little problem here, a while back. I think I can help, dude."

When the adjoining door was opened to her knock, Tannis could see a flushed Cal and Josie had just finished their showers. Cal lounged on the bed in his robe and watched in fascination as Josie applied her make-up. After a cheery greeting and chuckling "you must have found something to do while I was out," Tannis shut the door again and began her own ablutions.

Feeling much better after a brisk walk and hot shower, she applied her own light make-up and dressed. Then she placed the headband firmly on her halo of curly hair. Standing back, she admired her reflection in the full length mirror, delighted by the silver glints that danced over her with every turn. When Josie knocked and tottered into the room on her new spikes, they stood in silent appraisal of each other.

You look absolutely magical," Josie pronounced, truly impressed by the vision standing before her.

Blushing a little, Tannis replied, "Thanks. At times the dress does make the person. And you definitely give Audrey Hepburn a run for her money," she added. Josie appeared surprisingly svelte and much taller than she was. Her signature braid was looped twice around and held above her ear by some invisible pins. She had removed her bell and the sparking earrings added a touch of whimsy to her sophisticated look.

"An exaggerated "whoo whoo' followed by a series of wolf whistles assured them of Cal's appreciation. He leered at them as he gallantly reached for their long black capes and draped them over his outstretched arm. "I am the luckiest man alive," he exclaimed, as he ushered them into the waiting limo. He cut an elegant figure in a burgundy silk jacket over a cream shirt tucked into crisp navy slacks.

Quaglinos, a favorite of the Royals, particularly Princess Margaret, was reputed to be one of the finest restaurants in London. The brass staircase with the letter 'Q' interspersed along its gleaming rails, led them down to the bar level. A gentleman in tails softly stroked the keys of a grand piano, adding a classic touch to the genteel opulence of the main dining area. Crystal, china and silverware sparkled on the red linen table-cloths, and blended with the art deco motif of creamy marble, etched mirrors, and hanging wrought-iron lamps; an atmosphere of refined elegance.

"How on earth did you manage reservations on such short notice, babe?" asked a very impressed Josie as her eyes darted around the room in search of royalty.

"I too can make magic, on occasion," Cal responded, warmed by the many glances discreetly directed towards them. He was a little nervous about the tricky events to play out later but Josie had assured him all would be well. She gave his arm a reassuring squeeze. It was as if she had read his uncertainty, which she had.

After their dinner orders were placed, Tannis twirled the stem of her champagne flute as she listened to Josie recount their tour, discuss Stout, and the upcoming trip through Wales.

"I don't want Stout winding through the whole of England to get us there," she interjected. "I want to go straight to Wales so I, rather, we have time to really see it," she added, all the while looking intently at the bubbles in her glass. For Cal's benefit, she hoped she'd camouflaged her intensity.

Cal and Josie exchanged a furtive look she didn't notice. "Can do," Josie agreed. "Remember that place I told you about, the Le Node project in Ireland? Since we're going to the Welsh coast anyhow, why not go north to Holyhead after and take the ferry across to Ireland? Le Node is just south of DunLagohaire where we dock on the other side. We can do a leisurely tour, and maybe Cal can get away long enough to meet us there for a day or so." Cal nodded his agreement.

"Ley Node? Oh yes, I remember. Why not? Maybe I can pick up some useful tips for my garden," she responded and missed the looks of relief that washed across the faces of her companions as she took another sip of champagne. Further conversation was interrupted by the arrival of their appetizers: pate fe grau, caviar, and a delicate endive salad with nuts and gorgonzola cheese, lightly topped with a creamy dressing.

After their plates were removed, Josie speculated on the identity of several possible semi-Royals. Tannis, disinterested, watched a cigarette lady's progress between the tables. This charming touch from another era, accompanied by the light classical melodies drifting through the air, held her attention until dinner arrived. She eyed her roast duck in anticipation and inhaled the spicy aroma of the seasoned sauce. Josie, who had ordered only a light meal of pan fried scallops with artichoke dressing, a delicacy of the house, just picked at her plate. It was delicious but her dress was snug and excitement at what was to come churned in her belly. Cal had no such reservations and dug into his crown roast of lamb with relish.

After dinner, coffee was accompanied with cordials: Absinthe for Josie, Amer Picon for Cal, and Tannis' favorite, Drambui. They sipped their beverages and enjoyed the ambiance while waiting for dessert: Passion Fruit Pavlova, another specialty of the house.

Their decadent dessert leisurely consumed, Cal announced he'd go fetch their capes and have the limo brought around. As he got up, so did Tannis, to look for the ladies' room. Both paused when Josie exclaimed, "Wait, you two. I'll go with you babe. I have to talk to you. You don't mind Tannis, do you?" she asked, adding with a flourish, "Just wait out front for us and pretend your magical coach is on the way to carry you off to Camelot."

Tannis was puzzled, but agreed. She wondered what was so important it couldn't wait until they got back to the hotel when both would be alone. After her lipstick was freshened, she paused at the bottom of the stairs to listen to a melody she particularly liked. Then she strolled up the stairs and out through the main doors, expecting to find the car waiting. Seeing neither the limo or her pals, she breathed in the warm evening air and scanned the street blindly, her thoughts on a more ancient piece of real estate.

As his limo slowly moved past on the other side of the street, Bryan saw her. He had driven around once already and on impulse had taken a second turn. The brief glimpse of her face framed within a halo of ebony curls and the secret smile on her lips immediately reminded him of the Enchantress. Like her, she also appeared golden and magical as evening lights winked over her undulating dress.

He felt his heart sink as a sleek limo pulled up in front of her and she vanished into its depths. Before he could properly register what he had just seen, the limo moved up the street away from him and turned the corner. It had all happened so fast, he wondered if he had really seen her at all.

But it was her—his Enchantress—and she was real. Of this he was certain. His heart pounded in his chest and his mind reeled at the sudden encounter. He knew there wasn't time to follow the limo which had whisked her away. But excitement rushed through his body and the words 'she's real' reverberated in his head.

Then reality set in and he groaned in despair. How would he find her? Suddenly London felt very large, and he very helpless; a feeling he hadn't experienced since boyhood on the estate. He didn't know which was worse, thinking her a dream and yearning for her to be real, or knowing she was real and having little hope of finding her in this massive city. Unless . . . someone knew who she was.

Cal. It was because of him he was here tonight. He had implied he might have some news and would meet him outside Quaglinos at a specific time. Bryan was to drive by and pick him up if he was there, or await his call tomorrow if not. Cal had not been there, but she had. It was the Enchantress who had stood outside the restaurant. Perhaps that was Cal's answer.

Bryan ordered the driver back to the hotel. He would call Cal to find out what he could of the artist and her mysterious model, obviously the woman he had just seen. It was a strange way of giving him a message, but effective. It had to be her. Satisfied with his deduction, he brushed aside his impatience to find out who she was and sat back to replayed his brief glimpse of the Enchantress in his mind, over and over again.

Tannis had slipped into the limo, unaware she was being observed from across the street. As she did, she reeled at a sudden quickening in her belly, her indicator something of note had just happened. Only this time a rush of heat flushed her skin and stayed with her as she settled back into the seat. She took several quick gulps of air to steady the woozy feeling which still persisted, surprised when Cal suggested they drive along the river, past the Tower of London. He knew they had already seen it. Before she could comment, she was enveloped by an unexpected sense of longing that reached out from the core of her being and drew her into a sea of sensation so poignant, she rode its waves to another place.

Chapter Nineteen

ER DREAMS THAT NIGHT gave no clue to her longings and when a flushed Josie chirped her a spry morning greeting, Tannis only mumbled a fuzzy "Ummm." She eyed the gurgling coffee maker and inhaled its enticing aroma as if willing it to evaporate her stupor. Stifling a yawn, she sat up and peered at Josie with bleary eyes. "Considering your rosy flush, I gather you thanked our host most vigorously for last night," she commented dryly.

"You bet. And sent him off with a big smile. So when's Stout whisking us off to your lands?" Sobered by the task ahead, again of what to pack and what the unusually grumpy Tannis would insist she leave behind, Josie made a face.

"Around lunch time. And remember, only one suitcase."

Josie stared at Tannis belligerently as she gulped down her first scalding cup of coffee and stated, "May I say you're nasty this morning."

"You may. Doesn't change a thing. Only one case," was the tart reply. Then she vanished into the bathroom.

Tannis' one and Josie's two cases plus an array of totes were placed into the trunk by Stout. He beamed with self-importance as he waited for them to settle in the back seat. Then he slipped behind the wheel of the Merc, ready to set off on his carefully planned tour. But it was not to be. Even before they cleared the center of London, a voice piped up from behind.

"Change of plans, Stout. We want to go straight to Wales. Just get us somewhere around the north end of Breacon Park by tonight," Josie instructed airily.

There was nothing for it but to comply. Being both pragmatic, and well-paid to ensure these two got what they wanted, he quickly scanned his options. The quickest and most direct route was on the M4, but they would see nothing along the way. He wanted them to see the best of what had been missed on their tour. He would take them past Alfred's Castle in Berkshire and South Cadbury Castle in Somerset, claimed by the locals as the real location of Camelot. They'd also pass near Arthur's Stone in Herford before they crossed into Wales around Hay on Wye and arrive at Builth Wells by dinner time.

The closer to Wales they got, the more excited Tannis became. Her eyes greedily embraced the summit of the pass at Hay where the great hills of the Black Mountains sloped into the valley of the Wye and lonely moorlands further west. As they wound through Builth Wells, Tannis felt a slight shift of consciousness, and perception. As they crested a particular ridge, she reached forward to grab Stout's arm and demanded he stop. She pulled a bemused Josie from the back seat and strode to the edge of the outcropping. She felt herself transported through time. After a moment of silent observation she waved her arms expansively across the vista.

"This is my home," she said with obvious pride. In a strong but slightly sing-song cadence she continued, "Wild and dramatic she shows many a face, my land. Rolling hills cradle jetting falls I've sat by, great fortress peaks accompany stark crags upon which I've embraced the winds, and silent indigo lakes my horse and I have drank from nestle amid warm green valleys I have ridden. How many times I trod this land I cannot say, but love it I do, and with all my heart." The last was said in almost a whisper, with a noticeable lilt to it.

Startled by the change in Tannis' demeanor, Josie recovered, and replied smoothly, "I can see that. Somehow it feels more mysterious than England; more like Scotland. Untamed and uncontrived." She crinkled her eyes and looked off to the left. "If I pretend there's no roads or cars, I can look down that valley and see it as Taenacea might have." For this was obviously how Tannis was seeing the vista.

"Ummm," came the dreamy response, for her mind was not here, but in the past. Suddenly struck with an incredibly wonderful idea, she spun towards Josie and with eyes a' gleam, said, "I know. Let's travel through here on horseback. I'm sure we can let some horses somewhere around here. The land is riddled with trails and it would be an adventure of the grandest kind. Are you with me?"

"You bet," Josie exclaimed, her eyes glinting now too, but more in speculation as to how her pal would manage on a horse since she had never ridden before. It should prove to be a humbling experience and she did not intend to miss such a delicious opportunity.

When they returned to Stout and told him of their plans, he paled at the thought of getting on one of those beasts. The Stouts of London had ridden little other than lorries or trams for generations, and even the beast's great size from a distance put him off. Unsettled by this turn of events, he responded with some reluctance, "There's stables at the Dalynwyd Farm, a few miles from Builth Wells. We can get the beasts there and leave in the morning. And where to, is it?"

Tannis waved her hand negligibly and replied vaguely, "Oh, westward. To the coast," which made him pale even more. He'd thought they intended a day's ride at most. Bit it would take several days to get to the coast on horseback if they planned to take their time and stop when the mood took them.

Josie's mind was absorbed by timing of a different nature. She calculated how long it would take to ride there, check out Taenacea's lands, visit Ley Node, and still make it to the Estate in time for the grand finale. Their plan, hers and Cal's was still intact, but didn't include Stout. Sweet man that he was, his presence would prevent them from freely discussing Taenacea's life, the whole point of the trip.

"I want you to take the car and meet us on the coast, Stout. Consider it paid time off. You can visit with people you know, like you said. We'll decide later where we'll meet," she stated, and caught Tannis' grateful look, who hadn't considered Stout at all.

Bugger! Stout knew that once again he would have no choice but to comply. With a mournful sigh he resigned himself to ensuring they be properly equipped for their impulsive journey. In Builth Wells he contacted the pony trekking center and booked two riding horses, along with one pack animal to carry their provisions. They would be equipped for up to four nights, depending on how much headway they made each day. They should do it in three days, but you never knew what would entice them along the way.

When they reached Dalynwyd Farms, Josie was first out of the car. Being the resident expert on horseflesh, she not only chose their steeds, but also had her private 'chat' with each of them. Some of the land appeared treacherous and she had no intention of having her plans thwarted by an accident.

Settled into their B&B, a delightful little Inn where Stout knew the cook, they were treated to an authentic country meal: Welsh Rarebit followed by whole creamed leeks and roast lamb and potatoes. And what lamb it was! As explained by Bronwyn, the hostess and cook, the exceptional taste was due to its unique preparation. First marinated in rosemary and oil, the lamb was then placed in a clay pot which was then placed in a bed of hay on a larger pan. The whole tray was covered by a lid so the hay inside wouldn't burn as it baked. It was the baking hay around the pot that gave the lamb its unique flavor and tenderness. Tannis ate with the relish of a farm hand and took time to write down the ingredients and directions before bed. She had every intention of claiming this dish as a specialty once she got back home.

Early next morning they drove back to the barn under a blanket of mist, both appreciative of the warm capes they wore. After their gear was secured by Stout, they prepared to mount. Josie had been waiting for this moment with delight, and watched Tannis intently. She thought their journey might take longer than even she had calculated, what with her novice riding companion and had pulled Stout aside to make contingency plans in case they ran into problems along the way. She should have known better.

Tannis stood for a moment and stared blankly at her ebony steed. Then she squared her shoulders as Taenacea habitually did, and smoothly sprang into the saddle in one fluid motion. She reached for the reins as easily as if she had done this a hundred times before. Which she had, only not in this lifetime.

"I didn't know you could ride," whispered Josie as she jostled her horse closer so Stout wouldn't hear.

"I can't ... I mean, I can. Oh, shut up! Any idiot can sit a horse," she snapped in Taenacea's impatient voice, implying she had no tolerance for foolishness and wanted to leave at once.

"Well wuppty-do, and pardon me, oh Lady of these here parts," retorted Josie, miffed that she had missed what was anticipated as a hilarious start to their adventure. Pushing her disappointment aside, she realized Tannis was completely unaware of the change in herself, and was immediately intrigued at the prospect of riding through Wales with Taenacea at her side. She suspected she would set as brutal a pace as when she had lived in the saddle, in the past. As much as Josie accepted the mystical Taenacea's appearance, at times she was still disarmed by how fluidly the change in her friend occurred. One moment it was Tannis, and the next it was the other one. Much like a split personality, she would give this aspect of her friend's unpredictable transformation special attention in the book.

They waved a hasty good bye to the forlorn Stout and as instructed by Taenacea, walked their horses through the valley to get a feel for the saddle and the rhythm of their mount's gait. Wrapped in their warm capes to protect them against the chill, they began their climb up the steep and narrow trail which hugged the ridges of the nearest mountain range. They trudged under the dense cloud cover, dulled by their forlorn surroundings. It was nearly noon before Josie halted by a gorge from which cascaded a rush of icy water. She slid from her horse with a groan, and after rubbing her butt gingerly, knelt down to drink. Then she rooted through her saddle bag for something to eat.

Tannis had also dismounted, but didn't drink, or eat. She paced back and forth restlessly as her eyes scanned the mountains on her left. "It's there . . . just over the ridge. The Wailing Valley. Come on. I have to see it now, before the mists rise. We can rest and eat later," she commanded as she sprung back into the saddle and grabbed the reins of the pack animal. Without a backward glance, she headed up the trail.

Well, the lady certainly had no problem giving orders, and expecting them obeyed, thought Josie. She scrambled to catch up, and when she did, hollered at her back. "Slave driver. I hope you settle down after we see the valley. Since this trip is supposed to be fun, I'd like to see a little of the happy, carefree side of you. Besides, my butt's blistered, and I'm starving," she moaned. Her mock outrage received no response. She knew what drove her pal to reconnect with this place, but nursed her discontent anyhow.

Some time later they crested the final hill where Tannis stopped. Both looked down at the place Tannis, or rather Taenacea identified as the Wailing Valley.

The steely gray blanket of mist created a forlorn stillness, wherein rose only the tops of the trees dotting the valley floor. Moving to its own sluggish dance, the undulating swirls offered only brief glimpses of what lay beneath as it appeared and vanished within the eerie and breathtaking landscape.

Tannis sat her horse rigidly and listened intently for the sound she almost dreaded hearing. Not even a faint whisper or lone bird call penetrated the utter silence. As memories of this place snaked into her consciousness, then rushed to engulf her in one swoop of sensation, a bank of mist lifted across the valley. She recognized it as the rise from which she had first seen the aftermath of the slaughter, as Taenacea. That meant that from this location, on the other side of the valley from which Taenacea had arrived, Giles and his men had spied on the Gathering. The icy fingers of panic snaked through her at the thought of standing on the very spot from which Giles had given his deadly orders.

Pulled into the past, she saw clustered troops of men lying in wait beneath the scanty cover of brush which rustled faintly in time to their furtive movements. She heard them speak softly amongst themselves, so their voices would not carry into the valley below even though their stealthy movements along the length of the ridge were hidden from view. That's how so many of her people could be killed at one time, that and the fact they would not suspect an ambush. Giles had about a hundred men scattered along this ridge, not enough to do much damage had her people been expecting an attack, or been armed for one.

She felt Taenacea settle into her body beside her. Tears slipped silently down her face as they both relived the events, but through strange eyes: the eyes of Giles Kaylon. Yes, it was a good plan, she thought, as he obviously had. They watched the swift and silent attack. If she had been inclined, she too would have done the same and seized such an opportunity. And were she embroiled in the politics of helping Richard claim the throne, she too might have wiped out this unsympathetic gathering of countrymen.

Like most powerful men from that era, Giles had been greedy, ready to seize every opportunity. She had been greedy too, she saw now, for the first time. Greedy to protect her holdings, and willing to slay anyone who threatened her lands. As her own battles flashed before her eyes, superimposed on the dismal backdrop below, she saw them from these same alien eyes. She watched battles fought only with her men, and others with Garth at her side. Shocked at how easily and viciously she had herself slain many of her countrymen, she felt a surge of justification that their deaths were essential to the protection of her people and lands. But an inner sickening, one she tried to push aside, demanded attention.

Tannis felt very odd, disjointed as her focus alternated between the three of them; Taenacea's view, Taenacea watching the events through the eyes of Giles, and then through her own, aware of each point of view as seen from her own era and perspective. The scenes and perceptions shifted and melded until she understood their purpose. Then she heard the chimes clearly, heralding the significance of the awareness that had taken place. Drained by the experience but mesmerized by the scenes which had played out in her mind's eye, she saw a change within the shifting shroud. She could see her people as she had in her first flash of vision at the professor's. She saw them alive and vital, then dead, then alive again; and was hit with an immense realization.

"Karmic lesson learned, Josie," she stated bleakly to her silent companion. It was definitely Tannis speaking now. "I just watched the entire slaughter from three points of view, out of three different eyes. Giles did what he needed to meet his ends, as did Taenacea. Both had blood on their hands, only the blood on her hands was justified in her own mind. Her guilt at being responsible for the slaughter and the constant denial of her own butchery, made her direct all her self-loathing towards Giles, who mirrored the worst in her back to her." Josie's compassionate look encouraged her to continue with her revelation.

"She could have prevented all this, you know. If she hadn't been so blinded by her hate for Giles, her own willfulness and need to absolve her guilt in the eyes of her people. She would have scrutinized the Writ. She'd have remembered there were two, realized something was wrong, and taken troops along with her to the Tower. If she had gone at all."

"Well my Lady of Lianarth, you have just had a tremendous halogen moment. And I'm immensely proud of your courage. I know how hard it must be for you to admit all this, and I applaud your willingness to embrace your own accountability and human frailty, even if it's Taenacea's. I would surmise your awareness has finally released Taenacea from the grip of her eternal torment," Josie said, and bowed in formal acquiescence.

As if in celestial agreement, the sun broke through the clouds and quickly burnt away the mists, finally revealing what lay beneath the valley's shroud. Both caught their breath in surprise. The valley was carpeted with tall swaying grass amid outcroppings of rocks scattered among a sea of wildflower in shades of purple, blue and yellow interspersed with white. Normally sheep kept the grass cropped close throughout Wales, but this valley, as if by divine decree, had stayed immune to normal practice. Thousands upon thousands of blooms swayed in friendly clusters, reminiscent of the clans that had once gathered here. Nature and time had transformed the slaughter of a thousand into a celebration of renewed life.

The mantle of tension and gloom that had shrouded Tannis since dawn also faded under the warm caress of the sun. Not that she would ever forget the horror, but her counterpart's guilt at not preventing the slaughter was gone and left her with a lighter though no less powerful demeanor. This emotional catalyst had truly brought Taenacea to life within herself. She knew she would relive the events again and again, but more objectively now.

They urged the horses down the slope, Josie as eager as she to enter the flowering valley. In the middle, in a moment of sheer celebration of her emotional release, Tannis impulsively danced her steed in a circle. He pranced with light hooves in time with her gleeful laughter as if the steps had been long-practiced. Her pent-up emotions spent, they climbed the hill on the other side. There Tannis pointed to a huge oak tree that rose like a monument to guard the valley below.

"That's where Garth sat me down and tried to comfort me. But I was a complete zombie, oblivious to everything around me, even his shock and misery. Gawd, I never gave him a thought, you know that?" She dismounted and looked down into the valley for a time and added with a chuckle, "I must say, I enjoy the view much more now than I did then."

A more carefree Taenacea was now in her element and took Josie on a tour of the world she had loved. As they wound their way through a green desert of gently rolling hills dotted with small isolated homesteads and grazing sheep, she pointed out several spots and shared cherished memories of Garth at each. There was the unexpected wild gorge where they had helped birth a wild mountain pony's foal, the open rolling hills where they had raced with the wind on her steeds, and between those ridges over there, the sudden hidden pocket of lush meadow where they had romped naked in the stream, later to warm themselves in passionate embrace on the virgin grass.

It was by this stream, now wider and more shallow than she remembered, that they finally stopped to rest and eat. Tannis looked around to orient herself through Taenacea's eyes, and smoothly moved into her consciousness to speak of the past. "The land was extremely fertile then, but only because of the people. Their loving hands and hard work made it so. Unlike England, there was no lording and bossing around here, and the land thrived as community spirit rooted and grew. There's a Welsh word, 'gwerin', which doesn't translate into English, but if it did, would loosely do so as 'common folk'. It's more a description of a spiritual essence. The Welsh meaning expresses the warmth, dignity and spirit of the people themselves. That's why it was so easy for me to work with them, and why, in spite of some resistance to my land management style, the land prospered."

"Sounds unique from a cultural point of view, although I suspect your magical interventions not only influenced but greatly enhanced the results," Josie commented dryly. She squinted again and imagined her surroundings as they might have looked then: lush with fodder, foodstuff, and the activities of content people.

The horses grazed nearby as they lay on their sides and idly munched on their lunch. Tannis had discovered that unlike most Welsh ponies, theirs did not head for home when uncobbled. Josie's 'chat' had temporarily altered even their instinctive behavior. Taenacea joined them again and shared other aspects of daily life in medieval Wales. Prompted by a sudden yen for more than the simple bread, cheese and fruit they were eating, Josie asked, "What did you eat back then?"

"Bread, cheese, butter, eggs, fish and meat; usually a lot of fresh roasted poultry or boiled meats smothered in spicy sauces."

"More details please," Josie demanded, salivating as Taenacea continued. It didn't strike her as weird that she was conversing with a woman over five hundred years old, albeit through her counterpart's voice and mix of both speech patterns.

"Lots of fresh bread. The course whole wheat Cocket loaf was the most common. We at Lianarth also ate Wastel, a light white bread usually reserved for the finer meals like celebrations or when entertaining guests. The broth I gave Garth when he was ill was of dried beans and bacon, onions, leeks and saffron for color."

"Saffron? I thought saffron was a middle eastern spice."

"Not at all. We used a lot of saffron, as well as nutmeg, ginger, and cloves, or galingale, which is like cloves, only with more healing properties. We liked our meat sauces spicy. Besides, at times the meat was spoiled, so the spicy sauces disguised the fact. I also used a great deal of anise and fennel for medicinal purposes, generally as a watered-down herb wine we drank in the morning. We drank ale too."

"What about milk or water?" Josie asked curiously. Tannis had always been a huge consumer of milk, buying it by the litre, and she drank water constantly.

"Not usually. We used milk and eggs liberally in our cooking, but only drank water from fresh mountain streams while traveling, at least I did. Well water could be contaminated and was used mainly for cooking and washing.

"Bingo! I now know why folks were considered fey and mystical in those days, and why there's so many legends filled with magical events. You guys always had a buzz-on!" Josie chortled. She could almost see everyone totter around half drunk.

"I think not. Keep in mind our bodies were used to a regular infusion of wine and ale, just like yours is used to coffee. Consider what a buzz strong coffee or a good cappaccino can give you. Yet, you drink it every day without being considered impaired," Tannis responded as she twitched her nose in disdain. They giggled as they threw despairing comments at each other while they packed up.

Lianarth lay on the other side of the ridges of the upper Teifi Valley which shimmered in the distance. As Tannis gazed at them, she had another inspiration, prompted by Josie's keen interest in her other life. Their chatter had also prompted a desire to recapture the magic of the past before they reached the coast. For here she had spent some of her happiest times. With eyes a' sparkle, she turned to Josie. "How would you like to spend the night under the stars in a very special meadow," she asked as she pointed to a ridge in the distance. "And ... then go on a magical journey?"

"Yes, and where to." Josie shot back.

"I know a perfect place to make camp. And then, dear friend, I will take you back in time."

"Can you really do that?" Josie asked, her heart beating in anticipation. "I thought you were done with magic. Never mind, forget I said that. What do I have to do? Holy Moley, what a rush as Linka would say," she exclaimed. She urged her horse to quicken his gait, as if she couldn't get there fast enough.

"To answer your questions; yes, this is an exception, forgotten, nothing, and I'm sure it will be, but now, would you please slow down. You're pushing me off the ledge. I'll just use a spell from the Magik Book to transport us there," she added casually, unconcerned at the prospect of using magic to propel them back in time, something she swore she would not do again when she had de-materialized the book. But it seemed important that Josie both experience and verify her past for herself.

It took longer than expected to reach their destination, a meadow nestled high above the hills and crags. Once there, Tannis headed for a clump of trees that made a perfect canopy for their pup tents. Enough scrub and dead branches lay around to feed a small crackling fire. She could hear the merry gurgle of a brook nearby which would provide them with fresh water to cook, drink, and wash.

The horses were unsaddled and given a quick rub-down, then shooed away to graze. There was no need to cobble them for Josie's 'chat' was remembered. Besides they had nowhere to go. They prepared and ate their simple meal in the crisp evening air and had everything cleaned up before the last rays of the sun dropped behind the horizon. Distracted by her anticipation of what was to come, Josie was more of a hindrance than help in the food preparation and clean-up. She was just as useless in erecting their tents. Tannis finally sent her to collect wood for their night fire, something she could handle without mishap, and hopefully without falling down a gorge.

There was no need for a relaxation cycle or any ritualistic preparation. They had been lulled into a semi-altered state of contentment by their surroundings. Lightly covered by their cloaks, they lay on their sleeping bags which they had laid out in the middle of the meadow. Soothed by the night, they welcomed the new stars that seemed to wink in anticipation of their intended journey. After inner preparation, and when she was ready, Tannis reached over and took Josie's hand. She crooned softly, "Now, just let yourself go. You'll feel some uncomfortable sensations, but if you don't resist them, they'll pass quickly. Ready?"

A confirming squeeze and nervous giggle was followed by a whispered, "Beam me up, Scotty," Josie was more jittery than she let on, but she forced herself to relax, taking long and deep breaths in readiness for she knew not what.

Tannis focused on her intent, and softly chanted the magic spell.

At first Josie felt nothing but the quiver of her own anticipation. Then a slow but steady rush of tickling warmth surged from Tannis' hand into her own. It moved up through her arm and dispersed throughout her body. A vibrating surge followed which raced through her until it settled in her solar plexus to trigger a succession of sensations that completely caught her off guard. After a sudden and sickening crunch she could feel and hear, she felt herself being ripped from the ground and flung upwards with dizzying speed. She spun through a swirling vortex of colors and blinding shards of light, all the while hearing a noise that sounded like the rush of an oncoming tornado. Then she spun down into total blackness and silence. Gawd! she must be dead for sure.

Completely disoriented, she lay very still and began to sense light around her. As it brightened and pressed against her eyelids, she felt compelled to open her eyes. Inwardly she braced herself for whatever she would see, aware she was experiencing some very real physical sensations.

Her first impressions were a crunching sound, waves of warmth on her face, and something pricking her back. She opened her eyes, shocked by what she saw. She was lying in a nest of hay beside a few placid ewes, one of which stared down at her with baleful eyes as it chewed on its fodder.

"Holy Shit!" she exclaimed as she scrambled to get up, startling the ewes around her. They shied away, but continued to watch her from a safe distance. She looked down at herself and noted she had a body, and was still wearing her own clothing: black tights, a fleecy sweatshirt, and thankfully, socks and runners. Was she actually in the past? If so, her clothes would give her alien presence away. Even the ewes seemed to look on them with disapproval. Her mind a' whirl, she heard a throaty laugh and stomach tightening with panic, watched Tannis stride towards her in clothing from another era. A second glance revealed it wasn't Tannis, but Taenacea; a woman a little shorter and fuller of figure, but with a face almost identical to her friend's.

My Gawd, it was really happening. She really was in the past! She opened her mouth to greet her, and gaped as Taenacea walked right past her as if she were invisible. Behind her trooped several cats and a puppy who tried to intimidate the composed felines with his high-pitched yips. They ignored him as they stalked behind their mistress, stiff-legged with disdain. However, they did pause briefly to look at her.

"Am I a ghost or what?" she exclaimed outloud and noted the troupe which had just past her, pause again at the sound of her voice. But Taenacea didn't. She pinched herself to see if she was real. "Ouch." She was real all right, only no one here could see her. Or could they? The ewes obviously had, since they had shied away. And the cats had too, or at least sensed her presence. She turned towards Taenacea's retreating back and yelled, "Hey, girlfriend, over here!" There was no response from the woman, but two of the cats stopped and looked back at her curiously again. Well. It seemed she was invisible to people, but not to animals.

With only a cursory glance about, she hurried after the retreating figure as it headed towards the massive walled Keep. She wondered if she was at Lianarth, or Aberayron. Since there was no distinctive sea tang to the air and the land was too lush for the coastal holding, she knew she must be at Lianarth, the seat of Taenacea's holdings. Her eyes darted left and right to absorb and memorize everything she saw. But she wished Tannis was here with her, or at least that Taenacea was aware of her. She wanted to share this strange experience with someone. But if this was her one and only chance to experience Taenacea's past first-hand, she intended to relish and remember every minute sensory detail of what her photographic memory recorded. That it was fully sensory hit her with a vengeance, for in spite of the idyllic scene, the stench of rotting earth and animal droppings filled her nostrils.

Taenacea had stopped to talk to a round, freckled-faced girl with burnished copper hair which hung down her back in one thick but messy braid. She immediately recognized her as one of the dancing girls Tannis had sculpted, the one she called Nellie. Her clothes were similar to those worn by the women moving to and fro inside of the Keep. They wore similar coarse tunics with surcoats over woven skirts in the raw colors of natural vegetable dyes in lovely muted blues, grainy yellows, and murky reds. Though coarse, their clothing was relatively clean excepting the hemlines.

Slit up the sides, the tunics reached either to the knee or hem of their skirts. Most were loosely bound at the waist or hip by braided cords or woven belts from which hung small pouches that bulged with hidden essentials. From beneath the wide, loose sleeves peeked the tighter sleeves of their blouses made of coarse linen or a finer lawn. In Taenacea's case, a delicate muslin encased her arms.

Fascinated by the clothes, Josie noted most of the women wore wimples or crisp linen head scarves pulled back behind their ears and tied to form a puffy cap which kept their hair out of their faces. Taenacea wore no such head covering. Her long hair was braided, and the thick plait looped several times and held by a leather thong at the nape of her neck. At her temples wisps of the distinctive silver wings had escaped her bound hair.

What truly amazed her was that she could understand everything being said, even though she knew they spoke the ancient Welsh tongue. She listened attentively as Taenacea spoke to several men about livestock and other farming tasks, then turned to instruct the women in the washing and dyeing of the shorn wool heaped in dirty piles beside the steaming caldrons. Nearby were rows of racks made from sticks crudely tied together with leather strips. A group of youngsters draped sodden bats of colored wool to dry on these, but not without playful swats at each other and sharp reprimands from the women stirring the caldrons.

Josie scrutinized Taenacea's face as she spoke to a woman at length and noticed the subtle differences between her and her friend. Taenacea had slightly larger and darker violet eyes and more angular cheekbones. There was a definite hook to the end of her slightly longer nose and her bottom lip was wider and fuller, and slightly cracked. Weathered by constant exposure to the elements, her skin was also darker and more leathery, and she was a good two inches shorter than Tannis. Nevertheless, she towered over the people around her. Fuller breasts and more cushioned hips expressed a lush femininity within a steely demeanor. In spite of these differences, the resemblance was uncanny. What set them apart was her manner.

The woman before her stood staunch, as if staring down an opponent, and walked with a confident briskness rather than her friend's catlike fluidity. There was a hard edge to her husky voice, a tone she'd heard Tannis use recently: the tone of a leader expecting instant obedience. Yet when she spoke with the women, children, and her animals, her tone softened somewhat, and a small dimple below the corner of her mouth danced with charming regularity.

It looked like Taenacea would be occupied with her instructions for a while, so Josie explored the Keep and studied the sturdy little people at their tasks. She was careful not to bump into anyone in case they could feel her ghostly presence. Rounding a corner when she first began to explore, she had bumped into a woman who started as if she had felt her presence. The woman had quickly crossed herself and mumbled a prayer before she hurried off, throwing frightened glances behind her. She wondered how many incidents of sensing ghosts or a presence of some kind were intuitive reactions to time travelers, as she was. After the encounter, she tried to stay well away from the center of activity, particularly after she had once again almost fallen over a small child, who after looking up at her had shrieked in fright, and was still being comforted by an older girl as she babbled about her strangely garbed apparition. What impacted her immediately was the weathered faces wreathed in smiles as they threw loving barbs at each other in the melodious lilting voices exclusive to their race.

Taenacea had now moved into a stone-walled kitchen garden filled with herbs and vegetables. Josie followed, and recognized some of the herbs. Others, like fennel, dittany, hyssop, borage and porray, she didn't but heard Taenacea point them out as she named them for her young helper, the copperhead Nellie. The rich scent, spiced with the bite of freshly turned soil and steaming manure, tickled her nose when young Nellie pulled greens from the ground, placed them into her basket, then carried them through a stone archway into the kitchen.

Curious, Josie followed her into a huge cavernous kitchen. It quickly became apparent why the mortar and pestle had been such a dominant item during medieval times. The sound of pounding dried spices was accompanied the general din as aproned women scurried about. She watched cook ladle large quantities of ground spices into several huge cauldrons bubbling on the hearth with a wooden spoon stained to an almost ebony sheen. Spicy and tangy aromas wafted from the steaming cauldrons, but she couldn't get close enough to see what was bubbling in their depths. She followed the sound of sporadic sizzling and hissing and watched the fat drip onto the fire from a dozen roasting chickens in a hearth at the other end of the kitchen. A young boy turned the spit upon which these chickens were skewered. Josie chuckled as he paused to nimbly pick at the crisping skin when cook's back was turned.

She could hardly wait. It was nearly supper time. During the meal she saw the results of cook's efforts quickly disappear as the household sat down at the long trestle tables set up throughout the Great Hall. Wooden platters of steaming food were passed down the table length from hand to hand, and the individual trenchers from which everyone ate were emptied and filled time and time again. There appeared to be more than enough food to satisfy their lusty appetites. Some pierced pieces of meat dripping with sauce from the serving dishes onto their trenchers, and others used chunks of bread to scoop up the spicy thick sauce directly from the serving dishes. Throughout the meal, everyone drank deeply from their ale gourds or wooden wine pestels.

Josie was captivated by the easy camaraderie and obvious enjoyment of the food they all helped produce. A quick head count indicated over fifty people were seated in the Great Hall, with at least a dozen in the kitchen: all eating and talking loudly. Several times young serving girls dashed into the kitchen with empty platters and staggered back with heaping new ones. The noise was deafening in spite of the lyric lilt of the conversation. The smells, heat, and noise nearly overwhelmed her. She leaned against the huge hearth at one end of the Hall and closed her eyes to still this sensory onslaught. But she opened them again quickly, afraid she might disappear or miss something.

Once the hall had been cleared and the trestle tables and benches leaned back against the walls, Josie followed Taenacea up the stone stairs. It was much colder up here away from the roaring fire below. She glanced back down at the hall where the hounds were rooting through the rushes on the stone floor for discarded bits of grizzle and bone. She trailed Taenacea through a cold hallway into what was her bedchamber where a fire had somewhat eased the ever-present chill emulating from tons of stone wall. She followed her to the archway of a small room off her chamber: a room filled with wooden boxes and hanging pouches of medicines and herbs. This must be her private healing and magik room, she thought. She looked on curiously as Taenacea sat down on a stool, placed a smooth linen cloth onto the bench before her, and reached for an ornate chest sitting to her right. She drew it closer, opened the jewel encrusted lid, pulled out the piece of parchment on top, and lay this single sheet on the table in front of her.

Then she lit the cluster of candles along the back of the bench. Soon their honeyed sweetness mingled with the tang of herbs hanging from two rows of wooden rafters above her head. Josie crept closer, surprised Taenacea could not sense her presence. Standing slightly to her right, she could see her face clearly. For a moment Taenacea sat unmoving, eyes dilated as if in trance. Then she reached for her quill, dipped it carefully into a jar of ink, and began to write in a neat tight hand.

Josie peered down at the parchment and watched her script several new lines below the previous entry with dawning amazement. She remembered reading this particular page dealing with joint ailments before. Only then the page had been bound within the covers of the Magik Book at Tannis' house, in another time. Now she stood in the past and watched as Taenacea wrote what she would read five hundred years later. At one point Taenacea got up, rummaged along a row of hanging pouches at her left, and pulled one down. She drew out a gnarled root and held it in her hand for a time, turned it over, and felt its weight. She got up and pulled a delicate scale from behind a cluster of small wooden boxes on a smaller bench along the far wall. With a small knife she pulled from the pouch hanging from her belt, she carefully cut off a sliver of the root. Then she weighed it, and thoughtfully added several more slivers to the wafer thin piece resting on the scale. She then tied the root back into its pouch, hung it up, and recorded her measurements on the page.

Josie was awestruck and wondered what she would do next. But she would never know. Suddenly the dizziness she had felt earlier washed over her again. Then she felt that sickening tug at her solar plexus. She only had time to utter *"Uh Oh,"* before she felt herself wrenched upwards so abruptly, a yelp of protest escaped her lips. Once again she felt herself rush through a vortex of wind and colored shards of light and sucked back into a black void. Spiraling downward at neck-breaking speed, she landed on her back with a sudden, sharp thud.

It had happened so fast, it took a while for her to recover and orient herself again. Although it felt like every bone in her body hurt, she felt no real pain. Gawd, she thought, Tannis must go through this every time she traveled to the past. She hadn't realized how hard it was on the system. Her head was still spinning as the hand she held slowly disengaged itself from her. Warily she opened her eyes and focused on her surroundings. Still dazed and disoriented, she looked up at an ebony sky filled with twinkling stars. Then she became aware of Tannis' heavy irregular breathing at her side. She turned her head towards her, concerned over her friend's labored breathing. Her "Are you OK?" came out in a hoarse croak, as if her voice had gone long unused. A nod confirmed Tannis was.

"Was I dreaming, or did that really happen? No it couldn't have. But what a dream it was." Right now she couldn't comprehend the possibility that she had really gone to the past. This was nothing like her own past-life regressions. Not knowing what to believe, she waited for Tannis to say something.

Tannis didn't respond, so she lay silent to let her experience settle in her mind. Finally, in a voice shaking with emotion, she said, "I will never forget this Tannis. Thank you, my dear friend." Suddenly her face crumbled, and she burst into tears. There was no other way to express how profound her experience had been.

Though pale from her efforts, but breathing evenly now, Tannis waited until the last tear was shed and wiped away. Then she reached towards Josie and plucked something from her hair. "If it was a dream, why would you have bits of straw in your hair?" The shadow of a dimple danced by the side of her mouth as she handed several pieces of straw to her startled friend.

Josie twirled them around with her fingers, then bit down on one to confirm it was real. She stared mutely back at Tannis. For the first time in their years of friendship, she was truly speechless, a condition that lasted a considerably long time.

A cryptic smile lit Tannis' face, and she chanted softly, "The poet Coleridge once wrote:

'*What if you slept?*
And what if, in your sleep
you dreamed?
And what if, in your dreams
you went to heaven,
and there plucked a strange and beautiful flower?
And what if
when you awoke,
you held the flower in your hand?
Ah,
What then?'"

* * *

Charles' punishment was worse than anything he could have imagined. Instead of booting him out, Marjorie had evenly informed him everything would remain the same, in spite of the wicked urges he'd succumbed to. That was it. She had placed his soggy dinner in front of him as always, and prattled on about the doings of their neighbor on their left and right, as always. This daily reminder of his transgression on the pained face of his disappointed wife was by far the most lethal punishment, and she knew it.

On Monday, distracted by his displeasure at the turn of events, he gathered together his previous file on the Lagohaires search and continued to plot their descendants from where the file had left off over twenty years ago. A gap in the lineage irked him. Still distracted, no matter how he approached it, he reached a dead end. He butted out his cigarette carelessly and amid the smoke still spiraling from it, carefully checked the old data again. Then he re-read the letter from Mrs. Wilde. She wanted him to go both back, and forward in time. He scanned the ancient O'Finn file again, dog-eared from countless searches for many other hopeful clients. Most common in county Cork in modern times, the name could be a branch of one of the old families, or an entirely independent family. He must determine which, or if there was a connection at all to the legendary hero Fionn mac Cumhaill. After several hours, he decided it was a dead-end like the other searches, and looked no further.

Ancient files had long been destroyed and any link to the third century AD Fionn, known as the Finn, were only legend now. The MacCumal line was suspect in spite of the fact an old line of the family originated in Ulster, rumored the real seat of the Fionn line. He then investigated the Collum family lines. The Mac prefix usually denoted the province of Ulster in the north, but he knew Cumal to be a derivative of one of the two primary Collum lines, one being the Cumhaill line.

Two weeks later he found the missing link to the MacCumal and Lagohaire line. The link had almost been obscured by either accidental or purposeful misspelling of a name on a fourteenth century marriage record in Wales. It would have gone undiscovered had he not been so enthralled with the emergence of a noticeable pattern. Nearly all recorded births were of male issue. The few female births recorded were followed by a record of their deaths within a year or two of their birth. He had also uncovered an unusual legal contract between these two families going back to the eleventh century, a contract, surprisingly still legally binding to this day.

His report on the MacCumals was as complete as records and his own inclination permitted. There was no definitive proof of a connection to the legendary Finn, but going back so far, there rarely was. Barons and Clan Leaders often took on the name of the landholder they conquered if it suited their ambitions, and nearly every family whose name remotely resembled legendary heroes, lay claim to their ancestry. He'd concentrated on the more current lineage of the Lagohaires and MacCumals as requested by Mrs. Wilde. Apparently her book would only elude to the earlier connection and focus on more current ancestry, where he had done a thorough job. He handed the file to the typist and instructed her to courier it to the attention of Mrs. Wilde at the London hotel.

* * *

Osmond Harcourt wished again he had not given in to his impulse. His older brother Gerald had not been pleased to see him on English soil, let alone at his doorstep in Birmingham. As always, they had little to say to each other after initial inquiries into their latest projects. Once again, Gerald had made him feel like he would never measure up, no matter what his academic achievements.

"You must consider your reputation, Osmond, as well as mine. Stop this questionable regression pursuit," Gerald admonished with a disdainful sniff of his sharp nose, a legacy of their equally sharp-natured mother. His own more bulbous protrusion and redundant stature had come from his more congenial father.

No matter what he said, Gerald would imply he was just off the mark. Like himself, Gerald was a bachelor, and like himself, a historian, but one with a long list of accolades, and the arrogance to remind him that he, Osmond, had none of significance. His inability to follow suite was more of a stain in his brother's mind than his own. It was why he had left Birmingham in the first place, to make his own mark as far away from his brother as possible. Stirred by his sibling's derogatory comments, he retorted, "My reputation is not in question, Gerald. Neither is yours. Including my past-life regression experiences in my book on the 'Witches of the Medieval Era' was as reputable as your last dissertation on the 'Rituals of Silent Monasteries', based almost exclusively on the visions of a fanatical friar."

He knew this last comment would sting, but felt a small satisfaction at pointing it out. "Besides, as a result of this regression, I have uncovered an item of proof never before imagined possible." He didn't know why he had added the latter, for Gerald was only momentarily impressed when he told him of the Magik Book.

"Nevertheless, reincarnation is not a reputable source. What does it prove? Mostly that your subconscious is actively creating these dream-like probable experiences. You'll be laughed at and so will I. I won't have it, Osmond," her stated emphatically.

"You're over-reacting. Within your circle of associates, perhaps. As I told you, I have assisted in several documented case studies, proven authentic. I don't intend to make myself the primary source of information, just to include my personal perspective as a possibility. I didn't believe in reincarnation either, but my own subjective experience proves otherwise. Of course I intend to follow proper procedure and authenticate all my data." He'd said the latter with the frustration of being treated like an idiot child.

While Gerald continued to rail at his unorthodox methods, he let his mind wander. He would go to Wales tomorrow instead of next week as originally planned. Gerald was sure to be as pleased to see the last of him as he was to leave. He had almost squashed his initial enthusiasm at discovering if anything of the Kaylon holdings remained. Were he to stay here longer, he was sure to give up on the idea entirely.

But once in Wales, his hopes of finding relics from the past were squashed as well. Not even a wall of his Keep remained. Since all signs of his existence in that life had been wiped away as if inconsequential, he decided to cut short his holiday and return home. He felt nothing for the land itself. Even standing on the site of his own Keep, he felt only a faint familiarity. He thought his past-life regression should have stimulated a more noticeable response. He drove past a valley of flowers which could well have been where the Gathering and subsequent slaughter had taken place. But nothing distinguished it from other valleys excepting the absence of sheep and much longer grass.

He hadn't know what to expect from this impulsive jaunt but felt it was less than he had hoped for. His spontaneous visit with his brother had also been a disaster, as had his visit two years earlier. The Welsh records, particularly the chapel records in the counties surrounding his ancient lands and hers had also not revealed anything of note other than to confirm Lord Kaylon's date of birth and death. He realized there was only one other place which might trigger a more vivid memory: the Tower of Aberayron. He would go to the coast in the morning.

Chapter Twenty

THEY AWOKE TO THE PROMISING CARESS of the sun's finger on their cheeks. The morning chill quickly dissipated as Mother Earth showed yet another of her many faces: a bright day dancing with the anticipation of seeing Taenacea's lands at their golden best. Tannis quickly prepared coffee while Josie, unusually alert after her night's travels, darted around and commented on everything with enthusiasm.

"I am infused with magic," she exclaimed, wincing only slightly at the aches from the previous day's ride. Tannis, the novice rider, seemed unaffected. But then, it had been Taenacea, accustomed to riding every day, who claimed possession of her body while in the saddle. Josie still couldn't figure out how *that* worked, how a body could be used by another without any residual effects, unlike when Taenacea had bitten her lip at the Tower and Tannis had sported the abrasion for several days.

After their coffee Tannis tied the packs back onto the horses and they ascended the last of the mountain ridges to view a very different terrain. At the crest, they looked across the vista of softly rounded hills that stretched all the way to the coast. Only the occasional small village and stone farmhouse dotted the grazing pastures amid these open heathlands. Civilization's encroachment was minimal and the timeless scene of cropping sheep was dated only by telephone and power lines.

Tannis reined in her horse as they rode by one of the small hamlets. She looked around intently then moved towards a slightly isolated farmhouse near the far end of the village. A diminutive man paused in his tasks and leaned on his pitchfork to watch their approach. Even close up he didn't get much bigger and remained a little gnome who hobbled towards them with a rolling gait. As Josie watched open-mouthed, Taenacea greeted him in the language of his ancestors. *"Bore Da."*

A near toothless smile of welcome spread across his craggy face as he responded in kind. *"Bore Da.* It's not usual for riders to speak the tongue of the land," he added in English.

344

"Unless they are of the land," Tannis responded. After an animated conversation about the changes in the area and what remained of the relics from the past, she asked, "Would there be anything of the old Keep hereabouts?"

He waved his arm in the general direction of the barn as he answered. Then he scuttled along the rocky road like a little crab and disappeared into the farmhouse.

Tannis turned to Josie. "There's breakfast for us after he sees to the horses. He's just letting his missus know. But first I want to feel the stones." She dismounted and strode towards the sturdy stone barn to their left. Amid the rooting pigs, enclosed sheep and squawking chickens, Tannis laid her hands on the thick stone walls. Then she moved to several low stone fences that enclosed the adjoining paddocks and did the same.

"Most of these are from the Keep at Lianarth. I can feel it. Elwyn, that's his name, said there used to be large medieval ruin here in his great-grandfather's time. It's where his ancestors hauled the stones from for these out-buildings. Nearly everything you see here was built from the stones of Lianarth's Keep," she said dreamily, satisfied some remnant of her home had survived, albeit as foundations for someone else's humble abode.

"Did he say anything about their history or about Taenacea?" Josie asked.

"No, but he said his missus was knowing of these things and will tell us while we have a meal. Friendly folk, eh?"

"Yeah. Especially when you speak their language," Josie pointed out dryly.

"Ah, wel … it's for the questing, as needed," Tannis quipped, her dimple dancing in confirmation of just who was answering.

At breakfast the beaming missus, Meinir, recounted the legend of their beloved local Sorceress, still much alive in the hearts of those hereabouts. Her legacy of mystery, benevolence, and what remained of the old beliefs was translated for Josie by Taenacea. Since most of the buildings for miles around were constructed from the stones of Lianarth, her memory was scattered around the site of the old Keep where the barn now stood.

After their simple but hearty meal and warm farewells punctuated with thanks to Meinir for the bundle of fresh bread and other foodstuffs she had pressed on them, a pensive Tannis rode in silence for some time. "I'm surprised I don't feel as impacted here as I thought I would. There's more of a feeling of familiarity with the land than any deep resonance with the stones themselves. Interesting," she added.

"Maybe the clue to your disappointment is emotional energy. Since more of your emotional energy was tied to Aberayron, maybe you'll feel more connected there. After all, it had a greater affect on your life and the strands appear to be based on emotions," Josie suggested.

"Ummm, could be. I just had a thought along those lines. Maybe ruins that survive are intended as a monument to both the life energy experienced there, and the earth's energy grids on which they rest. It's possible the intensity of emotion experienced on a given site is what preserves the ruin itself." She squinted against the sun as she peered to her left, and exclaimed, "Over there. Come. I have a treat for you."

Still feeling the effects of her last treat, Josie eagerly followed as Tannis led the way to a large forested area in the distance. When they reached the edge of the weald, she tied her horse to some scrub and tracked Tannis into its depth. She worked her way carefully through the prickly brush under the trees and almost ran into Tannis, who had stopped at the edge of a small clearing.

"The Faery Ring," they exclaimed in unison. Josie had all but forgotten about this spot. The soft mossy grass beneath their feet was in stark contrast to the brittle gorse surrounding it. Hushed by the magic of this ancient site which had particular significance for Taenacea, she tried to envision what had transpired here.

It was so hushed in the clearing she could have been standing in a chapel, an impression reinforced by the leafy interlocking branches of the oaks which formed a canopy over the sacred site. Extending her aura and consciousness, she heard faint murmurs between the silence, murmurs which spoke of secret rituals. She watched Tannis walk to the center of the circle and in silent homage, raise her arms and turn first north, east, south, and finally west.

Tannis stood transfixed as her mind flooded with memories of the moonlit birth of little Faye, her own mystical awakening, and the many other nights when she had slipped from the Keep for private rites. It was here she had first introduced her daughter to the Mother, and shared silent knowings with her child. And under her watchful gaze, Faye had played at making Magik: changing the colors of flowers at will, playing peek-a-boo with shy wood spirits, and hovering above the ground with darting Faeries that encouraged her floatation with frenzied delight.

Here she felt deeply connected. Trance-like, she whispered, "It was much larger then. But even after all this time and the encroachment of the brush, I feel its power. Though held in abeyance now, it awaits the awakening of another. For there will be another, in time."

Josie was stirred by her friend's words. "In daylight it's hard to imagine that all those profound things happened here. Yet ... I do feel an aura of waiting," she said as her hand strayed to her lower belly.

"It's only when we're connected to the Mother, and know so and honor her, that we have this invisible world and all the power coiled therein available to us. Then all is possible. It was always there, was meant to be used, and always will be." Taenacea mumbled something in Welsh, then continued in English.

"Absorbed by the drama of our lives, most of us search for celestial guidance from a god that seems separate and distant from us. We don't see the Mother's face in what lies around us, or feel our connection to her life-giving and sustaining energy. She asks for nothing but faith, and acceptance of our natural heritage."

Tannis settled back into her body as small birds began to rustle and twitter in the branches overhead, then glide downward and swoop past their heads before bursting into song on the overhead branches. The sun was directly overhead now and beamed shafts of warmth through the swaying canopy as it dappled their bare arms with the ever-changing design of fluttering lace. Bees buzzed past their faces, followed by a host of other insects which whizzed by in erratic dance. The ancient haven seemed suddenly to crackle with life. They stood mesmerized by the Mother's vibrant display. When the activity wound down, they left the forest and its secrets behind.

Josie was entranced by the spontaneous experiences Taenacea had triggered within herself and wondered if she would feel something at Aberayron since her own sensitivity had become more acute on this journey into Taenacea's past. She had never felt so in tune with, or aware of the slightest nuances of her surroundings. Riding in a north westerly direction, they tasted the faint tang of the sea long before they reached the rugged coast and its small inlet coves. As they rode along the plateau of the cliff towards one of these coves, they caught glimpses of the pristine seaside town that lay to the north.

Tannis stopped near the south end of just such a sheltered cove beyond whose northern cliff lay the wide bay of the town they had just glimpsed.

The windswept mesa on which they dismounted was strewn with ragged rocks. Coarse grass and thistles sprouted amid them, pressed almost flat by the constantly gusting winds on this, the high point along the coastal cliffs.

About forty feet from the edge of the cliff loomed a dark shape surrounded by piles of lichen covered boulders. Banked by a grouping of trees and gnarled gorse on the inland side, they could not see the ruin itself clearly. Propelled by a sudden tension that quickened her stride, Tannis, her heart pounding in time with each step, skirted the trees and stopped in astonishment at the little left of the Tower of Aberayron.

At its highest point it stood only six feet tall: a thick curve of ancient stone. At its base amid the tall grass and weeds emerged the remains of three stairs, with only the bottom step intact in its full width. The others had crumbled to half their original size. Her face waxen as she looked at the stairwell that led nowhere, Tannis ran her shaky hands over the stones. What she felt made her crumble to the ground beside them.

Josie watched her dazed approach to the innocent looking rubble. This was a very private moment and she could just imagine the memories that must be surging through Taenacea. She also wondered what cataclysmic event could reduce an eighty foot tower to a six foot memento of secret treachery and death. She didn't realize Taenacea had moved until she had almost reached the cliff's edge. She stood there frozen, her gaze fixed to the sea as it had been so many times before.

Taenacea gazed out to sea and waited. Almost reluctantly she peered over the edge expecting to see a churning flux below. In her mind she saw the bodies of Faye, Garth, and then herself, sucked into the maelstrom by the undertow's greedy clutch. She scanned the sandy shore of the little cove. Pebbled with smooth stones under the undulating waves lapping its edge, it looked harmless, now. She turned quickly and strode back to Josie in brooding silence.

"I'm waiting, always waiting. It was here I came, following my inner urgings, and here I trod the stairwell to my death on that fateful night," she said. A shudder rippled over her body. Then her face cleared and another voice added, "Let's see if there's anything left of the Keep at Aberayron."

The transition between Taenacea and Tannis was so fluid now, it was almost unnoticeable unless you knew what to look for. Josie did. She was fascinated by the swift succession of expressions which chased each other across her friend's face, but said nothing as she silently followed Tannis. All they saw was the fringe of the town sloping into green pastured fields with an air of restrained good manners. Dotted with neat homes and gardens, the valley, ringed by its protective ridges, reflected nature's surrender to man-made order.

Tannis recognized the familiar ridges. Oddly enough, she had expected to see remnants of the newer Keep on the edge of this slope. Instead it was the old Tower, the site of her traumatic demise that had survived. Her earlier speculations confirmed, and feeling more rooted in the present, she said, "It *is* the emotional intensity of a place that makes it durable. I suspect this Tower ruin will still stand in another hundred years."

"Perhaps. How does it feel now that you've come full circle?"

Tannis shrugged. "Strange. It's almost a let-down. It'll take a while to digest everything. I still see flashes of what was and what is, depending on who's looking out of my eyes; me or her. Sometimes it's both, which doesn't feel as strange as it first did."

"Yep. I kinda noticed your shifty personality on this here trek," Josie sassed back. Tannis responded with a chagrined smile but deftly changed the subject.

"Have you noticed how isolated and intact this site is, in spite of the town right down there? Almost as if an invisible force prevents the town from encroaching onto this spot. What really changes the flavor is all the trees here now. It looks so neat and elegant; not at all like I remember it."

"Welcome to the 20th century. Not that I mind Taenacea, but it's nice to have you back, more or less," Josie said dryly. She suspected the shifting wasn't entirely over yet.

Tannis ignored her insinuation. "She's more settled in me now that the Quest is almost over. I thought I would find the last strand, the 'Firmness of Rock' here, but I haven't heard the chimes, and nothing out of the ordinary has happened, yet."

Josie was certain the last strand would come with the reunion of Garth and Taenacea, rather Tannis and Bryan representing the intent and conclusion of the Quest. But in breezy innocence all she said was, "Oh, not to worry. I'm sure it'll come when your soulmate claims you as his own. Have faith. The journey's not over yet." She hoped she hadn't sounded too certain, relieved by her friend's frustrated response.

"Yeah right. When I'm old and gray, sitting on some rickety porch swing, a little old man will hobble up to me and identify himself as my ancient lover. We'll gum kiss passionately between cat naps, and probably die of a stroke from the thrill of it all. Then we'll be buried side by side holding each other's gnarled hands, reunited at last." The visual made even Tannis laugh. "Come on, let's go check out the town."

They ran their fingers through their wind-tossed hair. They would leave the horses here on the buff while they walked down to the town. Neither heard the approach of another person on the desolate bluff. Tannis, still laughing at her ridiculous visual, felt a sudden wash of coldness up her back and spun around quickly. She froze. Memories thought forgotten replayed the horror of her death. For before her stood her nemesis, none other than Giles Kaylon. Her heart pounded her dismay and disbelief, and she heard a ringing in her ears that had little to do with the soft tinkle of chimes.

"What are you doing here," she hissed in indignation at the unwelcome trespasser on *her* lands.

Josie froze and looked from one to the other. This would be it, their confrontation. She almost laughed at the rumpled discomfort of the professor. But she knew this to be an opportunity for resolution and kept silent. His wisps of hair blew in the wind and the knot of his tie had been loosened. Still puffing with exertion from his climb he stood panting, a look of shock and confusion on his face. He too had not expected to meet with her here on the wild coast of Wales. Destiny had forced Tannis' hand and drawn him to this place.

"Oh. Uhm, visiting my brother in England, and ... checking some local archives, to do with my work," he lied hastily. The proprietor of the B&B where he had spent the night had directed him up the narrow trail leading to the outcropping where an insignificant ruin was said to have sat since ancient times. She didn't know much of it's history she had said, only that the stones were very old, a relic of what must have been a tower overlooking the sea. A relic, she added, people shied away from for some reason. Oddly enough, as he had struggled up the buff, he had felt his first faint stirring of familiarity, quickly followed by a cold knot in his stomach. He had been here before, and knew it. The cold knot in his stomach persisted. The memory of his deed on this site washed over him, a memory obviously shared by the woman who faced him now: a woman whose own memories were fraught with emotion, the greatest of which being hatred towards him. Not knowing what to say or do, he remained mute, expecting an outburst even more disturbing than what he had experienced when he had visited her home.

But his heels ground into the caked ground in readiness for battle, a battle remembered from another time.

After a long silence she said, "I know what you did here. And how it was done." Her statement held none of the venom he expected, only a flatness. He could not tell if it was from a sense of defeat, or acceptance.

They looked into each other's eyes and remembered. The professor and Tannis looked on curiously, suspended in the consciousness of the two adversaries as Taenacea and Giles relived their past. Then, to his surprise, she grinned and said, "We battled well, did we not?"

Her comment was so unexpected he didn't know what to say. He cleared his throat and nodded, still dazed at not being struck down in some cataclysmic manner. She still looked to him like the demon Taenacea he had briefly encountered at her house.

"It seems silly now, all this fighting over small strips of bordering lands, rich as they were. Although, if memory serves me correct, you had your eye on the whole thing not just the borders, did you not?" The latter was said conversationally, but pointedly.

"Yes." There was little else to say, and she had struck the truth of the matter. Surprised by her almost playful discourse, he hoped this encounter would put an end to their animosity. Emotional intensity was most difficult for him. He had liked her on first meeting her, and still did, excepting their brief conflict and his own surge of past-memory resentment. Nevertheless, he readied himself to defend his desire to use her magic book as a resource and mentally formulated how to ask without further enraging her. Calm as she appeared, he suspected her anger could quickly resurface. Before he had a chance to say anything, she did.

"Though you may have defeated me through my death, you do not defeat me in life. Taenacea lives on through me, and so does the book—but not in this reality. In the safety of another realm."

She felt strange. Resolution and understanding had come so simply and swiftly, it felt anticlimactic somehow. When she'd first been engulfed by the memory of her demise at his hands, she thought she would rant and rail at him all over again. But as if from a great distance, she saw herself in a paradoxical light. For as important as the events of that time and what had taken place on this site were, they were also inconsequential. She had not known what she would say, and had surprised herself at the ease with which peace had been made with the past. For as spoken in her words, Taenacea would live on, through her link with her present-day counterpart. Therein rested the continuance of the past. The enduring essence of herself far outweighed the trauma of one demise in a continuum of births and deaths within the timelines of physical experience.

In light of this awareness, the professor changed before her eyes. No longer did Giles Kaylon stand before her, rather a perplexed and very rumpled little man who again appeared sweet and completely befuddled over what had just occurred. He also looked quite terrified of her.

Josie cleared the awkward but no longer volatile aura around the two. "We were just heading down to town. Care to join us?"

Startled by the unexpected invitation, Osmond glanced at Tannis quickly to assure himself of her agreement. She shrugged her shoulders and led the way, but said nothing to him directly. As he scrabbled behind the two, he felt somewhat relieved.

Stubborn to the end, Tannis knew she had cleared something between them. Whether it was from relief or just to establish a more companionable relationship she did direct a few comments his way, but about everything but the past. The professor gave them a brief history of the charming Regency style town. Sailboats bobbed in the cove ringed with tall square buildings tightly sandwiched along the bay. Tall Georgian houses could be glimpsed as well along the slopes that led to a fairly heavily wooded, yet discreetly inhabited Cliff-top at the other end of the bay.

When they left the professor at his B&B, Josie assured him they would call him once they were back home. Although he would never see the Magik Book again, Tannis indicated she would be willing to provide limited information from memory. It was much less than he hoped for, but more than he had a right to expect. As he watched them depart he had a sinking feeling he would never see this woman again. He almost expected her to dissolve into a mythical past, just as her counterpart had. He shook off this strange premonition and waved the pair good-bye.

When they reached their horses, they mounted and ambled south towards New Quay. Stout had instructed them to leave their horses at the stables near the edge of the old-fashioned town. From there they were to call the number he'd left with Josie and wait for him to pick them up. Having done so, they milled around the stables until the silver Merc arrived.

Elated by their arrival a full day earlier than expected, Stout beamed his welcome. "Alo' luvs! You both look smashing. How was the ride?" he asked, relieved his charges would once again be safely tucked under his protective wing.

"Just Awesome," chirped Josie as she slid from the fence where she had perched. She had several stableboys enthralled with the telling of her experiences with beasts of burden in other parts of the world. As she slid off the fence she had caught a whiff of her armpits. "What I need in the worst way is a bath and a real meal, in that order. Lead on Stoutheart! Over dinner and drinks I'll spin you tales of mysterious Wales as seen through my unique eyes."

Stout loaded their gear into the trunk knowing Josie would take the mickey out of him again, and relishing it. In the Merc, aware of the strong scent of horse sweat clinging to their clothing, they made disgusting faces and choking noises as they joked about their body odor. Stout rolled down the windows and chuckled at their spirited horseplay as seen through the rear view mirror, especially when they waved their arms wildly in efforts to disperse the stench. But all they succeeded in doing was wafting more of it his way.

Refreshed after a bath and change of clothes in the rooms provided by Stout's cousin Ellie, they clattered down the narrow stairs to meet him in the pub. Over drinks, Josie teased him mercilessly with hints of mysterious events peppered through hilarious descriptions of their trek.

"Wales will do that to you, luvs," Stout said emphatically. "It's the darkness and secrets kept under mists that have you thinking of ancient times," he added sagely. He wondered what the furtive looks and giggles were about but knew better than to ask.

"True. I swear, Stout, there was a time I thought I was right back in the 15th century," Josie intoned. She winced when Tannis kicked her under the table and shot her a 'be careful' look.

After dinner Stout led them through the town to nearby Craig-yr-Adar, or 'Bird's Rock' as it was called. Several hours later, both gals finally fell victim to fatigue and surrendered their aching bodies to their narrow but inviting little beds.

Surprisingly refreshed, they were raring to go the next morning. Their drive wound through the seafront of Aberystwyth where Josie, always drawn to water, insisted on a stroll along the shallow rocky beach. Turning north they traversed the B roads through the wilder country of Anglesey. Often called 'Mon, Mam Cymru', Stout informed them the name meant the

Mother of Wales. They looked back at the famous hundred foot high cliffs of Holyhead Island, known for its fertile corn fields and free ranging black cattle as Stout continued to expound on the history of the area.

It was from the Court at Aberffraw on Anglesey that the Princes of Gwynedd maintained the independence of Wales during the 13th century. The history of this land may have changed drastically had they been left to develop on their own, instead of being squashed by the English.

Stout's recount of stories from that era was interrupted by Tannis' tart, "History is known more for the changing than the keeping of what is good," but his good-natured shrug indicated he did not take his ancestors' failings personally.

They had boarded the car ferry that would take them the 53 miles across the Irish Sea to Dun Lagohair. Still called Dun Lagohair by the locals but now known as Dunleary, the port was situated at the southern tip of Dublin Bay. Tannis knew it was most likely from this ancient port that Garth had set sail in another time. Disembarking on the Emerald Isle, they drove by Ireland's principal yachting center which held no interest for them, and past the hills reputed to be the boyhood home of George Bernard Shaw, which did. Then it was on to Dalkey where they would spend their first night on the soil from which the Quest had sprung.

* * *

Bryan MacCumal tossed and turned in his sleep. His dreams were filled with disjointed scenes of fighting and loving, both with his Enchantress. In the sequence of images which blended into each other, they were always together: loving, battling, or laughing while attending to the needs of the land. First his arms would tenderly hold a small babe, then swing a heavy sword, then strain with the tension of reining in his powerful ebony steed, only to soften again as he gently caressed his Enchantress. He could not get enough of the touch of her.

The satisfying visuals then turned melancholic. Mournful wailing trailed from a misty valley of death through which floated a figure in muted gold: a vision of doleful loveliness but immense sorrow, wandering aimlessly amid a carnage of bloodied bodies. Then screeching winds encumbered his own ascent up the winding steps of a tower, as blazing darts of lightening shook the stones beneath his feet and thunder boomed in celestial rage around him as he felt an immense pain in his back.

Amid a replay of similar flashes appeared the face of his father and mother, superimposed on that of his Enchantress and himself. A sickening replay of disjointed events he still remembered raced over the backdrop of his earlier visions. He heard a great roaring in his ears as the scenes vanished into blackness.

He awoke with a heart-thudding start. Disoriented, he didn't know where he was. It was three a.m. and he was in a hotel room somewhere in London. Confused by the fading images, he somehow knew they were related, and that he should know why. He sensed there was something he should remember. Then the feeling was gone. Suddenly he was sick of the succession of hotel rooms and suites which had been his nightly home these past twenty years. There had been so many, he hardly cared where he was anymore. He longed for the stability and comfort of familiar surroundings. He longed for his home.

He thought about his dream again. He almost felt like they were about a past that should be familiar, much like an ancestral memory. He wished he could return to a time when the Enchantress could have been part of his life. Fueled by longing, he forced himself back to sleep. But sleep and the past eluded him. Instead his mind just replayed the disjointed scenes from his dream. Could he now be so obsessed that he had created a dream past just to be with her? And how did the images of his mother and father fit into these dreams? What they brought to mind had been safely locked away into the deep recesses of his mind.

Attempts to contact Cal had been unsuccessful until yesterday. The result of that call was less than satisfying as well. Cal had accepted his offer of a visit to the Manor this coming weekend, confirmed his wife's friend would accompany them, and assured him he'd solve the puzzle then. His delivery had been hurried, and he had rung off so quickly there had been no time for Bryan to ask about the artist or to bring up the matter of the model he'd seen outside Quaglinos.

Frustrated, he thought some time at the Manor before his guests arrived would give him a chance to clear his head. Walking the land, and Seamus' calming presence always had a settling effect on him. After these stirring dreams and their residual longing, he needed to get his head together or he'd be greeting his guests like some demented Lord of the Manor whose eyes burned with inner madness. He chuckled bitterly as he lay down again. Surprisingly, he quickly fell into a deep dreamless sleep. At least his restless spirit had allowed him this small respite.

* * *

Fortified with a traditional breakfast of rashers and eggs, freshly baked wheaten bread and a few slices of fried soda bread which made their arteries tighten in protest, the gals picked their way through Dalkey for an Irish ABC day. The mansions and church ruins they saw were remnants of a time when the town had been the principal landing place for English visitors, thus held a mix of English and Irish remains.

Tannis commented on how much 'lighter' Ireland felt than Wales. "Though as steeped in history, this landscape lacks the brooding depth of Wales. Its Celtic annals are open to the skies, rather than obscured within dark gorges and mysterious valleys, hidden from a scrutiny they didn't care to share. Even the mists here lack the brooding quality of Wales." Having said that, she took inner satisfaction in the mysticism of her beloved Wales. It would always be a special place to her.

The landscape around them was strewn with broken Abbeys, churches, and distinctively Irish Celtic Crosses and round towers as they headed into county Kildare. Scattered amid hills and plains, rivers and coast, by lakeside and in towns and villages, their ruinous splendor was a continual reminder of the island's devout heritage. In this, the flattest part of Ireland made famous by the grassy Curragh, and boasting the largest part of the Bog of Allen, they drove along its eastern border fringed by the foothills of the Wicklow Mountains. Turning south to Athy, the road skirted the borders of Kildare, Laoighis, and Kilkenny.

The village of Ley Node was nestled at the southern edge of an estate surrounded by pastured hills ringed by wooded parklands. The Estate itself was a distance away, sequestered at the center of its own large acreage. Into its fourth year of operation, Josie informed them, the village was originally built to house only the Foundation members in thatched cottages that cost a fortune to build and fit with modern amenities. Since, Ley Node had grown into a prosperous tourist attraction. With self-sufficient cafes, pubs, and gift shops, it also boasted several quaint B&B's booked year-round.

Now at the end of June, the little gardens surrounding the cottages blazed with riotous color. Roses, the predominant flora, flaunted extremely large blooms in shades that ranged from the most delicate pastel to the deepest crimson. Alongside the brightly painted shop doorways sat benches and large pots which spilled their flora onto the flagged sidewalk, and wafted their sweetness over foot-sore visitors. For the more aged locals, the rustic benches provided a perch from which to comment on the oddities of the steady stream of foreigners.

Shops on both sides of the street housed craftspeople who not only sold, but actually produced their wares on site, often right under the eyes of the prospective customer. You could watch dyers and weavers, silversmiths and other artisans busy at work, yet willing to smile a greeting or answer a question in their lyric voices. They planned to visit the shops tomorrow. First they would drop their luggage off at their B&B, then check out the agricultural center that lay a little west of the village. They could see the open produce market down the lane was already swarming with customers. They hadn't anticipated that getting away from their gregarious landlady, Mrs. Betty O'Keeley, would prove so problematic.

"For sure yeh'll be after a bit of tea 'afore yeh see the greens growing. And almost seeing them stretch their wee faces to the sun, yeh can. It's what we're famed for. From the Wales yeh say ... ach, it's a terrible dark place, that. So would yeh be after gettin' these few greens for meself then, at the market like?" she asked, waving a list at them. "O'Neal will be knowing what I'm needing, so tell him was Bett that sent yeh. But watch him," she lowered her voice to a whisper and admonished, "He be likin' the drink, poor man, what with the missus just passed away not three years since."

Only one small breath, barely discernible interrupted her prattle, "It was the colon, yeh see. Pity that, such a fine church-going girl she was . . . may the saints preserve her soul . . . only just past seventy she was." She shook her head morosely at such an early demise, but instantly brightened and shooed them out with a "Go way widya now, d 'yeh hear. I'll not be keeping you, and mind O'Neal be pulling only the best for Bett."

They would soon realize every conversation with Bett, and they were given permission by herself to call her Bett, would be filled with darting changes of topic, for the Irish liked the telling of their tales with passion, but in their own way and time.

"If Bett's any indication, we won't have to open our mouths unless a question is asked at least twice, or thrice. Only then is an answer expected," chuckled Tannis as they darted through the open front door and strolled towards the market.

"I was so fascinated by the sound of her rattling dialogue, I missed most of what she actually said. I didn't realize how fast they can talk. I can see why they have a reputation for the blarney," Josie said, then added with amusement, "Half of what she said had nothing to do with anything. You end up charmed, but totally confused." Tannis agreed. At the market Josie handed the list to the man pointed out as O'Neal. She told Tannis she'd catch up with her after she dutifully delivered the produce to Bett.

Tannis, relieved to be left alone, hurried to the entrance of the agricultural centre. She was immediately claimed by Jamie, a little leprechaun of a man straight out of a storybook. He had watched her approach, and for reasons known only to himself, proclaimed himself her personal guide.

"Yeh'll be wanting to see the growing center, then?" he asked as he squinted up at her great height and took a few smacking pulls from the knobby pipe protruding from one side of his mouth. An aromatic cloud of smoke wafted behind him as he led the way. Weaving a tale for every aspect of this unique project, he led her through rows of enormous plants and into greenhouses filled with seed beds, bedding plants, cuttings and some rather unusual grafting experiments of his own. Tannis was in heaven. She asked a stream of questions and strained to understand Jamie's speedy answers. What tickled her the most were several unusual suggestions of his own, reminiscent of Taenacea's methods, but difficult to extract from the streams of unrelated trivial information surrounding these pearls of wisdom. Listening to Jamie was much like listening to Bett, leaving you never quite sure what was being said, or meant.

When a tall gaunt woman joined them, he introduced her as Mary, the founding Director of the project. Mary had not only known of her arrival, but had sensed her uniqueness while she had covertly observed her arrival from afar. In recognition of a kindred spirit, her narrow face sprang to life with a brief show of ephemeral joy. Then her face settled back into its serious visage as she responded to Tannis' questions in a soft English accent.

"When I worked at Findhorn, I discovered that much of its success, outside of the use of resonance energy, was due to the energy of the site itself, beneath the earth. Fascinated by that concept, and after some exhaustive research, I came to believe there are key lines of energy called 'leys' in many parts of the world. These lines link all over the planet in fact, but are particularly predominant on these islands. Aligned with astrological intersections and defined by the barrows or 'nodes' as they're called, these intersections represent powerful energy conduits that can be utilized in ways we've long forgotten."

"Like Stonehenge?" Tannis asked, intrigued by what she suspected had contributed to her experience there, and most likely the root source of her own land's prosperity in Wales.

"Yes," Jane said, tucking a stray lock of lank hair behind her ear. "These spots, some of which cover many miles, seem to preserve antiquities. Several are more localized and therefore stronger, like at Stonehenge. However, with the right stimulation and through the use of sound and vibrational resonance, they can promote unusual growth of organic material, providing only organic methods are used, of course. That's why the name Ley Node was chosen for this site, in deference to the energy which makes this all possible," she added as she looked around with obvious pride.

"How do you stimulate the energy here?" Tannis asked.

"Through energy synchronicity and resonance. Everyone who works here possesses a natural empathy and love for the land. We use psychic methods to qualify people before we hire them," Mary said in a matter-of-fact tone. "We then teach them techniques to develop resonance with their surroundings and the land itself. As well, at dawn and dusk, a group of us form an energy circle. We alternate locations each day, and channel energy through us, into the ground and surrounding areas. Some of us who have had more specific training, chant and facilitate the proper focus of the group's energy."

As if to qualify what may sound far-fetched, she added, "It's not as strange as it may sound. Many of our primordial cultures did the same thing, in reverence of Mother Earth or a Provider God. Whether they believed in a female source or a male deity, they resonated and worked with universal energy, as we do here."

"Ummm . . . I know what you mean," Tannis responded dreamily. Her own light teachings as Taenacea confirmed what Mary said, as had her father in his research of Celtic customs and their unique bond with the natural elements around them. They walked in companionable silence towards the livestock center where young kids, lambs, calves and colts romped in their fenced paddocks. The huge barn attached to the paddocks served as a nursery for those just born. Josie was waiting for Tannis, still chuckling to herself over her latest encounter at the market.

"I swear, O'Neal has had a wee dram or two already, as the Irish say, if the whiskey fumes clinging to him are any indication."

"Probably," Mary responded calmly, giving Josie a quick once-over. "The fact that he wears the same clothes for at least a month may also account for that. In spite of it, there's no man around excepting Jamie who handles the Market and greenhouses as well as he. Spirits may course through his veins, but they also fill his heart and hands. He more than earns his keep with his green thumbs."

After introductions were made, Josie craned her neck to peer into the surrounding paddocks and exclaimed, "Now, *this* is what I want to see! I have a ranch in Montana, with livestock. No sheep yet though," she added in a speculative tone. She envisioned thousands of fluffy-wooled sheep contentedly grazing her Montana pastures. "They're so healthy looking," she commented.

"We use the same methods with the animals as we do with the vegetation. Tannis can fill you in on that later," Mary instructed. "The people working with the livestock have a natural affinity with them, and utilize and develop their innate understanding. Of course, the natural fodder grown right here goes a long way towards maintaining their good health, which in turn creates a growing demand for their meat."

"You sell the meat?" Josie queried. She knew they sold produce, but never thought about the livestock itself.

"Only to local butcher shops and select restaurants in Dublin and the yacht club at Dun Lagohaire. Those living in the immediate area can purchase fresh meat and produce at a reduced cost. Employees get theirs free, in lieu of a higher salary. It encourages them to maintain a consistently high standard in their work, as the product ends up on their own tables."

Conversation quickly turned to horseflesh and breeding selection, where Josie was in her element. She asked about horse racing, a passion on the Emerald Isle, then launched into an account of her Arabians in Montana. Mary quickly excused herself and invited them to wander the pastures surrounding the paddocks.

The overcast morning had transformed into a glorious afternoon. The sun blazed in a crystal blue sky that held only a few puffs of cloud. They watched the happy antics of the young animals amid the placid elders who contentedly cropped the grass. It was nice to do nothing other than enjoy the peaceful cycle of nature. Conversation between them was stilled by the sheer beauty of their idyllic surroundings. The faint sounds which drifted their way from the village only emphasized the tranquillity around them.

Jamie found them sitting under an oak tree making daisy chains to add to those already circling their heads, necks, and arms. He suggested they head back for the evening meal, adding, "Bett will be after screaming like the harrag she is at having her meal spoilt like, having 'specially made her favorite just for yeh two."

The simple but delicious steak and kidney pie covered with a flaky crust was augmented with a variety of surprisingly crunchy veggies, her concession to the 'veg-o-tarion' trend Mary hoped to encourage throughout the village's permanent occupants.

"How's a body to survive at all, wid just veggies, if you ask me," which they hadn't. She clucked her disapproval as she scooped more on their plates as if quantity would compensate for lack of substance. "'Tis the wholesome grains and meats of the land that be keeping a body strong since time began, not a feather in the wind such as Mary is ... what with her thin face and bones sticking out like a waif from the potato famine." She quickly scanned the girls as if to reassure herself they wouldn't succumb to the same fate, then sang the praises of her own three girls, or two of them at least.

"Now there's the making of stout lassies. Maggie bein' the black one, takes after the father. Mother of five she is, in Finglas West now. A little wide in the hip I'd say, not to criticize mind yeh ... but 'tis to be expected after birthin' the likes of the last one ... he being just under a stone and all in the coming out."

She scooped more meat pie on their empty plates, ignoring their objections. "The middle one, my Colleen ... carrot top the lads were after calling the poor wee thing. She's nursing at the Royal Hospital she is, caring for the unwell like, and soon to be wed to a fella from Dublin. A professional man, but the mother's a fine girl at that, for being city-bred, like."

In spite of her apparent attentiveness towards them, she caught a movement through the open front door and darted by the table to yell after someone, "Yeh be walkin' the streets with your apron on, Jenny O'Keef, yeh dotty eggit! Where's that worthless daughter that can't be keeping her eyes on yeh?" Not waiting for a response, she turned back to them and picked up right where she left off as if her dash to the door was a normal occurrence.

"We all have our burdens, like, as I do with me Corey. Now there's a child to break a mother's heart, traipsin' around single like with no intention of settling, she says. Brought up right, mind yeh, just in need of some babies to settle the wandering blood ... it came from the father yeh know." She lowered her voice and sighed, "Fifteen years in the grave now, God rest his worthless soul, and meself left with the care of three little ones. Kicked in the head by a bullock he was, and dropped like a stone he did, just before tea." She gave her eyes a quick wipe and after making the sign of the cross, whisked away their plates and disappeared behind the swinging door.

She returned from the tiny kitchen with tea, scones, and a rundown of all the local inhabitants for miles around. Tannis and Josie could barely sip their tea they were so full, and refrained from laughter as a long list of the villager's secrets were scooped out as freely as the thick cream which almost smothered their huge scones.

Bodies leaden from their enormous meal and head swimming with the histories of those for miles around, they excused themselves and strolled around the village and recapped Bett's monologue.

"Well, we now know everything there is to know about these folks. Fine fodder for blackmail. But I for one am sorry that Jenny is both an eggit and not right in the head, wary of Mary O'Donnel since she's the town gossip, not surprised the 'devil drink' took most of the menfolk, and shocked by those two youngsters of twenty-something even considering contracepshon. They'll be dammed to hell for sure." Delivered by Tannis in an Irish lilt with appropriate facial expressions, her accent was so good, Josie wondered if she'd be speaking Gaelic next.

They met up with Mary again at the chicken coop, where clucking fat hens pecked greedily at the grain she scattered from a bag slung over her hip. One look at them, and she said dryly, "I see you've been treated to Bett's fine cooking as well as a few comments on the villagers." Seeing their nods she added, "She's a dear really. She came to me insisting I rescue her from a fate worse than death, going into a home. She was convinced she'd be struck dead the moment she stepped over the threshold of such a place. She still lives in terror of not being useful, and useful she is. Outside of the fine B&B she runs, she can bully anyone into doing anything she fancies needs doing. So, unofficially, she runs the village as its honorary Mayor."

She asked, "Would you two be interested in joining us at our energy circle at dawn tomorrow? I sense neither of you are strangers to such an experience, and we would welcome the addition of your energies." She received an enthusiastic yes from both, who realized it was an invitation not usually extended to visitors.

They arranged the time and on leaving, Mary paused and threw another invitation over her shoulder as she entered the barn. "Interested in milking a cow the old-fashioned way?"

Josie immediately responded. "Me. I mean, I am. I've never done that before." Her enthusiasm had her knocking over the stool several times before she was even properly seated. The cow's udders were bursting for release and milk already dripped from her teats. She lowed in wide-eyed protest as little hands grabbed her and pumped away furiously, almost pulling her teats to the ground in her efforts to extract more than a pathetic dribble of milk.

An amused Tannis watched as Mary showed Josie the hold and motion several times. But to no avail. By this time the poor cow was flicking her tail in agitation. The last swish caught Josie across the face as she turned her head to say something to Tannis, and left behind a streak of something dark and pungent.

"*Shit!*" shrieked Josie as she jumped up and knocked over the bucket. A little puddle of milk dribbled from the shiny bucket, all she had managed to extract for all her efforts.

"Yes. It probably is," Tannis said with irony before she burst out laughing. "Perhaps you'd like to try a goat instead? Smaller teats, you know."

"Righth. And get a butt in the head on top of shit on my face. Not likely!" she spat, further frustrated when Tannis, or rather Taenacea, calmly sat down and began to smoothly draw streams of steaming milk from the grateful beast. Josie looked on in resentment for a moment, then stalked out of the barn to vent her frustration on the unsuspecting chickens by strewing their grain just outside the enclosure's mesh fence. Sorry for her spite, she was soon back, her happy self again. Mary, seeing her frustration, had let her collect eggs from the coop, something she could manage without mishap.

Dusk fell gently around them as the livestock settled for the night and they meandered back down the street to their little home. As they passed the pub on the corner, they could hear the sound of singing and laughing, but as much as the merriment enticed them, they continued on to their B&B. Transported into this gentler place, the natural rhythm of the land dictated it was time to rest. Besides, they had to be up early for the energy circle at dawn.

During a mandatory 'wee dram' by the fire, sipping on Bett's stingily poured Sherry 'to help the blood circulate like', they got the scoop on all the residents missed earlier and some of the good-for-nothing relations Bett would not discuss but did, from the father's side of course ... god rest his soul.

Unable to stifle her yawn, Tannis rose and said a firm good night. Josie followed suite and joined her for a hasty wash in the icy little bathroom.

Then, nestled between crisp linen sheets that smelled of fresh summer air and the iron's steamy swipes, they drifted into sleep. Tannis' last thoughts were what a delight these people were. So unpretentious and funny. She wished Linka could be here with her, but was thankful she wasn't. Having Josie around was excitement enough. Her thoughts strayed back to the people she had met today. Much like her folk in Wales, the people here moved through life with a richness of expression, in sync with the natural elements around them. Today she had experienced the earthy aspects of this land, and tomorrow morning with luck, the mystical.

Chapter Twenty-One

THE NARROW STAIRS CREAKED in the pre-dawn stillness as they crept downstairs. They were startled by Bett who suddenly flicked on the kitchen lights. "'Tis off to the dawn circle, I see," she said, and sniffed her disdain.

She looked ridiculous. Her hair was flattened to a skullcap of messy pin curls that ringed the round little face perched on her sunken neck. With her body wrapped in a pink chenille dressing gown, arms firmly crossed under the weight of her sagging breasts, she looked like a fat, worried little turtle.

Undeterred by her appearance, she admonished, "Whel ... 'tis not for me to be telling yeh the foolishness of such doings ... may the saints preserve yeh, but yeh'll be wanting a bite when yeh gets back. So mind, come right quick, d' ya hear, what with the bread I'll be putting to bake shortly." Having had her say on the matter, she vanished behind the swinging kitchen door.

"Not that I'll be telling yeh the foolishness of such doings," Josie mimicked as they adjusted their eyes to the dark and crept to the gardens to join the small group waiting there.

Nine hushed figures filed carefully through the dew-kissed vegetation to the middle of a field. They stopped and formed a circle small enough to loosely link hands. Under Mary's whispered directions, they stood silent, breathed deeply, and focused on their connection with the seemingly sleeping earth. The sun sent its first shafts of watery light over the horizon as they stood in the light mist that cloaked their surroundings.

Tannis felt a now-familiar shift within her as a surge of energy ran through her body. She glanced at Josie and sensed she too felt the tingling warmth passing through their linked hands. Connected deeply to the ground beneath her, she heard the first faint strains of a hum vibrate in her ears, similar to what she had heard at Stonehenge after the clicking sound emitted by those ancient stones. As the sound grew stronger, she observed an unearthly glow around the plants; a halation of expanding and contracting white light that shimmered around each bud, leaf and stem.

She felt the confirming squeeze of Josie's hand in hers. She too saw the pulsing halo. Like a celestial light show accompanied by a pure oscillating strum, they were drawn into the magical dance of energy. As instructed by Mary's soft voice, Tannis extended her aura along with the others and before long, the rings of light expanded slightly in response to their energy infusion. And when Taenacea extended her aura, everyone within the circle was both witness and participant of the effects of directed energy.

Through the Plains of Silver and utilizing the power within the ley lines beneath their feet, a slow whirring began to swirl around Tannis, a whirring like at Stonehenge. The whirring brought visions of ancient rituals on this very spot. But unlike before, the column of light around her extended itself to encompass the whole circle in its undulating pulse of palpitating light and sound. For there was an indescribable sound to this experience, one which could not be voiced. As the humming and spinning crested, those within the circle were gently lifted a few inches off the ground. As they hovered, memories of a deep connection with the earth's pagan consciousness flashed through each mind. When they lightly drifted back, they were uncertain if their feet had truly left the ground or if they had just imagined it to be so through desire.

But Tannis, Josie and Mary remained afloat a little longer and descended under the awe-struck eyes of their befuddled companions. Tannis was the last, and with her descent, the humming and whirling that had encased them slowed, then stopped completely.

Under the early morning light, the glistening dew and glow that girded every leaf and surface sparkled with an incandescence of vivid colors that drew a collective gasp from the group. Still giddy from their levitation, they gaped at the shimmering motes that swirled in the rhythm of a frenzied dance of exuberant life, then settled back into a subtle white glow, and smoothly faded away to leave just the kiss of dew on nature's mantle.

Like an illusion, the experience had been too brief and fluid to be believable. Had it not been for the flashing visions imprinted in their minds, they would have thought it had not happened at all. They shot Tannis an appreciative, but somewhat fearful look, and slowly dispersed, murmuring amongst themselves to see if they were the only ones that had imagined what they believe had happened.

All except Mary, who stood where she was and appraised Tannis silently. Finally she spoke. "The closest I've come to experiencing something like this was reading about the oscillating aura of plants in the book *The Celestine Prophecy*. Thank you." Then she added wistfully, "I suspect you could teach us a thing or two were you to stay here a while."

"Thank you, Mary. It was a wonderful experience for me too. I've had a little 'special' training, that's all. But your channels are fully open now and you can do this again," Tannis responded modestly.

"Tell me, did I imagine those flashes of other times, of the elemental rituals?" Mary asked.

"No. The name you chose for this place is most appropriate. It does lie on a ley conjunction, a 'node', one which holds a vast storehouse of energy you've already activated, and can utilize more fully now. Earth memories are now awakened to their past on this spot. You've all been here before, you know, as I have. You'll begin to remember now. Use that knowing, for it's ancient and true." And with a very outwardly smug, but inwardly awed Josie in tow, she briskly strode back towards town. She suddenly felt very hungry and anticipated what was sure to be another fried nightmare of a breakfast. She could hardly wait.

"How can you just do that, like it's no big deal? I'll never get used to it. I bet Mary never expected us to levitate when she asked us to join them. Neither did I, come to think of it," puffed Josie as she scrabbled to keep apace of her friend's long stride.

"And neither did I. It wasn't me back there, you know. Like I said to Mary, I've been here before too. I can feel it," Tannis said. She offered no further explanation. She needed time to mull over her introduction to yet another powerful conduit, Mauve, so she changed the subject. "Weren't the colored auras around the plants wonderful? I don't remember having seen that quite as clearly before, even in Wales."

"Should we tell Bett?" Josie asked with a twinkle in her eyes.

"Lordy, no," retorted Tannis. "For all that she embraces the fey of this land, she'll be dragging us to Mass and setting the church 'afire with all the candles lit in hopes of saving our souls if she hears about this. Though I suspect she's really a pagan at heart."

There was nothing pagan-looking about Bett when they arrived for breakfast. Corseted into a fifties sweater set over a plaid skirt, her previously flattened hair now bristled around her face in a springy fluff of curls. She ushered them to the table where a freshly baked loaf of Wheaten bread scored with the mandatory cross sat surrounded by little pots of preserves and a dish of fresh creamery butter.

"Well . . . yeh be bringing in the dawn with some strange doings then?" she asked as she peered at them intently. This time she waited for a response.

"Just as expected. Levitation and floating around the garden for a while," breezed Josie, ignoring the expected kick under the table from her pal.

"Sweet Jesus, Mother of God! Don't be feckless about these things or the wee folk'll be right annoyed, they will!" exclaimed Bett. Her eyes darted heavenward in an appeal for absolution as she scooped eggs and sizzling rashers onto their plates. "They mean well here, mind, and there's no denying the growth of things, and wid that, yeh be slicing the bread there now," she said as she handed Josie the big knife. "Now, what will yeh be doing with this fine day, then?"

"Checking out the weavers and dyers is what I'm doing," Josie announced promptly. "I may take up weaving myself. I want to try it out here and observe your dying methods."

Tannis immediately envisioned endless Christmas gifts of poorly woven wraps should her efforts prove successful. Inquiring looks were thrown her way. She hadn't thought what she would do, but heard herself say, "I'm going to buy something quaint to wear and play the country maiden. Then I shall explore the surrounding area ... alone."

"A picnic then. I'll be packing a wee basket my Corey used, to collect flowers before she took to wandering more than the fields," Bett said. Reminded of what a vagabond her wee Corey was, she launched into greater detail of that particular misfortune while the girls ate.

Stuffed to the gills, they groaned with satisfaction and thanked Bett with appreciative hugs. Her embarrassed, "go way wid you. Off yeh go now," was followed by tender little pats on their backs before they left. Under her now misty gaze, they sauntered down the road to the shops that had just opened their doors for business.

"So what's this country-maiden-walking-the-lands bug that just nipped you?" Josie asked as soon as they were out of earshot of Bett who lingered at the front door and peered after them.

"Why not?" Tannis shrugged, ignoring the sudden attack of butterflies in her belly. "I feel a resonance with this land and since this morning's experience, want to find out if I have any other memories of Maeve. Besides, I need some time alone to think about everything that's happened here. You can understand that?" She raised her eyebrows in mimic of Bett and asked, "Weaving is it now? Come on, let's find the perfect country maiden outfit before looms and skeins claim all your attention."

With Josie's help they achieved the perfect country-maiden look. A muslin slip fringed in delicate lace peaked from the front opening of a lightweight, buttoned green linen skirt. The skirt was topped with a creamy muslin peasant blouse with a low drawstring neckline and sleeves that gathered at the elbow. Since the blouse was semi-transparent even in its fullness, Josie had insisted on a light dusty rose shawl draped over her shoulders and tucked into the front of her wide belt, as was the Irish custom. The shawl was less for decorum than to offset the look of her costume, but would keep morning or evening chills at bay.

With her hair flying loose and bare feet in braided sandals, Tannis looked the picture of an Irish colleen from yesteryear, thought a somewhat taller colleen than most in these parts. She collected the picnic basket from Bett, reportedly containing a thermos, tidily packaged food and a 'wee cup to drink from the streams' as Bett put it. Then she stood at the edge of the village, undecided which way to go. She would let her impulses lead her where they may. She closed her eyes and when she opened them again they seemed drawn to the west. The west it would be. So she headed through the grazing pastures towards the rolling hills in the distance.

* * *

Bryan had arrived back at the Manor in time to watch the sun set on his Enchantress. Up early again this morning, he sensed a particularly magical aura around the sculpture. As the sun's rays caressed her form, she appeared to be ringed with a pulsing golden halo he had never noticed before, a halo which seemed to contract and expand as if breathing life into her stillness. As the golden ring slowly faded, he felt a now familiar glow of warmth surge through his own body. It left an unusually restless longing in its wake. Not knowing what he yearned for, he went in search of Seamus.

Seamus was giving the gardener some final instructions for the rose beds out back before he would head over to the building site of his new home. The plans had been drawn to Nell's specifications many years before. He was to meet with the 'lazy good for nothing drinking sods' as Nell called them, and check on the progress of the foundation. He greeted Bryan and handed him the drawings of the 'barn' as they now took to calling it, and said, "Yeh'll be looking these over then, and wid that I'll be taking meself off for the day. Yeh ken play Lord of the Manor for a time, to get a feel for it, like." He had things on his mind other than the love-mooning of his brother. Nell was driving him mad as to what she wanted. She said it made no mind to her as long as she had a good working kitchen and the children a room each, as far from theirs as possible. Yet, the kitchen had already been moved from one end of the house to the other, twice. He strode across the lawn towards the site of his new home, mumbling about the irrational opposite sex.

His abrupt departure left Bryan at loose ends. Thinking he might drive to Ley Node and check in with Mary, he was hit with a sudden impulse to just walk his lands. He could see Mary another day. It must have been Seamus' comment of playing at Lord of the Manor. His yearning called for the soothing hands of nature and his restlessness for a long, brisk hike. Clad in stout walking shoes and accompanied by one of the young hounds he was partial to and vice versa, he ambled down the crushed stone drive. Near the gates, he cut under the canopy of oak trees and decided to follow the perimeter of the estate to the back quarter. He hadn't been that far afield for some time.

Tannis, her shawl and belt long since discarded and wound around the handle of the basket she carried was ready for lunch. She looked around and thought the trees at the top of the slope directly ahead looked a likely spot. Choosing a shady patch under the young oaks, she set her basket down and prepared for her private picnic.

She munched on a chicken leg and piece of crusty bread slathered with soft butter, savoring both her lunch and surroundings. It was a perfect day. The sky held not a cloud under the heavy heat of mid-day. The panorama of gently sloping hills was slumberous, as if the earth too was resting, temporarily defeated by the oppressing heat. Only the hilltop upon which she sat caught the occasional breeze. Below, the dells and gullies lay torpid. Even the few insects that buzzed around the clover and wild flowers did so lethargically, more to cool their heated little bodies than to gather pollen.

She swallowed the last bite of a half soggy ham and tomato sandwich, brushed the crumbs from her skirt and packed the food away. Then she impetuously undid the buttons on her skirt and pulled her slip right up to the top of her thighs. Sitting splay-legged, she allowed the shade and breeze to tickle her naked limbs. She wiggled her bare toes with delight and marveled at how familiar this land felt to her, almost like her Welsh lands, which was unusual since she'd never been here before. For even if this was Lagohaire land, Taenacea had never traveled to Ireland. It must be a trace memory of Maeve's life here, a residue of this morning's quick flash of memories of her life.

She opened the tie on her blouse and pulled the bodice down a little, her mind on the ancestral women with whom she shared a timeless bond, but knew so little about. She felt wild and free, unfettered by the constraint of a companion, time, or purpose. There was no one to see how she relished the breeze as it licked and dried the sweat that ran between her breasts, or know of the light shiver that snaked from her groin and puckered her nipples in sensual response to nature's caressing hands. She leaned back against the tree trunk closed her eyes, and playfully pulled a four leaf clover from the clusters growing around her.

Several hills away, a larger male hand plucked at the clover as well. Only he had no sandwiches to assuage his hunger, soggy or otherwise. Having trekked stoically until noon, Bryan rested in the shade of a small gurgling brook and watched the dog root in the shrub for something to chase. The young canine was unaware that at midday even the bravest of rodents would seek respite from the heat.

Bryan surveyed his birthright with pride, a heritage stretching back to the time of tenacious Norse invaders and stalwart Celtic defenders. Since he had only visited his home sporadically over the past twenty years, he had taken ownership of what he viewed for granted, and forgotten the beauty of what was his. All that would change now, and he would truly become Lord of the Manor by fall. The foundation was already laid for Seamus' and Nell's house. The Tudor style house Nell wanted would be livable by fall with only the interior requiring finishing and furnishing. Nell had already laid claim to many of the good old pieces of furniture cluttering the attic at the Manor.

His back pressed against the tree trunk he grasped a handful of clover and thought idly how the charms of the four leaf clover had woven itself through the heritage of this land's people and its culture. His countrymen believed wishes would come true with a four-leaf clover, if the heart is open and pure. Right now he wanted very much to believe: to believe his

Enchantress could be part of his life, whoever she was. He looked down at the fistful of green he'd plucked.

Should he find a four-leaf clover in this handful, he would meet his Enchantress, and with her at his side, dedicate himself to his lands and leave the affairs of business in Lorne's capable hands, excepting any necessary participation on his part. And if there was no four-leaf clover, well . . . he would be right where he was now. He would do the same, but alone.

His intentions clear, he felt a not-unpleasant constriction around his heart, as if an invisible hand had gently given it a reassuring squeeze. Almost fearful, he opened his fist and scanned the contents. Right in the middle, as if placed there by the force of his own will, lay a perfect four-leaf clover. He plucked it from its nest and twirled it around by the stem. Engulfed by a childish rush of hope and relief at finding this little bit of green, he made his wish before he could change his mind. Then he waited.

Nothing happened of course. Sighing deeply he knew it foolish to expect her to instantly materialize just because he had wished it on a four leaf clover. But then, he had experienced many foolish desires of late and one of them had materialized. He had seen the living counterpart of his Enchantress with his own eyes in London. He shook his wistful thoughts from his mind. It was too easy to let the magic of the land creep into the desires of the heart. Almost against his own volition, a long-suppressed sensitivity had once again unfurled and crept its way into his consciousness. It felt as if the land itself and nudged that aspect of himself into wakefulness. But with it came the painful memories he was not yet prepared to examine. Pushing those thoughts firmly out of his mind, but still holding the four-leaf clover between his fingers, he rose. He would go a little further before heading back to the Manor.

As he scanned his surroundings from the top of a knoll, his eyes were drawn to an inviting copse of trees. He had walked for some time now and was hot and tired. From where he stood he could see a dark shape through the opening that formed an entrance into the shaded tree and brush encased haven. Curious, he headed down the slope. The only ruin he remembered on these lands was the rubble left from a small private chapel at the back of the Manor house, beside which he had constructed a gazebo.

As he drew closer, the babble of a brook in the gully skirting one side of the little dell reminded him of his parched lips and the sweat slicking his forehead and chest. It also triggered rumblings in his stomach. It had been many hours since he had eaten his sparse breakfast.

He took only a few mouthfuls of water then scrabbled up the gully and entered the dell. Up close, the shadow seen from afar proved to be a small ruin all right, and a very ancient one by the look of the cracked stones cloaked with age-brittle lichen. The arched high back was still intact, but the front and one side had crumbled and left a gaping hole beneath the rough altar. A profusion of wild flowers sprouted from the cracks like a fresh offering for whomever this shrine had been intended. When he touched one time-worn side the rocks shifted beneath his hand. It would take little to send them crumbling to join the pile which jutted from amid the grass and flowers around its base.

Grateful for the cooling shade this haven provided, he stretched out on his side, his back near the front of the altar, his head supported by one bent arm. Feeling as if he'd just receive a whopping shot of Demerol, he was moments away from a hazy snooze when the hound loped towards him and lay down at his side. A deep moan of contentment escaped the canine as Bryan's hand idly rubbed the back of his ear. Under the blanket of stillness shrouding the silent haven, they both closed their eyes and surrendered to afternoon dreams.

Tannis still held the four leaf clover she had carelessly plucked in the hand also holding the weighty basket. In her other hand she held her shawl, belt, and sandals. She contemplated removing her skirt, but then she would have to carry it too. Drooping under the blazing afternoon sun, she felt a dizzying wave of vertigo and looked for a shady spot to rest.

Since the whole day was hers to do with as she pleased, she had walked at a steady but easy pace, stopping here and there to relish some particular delightful nuance of memory. Sticky now, she tugged at the neckline of her blouse until it hung askew, leaving one shoulder bared. She trudged to the top of another hill where a passing breeze lightly teased her with a moment's relief. She spotted a small brook in a gully beside a cluster of trees down the rise a little to her left. It looked an inviting, shady place. She would go there and rest, for even Mother Earth had slowed her pulse for a time. But when she skirted the trees and glanced through the opening into its center, what she held slipped from her hands unnoticed. She stood frozen in time.

Her eyes took in the crumbling little altar. But it was not what held her gaze. What had rendered her immobile was the man who lay propped up on one elbow in front of it, one hand resting on the head of a hound. As if sensing her shocked presence, he slowly opened his eyes. Two pairs of eyes locked in timeless recognition.

She stood motionless for what seemed an eternity, aware only of a persistent ringing in her ears. She barely felt the shift and increasing sense of fullness as the consciousness of another settled within her. Both peered out of her violet eyes into the deep, unfathomable blue of the man's lying there; their Garth! It was as if she knew him, had always known him, and would know him forever.

A profound feeling of relief washed over Tannis as she realized here was the man both of them yearned for; the man who had come to her in a dream; who had been life itself to Taenacea and now heralded a new beginning for herself. Caught in the immobility of disbelief, it was Taenacea who broke the timeless rapture with the echo of a greeting from another time. "I see you have met with the approval of Ruftar, our most ferocious hound."

Tannis remained frozen as Taenacea looked upon her beloved Garth, who lay before her now almost as he had then by her hearth so long ago. Hungrily she scanned his face, the breadth of his wide shoulders, the well-muscled chest, and his lean waist. He was as she remembered, even to the dark wavy hair tied back at his neck.

She drank in the strong clean lines of a face she had loved. Her eyes lingered on the wide mouth that had kissed every inch of her body and murmured sweet words of love in her ear and against her hair; a mouth used both tenderly and with passion. His long expanse of leg was covered with a strange trouser, but beneath the odd cloth she recognized the graceful shape and taut muscle her hands knew well. Memory of his manhood brought a flush to her face and sent an immediate quiver of desire through her body. Reluctant to release the heat of remembered arousal, she relished him for a time, then slowly retreated into the folds of her counterpart's psyche, knowing this time was now hers.

Tannis absorbed the rock-hewn symmetry of the face that spoke of strength and firm resolve before she felt drawn to his eyes: eyes that held both ice and heat, like in her dreams. With the eyes of a professional, she noted her sculpture of Garth was a true likeness. His dark wavy hair was a little shorter at the top and sides as was the fashion now, but the face it framed was the same, one imprinted in her heart. And she could finally see the burnished tone of his skin remembered from her dreams, but only implied by her sculpture's patina.

"Thank you, Mother," she mouthed silently. She glanced quickly at the four leaf clover her grasp had crushed. Whoever he was and no matter what had brought him to this magical place, he was for her. Caught in this dream that was not a dream, caught within the perception of the past and the present, she waited in a timeless limbo for his answer to a question she had not yet asked.

Bryan, lost in dozing dreams of his Enchantress, sensed something and propelled by some unknown force, opened his eyes. Before him stood the vision from his dreams, so he knew he was still dreaming. He blinked several times, but she was still there.

With the sun behind her, she appeared to shimmer around the edges. The long skirt that flapped gently against her legs was of the same shade as the grass, giving the illusion she had risen from the earth itself just for him. His eyes followed her form upwards and stopped on the one bare shoulder then moved back down to where an almost transparent blouse stuck lightly to the swell of a breast. The damp blouse defined one nipple, whose point and surrounding darkness was evident through the moist fabric.

He forced his eyes away from this enticing sight and gazed into the face that had haunted him since he first laid eyes on the Enchantress: a face framed by a halo of long ebony curls which clung to her shoulders in moist disarray. He wanted to touch the curl that lay stuck to the pulse of her throat, and almost reached for it, but became entranced by the silver streaks which snaked from her temples. She looked a pagan Temptress, and for a moment he was almost afraid of her.

Her enormous eyes stared at him unblinking, almost as if she was cationic. Then a swift shift of expressions raced across her face, a fluctuation of recognition and blank appraisal. When she spoke in a husky lilting tone a dimple danced by the side of her mouth, a mouth she had moistened with the quick flick of a pink tongue. Her action stirred a memory and a tingle of desire in his groin.

He had thought her a dream when his eyes first opened, a mirage conjured up by his desire and the shimmering heat of the day which was known to play tricks on the eyes. But she had spoken to him, and mirages don't speak. A surge of something coiled deep within him began to unfurl and without knowing why he answered her, surprised at the ancient lilt in his own voice. "Aye, he be that for sure." He immediately felt the ecstatic quiver of pleasure under the hand still draped over the canine and smiled a slow smile, then asked, "And how would you know his name?"

Tannis' confusion was apparent on her face. She recovered somewhat and said, "Aren't all ferocious Irish hounds called Ruftar?" Her dimple danced again, or was it Taenacea's?

A slight shiver raced over her body, but so quickly he almost missed it. She looked as if she was about to ask a question. Then, as if the action was not of her own volition she slowly lifted one hand and reached it towards him in silent appeal.

As she stood posed, almost like the sculpture itself, Bryan was over-whelmed by such a poignant rush of feeling that his breath caught in his throat. His ears rang loudly and he felt as if time had shifted somehow. He saw his Enchantress through dream eyes. She was a woman he knew well: a woman waiting for something he had willingly given before. He fell into her eyes and read her soul, seeking confirmation of his own feelings. An understanding had been presented, explored and accepted, all without exchanging one word. Not knowing why he reached his hand towards her in confirmation of an agreement reached eons ago.

Hypnotized, they reached for each other, two souls who had traversed the illusion of time, impelled by the burning passion of an ancient love cut short: seeking completion.

He watched her glide towards him, lower herself, and kneel on the ground before him. As if it were the most natural of actions, he gently lifted a stray curl from her neck, held it a moment and then let it fall. He had done this many times before. Compelled by a deep desire arising from an ancient habit, he gently took both her hands in his, turned them over palm up, and placed a soft, lingering kiss on each wrist.

That small action, so simple and yet more intimate than anything either had experienced or could imagine, sealed the knowledge their lives were now linked forever.

Bryan reeled from the impact of this awareness and shifted his gaze in momentary confusion. He caught a glimpse of a nipple as it peeked over the edge of her blouse when she leaned towards him. His blood stirred and his mind filled with the thought of crushing her to him and having her right on this very spot. But reason overruled his desire. He knew she was neither a country maiden in search of such attentions, or a dream. She was the woman he had just claimed as his own, and he would do nothing to dishonor the miracle of the covenant just made.

For a moment he was completely confused. What was he doing? It felt as if he were under a spell, but willingly, as if following a script, as if his actions had been ordained. But how was this possible? His momentary fight for control was quickly diffused by his need to see what she would do next.

Shaken by his gesture and the déjà vu impact of their unspoken pledge, Tannis foundered under his passionate gaze. Whoever this man was, he was the most delicious specimen of maleness she had ever encountered. And every inch of her body strained with a remembered desire for his touch. She didn't feel like herself at all, and could barely contain an urge to fling herself into his arms. Desperately she grasped for something to divert the lascivious thoughts she suspected may not be entirely her own. She forced herself to regain her identity, and focused on the shrine behind him. She hiked up her blouse in one graceful but unconscious motion and asked, "Is that a child's shrine?" relieved that for the moment her voice was her own and didn't reveal either her own sexual tension, or her counterpart's obvious desire.

"I don't know. It's the first time I've seen it. Yes, it does look as if it was meant for a child," Bryan answered, embarrassed by his keen observation of her unconscious action. Grateful for the diversion of her question, he pulled himself together with effort. "There are so many legends in these parts. I'm sure there's a story behind this little altar too," he managed to say, feeling a little like a tongue-tied adolescent.

"Yes, there would be." Tannis had no idea what to say, or do now. The gurgle of the brook nearby punctuated the surreal stillness between them and reminded her of the heat and her reason for being here. Her whole body felt flushed and now burned with lust as well. She jumped up, went to the basket she had dropped by the dell's opening, grabbed the cup, and ran to the brook without a word. She drank deeply herself, feeling more grounded by the mundane action and cool water. Still feeling like this was a dream, she filled the cup again and returned to the dell to offer its coolness to her nameless companion. Only a slight tremor of her hand betrayed her inner turmoil.

She watched as he drained the cup and held it out to her with a boyish 'more please' smile, a smile that crinkled the sides of his eyes and sent another snake of desire through her groin and up into her belly. Lordy, but he was gorgeous. She just managed to stifle a torturous groan and rose again to refill the cup, wondering only briefly at the absurdity of her actions. She stopped to pick up the empty thermos from the basket this time. This was insane! She couldn't just dash back and forth, refilling this one little cup like a lunatic. But then, she hardly knew what she was doing. Somewhat more composed when she returned, she grabbed the basket and sat down across from him and if a picnic had been arranged. She handed him the cup and thermos now filled with cool water.

Eyes on her task, she brushed a ringlet of hair off her face and pulled food from the basket. "What's left is a little soggy, but I'll share what I have. Breast?" she asked, and handed him a piece of chicken before she un-wrapped the remaining sandwich.

Mind on other than the breast in his hand, Bryan first nibbled the edge of the piece of chicken. Then, realizing his hunger, he devoured the whole thing with relish, smacking his lips as he pulled the last piece of meat off the bones and popped it into his mouth. He then reached for the sodden sandwich and made short work of it as well.

Tannis watched him, mesmerized by the remembrance of another lusty appetite. Yet this time she felt like it was her body he had devoured with those lips. Embarrassed by her thoughts she busied herself by gathering up the small bones and wax wrappings to stuff back into her basket. Suddenly the tension of this unexpected encounter, its implications, and the myriad of feelings which raced through her was just too much. She had to get away before she imploded or became crushed by the intensity of a five hundred year old passion.

She glanced at him and blurted, "Same time tomorrow?", then picking up her basket, she rose quickly. She paused only long enough to scoop up her other possessions, then rushed through the opening of the dell. So urgent was her sudden need to escape, she kept going until she had crested the second hill. She paused a moment to catch her breadth and continued blindly, chased by the images that raced through her mind. Finally her body screamed for release from her punishing pace. Her legs began to quiver as she stumbled down another slope, then gave way entirely. She crumbled to the ground and began to sob, both from the exhaustion of her mad dash, and the emotional impact of her encounter.

After a time her sobbing abated. It occurred to her she was either out of shape or getting too old for such a strenuous dash. Slowly, both her rasping breathing and jumbled thoughts subsided, and she realized what had just occurred. Never in her wildest fantasies had she thought she would meet him like this. It was one thing to dream of such a man and relive a love from the past but quite another to stumble upon his likeness in an isolated glen. And not only did he resemble the Garth she had come to know so intimately through Taenacea, he *was* Garth in every way. This she knew instinctively.

In spite of wistful thinking she hadn't expected him to look exactly like Garth, thinking she would find a man who would trigger a similar attraction, not the physical incarnation of Garth himself. Inwardly she was thrilled beyond belief. Replaying the scene in the dell she also remembered her reaction and cringed. What a total nit she had been. She hadn't even asked his name, or told him who she was. He must think her mad, gawking at him like a schoolgirl, then almost falling into his arms. And what had she said? "Lordy," she groaned, as she remembered Taenacea's out of place comment about Ruftar. Now, this was a time warp if there ever was one, especially since it really was the dog's name, or so he had said. Coincidence, I think not.

Then the heat of another memory flushed her cheeks. The whole time she had knelt before him, one of her breasts had hung out of her blouse, as if in offering. No wonder he had looked at her as if he was ready to pounce. Any man would consider a bare breast in an isolated spot an invitation, and her a slut for presenting it so blatantly. But he hadn't taken advantage of the situation as many would, which was something to be said for his character, and brought her thoughts back to what had passed between them.

She had experienced the same recognition Taenacea had with Garth, the certainty of two halves of one perfect whole united at last. But, instead of responding with some maturity as Taenacea had, she had run off like a lunatic, after a breezy 'same time tomorrow'. Gawd, she didn't even know where she was! Yet, she knew he would be back tomorrow, as she would. All she had to do now was relish her delicious experience for a while, then collect herself and get through the rest of the day and evening with some semblance of normalcy. But nothing would ever be normal again.

It was a simple plan, until she remembered. They were to visit an estate tomorrow owned by a fellow Cal had met overseas. Thankfully not until the afternoon or evening since Cal wasn't due to arrive until noon at the earliest. The afternoon; when she'd planned to return to the dell to find out who he was and where they would go from here. She wasn't blind to the parallel, for an ocean lay between them as it had between their ancient counterparts. She knew they would find a way to be together like Taenacea and Garth had, but she lived much further away and this was another time. She did not relish standing on some symbolic cliff-top, waiting for her lover. Unless ... She left her thought unfinished. It was too premature to think of those things.

Before she could return to the village, she also had to decide how to deal with a more immediate problem: Josie. What would she tell her? The answer came swiftly. Nothing. She would keep her encounter a secret, at least until after her tryst tomorrow. Once she knew who he was and their future was somehow clarified, she would share the wonder of her prize with her best friend. It was not that she was being mean-spirited, but this was her special experience, and she wanted to relish it, just as Josie had with her secret marriage.

She would slip away in the morning. What concerned her more was how to fend off Josie's radar once she got back today. They were supposed to spend this evening in the singing pub. Common sense told her if she didn't return on time Josie would assume she was experiencing some evening earth ritual and go to the pub without her. All she need do is slip by Bett and pretend to be asleep when Josie got in. Tomorrow after breakfast she would casually go for a walk and . . . just not come back. They'd have no choice but to wait for her. Besides, they weren't expected at the estate until late afternoon.

Problem solved, she wiped the grimy tear stains from her face with the last dribbles of water from the thermos. She lifted her sodden hair and wound it into a knot at the top of her head. She looked at the ground and found a stick she pierced through her knot to hold it fast. Nature always provided. She adjusted her blouse and let her bare feet lead her back to Ley Node while her mind replayed the wonder of her meeting.

Stunned by her abrupt departure, Bryan's head reverberated with her parting words, 'same time tomorrow'. Had she not said that he would have thought the meeting a dream in spite of having spoken with her, in spite of having touched her curl, and in spite of having kissed her wrists. As he glanced at the ground he saw a small chicken bone in the grass. If it had been a dream, it was one during which he'd eaten a piece of real chicken and brought the bone back into wakefulness.

The fact she had said 'same time tomorrow' implied she came from nearby. He would have heard of someone like her. Then again, he hadn't been here much. Although she could be a guest of a nearby estate he immediately thought of Ley Node. He recognized her clothing as similar to what the village produced and sold as their standard 'Irish' look. As much as he wanted to go to Ley Node and find her, instinct told him not to act rashly or appear more foolish than he already felt: foolish because he had let her just vanish without asking her name or making any attempt to follow her.

He should have followed her and couldn't fathom why he had not done so. Thankfully she would be back tomorrow. Then he would find out who she was, and make sense of this deep recognition he had felt the instant their eyes locked. If he were a wistful man, he'd think wishing on the four leaf clover had caused her to appear. And as much as logic propelled him to dismiss the possibility, he didn't. Meeting here instead of in London seemed a portent that she was suited to these lands, and to him. Surprised by her sudden departure, he was comforted by the thought that he would see her again tomorrow, after which she would be his forever. Of this he was certain.

As promised when he made his wish, he would honor his birthright, but now with her at his side, with the woman whose silver streaks glistened in the sun, but whose name he didn't even know. Filled with a swell of desire as his mind lingered on the glimpse of her one exposed breast, he groaned at the memory of his doltish stare. But it had confirmed that her breasts were like those on the sculpture he had covertly caressed. He jumped up quickly, aware of an insistent pressure at the front of his trousers. Embarrassed at his obvious arousal he whistled for Ruftar. The canine had quietly slunk away when the Enchantress had entered the dell, as if an interaction so profound could not be shared even by him.

Setting a brisk pace, he turned his mind to the dream images which wavered at the edge of his mind. Their substance remained as elusive as their meaning. Yet, he sensed there was a connection to the sculptures. The arrival of his likeness, the Enchantress, and the fairy child holding his ancient family crest was no accident, as much as he'd like to put it down to coincidence. Then there was this chance meeting in the dell. What of the sense of knowing this woman so well, yet at the some time, knowing nothing about her at all? Coincidence? Just as he knew nothing about the reclusive artist who had produced these wonders. And where did Cal fit in all this?

Unconsciously he slowed his brisk stride to a more even pace as he examined the chain of events set in motion by the arrival of the three sculptures. He'd had no idea that when he had commissioned the three pieces, his life would change forever. He felt out of his depth, faced with feelings his years of containment and control couldn't reconcile. He had never before met a woman who had such an immediate effect on him, be it in bronze or in the flesh. He instinctively knew she was the one he hadn't realized he was seeking. She possessed that elusive element which had kept him from forming a meaningful relationship in the past. With her at his side, he knew he would be complete.

Chapter Twenty-Two

KEEPING HER TRYST FROM JOSIE proved easier than expected. Tannis arrived back at the village at dusk with the flush of inner excitement still on her face. She had watched an exquisite sunset in solitude and felt blessed by the magic of this land. Bett's lights winked her welcome from behind Irish lace curtains as she opened the front gate. She entered quietly and received only a cursory scrutiny from a Bett more concerned over the eating of 'every crumb' of the packed lunch than the details of Tannis' wanderings, or her late arrival home. But she did shoot her a keen look.

"There's a flush bloomin' yer cheeks, what with the burn of the sun at midday yeh wouldn't be used to." Her tone implied only in Ireland did the sun burn at noon. "And now 'thother one is after going to the pub widout yeh. But a nice sleep will set yeh right I expect. Mind yeh wash the grass stains off yer feet before bed. I'll not have my linens smudged. Now, off wid yeh," she admonished as she shooed Tannis upstairs like an errant daughter.

Tannis made a lot of noise to assure Bett her feet were being properly washed, then lay in the tepid water awhile. She longed for the crisp linen sheets of her bed, and once there, dreamed of Garth and finally played out her pent-up lust in a variety of torrid scenarios that never quite consummated their love, but fed her desire to do so.

The trill of, "Hey sleepyhead. You missed a night of singing that would have the angels weeping, it would," woke her. Pulled reluctantly from her erotic encounters by the weight of Josie's body at her side, Tannis shot her a disgruntled "Morning."

Josie peered at her critically. She had noticed Tannis' heightened color right away. "Are you flushed from erotic dreams or is that a light burn on your cheeks? How was your country maiden day, anyway?"

"Hmmm . . . a bit of both, typically maidenly with my virtue still intact." Tannis hoped to divert the conversation away from details and stuck to the truth, at least as much of it as possible. "Kneeling at the foot of little altars

I was, and racing barefoot through the fields, I did. Then watched a fantastic sunset and did the earth mother worship thing." Said dreamily, she quickly tucked her aura tight against her body and crossed her fingers under the blanket as well. Better safe than sorry.

"We can't all have exciting days, can we." Fortunately Josie was too enraptured by her own adventures to question her further, or check her aura. Besides, she had no reason to suspect there was anything to hide. "I must be a born-again weaver. Talent from another life I suspect, another weaving-putz life most likely." She caught Tannis' baffled look, and explained. "When they sat me down at the loom. Remember my desire to learn to weave? Hello, anyone there?" Receiving a nod of comprehension she continued.

"Well, they sat me down with some reluctance at first, though I can't imagine why, and bingo! It must have been the same for you the first time you touched a lump of clay. I am a natural, instinctive weaver." She paused dramatically, waving her hands in weaving motions. "So, waddya say to that, oh talented friend of a newly-discovered-talented-genius—as in me?"

Tannis pulled herself onto her side and resting her head on her bent arm. "I always said you were talented, but you've leaned more to mental weavings, to date that is. Why shouldn't you be a wonderful weaver?" she responded warmly. Then catching her own pun, she giggled and asked, "Can we expect to have both ourselves and our abodes draped in the weavings from your loom from now on? Let me be the first to order a batch of soft, cozy, throw blankets for the couch."

"Yep! And so appropriate for long nights at the ranch. While the wind howls and the snow piles up against the windows, I'll weave while Cal sits by the roaring fire smoking his pipe as he watched my magical creations take shape." Caught in her own imagery, she added dreamily, "He'll throw me loving looks while reading fairy tales to the babies in his lap and clustered around his feet."

"So it's quarsixpletts you're after, is it? And Cal doesn't smoke," Tannis teased.

"Burst my bubble and mess with my fantasy will you? He can just hold the damn thing in his mouth then. I've already bought him one of those long-stemmed Irish pipes and the picture I just painted is a little further down the road. I'm still doing it one at a time, starting now," Josie shot back. There. She had planted the seed should it be required in the near future.

But Tannis missed the innuendo. Josie continued to spin her fantasy life while they dressed until wafts of frying rashers drifted upstairs to entice them down for breakfast.

As they clattered down the stairs, Bett stuck her head around the corner of the kitchen door and said to Tannis, "So, yeh be hearing about the weaving woman here? A natural she be, with a feel for the twine, Morag says." A moment later she came to the table with her sizzling pan in hand, and asked, "So what will yeh be doing with this fine day?" The question was obviously a daily ritual. "Did O'Neal, the filthy sod, sing Danny Boy for yeas all with tears streaming down his face?" A nod from Josie who's mouth was full of fresh bread prompted her to add, "He's after doing that when he thinks there's a dram to be had for it."

"It was wonderful," Josie managed between mouthfuls. She took a swallow of her scalding tea and added, "I've never heard such fine singing. Most of them were as butchered as I, but it didn't affect *their* singing any. As for our plans, my husband is picking us up today. We'll be staying at the estate of a man he met in Paris for a few days, around here somewhere. But we'll still want our rooms kept for us." Bett's face looked stricken so she added, "Don't worry, we'll be back." She didn't know if that was true, but wanted to reassure Bett.

"Well, do as yeh like. But nothing like the time yeh be having here. 'Tis the gentry that be spoilin' the land hereabouts. Most castles and grand houses have folk traipsin' about, to keep the taxes up. And sure it wouldn't do for me to speak of it," but she did, "but I wouldn't have folk poking in me own home. And wid them just living in a wee nook like, in those drafty places, I hear tell ... and taking money for to see the rest." She clicked her disdain as she glanced around her spry little abode.

A firm knock on the door was followed by Cal who had to stoop slightly to get through the low doorway. With a squeal of delight, Josie flung herself into his arms, one hand still holding a rasher and the other her third slice of fresh baked bread.

"Babe! You're early. Come, you have to have some of these rashers. They're to die for!" She turned to Bett and wheedled, "Bett, meet Cal, my husband. He's in desperate need of your divine breakfast."

Beaming her pleasure, Bett was already halfway to the kitchen as Cal threw Tannis a warm greeting which she returned with considerably less enthusiasm.

With sinking heart she realized her plans were shot by Cal's early arrival unless she could slip away while they were otherwise occupied.

"Say Cal, did you know your wife is a master weaver? She's a natural I hear. Josie, why not show him your skills at the loom?" More casually she added, "While you two are doing that, I'll take a walk. It's so beautiful here, I want to see everything."

"If it's beauty you want, you'll love the estate. Acres and acres of it I'm told, with an exquisite rose garden. You can wander to your heart's content while we relax and do some catching up," he said as he threw his bride a meaningful look. "We can leave after I've eaten and checked out my wonder lady's talent. Stout's waiting out front, or was. He's probably in the pub having his own breakfast, and a pint." The little pub Josie was at last night was open for breakfast and not adverse to offering a pint or two with the first meal of the day.

She had set herself up for that one. But there was nothing to be done about it now. Another excuse would look suspicious. Why hadn't she said she needed to see Mary? She could have slipped away from the pasture side of the agricultural centre without being seen. Then a thought hit her. Since the estate was nearby if it had horses, which any respectable Irish estate would, she could ride back to the dell. She would just have to pay close attention as they drove there in order to be able to retrace her route back to the dell, or at least to Ley Node. From there she could find her way. Mollified by her plan she excused herself to pack and arranged to meet them in the weaving shop later. Once there, she realized Josie had not exaggerated. She was a natural. As she watched her tackle a complicated pattern with ease, she could sense her intuitive focus. As an observer of Josie's trance-like state, she realized for the first time how she must appear to others while she sculpted. After the short demonstration, Josie arranged for several shipments of wool to the ranch.

"This should do me until we get our own herd. I'll fill you in on it later, babe," she stated to Cal. After 'babe's' initial shock, he took the new addition to his ranch stock in stride and reserved judgement on what his neighbors would have to say about bleating sheep invading sacred cattle country. He realized this as a major dispute in old cowboy movies, but pushed his discomfort aside.

As Cal had predicted they found Stout in the pub, having just finished his meal, enjoying his second pint as he chatted with the bartender. Josie immediately teased him about drinking in the morning.

"Don't you be taking the mickey out of me, girl," he shot back. "You were legless yourself last night from what I hear, trying to out-sing the locals, and doing a poor job of it at that."

Josie stuck her tongue out at him. He shook his finger at her as he left to load their luggage into the Merc. It was apparent to Cal the two had made a game of topping each other's quips.

They said their farewells to Bett who acted as if the uncaring world had swallowed up two more of her own. "Now yeh be taking care, mind. And it's expecting yeh back, I am. Yeh have the wee basket of eats I gave yer man there?" she said, pointing to Stout. "No telling what kind of fare yeh'll find at that place. Charging a week's wage for just a bite, I hear. And the basket is for the keeping. But only 'til yeh're back, mind."

Stout and Josie were still at it as they drove east, then turned north. Much closer to the village than Tannis expected, the road followed the fencing of a well-tended estate. The sweeping expanses of green boasted diligent care and lay like mossy carpets under aged mulberry, chestnut and hawthorn trees. The large flowering shrubs which created pockets of color between the trees blended with what nature herself had sown. Stout confirmed these were the grounds of the estate they would be visiting.

Elated it was so close, Tannis realized this was the very land upon which she had walked yesterday. She would have no trouble finding the site of her tryst on horseback now. Whoever owned this estate cared for it well. She felt the first stirring of anticipation at seeing more of it, especially the rose garden Cal had mentioned.

Off to their left they saw a large building under construction. The bulldozed drive leading to the site from the main road was an eyesore now, its raw slash through ancient soil a reminder of inevitable change. About half a mile up the road they turned into an oak-fringed driveway flanked by large stone pillars and open iron gates. Halfway up the drive she caught a brief glimpse of their destination through the trees. Her breath caught in her throat as the driveway curved to the left into an open expanse of grounds, on the right of which sat the Manor House she had briefly glimpsed.

The front of the large, rectangular two-story house was clean of line and almost completely blanketed with ivy, a subtle proclamation of its antiquity. Tall paned windows were ringed with a border of the same aged golden stone under the ivy. As they slowed to a stop in the cobbled courtyard, her eyes swept up the stone pillars that supported the portico above the entrance and jutted out over the wide shallow steps leading up to the carved oak doors. Her eyes swung to the left past a two-tiered fountain and down a rolling expanse of lawn ringed with trees and a variety of lush, leafy shrubs. She scanned the genteel surroundings with growing anticipation.

The beautifully designed picture of understated elegance brought to mind a time where long-skirted ladies alighted from carriages pulled by glossy, prancing steeds. Tannis could almost hear the whisper of their trailing skirts as they swept up the broad stairs and entered the Manor.

Stout had stopped the Merc near the flagged stairs. Tannis opened the door on her left and got out, shading her eyes from the glare of the mid-day sun. For a moment she couldn't see anything clearly. Overwhelmed by the heat as she left the air-conditioned Merc, she turned towards the fountain's cooling spray, and found herself looking at her sculpture of Faye.

She stared in shocked amazement, her legs trembling from the impact of seeing her work so unexpectedly. Her first thought was that her moon child looked perfect encased within the rainbow mists which gently lapped at her feet. The second was that she would murder Cal for luring her to the client's estate, the client who had commissioned the pieces, a client she never intended to meet. The image of the fat little upstart came to mind. She did concede he had the sense to place Faye in a perfect setting, but hurt by Cal's deceit, she felt a surge of resentment. How could he! He had spoiled everything. Whirling around, her mind only on confronting Cal, she skirted the car and strode towards the group of people clustered at the bottom of the steps. Blinded by what was now outrage, she was hardly aware of the silence as she descended on the group of people who had their backs to her, intent on something directly ahead of them.

"How could you!" She said as she poked Cal between his shoulder blades. He turned, surprised at her angry tone. "You planned this, didn't you? Well, if you think I'm going to play 'artist on parade' for some fat little upstart, for whatever bizarre reason you had in mind, well you ..." her words trailed off as the loud, lilting brogue from a man at the top of the steps interrupted her tirade.

"Now what fat upstart would yeh be meaning, lass?" Seamus asked as he slowly descended the steps.

She glared at the large burly man who had addressed her. A mass of screaming red hair ringed an open freckled face. His eyes were round with amazement as he stared at her then looked to his right, and then back at her in puzzlement. Embarrassed by her outburst in front of this stunned Irishman, she followed his gaze as it once again shifted to his right.

Her heart almost leapt into her throat as she found herself staring at herself. Rather, at the sculpture of Taenacea, mounted on a block of golden stone which jutted from the side of the steps. Instinctively she followed the line of her beckoning hand and her eyes fell on the other figure across from Taenacea. It was Garth. She shouldn't have been surprised, after seeing Faye, but their positioning was so dramatic, it caught her off guard. In the daze of drinking in the whole panorama as they entered the courtyard, she had not looked at the sculptures closely. Why would she?

There was no denying her surge of satisfaction as she looked from one to the other, then over her shoulder at Faye, mounted in ethereal serenity within the fountain's spray. This was exactly how she had envisioned them. Her anger evaporated at the sheer beauty of their placement, she walked back and forth between them, thanking the hands of fate for placing them where they seemed to belong. Placed as they were, they looked like antiquities designed specifically for this beautiful Manor House.

Saemus still waited for an answer from the fiery version of the Enchantress who was now scrutinizing the sculptures with a look of what could only be dreamy satisfaction. Jesus Murphy, Muther of God! She was real at that! Wearing a dusty rose dress whose gauzy calf length folds rippled against her slender legs as she paced, she was her golden counterpart come to life. When he had first seen her he was in awe of the power she exuded. The flashing eyes framed by a mass of dark curls bounced their own indignation and gave her the wild look of a gypsy. And the silver wings that fanned from her temples seemed to him to almost glint like sparks. She was magnificent in her ire, whatever had caused it. Although her temper had quickly abated on seeing the sculptures the impact of her powerful presence remained. He could hardly wait to see what Bryan would do on seeing her. Further speculations were interrupted by a fireball of another kind: his Nell.

Her voice trilled with motherly admonishments for the gaggle of children which spilled through the door behind her. They scuffled past their parents but came to an abrupt stop in front of the group of adults by the shiny silver car. Nell moved to Seamus' side and continued with her motherly admonishments, unaware of the tension around her.

"Now don't be trooping in Uncle Bryan's garden, and watch yeh don't fall in the lake or there'll be none but the fairies to fish yeh out. Mind the little ones, Nellie, and Jamie ... yeh be keeping yer hands off wee John or it'll be Da's hands that'll be warming the seat of yeh pants, d'yeh hear now." She brushed a wisp of hair even more fiery than her partner's off her forehead, and swiftly took in the tableau before her. Surprised but not showing it, her gaze rested on the tall dark woman who stood at the center of a circle of her curious offspring.

"Sweet Jesu! It be her come to life!" she exclaimed before remembering her manners and the guests who weren't expected until late in the day. "Pardon my start. 'Tis Nell I be, the muther of this here pack of hellions ..." and before she could say more, a small excited voice piped up. "Maa! The statue. 'Tis the lady here, and 'tis her titties yer're after seeing."

The 'out of the mouth of babes' observation by the shrill little voice drew six pairs of eyes towards Tannis, then to the statue, and then back to her again in solemn appraisal. A few nervous titters danced in the air around Tannis, who didn't know quite what to say, and competent Nell, who did.

"'Tis art. And many a fine establishment has naked women, and men for that matter, carved by the best. If yeh were to attend to yer lessons like yeh do to yer squabbling, yeh'd know it, and not be gaping like the ignorant little snots yeh are! She be the model for the work most like. Now ... off yeh go, or I'll be finding some chores to put an end to yer ranging, d 'yeh hear."

The adults chuckled at both her explanation and the bobbing figures who scattered in all directions. Their curiosity satisfied, they were intent only on getting away.

"This is my friend, the artist and model, Tannis MacCrae," stated Josie as she gave Tannis' arm a squeeze, relishing the looks of surprise on the faces of the pair on the steps. "And I'm Josie, Josie Wilde. This is my husband, Cal, Tannis' agent."

The flame-headed duo stood in synchronized shock for a moment, both wondering what would happen when Bryan returned to find his Enchantress in the flesh. Better yet, to discover she was the artist as well. They shared a time-worn look of understanding and relished the seeing of Bryan's first encounter with this lovely woman.

During Josie's introductions, Tannis appraised the earthy couple who lived in such genteel surroundings with such a lively brood of children. She couldn't reconcile the picture until she caught the answer in Nell's prattling, a characteristic of all the Irish met to-date.

"'Tis business that be keeping Bryan away, he being the eldest and the Lord himself. My Seamus has just been doing the caring for his brother, 'til he sets his money-making shoes aside and takes his proper place here." She shot Seamus a meaningful look and added, "It'll be soon enough now, so we can be wed. Then a married woman's name I be carrying with pride, after the smirching of birthing this brood without the blessing of the church." She sounded fierce about the first, unconcerned by the lack of the latter sanction, but intent on having her views on this private matter known.

Having said her piece, Nell's eyes darted to the pile of luggage Stout had brought to the bottom of the steps. Briskly she said, "We'll be after getting you settled then. Yeh can see the gardens out back afore dressing for dinner. 'Tis formal," she stated, "so you'll be wanting to wear yer best. Eight sharp for the meal, and drinks afore. Yeh'll be finding some tea and eats out back on the terrace shortly, after yeh're washed up." He parental tone implied there was grime on their hands and faces that best be attended to before they would be fed.

Tannis found the foyer delightfully spacious. There were no shadowy nooks here. Light streamed down from a domed glass skylight set high above the wide curving staircase on their left. The stairs led to a wide balcony that ran along the back wall of the house high above them. The only two nooks along the foyer walls each held large Celtic crosses of intricately carved stone. Directly ahead, under the canopy of the balcony, tall glass paned doors framed by a row of paned windows on either side opened onto a huge flagged terrace beyond which could be glimpsed an inviting pastoral land-scape.

They treaded up the staircase behind Nell and followed her along the balcony whose outside wall was also interspersed with large paned windows. Josie and Cal were the first be led into a large double suite. Decorated in soothing tones of hunter green and cream accented in burnt umber, the adjoining bed-sitting room was furnished with graceful antiques.

Tannis was ushered down the hall through the next set of double doors into what Nell dubbed 'The Rose Room', a dream in pale green, pinks, and muted rose. The drapes danced with a profusion of blooms around the silken couches and chairs, accented with the same colorful cushions as lay scattered on the bed. After showing her the attached bathroom Nell excused herself to arrange for their unexpected luncheon.

Tannis put her things away and saw any telltale smudges of grime were washed away. She strolled downstairs, taking time to appreciate the tasteful decor and fondle a few particularly intriguing relics placed on several antique tables. She admired the sparking chandelier hanging from the center of the domed skylight and childishly fingered the spray of rainbow glints that danced on the wall beside her as she descended the stairs.

To her delight she found the flagstone terraced led down to a second level, and then a third. All three overlooked a gardener's paradise which sloped gently towards a tranquil lake slightly off to the right. The lake was close enough for her to see several white swans glide along the lightly rippled surface and hear the quack of the ducks which bobbed between the lily pads along its edge. A dingy tied to a small wharf at one end of the lake, and brief splashes of brightly colored heads amid the rushes confirmed this was the children's favorite spot. She remembered Nell's admonishments, and smiled.

But it was the garden which beckoned her. Everywhere she looked the panorama was filled with a glorious variety of roses. Tree roses lined pebbled walkways that meandered around flower beds filled with hybrid tea roses. The rose beds themselves were fringed with dwarf daisies, alyssum and a dotted with tangy lavender bushes. There were rose beds of grandifloras, beds of old English roses and charming little pockets of miniature roses. Everywhere she could smell the heady scent of lavender. Azalea, Boxwood, and Hydrangea bushes alongside English laurel, Irish heath and Pieris ranged in graceful clusters along the walks. Further back, the walks disappeared into hidden alcoves screened by shade trees. She caught the faint gleam of sun-kissed water in one or two spots indicating the presence of a hidden pond.

Several small spouting fountains wafted their rainbow mists across the surrounding flora with each light gust of breeze. And near the rippling lake sat a romantic gazebo, charmingly screened by a mixture of climbing roses and honeysuckle.

Off to her left, fanning out from the stables attached to that end of the house by a stone-fenced courtyard, lay white fenced pastures where she could see several horses crop the lush grass. Drunk with the sheer beauty of her surroundings, she caught Josie's approach out of the corner of her eye. She turned to her and said grudgingly, "Say what you will about the brother being a fat little upstart, but he sure has a beaut of an estate here."

"So all's forgiven?" Josie asked hopefully, knowing Tannis' silence meant she was really miffed.

"I didn't say that. I just mean that seeing this place is worth having to put up with the upstart at dinner. But Cal will hear about it, for sure. I'm truly surprised and disappointed by what he did," Tannis stated as she turned and sauntered over to the tables where Cal was already helping himself to tea and a variety of small sandwiches, baked goods, and fruit.

"You could be surprised. You might even like him," Josie said as she trailed after her. "Besides, he can't be all bad having that teddy bear Seamus and Nell and their brood in the family."

Cal had overheard and attempted to get Tannis to see their host in a more receptive light. "See how he mounted the sculptures? He does have an eye for placement and these gardens certainly reflect his appreciation for beauty. Besides, it was he that funded Ley Node. He must have considerable fondness for the land to finance such a controversial project. Tells you something about the man, don't you think?"

The couple credited her slightly quizzing look to a re-evaluation of their host's merits. Little did they know the thoughts that had actually prompted her puzzlement. She wandered back over to the railing with her tea and plate, set down her cup and saucer, and munched on a sandwich as she scanned the rolling hills in the distance.

A familiar feeling had washed over her. She knew she had met her 'Garth' on this estate and wondered who he could be. Since he didn't look anything like the redheads living here, he might be a gamekeeper, neighbor, or tourist out on a walk like herself. She blushed with the memory of the clean hands that had held hers, and the lips that had kissed her wrists in the same intimate yet profound gesture Taenacea had experienced with Garth. Then she remembered his answer to her query about the shrine and decided he was most likely a neighbor, one she must somehow contrive to meet.

Damn! It was well past noon now, and she had missed her tryst. Completely enthralled with the gardens, she had forgotten all about her promise to return to the dell. Even if she jumped on a horse this minute and raced over the hills like a lunatic, he would be long gone before she found the dell. All she could do to salvage the situation was to slip away tomorrow on the off chance he would return again. Perhaps she was testing fate in hopes he would. But how was he to know where she was? Well, she was here now, and it was beautiful. She decided to follow the paths through the gardens, barefoot, and discover what lay within the secret havens of lush shrubbery.

Cal and Josie were lost in the privacy of their own whisperings when she took her cup and plate back to the table. She would not be missed, so she removed her sandals and left them on the patio. As she wandered along the pebbled paths she relished their smooth warmth against the soles of her feet. She inhaled the sweet fragrances that clung to her skin as she meandered alongside rose beds and trailed her fingers lightly over individual blooms that caught her fancy.

Much later, as the evening air teased a final wave of scent from the garden, heady with nature's sweetness, Tannis returned to the Manor to bath and dress for dinner, prepared to pay the price of her wondrous afternoon. When she entered her room she was surprised to find her golden dinner dress lain across the bed with the headband beside it and matching shoes placed on the floor. Her silent query was quickly answered by a voice behind her.

"Thought it most appropriate for a great Manor dinner. It suits the setting, don't you think?"

"And just how did you know it would be, may I ask?" Tannis asked suspiciously. She watched Josie's face carefully. There were entirely too many surprises forthcoming from her pal lately.

"Just a psychotic moment, I guess. Gotta run! But hey, I'm wearing something flowing and romantic too, for tonight we play the ladies of the Manor. Humor me. Besides, Nell said formal," was the light response before she dashed down the hall to cut short any further interrogation.

"I swear, that gal takes far too much for granted," Tannis muttered as she ran her shower. She lathered herself with the rose-scented soap provided, reminded of her afternoon amid their blooms. She felt a slight quiver in her belly, but chalked it up to apprehension at meeting the client, something she just hated doing. Especially in this case, since it was her naked likeness which sat outside his front doors. Hopefully her shimmering dress would detract from what he could envision it covered.

In the master suite at the other end of the Manor an irritated Bryan vigorously scrubbed dust and sweat from his body. His irritation was directed at himself, for feeling and acting like a love-sick fool. He had gone to the little dell with a flush of desire and hope after a turbulent night of dreams in ancient times.

In lands darker than these, he had played out overlapping scenes with his Enchantress. When she wore anything at all, an obvious Freudian implication, it was a green skirt and transparent blouse which always exposed one luscious breast. He replayed battles where she fought ferocious as any man by his side. But there were also torrid lovemaking scenes, actualizing his desires in the dell, but always fading before consummation. So torrid in fact, that even now under the shower's blast of cool water his genitals responded to the images in his mind.

He'd rushed to the dell, but she wasn't there yet. So he had waited. Hours later, his picnic lunch lay wilted in the shade, wilted just like his hopes. He had paced the perimeter of the dell and even crested several surrounding hilltops in hopes of catching a glimpse of her approaching figure. But by late afternoon she had still not come. His emotions had run the full gamut from hope to worry, then anger at his hopeful stupidity, and finally dejected defeat. Even his faith in the certainty she was for him was shaken. Whatever the reason, she had not come as promised. He began to wonder if his certainty was a mere illusion, if it had all been a mere illusion.

He wished now he had never extended the invitation to his weekend guests. He'd lost all desire to entertain anyone, even Lorne. He wanted only to scour the hills and surrounding villages to ask if anyone had seen her. For a moment he had the urge to drown his sorrows in a bottle of Scotch, but breeding and self-discipline won out. Oblivious to the picnic basket and blanket still on the ground, he had left the dell and trudged back to the Manor, his confidence oddly shaken. Her absence felt like rejection. The one time he had allowed himself to open to his desires, to allow his feelings free rein, his hopes had been crushed. An uncharacteristic bitterness washed over him for a moment which he quickly pushed aside. He braced himself for this evening's ordeal, of playing the gracious host while all he could think of was his Enchantress and why she had not come.

As he skirted the north end of the house on his return, he had seen a silver Mercedes and Lorne's red jag parked in the courtyard beside his own green jag and the help's various vehicles. Feeling he couldn't face anyone yet, he had dashed unseen up the private stairwell leading directly to his suite. He had ripped off his clothes and jumped right into the shower in hopes of scrubbing away his turmoil. Instead his mind replayed the events of yesterday adding to his frustration.

After a much gentler towel rub, he grabbed a silk shirt, pair of crisp linen trousers and dressed quickly. As he ran a comb through his hair before tying it back in his signature ponytail, he stopped to scrutinize his reflection in the mirror. Thankfully he didn't look nearly as haunted as he felt. He clipped on his Rolex, slipped his bare feet into soft leather loafers and headed down to the library for a drink before greeting his guests.

Lorne and Seamus were already taking lusty draws from their highballs when he entered the library, but stopped talking when they saw him. Both looked guilty, as if he had caught them flinching the family silver.

"Hey buddy, where the hell were you today?" Lorne asked, trying to mask his excitement. Cal had told him what was about to transpire. He shot Bryan a speculative look and raised his glass in a silent toast. Beneath Bryan's apparent composure he sensed a slight tightness of jaw cloaked some inner tension, so smoothly added, "Say, that's some dame at your front steps. No wonder you're besotted. A wild babe like that could induce even me to give up my bachelor status. Oh, and not a bad job on your mug either. The artist certainly stretched artistic license by making you look like a Fabio or one of those other romantic buccaneers the ladies drool over," he added with a sardonic grin.

A haunted look passed over Bryan's face before he collected himself and retorted, "Thanks bucko. Glad you're on my side of the negotiation table. And do help yourself to my best Scotch." He turned to Seamus and asked, "Are the guests settled? And what's Cal's wife's friend like? Some barracuda who'll sink her teeth into Lorne I hope."

His barb caught Lorne off guard. Seamus was saved from answering by Nell's voice from the doorway.

"Sure I'd be finding you louts swilling the spirits in here, what with the guests ready to come down. Drink up, and mind yeh have no more before the meal, what with the dinner wine and all. They'll be thinking there's none sober on this Isle, d'ya hear. There'll be champagne to sip in the foyer 'afore they come down."

Nell stood with hands on hips. Her bright pink satin blouse clashed alarmingly with her flaming halo of hair from which several springy curls had already escaped the tight topknot designed to control what took to no taming. She waited until they had drained their glasses, then shooed them before her like a gaggle of giant geese, her long green velvet skirt buffing the hardwood floor behind her.

Her voice had carried up to the balcony and brought a smile to Cal and Josie's lips. They stood looking down at the gardens while they waited for an unusually tardy Tannis. Cal, elegant in a dark shirt and pale trousers shot his bride appreciative glances. A wispy froth of rainbow colored chiffon cascaded from her tight empire bodice. The pointed layers fell in a whisper of movement around her feet, and the long sleeves caressed her wrists with a fall of soft ruffles. She looked like a spring garden in bloom. Her braid was charmingly looped and held with a bevy of flowers above her ear, and except for a cream velvet ribbon around her neck from which hung a porcelain rose, she was unadorned.

"You're like a breath of the garden, babe. My own Irish rose," crooned Cal as he planted a tender kiss on the top of her glossy hair. Just then a bent-over Tannis wobbled down the hall towards them, trying to extract the bracelet she had caught on the edge of her dress.

"You go ahead. I'll be a minute to untangle this. Besides, I forgot my headband," she wailed as she hobbled back to her room, careful not to rip her dress on the attached bracelet.

"It's not like her to be so dithery. It's almost as if she senses what's coming and is avoiding the inevitable," breathed Josie, adding, "Lights, cameras, and action." The scene soon to unfold was so dramatic, she felt like its prelude should be announced. It was.

"Ah, 'tis the Wilde newlyweds. And a lovelier pair has never been seen gracing this stairwell," exclaimed Nell, chuckling at her verbal pun as she lifted her champagne flute in greeting. Beside her stood Seamus and two other men who paused in conversation to look at the descending pair with interest. One was blonde with distinctly Norse features above a sinewy body, the other, the spitting image of the sculpture of Garth.

Josie's knees weakened for a moment and she faltered as she stared at Bryan MacCumal, the dashing Lord of Lagohaire. She couldn't begin to imagine how Tannis would react on seeing him, based on her own reaction now. He was absolutely gorgeous! She smiled a crooked hello, eyes still glued to him as Cal pulled her towards the little roll bar by the drawing room doors. It was positively eerie seeing a statue come to life. After the men shook hands, she accepted a champagne flute from the hands of the impressive Lord himself.

The resemblance was uncanny. Even she had not imagined he would look exactly as Tannis remembered from her time travels, and duplicated with her sculpture. She barely heard the buzz of voices around her, but felt the collective restlessness triggered by the tardiness of the last guest.

Bryan asked what she thought of an artist's ability to create such a likeness, sight unseen. But his need for an answer evaporated as some primal instinct drew his eyes up towards the balcony. Between the wide-spaced railings he watched a pair of slender silken legs move briskly along the landing, then pause at the top of the stairs.

The murmur of conversation around him dropped to a hush that sizzled with electric anticipation as his eyes moved up the legs, along the slender length of silk and lace twinkling with beads, and rested on the woman's halo of curls. Her head was bent as she carefully stepped off the landing. He watched one graceful hand slide lightly down the curved banister as she descended, a hand which looked very familiar.

Tannis, intent on the small thread hanging from her dress where she had extracted her bracelet was alerted by a deadly silence. Puzzled, she raised her head and scanned the faces below. As if swept there by an unseen force, her eyes locked with a pair of brilliant blue eyes, blue like ice and fire. She faltered and clutched the banister to steady herself. This was not possible. Stunned beyond belief, she said, "It's you!" just as the party in question said exactly the same thing.

Bryan felt as if the ground beneath him had shifted as she raised her head and he looked into the face of his Enchantress! In that instant of recognition, he couldn't even begin to fathom what he felt. His ears rang, and a wave of delicious heat flushed his body as he heard Josie announce with relish, "In answer to your earlier question, why not ask the artist herself?" There was no response, so she prompted, "Bryan MacCumal, meet Tannis MacCrae, sculptress extraordinaire, and my best friend," the latter added with undeniable pride.

Tannis stood frozen as she looked into the face of the man from the dell, the face of her Garth. Bryan, Josie had called him, a delicious name. Bryan. Still numb with shock, it took her a moment to grasp that he was the buyer of her sculptures, as well as the owner of this estate. She shut her eyes, then opened them again. It was no dream. She could see he was as shocked as she. As if in slow-motion, a kaleidoscope of images undulated before her eyes.

A surge of warmth rose up her body and flushed her cheeks, a warmth so sweet, it nearly pained her. Imprisoned in the silent tabloid, she heard the tinkle of chimes all around her; a sound which danced with the delight of this moment of sweet completion. 'The Firmness of Rock' was realized, for she now knew she was home. Home, with the man whose soul had followed hers through the planes and dimensions of time to complete a cycle begun long ago, a cycle completed in the very place it had begun. So firm was this passion, so rock-like its intent, its will would be done.

As the vision of her whole Quest raced before her eyes, she knew she would live here on the lands that Taenacea's feet had never trod, and claim for her her birthright. With her certainty came the awareness of Taenacea's presence, and her caressing look at Garth. An audible sigh of satisfaction escaped her lips. She knew her task was done as she faded into the recesses of Tannis' heart.

Tannis said her own farewells: to the mystical Quest so trustingly begun and now completed, and to her unknown yearnings for love kept hidden even from herself. She felt the grounding warmth of the Mother around her and knew she had justly won her prize. Those thoughts foremost in her mind, she graced the waiting group with a dazzling smile, punctuated by the dimple that danced by her mouth, a small remembrance of who she had been.

Bryan stood frozen in his own timeless place and saw many women within the one. Whatever doubts he may have had, even moments before, were instantly washed away. Mesmerized, his eyes were all that moved as they swept up and down the golden vision before him. The Enchantress, the country maiden, a dream, an artist, and a very real Tannis MacCrae, who had created the wonders mounted outside his front doors: all one and the same woman. It was almost too much to absorb. A coil of heat held him captive, a heat that flushed him from head to toe, a heat that ringed and stilled his hammering heart, and a heart that awakened erotic images he found difficult to suppress. If there was such a thing as destiny, it was this moment.

He watched waves of emotion wash across her face. Curious. First there was a look of deep glowing love solidifying into strength of purpose, then a softening to a dreamy glaze, as if lost in some cherished memory. Then her face cleared. She locked eyes with him and threw him a smile so dazzling, he could almost feel its warmth. As the dimple beside her mouth danced, he waited for the witticism he knew she was about to toss his way. He wasn't disappointed.

"You're not a fat little upstart after all. Good. I wouldn't want such a man to see me half naked," she said with a husky giggle as she drifted down the stairs towards him.

Chapter Twenty-Three

INNER OFFERED A GREAT DEAL OF FOOD FOR THOUGHT, but left most of the delectable fare untouched. After the stunned silence during Bryan and Tannis' introduction and departure through the terrace doors, everyone began to stir. You could almost hear the air buzz with questions as they followed the couple outside, especially after Tannis' unusual comment.

Cal held Josie firmly by the hand in order to give the pair a little time to themselves. "You did well, babe," he said. He then voiced the question that puzzled him. "Your plan was certainly climatic, just like you said it would be. But I can't help feeling they've already met," he said, as he glanced over her head at the pair now deep in conversation.

"I don't see how," Josie responded, certain she had events under control.

Seamus refreshed their drinks with outward calm. He too gravitated towards Josie, for her satisfied grin told him she played no small part in whatever had brought these two together. "'Tis like a tale of old, this wonder that be happening to him," he whispered to Nell once drinks had been disbursed.

"And time too. She'll not be letting him out of her heart to my mind," she responded with satisfaction.

"Well, I'll be dammed," stated Lorne. It almost made him believe in love at first sight. Four pairs of eyes looked to Josie, who raised her hand to silence the barrage of questions she knew would come. Judiciously, she said, "Hear, hear! It is a tale of wonder, one you'll hear over dinner. It's a story that'll stretch your concept of reality as well." She paused dramatically and turning to the pair by the railing and toasted them with a, "To true love, through time . . . and to magic," which further peaked her companion's curiosity.

In lieu of the unexpected events, a quick seating shuffle placed Tannis, Seamus and Nell at Bryan's right, and Lorne, Josie and Cal on his left. Bryan, seated at the head of the table, waited for everyone to be seated before he turned to Tannis and asked the question Seamus had not yet received an answer to. "And just who is this fat little upstart you referred to, Tannis?" He relished the sound of her name on his lips, still hardly believing she actually sat beside him. She was so close, he could lean over and touch a silken curl.

A sudden burst of laughter from Josie and Cal accompanied her own embarrassed laugh as Tannis replied, "I made him up." In response to the quizzing looks she tried to explain. "I always make up stories when I sculpt. In order to see them clearly in my mind, I invent who they are, their personality, what they feel and such. It brings them to life for me, and I can then capture a mood based on how I think they would feel." Her audience attentive, she continued.

"I try to get a feel for the client too in order to envision what they would like. Since I didn't know anything about who the buyer was for these three pieces, I decided he was some fat little upstart who made his millions on the commodity market and bought himself an estate and title. The image was triggered by having just met somebody who looked like that and the persona stuck." She threw Josie a smile at the memory of her first encounter with Giles, then continued. "I even imagined the pieces would collect dust in the nooks of some chilly castle and decided it wouldn't matter much if I took advantage of artistic license. I had personal reasons for sculpting these three pieces and thought I could kill two birds with one stone." Her explanation sounded odd even to herself so she shot Josie a 'help me out here' look.

Josie, impatient to launch into the tale of the Quest, knew she needed permission and felt Tannis' appeal had just done so. But before she did she looked at the auras around the table. It was clear everyone seated here tonight was linked to the story in some way, she was sure of it. The how would reveal itself later.

"Everything that's happened is tied to a very unique Quest. The issue of the sculptures and likenesses are all part of the tale." She looked around the table and asked, "Do you know the history of this estate?"

A puzzled Seamus answered. "Aye, a bit of it. 'Tis very old, built on the site of the original manor from what the family records be saying. There's a telling of some ancient bond wid another family that goes back a'ways." He wondered how this connected with the sculptures from across the seas as he leaned back to let the maid ladle the Vichyssoise into his bowl.

"That's an understatement. The story actually begins right here in Ireland, with the legend of Fionn mac Cumhaill, Warrior Chief of the Fianna," Josie said slowly, relishing the impact of her statement. Careful to avoid the intimate aspects of Tannis' experiences, she emphasized the connection between the Quest and Tannis' studio experiences while the main course was being served. She brought to life the memories of the successive strands, including Linka's tale confirming the authenticity of one of Ireland's most beloved legends, but down-played the magical aspects of Tannis and Taenacea. It was for Tannis to decide how much of her magical abilities she would share with Bryan. Josie noticed that even the men paused in their eating when she exposed the evil connivance of the despicable Giles Kaylon.

At first Tannis watched Bryan's face covertly, wondering what he must be thinking. She had no idea if he even believed in reincarnation, but his attentiveness was encouraging. Then she felt herself drawn into the story, her story, and relived the events with the telling. Privately she relished the unspoken and intimate aspects, knowing the cause sat at her side.

Bryan was attentive, as fascinated by the ever-changing landscape of Tannis' face as by the story itself. As strange as the tale sounded, a trail of remembered history gave it credence. And within this setting, after their magical meeting in the dell, the story seemed somehow fitting, adding a mystical depth to the woman by his side. Occasionally, as if overwhelmed with emotion stirred by something remembered or said, she would drop her eyes and give cursory attention to her food. He suspected it was more to hide her feelings than to relish the fare. And at other times, he could almost see the other one, Taenacea, peer from her eyes, emulating a power that strengthened Tannis' features before they again settled into those he already cherished. Several aspects of the story brought his own dreams to mind, but he would discuss those with Tannis privately.

Response to Josie's tale ranged from sighs, oohs, and ahhs, punctuated by the occasional laugh and misty eye. The sighs came from Lorne who relished the ingenuity of the Writs and family coalition, the 'ahs' from Seamus as Josie described the progressive land-husbandry of both the Welsh and Irish Estates, the misty eyes from Nell as the magic of the faery ring and little Faye was shared, and the laughter from all when Josie recounted Linka's antics.

The conclusion of the tale was accompanied by the arrival of coffee. "So, the desire to reunite sat in abeyance on a spiritual level for over five hundred years, waiting for the most auspicious circumstances to ensure completion." The latter was stated in a tone implying these two would unquestionably marry and set things right. Josie sat back smugly and sipped her coffee with satisfaction. She had told the tale well, and now waited for the questions that danced on several pairs of lips.

"So yeh're after sayin' we go back to the Fionn? How could that be?" Seamus was the first to ask.

"It appears so, from a reincarnational point of view. And perhaps historically as well," Cal responded. He relished Tannis and Josie's startled looks, and explained. "After Josie told me the story, I contacted a Vatican Historian I had some previous dealings with, and the lineage is being examined even as we speak. The preliminary report looks good, better than efforts by others to lay claim to the same heritage. There are gaps in the records, of course, particularly between the sixth and seventh century, but it's surprising how far back the church's registry of births and deaths do go."

"How so?" asked Lorne.

"It seems a duplicate of local records was always sent to the central church library. Such records were collected when the church's foothold strengthened. They're still stored in the Vatican, like so much else we're unaware of." He smiled at Josie triumphantly and added, "Linka is already working on her grandparent's connection to the Lagohaires." He turned to a startled Tannis, adding, "By the way, the kids are fine, and so's the garden."

Bryan paled slightly. Kids? He turned to Tannis. "I thought you only had one daughter?" Not that it mattered, much, but he suddenly realized he knew nothing personal about this woman outside of the Quest and her artistic abilities. He held his breath, awaiting her answer. Then he panicked. He wondered if she was married.

Be it from the strain of reliving her personal experience or the aftermath of her surprise at meeting Bryan in the flesh, she felt like she needed to break her inner tension. A good laugh would do it. "Oh, he's talking about the three boys and my little girl. Of course, they're much younger than Linka, all between one and eight years old," she said casually.

Josie, quick on the uptake, added mischievously, "Oh, they're so adorable, but Zoie is a real little terror."

Cal, knowing they would play it to the hilt, jumped to defend his gender. "They're talking about her cats, not kids. These two will have you going all night. They do it to me all the time," he added with a 'that's what you're in for' look and dramatic sigh to punctuate his point.

Inwardly Bryan was relieved and amused. She had a sense of humor. But he was more interested in an answer to something else. Turning to her, he asked, "So Tannis, you didn't know I was the owner of this Estate or the client of your pieces when we met?"

"No, I didn't. I was so flustered at meeting you in the flesh I was dazed. Especially after I ran away like I did," she said, smiling in embarrassment. Although she spoke softly, Josie had caught her response.

"You two met? When? You mean I missed something," she gasped. Her look of disbelief set off a ripple of laughter around the table. Then all heads turned to Bryan for an explanation.

"Yesterday, on the estate," he said and proceeded to tell of their chance encounter by the altar. He omitted the more delicate aspects of the meeting, and sensed Tannis' silent gratitude. Her comment about Ruftar made sense, now. It would have been Taenacea who had addressed him then, if that was possible. It must also have been she who had partnered him in his dreams. Whether he believed all this was real, or possible, he couldn't deny his own experience. But he would have to give this amazing story some thought. Further musings were interrupted by Josie's, "Well, I'll be damned! And I never picked up on anything, you witch. And what's this about an altar?" she asked.

"I wonder if it be the altar spoken of in the old tales the grandfather told, to the faery lady, Fiona," Seamus interjected. "If this tale be true, 'twould be hers, the intended bride of William MacCumal that the shrine be for. This was her home by the records. And that I do know, if not of the tie to the Fionn." He would have to give that remote and unbelievable possibility some thought. If true, it would be a pride he would carry willingly.

Another round of coffee accompanied speculations about the family connection, the shrine, and other such ruins, prompting a telling of that tale, as Seamus had heard it told. When he was done he assured them he would check the older family records, now crammed into the top shelves of the library, to verify what he could of their lineage.

It was Nell who asked the question the others had been wondering about. She had taken in all she heard, enchanted by the mystical aspect of the story. She was not at all skeptical of the succession of events that would have most questioning their sanity. But one question burned in her mind, only she didn't know how to broach it. There was nothing for it but to blurt it out. "It's bursting I am to know what it feels like, this having of another inside yeh, or living the life of another, and the knowing of it. Sweet Jesu . . . it must be a daft feeling." She shivered slightly just at the thought of it, and wondered how she would react. It was one thing to dally in the mind over it, another to have it happen to you.

Tannis paused to choose her words. The credibility of her story hung on the line, as did acceptance by these lovely people. "At first it felt like a vivid dream memory. Then it was like being sucked into a tunnel and coming out the other side into a life you recognize and know is yours. There's no other way to explain it. You know you're real, and you can feel everything, the sun warming you, your own thoughts as that person, what you smell and touch. You know who you are, just like you do right now, here." She crinkled her forehead and continued. "The difference for me, was the more experiences I had as Taenacea, the more we blended with each other. That's what took some getting used to. Even though she was me in another time and place, experiencing a different life to my own one right now, we are aspects of the same soul nonetheless, and her experience is mine too."

Silence as they digested her words induced her to qualify with some defiance, "I believed in reincarnation before, but only in an abstract way. But experiencing this Quest and the residual proofs of my time travel confirms its validity, for me at any rate. Especially after I went to Wales," she added, giving Josie a meaningful look.

Nell nodded her acquiescence, but wasn't done yet. "And so, would you be recognizing another from that life, here like? Other than the brute beside yeh. What with Josie's saying the eyes be the windows of the soul, and yeh knowing the professor was Giles then, through his eyes."

Surprised by her question Tannis thought for a moment, then said, "Yes. Yes I think I do." She looked into each pair of eyes around the table then returned her gaze to Nell's. "You were little Nell then too ... and Seamus the shy stable boy, Liam," she added with sudden insight, and obvious delight.

"And were we wed then?" Nell blurted out, oblivious to the laughter around her. The issue of marriage was obviously foremost in her mind.

"Considering you were just eleven years old, I don't believe so," Tannis chuckled, "at least not while I was alive. But you can go back yourself, if you wish, and find out. Josie can show you how," she added.

"Ah no! I'll be after thinkin' on that awhile. My Seamus was my heart's own then too, yeh say?" Her expression confirmed she had already decided to take this bold journey. She was somewhat relieved when Cal entered the conversation and diverted attention away from herself. She needed time to think on this.

"I'm intrigued by Henry's part in this. If history serves me right, Edward was King at the time. Why would Garth seek Henry's signature and seal for the Writ?"

He had made a good point. "Magical foresight," Tannis stated. "Taenacea knew from her visions Richard would be defeated at Bosworth, that Henry would be crowned. Only his signature could honor the Writ and protect her lands." Then, clarifying her statement, she added, "Although most events in life are probabilities based on choices and the variables of free will, any of which could play out as reality, there are some 'givens', or destined events, events an Auger could foretell. Taenacea had this ability."

"What intrigues and amazes me is how this story weaves through historic events, and is supported by them," Cal mused out loud. "Henry landed at Milford Haven in south Wales after his exile, I believe. It was King Charles of France who financed his march to battle, through what would have been Taenacea's lands, en route to Bosworth. I find it odd however, that he would take that route. It was certainly not the most direct to the east coast of England."

"I never thought of that," Tannis said. "Garth knew he was marching somewhat south of our lands from what the messengers had reported. But while I was alive, I never saw or met him, so it must have been after my death that he actually crossed my lands, if he did, that is."

"It was, and he did," came the quiet response.

Eyes swung towards a slightly abashed Lorne, who said, "As King Henry's royal chamberlain, I watched him sign the writ for Garth, knowing his offerings of gold and food would help ensure Henry's victory. It was on his invitation that Henry replenished his supplies from the Lianarth holdings. That's why we swung north instead of moving more directly east, where we would have missed Taenacea's lands completely. In fact, Henry was sorely saddened on hearing the news of her death. Her reputation had preceded her and he had wanted to meet her for himself."

Bryan's look of amazement was the most incredulous of all as he turned to his partner and said, "Why, you never told me you believed in past lives, or anything like that. And you . . . as King Henry's, what was it? Royal chamberlain?" His obvious doubt hung in the air between them.

"You never asked," Lorne said, quite unruffled by Bryan's skepticism. "Us cerebral types don't think numbers all the time, you know. What makes you think you know everything about me anyhow? Besides, look who's talking," he shot back with an implication that what Bryan had shared with him was just as surprising. "I've discovered some rather interesting new things about you too, mate."

"But, chamberlain to King Henry. That's a bit of a stretch," Bryan queried. This revelation, following Tannis' mater-of-fact statements spoken from another time had him feeling a little skeptical. Had he overheard this conversation from lips other than those he loved and trusted, he would have thought them all mad.

"Maybe, but I've had three regressions under hypnosis, I may add, that have confirmed it."

"Why?" Bryan asked, curious.

"Because I've had strange dreams since I was a kid. All the same; battles and marching, and then always being beside a king and the throne of England. That's fine for a kid, but not something you expect to continue as an adult now is it?" was the sardonic response.

Everyone tossed in their two pence, with questions about what it was really like back then, and what it had felt like to him compared to what Tannis had described. As the animated discussion continued, Bryan, reeling from the disclosures heaped on top of each other, signaled a breather by rising and suggesting they adjourn to the terrace. He automatically reached for Tannis' hand, pulled her up, and bent close to whisper in her ear. After her nod of agreement, they walked out, still hand in hand. Instead of staying on the terrace, he led her through the rose garden and along the subtly lit paths towards the gazebo. Within its sweet scented shadows, they sat side by side, grateful for the evening stillness that still held a trace of the day's lingering warmth.

Tannis was silent, content to allow Bryan to absorb the disclosures of the evening, thankful for the opportunity to quietly enjoy his presence at her side. Although deep in thought, his fingers ran lightly along her arm and stopped to trace a light sensual pattern on her wrist. His unconscious strokes were so erotic, she relished the shivers of desire which rippled over her in a succession of heart-melting waves. She could sit here all night beside this man, saying not a word but feeling the impact of his presence all over her body.

When he finally stirred and turned towards her, his gaze was even, but burned into her very being. Then, with a twinkle in his eyes, he said, "I asked for one, and got two. The luck of the Irish." She looked puzzled. He didn't enlighten her, but added softly, "All I know, Tannis MacCrae, is that I fell in love with you the moment I set eyes on you. If it started with my obsession with the sculpture, it's because she *is* you, and everything you are, including this Taenacea of bygone days. I don't understand much of that or what brought you here, but it's *you* I love and want to spend the rest of my life with." With a worried frown he added, "If you'll have me?"

Her answer had been formed so long ago, it slipped out smoothly. "Yes," she said simply.

They searched each other's eyes, strangers to be discovered as friends just met, yet with the assurance what would be discovered would confirm what was already know and deeply felt. There would be many conversations about today's revelations, and many others to cement and expand their heart's ties. Enough to last a lifetime—or more. But for now, the commitment made, they could begin the delight of discovering each other.

Assured by her certainty, Tannis asked with a lilt in her voice, "And will yea be crossing the seas to bed me every few months then, like 'afore?" Her dimple danced in time to her saucy smile.

"Not likely," came the unexpected response, delivered in a bantering lilt that matched hers and brought back heart-wrenching memories from his dream flashes. In an even thicker brogue he added, "It's never leaving me side yeh'll be, woman of mine. Unless to catch a breath of air from under the covers now and then, and to have a bite to eat, for a man has other hungers too, if naught but to keep the body able."

He delighted in her throaty laughter. He took a deep breath of the fragrant night, then sobered by the jesting implication, became aware of what could create a very real obstacle. "Where do you want to live?" So much depended on her answer.

"In my home, of course."

He sensed it had all been too good to be true. Her answer didn't clarify anything at all, and with sinking heart he persisted, "You want to stay in

Canada then?" He looked around quickly as if in farewell to the lands so recently reclaimed as his.

His saddened look tore at Tannis' heart. This was obviously not a moment for levity. She cupped his face in her hands, smiled at him tenderly and admonished as she would a child, "No, you nit. Not Canada. Here. Your home, the home of our ancestors, and my home now." His relief was so blatant, she had to chuckle.

"I can work anywhere, Bryan." Lordy, how she loved the sound of his name, "and I can't think of a lovelier place than this. I think I fell in love with this land the moment we drove to Ley Node. Only not right away. I mean my living here. There's a few things that need attending to first, like telling my daughter, you meeting her, disposing of my house, and getting the cats over here without that awful quarantine. You don't have a problem with the cats, do you? I couldn't bear being away from them for six months." She was amazed at the enormity of what she had just said, as if discussing a grocery list. A few months ago she could never have even contemplated leaving her home, or Canada, least of all for a man just met. But here she was, doing just that. The ancestral memories awakened her recognition of where she belonged. There was no question it was here.

"Of course, you do have to pass muster with my daughter and the felines, or the whole deal's off, you know," she chided. Although her tone was light, he knew she meant it. He could already recognize the steely undercurrent in her tone. Privately he identified her unbending will as 'the other one', and thought it would prove interesting to live with this duality within one woman. He marveled at how casually he had accepted what would be considered rubbish not long ago. When he was with her, there was no question it was all real, even their reincarnational connection. Besides, she had done nothing to try to convert him, just explaining what it was for her. He liked that. Then another reality hit him. "You'll have to go back then, won't you?" he asked, unable to mask the dejection already felt at the thought of a separation so soon after finding her.

"Yes. So, let's sort out the most important details, and then . . ." Her voice trailed off with an implied question and promise, should they reach a speedy agreement. They did.

Both could feel their longing and desire spark the air between them. Finally Tannis voiced what both had been thinking and said, "I want it to be outside, under the stars. In these gardens. Tonight, under the moon." She rose, and still holding his hand, led him back to the house.

The softly lit terrace was deserted now but they could hear animated conversation through the open library window. They would not be missed. Bryan led her up the stairs and arranged to meet later by the lower terrace in case the others decided to take a breath of air outside. This was one tryst neither intended to miss.

Bryan was waiting for her when she came back down wrapped in a long black cloak. The intent of the blanket slung over his arm sent a quiver of excitement through her, followed by another as he took her hand and whispered, "I know the perfect spot." He led her down the paths towards the far edge of the garden. They crested a gentle rise behind the lake and descended into a small dell surrounded by trees, not unlike the haven where they had first met. Eyes used to the moonlit night, she scanned the intimate setting, perfect for what was intended. She suspected there were many such secret hide-a-ways between the low rolling hills which held the sensual secrets of similar trysts through time.

Under the smile of the full moon, Bryan spread the blanket on the ground. Separated by the width of cloth, he stood before Tannis in silence, his heartbeat accompanied only by a slight rustle of anticipation from the leaves.

Tannis took her time and really looked at the glorious man before her. There would be no haste in this encounter, for it was timeless. Shadowing from the moon accented the strong clean lines of his face and reflected an ancient appeal: that of a man's desire for the woman of his heart. In ageless seduction, as others had before her, she reached for the clasp at her neck, and slowly let the cloak fall from her naked body.

Bryan drank in the unabashed beauty of the woman who stood proud and still before him, offering herself to him without coyness: a woman in the full bloom of maturity and desire.

He took his time as he ran his eyes over her, to forever imprint this moment in his heart. The silvery glow of the moon lay on the fullness of her ivory breasts, the nipples raised in expectation. The line of her waist was lean, but fanned into softly rounded hips. His eyes paused a moment at the dark vee, then continued down her long and shapely legs. Even more slowly than his downward gaze, he caressed her body with the hunger of his desire as his eyes moved back up again.

He paused at the steady throb of the pulse at her throat, the only indication of excitement in her stillness. Were it not for her taut nipples and the pulse, he would have thought her a statue. With tiny silvery glints in her dark halo of hair, she looked magical and mysterious; a goddess risen out of the earth itself, both ethereal and ripe with promise. Hypnotized by this surreal illusion, and in the spirit of her primal offering, he removed his own clothing until he too stood naked, open to her scrutiny.

He was everything she could imagine, and remembered. Her eyes scanned the powerful torso with its wide shoulders and broad chest tapering to a lean waist and long, well-shaped muscular legs. The dark matting of hair on his chest narrowed to a trail across his taut belly, then clustered more heavily around his manhood, but only lightly dusted his thighs and calves. She raised her eyes to his, her mouth slightly open as she silently asked for more.

He sensed her smoldering request and closed the space between them. Before he raised a hand to touch her, he took a deep calming breath. A moment like this must not be rushed.

She felt him gently cup her breasts in his hands, then gently run his thumbs over and around her nipples. They tightened in response and sent a snake of fire into her womb. He continued to touch and stroke, but lightly, like a silk feather dancing on her skin. When he lifted her hands and pressed his lips lightly to her wrists, first one, then the other, she knew this would forever be their private signal. And when he followed the gesture with a slow, lazy circle of his tongue, she expelled her breathe in an low moan. She felt as if the night itself had joined him as soft wafts of air encircled her body, landing for momentary caresses of their own.

The flush on her cheeks and promise of her response fanned his own desire, but Bryan held himself in check. He would not rush, in spite of his arousal.

When he lowered his head and gently cupped her breasts in his hands again, Tannis could hardly breathe. She felt the heat left by the trail of his fiery tongue as it deliberately circled first one nipple, then the other. He paused and did nothing until she arched towards him in encouragement. Then he took first one nipple into his mouth and drew on it, then the other. Tannis could not suppress another moan at the agonizing delight of his erotic touch. Her growing lust had fed his own, for she felt him brush against her belly when he straightened.

Eyes closed, she ran her hands over him as she had done with his clay torso. A feather light trail down the arms, then a gentle kneading along each quivering muscle as she moved back up his arms. Her fingers raced more surely over his chest, more boldly down his torso, and rested light and brief on the tip of him; so light it might never have happened. Then upwards again until she stopped at his nipples. She grasped each bud tenderly then rolled them gently and slowly between her fingers.

When she leaned over and put her mouth around one bud, he gasped in surprise, and as her tongue circled slowly then flicked the end, he expelled his breath at the torturous delight of her actions. She stopped in smug satisfaction and looking up at him, said, "Ah, we like this too then." And when she lowered her head again to the other nipple and did the same, only more slowly as if testing his fortitude, a beam of fire raced to his groin. When her fingers trailed over his abdomen and then her hands snaked around his waist and lightly squeezed his buttocks, he felt himself lose control. Then she rolled her palms across their tautness and trailed her fingers down his back legs and around his upper thighs where they paused to circle a lazy design. Her feathery touch moved up to his belly, stopped, and than snaked further down. Aware of his tension, she pressed against him tightly as she circled his neck with her arms.

He could take no more of this teasing, and crushed her to him, grasping her buttocks as he rained kisses on her brow, her lids, her neck, her ears. Finally his lips pressed on hers lightly, but with the firm intention of staying there forever.

Tannis was overwhelmed by the sweetness of that first kiss, a sweetness that grew insistent in its demand, urging her compliance. She did so willingly. Both tasted of each other for the first time, a taste that compelled them to seek more. Standing pressed against each other for what seemed an eternity, their lips teased, demanded, nipped and urged.

Tannis knew it was time. Her lips were swollen and her legs trembled so hard, she felt herself slip to the ground. Her body was afire and she could endure this torturous ecstasy no more. Bryan too had become tight with urgency and she felt his body quiver under her hands with the strain of holding back. His own thighs shook visibly as he lowered himself on top of her.

There was a moment of absolute stillness, a moment where their eyes locked in timeless accord. Then she opened her thighs and welcomed him into her heat. For a time he lay still, and she felt the wonder of being so filled, so complete, she never wanted to move again. But her body, so long denied, urged him into motion.

The slow rise and fall, withdrawal and thrust, an eternal cadence of joining within her silkiness washed wave after wave of pleasure through their bodies. Higher and higher they rose, deeper and deeper they sank, as they moved in perfect attunement: asking for more, and giving more while their eyes read each other's hearts.

Her thighs began to quake with the need of release. She arched towards that final primal thrust that catapulted her into a vortex of such excruciating pleasure she felt herself drawn out of her body into eternal bliss. The last thing she remembered was the warmth of Bryan's release. With a smile of satisfaction and amid the blinding brilliance of colors shards that danced behind her eyes, she followed her lassitude into oblivion.

When she came to, it was to drift in the delicious aftermath of the warmth of Bryan's body still atop her. He had pulled a side of the blanket over them. She squeezed her inner muscles in slow delight of her afterglow, and realized he was still inside her. Not only that, but responding to her subtle movements. She opened her eyes in surprise and felt his slight shift as he raised himself onto his elbows, his eyes never leaving hers. "Oh Bryan," she whispered with wonder as he smiled his own satisfaction. "I thought I had died with pleasure." She responded instinctively to his movement with a slow roll of her pelvis and throaty chuckle.

"Me too, which would really spoil a rematch," he whispered hoarsely, his face reflecting his delight at her obvious pleasure and resurrection from death. His rekindled desire was unmistakable as he lowered his lips to hers again.

Tannis thought she would die with the love of this man, as another had before her, and surrendered to the slow swell of desire she knew to be completely her own. And this time, she drew them to a completion so fluid, they drifted to another place together.

When Tannis finally rose, her slight stagger and wince did not go unnoticed. Immediately solicitous, Bryan asked, "Did I hurt you, pet?"

Touched by his concern, she replied smugly, "Nope, Just rubber-kneed is more like it. I can't remember when I've had such a delicious workout, if ever." She could see her answer pleased him. As they walked back to the manor, his arm clasped her around her shoulder, he leaned close and whispered, "Well, my lady, I believe I have a cure for your years of neglect." She smiled softly as they crept up the private staircase and into Bryan's suite.

Under the hot spray of the shower, they soaped each other amid light kisses and tender fondles that quickly became more sensual and intentional. Feeling the rise of his soapy desire in her grasp. Tannis shook her head in disgust and said, "Pervert."

He grinned wickedly and replied with relish, "It's of your own doing, and now you must pay the price."

They aimed half-hearted swipes at each other's bottoms while they towel dried their hair, then wrapped themselves in bath towels and strolled to the king size bed.

Tannis quickly whipped off her towel and spread it onto the bed. She wiggled her bottom at him then lowered herself on the towel and positioned herself provocatively on her side. With one leg slightly bent, she traced circles on her inner thigh and teased him with a 'strumpet' look as her fingers continued their sensual upward journey. She dropped her voice to a husky whisper and said, "Now, let's see if you can pay the price." Although it had been many years since she had been with a man, let alone experienced such intense lovemaking, she felt no shyness. Rather, she felt liberated by how naturally she could express her desire with this man; a man just met, yet known as intimately as if a lifetime had been spent together. Perhaps it was her experiences as Taenacea which made this so easy, for she had known him intimately. Without that, she would never have made love after just meeting, no matter how desirable he was. The Lady Taenacea certainly was cunning. But further musings were interrupted by her body's arousal at the hands of her beloved.

Leisurely they explored and feasted on each other in shameless delight. Moans and groans, and soft encouragements drifted through the room as no part of them went unexplored or untasted. It was as if they could not get enough of each other and their final caress was exchanged under dawn's dim glow. Bryan was the first to wake. Extricating himself carefully, he rose and stood naked by the window to breathe in the fresh morning air and relive their night of lovemaking. Never had he experienced a woman so gracefully willing to share herself, whose curiosity was almost innocent, yet possessing a passion and wanton enthusiasm as fulfilling as any man could desire.

Her passion had carried him to places he'd never imagined, and drew from him a tenderness and intent to please that surprised him. He could not get enough of her and he could not take his eyes off her during their joining.

He loved her unexpected sauciness; a humor that sent them into giggles of delight, adding spice to their desire. She was rare, this woman; one he sensed he could be quiet beside, talk to, laugh with and explore the mysteries of love expressed in a way that felt almost spiritual. She was a woman who in just one night had drawn from him what he suspected was the best within himself; expecting as her due what he gave so willingly. And with her eyes alone, she had drawn him into a new state of spiritual merging he had never experienced before, or completely understood. He knew only that he wanted more.

He winced as he ran his tongue over his lips. They were tender and swollen, like that of a teenager after a night of heavy necking. He grinned his pleasure as he picked his watch off the night table. It was already late morning. They would have to go downstairs sometime soon. He walked back to the bed with the intention of waking Tannis. Instead he stopped beside the bed, and just looked down at her; this Enchantress who would be forever his. He would never tire of her; the spill of messy curls, one of which lay across her cheek; the puff of lips swollen by tender use and sleep; and the telltale marks of love on her neck and breasts. The sight of one inner thigh lying exposed to his gaze stirred him. "Good god," he mouthed as he sat at the edge of the bed, "you are so beautiful." Bending towards her, he began to wake her gently with his lips. His intent was quickly forgotten as she reached for him in sleepy welcome.

* * *

James Sanders was passionate on a career in the hospitality industry. He would do just about anything to ingrate himself in the eyes of his mentor and idol, Mr. Nigel Holmes. When a large bulky envelope had come for Ms. Josie Wilde, he had just put it with the other mail in her slot. Then, as he rifled through her growing bundle of mail, he caught sight of a note which said any mail from Braith & Timms was to be given the highest priority and forwarded to her immediately. He knew she was on tour and their things held in a special storage room for he had been on duty the day they left.

His Adam's apple bobbed in agitation. What to do? Nervously he picked at a pimple on the side of his neck. The large envelope was obviously important, and looked official. The note said it was to be forwarded. He also knew these clients were indexed for special attention by Mr. Holmes. It was his duty to comply. Besides, such an action would result in a commendation on his work record. He found the address of the village they were visiting and sent the package on by special delivery.

* * *

It was past noon before Tannis and Bryan were showered and dressed. Shakily they descended the staircase and paused at the bottom for a reassuring hug to brace themselves for the jest they knew would come. Then they casually sauntered onto the terrace where lunch was being served.

"So, it's finally seeing the light of day, are yeh?" teased a jovial Seamus. He noted the puffiness of his brother's lips and added, "I was after asking you to work the land wid me, but it seems yeh've done some plowing of your own already."

"For shame, Seamus," retorted a blushing Nell as she poked him in the side. Her eagle eye hadn't missed the bruising on Tannis' neck, poorly covered by a dab of powder. "Tis making her out to be a strumpet, yeh are."

Josie had waited impatiently for their decent from what she knew was a night of rapture. She wanted to be the first to see Tannis' face, but had her back turned when they arrived. "Ah no, not my friend," she said as she plopped another spoonful of potato salad on her plate. "She must have run into something in the night . . . and more than once from the look of it. Welcome to the club, and you know which one whereof I speak."

Tannis' blush and momentary discomfort indicated she remembered their conversation during the ride to the foundry.

Lorne, who leaned against the railing as he munched on a sandwich, looked on with envy. Cal shot Bryan a 'now you're screwed and hooked, buddy' look before he turned to Tannis and innocently asked, "Ran across a lump of clay that gave you a little trouble, did you?"

Knowing there would be no escaping the jests, Tannis replied, "Stiff at times, but no trouble if you know what you're doing. Quite pliant if you work it properly."

Surprised by her candor Cal looked so embarrassed, Bryan's eyes crinkled and he laughed outright.

The women exchanged one of those knowing glances that baffle and irritate men. Lunch was interspersed with more good-natured snide remarks, but delivered with genuine affection. Secret looks passed between the other two couples who made vague excuses and departed, leaving Tannis and Bryan alone. They each had phone calls to make.

After Bryan made a few business calls, Tannis rang Linka. She felt surprisingly nervous while she waited for the familiar voice to answer, one she suddenly realized she missed sorely.

"Hullo." Linka's voice was soft, but not sleepy. She sounded as if she might have already been up even though it was six a.m. on the west coast of Canada.

"Hi, sweets!" Tannis leaned against Bryan's chest and unwittingly squeezed his arm, reassured by his responding squeeze and light kiss on the back of her neck.

"Moom! Is that you?"

"None other."

"Man, I'm *sooo* glad to hear your voice. Not that there's anything wrong. It's just that I miss you. I just knew you would call, 'cause I woke up a while ago and couldn't get back to sleep. So how's the holiday? Did you go to Wales? Where are you calling from? Hey, I love the cards, and especially the outfit. Its choice, and fits perfect. The cats are fine and Sam's got the garden looking just like it should. When are you coming home?"

Tannis heard a scuffling sound as Linka hollered, "Babe! It's mom!" Then she came back on the line with a casual "What's up?" as if this was just a regular check-in call.

"The holiday is lovely, I'm glad the outfit fits, yes I did go to Wales, and what's up is that I've met him."

"Met who?" Linka asked, as she tried to pull Mr. Muff up to her face so he could hear the mamma's voice too.

"Garth. I mean Bryan, his name is Bryan and I want you to meet him. He, as it turns out, is the mysterious buyer of the sculptures. I'm calling from his estate in Ireland. Can you get away for a while and come over, Both of you, and the cats too, of course. Bryan will send his private jet for you once the date is set." It had all rushed out in a quaking voice she didn't care for at all. Her daughter's approval was more important than she'd realized. Further speculation was cut short by a deafening shriek at the other end of the line.

"Nooo Wayyy! You mean he's real? Is he a hunk like Garth? Are you getting married? Not without me I hope. OhMyGod! Yes, yes, yes. I'll talk to Sam and let you know when we can come. What's the number there. I'm sure we can swing it, even though I'm up to my ying-yang with work just now. I can burn the midnight airbrush and have them cleared up zappo! A few days, maybe. Do we need passports? Are you in love, mom?"

Tannis barely heard her last question since she held the phone away from her ear during Linka's screaming questions. From the jiggling of the chest she leaned against, Bryan had heard as well. Tannis gave her the phone number and several farewell kissy-smacks, then hung up, relieved at her daughter's acceptance of the unexpected news. She could cover the details of tranquilizing the cats with Sam when Linka called back. She turned to Bryan and saw his raised eyebrows above a 'what have I got myself into' look. She smacked his stomach lightly and said, "I never said she was like Faye, I just said that she had been Faye."

"She sounds ... most ... er... vibrant," was his diplomatic response.

"Just be ready for a space cadet, but a delightful one. As I'm sure you heard, she'll call back and let us know when they can come." Bryan had been the one to thoughtfully suggest they come a few weeks before the wedding. My God, she was really getting married. Caught up in the momentum of what had occurred, she knew she had to take some quiet time to let that one sink in. Changing the subject, she asked, "Now then, does the Lord of the Manor wish to take the prospective Lady of the Manor on a tour of her new home?"

"Ah yes, he does that," Bryan responded laconically, but with a thrill of inner pride at not only being able to show off his family home, but her eagerness to claim her place at his side. Their grand tour was not finished until almost dinnertime due to the necessity of having to stop in several secluded spots to exchange tender caresses and ginger kisses.

All that Tannis viewed was tasteful and inviting, speaking more of use than showiness. Although only slightly shabby with natural aging, the furnishings proclaimed loving use. The house looked lived-in and the modernizations was done with such ingenuity they blended into the overall flavor of timeless elegance. It was Bryan who had added the skylight dome over the staircase, as well as the long row of windows along the back wall of the house and upper balcony. And as if knowing the taste of the future Lady of the Manor, he had added the large airy sun room along one side of the terrace, opposite the library.

Filled with lush tropical plants, hanging plants, and flowering potted plants in charming clusters on tables and even on the ceramic floor, the room provided cozy seating groupings of white rattan cushioned with a watery lemon and green leaf-patterned fabric. The whole room was dappled now by filtered sunlight that danced through the partially screened skylights and shuttered windows. Tannis knew this room, which provided both morning sun and evening shade, would become her personal favorite. The only change she could envision was to replace the rattan furniture with her own comfortable couches and tables. She could picture it in her mind as the cat's favorite room too, filled with familiar and well-marked items.

She was thrilled when Bryan suggested they build her studio off this sun room. Banking the east side of the second and lower level of the terrace as it sloped towards the gardens, its placement would give her a spectacular view of the rose garden and also provide good working light.

Her mind swam with their plans while they ate dinner on the terrace; a bountiful buffet that included delectable dishes from last night's sparsely sampled meal. Bryan scooped several helpings onto his plate and ate with relish while they discussed the Quest, still the primary focus of everyone's conversation.

Lorne felt somewhat left out. Stout had left in the morning to run an errand for Cal and wouldn't be back until late tonight. He listened to Nell, who had cornered Josie with questions regarding the 'living afore' matter. Cal and Bryan were deep in conversation, as were Seamus and Tannis. Thinking Nell and Josie's metaphysical topic the most interesting, he sauntered over to join them.

During a pause in her conversation about land husbandry in Wales, Tannis sat back in her chair and looked around at the faces she loved, and those she was quickly coming to love, Nell, Lorne, and particularly Seamus.

He felt the warmth of her scrutiny and bent towards her. "'Tis a wonder to be seeing Bryan with such joy about him. I thank yeh for that. I don't wonder yeh'll be keeping his interest in the land alive with yer own, if I be a judge of such matters. I meself, and Nell be welcoming yeh into the family, Tannis."

Touched by his simple declaration, she smiled and squeezed his burly arm lightly. "Thank you," was all she said, but the light, fragrant kiss she planted on his cheek reddened it noticeably. Embarrassed, he rose and walked over to his brother. He whispered something in his ear as he lightly punched him on the arm, their personal exchange of affection.

Tannis sensed a new feeling settle within herself, that of belonging, not just to the land, but to these people. Isolated from the normal interchange between families most of her life, she relished the embrace of this family. She had tried to create her own family circle with Linda, Cal, and Josie, but it wasn't quite the same. As an only child and finding little warmth in Brad's snooty family even before their divorce, she had convinced herself she did not need or yearn to be part of an interactive family. But that had changed. She now yearned to be part of this one, in spirit, if not in actuality yet. Knowing she had just passed some unspoken muster and was welcomed with genuine kindness warmed her heart. She was home now, and knew it. With a new feeling grounding her actions, she got up and joined the ladies, if you could call these two firebrands that.

As the velvet cloak of night settled around them, Tannis felt the aftermath of her sleepless night of lovemaking. She stifled a yawn Bryan had seen. He responded immediately, as if already attuned to her thoughts. After warm hugs to all, which Seamus and Nell received with a blissful 'goway wid yous', they left arm in arm. And just in time, for the hellions who knew to be back from their wanderings by dark came racing up the terrace for their late and noisy dinner.

In the master suite, there was no sign of their earlier tussles. The maid had folded the bed coverings back several times, right to the foot of the bed in fact, as if in resignation of a repetition of the previous disarray. While Bryan was in the bathroom, she went to collect some toiletries from the Rose Room, a room which had seen little of her since dressing for her monumental encounter. Clothed only in an electric blue satin robe, she returned to Bryan's room but found it empty. She heard the sound of running water from the bathroom, and looked through the open door. Brain was bent over, stirring the steaming froth of bubbles in the deep sunken tub.

Sensing her presence he looked over his shoulder and drawled, "The bath is drawn, milady." He dropped the towel from around his lower body and gingerly stepped into the tub. He lay back amid the earthy waft of herbs and with legs bent and splayed wide under the froth, asked, "Care to join me?" as he patted the bubbles in front of him.

The invitation was too delicious to decline. A hot soak was just what Tannis needed. She sashayed over to him and dropping her robe, said laconically, "Well ... if I must." Settled in front of him she lay back, head resting against his shoulder, breasts cupped by his hands. She floated in frothy daydreams until his sensual strokes under the water grew more insistent.

Glowing with heat, they fell on the bed and lay indolent as their fingers lightly traced trails of moisture on each other's bodies. It was Tannis who stirred first. Propelled by the memory of that morning's tender awakening, she rolled over and straddled Bryan with calculated wantonness. Her damp hair hung over her breasts and tickled his chest as she swung it gently to and fro.

She rolled her hips in a sensual revolution and said with mock severity, "It appears the hot waters may have done some damage, milord, sad as it looks." She shook her head and giggled at his concerned glance downward. "But being a healing woman of old, I have the cure. However," she paused to raise her eyes heavenward, "being a cure of my own making, I must proceed with the first of what I fear will be many a 'required treatment." She slowly snaked down his body to dispense pleasures that soon had him gasping.

Bryan's last coherent thought was that this woman would either be the death of him, or cause for him to be written up in the Guinness World Book of Records. There was certainly something to be said for her holistic approach to quenching the fevers of passion.

Much later, after several journeys into blissful release, they surrendered to sleep. Bodies intertwined, their soft breathing drifted into the night through the open window. Outside, the caress of the moon's glow and the shadow from the portico cast hidden meaning on the looks Garth and Taenacea exchanged as they reached to each other.

Chapter Twenty-Four

WHEN JOSIE WENT INTO THEIR SUITE to change her shoes, she saw a bulky envelope propped on the desk. All thoughts of a visit to the stables flew from her mind when she saw the Braith & Timms Crest. The genealogy results. She wondered only briefly how it had found its way here, but thrilled it had, ripped the envelope open and pulled the contents out. A quick scan of the two pages brought a satisfied grin to her face.

Yes. It was just as she'd thought. Everything was falling into place. Papers in hand, she headed downstairs to the sun room, glad it was empty of guests so she could relish the contents in private. Tannis was indisputably the legal issue of the original Lagohaires, through her father's line. It took a moment to sink in. She laughed with delight. She was sitting in Tannis' house, on Tannis' estate. A delicious bit of news, but no one to share it with.

The men had left early this morning to sail the Enchantress and Nell was preparing a room for her friend Iris, who was to arrive later that day for an extended visit. Nell had shared her match-making plans with Josie at breakfast and also her reasons why Iris was perfect for Lorne. Love was in the air and she intended to utilize this visit to get the two together. Josie offered a few of her own Astrological opinions. But right after breakfast Nell had bustled off to attend to domestic matters. Since Seamus was over at the site of their 'barn' and Tannis was still asleep, Josie had intended to check out the resident four-legged champion racers and perhaps go for a ride. But now all thoughts of horses and riding flew out of her mind.

Some instinct prevented her from bounding upstairs to share the news with Tannis. Instead, she went to get her laptop. This was a perfect opportunity to work on her book. Since the book would be written as a novel, she needed to backtrack and weave hints of this ancient connection throughout her story. The snippets offered would leave the reader in doubt as to her heroine's claim until the very end.

Her initial contact with Amora Publishing had been arranged by an enthusiastic Bernie, a friend of the publisher, and author of his own book on reincarnation. Her submission had resulted in a contract based only on an outline, synopsis, and draft of the first three chapters. Although the story was incomplete and its ending uncertain, they knew scandal among the titled, based on a real story, would sell. She had insisted the privacy of her 'heroine' be respected until the tale had played out, and that the same courtesy be extended to the 'hero', a man named only yesterday during her phone call to her editor, Alan Bean.

* * *

Alan Bean gulped down his martini and automatically ordered a fourth. His companion Harold, was deep in conversation with a reporter from 'See', London's competitor of 'Star' Magazine. Frustrated by his promise to keep a lid on his new project, particularly since the call from Josie, he turned his attention to the redhead on his right. He had been eyeing her for some time, and when her friend, a slightly frowzy blonde had staggered off with a chap, he had seized his opportunity.

"I say, can I buy you a drink. Alan's the name and publishing's my game. After three of these dynamite martinis you may consider me mellow and no threat to a lovely lady as yourself." He detected no slur in his speech as his eyes covertly raked her luscious form. Her softness was not his usual style, but mellowed with drink, she looked inviting to him now.

Lori was in need of distraction. Her editor had been on her back all week. Bottom line; shape up and get a good story, or its back to reporting community events. The fellow on her left was a right handsome bloke, in a pale, taut sort of way. Tired of being pumped for inside info on the outrageous stories published by the weekly Rag, she decided to adopt an alias for the night. Even if she left with him she'd never see him again so it wouldn't matter who she said she was.

It was always the way. They gorged on her lushness and after feasting, forgot her. She lowered her lashes over her pale green eyes and smiled what she thought to be a seductive invitation. It was better than being bored, or alone.

"You look trustworthy amid this sea of beasts. Lori's the name, and yes, I'll have a vodka. On the rocks would do nicely, ta."

"Are you in the business, then?" Alan asked, assuming she was. The Crocket was a popular hangout for the press and publishing related crowd.

"Actually no. My friend is. Community events is my area," which would be true if she didn't get her act together. "I just joined her for a bit of fun. It's my first time here," she lied. You never knew what you could stumble on when a man's guard was down and his pecker up. She feigned disinterest when he pointed out several well known reporters and pressed her straining breasts against his arm accidentally, several times. Her ploy worked. It always did, even if they preferred the skinny ones. After some light but snappy small-talk and another drink they both downed quickly, they left.

"That was nice," Lori said as she handed Alan the cigarette she had lit for him and placed between his lips. And it was, even if the room wasn't. For a wiry fellow, he was more tender than she'd imagined, or more butchered. She might even hear from this one again. His mention of 'the next time' almost rang true.

Alan was mellow. Lori had been surprisingly sweet. Unlike the bonkers he'd grown accustomed to with bar-birds, all quick and slick, hard-bodied and performance minded, she was comfortable and comforting, a bonus that. He hadn't realized he needed comfort. To thank her, he talked to her. In fact, suddenly he wanted to impress her, to have her think him worth another go. Over a year it had been since his last steady, a placid, mousy gal, Gail had been. He'd sent her packing, thinking her too bland for his fast life, but now regretted it. He missed her adoration. Lori reminded him of her in that. Besides, she was much more attractive than Gail and would do nicely.

"I'm on a good story, a scandal in the gentry when it breaks. Then we can do the town proper," he intimated and watched her reaction.

"That's nice for you Alan," was all she said, warmly, not overly impressed.

"You know, once in a while you get on something you know is big. This could be it for me." Still nothing but polite interest. It was nice not be pumped for more, or asked to look over a story they had written which usually turned out to be crap. But he was almost disappointed by her lack of interest. "Yes.. And most surprising. It could blow the lid off one of the best kept secrets in titled Irish circles. A bit of a mystery at that."

He had certainly caught her attention, but Lori was careful to cloak her growing excitement. "That important, eh?" was all she said.

"It is when the key player has made it a mission to keep a low profile," Alan retorted importantly.

"To do with the Royals, then?" she asked. All Britts assumed the juiciest stories had to do with them, especially the Princess of Wales. Reporters made it their personal goal to keep abreast of her doings in particular.

"Nooo ..." Alan drawled, "but you could say it would cause as much stir in financial circles." It was a bit of a stretch, but he had her attention now. "One of the most eligible bachelors that's dropped out of sight some time ago," She had probably never heard of him, so Alan knew himself safe. Besides, he was bursting to tell someone. "He's about to have his estate pulled out from under him, his title with it," he embellished with enthusiasm, only briefly wondering if he'd gone too far. The book would be written as a novel, so some embellishment was allowed. "What's his is not, apparently. It belongs to an heiress who's come across from Canada to hunt up her past and claim her birthright. Legally hers it is. It'll make his stocks drop a bucket or two when the financial world finds out, and his investors in an odd Irish project of his. Something to do with witchery, pagan rites, and reincarnation it seems." He knew he should have stopped, but couldn't. She had begun to fondle his genitals, with pleasant results. He didn't want her to stop now.

"I think that's so romantic," she gushed, completely attentive now. She alternated between steady strokes and some titillating fondling. "Have they met and had a go of it yet?" she asked, as if caught up in the romance, not the detail of it.

"Don't know. She's on his estate in Ireland now, and neither ... oh yes ... know of it apparently. It's her writer friend that's found it out. She's a sculptress, the Canadian heiress, and had past life memories that ...." Whatever else he'd intended to say died on his lips. She was hot one, this Lori.

Temporarily distracted herself, Lorie mentally filed the information and settled herself atop him. Their chance meeting had definitely proved profitable. She'd search it out, but for now, well, she'd show her appreciation. He wasn't half bad. He'd treated her nice, not shy about giving her a little pleasure too.

* * *

The courtyard lay before her like a magical setting. Pots of tree roses lined a gold carpeted path from the doors of the Manor to the wedding arbor in front of the fountain. It too was circled by rose trees in beribboned clay pots. Hybrids, miniatures and more tree roses lined the courtyard and formed clusters behind the two statues at the bottom of the steps. Even the pillars were wound with garlands of flowers amid live ivy. The air was sweet with their scent and light breezes gently wafted over the contingency from Ley Node who wore Celtic costumes in tribute to the joining of these two ancient families.

Poignant strains of Celtic melodies drifted from three harpists positioned beside the fountain where Bryan stood waiting under the rose clad canopy of the arbor. Beside him stood his best man Lorne, and Cal, who would give Tannis away. Bryan, resplendent in a creamy white tux, stood facing his guests. He looked every woman's dream of a knight in shining armor; the romantic Lancelot, waiting to claim his lady love.

A hush fell over the crowd as the bridesmaids appeared at the front entrance. The four looked like long-stemmed roses in their empire dresses topped with a froth of sassy ruffles that spilled from low necklines and draped the top of their bare arms. Each held a bouquet of roses a shade deeper than their dress, and as they stood together, they looked like a live bouquet. They reached the bottom of the stairs and turned to wait for the bride.

Tannis stood framed in the doorway a moment before she stepped into the sunlight to a collective gasp. Only the haunting strains of the harp quivered through the air as the sun set her gown a-shimmer and she began her solitary walk towards the groom. Like a golden flame, her dress rippled with every step as she walked from the past into her future.

Her hair lay loose over her shoulders covered by a gauzy-netting veil that trailed lightly on the ground behind her, held on her head by a simple but stunning headband, intricately braided in gold and silver. What created the shimmer as she moved was the long medieval tunic that covered her gown; a tunic made of the same delicate netting as the veil. Adorned with embroidered silver and gold flowers at the high neck of her dress, the gossamer sleeves and rippling hem of the tunic were stitched with the same flowery design. A woven gold and silver belt that matched her headband hugged her hips, its long strands caressing her thigh in time to destiny's tread.

So it would be, to the haunting strains of Celtic harps, the lilting words of bonding from the little priest, amid the cluster of their dearest friends, and fringed by the whole village of Ley Node, she would be wed. She looked at

Bryan, and caught her breath. Something was wrong. He seemed indistinct for a moment, so she blinked to clear her vision. But he continued to waver and fade into a growing darkness, a darkness that swallowed up her dreams and future in a vaporous cloud of black that threatened to obliterate her as well as it churned towards her. She felt an icy grip clutch her innards before all went black.

* * *

Tannis' eyes flew open in panic. She lay in Bryan's bed and knew it had been a dream. A dream of perfection, at first. Enthralled by the vividness of the setting and her gown, a vision from days gone by, she knew the dream was intended as a preview of her wedding day. The sweet scent of roses still hovered around her, so real had it been. That Bryan had faded into the dark vapor was disturbing, as was the icy grip of panic she had felt before she woke. But it was exactly how she had envisioned her wedding day. The ending could just be an enactment of fear, the fear of losing him now that he had been found. This dream was different in that it was just a dream, not a journey in time. Yes, that must be it. For nothing could mar the perfection of that moment. This reassured her somewhat and dissolved her concern over the ending. Her Quest was finished now. She could leave behind those unexpected journeys to the past.

Bryan had not proposed formally, but a wedding date had already been set. Everything had happened so fast, there had not been time for a ring or formal proposal. With the dream, she now had a clear picture of what she wanted and could set the wedding plans in motion. She would ask Nell about a seamstress to make a wedding gown just like the one she wore in her dream.

As she rolled over she caught the faint scent of Bryan, amid the wafts of roses from the large cluster set on the night table. Ah, that must have been what she had smelled on awaking. The thought of Bryan sent a wave of longing through her. She wanted to stay right where she was in his bed, their bed now, and moon the day away, but the shafts of sunlight which danced along the opposite wall enticed her to rise. If she hurried, she'd be in time for lunch with Josie, whom she had seen little of since their arrival here.

She found her in the sun room, busy at her laptop. Brimming with a desire to share her wondrous dream, she smiled indulgently at the piles of papers Josie hastily stuffed away. Disarray always materialized around Josie, and spreading her stuff around somebody else's house didn't bother her one bit.

"Catching up on your charts, eh?" she asked, paying scant attention to Josie's mumbled response or how quickly she shut the lid on her laptop. She was hungry and wanted to eat. "I thought you'd be in the stables. Come on, let's eat, then the two of us can check out the famed horseflesh." She grabbed Josie's arm as they left and added, "Have I got a dream for you. No, not time travel. Precognitive you'd call it, but the best kind. Makes planning a wedding a breeze when you've seen the end result."

* * *

Lori's eyes burned as much from lack of sleep as staring at the computer screen these past five hours. She rolled her head and shoulders to ease her tight muscles. She had rushed to her desk, straight from Alan's bed to scour the Internet. If she found nothing there, she would try the micro fiche downstairs.

Between bouts of sex which had lasted well into the dawn hours Alan had dropped a little more information, enough so she had the gist of the story, though not the players. Satisfied, she had agreed to meet him again tonight. But for now Alan and her bodily needs were forgotten. She could smell a story.

Her first lead was found in the financials: The Emerall Corporation of Ireland, whose international umbrella of companies represented communications, industrial, and manufacturing interests. The name also came up in mining ventures when she scanned the stock market press releases. She had honed in on Emerall because it also funded an agricultural project in Ireland called Ley Node; some odd alternative agricultural center with its own website. It proved to be the only conglomerate which had such a tie to Ireland. She knew she was on the right track when Bob from Finance confirmed a reclusive Irish Lord with the Midas Touch was rumored to be the silent partner and prime initiator of this lucrative venture. He suggested she check magazine articles, particularly *Fortune,* that there were several articles over the past ten years about the Emerall Corporation.

In the ladies room she felt a wash of panic. She had to find something that would confirm the identity of this Irish Lord. Her life was a mess, her job on the line, and her landlord ready to turf her out if she didn't come up with the back-rent. This opportunity had come like a last-ditch omen. What she needed was a bit of Irish luck.

It was Rodney, the sports editor, who provided it. On his silent trek past her desk, a daily ritual in hopes of a glimpse of her spectacular cleavage, he had triggered a question, a question that might just lead her to what she sought. Usually she ignored him, but played the tease and allowed him a few moments of pleasure, the sick sod. Sometimes she even enticed him with body movements that thrust her breasts out even further. But never before with intent other than to taunt.

"Rodney, a moment please," she said, cloaking her amusement at his look of shock at being addressed. He attempted to straighten his rounded shoulders as he came closer, and vainly tried to pull in his protruding belly, a low hanging paunch that looked ridiculous on his slight frame.

"You're in the know on the races aren't you?" she asked, coyly bending forward for his benefit. An nod indicated he was. "In Ireland too?" she asked. He nodded again. "So you would know of the Lords that race regular and are in the running for the big purses?"

Comfortable on his own turf and enthused because she needed something from him, Rodney nodded again. "Yes. I know most of the stables where money's made. I spent some time in Ireland, for a story on the Ballsbridge Show in Dublin."

"Not much about the owners, then?" she asked casually. She registered his quizzing look. To set him at ease she made up a reason for her inquiries. "Just a background check for a story I've done. His nibs wants it," she said, rolling her eyes towards the Editor's door at the far end of the office.

He understood. "Who's it you're after?" he asked, eager to be of assistance.

"Some bachelor Lord. Don't even know where in Ireland, but rumored to have stables. An old family line, private owned estate not in debt, and maybe connected to an international conglomerate. Something about an odd project he funds. I don't know what," she added, shrugging her shoulders as if she didn't care.

Rodney pursed his thin lips and thought about it for a moment. There would be only two she could mean, if she was talking Ireland. "Lord de Lacy of Wexford, but he's going on seventy-one. The only other would be Lord Lagohaire, Bryan MacCumal. His stables show and race. They generally

place in the grand National in England. You don't see anything of the Lord
himself, I hear, even at the Ballsbridge Shows in Dublin. His horse, Laogson,
won out over Regis, the UK favorite at the races again this year. A bit of a
mystery about him, the Lord I mean. Very private. Gets his money from
overseas. Try the Irish Archives if its history you're after. The title goes way
back but his name is different. You'd mean Ley Node, the odd place where
they use psychics to grow things."

Lori batted her eyelashes and dimpled in thanks them mumbled she had
a call to make. As of that moment, he no longer existed. He stood by her
desk, hopeful for continued conversation, but her pretty shoulders were
hunched over the phone as she scribbled on her notepad. He left, pleased
she had even spoken with him. After two years, perhaps he had a chance.
If he took it slow, she just might agree to a pint after work sometime soon.
The possibility lightened his step.

Bless the sod: she now had a lead. Lori pulled up the society page first.
Nothing there, like she thought. She was about to close the window when
a name caught her eye. A sizable donation made to Ley Node by a well-
known socialite, rumored to have her eye on the Lord of the Estate, Bryan
MacCumal, who had funded the project. Good. She had a geographic
location, and more important: a name. Now all she had to do was find what
she could on him and connect him to the Emerall Corporation.

Next she scanned the back articles in *Fortune*. The name Emerall came
up several times and implied a mystery to its ownership. There were pictures
of Lorne Stonebridge, but none of the rumored silent partner. A few hours
later she found a few grainy pictures in the Dublin Herald archives. One was
of a young Bryan MacCumal beside his brother at his father's funeral, the
late Lord Lagohaire. A small article said the twenty-one-year-old Bryan had
inherited the title of the heavily debted Lagohaire Estate and possibly his
father's curse as well. It implied he would most likely lose it to back taxes.
Uncertain whether to backtrack and get a line on what appeared to be
another dark family secret, she scanned the rest of the article and the
second picture, of him in his thirties on the deck of his newly purchased
yacht, "The Enchantress," with his partner Lorne. A handsome fellow,
there was inference of the immense growth of their corporation, Emerall,
and speculation as to why such an eligible bachelor chose not to be
photographed or interviewed. There were no other pictures of him that she
could find. What she needed now was more background on the title and
how someone from Canada could lay claim to it.

A few calls to Dublin, one to Braith & Timms and she had enough to draft a story, one she intended to take either to *See* magazine, or the quarterly London publication *Reincarnation International*. That's where she had found a comprehensive story on the Ley Node Project and a brief history of the Lagohaire lands which had been owned by the family for over five hundred years. They seemed an odd lot, one brother playing grounds-keeper with a bunch of bastard kids on the secluded estate, the other a dark horse, rarely seen but with an unlimited source of wealth. The big question of course was what Bryan MacCumal might be hiding to cause him to seek obscurity. Witchcraft? A bit of a stretch, but devil worship and covens were alive and well in jolly old England.

She hoped the story would interest *See*. She'd done free lance work for them before but wanted on staff full-time. The Editor knew her, had boffed her, but still wouldn't hire her. He'd just put one of his own reporters on the tips she'd submitted. *See* usually didn't print a story unless it had already been picked up by one of the other papers. She'd done a good day's job of sleuthing and had enough checked out to write a solid story. Perhaps this time their Editor would take her seriously. She paused, hit by a momentary pang of guilt. Alan would be wild. She would have to make a decision here, the certainty of a well-paid front page story or a relationship that could stick.

She drummed her fingers on the mouse pad. Maybe she could have both. She'd be seeing Alan again tonight. Hmmm . . . things were looking up. It was time to get out of this Rag-hole. The book would take ages to hit the bookstands anyhow. It wasn't even finished yet from what he'd said. She could see no problem. Considering the books published on Princess Di in response to media allegations, this story of hers would either boost book sales when it did hit the stores, or be long forgotten by then.

Excited by the prospect of another evening with Alan, her flush of anticipation was enhanced by a sudden rush of power. She had never had the heady feeling of exposing something of this magnitude. She was about to shatter a recluse's anonymity and it felt grand, grander than anything she'd ever felt before. Possible headlines danced through her mind as she envisioned herself in her new job at *See,* after they bought her story. She drifted in the imagery of her new job and relationship with Alan, then double-checked her information and refined her draft. It was a spicy piece.

* * *

Moira carried the mop and bucket into the sun room. Rarely used, it needed more the watering of the plants and a light dust than any heavy cleaning. But she'd mop down the floor anyhow, what with the guests using it now. She caught sight of something white out of the corner of her eye as she mopped between the big ceramic pots by the settee, and bent down to pick it up. The paper, fallen between the leg of the settee and the plant pot, had Braith & Timms embossed along the top of creamy vellum paper.

She assumed it was for the Lord, being page two of a letter. Best to put it on his desk, then. She took it into the library and tucked it on top of some papers stuck under the side flap of the desk pad, and humming a merry jig, went back to the sun room to finish mopping the floor. She loved this room, this house. Her four years on the estate had been good. She had a lovely little room, and the work was light mostly, what with the mistress Nell doing much herself and hiring out regular for the heavy work. Rumors of a new mistress, the dark one from overseas soon to wed the Lord, had her wondering of the changes it would bring. She liked how it was now.

Josie was deep in conversation with the horse trainer. Bored with talk of races, Tannis excused herself. Her interest in horseflesh was minimal. In the flush of love, her romantic wedding dream still fresh in her mind a pang of nostalgia made her think of the dell where she and Bryan had first met. She would go there again.

Her feet led her to the spot as if the route had been trod many times before. Once inside, she noticed the altar sported a fresh cluster of blooms as if just placed there that very morning. She also saw a large picnic basket and blanket under a tree and realized Bryan must have brought it with him for the tryst she had missed. Its poignant presence tugged at her heart. He had come prepared for a romantic picnic, and been distraught enough to leave it when she hadn't showed up. She sat cross-legged in front of the altar, and opened herself to the energy of this ancient place.

She felt a subtle shift in the air around her as a swirl of light began to materialize behind the shrine. It moved towards her and encased her in a familiar warmth. Then she heard a soft voice, a whisper in her ear.

"William carried the stones here, each by one. He built this shrine with his bare hands in tribute to our love. Then he left, mad with grief." A deep sigh seemed to undulate through the dell before the voice continued. "This magical dell was the place I loved the most. His spirit is within the stones which carry a trace of the tears he wept as he built the altar. He loved me fully, but alas ..."

Tannis felt her throat constrict and her belly tighten. It was Fiona, speaking from behind the veil of her spiritual self. And she was immensely sad. A halo of light formed around the altar, obliterating what had been there a moment ago. Within it, the holographic figure of a man appeared. This man was shorter than both Garth and Bryan, but just as handsome. When she saw his ravaged face more clearly, she knew it had to be William. She watched as he built the altar, stone by stone. As he set each upon the other, his heart poured out his sorrow with a torrent of tears that marked each rock with his pained love. She could almost hear his thoughts. "Why did I wait, why did I wait," seemed to echo around her, but mournfully so.

Mesmerized by the dolor vision, she wondered at its meaning for her. As her focus shifted, he began to fade and another figure replaced his. It was Fiona herself. She hovered over the shrine, her transparent eyes seeking, and finally locking with hers. It was a discomforting feeling, in spite of the many strange events she had become accustomed to these past few months.

Fiona stroked her thoughts with her own, tentative at first, then with more assurance as she sensed Tannis' compliance. She transferred an awareness of her timeless essence to the corporeal woman before her; spinning the tale of her life, of her love for the land, and of her love for William. And she also transferred her sorrow at opportunity lost because they had waited. She urged the woman before her to reap the fruits of the love denied her through her early demise, no matter what obstacles lay in her path. The latter was said emphatically.

A shadow appeared behind Fiona, a momentary darkening like the sudden wave of a giant black cloak. It reminded Tannis of something, but before she could grasp what, it was gone, and with it the apparition of Fiona. Just before she faded away, Tannis saw her take one last sorrowful look at the shrine beneath her. Then she melted back into the mists of another reality, taking with her the warmth which had enveloped Tannis, and the magical aspects of the dell itself. She left behind only a crooked little altar, broken at the front and side, through which grew wild flowers in blue and white.

Tannis was deeply moved. She couldn't help but wonder if it was an omen. This was where she had first met Bryan and realized an opportunity for a rich future. But this was also a place of great loss. Was she, in a lasting union with Bryan to wipe the ancient tear stains from these crumbling stones? She hoped so. But the shadow disturbed her. Was it too an omen? About to examine its meaning, the spirited neigh of a horse drew her to the entrance of the dell. She looked down the slope and saw Josie and her glistening mount drinking from the little brook.

"Hey how did you find me? By accident or design?" she asked as she approached.

Startled out of her private thoughts, Josie was relieved to hear a familiar voice. She had gone riding more out of boredom than anything else. As much as she had enjoyed her time in the stable chatting with the groom, trainer, and prize steeds themselves, she felt at loose ends and restless, as if waiting for something to happen. She recognized the feeling, but hated not knowing just what was about to happen. She had put in a quick call to her editor, Alan, but he was out and not expected back for some time, so she left the number and decided to look for the dell where Tannis and Bryan had met. She would invent a most romantic meeting once she saw the site since she had received no particulars from Tannis herself.

"In answer to your question, a little of both. Iris, Nell's friend must be here by now. Let's go check her out. Nell's all fired up about setting her up with Lorne. Apparently she's been trying to do so for a while but could never coordinate their visits. Funny, they've missed each other for years, just like Cal and I did. Doo-doo-doo-doo! she says your match with Bryan is a lucky omen since they're finally both here at the same time."

Tannis thought it odd she would use the word 'omen' as she had moments before. "Lead on, but tell me, am I to run behind your steed like some lowly peon?" she quipped.

"I'd love to see that! No, we'll walk the horse back," Josie retorted, "in deference to your ancient status, and in fear of reprisal. You might turn him into a frog and me into a fly," she quipped, glad of the company. Riding lonely landscapes was not her thing.

Tannis batted Josie's bottom, then gave her arm an affectionate squeeze. "It's proper you're in awe of my power. But as a fly you'd be far too pesky. Now, let me see, I think a ..." She presented several silly options and forgot all about her earlier dis-ease in the dell, or the omens.

* * *

As much as Bryan enjoyed sailing, his mind was on Tannis rather than the sea. He wondered what she was doing right now. Cal was expounding Josie's passion for shopping and disregard for the cost of anything, or accumulated totals. Although she had money of her own from her trust, he felt a need to cushion his own substantial income with profitable investments. He would suggest she do the same. Lorne was more than happy to provide him with potential investment tips, based on their own lucrative portfolio, no charge.

"The Yellowknife mines in Canada will double their share values over the next two years. They've begun drilling already and the gold veins show the potential for substantial extraction based on their latest Survey on three claims. They're looking at about 664,950 ounces of potentially recoverable gold. Figure it out at the US price of $305 per ounce."

"I've steered clear of gold, diamonds, and other minerals," Cal said as he adjusted the cap Bryan had given him when he came aboard. "I figured the big loads were played out already."

"New processing techniques have created a whole range of metallurgical potentials for both existing and new mines. Extraction is more refined now, like resin extraction and the LPF—leaching precipitate-flotation process, for copper and cobalt metal, for example. They're getting all kinds of 'free-riders', like zinc. It's now being considered as a value-added product, like manganese. Manganese sulfate now has lucrative agricultural applications, another potential for profit." A potential he enthusiastically shared.

Bryan barely listened. This was Lorne's territory, not his. And now, more than ever, he had no desire to know what they were mining in China, South America or the North West Territories of Canada. The waves seemed to swish the name 'Tannis' as the prow of the yacht cut through their chop. Tannis, the woman he'd been waiting for all his life, and longer it seemed, according to Josie.

When they got back to the Manor, he could barely contain himself. He stayed right beside Tannis while they had drinks on the terrace, and touched her at every opportunity, seeing in her every glance or smile an invitation. Finally he drained his drink and grabbed her hand, saying, "We'll be back," as he pulled her upstairs with obvious urgency. He slammed the door, locked it, and in three strides scooped Tannis into his arms. She squeaked her protest as with another three steps he fell onto the bed with her beneath him.

His desperate and intense kisses, the hunger of his lips as they devoured hers, and the insistence of his hands as they scoured her body took her breath away. But the fires he ignited with his searing attention soon had her returning his passion with fervor. Gasping for air amid their torrid writhing, she implored, "Get off, you oaf. You're squashing me flat."

Bryan paused a moment and breathed, "Oh darlin', my treasure. How I've missed you," as he cupped her face in his hands tenderly.

Tannis tried to stifle a giggle. He acted as if they had been apart for weeks, not hours. But secretly she was thrilled. Bryan rose up on his knees between her legs, and with a devilish leer, grabbed the hem of her dress in each hand. With one deliberate move, he ripped the dress open.

Buttons flew in all directions as he leapt off the bed just long enough to pull off his shirt and drop his pants. He raked her waiting nakedness between the ragged edges of her dress with smoldering eyes, then covered her with his own warmth. After a long, tender kiss, he plunged his tongue deep into her mouth with a desperate moan. He rose on his arms, and without ceremony slid into her waiting heat. A gasp of excruciating pleasure escaped both their lips as they hung in suspended rapture. A few thrusts more, and they were spent.

Dazed by the intensity of this short coupling, Tannis felt her heart hammer in time to her contracting muscles. Shakily she gasped, "Now look here, look what you've done. You've ravished and compromised me." Then with a Cheshire grin, she added, "Well, you'll just have to make it right and marry me."

He responded with aghast dismay, "Well, if I must." Somewhat coherent again, he realized she had worn nothing under her dress. "And what would my bride-to-be be doing, traipsing around without even panties, may I ask? I'm marrying a wanton, it seems."

Feigning disappointment Tannis responded, "And what of this schoolboy who spills his seed with just a thrust or three? I thought I am to marry a man of stamina." She pretended to rise, and added, "Alas, I must be in the wrong Manor." His forlorn denial prompted her to giggle, then sigh dramatically. "No? Then best I be teaching you the proper ways of loving. With a contented sigh at the prospect, she applied herself to doing just that. Before she was swept away, she chuckled at her own foresight in purchasing several of these front-buttoning dresses. She suspected they would become a recycled staple in her wardrobe and made a mental note to get more.

Their sheepish arrival on the terrace during the buffet dinner was greeted with understanding smiles. Lorne looked relaxed standing beside a beautiful tall blonde. This must be Iris, Tannis thought. She looked like a Norwegian Ice princess with her blue catlike eyes above high cheekbones, and platinum hair which hung straight down the back of her delicate frame. The lightness of her laugh reflected an inner warmth and gentleness, in contrast to her cool exterior.

Lorne was obviously captivated by her. By all appearances, Nell's match-making efforts had proved successful. After their initial appraisal, Lorne and Iris gravitated to each other without prompting. They now spoke companionably, as if continuing a relationship begun a long time ago.

After they ate, Bryan asked, "Do you want to come to the library with me or have a bath while I return these calls?" He was already tuned into her love of candle lit baths. A grouping of beeswax candles had appeared overnight, waiting to mingle their sweetness with the herbal bath oils Tannis loved.

"Oh, a soak I think," she said. She stretched like a content cat and added, "I'll be in the sun room after my bath, updating my journal. I just love the way moonlight turns the room into a magical haven. We can have cordial there when you're done." With a backward smile she blew him a kiss and left.

Chapter Twenty-Five

BRYAN WOULD HAVE TO RETURN most of the calls in the morning. He could only get hold of two of his clients, and was now speaking with Graham, his Investment Advisor. As he jotted down the trading symbols for the companies he was to watch on the NASDAQ Stock Exchange, his hand fiddled with the papers tucked into the side of his desk pad. A few words on a page of correspondence jumped out at him. " . . . claim to the MacCumal lands . . ."

A cold knot tightened his stomach as he pulled the sheet out. He'd never seen this before and was puzzled. His conversation forgotten, Graham's continued update became just a background murmur. What registered was the content of the paragraph he had just read.

"After exhaustive research, and further to our previous correspondence, I am pleased to inform you that Tannis MacCrae, as a direct descent of the Lagohaire line, does indeed hold legal title to the lands of Laoighis. Her claim is valid. However, to pursue her claim would most certainly entail a costly suit against the current owner of the property, Mr. Bryan MacCumal, but would most likely be upheld by the courts as legitimate, based on supporting documents enclosed."

What? Bryan's ears rang. This could not be. As if to reassure himself this was a huge joke, he read further.

"The Editor of Amora Publishing whom you have indicated has contracted for the completion of your book, may contact me for supporting confirmation of any of the data enclosed.

I wish you well with your publishing venture, and am at your disposal should you . . . "

He had reached the bottom of the page. Should she what? He realized Graham was still on the phone, prompting him for a response. He cut him off with a hurried, "Gotta go," and promised to call back. Slowly he re-read the whole page. He didn't know what had come before, but the words '*does hold legal title to the lands*' rang through his brain, over and over again. For a moment he didn't know what he felt. A book . . Tannis MacCrae had title to his lands . . . a publishing contract signed to tell the story. He threw the sheet down on the desk as if it burned his fingers, its contents seared into his brain. Then he knew what he felt. Rage; the cold rage of betrayal.

He walked with deliberation to the sideboard and grabbed a glass and the bottle of Scotch. Then he sat himself in the high-backed armchair facing the terrace window. He filled the glass and drank it all down, oblivious to the burn of disgust as the fiery spirits raced down his throat.

He'd been duped. Tannis MacCrae, his love, his Enchantress, his soon-to-be wife and Lady of the Manor had duped him. All the chance incidents leading up to their meeting suddenly were not chance at all. She must have orchestrated it all. And for what? To take away what was his: this land, his title, everything he loved.

He didn't want to believe it, but the words on that sheet of correspondence danced before his eyes, taunting him. He'd been a fool. Her lineage had been researched and confirmed. Suddenly all manner of small incidents flew through his mind to confirm a plot so subtle but deliberate, he was shaken by its cruelty. Only for a moment did he wonder why she would do this. Why the seduction? Cal and Josie must be in on this too. Her agent and best friend, now husband and wife. Disjointed connections clicked in his mind. He didn't want to believe it. But the evidence of deceit piled up: Cal playing hard to get, then luring him to Quaglinos to catch a glimpse of her, Tannis' reference in the gazebo of wanting to live in 'her home', and the sculptures. His likeness in bronze to lull him with the ancient legend of destined love as he responded to the allure of her own half-naked form. Then there was the child holding his family's ancient crest, to authenticate their legendary connection. Of course. She would have researched thoroughly in order to be able to duplicate the ancient crest, which only confirmed the subtlety of the plot. My God!

He didn't want to believe it. He remembered something said on the terrace just yesterday. Cal had asked something about him giving her trouble, to which she had answered, "No trouble if you know what you're doing." They'd been brash enough to refer to their devious plan in casual conversation.

He didn't want to believe it. He refilled his glass and swallowed the burning liquid without flinching, though his eyes stung. Unthinking, he filled the glass again. But he couldn't get the image of his beautiful Enchantress out of his mind. The lands she coveted would have been hers shortly, through marriage. Had he not seen the letter, he would never have known, and thought himself the luckiest man in the world. But he did know now.

He smirked. So much for his gut instincts. He had fallen for her hook, line, and sinker: fallen prey to the oldest trick in the book—sexual allure. A small thread of reason wound through his bleak thoughts. His heart reminded him of their unity and told him she felt for him what he felt for her. Such an attraction could not be faked. Or could it? What of their first night together under the moonlight? Had it all been a ruse? Numbed by pain and the effects of the spirits heating his belly, he doubted even his own instinct.

Images flashed through his mind. She was by far the most gifted of whores. Suddenly all her actions appeared calculated; calculated to entice, seduce, and have him panting for more. He knew the pleasure of the game, any game, be it finance or seduction. And she was master of her game, as he was of his; his Enchantress, now a devil in disguise. The strength he had seen in her face, what he called 'the other one' seemed now to reflect her true nature, that of a manipulator. In light of the letter, the whole story of their supposed reincarnational past appeared a foolish fabrication. Romantic yes, but ridiculous.

And he had believed it. Their first accidental meeting and her assurances that she did not know it was his land seemed contrived now. Everything she had done since they first met seemed contrived now.

He wanted to confront her, but pride won out. Doing so would mean admitting he'd been taken for a fool. There had to be another way. Twenty years of his life, twenty years of staying away to maintain and keep what he loved. Down the tube. Just now, when he was ready to reclaim it in name and heart, she not only intended to snatch it away, but write a book about the rape of his birthright. Enraged by the blatant commercialism of her intent, another thought made him pale.

Seamus: Seamus who was finally building his own home on land that might be snatched away: Seamus who had dedicated his life to the care of these lands. Not only Seamus, but Nell and their six children. What would become of them if she took it all away? He realized he could never tell Seamus. He must fight her legally to retain what was his, to protect his brother and his family. Thankfully he had the means, but would need Lorne's help. Seamus must never know what a fool he'd been.

For almost a hour he sat, poisonous thoughts chasing each other in his mind as he drained the bottle. Tannis had called this her home already, so must intend to live here. She'd been brazen in speaking the truth, even then. He had to talk to Lorne.

Then he remembered she was waiting for him in the sun room. He knew he had to confront her eventually, but not yet. Until he knew just how to proceed, he'd have to appear as normal as possible. This would be by far the hardest thing he'd ever had to do. But he could not touch her. The thought was so painful he began to shake as much from revulsion as the truth that he wanted nothing more than to lose himself in the scent of her, in spite of what he now knew she had done.

Desperately he tried to pull himself together. He disgusted himself. But it was true. In spite of his discovery, he still wanted her. The ache of betrayal was threaded with the treachery of unabated desire. It would take every ounce of willpower he had to distance himself from her heat. She was waiting for him. He was supposed to bring her something. To bring her, what? Oh yes, a Drambui.

She'd be all aglow after her soak. Her skin soft and velvet, and fragrant. His mouth dried at the thought, and he groaned in despair at his anticipation. It was just an act he told himself. She cared nothing for him. It was only the land she wanted, her legacy. Everything she had done was towards that end. It was easy to feign caring when your efforts brought you such a prize.

Frantically he mouthed the words in the letter and felt his desire wan, a little. He steeled himself against its intrusion and rose unsteadily. He had to do this now, while he could still walk, or reason.

Tannis, lost in the vision of her dream wedding did not see Bryan's controlled approach. She caught a whiff of Scotch as he bent to hand her the Drambui and thought the men must have had a nightcap in the library. She looked up at him lovingly and noted a tightness of jaw which gave his face a cold, pinched look. His business calls must not have gone well. Impulsively she reached to caress his hand. "You look strained, my love."

Bryan flinched as her fingers lightly caressed his hand. "Yes," he said as he stepped out of her reach. He registered her startled look and rubbed his forehead as if it had been his intent to do so all along.

"I've a beast of a headache. Business. I don't usually have headaches. When I do, I'm unbearable," he said in a tight voice.

Full of concern, Tannis placed her cordial on the table beside her and said, "I have a remedy for headaches. Night air would help too."

"No!" he exclaimed, surprised by the sharpness in his voice. Images of their moonlight lovemaking shot through him like liquid knives. "I mean, I'm not good company right now. You go on up. I'd rather go alone."

"Oh, of course." Tannis was puzzled, but only for a moment. She too liked to be left alone on the rare occasions when she felt unwell: something else they had in common. Her disappointment was mainly because she had looked forward to another night of leisurely lovemaking. She'd go up to bed and wait for him there. If his headache wasn't gone when he got back, she'd use a remedy guaranteed to work.

Bryan decided on one of the benches at the far side of the rose garden. He'd intuitively headed for the gazebo, but memories of their conversation within its scented enclosure now repulsed him. He headed in the opposite direction and now sat and looked towards the back of the softly lit Manor House. His stomach churned. Was it possible he was about to lose it all? No, he could not let that happen.

An hour later he'd decided on his course of action. His heart hardened. He'd all but told Tannis to go ahead with their wedding plans last night. He would do or say nothing to change that, for now. But what he would do was call his lawyers first thing in the morning. He had to know where he stood. And Lorne, Lorne would understand. He'd been snookered once, not quite so dramatically, but none the less had felt as devastated. Besides, he needed his sharp mind. Whatever it took, he would fight to keep what was his. And when his legal position was clear, he would repay her for what she had done to him. He would humiliate her in the most publicly devastating way a man can humiliate a woman, by leaving her at the altar. With the media sure to be there, the disgrace would follow her all the way to Canada. In the meantime, he'd try to act as if nothing was amiss. It would not be easy as discovered by his trip to the sun room. It had been hell. It would be as difficult to pretend normalcy with Seamus and Nell. Cal and Josie, he gave nary a thought.

A sudden impulse to just confront Tannis hit him again, but he squelched it. He had to stay as far away from her as possible. If he so much as touched her, he would be lost. Leaden with humiliation and the after-effects of nearly a bottle of Scotch, he dragged his feet back to the library. He placed the treacherous sheet of paper in his desk drawer, locked it, and lay down on the leather couch. Eyes closed, he surrendered to the nauseating swirls of gray that steadily pulled him down into a darkening vortex. Just before he passed out, he felt the heat of an unbidden tear as it trailed down the side of his face.

Tannis awoke alone, confused. Bryan had either not come to bed or had got up very early and very quietly. She remembered a moment of dis-ease last night as she lay here waiting for him. For just a few seconds the image of the dark cloak had flitted past her vision but she had quickly chided herself for her paranoia. She was getting as bad as Josie had been in the heat of her many past love affairs—possessive. She had probably fallen asleep and he didn't want to wake her, that was all. Besides, her body still held the flush of their earlier lovemaking. She was too greedy for his touch, was all. He probably knew if he woke her, there'd be little sleep to be had.

She glanced at the clock. It was only 6:30 a.m. Then she caught sight of the note, tucked under the base of the lamp.

"I have to go away on business for a few days, with Lorne. Amuse yourself, my love. Bryan."

The note was rather terse, but explained his absence. She knew all about commitments, and was prepared for business calling Bryan away. He would also have to deal with her sequestering herself when in a sculpting frenzy. Unconcerned, she intended to use the time to finalize her wedding arrangements. They'd go to Le Node, her and Josie, and share the news with Bett and ask her assistance. She chuckled as she envisioned Bett putting all of Ley Node to work on her behalf.

Hopefully Iris, a floral consultant, would participate as well. She owned several exclusive shops, one of which was in Dublin. That's how Nell and her had met. Nell had worked in her shop until her first son was born, and still helped out for special occasions. It kept her sane, she'd said, when up to her gullet with the little bastards.

The next two days passed in a happy flurry. Cal had also left for the continent for a few days and poor Seamus, confounded by the incessant chatter of women making and changing plans, escaped to the sanity of the outdoors and only joined them for meals. His absence was appreciated, since he took the children with him.

Bett was elated at the news of Tannis' impending marriage, and credited herself with foresight of the blessed event. She had known, she said, that were the two to meet, they would be besotted with each other.

The village would all attend, according to her, and be pleased at being dressed in costumes of old, if she had anything to say about it. As to the feckless O'Neal, "He'll dress up for me or I'll curse his vegetable patch and sour his whiskey." The wedding had been set for August 24th, plenty of time to do it right, she'd added.

Jane solved the problem of materializing a wedding dress in a short period of time. Thrilled that Tannis would soon reside nearby, she had called her sister, a seamstress for Forthington, an exclusive designer in London. The wedding dress was to be a gift from the Foundation, made by her sister's own hands. She was expected this very afternoon with fabric swatches.

Reporters from local and surrounding community papers were already taking shots of the courtyard where the ceremony would take place, and the terrace and rose garden, the site of the outdoor reception. In fact, reporters had already taken shots as they skulked around the grounds, but no one paid them any mind as a whole brigade of gardeners and house-cleaners had been hired to spruce up what Nell called 'the general filth of the place'. There were so many strangers about, it was hard to know who was who. Although they intended to keep the event as private as possible, it was to be expected the marriage of Lord Lagohaire would draw local, if not regional attention.

Nell volunteered to arrange the wedding feast, suggesting it be spread buffet-style, on the upper terrace. Tannis loved the idea, particularly since she intended to have canopied tents out back. The only thing left undone was confirmation of Linka and Sam's arrival. Linka had called last night and Tannis just needed to check with Bryan about transporting the cats. His Challenger jet would be sent to collect her daughter, Sam, and her babies, whom she missed desperately.

Three days later Bryan had still not returned. Seamus had received only a short call from Lorne saying he was held up. In fact, Bryan was not held up, but holed up; in a discreet, leased residence in London. Only Lorne knew where he was and had gone to see him several times under cloak of darkness. Both were agitated at the need for such measures, and rightly so.

For the cover of the front page of the latest issue of 'See' held a picture of the statue of Taenacea, her hand extended to the dropped headlines which read "Tycoon Loses all to Statue of Victory!" The taunting smile on the statue seemed to reinforce the headline. When Lorne slapped the tabloid down in front of him at the office, Bryan couldn't believe his eyes.

His disbelief turned into anger, then grew into rage as he scanned the rest of the article. The implications were libelous. A host of corporate and land lawyers had already been dispatched in both London and Dublin, to search out his land rights in preparation for what was hoped to be a private action.

The headlines shattered his hopes of a discreet litigation and ruling. By the next day, other London tabloids including the *Tribune* had picked up the story. Scandal in the ranks of the titled was eagerly consumed by those wishing they had as much to lose. That he was a financial tycoon as well only spiced public interest. Lorne had arranged his escape to this hideaway and dealt with the reporters that hoped he would lead them to their quarry. Bastards! But they hadn't found him yet.

The anger Bryan felt before was nothing compared to his fury now. It would not be long before someone picked up a paper in Dublin and Seamus and Nell found out about it. Thank God they rarely watched the telly. In spite of his money, there was nothing he could do to protect his own from this ugly absurdity.

In spite of his determination not to do so, he glanced at the front page again. As intimately as he knew the face, in this picture, her smile looked both taunting and victorious in a calculating way. He had read the story, a story based only loosely on the truth, truth as he knew it. The story told of her search for her legendary lands but also of his efforts to keep it from her. It also implied this was the motivation for his own seclusion, particularly when it came to his business ventures. He had kept himself hidden because he had something to hide.

"This is plain crap!" he had shouted, as he paced before Lorne. He pointed at the growing pile of tabloids on the coffee table between them with disgust. One story was more ridiculous than the other. Well-written and using the bizarre logic of the press, it would be difficult to call their statements outright lies.

"Of course, but any rebuttal of denial now will just put *you* on the front page. That's what they want, to flush you out. Pull yourself together and think. Let me handle the press. But I'd go talk to Tannis if I were you. Maybe she'll retract the story for the papers," Lorne suggested, at a complete loss.

He was torn. He found it hard to believe Tannis had done what was implied, but realized Bryan did. What was he to do? He'd known Bryan almost all his life, and her only since the weekend. But he also remembered how Bryan's own father had sealed his mother's fate through an unwillingness to seek the truth of a matter. He too had jumped to conclusions and, when he had falsely accused her and turned her out, his actions had set into motion events which inadvertently caused her untimely death. The incident had happened not long before he met Bryan, and he still remembered the torment caused by misplaced pride and an unbending will. History appeared to be repeating itself in Bryan's current attitude. There had to be an explanation for this, and he intended to find it. In the meantime, he had to stop Bryan from doing something stupid.

"I'll confront her all right. But not just yet. Not until I've slapped the biggest libel suit against her and her co-conspirators, Cal and Josie. She's chosen to keep a low profile herself until now. Let's see how she likes having her life plastered all over the papers. Let's see how they all like having innocent events twisted and distorted by dark implications."

What had irked him the most was the implication in one story that he had coerced Seamus, his own brother, into the equivalent of a modern day bondage. Other papers had embellished the point and implied Seamus lived on the estate like a pauper, stripped of his inheritance, living hand to mouth by the grace of his absentee brother. It also implied Bryan had disallowed his marriage to Nell, because, possibly he was the father of two of her children, the two with dark hair.

The next night, Lorne went back to Bryan's hideaway. But Bryan was gone. Now where the hell was the bastard? Jesus! In his current mental state, he could do just about anything. A quick call to the Estate assured him he wasn't there yet. Again he made excuses, to Nell this time, and implied they'd both be back shortly. Then he reached a decision. He had to tell them, even if Bryan didn't. Caught up in wedding preparations, and isolated by choice from mainstream news, they hadn't yet heard of what had become public knowledge elsewhere. He could at least prepare them for the worst.

* * *

Lori was elated. Not only had she received payment for her scoop, but also a one-year contract from 'See', and carte blanche to follow up on this juicy story. They had even given her a photographer and endorsed her plans to fly to Canada and get more background information on Tannis MacCrae. Her attempts to locate Josie Wilde the author, had drawn a blank. She still intended to track her down. This tidbit had fallen into her lap when she had first called Amora Publications. The receptionist was an old school chum of hers, and disgruntled as usual, being a whiny sort if memory served her, was eager to make things just a little sticky for her higher-ups, particularly Alan. He had dumped her last year after a far-too-brief relationship, in her eyes.

Lori's mind brimmed with plans. After her trip to Canada she would give her landlord the finger and get a new place. The only fly in her ointment was that Alan had not returned her calls. Ah well, the circles she would travel now would offer finer pickings than a loose-lipped Editor. Besides, she had known the chance she took and was prepared for the worst. She had no regrets.

Alan regretted his loose lips. He was both pissed-off and guilt-ridden. He'd been raked across the coals by his publisher then told to set up a meeting with marketing to see how best to utilize this unexpected disclosure. The publisher would contact the legal department to prepare for a breach of contract suite in case the author chose to file suit.

Ideally they would circumvent a lawsuit, and it would be Alan's responsibility to convince Mrs. Wilde not to take action, his publisher had said. What Alan feared more than a suit was facing Josie Wilde. She had been specific about keeping the identity of her subjects secret. He suspected his upcoming encounter with her would not go as well as with his publisher. There was something about her that made him fearful of reprisal.

As to Lori, he never wanted to see that bitch again. She had lied to him. In spite of his good instincts in ferreting out the press, she had been a reporter after all. And he, stupid drunk and full of himself, had spilled his guts—all for a piece of soft ass, and not a very good one at that. He was done with her of course.

* * *

Charles Thornton had seen the papers too and preened. He had been the one to make the connection, and had said so at coffee break. He didn't know why. Usually he was silent, but this time he felt a need to assert himself.

The file clerk Anne had heard, and eyed him speculatively. Perhaps he wasn't such a dolt after all. As bland as their one night had been, it was the only one she'd experienced in more years than she cared to remember. She may be young, but she knew she was plain, and already felt as old and used up as her ailing mother. Besides, were she to see him again, him being married, her encounters would be irregular and in her control.

Better an affair with a mediocre man than endless nights of nothing but the company of her mother's silent suffering. She smiled at him with renewed interest, intending to slip him a note saying she'd enjoyed the last time, and asking if he'd like to join her for a drink. She could do worse, and had. Being alone was worse. Quickly she wrote the note before she could change her mind.

When Charles received her note at lunch time, he was elated. His small part in the scandal had captured her unexpected attention. Suddenly he realized the situation at home was still unbearable, and Majorie's pained looks difficult to ignore. He knew she wouldn't let up. Impulsively, he decided if he was going to be punished for it, he might as well do it.

He'd do it. He'd invite Anne for a drink after work and propose a continuation of their relationship; covertly and only occasionally, of course. But his analytical mind already searched for a place to meet. And Marjorie, cow that she was, intent on everlasting punishment, would never suspect he'd do it again. Funny that. Had this story not broken, he'd never have thought to approach Anne and find small solace with someone else. With her renewed interest, he felt a man again, at least more so than before.

* * *

Josie entertained a captive Iris and Nell on the terrace with stories of her continental treks. Tannis, stretched out on a lounge chair beside the three had heard them all before. She was exhausted. Her first marriage to Linka's father Brad, had all been arranged by her take-charge mother-in-law. All she had to contend with then was to pick one of the three dresses her mother-in-law had chosen and show up for the countless rehearsals. This time was different. This was her experience, and for the first time she understood the obsession brides had over having everything just perfect. It would be the ultimate celebration of her life. There was so much to decide. And her dress was of prime importance.

Jane's sister, Ellen had come as promised, with a full case of delicate fabric swatches. Since Tannis knew exactly what she wanted, it hadn't taken long to choose a creamy shantung silk for the dress, and gossamer gold netting for the tunic. Ellen would use the sketches she had made from her dream for the pattern. Her measurements taken, Ellen left with a promise to return with the muslin mock-up for Tannis to try on by the end of the week.

Tannis had just reached for her glass of lemonade when she heard the front door crash open. From where she lay she could see through the paned doors into the foyer, and Bryan's determination as he strode towards them. She half-rose in anticipation, but paused as she saw the scowl on his face. In fact, his face looked chiseled from stone as he bore down on her. Without a glance at her companions, he tossed an armful of tabloids onto her lap.

Some slid to the ground, but one landed in her lap, straight in front of her. She looked down at it and found herself looking at a picture of herself, rather her sculpture of Taenacea. Her heart sank as she followed the sculpture's hand which pointed to the headlines dropped to the bottom right of the page. As the headlines registered, *"Tycoon Loses to Statue of Victory,"* she thought it a joke, and laughed. When she looked up at Bryan, she knew it was no joke. Good God! He believed this. The enormity of what she had responded to with a laugh suddenly hit her.

It was like a nightmare. She opened her mouth to say something. But what? So she shut it again and looked down at the picture in her lap. As if in slow-motion, she picked up another paper and read the headline, then another, and another. Book, what book? She felt like she had been whisked into someone else's bad dream and looked over at her now-silent companions, pleading comprehension. Before she could utter a word, or even properly register what was going on, she felt a painful wretch on her arm. Bryan had reached down, pulled her up by the hand, and was forcefully dragging her behind him. He pulled her into the library and slammed the door behind them. Then he let her hand go and stood back, hands clenched at his side, eyes flinty with rage.

"The wedding is off and I want you out of here. If you publish your book, I will see you in court. Now . . . get out!" Then he turned and strode to the window. His back to her, he stood rigid, as if carved in stone.

The horror of his words registered, each piercing her heart like an icy dagger. Yet a part of her didn't really understand what he had said. The wedding was off. Why? What book? What was this book the paper and he alluded to? This could not possibly be happening. About to protest, she opened her mouth, but not a sound escaped. In disbelief and discomfort, she had the most inappropriate urge to laugh again. This was the most horrible, yet silliest thing that had ever happened to her. And Bryan, her Bryan could not possibly believe what these rags were saying. Could he?

It must be a dream. Yes, that was it. She had fallen asleep on the lounge chair and was having a nightmare. Hopefully, she would awaken any moment. Her reality had merged and blended with others so naturally during her Quest, why, she probably didn't even realize she was dreaming now. Yes, of course. That was it. It was just some sort of very real dream.

The nervous laugh she held back escaped. But it sliced the air in a cruel and cutting sound, not at all what she had intended. She saw Bryan flinch and rushed forward, to explain. Her hand only inches from his back, her words of explanation died on her lips as he twirled around and pushed her aside brusquely. She staggered against the desk and managed to say, "Listen . . ." Whatever else she might have said was cut short by Bryan's look of utter loathing. It sent a shiver of cold up her spine.

She watched him stride to the desk, unlock a drawer, and pull out a sheet of paper he then thrust in her face. Suddenly she knew this was no dream. It was real. For the love of God, she didn't understand what was happening, but it was real.

"Haven't you done enough? I think this explains everything," he said coldly as he let go of the paper as if it would infect him with its message. She watched it flutter to the ground between them. Suddenly she felt a surge of indignation. What the hell! What was going on here? What right did he have to attack her, without giving her an opportunity to find out what she was being accused of. He couldn't think she had anything to do with those horrible tabloids, could he? The moment she thought it, she knew it to be true. He did.

She looked around desperately, as if to seek aid from her surroundings. She registered the glow of gold lettering on the rows of leather-bound books around her; silent witness to her humiliation. She was on her own it seemed. Incapable of dealing with the situation, she silently called for help and immediately sensed the presence of her counterpart slip into her consciousness. This was absolutely ridiculous. Whatever he thought she had done, it needed to be addressed. She would not be attacked so. In a voice that more than matched his own coldness, she said, "You accuse, but without cause. So be it. I'll go." Only her heart knew how the ice of her words burned.

Pride wounded, she would not defend herself. She picked up the sheet of paper and with great dignity, turned and walked out.

Angry now, she went back on the terrace and picked up every one of the tabloids. She refused to meet the eyes of the three silent women. She knew they must have seen the headlines, probably even read the stories, but didn't care. This was all a big misunderstanding, a horrible mistake. Whoever was responsible for this ,it was not she. Bryan may feel justified in his rage, but she too had been maligned, her privacy compromised as well. She left the terrace and went upstairs into her room, the Rose Room. The door locked against interruption, she spread the tabloids out on the bed and began to read.

Much later she stood by the window and stared unseeing at the panorama. She had read every word and thought she knew what must have happened. That she was faced with the result of coincidental events, phased her only a little. That it was her best friend who had initiated this horror hurt. But that Bryan did not trust her, and believed her capable of such vile motives, was devastating. She would have never believed him capable of this.

Of course, she would never forgive Josie for this, and their friendship was over. But that her one chance of happiness would be snatched away by Bryan's open lack of trust in her was more than she could bear. Why had he not come to her and asked her about it? Why had he so easily assumed she had done this? Did he think her capable of such duplicity? Was their attraction only a sham? As deeply as she had felt their connection, was it only sexual attraction after all? Had this newly discovered love been only a lustful interlude on his part?

Suddenly the whole Quest seemed a dream, or worse yet, a fantasy, an illusion she had created. That was it. She had made this all up, this aberration of her mind, and this was her reality check.

Another thought hit her. How could she face any of them now? In spite of her innocence, they must all think her guilty. And it mattered. For the first time in her life, it mattered very much. She couldn't face them. She had to get away. That was it. She would leave. A darkening had gathered around her, a leadening of her limbs, a hardening of her heart, just as Taenacea experienced when faced with the ruin of her gathering. It was happening all over again. She knew she was about to travel to the same dark place as her counterpart. But not yet, and not here. At home, in her Canadian home. Once there, she could let go, but not until then.

With robotic precision she pulled her case out of the closet, and carefully folded her belongings into it. When it was half-full, she stopped.

Why was she even bothering? Every article she had purchased would just remind her of her humiliation. She couldn't bear that. She left the room, her case still open on the bed behind her. Quickly she stuffed her wallet into the pocket of her jacket, then remembering her passport, grabbed her purse and left the room.

She reached the courtyard undetected. As she tiptoed past the closed library doors, she had heard the rise and fall of agitated voices, and instinctively hastened her steps. Stout was nowhere about, but thankfully, the keys were in the Merc. With thought only of escape, she got in, started it up, and quickly drove away, barely registering that she was driving on the wrong side of the road. When she got to Ley Node, she parked the Merc under the shade of a sprawling oak tree by the entrance to the growing center. She let out the breath she felt she had held since her departure. Now what?

She saw Jamie wave at her from the nearest greenhouse, a smile on his face. He must not know. He would help her get away. She hurried over and explained the need for a quiet and secret departure, citing a private emergency as the cause. Jamie was willing to help and kept his questions at bay on seeing her stricken face. No matter. He'd call the Manor later, or better yet, ask Bett. Jamie's nephew would drive her to the airport.

But at Shannon Airport she discovered there were no flights scheduled for departure until the next day, and then only, weather permitting. Planning to purchase a ticket anyhow, she reached for her wallet and credit cards. OhMyGawd! The wallet was not in either jacket pocket. Quickly she searched her purse, but knew it was not there either. Well. It appeared she would not be going anywhere, either today or tomorrow. Automatically she pushed her hands back into her empty pockets. The wallet must have fallen out in her room, or in the car. Quickly she excused herself and dashed back outside, relieved to find Jamie's nephew still parked at the curb.

"There'll be no flights out til the morrow, if then," he said pragmatically as she pulled open the door. "Where to then, back to the village is it?"

Yes, where to? Tannis had no idea what to do now. She could not face Bett at the B&B. Mary perhaps, but no. She would not share her humiliation with a stranger. And she couldn't go back to the estate, or stay here either. Without wallet and credit cards, she couldn't get a room in Dublin, or leave the island for that matter. The sound of fingers drumming on the steering wheel cut through her numbness. She's have to decide something.

"Yes, Ley Node." It would give her time to think of something else.

* * *

Josie was in shock. When she saw the tabloid cover after Bryan had dragged Tannis away, her stomach dropped. OhMyGawd! Someone at Amora had leaked the story. Whoever it was would pay. But her own outrage was quickly replaced by fear, fear of what Tannis would do. For like it or not, it was her fault. She had covertly done what she knew Tannis would not willing endorse. With a sinking heart she realized she was responsible. She had gone too far this time.

The look on Bryan's face bode no good. Nell and Iris had also thrown her odd and speculative looks. But she gave them no chance to say anything. With righteous indignation, she excused herself and hurried upstairs, intent on speaking to Tannis right away, then placing a scathing call to Alan at Amora. She tip-toed down to Tannis' room and quietly tried the door, but it was locked. She knocked several times, but there was no response, not even when she identified herself. Tannis must really be furious. Best to leave their confrontation until later, for a confrontation there would be.

Her call to Alan proved unsuccessful as well. He was out. She had to think. Cal. Gawd! What would he think? He knew she was writing the book, but had assumed Tannis had sanctioned it. She wondered if he had seen the papers already. Gawd . . . what a mess. She had to try and straighten this out. She left an urgent message at Cal's Paris hotel to come to the estate immediately.

Her message was answered sooner than expected. She had taken a quick shower to distract herself and was just drying herself when Cal walked in. He had seen the tabloids in Paris and booked a flight back. His face told her he had seen the papers, but his concern was all for his bride. "Are you O.K.? Oh, babe, what a mess. So, tell me, how did this happen?" His apparent calm reassured her somewhat and she filled him in on what had transpired.

They agreed it was best to leave Tannis alone for now. An accounting of her actions was bound to come, and both faced that eventuality with trepidation. Cal was not insensitive to the fact that the end of their relationship could well seal his fate as Tannis' ex-agent. There was no wrath like that of a Leo maligned. But other than knowing with certainty the leak had come from Amora, they had no idea how, or why. Cal endorsed Josie's decision to sue the publishing company. Of course, the book would now not be written. Josie also knew she had to own up to her part in this. She did not relish facing Bryan just yet either, and decided to talk to Nell first.

"I'll go talk to Bryan first, Babe. You've got enough on your plate without getting the full brunt of his anger," Cal said.

Josie was relieved and gave him a tight hug. "God, I love you. Thanks for not beating on me for being stupid, stupid, stupid. After this gets all straightened out, remind me never to mess with anybody's life ever again." She meant it. But first she had to salvage this situation.

Cal stepped out into the courtyard and looked for Bryan. The house had suddenly felt hushed by a blanket of doom. Outside, clouds now obscured the sun as if in response to the drama being played out beneath their rolling disquiet. A few drops of rain splattered on his head and he sought the shelter of the Portico. About to go back inside, he caught a speeding streak of red flash along the oak banked drive.

Lorne's Jag screeched to a stop, and its agitated driver leapt out. Lorne hesitated a moment when he saw Cal on the steps. His first reaction was to avoid him. Then reason set in. Just because Bryan suspected everyone didn't mean he had to. He cared more about getting to the bottom of this than who was to blame. Besides, Cal might know how this had happened.

"Come on, we have to talk," he said and beckoned Cal to follow him to the stables. He took him into the trainer's office, closed the door, and faced Cal, his back to the wall, arms crossed over his chest. "Now, how about you tell me what you know about all this." Cal did. An hour later both men were partnered in their mission to make Bryan see that Tannis had done nothing, and was as much a victim as he.

Lorne knew his partner well. "I'd better talk to the poor bastard myself first. He's liable to shut you down. I know him, and right now he's so hurt, he's lethal. I've never seen him quite like this before." They agreed it was the best course of action. It seemed history had repeated itself, but hopefully not to end in tragedy. Bryan, just like his father before him, had sent the woman he loved away, and for the time being, no one knew where she was. Since there was only one flight out of Shannon Airport a day, at least she could not leave the island until tomorrow.

Lorne's task was difficult. At first Bryan didn't even want to hear Cal's name, let alone Josie's or Tannis'. It almost took a personal ultimatum to get him to see Cal. He wasn't ready to see Josie, or Tannis for that matter, but reluctantly agreed to let Cal and Josie have their say after dinner, in the library.

Only after Cal assured him Josie would contact the media, and publicly claim she had made it all up, did Bryan relent. With a bit of luck, her admission would diffuse further interest. But he still refused to address Josie directly. For the first time he questioned his own conviction Tannis was responsible for this nightmare. That Josie was willing to expose herself to public ridicule made Bryan think perhaps Tannis didn't have anything to do with this after all. What Lorne and Cal were trying to drum in his brain was possibly true. It was possible that Tannis had not even known about the book Josie was writing. It was beginning to look like he could have misjudged her. But then, Josie's actions could be based on nothing more than blind loyalty towards her best friend. Perversely, his ears still rang with the sound of Tannis' harsh laugh.

He didn't know who to believe just yet. He had to think this new development through. Uncaring of the rain, he headed for the stables. Weather be dammed, he would go for a ride. Perhaps the wind and rain would wash fiction from fact. It didn't.

The evening was a disaster. Josie knew that Bryan did not entirely believe her and didn't known what to do. Seamus, bless him, seemed the most pragmatic and had just said, "Well . . . there's naught to do about it now but weather the storm that be gatherin' around yeh, together." But she felt his pain at being besmirched just the same.

And Nell, unreadable polite, but unusually silent, was fighting her own demons. Her outer concern seemed to be only for the children. "I'll not have them branded bastards. I'll be taking them to me sister's in Cornwall. We'll go first thing in the morn," she had said curtly.

Her look brooked any objection Seamus may have voiced. Inwardly, and beneath her motherly concern, stirred an uncomfortable awareness, one she knew she must address. Her own stubbornness in resisting marriage had been based on what? Her will to have her own home first. She had known what was to be when she had first decided on Seamus as her man. He had made no secret of his commitment to care for the land, however long, before Bryan took over. Used to having her own way, she had dug in her heels in what area she could. For it, her children were now branded. This was a truth she must come to terms with. But in Cornwall, under the salve of her sister's comfort.

Lorne remembered something that would make the situation even stickier. "We have another problem. Linka, Sam, and the cats are arriving in the morning." His words fell on an uncomfortable silence. Bryan did not look pleased, and everyone but Josie looked discomforted.

It seemed to Josie there was no end to new complications. Well, she would do what she could. "I'll go with Stout to meet her at the airport and explain everything. Hopefully by the time she gets here she'll be prepared for a less than enthusiastic welcome, in spite of her own innocence, and her mother's for that matter." She couldn't keep the bit out of her tone. This was too silly for words. She knew it was difficult for everyone, but who had given thought to how Tannis or her daughter might feel? Frustrated, and defensive of her 'family', she rose.

"Well, let's get this over with. I'll be in the library, waiting for the jury's verdict. If no one comes, I'll just hang myself. It will save you the trouble. Then the press can dig up a bunch of dirt on me, and they're bound to find plenty. That will take the heat off you all. What the hell! Life goes on." She stalked out and left behind a stunned silence.

In spite of her ridiculous statement, Bryan squirmed. She had a point. He knew Linka was as innocent as Nell, Seamus, Lorne and Iris, yet all were caught in the ugly web of speculation and conjecture triggered by what had been printed.

Sensitive to how Tannis must feel right now, Iris had quietly slipped upstairs, intending to offer her some comfort. When there was no response to her knocks, she tried the door. The door opened on an empty room. She immediately saw the half-packed case on the bed. A quick scan of bathroom and closet confirmed her suspicions. Intending to leave with her luggage, Tannis had chosen to flee with nothing. She saw the tabloids on the desk, and the page of correspondence on top. She carried them downstairs into the library where Josie and Bryan stood eyeing each other in the centre of the room. "She's gone," she stated. She handed Josie the sheet of paper and asked if she knew anything about it.

Josie worked her bottom lip as she scanned the page. She realized what had happened. "I must have dropped this in the sun room when I was putting my papers away." She looked at the blank faces around her. "Don't you see, this is page two of a response from Braith & Timms to my inquiry on Tannis' ancestral line. Tannis knew nothing about this. I have no idea why they sent it here. I asked them to send their response, if it was done while I was here, to the hotel in London." She turned to Bryan and stated, "It's *my* letter you read, only *you* assumed it was written to Tannis." His face seemed to crumble, confirming the truth had sunk in. She turned to Cal and said, "Babe, go get my writing portfolio. I want Bryan to read the whole letter. Maybe then he'll believe me."

When Bryan had read it, plus her initial inquiry and her contract with the publishing company, which specifically stated the anonymity of her characters was to be kept strictly confidential, he finally realized what must have happened. He also realized what he had done.

Without giving her an opportunity to explain, he had jumped to the worst conclusion possible. He had accused and condemned her, and cruelly so. Now she was gone. God, he was a sick, judgmental bastard; uncompromising in his arrogance. How could he have even thought her responsible? True, he could have jumped to that conclusion, but along with their pledge of love, they had sealed a pledge of truth and honesty, a pledge he had broken, even before their marriage. Suddenly he paled. Now the appearance of his father and mother's face in his dreams made a strange kind of sense. Unwittingly, he had done the same thing his father had when he had wrongly accused her and sent her away. The horror of the past washed over him. His mother had gone to a neighboring estate, owned by an old chum of hers, to seek financial advice in saving the estate from foreclosure. Unfortunately he had also been her fiancée, until she had met and fallen in love with his father. His father, besotted with his mother, had jumped to the worst possible conclusion when he heard of her destination from the maid. Enraged and pained beyond belief, he had sent her away when she arrived home late that night, giving her no opportunity to explain. It was not until late the next day that they found her broken body amid the twisted ruins of the car which had plunged off the edge of a sharp turn on a nearby mountain pass. Though classified an accident, and the truth of the matter explained by her ex-fiancee, his father's remaining years were spent in guilty recriminations and bitterness over his rashness.

It appeared he had unwittingly inherited a character flaw from his father. To all intents and purposes, history could well repeat itself. The thought of Tannis fleeing in anger and hurt, and finding her broken body down some gorge, brought the bile to his throat.

Overwhelmed by revulsion at himself, he looked into each face in turn. He read accusation into each expression, but did not flinch from their censure.

"You're right. I'm a bastard, a fool, and a self-righteous prick who deserves to lose her, just like father. . . ." But his voice cracked and the words were never said. Suddenly he could bear no more and just walked out. He kept on walking, across the soggy fields, blind to a destination, blind to the wet as the puddles soaked his slippers. He ignored the wind and the sting of rain driving against his face, rain mingled with tears.

Chapter Twenty-Six

S TILL DAZED DURING THE DRIVE BACK, Tannis was no clearer on her course of action when she alighted in Ley Node. Mumbling her thanks to Jamie's nephew, she sought shelter from the rain under the big tree by the market place, barely registering the Merc was now gone. In a daze, it was sometime later she realized the merchants were closing down their stands for the night. She had stood there sightlessly for she didn't know how long. She had enough money to get a meal in the pub, but the thought of pretending all was well with the bride-to-be was too overwhelming. "The wedding is off and I want you out of here" reverberated in her mind and brought a flush to her cheeks. She had to think, but where? It had grown noticeably cooler and darker. She couldn't just stand here under the tree all night.

"What a pleasant surprise seeing you here."

Tannis turned around quickly and smiled wanly at Mary, who was shaking out the kerchief just pulled off her head.

"I'm so glad I ran into you before you left. The muslin mock-up of your dress is finished, and if you had the time, you could try it on here and save me a trip over tomorrow, if that was possible."

Tannis felt herself reel. The dress, for a wedding which would never be. She thought furiously. If she could manage it, it would take care of this evening. But it would by far be the most difficult thing she had ever done.

"Why, yes," she said, forcing herself to sound normal. "I'm a bit tired just now, but not expected back until late tonight." There, it would give her time to figure out just where she would go once the fitting was done.

"Then a cup of tea and something to eat wouldn't be amiss, would it?" Mary asked, adding, "Unless you've eaten already."

"Actually, no, I haven't," Tannis responded.

Tannis was surprised she not only enjoyed her cup of tea, but even managed to eat several of the tasty sandwiches Mary prepared in her tiny cottage kitchen. In her own surroundings Mary was eager to share her experiences at Findhorn and elaborate on her plans for Ley Node. Tannis, lulled by her thoughtful discourse and the soft Celtic harp music in the background, felt herself lulled into almost a state of well-being. She even forgot about what had brought her here in the first place.

But when Mary took the tray away and came back with the mock-up of her wedding dress, the truth of what had transpired washed over her in one huge wave of humiliation. Hiding her shaking hands by clutching the fabric to her body, she quickly turned and vanished into the small bathroom Mary pointed out at the end of the hall. Once inside, she took a few deep breaths. She could do this, in fact she had to. Mustering her will power, she slipped off her clothes and pulled the long sheath over her head. It was, of course, a perfect fit. When she returned she indicated as much and circumvented further inquiries by asking Mary to elaborate on a point she had made earlier.

Although Mary was puzzled by her obvious lack of enthusiasm or desire to talk about the wedding or the dress itself, she said nothing. This woman was different from most. A few well chosen questions kept Mary talking until her hastily covered yawns signaled Tannis of her fatigue.

"Well, I should go now and let you get your rest," she said, adding, "My ride should be coming for me soon. Oh, and please don't tell anyone I was here, Mary. I'm getting a little surprise gift for Bryan, and don't want him to know what I've been up to. I'll just wait outside if you don't mind. I love the stillness here."

Their farewells said, Tannis casually walked down the lane as if knowing exactly where she was going. Only she hadn't a clue. It was dark now and clothed only in her tights, a shirt and light jacket, chilly. Hastening along the almost deserted street, she felt the first splatter of rain on her face. She would have to find shelter for the night. Like others before her in more ancient times, the softly lit barn to the left of the lane beckoned her with its warmth. She slipped inside and quickly looked around to see if anyone else was there. The soft snorts and snuffles of animals in their stalls assured her she was the only human intruder.

On her way to the back of the barn she passed a tackle room where she spied a stack of horse blankets. She grabbed three, then she climbed the ladder leading to the hayloft above. It occurred to her that even in her past life, she had often slept under the stars, but never in a barn like a fugitive. Bone weary from the strain of this afternoon's shock, she felt her legs tremble as she hoisted herself up the last few rungs. Leaning against the center post of the barn, she looked around and picked a secluded spot behind some bales near the back of the loft. She scooped out a cradle, lay one blanket into it, and using her jacket as a pillow, curled on her side and covered herself with the other two.

When her heartbeat had stilled, she became aware of faint rustlings in the hay around her. Shutting her ears to their source, and with only the sound of faint shuffling and stirrings from below, she felt her iron-clad control slip. In spite of her resistance, her mind replayed the devastating scene in the library over and over again.

It was one thing to experience Taenacea's devastation, but quite another to experience her own. How was she to wipe away the scene of her last encounter with Bryan, and more importantly—deal with the pain of losing him, a pain so crushing, it prevented both rational thought or action. Why had she run away instead of staying to deny his accusations? If it was not her, rather Taenacea who had made that decision, then why? Her mind swirled with questions and unaccustomed doubts. She needed the respite of mind-blanking sleep. Once her body had warmed somewhat, she willed it to relax and detach from this unbearable reality. But her exit was not smooth. Several times she was startled back by an animal snort or the bleating of sheep, but accustomed to the sounds from her past, she finally escaped into nothingness.

* * *

Linka was concerned. She had expected a warm welcome from a joyful mother on her arrival. Instead an uncharacteristically subdued Josie had met them at the airstrip. Because of the bulky cat cages, Lorne had brought a panel van from Ley Node into which Sam had loaded the cages containing the sedated felines. Josie revealed the scandal on the drive to the estate and showed her the articles from a handful of papers she'd brought along. Meanwhile, Sam received a much shorter and more mas-culine version of the events from Lorne as they followed behind with the van.

It was just awful. Here she was with four groggy cats, about to meet people who now thought her mother had intended to, and still could, take away their home. All because of a scandal set in motion by Josie's thoughtless actions. She was also about to meet Bryan. Remorseful now, he had nevertheless responded to the printed allegations like an arrogant prick, and sent her mother away. That he would think her capable of such conniving behavior indicated he didn't know her at all and greatly diminished him in her eyes. Gawd! It was too stupid for words this chain of events with devastating results. If the effects were not so serious, the situation would be hilarious.

She had heard out the story in silent disbelief. When Josie finished, she couldn't help herself. "You really are thoughtless, Josie. What possessed you to contract a book deal before mom was even married. In fact, you should have _asked permission_ first. You know mom, or I thought you did. Man . . . she must be major pissed at you."

"How was I to know some idiot would be interested, figure out who Bryan was, and take it to the press. I didn't disclose his identity you know. In fact, I went to great lengths to protect it, and your mother's too," Josie retorted.

"Do you know who did?" Linka asked.

"It doesn't matter now, does it? Besides, it'll all work out, you'll see." Josie saw no point in laboring the past. Tannis would fume for a while, but being pragmatic, would eventually come back when she'd cooled off. Her daughter and cats were here. As to the effects on their future relationship—well . . . she wouldn't think about that now. If all went well, Tannis would soon be enjoying marital bliss, which would temper her anger considerably.

Linka didn't share her optimism. She suspected her mother's pride would prevent her from making any move to rectify the situation. It was her modus operandi. In spite of her otherwise forthright nature, she tended to be touchy about her innate integrity, assuming everyone knew it to be impeccable. She'd be devastated by Bryan's accusations and shamed by being sent away. No, she couldn't see her mother getting over this one in time for a merry wedding. Too bad, she thought. All they could do now was wait for her return. Laying her head back against the soft chair cushion, she closed her eyes and replayed the last several days.

Linka was overwhelmed by the impressive setting when she had first arrived. In fact, she felt like she had stepped on the set of an English period movie. The Manor House oozed breeding and the grounds seemed sculpted with an eye to artless balance, and a pocketbook to maintain such perfection. She looked at the sculptures of Taenacea and Garth mounted on either side of the steps, then back towards the fountain. A thrill of pleasure ran through her. She had seen Faye as soon as Stout pulled into the courtyard and thought her perfect in her watery setting. She deliberately took a moment to relish her mother's work before she turned to greet her hosts.

Determined to act as natural as possible under the circumstances, she smiled brightly. Seamus and Nell extended her what she considered a polite but somewhat restrained welcome. She was not to know their restraint was due to embarrassment over Bryan's actions. Originally excited to meet Bryan, to see the man who had swept her mother off her feet, she was relieved by his absence.

Nell had not gone to Cornwall as intended. Informed of Linka's arrival, she felt her own introspection could wait in light of the awkward situation here. Besides, she was curious about Tannis' daughter, and secretly pleased by the diversion of her arrival. She was much better at seeing the truth of a matter in others, than in herself.

It was her children who dispelled the awkward silence while Stout unloaded the baggage. Appearing as if by radar, they stood clustered around their parents and observed the new arrival with interest. Fascinated, they watched Linka remove her jacket and toss it carelessly on the hood of the Merc in a zippy swish that made her lop-sided pony tail bounce over one ear.

As captivated with her young audience as they were with her, Linka clapped her hands and asked, "Hey guys, want some goodies from Canada?"

They did, and sprang towards her as if launched from a cannon. She moved to the open trunk of the Merc and after asking their names, distributed the large, colorful gift bags to the correct recipients. She noted Nell's surprised look and said, "Lorne told me about the kids when I called to confirm our departure. I thought they'd like something uniquely Canadian, eh?" With her gesture, Linka not only endeared herself to the parents, but was declared worthy of worship by the offspring.

Sam, who had been viewing the spectacular grounds from beside the fountain, came round the van to join Linka. Wide-eyed and silenced by his sudden appearance, the children appraised his smiling face and declared it nice, like Da's. Satisfied, their attention returned to their packages. They emitted shrieks as they unwrapped Tomahawks, feathered and beaded headbands, necklaces, peace pipes, packages of war paint, and other items essential for a Pow Wow or war party.

Nell, taken back by the long-haired giant at Linka's side, couldn't help herself. "Jaysu Murphy! But what would they be feeding yeh out there in Canada! Growing like the oaks that's been here these last few hundred years, yeh are." She scanned his open, smiling face but was interrupted from further comment by some scuffling sounds from the opened back doors of the van.

Partially adorned by their gifts, the children dashed to the back of the van. Their feathers bobbed and necklaces rattled as they jostled to peer inside. Zoie's wail of indignation had not only captured their attention. The dogs, rooting in the shrubs nearby, loped into the courtyard to investigate. They eyed the caged spitfire warily, but quickly lost interest in the disagreeable newcomer and wandered off. All but Ruftar, who found this vocal feline fascinating. As childish hands and his wet nose pressed against the front grill of the cage, Zoie reinforced her displeasure with more hisses and throaty growls. Her sedation partially worn off, she was irritated by her confinement and noisy audience.

"Don't be tormenting 'em now," Nell admonished loudly. "Best we take 'em to the sun room, and yous lot, don't dare go in there until yer' told. I'll not have the wee pussies bothered or getting loose."

Stout, Sam, and Lorne each grabbed a cage and followed Nell inside, then brought in the other cages and cat supplies. Their faces pressed against the glass doors, the children watched as Sam set out some dry food, water and their litter box. Linka propped open each of the cage doors then tiptoed out behind Sam. She could hardly wait to change and check out this awesome old house and the grounds out back.

* * *

Linka sipped her lemonade on the terrace and watched Sam and Bryan's leisurely progress through the rose garden. It always surprised her the way men who just met, easily fell into casual conversation without the evaluating reserve most women express at first meetings. Sam was as comfortable with Bryan as with Seamus, Lorne or Stout.

When she finally met Bryan at dinner, she had been cool towards him, barely civil in fact. A gracious host, he offered them the use of the Merc while they were his guests and suggested they take in all the sights, especially Ley Node, of which he was extremely proud. Sam extended his thanks, but she had remained resentfully mute. During a walk around the lake the next day, Sam suggested she show Bryan a little more compassion. He cited Tannis' impulsive flight just as unreasonable as his actions. In his mind, they were two of a kind and said as much.

"They're well-suited, but both pig-headed if you ask me. I like him, as I do your mother. Besides, your mother, if I may remind you, didn't make any attempt to explain herself when unjustly accused. In any event, it's none of our business."

"Oh, isn't it?" Linka needed an outlet for her indignation. Her pleasure at having been warmly welcomed and accepted by the family occasionally made her feel disloyal to her mother.

"No. And punishing Bryan with your dagger looks solves nothing. Talk to him. You have a right to your feelings, but at least hear him out. Then let it go. As you so regularly remind me when I get stuck in judgment mode, 'pout and get over it'."

What he said smarted. She didn't appreciate having her own words thrown in her face, and continued to respond with biting sarcasm, or not at all whenever Bryan addressed her. With everyone else she was her usual cheery self, which only made her reserve towards him more obvious. Even Sam found her attitude tiresome. At dinner that night, Bryan, once again rebuffed when he inquired into their day's activities, banged his fist on the table and addressed the startled Linka in a steely but polite tone.

"I realize this is uncomfortable for you Linka, but we're all upset by the situation. You and I need to talk after dinner. I expect to see you in the library, at eight sharp."

Embarrassed at being dressed down in front of everybody, Linka mumbled a curt "Fine by me," but had no intention of showing up. Who the hell did he think he was anyhow—practically ordering her to appear?

Sam watched her fume as she stabbed at the remaining food on her plate, as if wishing it was Bryan her fork had pierced. She was definitely acting like a petulant child. Fortunately the real children, unaware or uncaring of the undercurrents around them, chattered like magpies and diffused the tension somewhat.

Determined to have his say, after supper Sam pulled her towards a secluded corner of the terrace.

"I'm disappointed in you, babe. You're not practicing what you preach. Being spiritual and all, I thought you were supposed to be non-judgmental, compassionate, etc., etc. Your behavior is not reflecting your beliefs."

"Point taken. I'll go already! Now get off my back." What Sam said was true, but it would take more than one forced conversation to convince her Bryan deserved forgiveness. At the appointed time, she flounced into the library, seated herself stiffly in one of the high-back chairs, and clasped her hands primly in her lap. She was prepared to hear him out, but also determined not to be swayed from her point of view. "All right. I'm listening." She hadn't expected his candor.

"Obsession warps our perceptions and makes us do unforgivable things. I never truly cherished this land, until recently," he began as he waved his arm towards the panorama outside the widow. "This land has been in our family for hundreds of years. However, when I inherited, it was so heavily encumbered, we were about to lose it. What I really wanted for myself was to leave here and build a financial empire, not look after a crumbling estate, which it was at the time. Seamus was always more suited to the land than I though myself to be. Nevertheless, I vowed to do what was necessary to keep it in the family. So Seamus and I came to an agreement. He would stay here for about ten years and handle the management of the estate while I would go overseas to make the money needed to keep the property.

"I spent the next ten years, then another ten, abroad, doing just that. With Lorne, an old chum of mine, I built my empire and established a private trust to ensure the estate's future solvency. But I got so caught up in the thrill of expansion, mergers and takeovers, I forgot to stop once I reached my goal. I continued long after the estate was safe and I'd secured my own private fortune." He walked over to the sideboard and poured himself a shot of scotch. Only the slight tremor of his hand indicated how difficult this disclosure was for him. He raised his glass in inquiry, but Linka signaled her denial.

"I intended to come back," he continued, "but there was always one last deal to close, one more opportunity to be seized. I can see now how selfish I was in assuming Seamus would continue to maintain the estate in my absence indefinitely."

Linka noted his eyes softened as he took a thoughtful swallow and continued.

"When the sculptures arrived, everything changed for me. They touched me in a way I still find hard to explain. And when I met your mother I knew she was the only woman for me."

"I fell in love with her and knew this was the woman I wanted to spend my life with, the woman I've been waiting to give my heart to without reservation. She stirred something inside me that completely shifted my priorities—for the better." He stopped and smiled in tender memory. Discomforted by the realization those moments would never be repeated, he paled, but looked her straight in the eye and continued.

"I also realized how deeply rooted I was to this land. She reminded me of that, your mother. It was as if the two, she and the land, were intertwined in some intrinsic way. I believed her story of our ancestral heritage, thinking it was destined to continue under our care."

He went on to explain how the possibility of losing the land made him panic when he found the letter. But the effect it would have on Seamus was what had pushed him over the edge. His reaction had been instinctive, partially to protect his brother, and partially in retaliation of his own shock and fear that it could all be taken away. What hurt even more was the possibility that she had never really loved him, that it had all been a sham.

Before he could say more, Linka blurted out, "Didn't it occur to you she would become joint owner through your marriage anyhow? What would be the point of marrying you if she just planned to take it away and throw you out? Why not just go to court without all your implied pretense?"

"I see that—now. But not then. In my circles, I've seen plenty of women do just that—in order to get a large divorce settlement or better yet, stay married but live a separate life, and have their estranged husband pick up the tab while they did so. How was I to know she wouldn't do the same? We hadn't known each other long, had we?" Although the truth, he could see by her expression that his justification sounded unworthy of the object of discussion.

"It wasn't just the scandal and its damaging implications. Scandals blow over and I have enough money to re-establish myself elsewhere. But Seamus doesn't. He would be left homeless if your mother took the case to court and won. Although I've made provisions for his children, I didn't intend to transfer title for the house and land until the house was built." Although Linka said nothing, she looked puzzled.

"Although Seamus can live here for the duration of his life as designated in our father's will, he has no legal claim to any of it. His inheritance had been a lump sum held in trust which he chose to apply to the outstanding taxes. It was his initial payment which prevented immediate foreclosure and bought me some time after our father died. But we were far from out of the woods, even with him giving up all his trust money. It took ten years to become solvent. As well, the house was crumbling, so a great deal of time and money was dedicated to upgrading, refurbishing, and restoring it. I always intended to deed Seamus the house Nell wanted built, as well as a chunk of land he could liquidate if need be. He'd earned it many times over. Instead, my selfishness has kept him bound to the Estate long after there was a need for it. Now I'm afraid I've done just what my father did." He proceeded to tell her of his mother's senseless death."

Well. This tidbit added a new wrinkle to the mess. Linka observed him critically while he spoke, and felt herself soften. That he had shared this private aspect of his anguish touched her, and reflected an innate sense of responsibility and character. She knew the courage it took to expose his shortcomings and share his failings. She also hadn't missed how everything about him mellowed, his tone of voice, expression, and especially his eyes, when he referred to her mother. He was all she had described, in spite of his one unforgivable action.

Suddenly, there didn't seem a lot of point in staying angry. It would change nothing, as Sam had pointed out. Besides, she could understand what had caused him to react as he had. She had no problem changing her opinion in light of this new information. Yet, she didn't mince words. "OK. I can see your point, but I do have to say this; you really screwed up as far as mom is concerned." She saw his jaw tighten as he nodded in agreement.

"Mom is proud—and trusting. What you did would have wounded her deeply. I can tell you right now, as far as she's concerned—you're dead meat. Nix, finito. No second chance, even if she loves you, which I know she does. That's how she is."

Her statement dissolved whatever hope he may still have harbored. A look of woeful resignation washed over his face and leeched it of color. He looked so pathetic her heart went out to him.

"Don't misunderstand me," she said as she rose and faced him in front of the window. "Mom is a reasonable and accepting person, in spite of her inflated sense of personal integrity. But I think she will be unbending over this injustice. Just ask my father," she added wryly. She hadn't intended to bring *that* up, but since it slipped out, she felt the example would clearly make her point.

"Mom walked in on him in delecato, with his secretary at the office one night. Zap, bang! The next day he was out of our lives forever. It took me a long time to understand why she refused to give him another chance. She's un-negotiable about some things and fidelity is one of them. Trust and doubting her integrity is another. Between her Leo pride, and now the influence of Taenacea's indomitable will, I'd say you're in a no-win situation."

Bryan winced. Linka certainly didn't pull any punches, but had reached out and given his arm a light squeeze which softened her harsh statement somewhat.

"I think it's intervention time." Her attitude became all business. "First we have to find her. Pride won't let her make the first move even if she wants to. It boils down to a choice of being right, or being happy. Unfortunately, mom likes to be right. You still want to marry her?"

"Of course," Bryan stated, surprised she would ask.

"I assumed so, but had to ask. You'll definitely need our help though. Josie and I know the nature of the beast we're dealing with. You, apparently, don't yet. Her pride can be a pain in the butt, but if you can help us figure out where she might go, you might have a shot. Are you game?"

"Yes." He was game, but had no idea how he could possibly make things right once they found her. "What do you suggest I do?" he asked.

Inspired by the vision of a grand concerted effort which would result in a happy ending, Linka's mind buzzed with possibilities. No way was her mother going to throw away this chance of happiness if she had anything to do with it.

"Call a family meeting. I'll tell Josie. She knows mom better than anyone."

Bryan's face reflected his lack of confidence in entrusting the solution in part to the very person who had created the problem in the first place.

"Don't be too hard on Josie. She's just . . . well . . . Josie. But don't underestimate her either. She says that you can't create a problem without already having the solution; they're two sides of the same coin, and you can't have one without the other. I know she's right. Remember, *everything* happens for a reason. We just can't see the whole picture yet and you just gotta have faith, 'is all."

Bryan raised his eyebrows skeptically. From where he stood, his chances looked mighty bleak. Then again, he'd often used a similar approach when confronted with business problems. Perhaps she was right. He realized he liked this off-the-wall young woman very much. Beneath her childish optimism, he sensed a strength of character and conviction of purpose reminiscent of her mother.

When everyone was gathered in the library, Linka jumped up and looking straight at Bryan, said, "I apologize for acting like an immature brat. I tend to get very defensive about my mom. I also want you all to know I appreciate your desire to help. Lord love her, but we're dealing with a strong willed control freak here. I give the floor to Josie, who knows her better than anyone."

Josie looked at Bryan pointedly.

"There's a definite parallel here. You're *both* control freaks as far as I'm concerned. You've *both* been living in your carefully constructed private worlds. That's all changed now. It appears the universe, via this scandal, has indicated you both have to change if you want a future together. Now, here's what I think . . ."

Nell and Seamus shared a long look. Josie's statement had touched a nerve, and a wash of red colored Nell's cheeks. The squeeze Seamus gave her hand reassured her somewhat. No matter your stubbornness, his eyes seemed to say 'I love you all the same'.

Her blush resulted from other than just embarrassment at her refusal to marry Seamus for so long. She didn't know why she hadn't canceled the wedding as she should have when Bryan sent Tannis away. It was the logical thing to do, and Bryan, enraged over the tabloids, wouldn't have thought of it. For some reason she hadn't. Perhaps secretly she had seen a window of opportunity for herself. The intended bride and groom could simply be replaced with Seamus and herself.

She could both save the day and have her heart's wish. Besides, denying Ley Node its eagerly awaited celebration was inconceivable at this point, and would not easily be forgiven, or forgotten. A lot of people had put a great deal of work into the preparations, and were still doing so.

While they were finalizing the catered buffet menu earlier that day, Iris had come to the same conclusion and had hinted as much. It could instead be her wedding, Iris had said, and one much grander than she could hope for. Nell's family had lots of love but little money and could provide no more than a simple ceremony in the little parish church with a boisterous, drunken celebration after.

During the planning of Bryan's wedding, she saw how unlimited funds could make real the most fanciful desires. Before long she could see herself walking down the rose-lined and carpeted path towards the arbor by the fountain, wherein she would speak her wedding vows. Later, on the terraces, the lace train of her mother's wedding gown draped over her arm, she saw herself glide amid the guests like a real Lady of the Manor. A part of her hoped Bryan and Tannis would resolve their issues, and a part hoped not. Ashamed, she pushed her selfishness aside and drew her attention back to the conversation. Although attentive she could not in good conscience actively join in.

She wasn't seen at Ley Node when we went to get the Merc," Cal said. He had driven over with Stout in the van when Jamie had rung up to say the car was there.

"And with no flights out, the only thing she could do is go to Dublin," Lorne stated, uncomfortable with the parallels to another family flight. "But why wouldn't she drive the Merc there?" Secretly he was glad she hadn't. The thought of Tannis behind the wheel of a strange car, driving on the wrong side of unfamiliar roads while distressed made him squirm.

"What about the ferry back to Wales? Do you think she would go back there?" Cal asked Josie, sensing she would know.

"No. Tomorrow maybe, but not tonight. Besides, the ferry doesn't run this late, does it?" She looked at the men in inquiry.

"No. But first thing in the morning, yes," replied Lorne.

"Well, there isn't much we can do tonight anyhow. Let her cool off, wherever she is. I get the sense she's around here somewhere and will probably show up in the morning. Besides, we can't just chase her down like a missing child," Josie added, rising as if to end the meeting. "I for one am exhausted, and I think we all need a good night's sleep. It's been an emotional day for everyone."

* * *

Tannis awoke slowly, wondering what was prickling her face and neck. She stretched her cramped arms, confused by the smells and her physical discomfort. As she stretched she realized she was not lying in Bryan's bed, but in a bed of hay. And then she remembered why. Never before had she felt so immobilized, not even when she had caught Brad with his secretary. As if she had unconsciously known his actions proved a weakness of character she had long suspected, she had felt hurt and anger, but not shame. His betrayal had not cut so deeply she could not function or make decisions. In fact, their breakup had been the best thing that had happened to her, the impetus which had freed her to express herself in a way she never could under his domination. It had also launched her career. Left to support herself and raise a daughter, she had done so with determination and joy. But that confident woman felt like another person, not her.

What she felt now was entirely different. She had no reason to pull herself together. The Quest was over, and so was her dream of a life with Bryan. With nothing to focus on, nothing to motivate her, she had lost all desire to do anything. She was neither wanted, or needed.

Maybe what she needed was a little help, just to get focused, to get herself back on track. She appealed first to Taenacea, who seemed to have disappeared into the folds of time, then Lil. Her whispered assurances didn't materialize either. Their lack of response weighed on her like censure, but censure for what? What had she done?

Grasping at straws, she pulled herself up into a sitting position. At first light the animals would be fed, so she had to leave quickly. She shook out the blankets and folded them. Quickly she crept down the ladder and to the tack room where she put the blankets back on top of the pile. Hesitating only a moment, she went over to the big utility sink and using the tin cup set on the narrow shelf above it, drank a few glasses of water. She spied a half package of dry biscuits on the shelf, and with only a momentary pang of guilt, grabbed and stuffed what would be her breakfast into her jacket pocket.

Only the baleful eyes of the milking cows followed her silent departure as she slipped through the barn doors, felt her way along the outside walls and hurried over the rise of the first pasture behind the barn. As least now she could not be seen by anyone in the village. Once past the newly tilled fields she slowed her gait. She drew two of the biscuits from the package and ate them abstractly as she picked her way over the sodden ground. She zipped up her jacket against the morning chill. Though her loafers were already soaked, her mind did not register this discomfort.

Her future, it seemed, would be determined by her willingness to purge in preparation for an undetermined transformation. Good god! How much purging was she supposed to do? And to what end? She'd lost her privacy, her lover, and her self-worth. She'd lost everything that gave her life meaning. What more could she give up?

It wasn't fair. Everyone else had found love but her. She had done everything asked of her. She had embarked on a Quest that sent her back and forth in time. She had relived another woman's life, helped balance an ancient karma, and opened herself to experiences others would consider insane.

She had also truly opened her heart and soul to a man for the first time. But her surrender had brought her only a fleeting rapture followed by the sudden and devastating pain of betrayal.

She remembered the shadowy cloak she had seen behind Fiona when she had appeared at the altar. Had the ominous cloak been a foreshadowing of what was to happen, what had happened? Bryan had turned out to be a shadow of what she had thought him to be. He had believed the papers and sent her away like a worthless piece of trash. His land and reputation had proved more worthy of defense than she. Unbidden tears sprung to her eyes, and she ached with pain. In spite of his betrayal, she loved him still. Rendered helpless by her heart, she fluctuated between anger, self-pity, and a longing she tried to suppress.

She was angry with Taenacea who got what *she* desired: the opportunity to relive her grand passion and resolve unfinished business. And she was angry with herself. How easily she had allowed Taenacea's will to direct her own actions. She could see that now. She was also angry with Josie. Like a parasite, Josie had leeched onto her very personal experience, and utilized it as an opportunity for herself. Well, she could have it, but at a price—the price of her friendship. In her own words, she would now reap what she had sown. But anger was laced with self-pity. She had lost someone else she loved. Angrily she pushed that thought away. Still, Josie's actions were unforgivable.

She knew her thoughts were mean-spirited, but allowed her mind to conjure ugly scenarios of retribution anyway, for everyone who had hurt her; Taenacea, Bryan, and Josie. Had they considered her feelings? No. So why not do exactly what she had been accused of?

She paused and leaned against a tree on the next rise, bitterly realizing it was the one under which she had eaten her picnic lunch. So, it seemed she was to retrace the day of her magical encounter with Bryan. Well, so be it. Although she felt her heart constrict, perhaps this was her ultimate punishment, after which she could purge him from her heart forever.

* * *

Linka loved it here, in spite of her mother's absence. This was her and Sam's first holiday together and they relished the Celtic essence of the land and its people. She could see why her mother had fallen in love with this place and why its owner's ancestors had protected it so fiercely. They had gone to Ley Node, where her mother had become the source of much speculation.

The forthright interest of the locals quickly became apparent. While having a drink at the pub, a little woman at the next table leaned over and asked, "I won't be breathing it to a soul, but yeh be the daughter from Canada, then?"

Linka wondered how word of her identity had spread so quickly. She had said nothing about who she was. Then again, since preparation for the wedding continued, there was much coming and going at the Manor, in spite of the bride's absence. Men were in the process of transforming the terraces into a magical setting for the reception and the house was getting a polish from floor to ceiling. Any one of the hired help could be responsible. She nodded uncomfortably, and leaned closer to Sam in polite dismissal.

"Yeh don't have the look of her, an' all. A shame, that. She'll not be marryin' him then. For the title, like," the woman asked, undeterred by her obvious dismissal. Linka wasn't sure what she considered a shame, that she didn't look like her mother, that there wouldn't be a wedding, or that her mother would miss out on a title.

She bit back her intended retort and just smiled blandly as she nudged Sam to drink up. Afterwards, as they walked back to the agricultural center to pick up the strawberries Nell had requested, she commented, "The Irish aren't shy about asking what they want to know, are they? In spite of all the tourists here, I imagine everybody knows who we are by now."

"They probably find this all very exciting. It's not every day a scandal breaks right in their back yard," he said, then added, "And your mother is the villain."

He was right. The tabloid stories had reached Ley Node that morning and set it a-buzz. Local reaction was mixed, with public opinion leaning towards indignation. Loyal to their own and suspicious of the authenticity of anything peddled by 'the bloody english', they nevertheless argued amongst themselves as they dredged up their own old family scandals over frothy pints and bubbly shandys down at the pub.

Bett had made it plain to those that would listen, and those that didn't give a care, that she knew for a fact there wasn't a bit of truth to it. But then again, Tannis *was* a foreigner and her motives suspect. Those who relished a mystery, which covered everyone with Celtic blood trickling through their veins, embellished what had been written with fabrications that grew wilder as successive pints were consumed. It added intrigue to the wedding still scheduled to take place the following week.

Their discreet inquiries produced no results. None they spoke to had seen Tannis either yesterday or today. Linka had a feeling she was close, but where? At breakfast the maid had handed Linka her mother's wallet, reportedly found on the floor behind the open closet door. Linka had quickly scanned her credit cards and declared none missing as far as she knew. Unless she had a large amount of currency on her, it looked like she couldn't go too far.

Stout had left for Dublin after breakfast, both to drive Nell and Iris to complete a large order at the flower shop, and to look for Tannis, in case she had enough money to get there. Cal and Josie had agreed to drive to the surrounding villages to look for her. The weather forecast was not good and Bryan had voiced his worry. He and Lorne had to attend to a business meeting after which they would check the airlines and ferry terminal in case she had managed to arrange a departure. It was obvious to all that Bryan felt as long as she was on Irish soil he still had a chance to make things right.

By early afternoon the air hung thick with a sulky heat in spite of the overcast sky. With everyone gone, Link was left in charge of the children. But even their shrieks were muted by whatever thicket their current adventure cloaked. After Sam and Seamus left for the building site she had demonstrated the stealth required by Indians on their scalping raids and since, had neither seen nor heard them. The hammering from the workers out back were temporarily silenced by yet another 'parched wid thirst' break. By the time they were done for the day, they'd be pie-eyed. She suspected they were under surveillance by her band of warriors and hoped for a surprise attack, anything for a little excitement. In fact, a good summer storm, with thunder and lightening and pounding rain would be welcomed. Although overcast, she could see no darkening clouds that might produce either a deluge or raging storm.

She decided on a cool shower of her own making before everyone came back. Dressed in shorts and a tank top when she was done, she stood at the open window and let the air dry her hair. From the Rose Room where Nell had put them, she could look down onto the courtyard and across the fountain over the picture-postcard grounds. She squinted and tried to view it through Fiona's eyes. Then it had been wilder, the old growth she saw now still young and tender among more ancient trees long since felled.

Bored with the game, she leaned out further and craned her neck to the right. She tried to identify Sam among the ant-sized people crawling around the building site but distance made it impossible. Still referred to as 'the barn', the structure was in fact a beautiful, two-story, multi-gabled country house. Time, wall-hugging ivy, and fragrant climbing shrubs would mellow and blend its bare stone exterior with its pastoral surroundings. Today they were laying the courtyard flagstones out front and the terrace out back.

As she leaned out even further, she spied a moving cloud of dust along the distant strip of dirt road. Since nothing else was happening, she followed its approach with interest. Too early for anyone's return, she assumed it was the post or delivery of another batch of wedding gifts. A steady stream of gifts continued to arrive and were placed unopened in the sitting room to await their fate.

Talk about denial. Wedding preparations blithely continued in spite of the absence of a bride. Only she seemed to find this odd.

"It's like the Twilight Zone," she had said to Sam. "Ignore the fact that . . ." she smiled wickedly and sang, "the groom throws out the bride, the bride has left the land, High ho-a Deere-oh—but the wedding is still planned."

Sam had shook his head and smiled at her silly ditty. "Why not—they can afford it."

The upside of course was that if her mother did return, and if everything did get straightened out, she would be married on August 24th as scheduled, in the setting she had envisioned for herself. Personally, she still thought it weird.

She stood back a little and watched the vehicle as it turned into the courtyard. Disappointed, she watched the young fellow who hopped out of the catering van carry in a bunch of boxes, serving dishes most likely. She had hoped it might be her mother.

* * *

Though overcast, it was muggy and sticky now. Tannis had long ago removed her jacket. Her pace began to falter as she half-stumbled down an incline. Unable to go any further, she came to a stop. Her head spun and she was breathing heavily. She blinked to clear her vision and looked around to see where she was. Her feet had led her to the little dell which sheltered Fiona's altar.

Somehow she wasn't surprised she had found her way here. An unexpected shiver ran up her spine and left her tingling all over in spite of the pressing heat. She didn't know if it was apprehension or anticipation. Everything around her suddenly grew quiet and became very still. Even the pounding of her heart grew silent as she seemed to stand in a place of timeless pause. She sensed the import of her next move—to enter or not. She knew her choice would determine her future.

Chapter Twenty-Seven

BRYAN HAD ARRIVED HOME to hear Tannis had not yet been located. Seamus, just in from the stables, stuck his head into the sitting room and with a twinkle in his eye assured him all vehicles were accounted for. Privately, Bryan thought his brother's attitude far too light. She wouldn't have sneaked back like a fugitive and taken one of the vehicles to make her escape. However, just to be safe, Stout had brought all the car keys usually left in the vehicles into the foyer. Were she to consider doing so, she could not escape as easily as the first time.

A frown creased Linka's forehead as she asked, "Anybody heard anything?"

"She's not reached Ley Node yet, if she meant to," Nell assured her. "But not to worry, I've seen to it they keep an eye out and ring if she shows up. She'll not slip away on us. Come, have a cuppa," she added as she reached for the crockery tea pot on the large tray in front of her.

"Shouldn't we *do* something? Go look for her?" Linka persisted, waving the offered cup away. She couldn't stand this waiting and had pestered Sam with her 'what-ifs' ever since he got back from the building site.

"We already did all we could and can't send out a search party like she's a lost child," Sam said. But he gave Bryan a quick look of inquiry. "Besides, she can't go too far if she's on foot."

Let's give it another few hours," Bryan said. If she's not back by then, I'll go out on horseback. It won't seem out of the ordinary to meet up with her while I'm out riding. In the meantime, try and relax. I'll be out back if you hear anything. Looks like we may get some rain," he mumbled as he looked at the darkening sky through the window. His heart was racing, but he wasn't sure if with hope or trepidation.

Seamus knew better than he what was to come. Years spent on this land enabled him to read approaching weather systems and he'd seen the makings of a storm gather on the way over from the site. "Best prepare for the worst. I have a sense there's trouble brewing," he said before he left the room to wash up. Last night had seen an unusually heavy fall of rain, and already some of the creeks were dangerously swelled.

Out back, Bryan looked up at the murky ceiling of gray, then towards the east where ominous clouds had begun to gather into churning clusters. The leaves rustled encouragement as a tentative gust of wind raced through the drooping foliage and nudged against the heat as if to test its resistance. Other gusts followed, and though they still blew warm, they carried a hint of cool. Out of the corner of his eye he caught a flash of sheet lightening from within the bank of darkening clouds. They'd had little rain these past few weeks; just a few light showers during the night to rinse the day's dust from the lush summer foliage. Last night's drenching and the churning skies seemed a portent that more was on its way.

Concerned about potential damage from the approaching storm, Bryan eyed the partially erected frames on the perimeters of the terraces. He watched the men secure the last of the support poles for the awning which would cover the main terrace and shield the buffet tables and courtesy bar to be placed beneath from sun or unexpected showers.

A large pile of piping designated for smaller carousel awnings, lay ready for assembly beside the lower terrace. Tannis had chosen a festive medieval theme with tented pavilions placed along either side of the rose gardens. White and green-striped canopies with scalloped edges would cover the dining guests and panels of white looped drapes and potted rose trees and bushes would camouflage the corner posts of the pavilions. The rest of the potted roses were intended for the front courtyard where the ceremony was to take place.

"Iris told the nursery to hold off delivering the potted and tree roses until early next week."

Stout's words startled Bryan as he came up behind him. He was just thinking about the roses. "Just as well," he said. Had they been here already, they could well be ruined. A hundred raspberry-hued tree roses and another hundred creamy white potted miniature rose bushes were not so easy to replace on short notice. He quite liked this spry little man and his way of attending to matters without giving offense. No wonder Cal relied on him so heavily.

He felt strange surveying preparations for a wedding that might never be and should have been canceled when he sent Tannis away. He didn't know why he hadn't told Nell to do so. Even during his initial rage, and later as he watched and heard Nell continue with the preparations, he had said nothing. Nell had thrown him several inquiring looks, but had said nothing either and just continued with the arrangements. Perhaps this was due to some celestial intervention. If so he was glad of it, and hoped it indicated there would be a happy resolution to the mess his attitude had created. He would find a way to make it right between them. It was the waiting that was excruciating.

The wind had picked up. He watched it pluck petals from the blooms in the garden and send them into a frenzied race through the air. During the stillness between gusts, the airborne petals and dried leaves caught on bushes or drifted to the ground in lazy spirals. Then another gust would pick them up again and whorl them to a new location. The bank of clouds in the east had darkened but not moved, as if still charting its course. Nature appeared to be waiting too, just like he was.

The electricians had run well-camouflaged cables everywhere power was needed, especially to feed the hundreds of lanterns which would illuminate the night dancing and festivities. Heedful of Seamus' warning, Bryan instructed the men to pack up for the day and suggested they leave-off hanging the actual lanterns until the storm had passed. The boxes of lanterns could be stored along with the tools and supplies in the old smithy by the stables in the meantime. As if in confirmation of the need for such precaution, the sky darkened and the churning black mass to the east began to move—their way.

The women were arguing over scrabble words when Bryan returned to the sitting room. The children, antsy over being confined indoors, stood clustered around Nell and whined to be let back out. It seemed everyone was testy, be it from the prickly heat, impending storm, or tension of just waiting for no one knew what.

Nell finally lost her temper. "I've had it with yeh snot rags. How's a body to think with yous gabbing in my face. I've a mind to let the storm drop a tree on yeh—to knock some sense into yer heads. Tell Da I said yea can watch television and play the computer games. Now goway 'wid yous."

Their TV and computer game time was strictly controlled and considered a rare treat, particularly in summer when they were generally outdoors until dark. The younger ones dashed off to their wing, but more interested in the activity out back, the eldest two, Seamus and Nevill, used the opportunity to slip out and see if they could give a hand.

"Wheel, I expect so," said Kenny, the electrician on the terrace. "One of yeh go to the bottom terrace and t'other to the post by the garden entrance there. Connect the plug end of the extensions when I signal yeh, but mind, not before," he said. The boys ran to do as they were bidden. The breaker to the outside outlet had been turned off, so rather than go and turn the juice on at the box, Kenny decided to test the line from a house plug. He knew the line worked fine, having already tested it once, but wanted to give the boys a chance to feel useful like.

With stopping work early as the man had said, he'd get to the local before his mates. He'd have time to give the boys a bit of fun and still have a quiet pint before his mates arrived. He tried the terrace door which led to the room filled with plants. He looked along the wall and found what he was seeking not far from the door and plugged in his cord. Then he went back out and signaled the boys. The test bulb on top of the farthest pole lit up as he knew it would.

"That'll do," he shouted to the youths. "Leave them plugged together mind. Yeh can help move the lantern boxes from the truck into the smithy if you like." He pulled out the cord and with his foot, shut the door behind him.

"Persuado is so a word," Linka said. "We use it all the time, don't we Josie?"

Her partner nodded sagely. "It means an extremely persuasive person, which Bryan will need to be to win back the tumultuous Tannis."

"Not when referring to the king's english, 'tis not," retorted Nell, stifling a giggle but still exasperated by her opponents' brash efforts to qualify non-existent words.

"I don't recall being on English soil, do you?" Linka inquired of Josie.

"Nope. So English rules don't apply. Our points." Josie made a great show of tallying up their lead.

Seamus and Sam paused in their Chess game to throw the women a baffled look. Linka and Josie had merrily cheated their way through the game, making up words and taking points even when proven wrong by their more serious opponents, Nell and Iris. Bryan smiled too as he walked over to one of the tall windows. Thrown wide open to catch the breeze, he felt the first few spatters of rain amid the cool gusts that now blew the curtains in his face. He turned and scanned the room. The cozy lamp-lit scene belied everyone's hidden concern. Although only five o'clock, it was almost dark as night outside. Wherever she was, Bryan hoped she would return before things turned nasty, or at the very least, that she would seek shelter within one of the protected dells. Then again, that could prove dangerous too.

He stopped in his tracks. Now, why was he so sure she was nearby, on this land? He closed his eyes a moment and allowed himself to become very still. Oddly enough it was the face of the "other one" which floated into his mind. She would not flee, not after having set this quest in motion. Somehow the clarity of that thought reassured him, and he sensed it was true. Tannis might, but Taenacea would not allow her dream to end in naught, in spite of his attitude. Garth too must have had his character flaws, but she knew he was right for her. And if he was the incarnate of this man, meant for Tannis, then perhaps he had the means to make this right. He had to go find her. Without knowing which way she was headed, he didn't know where to start looking for her. Stout was up in Cal's room discussing possible acquisitions from estate sales, and with Seamus and Sam engrossed in their game, he had nothing to occupy him but worry. Restless, he paced from window to window, wondering where she was and formulating what he would say when she returned.

The phone rang and startled them all. Nell answered and beckoned to him. It was only Lorne. Relieved at the diversion, he said, "I'll take it in the library." He knew what he would do right after the call.

* * *

Tannis steeled herself against the storm which raged inside her, oblivious to the storm gathering around her. Dizzy with exhaustion when she stumbled into the dell, she sank to her knees before the altar. She sat back on her heels, determined to sort out her feelings. Perhaps within this sanctuary she would find the answers she sought. A welcomed calm settled over her and the imperceptible earth noises outside the dell faded away as if the interior had been placed in stasis.

Within this sacred place, she knew it was time to examine what she had so deftly avoided addressing. All she had done up to now was wallow in self-pity and humiliation. But here, her mind felt cleared of such emotions. Was she willing to throw away her one chance at happiness because of her precious pride? But wasn't her sense of pride important? All right. She would examine these thoughts in a new way, since her habitual attitude had brought her no answers.

She was proud of all she'd achieved, she thought defensively. Through force of will she had kept her vision, goals and integrity intact for nearly two decades. Her will had enabled her to disregard the 'shoulds' of life and single-mindedly forge her own path at a time when a divorced, single-mother was not so commonplace. Her single-mindedness had led to success as a mother, and in her craft. However, it may have done something else as well. Had she kept more than distraction at bay? She may well have hardened her heart with the inflexibility of her will.

The trees rustled a response. Perhaps, they seemed to whisper—perhaps. It may well have been an inner yearning to express a stifled need for love which had made her receptive to the dreams and subsequently, the Quest. She had suppressed her need for love and diverted her sexual energy to her craft, convincing herself she was whole without it. But once she experienced Taenacea and Garth's passion, her heart cried out for its own fulfillment. And she had found it with Bryan—but only for a short while.

Where had it all gone awry? The library scene flashed before her. She felt herself tighten with the same prideful indignation she saw herself express as the scene replayed itself in her mind. She had refused to defend herself, refused to face the unexpected accusations. Instead, she had chosen to run off in righteous indignation. And nothing had gone right for her since. Was her ego so inflated she would surrender her happiness and a joyful future to its will? Just when had she become so arrogant—so rigid. In retrospect, it seemed a poor choice.

Of all the qualities Taenacea had possessed, accessible to her through their unusual meld, she had drawn on what was perhaps her worst quality—her indomitable will. She had allowed Taenacea to settle within her and handle her own uncomfortable situations for her. It had seemed appropriate, until now. She had given her power away. What she had overlooked was that Taenacea's power, directed by a lifetime of practiced Wicca skills, suited a more barbaric era; a time when a show of force was often essential for survival. As to pride, someone like Taenacea did not *have* to explain herself. She had earned respect by her ability to protect her people and safeguard her lands. Any weakness on her part could cost lives—as it had, and dearly so, in one case. And here she had blithely called on this tremendous power to diffuse what were essentially situations requiring openness and communication, not inflexibility.

Her altercation with the professor during his unannounced visit had resulted in no discernible damage by Taenacea's intervention. However, her actions had only deferred the inevitable. Tannis had still met up with him on the coast in Wales. It was intended for her, not Taenacea, to resolve the animosity between them. She smirked at the thought that were it left to her counterpart, and were she willing to cooperate, Taenacea would have promptly tossed him into the sea, and considered herself justified in doing so.

She sensed a subtle arousal in the air just before everything within the enclosure began to dissolve. Something was happening—shifting. She was in the same place, but somehow suspended, as if she and this enclosure had slipped between the folds of time. Although she couldn't describe it even to herself, the memory of a destiny she had scripted herself, long before this life began, awakened within her.

A thin film had covered her eyes during the shift, and when it lifted, the altar was gone. In its place hovered a milky void which quickly became a backdrop for a series of flashbacks from her own life: scenes wherein she saw herself exert an almost arrogant single-mindedness she would have found offensive had she viewed it in others. In her relationships, it was always she who set the criteria, she who stubbornly exerted her will and called the shots. The emerging image of a willful woman who protected her privacy with fanatical intensity, made her squirm. Briefly she marveled at the loving indulgence of those close to her, who allowed themselves to be manipulated because they loved her. There seemed a very fine line between strength of purpose and ego—a line in hindsight, she had carelessly crossed far too often.

The scenes faded but were immediately replaced by what appeared to be two separate scenes she could view simultaneously; the past and the present; Taenacea and herself. As they played out side by side, she was impacted by the parallels and differences.

While Lil gave Taenacea magical instruction in the practice of Wicca, Maureen introduced her to Celtic lore and the healing properties of herbs. But whereas Taenacea built her keep at Aberayron to gather her people around her, she had gutted and rebuilt her home into a fortress against all but the few she permitted entry. The two had chosen very different daughters, but both had found love with a similar type of man. Only Taenacea had experienced several fulfilling years with Garth, whereas her relationship was over before it had truly begun.

As other scenes unfolded, she noticed the parallels in events and actions. When she had her dinner parties, Taenacea entertained guests in the great hall, and while she worked in her garden, Taenacea was seen riding her lands and instructing her overseers in the care of the crops. The many times she lay in bubbly stupor in her scented bath, Taenacea would lie submerged in a much smaller tub in her chilly chambers. When seen side by side, time only thinly veiled corresponding actions underlined by a similar theme. Awed by the synchronicity, she felt a pang of disappointment when the visions faded and the two spheres of activity merged back into one. But the picture show was not over yet. After a few moments of milky whiteness, a new series of images emerged: only this time they were shadowy, and in black and white, in contrast to the previous colorful scenes.

They confused her at first; not only because they lacked color and a certain definition, but because clusters of different scenarios seemed to spring from points along an unending spiral of ever-diverging future events. Every time she made a choice, a new reality emerged from that point of decision and presented a visual of future events. This again changed her future, until another decision or action prompted a new series of probable events. My god! It was like seeing the blueprint of creation, of how one's life could unfold with each choice made.

In one probable future she saw herself win the estate from Bryan in court, evict them all, only to wander alone amid what began to slowly crumble because she could neither afford to maintain it, or marshall the energy to care. In another she watched her return to Canada, to a life which at first glance looked much like it had been before the Quest. But as bitterness leached the life from her creations and orders slowly dwindled, her self-imposed isolation and the growing cancer of self-debasement resulted in a lonely, painful death.

She watched other probabilities based on other choices unfold in endless variation. Fortunately the bleak were interspersed with more uplifting and interesting probabilities when she allowed herself to surrender to her heart. She saw herself as she had originally imagined, with Bryan at her side, then as a teacher leading new initiates through the steps of Wicca practice at Ley Node. Then she saw herself pregnant, anticipating the birth of their first child, which shocked her somewhat. She would have never thought of that probability. There were others as well which spun in unending design, but underlying each of these scenes was love. Righteousness and willfullness seemed less appealing in light of its price.

When the visions faded, she realized life was not just about the richness of living, but making spiritual choices. It was embracing the belief that she was a spiritual being having a physical experience, not the other way around. Taenacea had known this and lived accordingly, excepting the one time she had allowed her hatred to divert her from her spiritual intentions. As for herself, she wanted love in her life, but was unwilling to relinquish anything for it: not her judgments, control or self-serving attitudes. Basically she was alone and knew it. In order to protect her vulnerability, her arrogance had pushed away the very thing she desired. Only her willingness to release control, to surrender to her heart's nudging not her ego's will, would give her the love she sought. The alternative would be a prideful but lonely life.

She realized something else too: to experience love fully was not a capitulation as she had always thought, but a surrender, a surrender that embraced love above all else. She knew what her heart desired—to be with Bryan. She wanted a lifetime of the love they had shared so briefly. But how? Then a possibility came to mind.

In her studio, she did her best work when she let go of willful intention and surrendered to that invisible creative source which flowed through her. Was that not a surrender of will, a surrender to the higher power of spirit? If surrender worked in her art, would it not work in matters of the heart? She would have to just let go—of her need to control, her expectations—and trust in her own spirit's wisdom—as she intuitively did in the studio, but refused to do in the rest of her life.

A clarity of mind washed over her. The heart was the connective voice of one's soul. Denying love diminished spirit's expression. She had always loved her craft and approached it with an open heart, thus the universal source had provided her an endless flow of creativity. When she closed her heart, her channel of inspiration had been blocked. It was so simple really. What had brought her the greatest joy in life, raising her daughter, her art, and caring for her felines, had been fueled by a loving and open heart.

The brief view of motherhood, of a small child at her side replayed in her mind. This child reminded her of someone whose eyes reflected a similar disconcerting wisdom. She felt a coil of heat within her womb, a core of energy eager to unfurl, and knew the seed of this new life lay within her. And she knew why the child's eyes had seemed so familiar. The aged wisdom was Lil's: a soul awaiting expression in another time, but within the realm of what she had helped nurture. She could choose this chance to give back what had so unstintingly been shared with her.

Before she could give this possibility more thought, the scenes faded and the altar reappeared. She sensed another shift, an arousal in the way the aged stones sat one upon the other. She noticed their slight movement but was distracted by a sudden gust of wind which blew through the opening in the dell and hit her in the back with such impact she fell forward. As another gust hit her from the front and nearly knocked her flat on her back, she cried out for help. She felt as if she had been slapped by the universe. As she attempted to regain her balance, she realized her call had been answered. Taenacea and Lil materialized before her side by side, growing larger and larger until they filled her vision, and then the dell itself. They continued to expand until they lost shape and form, and merged with the turbulent skies she had not noticed until now.

Infused with wonder and an almost painful clarity, Tannis became acutely aware of her surroundings. She looked up at the churning ceiling of darkness wherein Taenacea and Lil had faded. Momentarily blinded by a flash of lightning, she heard the boom of thunder as it rolled and rumbled above her. Good god! How could she not have noticed the storm? She felt like she had undergone an initiation or rebirth while insulated within the dell, but couldn't remember exactly what had transpired, or how long it had taken. She just knew that she felt revitalized, and clean, as if purged of her heavy heart and dark thoughts.

She surrendered herself to the storm. Rather than cower at the on-slaught, she raised her head and with arms flung towards the heavens, embraced it. The shrieking wind tore at her hair and tried to pull the breath from her throat. The cracks of thunder vibrated through her bones and the downpour pelted her from above as if to demand her submission. She was soaked in a matter of moments. Blinded by another flash of lightning and with water in her eyes, she sensed a new comprehension within herself.

Another deafening roll of thunder transported her back to another storm in another time and she pushed down a wave of panic. There may not be a Giles waiting around the corner, but she felt like she could be picked up and hurled into the sky, or driven into the earth by the sheer elemental power around her. If ever there was a time for trust, this was it. With blind faith she surrendered herself to the care of spirit and knew she would be safe, relishing the immense and passionate energy playing out around her.

She heard a tremendous crack and saw a flash of light right before her eyes. Then the wind ceased as suddenly as it had begun, and for a moment all was still but for the sound of rain. Stunned, Tannis looked at what was now a crumbled heap of broken stones spread across the sodden grass in front of her. The altar might never have existed. Then it hit her. What had been built first as a tribute to love, had also symbolized one man's need to cling to pain and loss. Tannis didn't need any more inexplicable events to realize they had both been purged: she in body, and he in spirit. What now filled her mind was the power of love. She would hold fast to the certainty of creating such a destiny for herself, and let her heart guide her home to the man she loved.

* * *

"Maaa! The kitties is gone!" shrieked Jamie, his eyes like saucers as he came to a skidding halt in front of Nell. "It wasn't me—honest. I never was in there. I was looking for Nevill and saw the door open. To the patio," he added in agitation.

"Sweet Jesus!" exclaimed Nell as she jumped up and followed him into the sun room. That's all we need, she thought. Four cats loose on unfamiliar territory in a raging storm. The others were right behind her and joined in the search, Linka and Sam calling their names. The only cat found was Mr. Muff, pressed tight against the back of his cage. Nell sent Jamie to gather the children and look throughout the house if for no other reason than to keep them from gettin' underfoot.

Seamus checked the wide open door. "It's not been latched properly by who's opened it," he stated. He had meant to replace the old latch, but with all the activity lately, had forgotten. He saw the cable lying just outside on the patio and surmised what must have happened. He hadn't thought to tell the workmen the room was off-limits, assuming the patio doors were still locked. But the guests had used the room lately and anyone of them could have unlocked it during the past week.

"Mom will freak if anything happens to the cats," Linka stated, looking around frantically. "Come on Sam. We have to find them."

Bryan emerged from the library to the pell-mell of activity. His mind made up, and certain he would find her, he stated, "I'm going to find Tannis while you find the cats. I know she's close by . . . I can feel it." Oblivious to the startled faces around him, he added, "I'm going on horseback. I think I know where she might be." Although he wasn't certain, his conviction was apparent. He'd watched from the library window as the wind tore branches from the trees and bushes and sheets of rain pounded the earth with a deluge it could not soak up fast enough. He dashed for the stables, head bent against the wind and rain. Inside, he saddled his horse, donned a rubber riding cape and wide brimmed hat, and urged the reluctant steed outside.

Protected by rubber boots, slicks with matching hats, and clutching their battery-block torches, the three men began their search out back. It was slow going. Their torches bobbed in drunken dance as gusts of wind impeded their progress and snatched their calls right from their lips.

Seamus looked up at the churning ceiling. More like the storms that blew from the Arctic and battered the coastline, he'd not seen nothing like this so far inland in quite some time. It was still raining hard even though the thunder and lightening had moved off to the southwest. Two new beads of light bobbed towards him as Stout and Cal came to join the search. His shouts barely heard above the downpour, Seamus gestured them towards the stable side of the house. They all fanned out and looked under the bushes and in likely spots for a frightened and wet cat to hide.

Sam found Billy-Bob. The pile of pipes down by the lower terrace had shifted during the first onslaught of wind creating a protective tunnel on one side of the pile. Billy-Bob had dived into its depth at the first crack of lightening and stayed crouched within the shelter until Sam's flashlight picked up the feral glow of his eyes. Sam picked him up and carried him indoors to Nell and Iris, who quickly wrapped him in a large towel to rub the moisture off his sodden fur. The worst of the mud wiped off his paws, he was quickly deposited back into the sun room to proceed with his own toilet. The terrace doors had been firmly latched to prevent future escape, but Sam checked it from the outside again before rejoining the search for the other cats.

* * *

Bryan mounted his mare at the edge of the stable and let her get accustomed to the noise and rain. He had chosen her rather than his own stallion because of her reliable nature. Not much deterred her and she barely flinched as flashes of lightening lit up the sodden landscape. He could see the occasional stream of light from the search-party off to his right and hoped they would find all the cats. If nothing else, this unexpected distraction would keep them from helpless worry about Tannis' whereabouts.

He had his own problems. Where to go? Tannis could have headed in any direction. He cleared his mind and tried to think like she would. If she needed solace, where would she go? Rather than Ley Node as the others had assumed, he suspected she would seek refuge in a secluded but familiar place on the property. There were only two he could think of, and the first was too close to the house. Besides, she wouldn't go to where they had first made love, not after his cruel rejection of her. Which left only one other place. The shrine; Taenacea would lead her to her connection to a past which bound her to this land. He knew that's where he'd find her.

Lorne had told him the obvious on the phone after business was concluded. "Go after her man, and drag her back if you have to," he had said. "But for God's sake don't let her get away. Be that knight in shining armor all women expect us to be. Grab her, toss her on your horse and when you get her home, make love to her until she forgives you."

"There's a bloody storm out, you fool, and its pouring. We've got branches snapping off trees and flying around like match sticks. I've never seen anything like it," Bryan interjected.

"Nothing like a good storm to clear the air. When you find her, you can always grovel in the mud. Weep if you must, and beg her forgiveness. Remember, she's a romantic."

They had laughed at the image, but in his heart, Bryan was willing to do even that; grovel in the mud. He remembered his brash intentions as he rode directly into the eye of the storm. Moving at little more than a slow walk he was careful to avoid the trees. Lightening flashed too close for comfort and had already hit two clusters of trees just passed. He stared at the raw, jagged break on one huge oak. Still partially attached, half of the tree had split away and hung over the mass of smaller limbs beneath which had been crushed by its fall. He shone his flashlight in wide arcs in case Tannis, instead of waiting out the storm, had foolishly tried to return to the house.

By the time he ascended the last hill overlooking the dell, he was tense with anxiety. He wasn't even certain this was the spot, for it looked very different now. Lightening had struck the two tall trees beside the creek at the bend. They stood crippled, their severed limbs twisted across the gully to form an uncertain canopy that shifted with each gust of wind. Beneath, a tangled wall of branches, brush and clumps of leafy silt held back a wall of water. From what he could see, the creek was at least two feet higher than before, and much wider. The obstruction at the bend only temporarily dammed a much more dangerous flow. Already the water behind strained for release and sought to push through a weak spot.

He dismounted and walked the mare down the slope, his hand on the saddle horn to prevent himself from slipping down the slick bank. The wind pulled the hat off his head and drove stinging pellets of rain into his face. He could hear the rush of the swollen creek in the gully and felt a knot of anxiety tighten in his belly.

He paused to decide if it was safe to ride across or if he should dismount and wade across. He called Tannis' name repeatedly and strained for an answer. But he could hear no response above the sound of pounding rain and rushing water. He cupped his hands around his mouth and continued to call. Instinct told him she was inside the dell.

Tannis laughed as she twirled around in sheer exuberance, oblivious of her wet feet and transparent shirt plastered to her body. The jacket she had removed at some point now lay forgotten in a sodden heap nearby. She couldn't remember the last time she had relished being out in a storm as much. She felt as much a part of it as Taenacea and Lil's energy were. She sensed that all who had gone before—Fiona, William, Maeve, Garth, and the countless other souls which had been part of her journey through time—were all around her. She could feel their waiting presence and knew whenever she needed to, she could draw them to her with a thought. She could connect with their essence as it merged with hers upon a breeze, in the face of a flower, on the wings of a bird, or within any other aspect of nature. And she knew she was safe—lovingly connected to, and supported by this invisibly spiritual world.

She was ready to go back now, trusting she was again on destiny's path, and willing to embrace what was meant to be. Giving up control opened a delicious host of unexpected experiences.

She thought she heard her name called as she twirled near the opening of the dell, but it was raining so heavily she could barely see more than a few yards ahead of her. Then a movement across the gully caught her eye. Halfway up the hill she thought she saw a man beside a horse, waving his arms vigorously. Could it be? Yes—it was.

"Bryan!" She had instinctively called his name. Her heart pounded in time to her thoughts. He had come, he had come for her.

"Stay there. I don't know how . . ." She could see he was still yelling something, but the wind tore the rest of his words away.

She knew the next move was hers. Crossing the creek would be her act of surrender. Before she could change her mind, and eager to reach him, bent against the rain, she half-walked and half-slipped down the slope. At the creek's edge she hesitated a moment, wondering where all this water had come from. Most of the bank had fallen away and the creek was not only higher, but a great deal wider than before. It looked more like a broad and fast flowing river of liquid mud, but hopefully not too deep. She couldn't fathom how it could rise so quickly, unless she had been in the dell longer than she thought. It would have taken at least five or six hours of heavy rain to swell the creek to this level. But her mind was on reaching the man on the other side.

Cold water pressed against her legs insistently as she sought solid footing on the slippery rocks beneath. The current was much stronger than expected, and by the time she was up to her thighs near the middle of the creek she was seriously battling the flux. Then she became aware of a sudden rush of noise, louder even than the bedlam around her. Distracted, she lost her balance and instinctively threw her arms wide to steady herself. Something hit her from the left so hard she pitched forward.

For a moment she felt suspended in time. She flailed her arms in the air as she registered the wall of water rushing towards her. When it hit, she felt a sharp pain on the side of her head, a pain so intense, her legs buckled. Then everything turned into a slow-motion blur. Her mouth filled with gritty water as she cried out. Underwater now, and pushed by a force she couldn't resist, she tumbled along with the current. She managed to surface and gasp for air once before she was once again rolled under. Then she felt another blow on her head and all went blank.

Bryan was frantic. The immense relief at finding Tannis was quickly replaced by disbelief. Expecting her to wait at the water's edge after his warning, he was surprised when after a moment's hesitation, she began to wade towards him. He couldn't believe the stupid woman was trying to cross by herself! Her progress was slow but steady in spite of his shouts for her to go back. Although she probably hadn't heard his words, he thought his gestures explicit, particularly since the rain had eased and they could see each other more clearly now. She was up to her thighs in the murky flow when some instinct made him look up the creek towards the bend. Not knowing what to expect, what he saw froze him in horror.

The dam at the bend in the creek had burst, and a mass of churning silt and debris within a four foot wall of muddy water was rushing towards Tannis. He looked back at her in time to see her body jerk as it was hit. One moment she was there and the next she had vanished from sight within the churning mass. A large clump of debris and branches swept across where she had been moments before, then rushed downstream, to finally wedge against an outcrop of boulders.

His stomach lurched. He pulled his rain cape over his head and threw it down as he ran downstream. When he was opposite the wedged lump, he slid down the incline and nearly pitched into the water himself as the bank gave way beneath him. Quickly he picked himself up and waded in, eyes never leaving a small patch of white which bubbled on the surface by the brush caught on the rocks. The initial wall of water had passed, but the current was still strong against his legs. The dammed backlog of water seemed intent on pushing aside any obstruction in its path, including himself. He had trouble keeping his own balance and realized the force which must have hit Tannis.

Mind numb but focused on the bubble of white, he fought against the flow. Though he slipped, righted himself and slipped again, he waded steadily closer. The patch of white hadn't moved, and although he could see one leg bob with the swells, the upper part of her body seemed strangely immobile. When he got to her he saw why. A heavy branch lay across her back had pinned her down. Christ! She'd drown if he didn't get her out right away.

He tugged first at her feet then one limp arm, but she was held fast. Frantically he tore at the limb across her back and tried to dislodge it. It gave a little as he pulled and pushed, but not enough to release her. He'd have to pull her out from beneath it. Suspecting she might be wedged by something underwater, he reached under her body with his hands and found what held her. She was caught in the V of the thick branch. Although she was on the downstream side of the clump of debris where the current was not as strong, he'd have to move fast. If whatever held the clump released its hold, they'd both be swept under. By holding down the limb under the water with his knee, and pulling on her body from the side, he managed to shift her a little.

Finally, after repeating the action several times, he pulled her free. He had no idea how he managed to drag her inert form towards the center of the creek, only that he had done so just in time. He had only just safely cleared the clump when he saw it shift. He watched as it was lifted like a watery monster, then rolled over by a muddy swell, and quickly swept away. Worried about the possibility of more debris headed their way, he redoubled his efforts to pull her through the water. With chill-stiffen arms, he managed to drag her up the bank. It would have been easier to pull her up on the bank on the dell side, but they would still have to cross the creek later and he didn't know how seriously she was injured.

He lay beside her for a moment to catch his breath, then, still panting from exertion he rolled over and got up on his knees. The pounding rain had slowed to a steady drizzle and he could finally see her clearly. What he saw didn't reassure him at all. Her eyes were closed and she was deadly white. He winced when he saw the deep gash along her left temple. The ragged gouge was long and deep, its flesh swelled a grotesque blue-white from even the short submersion in icy water. But his concern was over her stillness. She didn't seem to be breathing.

"Tannis, wake up. Oh Lord . . . open your eyes my love, and breathe. Please . . . breathe," he pleaded in a voice cracked with fear.

She lay unmoving, like a broken doll dropped into the mud by a disgruntled child. He pressed his fingers against her neck to feel for a pulse, but his fingers trembled so much, he wasn't certain if what he felt was a sign of life or his own agitation. He quickly rolled her on her back and straddled her. He pumped her chest and breathed into her mouth; willing her to accept his breath. Finally some water bubbled from the side of her mouth and her chest heaved as if to cough. Her eyelids flickered and she raised a hand in a mindless motion of protest as she began to gasp and choke. Then she lunged sideways and a rush of water gushed out of her mouth. She gasped for air then expelled another gush of fluid. Weakened by the effort, she flopped onto her back and greedily sucked in rasping breaths of air.

Relieved, Bryan pulled her towards him and crushed her icy form in his arms. Clasping her tight, he buried his face in the wet tangle of her hair.

Suspended in a moment of profound gratitude, he whispered disjointed assurances and words of love.

"You're safe now. Oh God, Tannis . . . I thought you'd drowned. You silly, silly, woman. Why didn't you wait for me to come and get you? I'm sorry, I am so sorry. When I saw that wall of water rush towards you . . . then hit you . . . and when I saw you go down, I thought . . . oh Christ! I'm so sorry—for everything. Please, please say you'll forgive me. I can't live without you. I'll do anything you ask . . . just marry me . . . please say you still love me."

Tannis felt awful. Her head spun and her temple throbbed something fierce. She felt fuzzy and disoriented and her chest hurt. She freed a hand to touch her head and released an involuntary moan. Something had happened to her head when she pitched into the water, but she had no idea what. Numb with shock, all she knew was that one moment she was wading across the creek, and the next she was catapulted head-first into the water. A searing pain on her temple was the last thing she remembered before she blanked out.

Not all of Garth's words had registered, but his tone did. He'd said he loved her and wanted to marry her. That's odd, she thought. They were already married, only she didn't know why they were out here, wherever here was. What she did know was that her head hurt.

Shaking with cold she tried to concentrate but it hurt her head to do so. She moved her limbs gingerly, relieved to know everything worked. Then she realized her clothing was ripped off her shoulder and hung below her breast. She reached to pull the wet fabric across her nakedness, but Garth's hand stopped her. Too weak to protest, her hand fell away. She caught her breath as he gently cupped her breast in his hand and rolled his thumb slowly across the tight nub of her nipple. Then he pulled the damp fabric across it so smoothly, she wondered if he had touched her at all. The action was so unexpected and sensual, she felt an instant response in her groin. She moaned, and as she half-turned towards him, his lips met hers in a crushing kiss that left no doubt as to what he felt. She returned his kiss with matching ardor and for a short time, her aches and chills faded.

In spite of the heat of their embrace, her uncontrollable shivers finally impelled them to pull apart. Still disoriented, Tannis looked in bewilderment at the man who held her so securely. It was Bryan, not Garth. She tried to rise but her legs shook with cold and her head began to spin. Her realities were confused, mixed-up. Why'had she thought it was Garth who held her? But she was glad it was Bryan. She clung to him as he helped her up and clasping her tight, guided her up the incline towards the mare. At the top she collapsed against him hardly believing how weak she felt.

It had stopped raining. She could hear the rush of the creek below but without the sound of the pounding rain, the world seemed strangely silent. The departing storm clouds disclosed a ceiling of gray which began to lighten in spots, then separate to show an occasional patch of blue. When the sun broke through low on the horizon, she gasped in amazement at the emerging arcs of a rainbow.

The faint motes of color widened and deepened into intense bands of purple, green, yellow and red as the sun illuminated the colors to their full intensity. Tannis had never seen anything so beautiful. Anchored to the earth by mere illusion, it seemed a reminder of how fragile life was; a fact she truly appreciated in light of her near-death. As the skies cleared, the rainbow began to fade. Rays of sun cut through the ground-hugging mists, creating unearthly golden pockets of light which intensified the color and shape of the dripping leaves. After weeks of no more than light nighttime sprinkles, the bone-dry soil which had at first repelled the deluge, now swelled in welcome as it absorbed the life-giving moisture and released earth's ambrosial richness. The air was suddenly filled with joyful chirps, twitters and caws; in celebration of the departure of the storm and the richness it left behind.

She now remembered what had transpired before her accident and wanted to explain herself; to tell Bryan why she had run away, and about the incredible transformation she'd undergone in the dell. "Bryan, I have to explain . . . I . . ." She felt him squeeze her arm lightly as he nuzzled her ear.

"Shh. No need, my love. We have the rest of our lives. First we have to get you out of these wet clothes and home to have that nasty gash stitched up."

In spite of the setting sun's golden glow, its waning heat was further diminished by a light but crisp breeze. Bryan knew she had to get out of her wet clothes; they both did. There was only one way to stimulate enough body heat to warm themselves. Hopefully, he'd have the self-discipline to do no more than what was essential. Disgusted with himself for his lusty thoughts, he marveled than even under these dire circumstances, this woman so easily inflamed him. He had to get his mind off his bodily needs and attend to hers.

"Take off your clothes," he ordered as he felt another shiver skim over her body. He let her go and turned to pull the saddle from the mare. Looking around, he spotted a bramble patch over which he could anchor their clothes. The sun's waning heat and breeze would suck most of the moisture from the fabric. Voicing his intentions, he realized she hadn't moved or said anything. She just stood there and stared at him dumbly. She must be in shock. Quickly he peeled the clothes off her unresisting body, rung them out, and lay them over the bushes. He wrapped her in the horse blanket and rubbed her vigorously. She protested only once when he pressed on a tender bruise along her side. Then he removed his own clothing and spread them on the bushes beside hers.

Tannis inhaled the mare's sweat from the fold of the blanket. Stirred by the damp scents, she felt herself tremble; uncertain if from cold or in primal, erotic response to the sensory combination of scratchy blanket, animal sweat and dank soil. Momentarily lost in an aura of sensation, she didn't resist when Bryan pulled her down on the ground beside him.

Cold air hit her body when he pulled the blanket back and she automatically strained towards him for warmth. As he shifted to better embrace her, she snuggled tight against him. She continued to shiver, but slowly their combined heat dispelled her chill. As she warmed, she became acutely aware of his nakedness, and her own. There was something so elemental about surviving an accident, being rescued by her lover, and now lying naked together. He must have had similar thoughts, for she felt the beginnings of his arousal.

Embarrassed by his body's betrayal, Bryan shifted and gently pulled her up into a sitting position. He looked into her eyes; eyes that could hide neither her love or arousal. She strained towards him as he planted a series of soft kisses on her face. Her disappointment was so obvious when he pulled away, he stifled his urge to continue.

With a catch in his voice, he said, "I have to bandage you up. It'll be dark soon and we need to go. You're still in shock, and may have a concussion. Besides, everyone will be worried sick. Come." He rose reluctantly and pulled her up, cradling her tenderly for a moment before he released her to get their clothing. When he got back he cut a wide strip off the bottom of her shirt with his pocketknife and fashioned it into a band he carefully tied around her head.

Their clothes weren't dry, but with the lingering heat of her arousal, Tannis hardly noticed. Since Bryan had cut the bottom off her shirt and the buttons were missing on what was left of it, she pulled up the two ends and tied it in a knot under her breasts. Her damp tights were harder to pull up, but she managed. There, that would have to do. As it was, she was barefoot, her loafers lost during her watery tumble. Exhausted by the simple effort of dressing, she sank to the ground and tried to still a sudden wave of nausea.

Bryan wrapped the saddle in the blanket and placed it under the brush. It would be much easier to ride bareback and he could come back tomorrow and get the saddle.

Tannis sat watching him, absorbed in the efficiency of his movements as he draped his rain Mack over the blanket and saddle. When he was done, he helped her up. Bryan tried, but getting her on the horse without one jarring boost was impossible. Once on, she leaned forward and clutched the mare until Bryan mounted and settled behind her. She found her access to Taenacea's equestrian skills were somewhat diffused by her shock and she sat the horse more like the novice she was. Once she felt his firm clasp across her ribcage, she leaned back against him gratefully.

Her head was still spinning and she had to grit her teeth against the jar of the mare's gait. She had to will herself to stay upright and conscious. She knew enough about concussions to surmise if she did have one, it was probably a mild one. What she did have was a cut on her temple and horrendous headache from the nasty bump on her head. She must have hit her head on a rock underwater, which would account for her disorientation. Unable to fight it any longer, she allowed the fuzzy stupor she'd held at bay to envelope her.

* * *

"They're here! He's found her," Stout announced as he stuck his head into the library. He had gone back outside after the rain stopped, both for a smoke and to call Zoie, the only one of the cats still on the loose. The others were safely back in the sun room. Trix and Ginseng had been pulled out from under the big rhododendron bushes near the terrace by Sam and Linka. Soaked and muddy from having to crawl under the bushes to get them, the two handed their frightened and equally dirty charges over to a surprised Nell and Iris, declared in charge of speed-drying resistant cats.

"It's much like drying a squirmin' child," Nell had said as she grasped the first one awkwardly. "You'd best be quick about it 'afore it knows enough to fight you off." She had to admit that Iris's soothing murmurs helped. She had little patience for, or experience with coddlin' cats, her inclinations more to seeing to the needs of children, and recently to the comfort of her house guests.

"A shower and hot toddy will set yeh right," she said as Same and Linka made to leave. "I'll do up some Irish whiskeys for yeh in the library when yer down. Toss the rain gear outside. We'll see to it later."

"Don't worry about Zoie," Linka shouted out at the fellows through the doors. "She won't come 'til she's good and ready, even for mom. She's probably nearby, watching and laughing at us all," she added as she tossed out her wet gear as instructed and went upstairs with Sam to shower and change.

The others came in too, but when the rain stopped, Stout had slipped back out for a smoke. Although it was almost dark, he had seen the beast and its burden crest a hill over by the pastures and had gone in to give the news.

Showered and changed, Sam and Linka had joined the others in sipping a potent but delicious Irish Whiskey. On hearing Stout's news, Linka and Josie dashed to the side window and peered out, but the library was on the far right at the back of the house and they couldn't see past the sun room opposite them.

"I'd best go with you," Seamus said to Stout, and rose to do so. By the time the two reached the back end of the stables, the mare was plodding up the incline towards them.

"What happened?" Seamus asked. He noted how tightly Bryan clasped the deathly-white Tannis against him as if to prevent her from falling. She looked slack in his arms, barely conscious in fact, and her injury was apparent. Blood had begun to seep through the bandage around her head.

"She got caught in a flash flood trying to cross the creek and was hit by a wall of debris. The bend of the creek dammed, then gave way while she crossed. I've never seen anything like it. The river up-a-ways must have channeled into the gully. She's got a nasty gouge on her temple. Have Nell call the doctor. She'll need some stitching." Tension and fatigue were apparent in his voice.

Tannis was eased into waiting arms which held her sagging form until Bryan dismounted.

"I'll carry her up to my room," he said emphatically. "I don't think she can walk herself. Oh, and Seamus, have the mare seen to would you. She's earned a good rub and feed."

Linka and Josie were waiting by the front door when Stout came back. When they heard Tannis had been carried up the back steps to Bryan's suite, they raced upstairs to see if they could help. But the bedroom door was closed, and when their knocks went unanswered, they straggled downstairs and inundated Stout with questions. All he could do was repeat what little Bryan had told them.

* * *

Tannis was only faintly aware of what was going on around her, and had been in that state since they began their ride back. Her efforts to stay on the horse and still her waves of dizziness left her exhausted. All she wanted to do was lie down on something that didn't move—and sleep. She felt herself eased into a pairs of burly arms which held her upright until she was scooped back into Bryan's arms. Her protest died on her lips as another wave of dizziness engulfed her. She kept her eyes closed and tried to ignore the forks of pain which shot through her head with each step as Bryan carried her upstairs. Her eyelids fluttered open briefly when the motion stopped and she felt herself laid down on a bed. She lay very still and prayed for the pain to recede. Mercifully it did, as did she.

When she drifted back to consciousness she knew neither who or where she was. Then it slowly came back to her as she relived recent events, what she could remember of them. She was in a room, softly lit by lamps—Bryan's room, under a familiar beamed ceiling. For a moment she just relished the warmth of their bed within the comforting silence. Then she sat up slowly. Feeling only a little woozy she swung her legs over the edge of the bed. She rose carefully, and since her head didn't pound too much, wobbled to the bathroom.

Good god! The face in the mirror was bleached of color and hardly recognizable as her own. With the blood-soaked bandage drooping over her eyebrow and twigs caught in the tangles of her matted hair, she looked like a mud-streaked pirate, one who had survived a battle, but not unscathed.

She couldn't possibly greet the doctor looking like this. She would have preferred a bath but knew a shower was the easiest and quickest way to clean herself. She wouldn't be able to wash her hair with the bandage on, so gingerly removed it, careful to keep her actions slow and smooth. Any movement set off the pounding in her head. She pushed down a wave of nausea when she saw the long raw gash that would require more than just a stitch or two to pull the ragged edges together. Bad enough on someone else, to see this horrible injury on herself almost made her faint.

She had to hold on to the side of the shower stall, but awkwardly managed to wash her hair with one hand. She had to tilt her head sideways to avoid getting soap into the gash but couldn't prevent the hot water's sting. As for the rest of her body, since it hurt too much to lower her head to soap it, she just let the hot water do what it could. When she was done, she felt clean and warm, but exhausted. Her ears rang and her legs felt rubbery so she sat on the toilet seat for a moment to still her spinning head.

That's where Bryan found her; naked, with pink rivulets of blood running from her wound. He quickly grabbed a bath towel and wrapped it around her, then used a hand towel to staunch the flow of blood.

"Christ, Tannis. Here, hold this," he said as he raised her hand up to the bundle at her temple. "You shouldn't be out of bed. You could have fallen. And look at your head—the hot water's started it bleeding." He could barely contain his exasperation at her stubbornness and insistence on doing everything herself.

"Oh. I feel better. Really." Nauseated by the mere mention of the blood, she added, "I just need to lie down for a minute." But the quiver in her voice belied her statement. From a fuzzy distance she felt him scoop her up and carry her back to the bed, then prop her up against the pillows. She felt his gently hands wrap a bandage around her head, towel dry the ends of her hair, and button a cool, silky shirt over her nakedness. Then she was tucked in like a child and told to go to sleep, which she promptly did, but not before a smile at how lovely it was to be cared for.

Bryan had done all he could until the doctor arrived. For a moment he just stood and looked down at her, hardly believing she was safe and lying in his bed, if somewhat battered. She had to be the most beautiful, proud, stubborn, sexy, and trying but fascinating woman he had ever met. Right now her vulnerability cloaked her strength: her pallor pronounced by the dark silk shirt and raven fan of curls around the white bandage. He reached down and ran his finger down the side of her cheek and along her jawbone.

She was everything to him and now that he had her back, he would do all in his power to keep her. Although encouraged by the memory of her arousal while they lay under the blanket and what he had read in her eyes, he did not interpret it as automatic forgiveness. She might not even remember much of what had happened, or what he had said. Suddenly he remembered something else, what he had asked of Seamus earlier that day. He would go downstairs and see about it then slip into the shower himself before the doctor came. Now that she was safe, every muscle in his body ached. He was also filthy. But first he must take care of this matter. He would call Josie and Linka to sit with her until the doctor arrived.

* * *

"I've done a fine job, if I say so meself," said the grizzly little doctor as he carefully pressed the tape over her stitches. "Mind, but yeh'll have a fine mark to show for it, I suspect," he added, "unless yeh go see one of them plastic surgeon fellas, that is. I'll be back in a week to check on it. Yer head will ache some for a time, but yer lucky. A right bump and bruising yeh had, and yeh'll' stiffen up for a day or so. But there's no damage otherwise that I can see. Rest's the thing now for a day or two I'd say, d 'yeh hear?" He tidied up his instruments and put them back in his bag.

Tannis wiggled down on the pile of pillows behind her with relief, glad her stitching ordeal was over. Her head still throbbed, but more dully after the freezing. The Doctor had agreed with her own diagnosis; that she had only a very slight concussion. But he still insisted on bed rest for at least a day or two.

What had first discomforted her, and now amused her, was her captive audience. Everyone was in the bedroom, even the children. Apparently in this house, doctoring was a family affair. Fleetingly she wondered if the birth of Bryan and Seamus had been as intently observed, since Bryan had told her both were born at home, in this very bed. But what warmed her heart was their genuine concern, even through she was a little embarrassed by their hovering attentiveness. She'd better get used to it. The Irish were not shy about considering every aspect of one's life their business, especially family, which she apparently was. She also realized her vanity was completely unnecessary.

When the little gnome of a doctor had first arrived, everyone else trooped into the room behind him as if this was a social event; oblivious to the fact she was in bed half naked, waiting to have her head stitched. Worse, she was scared stiff. Unlike Taenacea, she was squeamish about seeing blood and flesh sewn, especially her own, and could never watch an operation on television. Knowing this, Linka and Josie had rallied to her side.

Josie sat on the other side of the bed and Linka cross-legged right beside her, patting her hand in maternal reassurance. Both delivered a much too graphic description of just what the doctor was doing. The children milled around the foot of the bed, making faces, nudging each other, and emitting exclamations during the more gory moments of her surgery. She had almost passed out when the doctor first inserted the needle into the wound to freeze it. The men hung back around Bryan's desk. She suspected it was as much to avoid watching as to discuss radio reports on the storm and unusual flash flood the two had encountered. Only Bryan was missing from the charming scene. Assured by the doctor that she was fine, he had collected some fresh clothes and slipped into the bathroom.

"Enough now," Nell proclaimed when the Doctor was done. "Best we leave her to rest for a bit. I'll send up some tea, and something heartier later. Come on, yeh heathens. I've supper to see to and perhaps a wee dram for the doctor and the men before. Yous lot can go pick up the branches from the courtyard until yeh're called. Now off yeh go, do 'yeh hear?" she admonished one and all. They complied, excepting Linka and Josie, who didn't budge.

Josie threw Tannis a look of appeal. "Can I speak with you alone for a minute? If you're up to it, that is?" she asked. Although Tannis had been polite, she had not actually spoken directly to her, only answered in a general sort of way when Josie had addressed her. She was relieved at Tannis' nod of assent and braced for what was sure to be a scathing rebuke. Might as well get it over with.

"I want to talk to Josie for a minute, sweets. Do you mind? I'll see you later. We'll have our own private chat then, ok?" Tannis said quietly as she squeezed Linka's hand.

Linka winked and said, "Sure mom. You need to have your *best friend* at your side. I know you're just dying to tell her everything that's happened—like you always do." Pleased with her parting dig, she scrabbled off the bed and left them alone.

Tannis smiled at her offspring's transparent attempt to remind her of the depth of her friendship with Josie. She watched through half closed lids as Josie sat herself in the chair the doctor had just vacated. For a few moments neither spoke. They could still hear the shower running in the bathroom but knew Bryan would be out soon and this moment would pass.

"So . . . are you major pissed at me?" Josie figured she might as well plunge right in.

"I was. But only mildly so now." Tannis paused. "You should have told me about the book though. Reading about it in a tabloid was a shitty way to find out, you know."

"I know," was all that Josie said.

"I swore I would never speak to you again." Tannis tried to sound disgruntled.

"Understandable. And what changed your mind?" Josie queried.

"In light of my near-death experience, my perception change. My rage lost its edge. I still want to discuss this 'book deal' with you, but it can wait. What I do want to say, however, is . . ." She remained silent for a time then her voice softened as she continued, "that I'm sorry for being so unbending, Josie. I realized a lot of things today, and one of them is that I've been a fool—a stubborn control freak like you always pointed out. Because of it, I nearly lost everything I love, including you, you opportunistic little psychotic, who, I might add, is forgiven, but still on probation."

Josie might have anticipated a variety of responses, but not this. As long as Tannis was calling her names, all was well.

"All true, but understandable considering the powerful energies of an ancient sorceress at work here. I must have been under a spell too," Josie intoned as she rolled her eyes heavenward.

Tannis laughed nervously. "Like me? No, I think your spell was self-spun. As for me . . . I think I've finally separated the two, Taenacea and myself. I can't ride on her coattails and live my life through her. Remember, I swore I would never get caught in the experience at the beginning? But I did—bigtime, and her life became more real to me than my own. I realize now that I'm responsible for my own 'orgasm' as we used to say. I just didn't think I'd need such a traumatic knock on the head to finally 'get it'."

"You're strong, like her, that's why. A little tap on the shoulders would have gone unnoticed. Sometimes our priorities have to be, shall we say— realigned. I know all about that, if you remember. The more resistance, the more impact is required. However, the point is—you did 'get it'—and right on schedule too. That's all that matters."

She leaned over and gave Tannis a warm hug. "I must say though," she added with a cheeky grin and sparkling eyes, "it's all bloody romantic. You have a horrendous misunderstanding, dash off in a rage and get caught in a flash flood and are nearly drowned. Your lover races off on horseback during a savage storm, he finds you in the nick of time and saves your life, then brings you home and lays you in his bed, in his lair so to speak, so you can't escape him, which you are too weak and in love to do anyhow. It that ain't true love, or romantic, I don't know what is."

Tannis chuckled. Their friendship would survive this. Sometimes it was better to just let things go, rather than rehash past actions and misunderstood intentions. As to her synopsis of today's events, Josie had a way of cutting to the chase.

"Now, fluff up your hair. Your man's on his way in. We'll laugh about this once you're Lady MacCumal and have me for tea in the drawing room," Josie said as if it was a foregone conclusion. She paused at the door, hand on her belly; her expression soft, but tone serious. "You know, I've pretty much been a ditz most of my life, so my advise may be questionable. But when I met Cal, a great many things changed for me. And when I found out I was pregnant, carrying a new life inside of me, everything changed." She saw Tannis open her mouth in amazement, and held up her hand. "I know, you don't have to say anything now. I'll be pregnant for some time to come. Let me finish. I realized loving life and living love is what we're here to do. It's what defines us as spiritual beings. Listen to your heart, Tannis." With those words, she quietly left. Tannis had no chance to comment on her disclosure.

She lay back and thought about the news of Josie's impending motherhood. She chuckled. A child raising a child; probably an ideal environment for the new baby who would not lack for stimulation or attention. She was thrilled for Josie and Cal. Then she thought about her friend's parting words. She too would start living more fully—from the heart. In fact, she already had by forgiving her irritating little friend for being just who she was; her unpredictable, ditzy yet immensely-wise, and gifted little psychic friend—soon to be a mother.

The sound of running water had stopped. Bryan would be out shortly. This was it. She sent a silent appeal to the heavens and stilled her fear. "If this is for my higher good, please make it so."

She smiled a greeting when Bryan came out of the bathroom and watched him approach with relish. It was so easy to love him when her attitude didn't come from a position of defense. He was not only gorgeous, but had proved his worth and caring. She just hoped he still considered her worthy of his interest after her lunatic actions.

When he was about a foot from the bed, he stopped. Her smile faded and her throat went dry. Why did he just stand there, looking at her with that unreadable expression on his face?

Suddenly she hadn't a clue what to say. He too was mute, or perhaps felt it was she who should say something. He cleared his throat and ran his hand through his damp hair. Then it hit her. Why, he was as nervous as she. It surprised her until she remembered his words when he had sent her away. She knew instantly he was remembering them too. Now that the trauma of her accident and his heroic rescue was behind them, she didn't know how to broach the past, or their future. Apparently, neither did he.

Maybe it wasn't the words as much as the tone that would bridge their mutual discomfort. Silence continued to stretch between them. She still didn't know what to say, but somebody else did. Before she realized it, she felt that recognizable fullness inside and realized her lips were moving of their own violation.

"It appears, milord, that I must thank you for saving my life. I consider myself forever indebted to you," she heard herself say in a husky whisper. What she had said was most unexpected, but after a moment she realized, also most appropriate. Thank you, Taenacea. She had left him an opening, an opportunity to recapture their previous lightness; to remind him of what was, and could be again. What had been needed was just a simple reassurance that all was well between them; that both were willing to commit to a future already pledged. The rest would sort itself out as things do when left alone to do so.

Her bantering and archaic tone had completely thrown him off. He'd rehearsed what he'd say, and how he would say it over and over again. That's why he'd stayed in the bathroom so long. He *could* read her statement as just a polite expression of gratitude, but her manner of address and tone of voice brought to mind past conversations in this medieval style of speech; a style used to playfully express their love for each other. Was she letting him know she was willing to forgive him, that she still loved him? He sensed her nervousness and suspected she found it just as hard as he to bring up their last encounter in the library. It was also apparent that she remembered little of what had happened after her accident.

But . . . if she wanted to approach it playfully, well . . .

O God! Now I've done it. He's walking out, Tannis thought when he turned abruptly and appeared to head for the door. Her heart did slow its hammering when he detoured to his desk and pulled something out of the drawer. He returned to where he had stood before, but she couldn't see what he held in his hands since he clasped them behind his back. She raised inquiring eyes to his, doubly perplexed when he slowly bent over and extended her a courtly bow, swishing the roll in his hand in lieu of a plumed hat.

"My pleasure, milady. However . . . I intend for you to honor your professed indebtedness. Are you prepared to do so, or are your words just empty platitudes of good breeding?"

Tannis saw the corner of his eyes crinkle, in spite of the seriousness of his expression. The huskiness in his voice had aroused her and she felt her nipples tighten under their silky covering. Oh, the beast! He knew she loved this titillating jesting, as Taenacea had, and considered it a maddening form of erotic foreplay. She made an effort to look demure as she peered at him from under lowered lashes.

"No, milord. 'Tis a genuine, and heart-felt desire I am prepared to honor . . . in whatever manner you deem fitting. I am at your mercy, milord." The latter was said with an appropriately submissive tone which nevertheless held an underlying promise he could plainly hear.

"Your gratitude may best be expressed two-fold," he said as he approached the bed. He knelt down beside it, one knee up in courtly fashion. "First, you must accept this Writ and honor what's contained therein, sight unseen." He handed it to her and waited, his hand over hers, eyes soft in silent appeal.

She looked down at the aged parchment, certain of what it contained and unsure of how to respond. Her fingers shook with what she instinctively knew she held: the ancient and still legal deed to these lands; a deed lawfully hers. There could be no greater sacrifice on Bryan's part than to hand her what he cherished most. Sobered by the enormity of his trust, she managed to whisper shakily "I accept, milord." Only then did he remove his hand and gaze.

Lordy! This was most unexpected. Of course she wouldn't keep it. He said accept it, not keep it. Besides, it was not she who had claim on this land, but the reverse. Wales had belonged to Taenacea, but Ireland had lain claim to her: this land which had not only spawned her line, but captured her heart the moment she set foot on it. But Bryan's gesture, of laying these lands at her feet, spoke of his love in a way words never could. She made no attempt to wipe away the tears that rolled down her cheeks.

"Now, for the second matter. You have run me a merry chase, milady. It seems you require something to occupy your time and attention, to prevent these . . . ah . . . unexpected urges to flee. As I am a reasonable man, I would find it abhorrent to shackle you. So, after much thought, I have come to the conclusion that the demands of an overly attentive spouse may distract you from such urges." He paused to pull a small velvet box from his pocket and opening it, handed it to her. "Milady, since you have enslaved me, I have no choice but to beg your hand in marriage. Only by complying is your gratitude proved as being forever."

"As I appear to have no choice, I must accept—forever," she responded, in a voice she wasn't certain was her own, although the answer was. Once again it was Taenacea who had voiced her desire, as if knowing she was again willing, but incapable. She had hoped for, prayed for, and even expected this proposal. But with the reality came such a rush of emotion, she was unable to respond. Thankfully, Taenacea had.

Curious, she pulled the ring out of its box and turned it slowly. It was obviously very old and hand-tooled, but so delicately, it might have been made by the finest equipment available today. The wide band consisted of two intertwined ropes, one of gold, and one silver. Inset along the top were three perfect opals, the central oval raised and somewhat larger than the two on each side. A narrower twist of gold and silver, matching the band's design, encircled each stone protectively. When she slid it on her finger, she found it fit perfectly.

"Oh Bryan," she breathed, all wordplay forgotten as she reached for him. "It's beautiful, and . . ." Whatever else she had planned to say dwindled as he bent over her and sealed their pledge with an excruciatingly sweet kiss that melted her heart as it imprinted itself onto her soul.

* * *

Sometime later, Tannis lay cupped in Bryan's arms. He looked down at her, hardly believing how tightly this woman was bound to his heart. She was a woman who had first bewitched him in the naked splendor of bronze, haunted him as her hazy image wove through his dreams, tantalized him in the flesh when they met in the dell, then claimed his soul with their first joining. She was his Enchantress, and would always be so; both sculptor and model who had breathed renewed purpose into his life. She was also a proud and willful woman who had run away when falsely accused, and nearly got herself killed in the process. She was a paradox; both as unpredictable as today's storm, yet as constant as the earth which had weathered all the storms through millenniums.

She was the woman who had agreed to marry him, whose mystical facets and fullness of being he would have a lifetime to discover, if not understand. She was his Enchantress—to walk with in stillness over their ancestral lands, to laugh with and to speak to about matters of the heart, mind, and soul. He suspected his jesting words of her 'running him a merry chase' would prove prophetic. But what an adventure it would be! For there would be their loving times; to tease her into wakefulness with his love and lull her to sleep with more; to embrace endless days with purpose and passion, saucy laughter and that deep, unfathomable wellspring of tenderness she drew from him. The thought of it made him tighten his hold on her as he planted a light kiss on the top of her head. "Ah milady . . . you have bewitched me," he breathed joyfully.

"Ummm!" Tannis snuggled deeper into the crook of his arm. Her lassitude, induced by the tenderness of a gentle lovemaking had miraculously dissolved her more persistent aches and pains. Bryan had resisted at first, concerned for her well-being, but she knew the joining essential, both as a salve for her recent trauma and to bind their pledge once more. She raised her hand lazily and admired the iridescent play of colors within the stones. Opals were considered mood conductors, both absorbing and amplifying the emotion of the wearer: a fitting augury to keep her rooted on a spiritual path.

"It's been in our family for hundreds of years and was always worn by the Lady of the Manor. There's an inscription on the inside, although it's nearly worn off now. *"In Ochi No Sharin,"* Bryan crooned.

Tannis slid off the ring and squinted at the inside of the band. She could see the worn markings but couldn't make them out. "What does it mean?" she asked, fondling the ring to feel the ancient vibrations captured in its design.

"It means *'Wheel of Life'*. My grandfather told me once that the women who wore it would come to know its hidden meaning."

She already did, thanks to the Quest. The inscription was most appropriate. Tannis had pledged her life to Bryan with this ring as others had before to their heart's choice. But the pledge ran much deeper than a pledge of physical love. By wearing this talisman she was adding her influence and energy to an enduring legacy of spiritual intention. She felt a quick shiver up her spine as she contemplated the ancient connection, the Quest, and events of the past few months.

It had started with a dream of a man whose undefined face gained substance with each dreaming, and stirred an inner yearning she wasn't even aware of. These stirrings had prompted her to embrace the Quest and subsequent journeys through time. And the Quest had changed not only the course of her life, but her very perception of reality.

The Quest had brought her an understanding of timeless love and earth energy, and given her a rare glimpse of not only history and ancient Wicca practices, but her own psyche as well. "*In Ochi No Sharin*". The picture of a wheel formed in her mind and brought with it a vision where Taenacea's and her life were each one spoke of the same wheel of physical experience. She had aligned with Taenacea because her life's spoke was directly opposite her own, connected by their shared soul at the wheel's center. That's why they could move along each other's life-line so easily. She wondered idly what personalities, in what time frames, lay along the other spokes: also aspects of themselves. With one spiritual channel opened within her, she could now access any of the others, but had no desire to do so. First, she would incorporate all she had learned into this reality. Then, perhaps . . .

She knew her experiences would be considered improbable by the scientific world, and definitely delusional by psychiatric standards. Those who did believe in reincarnation would also view her with skepticism, for most perceived the past, present and future in linear succession not simultaneous. Like a spiraling wheel of multi-dimensional aspects of one central soul, the lives of these personalities were separated only by the illusion of time. Each was in effect, a wondrous creative expression of their spiritual source. But this reality and her own *now*, was the point of focus she was responsible for living in a spiritually conscious manner, not only for her sake, but to uplift and influence all other aspects of herself, as Taenacea had done with her.

There was no question that the book Josie had drafted would be published as a novel. Even as a novel, such a book would fall into the category of fantasy. Yet the book could teach much; especially to remind women of their deep connection to an ancient life-giving energy; the very origin of creativity. Funny, she could have sworn Josie had know she would come to this conclusion eventually, but be unwilling to write about it herself. Enter psychic best-friend, would-be author with her trusty laptop sucking up bytes as her own experience unfolded.

As to the legend of the 'Finn' and her implied connection to him, well . . . it didn't matter if he had been a real person or just the dream of a wistful soul in another reality, planted into the hearts of the mystic Irish to incorporate into the dreams of their own past. In whatever reality, what the legendary 'Finn' and Maeve had set into motion had survived for a thousand years, and would continue.

The synchronicity of events she had experienced went far beyond coincidence. She fondled the cool opalescent of the three stones thoughtfully and smiled a secret woman's smile. They may be more significant than even Bryan realized. She would know soon. And their wedding would take place as originally intended. Perhaps that's what Josie had meant with her comment of "just in time too." But her elation was tempered with reason. She would not delude herself with a false sense of security, for there would be challenges ahead, times when both she and Bryan would forget their pledge. Both had lived alone too long, and their strong-willed natures could lead to conflicts lovemaking could not easily resolve. But their love and respect for each other would underscore and reinforce their intentions.

She needed a new philosophy for this next phase of her life. She would 'walk with her head in the clouds, but feet on the ground'; her interpretation of living a very physical life, but *through* spirit. All that was called for was some way to control her ego and prevent it pulling her off purpose. Silently she asked for guidance and received an immediate response—a sharp jab of pain at her temple. Her hand crept up to the plaster and she ran a finger along its length thoughtfully. Uhmm. Odd but appropriate. Instinctively she knew her scar would pain her when her ego became inflated. Her personal safeguard in place, she could now apply herself to her relationship with Bryan. She ran her fingers along his arm in feathery arcs, the arm leading to fingers which traced their own delicious circles on her breast. She sighed her contentment as their lazy dance continued.

With this man she would walk, talk and laugh with love. She would walk with him over their lands within the Mother's grace; talk with him of the mind, heart and spirit; laugh with him in the joy of pure beingness; and love him with all her heart. Ah, to love him!

To draw him with her love into each new day of togetherness, and to release him to his dreams with the glow of her love each night. And she would learn what it was to be Wicca. Once she was more practiced in her magical aspect, she would teach him to fly with her to the mystical Plains of Silver; the place of dreams and creation; the source of life itself. There they would nurture and feed their souls, and return to live their love with purposeful depth and richness.

There too, they would draw the skills required to nurture this land with honor, and protect it from the encroachment of a soul-less world. Unlike Taenacea, she would not become proprietary. She was but a temporary custodian of this piece of The Mother, and knew it. But through example they could remind others to reclaim their innate respect for the conscious-ness of earth. Ley Node—who's reputation was already wide-spread—could be expanded as a Center for Learning about more than how fruitful earth or healthy livestock can become with spiritual nourishment. The possibilities were endless.

She heard a familiar celestial tinkle of chimes, and knew her purpose had been redefined. She would continue with her craft of course. Here, in a land overlain with the richness of Celtic lore she wouldn't lack for inspiration—both through real people and the shadow souls of this land's legends. But there was much else she could do as well.

Tannis also knew she was not alone, and never would be again. She felt that subtle, familiar shift and allowed Taenacea to settle within her to relish the continuation of her own life's dedication to service and love. After a time, she felt her fade away, leaving her to experience the bliss of what was now her grand passion; a love born in a mystical place and swept through time, on silver wings.

The Beginning

ON SILVER WINGS
This tale is real.
The question is;
Is it real because I lived it in another time?
Or, because I made it up,
and live it now?

Acknowledgments

SPECIAL THANKS to Don MacGregor of *MacGregor Photography Studios*, the lovely and gracious Sofi Teleky and talented Claire Gandela *for bringing my vision of Taenacea to life, and to* Randy Aves *and* Michael Jacobs *for their digital contribution to the cover design.*

To those precious people who gave time, practical and moral support during the writing of this book, though you know who you are, I extend my heartfelt thanks to you again. For the arduous task of clear-reading my tale, I thank my daughter Jacqui Leddy, Katheryn Coleman, Sofi Teleky, Miriam Verstraelan, *and* Ritchie Veltheus *for not only this task, but faith in my ability;* Joanne Simons, *who gave her heart as well as invaluable help to the project;* Jill Parker, Ann Roberts, Howie Hoggins, Albert Finlay, my mother, *and the many others who knowingly or unknowingly helped and supported me. I appreciate you!*

513

ELFIE LEDDY lives in West Vancouver, British Columbia. Writing and story-telling have been a part of her life since she immigrated to Canada from Austria as a child.

She has worked in a variety of banking, accounting, marketing, and administrative fields. She promoted psychics and metaphysical instructors and also wrote metaphysical and self-development course material outlines and honed her understanding of people. She co-produced an Alberta Golf & Leisure Magazine and her poetry is featured in the *American Poetry Anthology, A Treasury of Poems,* and in a variety of community newspapers in Edmonton.

Elfie teaches private classes in figurative clay sculpting. Inspired by one of her own nude sculptures and the *Little Book of Celtic Wisdom,* which fell off a bookstore shelf and landed at her feet, Elfie began her first novel, *On Silver Wings,* in 1997. She has several other fiction and non-fiction titles in production.

Elfie is an intuitive people-oriented innovator of new ideas and has a strong conviction in the human potential for change through the healing of personal wounds. She believes that self-transformation becomes reality through the expansion of individual consciousness. She expresses her commitment to continued growth with directness and humor in her writing. In spinning her tales, she shares her own understanding of human consciousness and encourages others to explore their own innate abilities and valuable uniqueness.